Sarah Harrison became a household name in 1980 with the publication of her first novel *The Flowers of the Field*, an international bestseller that received unanimous critical acclaim. This was followed, with equal success, by *A Flower That's Free*, *Hot Breath*, *An Imperfect Lady*, *Cold Feet*, *The Forests of the Night*, *Foreign Parts*, *Be An Angel* and *Both Your Houses*.

Sarah Harrison lives with her husband and children in Cambridgeshire.

SARAH HARRISON

An Imperfect Lady

WARNER BOOKS

A *Warner* Book

First published in Great Britain in 1988
by Macdonald & Co (Publishers)

First paperback edition published by Futura Publications in 1989
This edition published by Warner Books in 1995
Reprinted 1996

A CIP catalogue record for this book
is available from the British Library.

ISBN 0 7515 1576 0

Printed in England by Clays Ltd, St Ives plc

UK companies, institutions and other organisations wishing
to make bulk purchases of this or any other books
published by Little, Brown, should contact their local
bookshop or the special sales department at the address below.
Tel 0171 911 8000. Fax 0171 911 8100.

Warner Books
A Division of
Little, Brown and Company (UK)
Brettenham House
Lancaster Place
London WC2E 7EN

For Carol . . . who else?

Acknowledgements

GRATEFUL ACKNOWLEDGEMENT IS MADE to A. P. Watt Ltd on behalf of the Executors of the Estate of Robert Graves for their kind permission to reprint four lines from 'A Slice of Wedding Cake' by Robert Graves, taken from COLLECTED POEMS 1975 (Cassell Ltd).

'Why have such scores of lovely, gifted girls
Married impossible men? . . .
Has God's supply of tolerable husbands
Fallen in fact, so low? . . .'

from *'A Slice of Wedding Cake'* by Robert Graves

Prologue

THE AFTERNOON WAS HOT. But then they were all hot this summer of the drought, 1976. A slow procession of brilliant, burning days. At the end of July the fields around Tarrford were already harvested, the tractors lumbered through clouds of reddish dust. Lawns were cracked and bleached, curtains kept drawn in the middle of the day, dogs and cats lay panting and slit-eyed in shady corners. They said if it went on for another week they'd be collecting their water from standpipes. The Devon countryside lay in a dry and breathless trance.

They were all under a spell. People rose early to walk dogs and do chores in the cool, damp dawn. In the early afternoon when the sun stood glaringly overhead, they kept to their houses and rested or slept. In the evening the village returned from the dead as people moved out of doors again, cooking and eating and talking and laughing on their tinder-dry patches of grass, unable to bear the thought of stifling bedrooms. Even the young children stayed up late, playing outside till after dark.. Everyone was magicked by the endless, eerie heat.

Adeline, too, was bewitched. This most un-English of summers had an hallucinatory quality. It was as if the suck-ing-dry of the ground, the fiercely lit days and the short, sultry nights had removed the signposts of ordinary life, its touchstones and talismans, so that no-one was quite sure where they were. The past seemed to stand very close to the present.

Adeline was well aware that this closeness of the past was one of the features of being old, and yet she had not been conscious of it before. On the contrary, every morn-ing as she got up she made a conscious effort to address herself to the present and the future. There was much to enjoy, and look forward to. Her year was divided between the two places she loved most, the island of Larme des Anges and Fording Place, where she had grown up. Her brother Frank and his wife had converted the house into three, the two large units for themselves and Adeline, the smaller one for a living-in couple. The nearby Dower House they kept as a holiday retreat for any friends and relations who wished to use it.

Usually her four months at Fording Place were the most crowded of the year. Apart from the mornings, which she kept free for painting, she was surrounded by people. Frank and Anne, family or friends who were staying, trips to London . . . there was almost a party atmosphere as she tried to crowd too much into a short time. More so than ever this year because her book, *Faces*, had been pub-lished, so she'd been tearing about giving interviews, talk-ing on radio, visiting bookshops. She'd loved every minute of it. The culmination of all this was her trip to London tomorrow to appear on what everyone assured her was '*the* chat-show'. She could not really believe that ten minutes' worth of superficial conversation with an Australian young enough to be her grandson was of any great consequence, but it was all going to be *fun*, an amus-ing new experience. She had had a day in town with her sister-in-law, Louise, in order to buy a dress for the occasion. Louise had excellent taste, but in the end Adeline had ignored all her advice and splashed out on a theatrical swirling long dress in red, black and gold, which she intended wearing with her biggest jet earrings and beads.

'They're expecting to see an artist, a colourful character,' she explained to Louise when she expressed doubt. 'So that's what I shall give them. Besides it's the *most* glorious dress. When I feel blue I'll put it on and it will make me feel better, instantly!'

Everything was ready. The dress hung on her wardrobe door, her case was packed, she was looking forward to it all immensely.

But that was tomorrow. Today, Sunday, the world seemed parched and empty. For one thing she was alone in the house for the day. Frank and Anne were on holiday in Scotland, Mr and Mrs Page had gone to the seaside at Tarrmouth for the day with their two young children and wouldn't be back until late. The dogs were in kennels. Fording Place lay in a heavy, heat-stunned torpor. Adeline's grandson, Patrick, and his girlfriend, were at the Dower House and had indicated that they might visit her later in the afternoon, but she knew better than to set much store by these casual verbal arrangements made by the young. She'd be pleased to see them if they came but she assumed, without self-pity, that she came well down their list of preoccupations.

Usually she gardened on a Sunday, or went for long walks, but today it was simply too hot and dusty to contemplate either. The heat, and the excitement about her television appearance made her restless. The inside of the house was dim and withdrawn, secretive. The part she occupied was what had been the library, the snug, the billiard room and the big downstairs cloakroom with its adjoining corridor. Upstairs, she had her own bedroom and bathroom, and a small studio. It was all absolutely ideal, but today as she wandered from room to room she felt as if the house had stepped back into its own past. She kept thinking she might catch sight of Frank, the boy, running past the window, or Bob, sitting in the corner with a book . . . when she glanced out of the window she half expected to see Richard wearing his straw hat, walking up from the woods with Trigger and Mark capering at his heels . . . or Elizabeth running and leaping round the tennis court in her long white dress, like a gigantic butterfly . . . .

It was not an unpleasant sensation, but, always wary of going a little potty in her old age, Adeline tried to ring an old friend, Toni Simpson, at lunchtime. There was no reply. All the world was out, or away, or sleeping. She turned on the wireless and listened to a repeat of the Goon Show, a favourite of hers, but the mad, piping voices and bursts of laughter seemed to accentuate the brooding quiet of her surroundings. When she switched it off the silence was almost palpable, a muffling curtain between her and reality.

She wasn't hungry. For lunch she had a large gin and tonic and a packet of peanuts, relishing it the more for knowing how furious Frank and Anne would have been with her.

Then she took her cigarettes and walked through to the library. Her comfortable canvas shoes made no sound, she might have been a ghost herself. The house seemed reflective, sunk in memories, its walls and floors warm with hundreds of past summers, its cool shady corners concealing people that she knew, watching unobserved as she went by.

Then the oddest thing happened. As she looked on the mantelpiece for her hated spectacles, without which she stood no chance of deciphering the print of *The Sunday Times*, she caught sight of someone outside the window. In the instant that she turned, her glasses in her hand, she saw that it was Charlie. He stood looking in, smiling at her, his light-coloured clothes rather dazzling in the bright light beyond the glass.

It was only the merest glimpse and then, when she put her glasses on, he was gone. She walked to the window and looked out, scanning the lawn that fell away from the house to the woods. There was nothing and no-one to be seen except the trees and the grass lying flat and languorous in the heat of the day; a complete emptiness, with no clues to time or place – no person, no animal, no building, not even the distant sound of a dog barking or a car on the road from the village. Just a kind of eternal Sunday.

Adeline was not shocked or afraid, for she seemed today to be inhabiting an element that was different from any other. She went through to the hall and out of the front of the house. To either side of the door the pear tree leaves lay still as glassy green overlapping scales, and the roses were wide, pale-centred, and furled back in their blowsy late summer glory.

But there was no-one there. And he *had* been there, his jacket slung over one shoulder, his hair falling on his forehead, his sleeves rolled up in the heat. Smiling. The impression she retained was that he was waiting for her. He'd asked nothing of her, hadn't beckoned or called her, nor intruded in any way on her life. He'd simply made his presence known.

Leaving the door open, Adeline returned to the library. She went over to where a collection of framed sketches of Charlie hung on the wall. She had never succeeded in painting a decent portrait of him, but now the sketches seemed full of life and immediacy, as if she had only just completed them, as if his head might turn a little further, or his face in repose might suddenly be lifted so that his eyes could meet hers. She laid her forehead against the smooth glass for a moment and felt how cool it was.

A little later, unable either to snooze, or to settle to anything constructive, she decided to brave the heat and walk down to the ford. It would be cooler down there anyway, and she liked to watch the swans. And if Patrick and Lindy did decide to come and see her they would walk that way and she could meet them.

She set off slowly over the grass, wearing her big straw hat, and carrying the folding canvas director's chair from Habitat which her daughter Dora had given her for Christmas. It was a godsend, light enough for her to take anywhere, and gave her back the support it needed these days, when she was occasionally afflicted with aches and pains in the lumbar regions.

Daringly, she went down the steep bank to the river, rather than take the longer and less precipitous way round. She climbed down crabwise, using the chair as a prop.

This summer the river had dwindled from its usual broad, sparkling self to a mere dawdling trickle, only just deep enough for the pair of swans who nested on the island to swim. The female and her single ungainly cygnet were sitting in the brittle brown rushes near the nest but the cob lumbered over the cracked river mud as far as the water and sculled towards Adeline, his wings slightly lifted. When she set up her chair and sat down he moved away again, satisfied that she presented no threat. Adeline closed her eyes, not from tiredness but because she was content to be here, with the hot sun filtered through layer upon layer of leaves, and the faint sound of the slow water. . . the company of the serene, monogamous swans.

When she opened them against she saw two things. One was that Charlie's headstone on the island, usually only visible in winter, had been exposed by the dying back of the long grass and reeds in the heat.

The other was that Lindy had appeared on the far bank, and was hopping about removing her sandals so that she could paddle across.

Adeline smiled at the girl's careless, athletic pregnancy, her red and blue striped cotton dungarees, swelled like a deckchair in a high wind, her cloud of crazily permed dark hair caught in a topknot of purple wool.

'Hallo there!' she called. 'Come and join me!'

'Hi . . .!'

Lindy pattered across the dried mud, squelched in the wet, paddled briefly in the shallow water that barely covered her feet. The swan paraded watchfully.

'Yuk!' She sat down on the shingle near Adeline's chair and began wiping her feet with handfuls of grass. When she'd finished she sat cross-legged, straight-backed, her fingers laced beneath her billowing stomach. She was an odd mixture, Patrick's girl, of unconventionality and stern self-discipline, with which Adeline felt entirely at ease.

'So how are you?' she asked.

'Fighting fit, thanks.'

'You certainly look it. You don't find this heat a trial?'

'Not the heat, no.'

'Where's my grandson?'

Lindy lifted her hands, still laced, and placed them on top of her head. She took a deep breath.

'I haven't the remotest idea.'

'I see.'

'Perhaps I shouldn't say this to you,' said Lindy. 'But I've had enough. I don't have to put up with all this, and I don't intend to.'

Adeline studied the stern, beetling profile that contained no hint of youthful uncertainty.

'What's he done now?' she asked.

'Oh! Christ! You wouldn't want to hear . . . he went off somewhere yesterday to take pictures – you know he wants to record aspects of the drought. I should think the entire countryside is crawling with photographers doing the same thing – at any rate he went, said he'd be back last night, usual story . . . it's the bloody predictability of it that drives me crazy!' She shook her head furiously. 'It's our last day and he knew I wanted to go to the sea, instead of which I've been stuck here – sorry – all day, with no car. He's so bloody thoughtless! And he could just as easily not turn up today either, and I'm due back at college tomorrow, so I suppose I'll have to get a taxi –'

'I'll take you to the station.'

'– and then fork out for a train! I'm sick of it. Sick!'

'What about him?' enquired Adeline cautiously.

'What about him?'

'Are you sick of Patrick?'

Lindy lay on her back with her knees drawn up. For the first time she looked directly at Adeline.

'I'm sorry, Adeline. Am I hurting your feelings?'

Adeline laughed. 'Good Lord, my dear, it would take a great deal more than that... .'

'That's what I thought. Can you see what it is that I'm saying? I feel as if I'm the one who makes all the moves, all the concessions, who does all the organizing, and the waiting . . . God, I sound like some put-upon suburban housewife!'

Adeline smiled down at her. 'No you don't.'

'We're not married, and I'm free to go. I think I must. I don't think I can tolerate any more of this being fucked about. I don't like what it turns me into. Hell . . .!'

She threw her arms over her face.

Adeline leaned down and touched the girl's bare, brown wrist. 'Poor Lindy. I do see, I do understand. Perhaps you shouldn't set so much store by your own dignity. After all . . . do you love him?'

Lindy shrugged, her arms still covering her eyes. 'God alone knows. . . .'

'Well . . . If you love him, and you value your independence, then you've got to accept that you're two different people with different ways of doing things. He's not going to change. You're the strong one. You have to decide. If you love him enough, then it's worth it. If not . . . you're free, as you say.'

A tall figure appeared on the opposite bank: cut-off jeans, red T-shirt, camera bag slung over his shoulder.

'Hallo!' called Adeline. 'We were talking about you.'

'Yeah . . . I bet.'

He crouched down, picking at the grass, in no hurry, Adeline saw, to confront Lindy.

But she had sat up at once, and was now clambering to her feet, taking the war into the enemy camp. Striding forward into the water, she yelled.

'You bastard! I've been waiting for you! I wanted to swim – to get cool!'

'Sorry. I am sorry. I drove right down to Cornwall . . . I got carried away. . . .'

'You could've rung! You don't give a shit, do you?'

'Stop shouting.'

'Don't tell me what to do. You haven't the right!'

'Who's talking rights . . .?' Patrick looked genuinely amazed.

Adeline closed her eyes.

'Can't you see?' yelled Lindy. She sounded perilously close to tears. 'Can't you see what it does to me? Can't you *see!*'

Part One

CHAPTER ONE

1909

ADELINE GUNDRY, nine years old, stood halfway across the River Tarr with her legs astride and her skirt tucked into her knickers. This was the river's fording place, but though it was shallow the water raced along with such force that she had to brace herself to remain upright. It combed and plaited itself around her ankles and swirled over her bare feet, which looked like two pale fish on the gravelly river bed.

'Hey!' she yelled to the boys. 'Look at me!'

Her elder brother, Frank, was sitting in the fork of a tree with his school friend Simon Charteris. They sat with their feet together, their backs braced against trunk and branch respectively, like handsome fourteen-year-old Siamese twins.

'Very good,' said Frank.

'What?' Adeline found it difficult to hear above the rushing of the water.

'Very good. Don't fall over.'

'Bob –!' Adeline shouted at her other brother, who was

whittling a stick at the base of the tree, his face a study in scowling concentration. 'Bob, look where I am!'

Bob glanced up, and then down again, without comment.

The water seemed suddenly to surge and Adeline flailed her arms to keep her balance.

'Bob, can you come and get me?'

'No,' he said, not bothering to raise his voice. 'You got out there, you get back.'

A large, billowy cloud, like a galleon, sailed across the face of the sun and its slow-drifting shadow stole the warmth from the air. The tugging water clung with strong, cold fingers to Adeline's legs.

'I'm going back to the house,' said Bob, getting up and driving his sharpened stick into the ground. 'It must be nearly lunch.'

He walked away between the trees, shoulders hunched, hands in pockets.

'Don't be mean! Give me a hand!' shrieked Adeline. Her feet and shins were numb. Her shoes and stockings on the bank looked considerably further away than they had five minutes ago, and the water in between dark and green, gleaming muscles of current flexing and contracting.

Bob had disappeared. Frank swung his legs off the branch and slithered down, hanging for a moment by his hands before dropping to the ground. Smiling affably at his sister, he said:

'I'm famished. Get a move on, Charteris.'

'Coming.'

'Wait for me!' shouted Adeline.

Frank tossed his jacket over his shoulder and began walking away with an infuriating air of unconcern.

'You'll have to catch up with us, Addy. We're not saving any.'

'Horrible beast!'

Simon Charteris jumped to the ground. He paused for a second. More than anything Adeline wanted him to help her. But all he said, hesitantly was:

'You'll be all right, it's not deep.' And then he, too, left, running to catch up with the others.

Adeline was mortified. The large cloud was followed by others, a whole fleet of galleons with rain on their sails. She shivered. The hem of her skirt had escaped in places from her knicker elastic and was wet. It whipped her legs in the stiffening breeze.

Furious, she turned and began to wade unsteadily for the bank. She understood Simon's predicament: he was a guest, after all, and male solidarity must outweigh chivalry in the circumstances. At least he had paid her some attention, tried to be encouraging.

It was a struggle but she made it, hobbling over the sharp, gravelly little stones at the water's edge to collect her shoes and stockings, and sinking gratefully down on the bank to pull them on.

As she did so she noticed the scab on her knee. It was a scab of some four days duration, large and scaly, but not quite ready to come off. Adeline examined it intently, her heavy, unchildlike brows drawn together in a scowl of concentration, her tongue curled up towards her nose, her damp, tangled black hair hanging around face and knee in a protective curtain. Breathing heavily, she slipped her thumb nail beneath the scab, and removed it. A gratifyingly extravagant rush of blood followed on this operation, and she allowed it to trickle down her leg, watching it fan out in a web of tributaries on the wet brown skin. She dabbed her finger in the newly opened wound and smeared her forehead with blood. Then, as the rain began to intensify, she set off for the house.

Richard Gundry and his wife, Elizabeth, with Frank, Bob and Simon, went ahead with lunch. They weren't given to standing on ceremony and neither were they much concerned about their daughter Adeline who, experience had shown, could look after herself.

'She was just showing off,' Frank said. 'She'll be here any minute. Don't let's wait, we're starving.'

Richard carved. 'Good appetite, Lizzy?'

Elizabeth flicked her napkin to one side and laid it on her lap. 'Certainly.'

'Simon?' Richard held aloft a slice of cold silverside between carving knife and fork.

'Yes thank you, sir, pretty hungry,' replied Simon cautiously.

'He's starving, too,' said Frank.

'Look after your guest,' said Elizabeth, indicating mashed potato and pickled beetroot. 'Adeline is naughty,' she added without much feeling. 'She doesn't make the slightest effort, ever.'

'She's only nine,' her husband reminded her in a conciliatory tone. 'She ought really to have been with Nanny, not tagging round after the boys.'

'Hear, hear,' said Bob.

'Nanny had sewing to do today, and it was a beautiful morning,' said Elizabeth spiritedly. 'I'd much rather she was out with her brothers than lounging about the house.'

'It's pouring now,' said Frank, with some satisfaction. 'She'll be soaked.'

Elizabeth was a tall, fresh-faced woman in her early thirties, with a fine bust and a good carriage. She was by no means a classic beauty, but men admired her for her figure and for her cavalier manner, and women envied her dash. She was proficient at tennis, drove a motorcar, and rode to hounds regularly and with conspicuous fearlessness. Her trademark was her spluttering, enthusiastic laugh which could be heard ringing out at social gatherings, giving the impression that wherever Elizabeth was, that was the best place to be.

She had been the elder Miss Lindsay-Smyth before she married Dick Gundry. The Lindsay-Smyths were affluent landowners in north Devon, and would have considered anything less than the same number of acres a comedown for their daughter. But fortunately the Gundrys of south Devon were comparable in both acreage and lineage, and their son Richard a young man of great personal charm and good looks, so there was every chance the match could be accounted one of love as well as expediency. The county attended the wedding and saw that the bride was radiant and the groom charmingly enslaved.

Richard, had been running the Gundry estate near the village of Tarrford for three years prior to his marriage, and when he brought Elizabeth home his mother, Sarah, moved into the Dower House nearby.

Fording Place, though neither the largest nor the grandest house in the area was universally acknowledged to be one of the prettiest. It was a Georgian building of mellow red brick, with white windows and a white colonnaded porch. It stood on a gentle rise in a quintessentially English country park, where the Gundry's herd of fallow deer grazed on lush grass between serene, widely spaced oaks and elms. To the south of the park were fifty acres of deciduous woodland through which ran the River Tarr with its unrivalled fishing and its natural ford, after which the house was named.

It was in these woods and on this river that Frank, Bob and Adeline spent their time. They were not gently reared children, as Sarah Gundry had often remarked. Many a distinguished visitor and house guest, strolling along the bosky footpath by the side of the Tarr, had been frightened half to death, on looking up into the overhanging branches, to see three grubby faces peering back, grimacing horribly. But the Gundrys were popular, and might be forgiven much.

It was raining hard by the time Adeline reached the top of the hill. Her skirt prevented the blood being washed from her leg, and she protected her face by pulling the neck of her blouse over her head so that the collar stuck out like a peak. She entered the house by a side door and almost gave Bryer, the butler, a seizure.

'In heaven's name, Miss Adeline, what are you playing at?'

'Nothing.' She adjusted the blouse.

'And whatever have you done to yourself?'

'Oh . . .' Adeline affected an air of restrained heroism. 'It's nothing. Have they started lunch?'

'Twenty minutes since,' said Bryer, with a hint of censure. It was wasted on Adeline who knew, instinctively, and without knowing why, that Bryer was not as other men were. And Bryer himself, in early middle age and as smooth and freckled as a bird's egg, knew that she knew.

Adeline went through to the front of the house, leaving a trail of damp footprints on the worn strip of red carpet with its green and yellow key pattern. Assorted Gundry forbears gazed down at her with pop-eyed hauteur from gloomy landscapes. In the hall her father's springer spaniels, Trigger and Mark, roused themselves briefly, wagging their tails and shaking their ears as she went by.

Outside the dining room door she paused. The muted burble of unconcerned conversation came from the other side, punctuated by her mother's robust laugh. Rage at their unconcern boiled up in Adeline, and along with it a longing for their attention, Simon's in particular. A burst of thunder made the dogs fidget and growl. The elements were clearly in tune with her vengeful mood. Firmly she grasped the large china door handle and turned it.

'Oh no, no, no,' Elizabeth was saying, 'you couldn't blame the poor wretched horse for doing what came naturally!'

She tipped her head back and laughed and the others, especially Simon and with the exception of Bob, laughed too, infected by her mirth rather than amused by her story.

'Now are we all done?' she asked. 'Frank, ring for Bryer, would you? Hasn't it gone most awfully dark?'

Frank rose, and was in the act of pulling the bell-rope when there was a terrific clap of thunder. The bilious yellow and black sky above the park was split by a white fork of lightning, and the rain abruptly grew heavier, pouring down in a sizzling curtain. The thunder, the lightning and the furious rain stopped all conversation for a moment, and it was into this lull that Adeline, with a nice sense of timing, now stepped.

She was soaked, and white faced. There was blood on her forehead, her skirt and her leg. Her thick, straight black hair hung in witchy, damp rat's tails. She wore an expression of the most profound resentment.

'Addy, *darling* . . .' Elizabeth at once got up and went to her daugher, half laughing, half commiserating. 'What on earth have you been doing? We've been wondering where you'd got to.'

'They knew very well where I was,' said Adeline, indicating her brother. 'I was stuck in the river.'

'And what's all this?' Elizabeth examined the blood-stains. But before Adeline could reply Bryer arrived to clear the table, and Richard put food on a plate and set it in Adeline's place.

'Thank you, Bryer.'

As Bryer left he favoured Adeline with a small, cold glance from his heavy-lidded eyes.

'Well?' persisted Elizabeth as her daughter went to sit down.

'I fell when I was climbing out,' replied Adeline composedly, sure of the rightness of her claim to sympathy and impervious to Frank's expression of comic disbelief.

'You might have washed,' said Frank. 'We had to, and we weren't caked in mud.'

'Oh let the child eat now she's here,' said Richard. It had been tacitly – and correctly – assumed by all present that Adeline's physical injuries were not serious. As Adeline ate hungrily, Elizabeth continued her hilarious horse story. Richard and Frank paid her smiling attention and Bob stared, preoccupied, at his lake of beetroot juice until the plate was removed. But Simon Charteris caught Adeline's eye, gave her his sweet, diffident smile and mouthed the word: 'Sorry.'

Of the three Gundry children, it was generally agreed that Frank had the looks, Bob the brains, and Adeline – well Adeline would probably settle down in time. Frank had his father's pure, fair English colouring and his mother's physical prowess. At school his work was adequate but his skill at games was breathtaking, and as everyone knew, which was more important, he was a hero. It was the breezy, unselfconscious, slightly callous charm of the physically confident which had drawn Simon Charteris to him. Simon was no slouch, in class or on the games field, and his family were staggeringly rich, so he was not unpopular. But he was gentle and shy, and somewhat hesitant, and his association with Frank Gundry provided him with a smoother social path than he might otherwise have enjoyed.

Bob – 'poor Robert' people would say in a pained, understanding way – was clever, and worked hard too, in a way which many thought rather dreary, and definitely un-English. But then, he needed to be good at something. Bob had suffered from a turned-in foot as a baby and, despite strenuous efforts to correct the deformity, still walked with a slight, lurching limp. He wasn't by any means a bad-looking boy, but he was so awfully *serious*, and his habitual expression seemed to be a frown. Elizabeth liked to think she loved all her children equally, but she had difficulty in understanding her younger son. Richard had the same difficulty but it didn't bother him. 'Just let him get on with it,' was what he said.

Adeline wanted everyone to be happy. She herself had a naturally exuberant, warm and loving nature, and an ability, unusual in a child, to empathize with others. She entered upon everything passionately, and whole-heartedly but with very little forethought so that where she was good she was very, very good, but where she was indifferent she quickly struck disaster. The friction between her two very different brothers caused her much real agony. She was at her happiest when the three of them went off along the river or through the woods on some elaborate imaginary adventure, a tight-knit family unit with Frank as commander, Bob as the brains and herself as chief cook and bottle washer. But now the boys were older these occasions were growing fewer, and when the three of them were together Frank and Bob usually struck sparks off one another. Sometimes they came to blows and fought, grappling and grunting and rolling over and over on the ground while she shouted at them to stop, and finally ran away when she could bear it no longer. In spite of Frank's advantage in age and size, Bob was a dogged and ferocious fighter and these altercations very often developed into marathon slogging matches. In the end, of course, Frank would win and would be, also predictably, gracious in victory, ruffling his brother's hair and suggesting there were no hard feelings before sauntering off, the matter entirely forgotten. But Adeline had once come across Bob after a fight. He had been sitting by the river, washing his hands and his face, and she had been going to sit by him and make some cheerful, encouraging conversation when she had noticed that he was crying, quite silently, his face contorted with shame and anger, tears pouring down his cheeks, his shoulders trembling. Shaken and appalled by this extremity of emotion she had crept away, not wanting to inflict the further humiliation of showing herself as a witness.

On that occasion she had gone to Frank and, screwing up her courage, asked: 'You don't hate Bob, do you?' and been only partly comforted when he had roared with laughter and said, 'Of course not, little silly, everyone has scraps from time to time! Where is the old fathead, anyway?' To which she replied that she had no idea.

As time went on she felt, with a mixture of fear and sadness, these cracks which moved like slithering snakes across the smooth encircling wall of family unity, and much of her considerable energy was spent in trying to shore them up, though she knew it was futile.

But the arrival of Simon Charteris to stay that summer of 1909 had taken her mind off her brothers' differences. At first sight she had developed a crush of epic proportions on this tall, fair, softly spoken and gently mannered visitor who called her Adeline and who blushed when their mother spoke to him. For the first time in her life the desire for approval from her family was superceded by the desire for approval from another. She wanted Simon not just to like her but to think she was wonderful. She displayed her skills and talents with fierce and sustained determination. Impervious to Frank's scathing exhortations to pipe down and stop showing off, she scaled trees, leapt ditches, did cartwheels, rode her pony bareback (and received a roasting from the groom for doing so), made funny teeth out of orange peel, fetched and carried slavishly and generally wore her heart on her sleeve. The result was that Simon, who was an only child, treated her with a kind of astonished but uneasy admiration, Frank alternately teased and vilified her and Bob and her mother either ignored or had completely failed to notice her turmoil.

Only her dear, dear father for whom (till now) her tenderest affection had been reserved, seemed to understand what she was going through, and to sympathize with her. Not that he expressed his sympathy in so many words – that would not have been Richard's style. It was his habit to demonstrate his feelings in a genial but oblique manner, as if protecting himself from emotional excess in others. But when he came across his daughter on her own, he would swing her up into his arms and nuzzle her cheek and ask her if she was all right and tell her to take care of herself in such a way that Adeline knew that he was on her side, as always.

The silent "Sorry" at lunch she regarded as a point on her side, and she awarded herself a further two or three when afterwards she heard Simon remark to Frank, thinking himself out of earshot: 'Your sister's a spunky little thing, isn't she?'

Frank's response had been one of perfectly proper fraternal disparagement, but that could not tarnish her pleasure in being the subject of such extravagant praise from the person who really mattered.

She considered her next move as she washed her knee in the nursery bathroom that afternoon. Mud and blood combined to turn the water a thunderous brown. As she applied soap to her face she saw, beyond her own face in the mirror, that of her nanny, Dorothy Sugden.

'I hope,' said Dorothy, 'that you are going to clean that basin when you've finished using it, Adeline.'

Adeline lowered her face to rinse it. 'Of course I am.'

'Not so much of the "of course",' said Dorothy smartly, inspecting the water with distaste, and herself applying a rough clean towel to Adeline's face and hands.

'And what's this blood?'

'My scab came off.'

'I told you,' said Dorothy reprovingly, lifting the hem of Adeline's skirt, 'to leave that scab alone. You'll have a scar.'

'I wouldn't mind that, as a matter of fact.'

'Oh wouldn't you now?' said Dorothy. She opened the cupboard in the corner of the bathroom and took out a clean towel and a cloth, handing the latter to Adeline and indicating the basin with its rusty tidemark.

Adeline wiped the basin while Dorothy put the dirty towel in the linen basket. Then, 'You're a fright, young lady,' said Dorothy and marched her into her room to change.

Adeline took all these ministrations in good part, for she liked Dorothy. The Gundrys' previous nanny had been ancient, cronelike and whiskery, and absolutely obsessed with the lavatory. In Nanny Dandridge's book regularity was next to godliness. The passing of half a dozen stools, twice a day, was the main tenet of her philosophy, and all three children had spent long, tedious, lonely hours trying to oblige and going to often quite bizarre lengths to make it appear that they had. Nanny Dandridge had not been intentionally cruel and she had come with excellent references but her regime of vigilance and syrup of figs had inflicted much mental torture. The boys had been too embarrassed to complain to their parents and Adeline had not liked to usurp their authority by doing so herself, but then one night Elizabeth had come to the nursery late to discover Bob, fully dressed, still perched on the lavatory, with the door wide open, and Nanny Dandridge hobbling back and forth exhorting him to try harder. Next day Richard himself drove the disgraced nanny to the station. She peered beady-eyed from the back of the motorcar, apparently unmoved by her disgrace. Neither did it occur to any of the Gundrys to wonder what would become of an old, single woman sacked without notice. It was like that with nannies.

Dorothy could not have been more different. This was her first post as a full nanny, after having been a nursery maid at a big house in London. In this position she had picked up all the jargon and mannerisms of the nanny, while retaining a sound core of humane good sense. She was a busty, attractive young woman in her mid-twenties with an air of coasting through her duties in the expectation of better things to come, though what they might be, Adeline had no idea.

She was too young to realize that Dorothy had no idea, either, or to comprehend fully that here was an attractive, lively, imaginative and naturally loving young woman in her sexual prime with virtually no social outlets and no opportunities for meeting young men. One of Dorothy's great skills was her ability to tell hypothetical stories about the glittering and romantic lives of past employers and their friends, to which the young Adeline listened enraptured. 'Oh yes,' Dorothy would say knowingly, 'he was after her, and she was blind not to see it. It was only a matter of time . . .'

'. . . till what?' Adeline breathed.

'Bedtime!' Dorothy would say, feeling, perhaps, that she had gone too far. Most of Dorothy's stories hinged on suitors who, in a white-heat of single-minded passion, pursued the object of their desire through thick and thin, letting nothing stand in their way. Wishful thinking, perhaps. A suitor would have had to be passionate indeed, not to say psychic, to locate and pursue Dorothy, cut off as she was not just by her position but by several hundred acres of rolling Devonshire farmland.

But now, with the dirty basin and the prematurely removed scab dealt with, there was something real to discuss. Dorothy followed Adeline into the nursery and, folding her arms, remarked with a little smile:

'So. And how is your Simon?'

Adeline leapt into a chair, hugging her knees. She adored these exchanges. 'He's not my Simon, Nanny.'

'But if wishes were horses, eh?' said Dorothy. She unfolded the gateleg table ready for tea. 'He's a nice-looking boy, I must say. Nearly as nice-looking as that brother of yours.' She meant Frank. Frank was the apple of Dorothy's eye, but Adeline would not be drawn into comparisons. Dorothy went on: 'You'd be surprised, in a few years' time, when you're a young lady, he could come after you.'

This last phrase made Adeline tingle with anticipation. She pictured herself dancing with one partner after another, the star of an already gay and glittering throng, perhaps at the Tarrmeet Hunt Ball . . . and Simon, his blue eyes fixed upon her, his face drawn with consuming passion, making his way towards her, elbowing people aside, claiming her . . . The fact that all the evidence suggested that Simon would never in a million years behave in this way did not mar the picture.

'Do you think so?' she asked.

'No doubt of it,' said Dorothy, sitting down and beginning to sort through a pile of clean washing, buttoning shirts with quick, assertive movements. 'Believe me, I know.'

That was the Wednesday. The day that followed was dark and drab and wet, the rain that had surprised them all having decided to stay and become thoroughly settled and boring. On Friday, Howard and Cynthia Charteris, Simon's parents, were due to arrive, to stay two nights and then to return to London, taking their son with them. Making those adjustments to time at which children are so expert, Adeline decided that three days was ages and ages. Never mind that he had been at Fording Place for three whole weeks, she told herself. If he had only been coming for a weekend this would be the very first evening of his stay.

Indoor pursuits having been exhausted during the morning, Thursday afternoon engendered in the younger occupants of Fording Place a sort of desultoriness. Had it been winter, fires would have been lit and chairs drawn round them cosily and they would all have resigned themselves to seeing out what was left of the day. But it was August, the air warm and the evenings still long, it might clear up in time for some kind of expedition after tea. This unsettled them. Frank and Simon became boisterous and volatile, charging up and down stairs and along corridors, laughing and skirmishing in a series of half-stifled explosions. Bob shut himself in his room with a book. Elizabeth, typically, defied the rain and took the dogs walking in the park, while Richard did something known as 'putting his papers in order'.

By ancient usage this activity took place in the Snug, a small room at the back of the house, overlooking the stableyard and garage. Other than Richard no-one was admitted except Trigger and Mark, and Bryer, who even today had banked the fire up to volcanic proportions. It was not part of Bryer's usual brief to heft coal and stoke fires, but he did so for Richard in the Snug because the room and the activities that took place in it were a tightly chauvinistic male preserve.

Adeline was at a loose end, feeling herself excluded by everyone, even Dorothy who had eventually tired of draughts and pick-a-stick and told her to amuse herself for a while.

As she came down the stairs, half sliding on the banister rail, she saw Bryer coming from the library with today's *Times* neatly folded on a tray, and heading toward the rear of the house. Adeline disliked his air of select privilege, and decided to storm the barricades of the Snug.

She flung her leg over the rail and slid rapidly down the last few yards. She loitered for a moment in the hall, waiting for Bryer to be out of the way. The heavy summer rain hissed and drummed on the gravel walk outside the long windows. In the corner by the library door stood a huge arrangement of overblown flowers – tea roses, larkspur, chrysanthemums, hydrangeas – with tentacles of greenery which swept the ground.

She heard the door of the Snug open and close, and Bryer's footsteps retreating in the direction of Cook's sitting room. Adeline went down the passage and knocked on the door.

There was absolute silence, and she opened it. Her father was sitting with his back to the door – and incidentally, to his desk – facing the fire, with his feet on the fender and yesterday's *Times* spread over his face. The small room was cluttered, hot, soporific. The paper which Bryer had delivered lay untouched on the desk.

Adeline closed the door gingerly behind her and went to Richard's side. His fingers were laced loosely on his chest, the newspaper rose and fell gently with his breathing.

Adeline took hold of the newspaper at its top and bottom edges and delicately removed it. Richard made a blowing nose through his lips and rolled his head on the chair back. He was a tall, slim, boyish-looking man and his sleep was deep and innocent. At this moment he could have passed for twenty-five. Adeline did not fully appreciate it, but the person her father most closely resembled was Simon Charteris.

She leaned on the arm of the chair, advanced her face to Richard's and gave him a 'butterfly kiss' with her eyelashes. He blew again and half opened his eyes, tucking in his chin to peer bemusedly at her.

'Oh . . . Addy, it's you. Run along, sweetheart . . . .'

'I thought you were busy,' said Adeline.

'I *am* busy,' said Richard comfortable, closing his eyes once more.

'Would you play cards with me? I'm bored.'

'Tut, there's no such word,' murmured Richard, with the complacency of the naturally indolent. Adeline gave his nose a tweak. 'Ouch! Addy! Can't a chap get some peace on a wet afternoon?'

'We can be quite peaceful playing cards, and you're not doing anything.'

'Yes I am, I'm doing nothing, which is something vitally important when you reach my age, as you will find out one day.'

Just the same Adeline saw that he was coming round. He took his stockinged feet off the fender, pushed his fingers into his hair and massaged his scalp and face vigorously. She went to the cabinet on the left of the fireplace, opened a drawer and brought out the cards. It was not the first time that Adeline had breached the barriers of the Snug.

When, three quarters of an hour later, Bryer put his head round the door to check the fire, it was to be confronted with the unwelcome sight of Adeline sitting on the hearthrug beating Richard at beggar-my-neighbour.

'Fire all right, sir?' he enquired softly, advancing as far as the desk.

Richard smiled over his shoulder. 'We're absolutely fine thank you, Bryer.' Adeline did not look up from her cards.

Bryer withdrew. But in Miss Purgavey's sitting room he found Dorothy Sugden standing by the table glancing through the *South Devon Gazette*, and could not resist commenting:

'That girl is a madam, Nanny. She's disturbed Mr Gundry in the Snug when he was trying to have forty winks. God knows the poor man has little enough peace.'

Dorothy did not lift her eyes from the *Gazette*. Thoughtfully she turned the page, scanned the new one.

'He gets little else as far as I can see,' she said.

'Some tea, Mr Bryer?' enquired Miss Purgavey, easing herself arthritically from her chair. She was that rare thing, a cook who admitted she was single, and who was not a tyrant. Indeed the Gundrys had her diplomacy to thank for the prevention of more domestic crises than they could possibly know about. Constant pain in her joints gave her a drawn, acid expression, and Richard and Frank called her Old Purgatory behind her back, but this was unfair.

'Thank you, Cook,' said Bryer. He removed his black coat and hung it on the hanger on the back of the sitting room door. He was fastidious about his appearance, even for a butler. 'She is not supposed to be in there,' he said.

Dorothy closed the paper and looked directly into his face for the first time with the wide, blue-eyed, slightly glassy half-smile she used to pull rank.

'It won't hurt Mr Gundry to be woken up.'

'She is disobedient, Nanny.'

'A child with character doesn't always do as she's told. Obedience isn't everything.'

Miss Purgavey clattered the lid of the kettle.

'It is an appealing characteristic in the young,' said Bryer.

'I don't set that much store by it.'

'That much is obvious.'

'Oh well, Mr Bryer,' said Dorothy, brushing imaginary specks from her white apron, 'you will have to allow me to be the best judge of what is, after all, my responsibility.'

'Now then,' interposed Miss Purgavey, 'let's have a spot of tea and not argue. It's the weather.'

Dorothy and Bryer exchanged a look of venomous mutual dislike. But Dorothy left the room, and an uneasy peace descended.

On Friday afternoon the grey Rolls, driven from the station by the Gundrys' chauffeur, Black, growled up the winding drive through the park, and disgorged Howard and Cynthia Charteris at the front door. Adeline had no intention of being a member of the greeting party and, having heard Dorothy pronounce that she 'couldn't be found', she sat on the first floor landing and watched the visitors through the banisters.

Cynthia Charteris was a woman of pale, ethereal elegance and her husband, in Adeline's view, was a bully. Everything changed when he arrived, everyone behaved differently, the very air seemed to scurry here and there to get out of his way. Where his wife was silvery and fragile, Howard was black and red and massive, with glaring, snapping dark eyes. It was his mighty bellow of salutation that could be heard before they had even entered the hall, whereas between the staccato outbursts of the boys, and Elizabeth's cascading laugh, and the roars and snorts of the men, Cynthia's gentle purr could hardly be heard at all.

Howard's verbal manner was as highly coloured as his complexion, and accompanied by gestures of bonhomie which bordered on assault, such as back-slapping, cheek-pinching and shoulder-crunching. He directed an amiable cuff at Frank and Bob and shook his own son's hand with a brisk, tugging movement. When Howard was in the house there was an undertow of violence, of hot and unpredictable energy which scared Adeline.

When the adults had gone into the library the three boys were left in the middle of the suddenly quiet hall. Bob sat down on the stairs, his chin in his hands.

'What shall we do then?' asked Frank.

Into the silence, Adeline heard Simon say: 'Haven't the faintest.' And then give, distinctly, a long wavering sigh.

The weekend passed. The weather returned from the dead in a riot of blue, gold and green, meals were taken outside and the children constructed an elaborate dam on the river and tried to swim in the resulting pool. Elizabeth tilted her face to the sun and declared that she liked to go brown; Cynthia remained cool and lily-like in dove grey and lilac netting beneath a ruched grey and white parasol. In the late afternoon the men played tennis (Elizabeth was precluded from playing by Cynthia's non-participation), and sometimes Bob, usually Adeline, ball-boyed. Richard was a talented sportsman. Any game depending on hand-eye coordination was easy for him, but he was sadly lacking in the killer instinct. His reaction to winning a point was to attribute it to 'the luck of the devil', and to losing one to say, 'another drink I owe you, old man,' and smilingly return to his place.

Howard, however, compensated for lack of flair with tigerish aggression. During a three-set confrontation his dark, perspiring features were never once lit by a smile. His few remarks were addressed to himself, and did not take into account the presence of a nine-year-old girl behind the baseline. Snarls of 'silly bastard' and 'bloody idiot' came thick and fast when the game went against him, but in the end he generally won, because he wanted to, and then he was at once the genial, open-handed guest, generous with compliments to the loser and thanks to the ball boys.

In church on Sunday morning, Adeline noticed first that Howard was extremely bored and secondly that he whiled away the tedium of the sermon by surveying the others of their party, and especially Elizabeth, with a faint, apprais-ing smile. Once, feeling herself watched, Elizabeth glanced his way and their eyes met. Howard's smile became more overt, he raised his eyebrows. Elizabeth at once looked away again with an abbreviated version of what, in another context, would have been a toss of the head.

Adeline had no talent for hatred, but she hated Howard.

On Sunday afternoon, after lunch, the adults sat beneath the chestnut tree on the brow of the hill that swept down to the River Tarr, and took their post-prandial ease. Con-versation was desultory, eyes were half closed, gestures few and lethargic. The deer grazing on the grassy slope came within fifty yards of the group. On the lawn at the front of the house, below the low wall that bordered the drive, the children played cricket, acrimoniously.

'Go on, hand over the bat,' said Bob to his sister. 'You were out.'

'It was a no ball,' replied Adeline. 'Wasn't it, Simon?'

Simon was put on the spot. He was a chivalrous boy, who had been brought up to do the right thing by the fair sex. On the other hand Adeline had plainly been out, lbw.

'It was a bit borderline,' he said carefully, as Frank moved in from the outfield to arbitrate. 'Perhaps we could give it her again.'

'Looked out to me, little sister,' said Frank with amiable but wounding sarcasm.

'Absolutely,' agreed Bob. 'Come on, Addy, hand over.'

'Oh please,' she said, 'I've only had three balls.'

'Why don't we give her another life?' suggested Simon,

with Adeline's shining eyes upon him, and his hosts could hardly refuse a guest on his last afternoon.

'All right,' said Bob, marching back for his run up, 'but no more chances *at all*!'

Adeline resumed her position at the crease, Frank went to long on Simon to silly mid-off. Bob stormed up to the wicket, his lurching run lending added menace to his approach, and let the ball fly.

It was a full toss, travelling at speed and in a direct line for Adeline's nose. She ducked and swung the bat wildly. By pure chance she made contact with the ball, the speed of whose trajectory caused it to shoot away towards Simon.

Exhilarated by her own exhibition of power play, Adeline scampered up the wicket and turned to come back. But astonishingly, Simon had scooped it up and Bob, baying for his sister's dismissal, stood at the receiving end, hands cupped.

'Simon! To me, quick!'

Simon drew his arm back at waist level and shied the ball. It was an excellent throw – hard, accurate and low. Unfortunately it was rather too good for Bob, who allowed it to shoot past his hands, and it hummed on its fateful way, seeming to slow down slightly to give the children time to appreciate the enormity of what was about to happen.

There was a crash, and the faintest tinkle of glass.

The Rolls was parked outside the front door while Black and Bryer loaded cases. The ball had gone straight through the back window.

Adeline stared at the dark, jagged hole, beside which there now appeared the face of Black, wearing a thunderstruck expression. She glanced over her shoulder. Simon was white as a sheet, his eye sockets a purplish grey.

'Oh my sainted aunt,' said Frank, almost admiringly.

Bob sat down on the grass, plucked a blade and put it between his lips. 'This wouldn't have happened if you'd been out before,' he remarked.

'I'm sorry,' said Adeline.

'That was unhelpful,' said Frank.

'True, though,' retaliated Bob. They glared at one another. Adeline stood, paralysed with misery. Simon was silent.

It was, of course, Howard and not Richard, who came round the corner of the house. His suffused face and agitated manner contrasted oddly with his casual, shirt-sleeved appearance.

'What the devil was that?'

Bryer straightened up, his cupped hand full of fragments of glass.

'I'm sorry sir,' said Frank, 'it was a complete accident.'

'What? What was?' Howard stormed round and took in the hole, the glass, the agonized cricketers. 'Who's responsible for this?'

He rounded on them. Adeline had her first, unforgettable glimpse of a truly violent temper coming to the boil. Howard's face was blotched and mottled, his eyes were bulging and red-rimmed, his big hands stretched and flexed as if crushing childish windpipes. What might he not do to any son of his who broke the window of their host's motorcar?

'Who did it? I want to know who did it?'

The other adults had appeared behind him, in attitudes of still slightly torpid concern, but they were mere chorus and spear-carriers to Howard's performance of towering, vengeful wrath. Simon walked forward, drawing level with Adeline at the crease. All his debonair grace and gaiety had deserted him and in its place was humiliating terror, ashen and faltering. It was more than Adeline could bear.

'I'm terribly sorry,' she said, in a voice strident with selfless bravery. 'I gave the ball a huge whack and it went straight through the window of the car.'

There was a silence, embellished with various reactions. Richard half turned away, putting his hand to his brow. Elizabeth and Cynthia put their heads together, stifling smiles. Black reached into the back seat and retrieved the ball.

'Here it is sir,' he said, handing it to Howard. 'The offending missile.'

Howard looked down at the ball in his hand as if it were an unexploded bomb on whose destination he was deciding. When he lifted his head to look at Adeline his heavy shoulders and thick neck seemed threatening.

'You hit this?' he asked, with a kind of cold snarl of disbelief. 'You are telling me you are the cause of the damage?'

'Yes. I'm afraid I am.'

Richard laughed: 'She's honest anyway. You've got to admit that, Howard!'

Howard lifted his head a little higher, like a stallion snuffing the breeze, spoiling for a fight.

'Boys, is this true?'

Frank, for once, was nonplussed. Bob, as the youngest of the three, was not being asked. All heads turned in Simon's direction. He, poor boy, being only human, opted for the proven expedient of telling the truth but not the whole truth. 'She did give it a tremendous swipe,' he said.

Now they did not look at one another, but stared straight ahead, like pieces on a chess board.

Howard said: 'Did she, by God!' and threw back his head and roared with laughter, displaying a big red mouth and huge teeth.

'Catch!' he shouted, and threw the ball overarm at Adeline. Scared stiff, she stuck out a hand at it, but missed. Simon, energized by relief, dived to his left and caught the ball on the half volley. Everyone clapped. Everyone was happy.

'I'm going to summon some tea!' called Elizabeth.

They drew stumps and began to drift in the direction of the chestnut tree, and refreshment, the adults murmuring and laughing, already consigning the disaster to the fund of amusing family stories. But the children still could not look at, or speak to, each other. Until just before they rounded the corner of the house Adeline felt a touch on her arm.

'I say,' said Simon, his face quite awestruck with gratitude. 'Thanks most awfully.'

She smiled at him. Black, still crouched on the drive picking up bits of glass, winked at them.

As they walked on Adeline felt her adoration for Simon coloured by two conflicting sensations. One was the warm, virtuous pleasure of having been of service to him. The other one was less comfortable. It consisted in the knowledge of how easy it had been to set him in her debt.

She experienced a momentary confusion. But she was only nine, and there was chocolate cake for tea, and a whole hour until Simon had to leave, so the confusion lifted and dispersed like clouds in the sun.

CHAPTER TWO

1914

WHEN ADELINE WAS thirteen and a half she was confronted by the irrefutable evidence that her parents were fallible. And developments in her own life helped her to understand why.

The shock of womanhood had diminished her natural confidence. Because after all, in spite of monthly inconvenience and a protruding chest, she still wished most of the time, to be an honorary boy, to ride and run and swim and climb, and this evidence of biological frailty was like the dead hand of maturity laid upon her. What, she would ask herself, was all this mess and alteration *for*? She admired Elizabeth for being the sort of woman she was: it cheered her immeasurably to see her mother thundering home an apparently untouchable overhead smash, for it showed that there was life after adulthood.

She had shot up, everyone commented on it. If she continued this way, she might even, the world said, grow into that awkward face of hers. All allowed that it was a face of strength, character, and a certain flamboyance, but no-one would have called it pretty. Adeline's hair was too bushy, her eyebrows too thick, her mouth too large (and all too often open). Her prominent nose was slightly but distinctly hooked. Howard had had Richard and Elizabeth in stitches by pointing out that their daughter's face, especially when she was out of sorts, needed only a cutlass between the teeth to complete it.

Adeline accepted these aspects of her appearance philosophically, since there was nothing she could do about them. Her height was another matter. She was now taller than Bob. This worried her, and she tried always to be sitting down or leaning on something, or doing up her shoe if he was in the room, so as not to be seen towering over him. At seventeen, he was the same height he'd been three years ago, and had only filled out slightly. In the autumn he would go up to St John's, Oxford, where he had won a scholarship to read history. He no longer seemed at all like a child. His pony (in which he had never had much interest) was long since sold, and in the holidays he was like a fish out of water, reading and studying and going for long, solitary walks and trying from time to time to answer his parents' polite questions about his work without either boring them, or appearing bored himself. For both Richard and Elizabeth were, in the nicest way, Philistines, who set little store by the things of the mind. They took their greatest pleasure in outdoor pursuits, for they had a lot of leisure. Richard painted a bit in a naive, highly coloured representational way, and Elizabeth could play a small repertoire of set pieces and songs on the piano. Sometimes Adeline would catch them looking at Bob as if wondering how they had come by this clever, aloof, scowling young man. Especially after Frank, who was all anyone could want in a son. He and Simon were both up at Cambridge now, and Frank's name had already been in the papers for scoring a century in the Varsity match. He did almost no work—he was reading modern languages— but he was always a fund of amusing stories about his escapades, and his parents would turn to him like sunflowers to the light after Bob's dry, cerebral discourse.

Adeline could see the injustice of this. Frank and Bob no longer fought, being altogether too grown up for that, but now she almost wished they would. At least the fighting had been real, it had been contact. Now they were cool, civil and distant with each other, going their separate ways, washing their hands of the whole thing and the slightly embarrassing blood ties which bound them. She still occasionally, and quite in vain, tried to bridge the gap by suggesting some activity in which they might all engage together, but it was hopeless.

She herself had discovered that she liked to draw. In fact it was more than a liking, it was a compulsion. Her parents insisted on treating the drawing as a dull but entirely suitable 'accomplishment', but she knew, she *felt*, that it was more than that. Nothing, just at the moment, gave her as much pleasure as getting down a likeness on paper, and she had a real facility for achieving that likeness in a few seconds. She was not in the least interested in landscape, or in the use of watercolour, but when other people were around her she felt lost without a pencil and paper to hand.

No-one took her drawing seriously but Bob. Once he came and looked over her shoulder as she sketched, and said: 'You're rather good, aren't you?'

'Oh . . . I don't know. I just enjoy doing it so much.'

'You're clever, Addy. Honestly. Don't let yourself be teased out of it.'

Touched, she had turned to thank him, but already he had gone, perhaps embarrassed at having started something of an emotional nature.

Simon still came to stay, once or twice a year, and these days Adeline would have died rather than show off. The memory of her earlier extravagances made her nearly sick with shame. Now, all her efforts went into appearing composed and ladylike, and generally behaving out of character, which was almost as exhausting as the exhibitionism had been.

She observed that Simon had changed, too. He had developed a sheen of cultivated charm and urbanity. He no longer blushed when Elizabeth spoke to him, and even

flirted with her in an innocent way, which made everyone laugh.

But he was two different people, Adeline knew that. He
liked coming to Fording Place. Here he basked in general
approval, in an easy-going atmosphere where there was
no hint of censure and where no-one expected anything
of him except that he be himself. But when Howard and
Cynthia came too, as they often did, Simon changed. His
manner became formal and restrained, his face seemed to
shrink, his mouth grew tight and his eyes anxious.

One day in April, when all the Charterises were there,
there was a scene at Fording Place, a scene of a kind so rare
as to be almost unknown: an unpleasant scene.

There were presages earlier in the day. During the afternoon Simon and Frank were teaching Adeline to dance.
They had rolled back the Chinese silk rug in the drawing
room and Simon was demonstrating ragtime. Adeline sat
with her legs bunched up on the window seat and watched
him take the floor with Frank. For once, Bob was with
them, winding up the phonograph and putting on the
records which the boys had brought with them from
Cambridge. He would never, ever even try to dance, but
there was a slight smile on his face, half mocking and half
envious, as if he were a much older man allowing the
youngsters to have their fun.

Simon, the taller of the two young men, led. His arm
encircled Frank's waist. Frank's large big-knuckled hand
rested on Simon's shoulder.

'Darling,' said Simon to Frank. 'Have I told you how
lovely you are tonight?'

'Dearest,' replied Frank, 'you are too sweet.'

'But now,' went on Simon, 'I must desert you for a
moment while I dance with the melancholy lady who sits
alone and has no partner . . .' He indicated Adeline, who
buried her face in her knees.

'Oh, cruelty! Do not go!' cried Frank, clasping Simon
in a vice-like embrace which pinned his arms to his sides.

At this moment the door opened and there stood
Elizabeth, with Howard. Elizabeth, who wore a mulber-

ry-coloured dress which matched Howard's face, hooted with laughter.

'But whatever are you doing? You absolute *fools*!'

Bob removed the needle from the record and leaned back on the wall, arms folded, staring at his shoes. Frank, entirely unabashed, executed a few prancing steps, his hand still in Simon's, and declared: 'We're demonstrating the ragtime to young Addy here so that she won't disgrace the family when she goes out into society.'

'Carry on then,' said Elizabeth. 'Show us how it's done.'

Bob replaced the needle and gave the handle a few turns. Frank was game, but Simon was now stiff and white with unhappiness. Adeline could hardly bear to look. Elizabeth laughed and clapped and even copied a few steps and Howard took his cue from Elizabeth and managed a bloodless smile, above which his eyes were glaring and angry.

'I can't imagine,' he remarked, 'why you two should feel it necessary to dance with each other when an attractive young lady like Adeline is present.'

Adeline knew very well that this was neither joke nor compliment, but a disparagement of all of them.

'Don't be pompous,' Elizabeth told him. 'Don't you remember what it was like to be young?'

In response Howard shook his head and offered his arm to escort her from this strange place where young men danced together. Watching them leave, Adeline was reminded of a bull being led to market, its ponderous muscular strength subdued and controlled by a slim length of rope.

The door closed behind them. The music was still playing and Frank clapped his hands together.

'Right! Addy, are you going to take the floor with this accomplished partner and show what you've learnt?'

Adeline caught Simon's eye, and he gave a little bow to encourage her. She went to him and he took her in his arms, but very chastely, with at least a foot between them. She hadn't needed the demonstration – dancing came as naturally to her as breathing – and she moved in a kind of ecstasy, feeling Simon's hand on her back, and holding her own hand. But when she glanced up at him, the light had gone out of his face and it was pale and closed like the face of a statue. He was gazing over her head and into some private place of his own. Disappointment swept over her, poisoning her happiness. Howard had spoilt things, again.

The record finished. Bob was sitting down, reading a newspaper, and the arm of the phonograph swam back and forth, hissing mesmerically. Adeline went to turn it off and the boys drifted to the window. As she removed the record she heard Simon say, in the flat voice he used when speaking of his father:

'. . . more than I can stand.'

'You don't want to let it get you down,' replied Frank.

'I can't help it. Whatever I do I sense it's wrong.'

'Rubbish, it's your imagination. You should stop worrying what he thinks.'

'It's all right for you,' said Simon. 'Your parents are so different. You don't know how lucky you are.'

They left the room, preoccupied. She and Bob might not have been there. Adeline closed the lid of the phonograph. Bob turned the page of the newspaper.

'I hate Howard!' she burst out. 'He's vile! As soon as he arrives, everyone's miserable.'

Bob laid down the paper and looked at her levelly. 'That's not just an exaggeration, Addy, that's a lie. It may be that he doesn't understand his son but then, that's not uncommon. My father doesn't understand me, that doesn't make him a monster.'

'But he doesn't make you wretched!' cried Adeline.

'How would you know?' Bob's tone was very dry.

Adeline was filled with remorse. 'I'm sorry.'

'There's nothing to be sorry about. I'm just pointing out that Howard may be unhappy too. Just because he's big and noisy that's not to say he's unfeeling.' Adeline was astonished by this defence of Howard from such an unlikely quarter.

'But he spoils things,' she insisted. 'We were enjoying ourselves until he came in, now everyone's upset.'

'Untrue.' Bob rose from his chair with an air of impatience. 'Simon may be upset, and you have upset yourself on his account. But Frank seems sanguine enough, I myself am unaffected. And Mother, you may have noticed, is never happier than when she's with Howard. You must learn to take a wider view, Addy.'

And on this superior note he left his sister with her sense of outrage unabated.

It was that evening that the trouble blew up, breaking the oily surface of apparent cordiality with alarming suddenness.

Adeline had been allowed to stay up to dinner, after which Howard, Richard and the two older boys retired to the back of the house to play billiards. It should still have been light at that time of year, but the sky had grown sullen during the early part of the evening, and now thunder rattled round the park and pale lightning flashed intermittently. Bob read a book, Adeline drew Bob, the two women talked. Elizabeth and Cynthia had absolutely nothing in common, which may have been the reason they got on tolerably well.

'No,' said Elizabeth, 'I couldn't take London any more, not for any length of time. I quite like going up with Dick now and again, but it's a great event for us now. I much prefer country life, it's what I was raised for, after all.'

'It is all what one is used to,' agreed Cynthia. 'Quite honestly, Howard is far better off in Town, he gets so bored and restless wherever he is. But on the other hand, you know, the notion of being a country squire . . . I think he's always envied Richard just a little . . .' She smiled faintly and looked into the distance as if enough had been said.

'Oh, Dick would be happy at the North Pole provided he had three square meals and a billiard table,' said Elizabeth carelessly. 'He is the most easy-going man you could wish to meet. And Chris Dance takes care of most things down here.' She referred to Christopher Dance, the Gundrys' farm manager. 'On the whole I can see us turning into a rustic Darby and Joan, growing staid and contented and unfashionable in the West Country and letting the world pass us by.'

'Come now . . . now, now,' murmured Cynthia, vaguely admonishing, not realizing that her friend was bragging. Adeline dropped her pencil.

'My goodness, Addy,' exclaimed Elizabeth, 'are you still here? You must go up at once, it's the middle of the night!'

'Where is Nanny?' suggested Cynthia, who rather thought the Gundrys allowed their staff to run rings round them.

Adeline leapt to Dorothy's defence. 'It's my fault. I said I'd go up at nine.'

'And so you should have done,' said Elizabeth. 'Go and say good night to your father and run along.'

As she collected up her pieces of paper Bob caught her wrist in order to take a look.

'Good grief, is that what I look like?' he said, but then added: 'No-one's safe, are they?' and gave her his grudging smile.

Though she would have liked to, she refrained from kissing Bob, because he hated it; she kissed Elizabeth from habit and Cynthia because she expected it, and left the room. As she came out into the hall there was a rustle at the top of the stairs and Dorothy's face, flushed with agitation, appeared over the banisters.

'My goodness, I was reading, I didn't realize the time!' Dorothy was an aficionado of the romantic novel. 'Hurry up, there's a good girl.'

'I'm coming – I'll just say good night to the others.'

'Very well, but quickly now,' said Dorothy, glad of a few moments' grace. She wouldn't be here much longer, for Adeline was due to go away to school in the new year. The governess, Miss Mortimer, had already been given notice and she could not see herself staying much beyond Christmas. She would need good references, and though her employers were nothing if not tolerant, there were aspects of her time with them which must remain buried deep. Every so often she would catch Frank's eye and her thoughts would make her blush so fierce and hot it was as though her skin had been turned inside out.

Back in the nursery, she closed the novel which had stirred her up so, and went to put Adeline's night things ready.

It was Adeline's intention to while away a few more minutes in the billiard room under the benign auspices of her father, who might even let her take a turn. She was quite a dab hand with the cue, and it made Simon laugh.

But when she reached the door of the billiard room, which was just ajar, there was an altercation in progress inside which prompted her to pause, and listen.

'I am simply pointing out,' she heard Howard say in his guttural, snarling voice, 'that that was an exceptionally unintelligent shot.'

'It was a mistake,' said Simon, rather muffled.

'What does it matter?' This was Richard. 'Frank, do something to consolidate our position here.'

Adeline now heard voices behind her, overlaid by the resonant descant of Elizabeth's laugh, and looked over her shoulder to see the two women coming down the corridor.

'Adeline, for heaven's sake –' Elizabeth took her by the shoulder and ushered her into the room.

'Ah, the ladies, God bless 'em!' cried Richard teasingly, 'You must watch the deciding game.'

'This lady must go to bed,' said Elizabeth, of Adeline.

'Oh, just five minutes,' protested Richard.

The upshot was that Adeline remained. She knew very well that her presence, and that of 'the ladies' generally, was useful as a curb to Howard's temper. A lot, apparently, depended on Simon's final turn. Adeline smiled encouragingly at him, but his face was stern with concentration. With brows drawn together and tongue protruding slightly, he lined up his and Howard's white on the red. But at the last his hand shook and he muffed the shot, miscued and missed both balls altogether.

'God almighty, what did I do to deserve it?' enquired Howard.

'Now then, it's only a game,' teased Elizabeth.

Howard did not look at her, but turned to Simon and said, with scarcely contained irritation, 'Only a game it may be, but it can at least be played properly.' He punctuated the sentence by hitting his son lightly on either side of his head with the butt of his cue, a gesture calculated not to hurt, but to humiliate. He then bellowed with laughter and the others joined in, knowing, in the way adults did, that this was the way to diffuse the acrimony. Even Frank laughed. Even Simon, white face and red-eared, managed a desperate grimace.

Only Adeline, like the boy who remarked on the Emperor's nakedness, did not fully understand the unwritten rules, nor care to abide by them. The rage she had suppressed for years boiled up inside her and she felt as if her head would burst if she didn't speak.

'Don't *do* that!' she shouted. 'Don't *do* it!'

Everyone but Simon glanced at her with the mild, disbelieving curiosity of those taken entirely by surprise. Simon's lips framed the word 'Addy –' but no sound came out. In any case he stood no chance of stopping Adeline who was now sailing buoyantly on a rip tide of righteous wrath.

'It's only a stupid game!' she yelled, sweeping her arm across the tranquil green baize and sending the balls over the cushion to thud on the floor. 'Nobody gives two hoots for it but you, don't you realize that? Nobody! It's common to care about winning, and that's all you care about – !'

Here the enormity of what his daughter was saying finally impinged upon Richard who, for once, took a firm hand.

'Adeline! Will you first apologize to Mr Charteris – our guest, may I remind you – and then go upstairs at once.

At once. I have never heard such rude and disgraceful behaviour.'

'Disgraceful . . .' echoed Frank, bending to pick up balls from the floor, but also to conceal a grin of unashamed delight.

Adeline began to march from the room but Elizabeth caught her arm.

'Adeline, you *will* say you're sorry.'

'No!'

Cynthia let out a little gasp, Richard glanced wildly over Adeline's head at his wife, Frank made a small, rude noise of suppressed mirth. But Howard . . . Howard simply bent over a table and fired a ball into the far corner pocket, with a noise like a rifle shot, and said casually: 'Off to bed, young lady, I don't want your apologies. Dick, another game?' He had never so much as glanced at Adeline as he spoke, and now he turned his back on her, one hand in his pocket, a study in complete unconcern.

Adeline wrenched free of her mother's grasp and stormed from the room. She tried to slam the door after her, but it had always been stiff, and merely half-closed with a little sigh. As she ran down the passage she heard Elizabeth say: 'I'll go and get her, we simply can't allow this.' And Howard's lazy reply: 'Nonsense, she's only a child.'

Adeline swept straight past the startled Dorothy and got ready for bed at high speed, still possessed by a fury which suddenly turned to desolation. She had made a fool of herself. She had behaved rudely and childishly in front of everyone. By standing up for Simon, as it had seemed then, she had probably humiliated him further. And Howard had brushed off her high-minded anger as though it had been no more than the buzzing of a gnat. Her only comfort was that she had been right, of that she had no doubt. It was her behaviour, not her response, which had been at fault. She smarted with a sense of injustice both on her own behalf and Simon's.

For about ten minutes she lay in bed in a tight little ball, fists clenched and teeth gritted, unable to relax, let alone sleep, and then she got up and went through to where Dorothy was sitting at the table doing some mending.

'Bed, young lady,' said Dorothy.

'It's no good, I can't settle.'

'Hm.' Dorothy gave her a knowing but not unfriendly look, and nudged one of the other chairs with her foot. 'I shan't ask what brought you flouncing in here like a nor' nor' easter.'

'I wish you would.'

Dorothy's needle hovered for a moment above the darning mushroom over which one of Richard's socks was stretched. 'Let me have it then.'

'I got absolutely furious with Howard – '

'Mr Charteris to you.'

' – and completely lost my temper. I was very rude to him, in front of everyone.' In spite of everything she could not hide some measure of pride and Dorothy was quick to notice it.

'I hope you said how sorry you were. In front of every-one.'

'No, I wouldn't. Why should I? I wasn't sorry for what I said . . .' Her voice tailed away.

Dorothy snapped the darning wool with her teeth and removed the sock. 'But now you feel very sorry for yourself for being silly.'

'Well . . . a bit, because I bet most of them agreed with me.' She watched as Dorothy laid the sock on top of its partner, rolled them up and turned back the open end to make a neat parcel. 'Aren't you going to ask me what I said?'

'I'm not the slightest bit interested.' Dorothy put away the darning needle and mushroom and threaded a smaller needle with white cotton.

'I just hope when I'm nineteen that no-one tries to make me look small the whole time the way Howard – '

'Mr Charteris.'

'The way he does with Simon.'

Dorothy, squinting, finally got the end of the cotton through the needle and picked up a pillowcase.

'At your age,' she said, at her most maddeningly mysterious, 'there's a lot you don't understand about the way things are done.'

Adeline shrugged extravagantly, to show her contempt for the adult world into which, all too soon, she must be dragged, kicking and screaming. 'I'm not sure I want to.'

'You will, my girl, you will.'

'Tell me, then. Go on, tell me something about how things are done.'

This was unfair and she knew it, for how could Dorothy possibly cast any light on what happened in the billiard room? Adeline simply wished to demonstrate that a few extra years did not necessarily make one an expert on human behaviour. But if she had hoped to discomfort Dorothy, she had also underestimated her. Dorothy had ample time to reflect on the ways of the world, and what she lacked in experience she made up for with a lively imagination and a sound intuition.

Dorothy stitched implacably and said, with a greater gentleness than she had used till now: 'You mustn't run away with the idea that because people behave in a certain way, that's how they feel, or how they are. Sometimes people behave in one way to hide the fact that they feel just the opposite. Older people do it more because they aren't as good at showing their real feelings, it makes them afraid. So life gets very complicated,' she concluded, 'and you must make allowances. You'll find it out for yourself one day.'

Adeline conceded that as a theory this probably held good, but she could not allow that it provided any excuse for Howard.

'I just think he's a beast,' she said.

'Perhaps,' said Dorothy, 'young Simon should try sticking up for himself.'

This was said so simply, without either implied criticism or malice, that it completely took the wind from Adeline's sails and she was, for a moment, speechless.

'Come along now,' said Dorothy, pursuing her advantage, 'to bed.'

Chastened, and with food for thought, Adeline climbed
into bed and lay more quietly this time, staring at the
ceiling. After a while her eyes closed, but only the thinnest
veil of unconsciousness settled on her, through which,
again and again she rose, disturbed by half-dreams, or by
small nocturnal sounds. Once the dogs began to bark and
she heard her father, remotely, silencing them. A little
later and it was Dorothy going to bed, the whisper and
gasp of cushions being plumped up, the click of the chair
being pushed into the table, the short hiss of the curtains
being adjusted, Dorothy's hand running down the join of
the two sides . . . the gentle final closing of the door.

The knowledge that the nursery was now empty, and
she the sole occupant, made her restless after that. The
stormy rain of earlier on had long died away and there
was absolute quiet except for a steady drip from the eaves
outside the window, and the occasional staccato cry of a
pheasant getting up in the park.

She got out of bed and went to the window and, drawing back the curtains, opened it wide. She inhaled deeply,
breathing in the smell of wet leaves and grass. On the edge
of the grass, against the deeper black of the trees, she could
see the pale shapes of the deer, one of them with its head
lifted as if it could sense her watching.

A door below the window opened, casting a wedge of
yellow light on to the gravel, and the deer melted back
into the darkness.

'. . . absolutely heavenly after rain,' Adeline heard her
mother say, and the four adults came out of the house.
Beyond the intrusive pool of light the gleaming, dark
landscape seemed to become secretive and guarded.

Adeline leaned forward to see better. It was thrilling to
be an unseen spy, though Dorothy had often pointed out
that eavesdroppers heard no good of themselves. Their
clear voices rose to her with the perfect truthfulness of
people who have no idea that they are overheard.

'You terrify us all, Howard,' said Elizabeth, laughing.

Howard snorted. 'Come, come, you're not that easily
scared, not you. Youth must be put on its mettle. Simon

has no brothers to rough-house with, so I do it for him. He may very well thank me for it one day.'

Richard laughed. Adeline knew they were all laughing, enjoying the privileged understanding of one another.

'I don't believe the child exists,' said Richard in his affable way, 'who ever thanked his parents for anything. Or at least not till it was too late.'

There was a general murmur of agreement. The four of them stood together companionably, looking out over the park. Adeline could smell Howard's cigar and occasionally the faintest whiff of the women's scent.

'He can be such a bear at times,' said Cynthia, laying her hand on her husband's arm.

'And so common . . .' Elizabeth's remark was broken by a chuckle, '. . . to care about winning!'

Adeline clapped her hand over her mouth to stop herself from yelping with outrage at hearing her own words quoted. She could tell by their manner that they were praising Howard.

'Yes, I approve of winning,' said Howard, 'and I like and admire winners. If that marks me out as common then so be it.' He sounded pleased with himself. If Adeline had had a bucket of iced water she would have hurled it over Howard's black head and broad, bullish shoulders.

'I think you should apologize to our hostess for being a disruptive influence,' said Cynthia. For someone whose usual demeanour was one of wifely acquiescence, she was being remarkably forthright, Adeline noticed. Howard must be in an outstandingly genial frame of mind.

'I agree,' said Richard. 'Howard, you owe Lizzie an explanation of your boorish and vulgar behaviour which has upset her badly, as you can see.'

'Rubbish, she enjoys it. You people could do with a bit more disruption in my opinion. A little excitement to liven up this bucolic retreat of yours.'

'Oh!' cried Elizabeth satirically. 'I feel an attack of the vapours coming on!'

'There you see?' said Richard, taking his wife's hand

and leading her towards Howard. 'Come on, man, where's your sense of form?'

'He has none,' volunteered Cynthia.

'That woman knows me,' said Howard.

'Apologize, sir,' said Elizabeth, more quietly. Adeline could only see the top of her mother's head, above a waterfall of oyster-coloured satin, but Howard had turned a little and she could see his face, dark and glaring, in the light from the house. Cynthia and Richard stood a little apart. Howard drew on his cigar, staring back impertinently at Elizabeth with narrowed eyes. Then he shrugged.

'Very well. I apologize.'

With his eyes still on her face he lifted her hand and kissed it with an abrupt, wolfish, biting movement. It was very far from being a kiss of chivalrous apology. It was not even, in Adeline's considered opinion, the kiss of a gentleman. When he let go her mother's hand Adeline half expected to see blood on it where his mouth had been.

Instead, Elizabeth threw back her head and laughed, her pale throat exposed and vibrating. Howard watched her without a smile, and then turned to the others and spread his arms as if to say: There you are, are you satisfied?

Richard clapped, a slow, uneven sound. 'Yes indeed. Honour is satisfied.'

The four of them drew together again. A narrow black shadow bisected the wedge of light. Richard clapped his hand to his brow in a characteristic gesture of mild distraction.

'Bryer, my dear fellow, are you still up? Please by all means go to bed. We were just enjoying the fresh air, now that it's cleared.'

'Is there nothing else I can get you, sir? . . . madam?'

'No, no, not a thing.'

'Very well, if you are sure, sir. Good night, sir. Good night, madam.' Bryer withdrew, but his brief interruption had broken some kind of spell, and Adeline sensed there would be nothing else worth watching or listening to.

'Shall we walk a little way?' Elizabeth suggested, and they moved off into the darkness, and out of earshot.

Adeline closed the window softly, and drew the curtains again. She climbed back into bed and slipped down under the covers like an animal regaining the safety of its den. Her heart was thudding and her breath rapid, her face, in the dark, wore an expression of fierce disapproval. They had let her down. It had all just been a joke to them. Bad was not bad, nor good, good. Only an hour ago Dorothy had suggested that Simon should stick up for himself. But what she had just witnessed persuaded Adeline even more strongly that he needed a champion, and that the champion should be herself.

The next day, however, Simon seemed quite restored, and Adeline once saw Howard clap him on the shoulder in a man-to-man kind of way which made her feel even more confused and angry. Her outburst was not referred to, though at lunch Howard suddenly leaned across and said to her:

'Tell me, Adeline, am I forgiven?' And everyone smiled indulgently, no doubt thinking him a very good sport for not taking offence. A little uncertain of her ground, she opted for what she hoped was an air of chilly detachment.

'I don't know what you mean.'

'Ah!' Howard sat back, raising his hands as if realizing he had touched a nerve.

'I see. I beg you pardon. Not another word.'

There was a little covert mirth around the table and that was the end of the matter, but Adeline knew herself to have been upstaged by an expert.

There was a dance that evening, a private party at the Carter-Hicks', who lived a few miles away, north of Exeter. Three or four couples were coming to Fording Place beforehand for dinner, and Adeline was allowed to be present during these preliminaries.

The people coming were a young married couple, the Armitages; Captain and Mrs Hyde-Latimer and their plain but amusing daughter, Anne; and Mr and Mrs Vale and their outstandingly beautiful daughter, Louise.

Adeline liked Anne, who always seemed friendly, and

always the same no matter what the company or occasion. In the drawing room she came over to Adeline, who sat perched on the arm of the sofa, and said: 'Hallo Addy, and how are you?'

'I can't complain,' replied Adeline, who would have complained at some length had it been appropriate to do so.

Anne recognized this, but mistook the reason. 'Don't worry,' she said, 'in no time at all you'll be going to dances, too, for what it's worth. I just wish you and I could change places. I should be happier at home with a good book.'

'Addy my love,' said Richard, coming up and putting his hand beneath her chin. 'Stop scowling, do, you'll wreck people's appetites.'

'Now, Mr Gundry,' said Anne, who spoke very freely to Richard, 'You should let Adeline scowl as much as she likes while she still can. Once she's a young lady she'll doubtless feel compelled to behave like a china doll, smiling sweetly and silently to impress brainless young men.'

'I hope,' said Richard, 'you are not casting aspersions on my sons?'

'No, no, of course not,' said Anne. 'Not before dinner at any rate.'

Richard put his arms across Adeline's shoulders. 'Addy will never, I hope, be that sort of young lady. If indeed she becomes a lady at all.'

Adeline grinned up at him. 'I shan't.'

'You'll have to work at not being one,' warned Anne. 'It will take a great deal of serious application.'

'She has a head start,' said Richard, 'with her mother's example before her.'

As if to corroborate this statement there was a burst of hearty laughter from the far side of the room where Elizabeth stood with Howard and the Armitages. Elizabeth held a cigarette in a holder and she was laughing at something Howard had said, for Adeline could see the recognition of his own cleverness on Howard's face, and the young Armitages were quite pink with thrilled amusement.

The cloud which Richard and Anne had succeeded in lifting descended once more on Adeline.

'Excuse me,' she said, and went into the hall. To her surprise Bob was already there, leaning on the banisters and looking cross and uncomfortable in his evening clothes. She sat down near him on the bottom stair.

'At times like these,' he said, 'I wish I'd paid more attention when those two idiots were showing us how to dance.'

'Anne's nice,' said Adeline.

'She's perfectly nice. It's the occasion rather than the company I'm at odds with.'

'You might meet some lovely creature and sweep her off her feet.'

'Don't be fatuous.' Bob pushed himself away from the banisters and took his hands from his pockets. 'I suppose I'd better go and put a brave face on it.'

Adeline watched as he went back through the drawing room door with the measured tread of an aristo approaching the guillotine. In a moment Simon and Louise Vale appeared in his place, framed by the doorway, talking animatedly. Or at least Simon talked animatedly, his head slightly inclined, one hand clenched and pounding an imaginary tabletop, while Louise demonstrated the absolute passive stillness which is the special property of the beautiful. She had only to *be,* in order to be fascinating. She was milky-skinned and cloudy-haired, youthfully slim but alluringly rounded. She wore an ice-blue dress, trimmed with white, and there were white flowers in her dark hair. Looking at her, Adeline seriously wondered if this could simply be dismissed as the 'china doll' behaviour so scornfully alluded to by Anne. Louise did not appear coy or vacuous. She simply offered up her physical perfection, and it was more than enough to cause a boyish flush to deepen on Simon's normally pale neck.

Then Frank appeared and said something in his exuberant, persuasive way, and took Louise's arm and led her away. Adeline saw that Simon was, just for a moment, nonplussed by her departure, all his charm and energy and attention had been focused on her and now she was gone.

She got up off the stairs and ran to his side.

'Oh. Hallo, Addy.' For the first time he used the brotherly diminutive.

'We're going on a picnic tomorrow if the weather's good,' she told him.

'That should be jolly.'

He was glancing over her head, not really listening, but she could forgive him anything.

'You look tremendously handsome,' she said.

Now, as if seeing her for the first time, he looked down at her and beamed.

'And so do you, ma'am!' He put one arm round her waist and took her other hand in his, and waltzed her for a few breathtaking steps around the hall, lifting her up for a final dizzying twirl.

'Oh, you must grow up quickly, Addy!' he cried, not really thinking about her at all, and kissed her.

He pursed his lips. The kiss he offered was a tease. But Adeline *had* grown up and he hadn't noticed. In an instinctive, clinging movement her arms flew about his neck and her legs, only slightly hampered by her taffeta skirt, about his waist. She pressed his face to hers with such strength that his lips parted and she felt, for a second the moist warmth of his tongue.

He spluttered and dropped her as though she were a troublesome puppy.

'Hey, steady on, what are you up to?'

On her dignity now she did not reply, but walked back into the drawing room as Elizabeth came to the door and called merrily:

'Simon, are you coming to take Louise in to dinner or must she starve to death?'

Bob offered Adeline his arm with a poor grace.

'Food? I need to keep my strength up for the ordeal ahead.'

As Adeline walked to her place in the dining room with

Bob she felt that she had crossed some small but important bridge of understanding, and that she now found herself in a country which, though not distant to the one she had inhabited a few hours ago, was different.

CHAPTER THREE

1914

THE DAY AFTER the dance, a lunch picnic had been mooted and agreed upon, weather permitting. Those who wished to ride would do so, and the others would travel by motorcar to the picnic site, which was a few miles to the west, where the steep Devon hills blended into heath, with gorse and heather and scotch pines threaded by sandy bridleways.

Adeline woke early, feeling excited, and saw that the weather was going to be everything one could possibly wish for a picnic. Unable to stay in bed with the morning so dew-drenched and inviting outside the window, she got up, saddled her pony, Beau, and rode over to the Dower House to visit her grandmother.

Sarah, the dowager Mrs Gundry, slept neither heavily nor long these days, so Adeline was confident of not disturbing her. And indeed when she reached the Dower House at a quarter past seven Sarah was already sitting in her window eating thin-sliced toast drooping with honeycomb.

Seeing her granddaughter she brandished the toast, indicating that she should come in and have some, and at once her terrier, Timmy, bounded on to the window seat and began bouncing on stiff legs, barking madly.

Adeline tied Beau to the gatepost. As she finished doing so Sarah Gundry's long-suffering maid Kathleen opened the front door.

'Miss!' she cried. 'Will you please have a care that animal doesn't eat the hedge? It's me gets the dressing-down from Collings!'

Adeline glanced over her shoulder. Beau had started on the hedge, pulling and tearing with his long yellow teeth, then staring benignly into space as he munched, with fronds of greenery sprouting from his mouth.

'Look, he's doing it now!' wailed Kathleen, and began running down the path, gawky in her black clothes like some large wingless insect.

'Don't worry, I'll get him,' said Adeline, but Kathleen was already at the gate.

'Stop it!' she shouted, making an ineffectual snatch at the pony's bridle.

Beau simply lifted his head out of reach, taking another huge mouthful of foliage as he did so. Timmy, realizing the front door stood open, scuttled down the path barking explosively, causing the pony to shy and almost wrench the gatepost from the ground.

Kathleen rounded on Adeline, attempting at the same time to grab the terrier's collar. 'Can't you do something, Miss?'

'I'll put him round the back,' offered Adeline.

As Kathleen scooped up the struggling dog, Adeline pushed open the gate and led Beau, still munching complacently, round to the back of the house.

The Dower House was no more than a pleasant L-shaped cottage. In the angle of the L was the kitchen door and here also was the patch of undistinguished grass, definitely not a lawn, where stood the washing line. Adeline attached Beau to the far post and he began cropping the grass at its base.

Kathleen appeared at the kitchen door. Timmy's barking continued in the background beyond other, closed doors.

Kathleen looked dishevelled: a few long wisps of her dry black hair had escaped from their bun, and a dusting of short white hairs from the dog lay on the front of her dress. She glanced at Beau with unconcealed disapproval.

'We don't have the place for a horse here.'

'He's only a pony, Kath,' said Adeline, 'and he's not doing any harm there.'

'I don't like him lumbering about in the garden, it's a responsibility.'

Adeline applied relentless logic: 'He isn't lumbering about, Kath, and he's not your responsibility. You really mustn't worry.'

This was an empty exhortation and they both knew it. Adeline entered the Dower House through the back door, a practice which scandalized Kathleen who liked to see the proprieties observed. On the kitchen table was the loaf and the honeycomb from which Sarah Gundry's breakfast had recently been hewn. Adeline took a chunk of one and a dollop of the other in passing, and stuffed the whole sticky, delicious parcel into her mouth as she closed the door behind her in the face of Kathleen's vociferous objections.

In the hall Timmy, seeing who it was, abandoned his barking in favour of a mad war dance of welcome, leaping and panting round Adeline's legs like a puppet on a string as she went into the drawing room to greet her grandmother.

Sarah Gundry was the kind of woman who was to be seen at her best in old age. Her three score years and ten sat easily upon her. She had led a sheltered and uneventful life: an indulged and sequestered country childhood had melted seamlessly into romantic courtship and early marriage. Years of blameless and contented union with Marcus Gundry had produced only Richard, the apple of her eye. She had subsequently lost two infants, one during pregnancy and another at birth, and had used this as a pretext for settling into a cheerful state of mild invalidity. Now, widowed for twenty years and 'put out to grass' as she herself described it, she found herself in the happy position of having no domestic or social responsibilities whatever and existing merely as a safe haven for whichever member of the family needed her at any given time. She was not concerned about having outlived her usefulness, for she did not delude herself that she had ever been useful. Here at the Dower House she was wonderfully looked after by Kathleen, whose slightly hysterical nature perfectly complimented her own benign and indolent one, and she was visited regularly, if infrequently, by the escapees from the more hectic atmosphere of Fording Place.

After Richard himself, her granddaughter was her favourite visitor. This was largely due to the complete absence of any common ground or similarity between them. Sarah had never been vain, so she did not look in others for a mirror image of herself. She found soothing any person who displayed fire, pride, anger, ambition – any of those qualities she did not herself possess. No wonder Richard was such a popular and good-humoured man: he had been presided over by a mother who adored and admired him but hadn't the energy for anything so active as over-indulgence. He had simply been allowed to wander unchecked into adulthood, pleasantly and ramblingly as a honeysuckle on a garden wall. Adeline in her turn found in her grandmother's house an atmosphere of uncritical and amiable attention which soaked up, like a warm poultice, the worries and irritations which she often brought with her.

'Hallo, my darling,' said Sarah now, peering round the wing of her armchair, her white napkin crumpled in her hand. 'Have you had breakfast?'

'I took a bit of bread and honey from under Kath's nose in the kitchen.'

'Now come along and have some of this, there's far more than I can manage. Come and sit down where I can see you.'

Adeline sat down in the window seat and Sarah waved her large, pale, beautiful hands over the little table where stood tea and toast.

'Help yourself, my dear. Do you want tea? Shall I ask Kathleen to bring another cup?'

'No thank you. I don't suppose she'd bring me one anyway, she's so cross with me.'

Timmy jumped on to the seat by Adeline and watched, rigid and unblinking as a black and white china dog, as she spread her toast.

'Now tell me when everyone is setting out,' said Sarah comfortably. She was going on the picnic, and was to be driven there in the Rolls from Fording Place.

'I think they're going to collect you at about midday. I'm riding there, and so is Mother and the beastly Mr Charteris.'

It was Sarah's great skill that she never latched on to the unkind references of others, and so avoided acrimonious entanglements. Though placid, she was far from stupid, and appreciated that her stock remained high in proportion to her degree of detachment.

'Well, it's going to be a beautiful day,' she said now, 'so I shall certainly be ready in plenty of time. Now that I wake so early I find waiting for the rest of the world to catch up with me very dull.'

'I know what you mean,' agreed Adeline. 'I simply couldn't stay in bed this morning.'

'Will they know where you've gone?'

'Oh I'll be back before they've even come down to breakfast. They all went to a dance last night.'

'It won't be so very long before it's your turn,' said Sarah, misunderstanding, as others had before her, Adeline's brusque tone.

'I don't think I'm interested in having a turn. They all behave like fools when they get their evening clothes on.'

'You'll enjoy it when the time comes, I promise you,' said Sarah tranquilly. 'I used to think dances and balls were a sort of heaven, I wanted the whole of life to be like that, full of music and gaiety and handsome men and lovely girls . . . I was a complete featherbrain – not like you, of course, my dear.'

This amiable humility, and the sweet smile that accompanied it, mollified Adeline. The honeycomb, the early sunshine on her back, her grandmother's unshakeable niceness, all made it hard to take a stand about anything. Now Sarah leant forward across the Crown Derby teapot and tapped Adeline lightly on the knee.

'Have you seen?' she enquired. 'Look.'

She pointed at the wall to her right. Adeline turned. There were a great many pictures on the wall, clustered close together like mosaic. They were in the main pale, tasteful, undemanding watercolours of the Devon countryside. But there in the middle, like a boisterous hoyden in a roomful of accomplished debutantes, was Adeline's own picture, mounted and framed and given pride of place.

Adeline bounced to her feet, a shower of crumbs sliding from her lap on to the floor where Timmy set about licking them up.

'Gran, you did it – it looks wonderful! You are an absolute *brick*!'

'I thought you might be pleased. Doesn't it look nice?'

'I wasn't sure you liked it.'

'I said I did, didn't I? I love it.'

'But –' Adeline was about to say that her grandmother always said that, but realized how it might sound and stopped herself. Instead she walked across to study her handiwork more closely.

The picture was a charcoal drawing of Sarah, quickly and decisively drawn with black, flashing strokes. It showed her sitting, as now, in the window, with Timmy on her knee, three-quarter face to the artist. It was no more than a sketch, not designed to stand up to the close scrutiny to which Adeline now subjected it, and yet it clearly conveyed something vital and idiosyncratic about the old lady.

These things did not at that moment cheer Adeline, who was suddenly crestfallen.

'How depressing. I'd forgotten how rough it was.'

'You're standing much too close.'

Adeline took a couple of paces backwards. 'And it's not very flattering.'

'Old ladies neither expect nor deserve flattery,' said Sarah, quite sharply for her. 'You don't make me look a doddering wreck, either. I should say it was a very good likeness. And it's excellent of Timmy.'

Now Adeline, who was always easily cheered, had to laugh as she went back to her seat.

'I agree, it *is* excellent of Timmy– and you've made it look much better than it is, all round. Bless you, Gran! The first time I've been properly hung.'

'You make yourself sound like a brace of pheasant.'

The two of them giggled.

'I'd better go back,' said Adeline, 'and have my second breakfast, but thanks for the first one.'

'You're very welcome, always. It was a lovely start to my day,' said Sarah. As Adeline bent to kiss her, she caught her hand and, looking up into her face, added, 'You know I wish *I* was an artist. You have just the sort of face that I should like to be able to paint.'

'Away with you, Gran,' said Adeline. 'I'm never going to be a famous beauty, thank heavens.'

But even as she made this remark she remembered Louise's imperious stillness and Simon's passionate attention, and realized she didn't quite mean it.

She collected Beau from the back of the house and rode back a different way to Fording Place, along the wooded banks of the river. Though she was looking forward to the rest of the day, she half wished the ride home might last for ever.

To extend the journey, if only for a few minutes, she let the reins lie loosely on the pony's neck and allowed him to amble through the barred shadows at his own leisurely pace, a pace of which Elizabeth would have heartily disapproved.

'Ride him, don't just sit on him!' had been her frequent exhortation when Adeline was first learning to ride. She would have been horrified now to see Beau's head nodding low as a seaside donkey's, his feet striking only the gentlest rhythm on the loamy ground. In the still-sparse, rustling canopy above them birds twittered and fluttered about their springtime business, but down here it was like being on a cool green riverbed, like being one of the fat, gliding trout who lurked under the banks of the Tarr in summer.

Adeline rode astride (Elizabeth maintained it was the only way to learn) and she removed her feet from the stirrups and let them hang. They reached a place where the path widened and became a small clearing. Beau put his head down to graze and she did not pull him up, but held the reins loosely in one hand and leaned the other on the cantle of the saddle and sat quietly. About a hundred yards further on between the bronze-coloured beech trunks she could see the smooth sheen of the ford. Across it glided the cob swan, decorous but alert, now that the nest was built and his mate installed there.

'Addy!'

The shout was sharp and intrusive, from further up the hill amongst the trees. Beau raised his head, ears pricked, jaws still for a moment.

Adeline looked, but at first could see no-one.

'Yes? I'm here! Who wants me?'

'Addy, honestly, you are a pest!'

Adeline recognized it now, the voice of fraternal annoyance, of the emissary sent out against his will to look for the miscreant.

'What are you doing hanging about down there? Don't you know it's breakfast and no-one had any idea where you were?'

It was Bob, running awkwardly down the steep slope between the trees. He almost overbalanced and grabbed a branch to save himself.

'Look, shall I say you're coming? Will you get a move on?'

'Yes, I'm coming. I just went for a ride . . . sorry.'

'It's time you started thinking about other people for a

change!' barked Bob, and as he turned Adeline could see that there was someone else with him, coming down the hill as he went up, someone in a white shirt and pullover, and with fair hair which glinted in the patches of sunlight: Simon.

As the two of them met she caught snatches of conversation: '. . . infernal nuisance . . . anybody but herself . . .' from Bob, and '. . . see her back . . . I'd enjoy the walk... tell them we're on our way . . .' from Simon.

She could at once picture the scene. Frank still in bed, Bob furious at having to come after her, Simon the polite guest offering to accompany him and, now, her.

She slid her feet back into the stirrups and hauled Beau's head up from the grass. Simon ran down the hill, hands in pockets, gracefully balanced, limber and at ease where Bob had been stumbling and awkward.

'Good morning!' he called. 'And isn't it glorious? It might be July.'

'It is lovely,' she agreed, 'that's why I came out. Sorry if I've caused a panic.'

'Oh I wouldn't call it a panic as much as a ripple,' he said, patting Beau on the neck. 'But I'm famished, and you must be too, so let's get going. Which way's quickest?'

Adeline nodded in the direction of the way he'd come. 'Straight up there, but Beau would never do it. We'll have to follow the path to the end and then turn back.'

'Fair enough.'

They began to walk forwards, Simon's head about on a level with her hip. For the first time she felt a little self-conscious about her boyish riding breeches.

'I went to visit Gran,' she said.

'Oh yes? How is she? She's a terrific old girl.'

'She's coming on the picnic.'

'Good.'

They walked in silence past the ford, the swan a silent, scowling outrider to their right.

Then: 'Did you enjoy the dance?' she asked, lightly.

'Yes, it was fun. A very nice evening.'

She sensed a reservation. 'Did you dance with all the ladies?'

'Hardly!' He smiled a brief, frowning smile, without looking up. 'Just a select few.'

'And were they as light on their feet as Frank?' she added, to show she took none of it seriously. And was rewarded by his looking up and grinning at her.

'Good grief, no! In the Terpsichorean field your brother stands alone.'

Then, of course, they both saw the funny side of that remark and burst out laughing. Fatally emboldened, Adeline was moved to enquire:

'Simon – what did everyone say about me after I rushed out of the billiard room the other night?'

'I'm sorry?' he said, not, she knew, because he hadn't heard, but to gain a little time.

Already regretting it, she was forced to repeat the question.

'Nothing, that I recall,' he answered. The back of his neck was pink. Adeline realized all too well that it was the spectre of his humiliation she was raising, and not her own extravagant behaviour.

'I'm sorry,' she mumbled. 'I mean, I'm not really sorry about what I said, but I am sorry for making a scene –'

'That's all right, just shut up about it,' snapped Simon in such a cross, querulous, unguarded voice that she went hot and cold with shock.

'Sorry,' she said again, reflexively. And now his neck was red.

They went the rest of the way back in a strained and painful silence which Adeline only felt confident in breaking when the house was in sight.

'Thank you for coming with me,' she said, in a voice gone quite meek with embarrassment.

'Not at all. I enjoyed the walk,' he replied, without looking at her. And then added, moving away across the grass, 'See you at breakfast.'

Adeline kicked Beau into a trot and reflected miserably, as she rode back to the stables, that it was obviously not always a good thing to take someone's part, for it got you precious little thanks.

The picnic was a great success. Dorothy Sugden, out for a ride on her bicycle, came upon it as she pedalled round the shoulder of the hill that overhung Tarrford, and stopped to talk to Bryer who was unloading the hampers from the back of the car in the shade of the pines.

The picnickers were scattered about on the tussocky grass in the sunlight beyond the wood. Looking at them from a distance of some hundred yards, as she propped her bicycle against the bank of the lane, Dorothy was put in mind of people on a stage.

Richard, Frank and Simon were throwing a ball about and catching it, while Trigger and Mark bounded and cavorted between them. Bob patrolled at a little distance from the rest, hands in pockets, apparently scanning the ground for something. Sarah and Cynthia sat in chairs, talking; Adeline was on the ground near them, drawing, occasionally looking up at the women and then down again, assessing her work. On a big plaid rug to the right of the group lay Elizabeth, flat on her back with her ankles crossed, her hat over her eyes, a stalk of grass protruding vertically from her lips. Next to her sat Howard, leaning on one arm, the other resting loosely on his up-bent knee. Once or twice he glanced at her and flicked the tip of the grass with his forefinger, but she appeared not to notice. The horses – Beau, and Elizabeth's Tulah, and Richard's heavy hunter Magnus – were tethered in the background, grazing peacefully enough but in accordance with a well-established pecking order, so that if Beau's head strayed too close to Tulah's the peace was broken by a shrill whinny of objection and the click of large teeth.

'Just so long as I don't have anything to do with horses,' said Dorothy to Bryer.

Black was sitting on the running board of the motorcar, his cap next to him, his hair smeared on his pale forehead with the heat. He grinned up at her.

'The horse isn't born would give you any trouble, Nanny,' he teased. 'They wouldn't dare.'

Dorothy smiled. But Bryer sniffed.

'You'd have an easier time of it with horses than you do with young miss,' he remarked acidly.

'Adeline?' Dorothy looked fondly at her charge. 'We understand one another, don't you worry, Mr Bryer.'

'She's turning quite handsome, I'll say that for her,' said Black.

'She's growing up,' agreed Dorothy.

Bryer hauled an earthenware wine-cooler from the car and let it down with a bump on to the ground. 'Yes,' he said, 'she appears to be spreading in all directions without acquiring the manners of a lady.'

'That's because she isn't a lady yet, she's still a young girl. When the time comes she'll be as grand and stately as the next person I have no doubt.'

Black chuckled affably. 'You're old-fashioned, Mr Bryer.'

'I am, and proud of it.'

At this moment the ball rolled in their direction with Frank in pursuit. He burst upon the three of them like a creature from another planet, flushed, perspiring and dishevelled, his face wearing a huge smile intended to be apologetic but which actually expressed only his own *joie de vivre*.

'Whoops – !' He scooped up the ball at speed, steadied himself on the bonnet and threw it back. He turned to them, shining the grin on them like a spotlight.

'Didn't damage the food, did I?'

'No damage, sir,' said Bryer.

Frank's warm and sunny stare took in Dorothy. 'Hallo, Nanny. Are you going to join us?'

'No, not today. I was just riding into the village on my bicycle.'

'Splendid day for it!'

He ran back into the sun. Dorothy felt a cool wash of loneliness and regret lap over her as he did so.

She must have said goodbye, for she heard, as she

walked quickly away, the responses of Bryer and Black, but she didn't look round. And it was only when she was once more on her bicycle and pedalling along the road that she began to take great heaving gulps of breath as though she'd been drowning.

'Bryer!' It was Richard, his Panama hat on the back of his head, his tie around the waist of his flannels. 'Bryer, rustle up the pâté, there's a good fellow.'

The wine had been poured. Howard and Elizabeth had vacated the rug for chairs and Adeline and the young men had taken their place. Adeline had drunk a tankard of hock and water rather too quickly and was mildly euphoric. The dogs lay facing them in a sphinx-like attitude, their eyes narrowed to slits, their long tongue depending from smiling jaws.

In deference to Sarah, and the Charterises, Bryer had laid a small table with china, glass and silver, though Elizabeth generally scorned such arrangements as not being in the true spirit of a picnic. In the centre of the table Bryer now placed a pâté, marbled with grains of fat and garnished with watercress.

'What about shrotted pimps?' enquired Richard blandly. 'Do we have any of those?'

Elizabeth ignored this, handing food to her guests, but Howard scowled and cleared his throat with a roaring sound.

'We do have some, yes sir,' said Bryer, and returned to the car to fetch them.

'Good, they are absolutely my passion in life,' declared Richard.

'And what a blameless passion it is, my dear,' said Elizabeth.

'How are you, Mother? Have you got everything you want? Is there anything at all anyone can do for you?' asked Richard, but Sarah's answer was drowned as the potted shrimps arrived. 'Ah! A great delicacy, tuck in everyone.'

The younger people collected food and returned to the

rug. Trigger and Mark, with a nice appreciation of where the pickings were to be had, advanced closer to them. Adeline was almost perfectly happy. She felt herself to be in one of those bubbles of peace and harmony (which occurred a great deal less frequently these days) when her whole family and even, she was prepared to concede on this occasion, Howard and Cynthia, seemed at ease with one another. The gentle chink of glasses and cutlery, the desultory, sun-slowed conversation, the buzz and rustle of minute natural life responding to the unseasonal heat – all these things, allied to Simon's relaxed proximity, contributed to her happiness.

Bob dusted his palms. 'Let's have a look at your drawing, Addy,' he said.

'Yes,' said Frank, 'come on, don't be coy.'

'I wasn't. But it's nothing much.' She picked up her sketch pad and flipped the cover back to display the drawing of Cynthia and Sarah, a study in two hats having a conversation.

'It's a joke really,' she explained.

'It's good,' said Bob. 'Shows a bit of wit.'

Frank flopped backwards, his plate resting on his stomach. 'Too clever for me,' he mumbled.

Adeline put the pad away again but Simon stretched out an arm and retrieved it. 'Hang on, I didn't get a look.' She munched furiously as he studied the drawing, then he covered it and handed it back. 'I honestly don't know how you think of these things,' he said admiringly, 'let alone draw them, but then I'm a complete duffer at art.'

'Hear, hear,' said Frank and they began fooling about, pushing and shoving and laughing boisterously while Bob moved fastidiously a little further away.

In due course Bryer removed the remains of the pâté and potted shrimps and brought cold beef and veal and ham pie and pickles and salad, and more wine from the cooler.

'Would you like me to pour the wine, sir?'

'No, no, Bryer, we'll look after ourselves. You go and do the same,' said Richard.

'Thank you, sir.'

Bryer retreated into the shade and poured himself a tankard of light ale from the stone flask. Black, who had been reading a newspaper, lay down on the ground, folded his arms, and covered his face with the paper, thereby advertising his unwillingness to talk, which suited Bryer. From the picnic, voices rose a little higher, laughter was louder and more sustained. They were enjoying themselves.

As he drank his ale and ate a slice of pie, Bryer considered, not for the first time, seeking a new position. He wished to work somewhere more . . . dignified. To work, perhaps, for older people, the sort of people who set store by order and decorum. Working for the Gundrys played havoc with his nerves and he could scarcely believe he had borne it for ten years.

'This is the life!' he heard Richard say. 'What man could possibly want more than this, eh?'

There were compensations, thought Bryer, but were they enough? Only his fondness for Richard had kept him here this long. He was still in his early forties and would certainly get good references. He thought it might be pleasant to work in a town or, better still, in London, perhaps in a good hotel. There was nothing to do down here for a man of his tastes. His spare time was spent in his room, reading the society magazines which Mrs Gundry passed on to Cook, or very occasionally at the Theatre Royal in Exeter, or in one or other of the less salubrious city pubs where he would sit in a corner, neat and straight and sour-faced, and watch the goings-on. The beauties of the countryside were lost on him, it was all mud in the winter and dust in the summer and he suffered from hay fever. He didn't care for animals, either, and everywhere you went at Fording Place it seemed you tripped over a dog.

'Steady on, Lizzie,' cried Richard, 'you'll have the table over – !'

Bryer sighed. A gentleman's gentleman was what he was at heart, and Richard was a gentleman of boundless charm. It was just a pity about the rest of them.

Dorothy Sugden only looked in the mirror once a day, and that was when she was pinning her hair up and her cap in place first thing in the morning. Even had she been vain she had no time to indulge vanity, nor opportunity to express it. So it always came as something of a shock if she suddenly caught sight of her reflection during the normal course of events.

This she did while dismounting from her bicycle outside the post office stores in Tarrford. Clear and transparent against the stacked cartons and jars of the shop window she saw a square-shouldered, straight-backed, untidy-haired woman with a trim waist and a set jaw. Her straw hat was skewered in position a little crooked and her clothes and boots were serviceable rather than smart.

It was a moment of truth for Dorothy. In that instant she saw what others saw every day and presumably took for granted: a nanny. Somehow, without her noticing it, she had taken on the look of a woman tailor-made for the role of surrogate spinster aunt, with none of that relative's claims to attention or affection. And, what was more, a woman fast approaching the end of her usefulness in this particular family. Today's was the first picnic at which her attendance had not been required. 'Have some time to yourself, Nanny,' Mrs Gundry had said. 'You deserve it.' Well, yes, she did deserve it, but it was becoming increasingly less welcome. Time to herself simply reflected back at her, as the shop window did now, an image of herself she could not quite come to terms with.

The only family she had was her older brother, Michael, who ran a hardware business in north London and had a wife and two children. She saw very little of him, partly because as real spinster aunt she did not want to be a burden, and partly because she did not care to lose face, which she felt she must do when confronted with his domestic and commercial stature.

She would get another job, of course, very easily: there was always a place for a good nanny. Every few years she would move on, the children getting younger as she got older, until at last, if she was lucky, she would finish up with a family who would be prepared to keep her out of kindness, pensioning her off and maintaining her in some little upstairs room while she dwindled into her dotage surrounded by photographs and memorabilia.

Dorothy shivered. She was so preoccupied that when the reflection of a second figure appeared at her shoulder she failed to notice it until a voice said: 'Afternoon, Nanny. Penny for them?'

She turned sharply. Because of the highly personal nature of her thoughts prior to the interruption, she suspected she was blushing.

The speaker was Christopher Dance. He smiled at her and repeated his question.

'They weren't worth even half that,' she said briskly. 'I was daydreaming.'

'A daydreaming nanny? Sounds like a flying horse,' said Chris. He was a bachelor of forty-three, with little time for socializing, but he thought Dorothy Sugden the deuce of a handsome woman.

'We're only human, for heaven's sake,' she said now, quite sharply.

'Of course, of course. I didn't mean to sound rude.'

Dorothy now felt that perhaps she was the one who had been rude. She was more than a little flustered, and annoyed at herself for being so. Chris Dance was tall, and broad, with receding fair hair above a bluff and open face, and clear, light blue eyes. He was a countryman, of course, through and through, who would probably have laughed at her novels and her fantasizing, but there was no denying his manly good looks.

'What wonderful weather,' she observed, in a more conciliatory tone.

'Glorious, absolutely glorious,' he agreed, adding in his downright way: 'And treacherous too, at this time of year. Brings everything on and then we get sharp frosts and that does for them.'

'Thank goodness I don't have to look on it in that way,' said Dorothy.

'It's part of a farmer's job, I'm afraid. Have you got a day off then?'

'Yes, they're on a picnic by the top wood so I thought I'd cycle down and get a few things I needed.'

'And I mustn't delay you any longer,' said Chris Dance, standing aside a little too elaborately, as if he might be teasing her, and replacing his battered old corduroy cap.

In the face of this extreme politeness there was nothing Dorothy could do but say goodbye and go quickly into the shop. There she bought writing paper and envelopes and a quarter of Devon cream toffees to assuage her dissatisfaction with life.

The picnic had progressed through predictable stages of conviviality, enthusiastic eating, and more serious conversation and now entered a phase of warm, digestive torpor.

Sarah had fallen asleep in the smooth, orderly way of those who are used to catnapping. She sat upright in her chair, her hands resting on the arms, a little smile on her lips, her head only occasionally giving a nod forward, as though agreeing with someone in her dreams.

Cynthia, next to her in the shade which had crept further across the grass in the past hour, would not have slept even if she had been utterly exhausted, so ingrained was her habit of control. Instead she displayed that art she had perfected, of doing absolutely nothing as decoratively as possible while maintaining an air of gracious attention. No-one would have guessed that beneath her enchanting hat with its red and pink roses, and her immaculately coiffed pale brown hair, her head seethed with nagging doubts and anxieties. Her calm gaze rested first on her son, then on her husband, then moved to the horizon. Her worries were for Howard, for only she knew that he was by far the unhappier of the two. But she would never voice them – to him, to the others, even to herself – for fear of bringing down some terrible retribution on them all. Instead she kept them locked in the Pandora's Box of her head where they buzzed and proliferated in secrecy.

Richard, Howard and Elizabeth still sat round the table.

Richard had sunk down in his chair with his legs stretched out, his arms folded and his Panama over his eyes. But he was not asleep: his lips moved as he hummed a little tune. Elizabeth and Howard were still conversing in a desultory way, though Elizabeth suddenly laughed aloud, making it seem to everyone else that their exchange must be very fascinating and amusing.

When her mother laughed, Adeline glanced up, but it was Howard she looked at. Of all those present he looked the most affected by the unseasonal heat. A long diamond-shaped patch of sweat darkened the back of his white shirt, and his thick black hair clung in damp points to his neck and his forehead. His face, in profile to Adeline as he looked at her mother, appeared irritable, although he was smiling, and he held a knife in one hand, blade pointing vertically upwards, the handle of which he tap-tapped restlessly on the table-top.

Frank, who had been lying on his stomach with his face on his arms, suddenly jumped up.

'Come on, who's for a walk?'

Trigger and Mark were the first to respond to this suggestion, hurtling on to the rug in an ecstasy of enthusiasm, bringing the others to their feet as they careered amongst them.

'Good idea! Good dog, Trig! Good dog, Mark! We're going for a walk!' called Adeline. In answer Richard raised one hand, rippled the fingers, let it drop again.

The four of them – Frank, Adeline, Simon and Bob – moved away, taking with one unspoken accord the path that led to the Lookout Point.

The top wood marked the site of a Stone Age fort. A huge, robust, commanding structure it must have been, set on the shoulder of the hill and protected on all sides by a great ditch and a rampart. Beech and oak grew along the gnarled ridge of the fortification but now, and the central keep of the fort, which local historians said would have housed several hundred people, was now dominated by tall pines which even on this fine, still day sighed and whispered together high above the walkers' heads.

There had always been flint arrow and axe heads to be found here and now all four of them instinctively moved with bowed heads, scuffing the peaty ground with their feet in case of treasure. Beyond the fort on all sides the lush wooded slopes and chequered hills basked in the bright heat, but here there was a profound and secret hush, and the cool shade was only lightly speckled with sunlight. They reached their destination, the furthest and highest point of the fort.

There must, during the fort's prehistoric heyday, have been a watchtower of some sort here, for the ground rose sharply to a concave plateau like a giant armchair. Where there had once been walls there were now trees, so the Lookout Point, as they called it, afforded both a commanding view and complete seclusion. They stood encircled by the trees, just as the ancient tribal warriors must have done, and looked out over the broad, gentle valley, with the dolls' house roofs of Tarrford away to the right.

'Seems odd, doesn't it?' said Frank. 'To think of all the battles that must have started here.'

They had this conversation, or something like it, every time they came here, because they fell under the spell of the place afresh every time.

'Imagine all the dead bodies,' agreed Adeline. 'All the blood and bones that must be sunk into this hill, right under our feet while we're standing here. We ought to begin a proper excavation and see what we can find.'

'It takes literally years to excavate a site thoroughly,' said Bob, automatically correcting her excesses, but not too crushingly. 'You'd be bored in five minutes.'

'It does make you think about ghosts, though,' said Adeline.

'Correction, it makes *you* think about ghosts, Addy,' said Frank. 'You and your over-active artist's imagination.'

'No, she's right,' said Bob. 'After all, terrible events must leave some kind of mark, scars or echoes, on their surroundings. Most of these trees were fed and fertilized by death. We all feel it. We all talk softly when we come here. I don't think it's specially fanciful to talk about ghosts.'

Frank gave a sepulchral laugh and waved his arms, fingers clawed, over Adeline's head. 'Ha! Ha! Ha! I see a hideous old hag draped in a tattered sheet and baring her toothless gums at us, warning us of a ghastly fate . . .'

But he wasn't wholehearted in his ridicule of the idea, and he fell silent.

Simon, who'd hardly spoken a word, put his arm around Adeline's shoulders, but addressed Frank.

'You should know Addy better than that,' he said. 'It'd take a lot more than your capering about to frighten your sister.'

As compliments went it was hardly extravagant, and the manner of its delivery was oblique, but Adeline knew it for what it was and could have stood there for ever, bearing the mild yoke of his arm and savouring those words.

Bob shivered. 'I've got a feeling this weather's going to break.'

'Rubbish,' said Frank.

'There's a wind getting up,' pointed out Simon, his arm still round Adeline, who felt that nothing short of a typhoon could have spoiled her happiness.

It was true. A warm southerly breeze, from across the channel, made the banners of the pines wave and sough above their heads, its invisible hand trailing a wake of ripples on the surface of the hill beyond, bringing, with the tang of resin in the air, a whiff of premonition.

CHAPTER FOUR

1914

ONE DAY IN early October of that year, 1914, the same southerly breeze skipped and scampered across from France, this time carrying a breath of Indian summer on its back. Dorothy and Adeline had gone into Exeter by bus to buy the last remaining things on the list for St Agatha's, whither Adeline would be going in January – vests, stockings, over-knickers and so on. The major items of uniform had necessitated a trip to London with Elizabeth, a night at Brown's Hotel and an evening at the theatre with the Charterises, at Howard's expense.

In between the two trips, war had broken out. Dorothy and Adeline came upon the popular face of the war as they walked down Southern Hay, in the form of a long column of raw recruits in mufti, with bright perspiring faces beneath bowlers and boaters and caps, all beaming and absolutely chock full of confidence and enthusiasm and the adoring praise of the girls who lined the route.

At home, Adeline had been left in no doubt that the war was a thing which wrought changes in people. Richard was suddenly purposeful and energetic and Elizabeth roared about like a steam engine. When Frank had spoken gaily of having joined up with a crowd of other jolly fellows it was the closest Adeline had ever seen her mother come to being really angry. It was the anger she chose not to vent on Richard, who had done precisely the same thing, and who would no more have stayed at home than missed the 'Varsity match.'

Now, Adeline and Dorothy craned over the heads of other people to watch the marching men. Adeline's view was better than Dorothy's, for she was a good half-a-head taller.

'Surely they don't actually want to go to war, do they?' she asked, in the piercing, unguarded voice of a fourteen-year-old. 'Surely no-one *wants* to be shot at, or killed – or to kill anyone else for that matter?'

Dorothy, pink-faced in the grey wool coat she wore outdoors from September the thirtieth onwards, laid a restraining hand on her arm.

'I don't suppose they're thinking about any of that,' she said. 'They're just full of the excitement of it all.'

Adeline heard the bright, clashing, thumping music playing 'There's Something About a Soldier'. But unbidden at the same time came a memory of the Lookout Point, and the tall dark trees that grew in a tilt of death, and the black-green banners of dry pine needles waving slowly as the breeze arose.

'But they're all smiling,' she said in a hard, defiant voice, 'and they're probably going to die. They must be mad!'

'Ssh!' said Dorothy automatically, but too late. A squat, choleric man with a crimson neck that folded down over his stiff collar turned and fixed bulging eyes on Adeline.

'Was it you said that, young lady? My word, I'm surprised at you. Those are brave, patriotic lads preparing to defend people like you.'

'And you,' snapped Adeline, who was not against the occasional low punch.

'We're on our way,' said Dorothy. 'Come along, Adeline.'

'Just a minute,' said the man, in a tone that was sufficiently nasty to turn a few heads and assure him of an audience, 'just a minute, miss. Don't you think that if I were young enough and fit enough I should be out there marching with the rest of them? Eh?'

'I really have no idea,' replied Adeline, resisting Dorothy's sharp tug on her sleeve. 'It's none of my business.'

'That's true!' The man looked round at his audience. 'That's certainly true! And let me just tell you something. Young ladies with no experience of life should keep their little opinions to themselves.'

'I'm sorry. Adeline, that will do,' said Dorothy. As the band and the marchers receded, so the audience for this small but piquant confrontation was growing.

The man turned his attention to Dorothy.

'Are you her sister, by any chance?'

'No – '

'She's just a friend,' put in Adeline firmly.

'Well if I were you,' the man went on, keeping his eyes on Dorothy's face, 'I should give her a piece of your mind. You look like a sensible sort of person, you tell her what's what. There are wives and mothers standing in this street who have waved their boys off to France so that England can do her duty, you – ' He pointed a stubby forefinger at Adeline. 'Should remember that.'

'I don't need reminding,' began Adeline. 'My father – '

'That will do, Adeline!'

This time Dorothy was not to be trifled with. She clasped Adeline's upper arm in a vice-like grip, gave her such a yank that she nearly overbalanced, and led her away. As they went, they could hear the fat man's voice, continuing to hold forth.

They turned into one of the small roads leading to the cathedral close. Dorothy stopped and pulled Adeline round to face her.

'Adeline! How could you?'

'I don't see why someone like that should have it all his own way.'

'But arguing in the street, with a man of his age – '

'I don't see what his age has got to do with it.'

'You may not, but believe me everyone else did. It just looked thoroughly rude and ill-bred.'

Dorothy's face with blotchy with agitation. Adeline felt some small stirrings of remorse.

'I'm sorry, Nanny. I didn't mean to embarrass you.'

'My feelings have got nothing to do with it. It's a question of decent, dignified behaviour.'

'Dignified? Oh, *Nanny* – !' Adeline let out a quite involuntary burst of laughter which she instantly brought under control when she saw Dorothy's expression. 'It's not as if anyone knew who we were. Or as if it *mattered* who we were.'

'*You* know, Adeline. It should matter to you.'

'Well I'm sorry, I said I was sorry. But it doesn't matter to me, and I wasn't going to let that horrible – '

'That's enough answering back! Come!'

Dorothy made off along the street at a furious rate. Adeline half expected to see her black shoes strike sparks from the pavement. She had never seen Dorothy so cross, it was quite unprecedented. She ran after her and fell into a step beside her. They continued in silence.

The uncomfortable atmosphere persisted during the selection and purchasing of the necessary items of clothing. Adeline refrained from even a token complaint about the hideous bloomers and the thick, uncompromising black wool stockings, and the whole operation was completed inside three quarters of an hour.

Adeline was perplexed. The last thing she wanted to do was to be on bad terms with Dorothy when they were to be parted soon anyway. She could see, with hindsight, that she had been a little forward, but just the same it wasn't like Dorothy to harbour annoyance for more than a few minutes. She was a cheerful, ungrudging person. Adeline was forced to the conclusion that there was more cause for this uncharacteristic behaviour than simply her own small lapse.

A slight thaw was indicated as they emerged from the

shop into the sunshine and Dorothy suggested a cup of tea.

'Yes, lovely,' agreed Adeline warmly. 'We could go to the place in the close.'

They sat at a table in the bay window and the waitress brought scones and strawberry jam and iced currant buns. Some distance away on the far side of the close the recruiting officer plied his trade, a salutory reminder both of recent misdemeanours and larger, more ominous events.

'Well, we got everything,' said Dorothy, stirring her tea. This small fluttering of the olive branch prompted Adeline to try again.

'I'm awfully sorry about – earlier on, Nanny.'

'Very well. Let's forget it, shall we?'

'Yes, only . . .' Adeline peered into her face, inscrutable as she stared out of the window. 'Am I forgiven?'

Dorothy put down her cup and looked Adeline straight in the eye. Adeline noticed, with an acute sense of embarrassment and shame, that she was upset. But she pushed the buns in Adeline's direction in a conciliatory gesture.

'Here, have another. I don't want one.'

'Thanks. Why am I always so hungry?'

'Because you're a growing girl.'

Adeline took a mouthful. Dorothy watched her for a moment, with returning fondness, and then looked back out of the window.

She said: 'I don't like the idea of your father going off to war any more than you do. Or Frank – he doesn't seem much more than a boy to me. All of you, you're like my family in a way. To be going on with,' she added more stringently. 'But I'm glad they've got the courage to go, that's all.'

Adeline thought about Frank, whom Dorothy had always seemed to be either spoiling or scolding, and realized that for Frank to go to war took very little courage. But this conclusion led her inevitably to consideration of Simon, whom she had not seen all summer. What would *he* do?

She put down what was left of the bun and pushed it away.

'I don't want any more,' she said. 'Let's go home, shall we?'

Not long after this, only a week before Richard (with what Elizabeth clearly considered to be indecent haste) was due to join his unit at Barnstaple, Sarah Gundry died. She had apparently suffered a massive heart attack whilst walking Timmy in the lane outside the Dower House. The dog, unlike those immortalized in popular fiction, did not dash back to the house for help, but bustled off happily into the woods on a rabbiting spree, not returning till some time after Kathleen had acted on her suspicions and found Sarah's recumbent form in the road. What bothered Kathleen most, as she confided to Adeline, was that old Mrs Gundry's skirt had become ensnared as she fell.

'It was up above her head, you could see everything, and she was always so pretty and smart . . . it was enough to make you weep – ' And she very nearly did, standing in the hall of the Dower House on the morning of the funeral, duster in hand, engaged in a ritual suddenly deprived of all purpose and meaning.

Adeline said helplessly: 'But she didn't know that, did she? Besides, you were the one to find her, so no-one else saw . . .' But she was very close to tears herself and her reassuring remarks died on her lips. She had been sent over to tell Kathleen that a car would collect her and take her to the parish church that afternoon. Adeline had borne up well so far, boosted by her father's constant reminder that Sarah had had a 'jolly good innings': but here, in the house which still seemed so full of her grandmother, and confronted by Kathleen's honest, red-nosed grief, it was very hard to bear. Timmy, silent and trembling, pined in his basket by the window.

'I don't know what to do with him, miss,' said Kathleen. 'He's that miserable.'

'We'll think of something, don't worry,' said Adeline,

'if you don't mind looking after him just a little while longer.'

In fact she had heard Elizabeth say that it would be best if Timmy remained where he was for the moment to give Kathleen 'something to look after' as she put it. But if ever a dog appeared to have turned his face to the wall, it was Timmy at this moment.

'I expect he'll perk up,' she said without conviction.

'I hope so, miss, I do hope so . . .' replied Kathleen and flew back down the hall to the kitchen, the door closing on a great, tearing sob.

The Indian summer had continued, a warm sun poured in through the window where Sarah had liked to sit and eat her early breakfast. Adeline sat in the window seat and bent to stroke Timmy's tense, shuddering back, as much for her own comfort as his. The time that she had sat here in April and talked about the picnic seemed years, not months ago. So much had happened, so much had changed. She felt a dreadful, desolating loneliness, and a sudden dread of going away to school, something to which until now she'd been looking forward. Her grandmother was dead, by January Richard and Frank would have left for France, Dorothy would be gone – when she, Adeline, went too there would be only Elizabeth left to keep everything going. She worried in case she were to return in the spring holidays and find that nothing remained of her former life. She realized, now that it seemed about to end, how happy that life had been, how much she had taken for granted, how little she knew of even the smallest and most everyday suffering.

Resisting the temptation simply to put her head down on the window seat and cry, she got up and took her drawing of Sarah from the wall. Then she went through to the kitchen, where Kathleen was scrubbing the table with fierce concentration.

'Goodbye, Kathleen. They'll be here to collect you at half past two.'

'Very well, miss.'

'I've taken this.' She indicated the picture. 'I don't think Gran would have minded.'

'I'm sure she wouldn't. Goodbye, miss.'

The funeral was well attended. The parish church of St Mark's, Tarrford, was packed. As well as Elizabeth's parents, the Lindsay-Smyths, there were the Charterises, the Armitages, the Hyde-Latimers, the Vales and a fair proportion of the county set. There was also a large contingent from Tarrford itself, old people who could remember when Sarah and Marcus Gundry were at Fording Place, and younger ones, shopkeepers and farmworkers, who had a good reason to be thankful for her generosity, and who simply liked her for the good-natured lady she was. Perhaps, too, there was a feeling abroad that the old order was changing, that the heart and youth were being sucked out of the village by the demands of war, and that Sarah had represented all that was pleasing and stable about the peace that had gone.

The staff from both houses, including Kathleen and Collings, sat in the pews beyond the side aisle. Chris Dance sat down next to Dorothy, his hat in his hands.

'A sad day,' he whispered loudly.

'Very sad,' agreed Dorothy.

Having regard to the seriousness of the occasion, Chris had to be content with that, though he would have liked to compliment Dorothy on her black straw hat with its grosgrain ribbon. Just as well he did not, for the hat was part of Dorothy's uniform for 'best', and was not what she would have chosen herself given the chance.

Adeline stood between her parents and her brothers in the front row when the coffin was carried in on the long black bier and set just below the chancel steps. She no longer felt that she would cry: there was nothing here to remind her of her grandmother, but she was very exercised in case either of her parents should do so. Elizabeth looked unusually proud and stately in full mourning, but Richard appeared slightly smaller, as though the worries and obligations of recent months had compressed him under their weight.

Frank wore his uniform, for he was already at a training camp near Dorchester and not even the obligatory gloom of the funeral could prevent him giving off warm waves of excitement. Frank alone, among all the men there, was the man of the moment, and he knew it. And Bob, as if he was conscious of this, allowed an appreciable space between himself and his brother on the pew.

They sang the first hymn and Adeline glanced sideways at her mother and father. Richard pulled his shoulders back and sang: 'O enter then His gates with praise' clearly and tunefully while Elizabeth, who was tone deaf, mouthed the words behind her smoky veil. When Adeline looked the other way, at Frank, he met her gaze and smiled at her encouragingly, but she quickly returned her gaze to the hymn book.

When they knelt to pray she was able, by resting her head rather sideways on her clasped hands, to see the Charterises at the far end of the pew immediately behind them. Howard remained seated, staring down at his large hands resting on his knees. When he fidgeted restlessly and looked up at the window, the soft rainbow of light illuminated his customary intent glare.

Adeline was surprised to see that Cynthia was weeping. A wisp of lace hanky showed between her gloved fingers, and her cheek glistened. Only Simon seemed completely absorbed in the service, his eyes closed and his lips moving dutifully, if uncertainly, with the responses.

When they went out into the churchyard for the burial, the warmth and light seemed to fall on them like a cloak. The sun beat on their backs and reflected dazzlingly off the rector's surplice. The coffin bearers were red-faced and streaming with sweat by the time they lowered their burden, bit by bit, jerking slightly, into the narrow hole.

Watching the small box descend with a bump, out of the balmy sunlight and warmth and into that dark ochre, fibrous, cold, domain of worms, Adeline felt a sudden sharp pulse of revulsion. It was impossible to believe that

Sarah's spirit – such a genial and ordered spirit in life – could conceivably fight its way up from that dark incarceration into any kind of afterlife, no matter what the rector said. It would be choked by the heavy red earth, and forgotten, too.

When a voice said 'Don't', quite clearly, she scarcely realized it was hers until she felt Elizabeth's hand on her shoulder.

'Addy, are you all right?'

'Will they bury it while we're still here?' she whispered.

'No, after we've gone. Now shush.'

Adeline swallowed hard on the lump that had risen in her throat, and blinked rapidly to dispel a stinging rush of tears. Standing opposite her, on the far side of the horrible hold, Simon gave a little smile, and lifted his chin slightly in the direction of the pile of rich red Devon earth that lay at the foot of the grave. She looked, and saw a wagtail, trim and clerical, who had found something in the soil and was picking at it furiously. Watching kept Adeline's eyes dry, her lips steady and her mind occupied during the remainder of the service.

When they left the graveside a few minutes later, Simon came over to her.

'I say, Addy.'

She looked up at him. 'Hallo. Thank you for pointing out the little bird. You saved my life.'

He blushed slightly. His skin was so fair that every emotion coloured it, like breath on a mirror.

'I'm awfully sorry about your grandmother, I know how fond you were of her.'

'Well –' She struggled for something appropriate to say, and resorted to Richard's: 'Well, she had a good innings.'

'Yes, she did, and a very happy one.'

They were all walking towards the gate that led into the road. Some local people who had not come to the church stood outside, bareheaded and respectful, greeting Richard and Elizabeth with solemn nods.

'Are you coming back for tea?' asked Adeline.

'I believe we're staying for a couple of nights. You know how it is with your parents and mine.'

Adeline was not entirely sure that she did know, but she nodded sagely. Frank stood near the gate talking to Anne Hyde-Latimer and the sight of his uniform prompted Adeline to ask, in a voice gone high and brittle with affected unconcern:

'Will you be joining up?'

'I should say so, and the sooner the better.'

'You sound awfully keen.'

'Well, that's because I am, in a way.'

Adeline looked covertly at him as he walked beside her, at his pale, set face and his soft, uncertain mouth, and wondered how that could possibly be.

'You don't have to, surely,' she said.

He put out his hand and gave hers a quick squeeze. 'I think I do, actually,' he said, 'but it's sweet of you to worry about me, Addy.'

Adeline's heart swelled and beat like a young bird trying out its wings. She had to agree with Simon: worrying about him was the sweetest thing in her life.

They all went back to Fording Place for tea. By four o'clock the October sun was westering, but even so it was still hot, faces were pink and shiny above heavy dark clothes, the brims of hats were surreptitiously lifted to enable a little air to reach scalps crawling with sweat.

In the hall and the drawing room, where the funeral guests milled about, it was cooler. Bryer and the parlour-maid, Mabel, presided over a long white-clothed table covered with plates of sandwiches and cakes, with two huge teapots steaming at one end and jugs of lemonade at the other.

The gathering soon broke down perfectly good-natur-edly into its component parts, with family and close friends, once furnished with tea, in the drawing room, and the rest remaining in the hall. After a slight initial shyness about the food, the Tarrford contingent, reassured that eating denoted no disrespect, fell on the refreshments, and the noise level rose perceptibly to a genial hubbub. Richard, Elizabeth and Frank circulated among the guests, but when Adeline took her lemonade outside on to the drive she found Bob, mooching as usual, sitting on the bank, his discarded jacket on the grass beside him.

'Do you want some lemonade?' she asked. 'Or food? There's masses.'

'No thanks, just fresh air. I couldn't breathe in there.'

'I'm glad it's over.'

'And me. All that best-bib-and-tucker piety sticks in my craw. And Frank acting the lord of creation in his bloody uniform.'

So that was it. Adeline's face burned with shame on Bob's behalf, and if she could have wished the clock back sixty seconds, with those words unsaid, she would have done so. With one sentence Bob had shown how insubstantial was the polite, grown-up veneer of the past two or three years.

She crouched down by him. 'Don't say that. He's not trying to . . . he doesn't mean anything.'

'I know *that*.' He shook his head at her as though shaking a fist. 'I know that perfectly well. I don't suppose Frank has ever meant anything in his entire life. It's all that effortless superiority that gets me down. Unworthy, I know, but there we are.'

'You're much cleverer than he is,' ventured Adeline.

'I know that too.' Bob's voice had suddenly lost its edge, and was gentler, as though he were tired of nursing his anger. 'But it doesn't make the slightest difference, that's the devil of it.'

'No.' Adeline entertained a fleeting mental picture of Louise Vale, as she had seen her the night of the dance. Of course she understood, and all too well.

'Come on, this won't do!' Bob got to his feet, his weak leg making him stagger slightly on the slope. 'Pass my jacket, Addy, would you? I must return to the fray.'

Relieved that the mood had passed, Adeline handed him the jacket. She was still clutching the now rather warm lemonade, and took a great gulping draught of it. Bob, shrugging his jacket on, gave a dry little laugh.

'Thirsty work, diplomacy,' he said.

By six o'clock everyone had gone, including the over-wrought Kathleen and the grand Lindsay-Smyths. In the drawing room there followed a loosening of ties and discernible relaxing of formalities.

Elizabeth, of course, gave voice to the general feeling as she lit a cigarette.

'We all know your mother would simply have hated everyone to be too glum!' she cried merrily to Richard, but addressing the company at large. 'And yet one has to appear suitably dismal in order to impress everyone else. It's too silly, but needs must . . . !'

Bryer arrived with the sherry decanter. Drinks were poured, and Bob, muttering some excuse, absented himself. Simon and Frank stood together near the window and Adeline sat on a footstool picking up snatches of their conversation. She dreaded hearing talk of Simon's joining up, but was no less dismayed to realize that they were discussing Louise Vale.

'She even manages to look devastating in black,' Simon was saying. 'She's quite the prettiest girl I know, but the trouble with creatures like her is that most of us common or garden fellows don't stand a chance.'

'I shouldn't lose any sleep over it,' replied Frank. 'If you want my opinion, she's a cold fish.'

Adeline, staring intently at the pattern on the carpet, warmed mightily to her brother. But before she could hear whether or not Simon was going to argue with him, Richard's feet appeared next to her.

'Well Addy,' he said. 'Time to run along.'

'Do I have to?' She looked up at him imploringly, but she could see Dorothy standing in the doorway, back to normal in her grey dress and white apron.

'Yes, Nanny's here.'

'It makes me feel like an infant, being sent off like this,' she whispered fiercely. Howard, who was sitting on the end of the sofa nearest her, transferred his cigar to his other hand and reached out to touch her hair.

'Come on, Dick,' he said, 'let her stay, for God's sake. She's practically a young lady these days!'

Adeline, looking up at her father, saw him hesitate at the same time as she felt the hated hand on her head. There was only one thing she wanted less than to be packed off, and that was to stay here, in Howard's debt.

She sprang to her feet, slipping sideways to escape his touch.

'It's all right. I'll go.'

'That's my girl. You don't want to sit about with us really. Come down and say goodnight a bit later, yes?'

'Yes.'

She left the room, hearing their voices sending her on her way with that note of affectionate relief that always accompanied the departure of children from the room. But as she closed the door behind her she caught Simon's eye and he blew her a small, light kiss.

'It's ridiculous,' she said, going up the stairs after Dorothy, 'being banished to the nursery at my age.'

Unseen by Adeline, Dorothy fought with a smile. 'There's not a great deal of banishing in this house, believe me. In Mr and Mrs Forsyth's house, Helen and Patrick only saw their parents for an hour each day after tea.'

This was one of Dorothy's trump cards, but it had lost some value by being played too frequently.

'But I'm fourteen, Nanny!'

'And don't we all know it?' replied Dorothy caustically, opening the nursery door. 'Methuselah, I must say. Now why don't you change out of that stiff smart dress into your blue and we'll lay up in here for a cosy supper?'

In spite of herself, Adeline found the familiar, well-worn comfort of the nursery and the prospect of a gossipy meal before the fire quite welcome. The term 'teenager' would not be coined for another forty years, but the raging biological storm was no easier to bear just because one had to remain to all intents and purposes a child, until the magical day when skirts went down and hair up and one emerged, overnight, as a woman. At present, Adeline's day was chequered by abrupt and apparently arbitrary changes from little girl to grown-up and back again. She was baffled and exhausted by them, and the nursery to which she had so vociferously objected was at least a safe haven where she was accepted lock, stock and barrel for what she was, and where small harmless rules fenced her in, protecting her from her own unpredictability.

Miss Purgavey, displaying her preternatural under-standing of the soothing and comforting qualities of food, did them proud, with cottage pie and buttered carrots, and blackberry and apple tart with cream to follow. When Mabel came to collect the things, Dorothy said: 'I can't believe they will have eaten any better downstairs than we have tonight.'

Mabel, a cottage-loaf-shaped Tarrford lass, pulled a face. 'Not near so good if you ask me, Nanny. All cold bits, chicken in jelly and that.'

'Chicken in aspic, ugh, I loathe it,' said Adeline. 'But tell Old – Miss Purgavey – that ours was scrumptious.'

'I'll certainly do that, miss. You got good appetites you two, I'll say that!'

Adeline waited for Dorothy to say 'She's a growing girl' but surprisingly she didn't, on this occasion. Instead she simply told Mabel to thank Cook, and put her hands on her waist as though reassuring herself that it was no thicker than it had been half an hour before.

The clear, metallic, early autumn dusk had given way to a chilly evening, and after supper Dorothy put a match to the coal fire in the narrow, black-leaded grate. Adeline sat on the hearthrug and watched the flames take hold. Dorothy got out the knitting, which was her practical response to the outbreak of hostilities across the channel.

'Do you want to get on with yours?' she asked Adeline. 'I've sorted it out for you.'

'I suppose I might as well.'

There again, Adeline was no great knitter, but it was comforting to work away at the uneven red scarf she had begun two weeks before, with Dorothy's brisker clicking in the background, and the heat from the grate making her cheeks and forehead glow. This small domestic activity, for which she had no aptitude, was at least free from the burden of other people's expectations, or even her own.

Dorothy glanced over at her.

'One thing I hope they do at this school of yours,' she remarked drily, 'is teach you some decent needlework.'

'I don't think they will,' said Adeline. 'It isn't that kind of school. They're much keener on science, and the classics.'

'It's a funny thing,' mused Dorothy, 'that school-teachers should have this idea that a bit of Latin will make a woman independent. Young women of your background can never be independent while they can't peel a potato or darn a sock, it seems to me.'

Adeline had to allow the logic of this observation.

'Yes, that's true. But you see if one wants a job, one needs a proper education and some qualifications, and peeling potatoes and darning socks wouldn't really fit the bill.'

Dorothy finished a row and changed her needles from hand to hand. 'You've got an answer for everything, haven't you?'

'No. I only wish I had.'

'What sort of job would you like, then? One like mine?'

Adeline knew she was being put on the spot.

'I don't know yet. I suppose I'd like to be an artist.'

'And I'd like to be Queen. That's not a job.'

'It's a calling.' Adeline, pleased with this, gave Dorothy a delighted, challenging smile. 'Something one does because one has to.'

'Like young men going to war, I suppose,' retaliated Dorothy.

'Yes, in a way, except it wouldn't be a duty, it would be a pleasure.'

'I think,' said Dorothy, laying down the knitting for a moment, 'that you should do your best to be whatever you want to be. There's no sense in settling for second best.' She knew that she herself had done exactly that, but this was said without rancour. She had had no choice: Adeline had one. She went on:

'I can see you as an artist. You're certainly not cut out to be anything else.'

'Nanny!' Adeline affected shock. 'I might be an extremely fashionable society hostess.'

'Pigs might fly,' said Dorothy.

After a while they abandoned the knitting and played Racing Demon and Pelmanism, and Dorothy did some of her card tricks. All the tricks were familiar to Adeline, who had admired them for as long as she could remember. They were Dorothy's only legacy of her own family life, and she'd had the good sense not to initiate her charges into their mysteries, so they retained a certain sparkle.

Then Dorothy announced that she must write to her brother (perhaps reminded by the card tricks) and Adeline, at a loose end, remembered Richard's invitation to go down and say goodnight.

'May I go then?' she asked Dorothy.

'Yes, but not too long now, it's late,' Dorothy was immersed in composition.

'I know.' Adeline went out of the nursery and closed the door behind her. The nursery, her bedroom, Dorothy's bedroom and the bathroom which they shared, were linked by communicating doors. Only the main nursery door opened on to the small second floor landing outside.

Everything about the landing marked it out as the boundary of a separate preserve. The banisters were painted white. The boards that showed on either side of the strip of carpet were not polished, as elsewhere, for fear of children (or nannies) breaking their legs. The carpet itself had once (Frank told Adeline, she had never seen it) been a pink and blue pattern of interlinking diamond shapes, but had now faded to a uniform dusty mauve, with parts of it so threadbare that the woven backing showed through. The walls were papered with a riot of floribunda roses which Elizabeth would never have countenanced elsewhere, and against this unlikely background, at regular intervals, were pictures of local fauna. There were herons, foxes, pheasants, stoats, hares and rabbits, all of them apparent posing for their portraits, and looking as if butter wouldn't melt in their mouths. It had always struck Adeline as odd that the nursery landing should be decorated with paintings of creatures many of which half the county pursued and killed.

There was a distinctive smell, too, about this corner of the house: a smell of good plain soap, and linen airing on the clothes horse, and carbonization from night lights and toast made before the open fire.

The white-painted banisters outlined the route down to the first floor landing and the adult world. Halfway along the top landing, the decorations changed to rather more sober cream and brown paintwork, and at the far end was the door to the back staircase, via which Mabel brought up the small brass coal scuttle morning and evening in the winter, and trays with nursery meals at regular intervals all year round. At the junction of staff and nursery quarters, for as long as Adeline could remember, there had stood a pale blue Lloyd loom chair and a wood and wicker table. On the table was a much-laundered linen runner decorated with lazy-daisies, and on top of the runner there lay a pile of dull but commendable children's books. To Adeline's knowledge, no-one had ever sat in the chair, nor read any of the improving books, but once a week, when she dusted, Mabel would put the top book to the bottom, for variety's sake.

Now Adeline followed the white banisters down the

first flight of stairs on to the first floor landing. Here, everything was different, as one might expect. The carpet was thick and brightly coloured, the walls were papered in a bold, broad stripe, and the pictures were mostly of sleek racehorses (Elizabeth's weakness) or glassy-eyed Gundry antecedents in landscapes where it seemed perpetually to be about to thunder. A few glossy, solid pieces of good English furniture stood about – a carved chest, an oak table on which stood an enormous Chinese pot full of potpourri, twin chairs with gold brocade seats and squat, curving legs. A scent hung in the air, the scent of the potpourri, and of ladies' clothes, and lavender. A trace of tobacco, Adeline noticed on this occasion, and when she looked over the balustrade into the hall there was Howard. He seemed to have followed her mother out of the drawing room, for she was there too, standing in the middle of the hall, looking back over her shoulder at him. Howard was holding the drawing room door to behind his back, but as she watched, he closed it and took a step forward.

'Allow me to help,' he said.

Elizabeth laughed teasingly. 'Don't be silly, I don't need any help. I know exactly where it is and I can manage perfectly well.'

'Just the same, I'd like to be of some assistance,' repeated Howard.

'Oh very well.' Elizabeth began moving away rapidly down the passage in the direction of the Snug, out of sight, but her voice floated back gaily. 'Come if you must, but put that thing out or you'll burn the place down, it's stuffed full of papers . . .'

Howard cast about for an ashtray, failed to find one, and stubbed out his cigar in the soil of the potted palm that stood near the door. Then he gave the points of his waistcoat a tug, and followed. Adeline heard her mother's voice again, and then a door closed, and she could only hear the muffled sound of conversation from the drawing room.

As she went down the second, curving flight of stairs

Adeline considered, briefly, two things. One was that it was a rare, even an unprecedented thing for her mother to be going into the Snug, let alone accompanied by Howard. The second was that she was conscious of having heard two exchanges, one with her ears and the other with her imagination. What Howard and Elizabeth had said was not what they had been talking about.

But these were only quick, glancing thoughts. Bursting with curiosity she determined to go the Snug first, to say good night to Elizabeth. She loved her mother best in the evening, when she had changed, as now, into evening clothes, and when she seemed softer, prettier, happier, than at any other time. Even after the depressing events of the day there had been something sparkling in Elizabeth's manner which drew Adeline like a moth to a flame.

More from habit than any sense of impending disaster, she walked quietly along the corridor, and paused for a second outside the door. As she stood there the handle turned and the door opened quickly, but only a few inches, as though someone had been about to come out. Startled, Adeline stepped back, expecting whoever it was to emerge, and perhaps nearly tread on her. But no-one did, and in the brief moment that she stood looking in she caught a glimpse of both of them, her mother and Howard, without herself being seen.

It happened so quickly, was over so soon, that later when she tried to remember she could scarcely rehearse it in her mind. It had been Elizabeth's hand on the door, in her other arm she held a large book. She was arrested in the act of leaving the room by Howard, whose arm, black in evening dress, was around her waist, and whose dark face was buried in her pale shoulder. Elizabeth's head was tilted back, her eyes closed, her lips smiling. But – and this was what Adeline could, and did, remember most clearly for the rest of her life – as Howard released Elizabeth and lifted his head, his eyes looked straight into hers as she stood there, an unwilling spy, in the dark corridor.

That was all. He showed no sign either of anger or anxiety and within seconds he had turned off the light and held the door wide for Elizabeth to go through, standing aside, then closing it after them. Perhaps he remained a little too long with his back to Adeline as he shut the door, making a business of testing the handle, but when he turned he put his hands in his pockets and smiled his usual scowling smile.

Elizabeth was carefree, knew nothing.

'Adeline! Hallo my darling, what brings you down here?'

'I just came to say good night.'

'And so you shall.' Elizabeth put her free arm across Adeline's shoulders and ushered her in the direction of the drawing room. 'We were talking about family matters,' she explained, 'and I told Richard his father had kept a family tree in the front of this Bible. Your father, of course, didn't believe me – just like him not to know! – ' (here she cast a smiling look over her shoulder at Howard) ' – so I said I'd show him, and here it is.' She tapped the enormous book.

'Here, let me take it for you now,' said Howard, and did so, moving quickly ahead of them to open the drawing room door. His composure gave Adeline a curious sense of dislocation. Had she really seen anything? And if so, what was it she had seen? The shock and outrage she had felt at that moment had been smoothly bounced back at her as if from the glass of a mirror, and her mother's sunny mood utterly precluded questions of an awkward and sensitive nature. Besides, here were all the others, sitting round in the drawing room, turning expectant faces as they entered.

'Here we are!' cried Elizabeth, releasing Adeline, and bringing forward Howard with the book. 'Give it to him, Howard.' Howard placed the Bible on Richard's knees. 'It's all there on the first page, it was right under your nose in the Snug all the time!'

Richard opened the Bible. Bob and Elizabeth went to look over his shoulder. Howard went to sit by Cynthia, brushing vigorously at the pale dust left on his coat and trousers by the book. Frank and Simon, who were still together near the window, looked across and then went on talking.

'Oh, yes . . .' Richard scanned the spidery black writing, the angular coathangers of lines, that covered the flyleaf of the Bible. 'Yes, here we are . . .'

Bob, leaning on the back of the chair, pointed. 'It's not up to date. Adeline's not here at all.'

'That reminds me!' Elizabeth caught Adeline by the hand. 'Say good-night, Addy, and run along. It's late.'

Richard glanced up with a look of pleased surprise. 'My favourite girl? Come on and give your aged pater a kiss.'

'And you'll have to put in the date of Gran's death,' added Bob, still absorbed in the tree. Richard set it aside, and invited Adeline into the curve of his outstretched arm.

She flew into his embrace, her arms round his neck, her face pressed into his collar to stifle the tears which threatened, with alarming suddenness, to overwhelm her. Her father seemed so innocent, so guileless sitting there, his pleasure in seeing her was always so open, his love so enveloping and unconditional. She remembered that he, too, was going to France, and she was afflicted by that same presentiment of loneliness which she had experienced in her grandmother's house that morning.

She wanted to say so much, but the others were all around, and all she could manage, somewhat broken-backed against the rising tide of sobs, was: 'Don't go!' He patted her back, stroked her hair, tried to prise her face from his neck so that he could kiss her, but she was locked on to him by her inarticulate distress. She heard voices above and around her, murmurs of 'Poor child . . .' and 'It's been a long day . . . too much . . . the funeral . . .' Then she felt Elizabeth's hands on her, exerting a gentle pressure, pulling her back, and she was obliged to stand, her wretchedness revealed in front of everyone.

'Poor little Addy,' said Richard, getting up too, and so helping to shield her from all those curious, sympathetic eyes. 'You mustn't upset yourself like this.'

'She's simply had enough,' said Elizabeth to him, over Adeline's head. 'She's tired out.'

Adeline had neither the will nor the words to dispute this. Let them think whatever they wanted, it was simpler.

Wanting only to escape, she pulled away from her parents and made for the door, hearing the chorus of 'Good-nights' and comforting endearments following her.

She was at the foot of the stairs before she realized someone had followed her.

'Adeline!'

She hesitated, fatally. In two or three quick strides Howard caught up with her.

'Hey, not so fast.'

She stood still, but she wouldn't turn or look at him, wouldn't show him her blotched, flushed, tear-stained face. Instead she stood very straight and stiff on the bottom stair, her hand clutching the newel post.

'I just wanted to give you something – not much – to spend on something pretty, now that you're growing up.'

She sensed that he was actually offering something, holding out his hand in a gesture of appeasement. She felt both disgusted and powerful. She would not look.

'And I don't know when I'll see you again,' he went on, perfectly calmly as though he hadn't noticed her scorn. 'You'll be off to this school of yours and we'll all be busy with this war . . . here, take it. Have fun.'

He stepped across and took her free hand, and pressed into it a coin, closing her fingers round it as though she were a doll. It was a gold sovereign.

Till that moment she had been unsure. No more. With his Judas money Howard had admitted his guilt.

Confident now, she turned and looked him directly in the face. His gaze did not waver or slide away.

Strangely, at this moment when she hated Howard most, he appeared almost likeable. But she wouldn't be bought.

'Thank you,' she said. 'But I shan't spend it. I'll keep it to remind me.'

He gave a tiny incline of his head, more like a bow than a nod. His unexpected gracefulness mocked her lack of sophistication. All she could do was go, quickly. But long before she reached the first landing she heard the drawing room door close behind him.

Dorothy was impressed by the money. 'Well!' she said, as she brushed Adeline's hair with long, crackling strokes. 'Lord alone knows what you'll find to spend it on, but I hope you were suitably grateful. Head back.'

CHAPTER FIVE

1915

BY THE TIME Adeline went away to St Agatha's, near Kingsbridge in January 1915, everyone else had gone. Richard and Frank were in France, Bob was at Oxford. Simon was at Shorncliffe, waiting to leave. He wrote to Elizabeth, with a special PS for Adeline: 'Tell Addy to write me some really funny letters all about her school – and perhaps a photo of herself in her ghastly uniform.' Adeline salvaged the letter from the library wastepaper basket and determined not only to act on its instructions, but to treasure it. She also decided that the very first amusing letter she wrote to Simon would contain a request for a photograph of him in *his* 'ghastly uniform'.

The going away was not as bad as she'd imagined it, partly because Fording Place was so profoundly altered that it was not like leaving home. Dorothy had gone to a new family, the Shelmadines, near Sidmouth, and Bryer had handed in his notice though not, it was noted, for any reason to do with the war but because he had applied for, and obtained, a job at a London hotel, the Piermont. Miss

Purgavey remained, and so did Chris Dance, because in
Richard's absence, and that of two thirds of the work
force, the farm could not have run without him. Black,
with his driver's and mechanic's skills, had joined the
Transport Corps.

The house seemed dull and workaday, as well as empty,
though Adeline noticed that her mother was in her
element. She had always been an energetic woman, and
had, too, a natural flair for organization which could now
be given free reign. She rose early, dealt with correspondence (including a rising tide of bills), conferred with
Chris Dance, and then launched upon a hectic round of
useful and patriotic enterprises, from initiating and running the local Red Cross to visiting families whose men
were away at the war. Black's absence meant that she
drove herself everywhere often at a suicidal speed of twenty-five miles an hour. She attended meetings – Women's
Suffrage, Food Reform, parish matters – as if she could
not get enough of them, while Adeline, who was frequently taken along, watched open-mouthed. She felt she
was seeing a completely new and hitherto unexpected side
to her mother. Letters arrived from Frank and Richard,
the former in a larky, must-dash vein, the latter more
concerned with how things were going at home. Neither
conveyed much of what life was like at their end, though
Adeline and Elizabeth read in the papers about a setback
for the British at Mons, and scanned the grey columns of
casualties.

At Christmas Elizabeth had suffered from a fit of phil-
anthropy which prompted her to entertain all the grass
widows and their children from the village to a gigantic
tea party. For the first time Adeline sympathized with
Bryer as he stared waspishly at the horde of red-faced
children, the runny noses wiped by frayed cuffs, the
harshly scrubbed hands with permanently blackened nails:
a ravening army laying siege to the tea table as if it were
the last food on earth. They were children she knew, nice
children, well but roughly brought up, and given
responsibilities at a terrifyingly early age. But presented

with Miss Purgavey's Christmas spread they changed into a single organism – a huge, ambulant appetite. The mothers, left behind in the stampede, attempted to exercise some restraining influence from the back, but it was a waste of time. Adeline had been deputed to help with the little ones, but as the youngest in her family she had no experience whatever of small children, and soon discovered that she had no flair for managing them, either.

These were not pampered, protected infants, but tough robust little animals, accustomed to fighting their corners and giving as good as they got. One after another they escaped her inept clutches and joined the fray, staggering, falling, wailing and rising again until they had got hold of a chunk of food and then, as often as not, going under the table with it, where the hanging cloth seemed expressedly designed to make a cosy house. By the end of the tea party Adeline was smeared with food and damp with spilled liquid, but her condition was as nothing beside that of Bryer. His immaculate trousers and gleaming black shoes had been an obvious and delightful target for the toddlers under the table, and from the knees down he was a sticky mess of cake, currants, crumbs and jam, some of it in a semi-digested condition.

'Oh – *Bryer*!' Adeline had exclaimed, as he stepped from behind the table to begin the awesome task of clearing up. She wanted to laugh, but his face was so ashen, and she understood so well the enormity of the injury to his person and his pride, that she controlled herself.

Mabel, however, was not so tactful. Her hand flew to her cheek, her eyes popped, her mouth opened in a great shriek of mirth.

'Oh Mr Bryer, what you been doin'?' she howled.

'Collect up the tea things, Mabel, and stop giggling in that hoydenish fashion,' said Bryer sharply. I am just going to my room to change, I'll be back presently.'

He left, and Mabel began clearing away the crockery, her plump shoulders shuddering with laughter. 'Poor Mr Bryer – he'll be happier at his hotel!'

Elizabeth returned from seeing the last families out of the front door.

'Well,' she said, 'I think we can account that a tremendous success. It's something I plan to do a lot more often!'

Adeline, pressing her lips together and thinking of the war, managed to keep a straight face as she prised the remains of a fruit scone from the carpet, but the remark was too much for Mabel who burst into another fit of uncontrollable giggles.

'It's all right for you,' Adeline said to Bob, later, 'you managed to get out of it.'

'I didn't "get out of" anything, as you put it. I had reading to do.'

'On Christmas Eve?'

'You're just jealous because I had better things to do than attend Mother's democratic bunfight.'

'She's going to have more of them, she says,' said Adeline dolefully.

'That needn't worry you though,' said Bob. 'You'll be away at school. Once you've experienced school meals I bet you'll remember today quite affectionately.'

Adeline didn't think so. By the time she was due to go there, in the first week in January, St Agatha's had taken root in her imagination as a place of almost mythical properties. At St Agatha's there would be learning, and opportunities for self-expression, and the company of other girls of her own age (of which, in the whole of her fourteeen and a half years, she had scarcely any experience). Though it hurt her to admit it, home wasn't much fun any more. For many years to come, when she heard the word 'war', Adeline was to think not of bloodshed and battles, but of the boredom and futility which had hung over her during that winter of 1914/15.

In sending their daughter to a boarding school, Richard and Elizabeth were ahead of their time. Good secondary education for girls was advancing apace, but the notion of schools dedicated to the development of the whole person, in the mould of the great boys' public schools, was new.

Not that Richard, in particular, was much concerned about matters of novelty, fashion or reform. He simply noted that the public school system seemed to have served both himself and his sons adequately well, and that if the same kind of institution were now available for his daughter he might as well stick with it, especially as it was fairly clear, even to his benignly uncurious eye, that Adeline was not going to make an early and socially advantageous marriage. He was wrong in this, but it was a sound judgement at the time.

He had taken Adeline to visit the school and they had both been much taken with the headmistress, Miss Daniels, who was enthusiasm personified. Tall and bony, with a face like an engaging horse, she had led them round her domain at top speed, keeping up a breathless stream of description and explanation. Up and down stairs, in and out of classrooms and laboratories (Miss Daniels was a keen believer in the sciences), round dormitories, and then outside to see the games fields, the riding stable and the kitchen garden (diet, too, was one of the headmistress's hobbyhorses). The pupils fell silent and stood up when they entered, but did not seem nervous or cowed, and when Richard remarked to Miss Daniels what 'very jolly girls' they seemed, she at once began to extol the system which had produced them.

'They are! Of course they are jolly! They have plenty to do, plenty of exercise and plenty of work, challenges and responsibilities. They are healthy and busy and they sleep like tops!' She might have been talking about sheepdogs. 'Girls are too often sedentary and passive,' she continued, sweeping through the downstairs cloakroom, 'but at St Agatha's we encourage them to be lively, active and enquiring, and they thrive on it!' She turned her bright, toothy, smile upon Adeline. 'I sense that Adeline would flourish here!'

Richard was enchanted by Miss Daniels and all her works. In the train on the way home he expressed his delight over and over again

'She was a really capital woman, didn't you think,

Addy? And I'm sure your mother would have felt the same, I'm sure she would. Now tell me what you thought to it all . . . .'

Adeline had been favourable impressed too. The proof of the pudding, however, was in the eating, and she was sublimely happy at St Agatha's. Apart from her infectious enthusiasm, Miss Daniels' most marked characteristic was a pleasing sense of humour, so that the regime under which the Aggies (as they were known) lived their lives contrived even at its most austere moments to seem like fun.

'Now girls,' Miss Daniels would say at Assembly, 'I know you have all been brought up as ladies, but here I want you to work and play like gentlemen!'

What this meant, in effect, was that the seventy or so Aggies were cocooned from social demands and encouraged in a state of wholesome tomboyishness. Miss Daniels believed wholeheartedly that the aim of education, especially the education of women, was to provide freedom, opportunity and choice. She was quite shameless about touching wealthy parents for money, and she had extended and improved the school's facilities with the funds thus acquired. There was a well-stocked library, two science laboratories, and a large studio for painting and pottery. Where drama was concerned she refused to be inhibited by the age and gender of her pupils, so that Adeline, by the time she left the school, had played Lady Macbeth, Mark Antony, Shylock and Tony Lumpkin in successive productions.

She also developed two passions. One was for lacrosse, a game only recently introduced to the school by Miss Brock (Games and Physical Training), with Miss Daniels' blessing. It was said to have been developed by the North American Indians (with which tribe some of the older staff thought it should have stayed) and had so few rules that it was considered daring to participate. The goalkeeper had to be padded more or less from head to foot, and to wear a wired protective mask. But Adeline played wing attack, with the run of the field – and how she ran! The speed and freedom of lacrosse, so unlike the laborious constraints of cricket or the intimate warfare of tennis, suited her exactly. She was fast on her feet, with good hand-eye coordination and the sort of fearless, ebullient disposition of which Miss Daniels heartily approved.

Adeline's second passion was for Naomi Keating. Naomi's christian name, with its connotations of languorous beauty, had been an unfortunate choice, for she was a stocky, muscular girl with a striding walk and a what-ho verbal manner. In the classroom she was dim and pedestrian, but Adeline, being nearly three years younger, was unaware of this. It was on the field of play that Naomi Keating was sublime: through her outstanding talent for games she even achieved a physical grace she did not normally possess and her manner was so pleasant in victory, so dignified in defeat, that she quickly took on heroic qualities in Adeline's eyes.

With her knowledgeable eye she quickly spotted Adeline's ability, and with a cheery 'Well played!' or 'Jolly well done!' she could give quite disproportionate pleasure.

One chilly day in March she sought out Adeline after games and walked alongside her back to school.

'Adeline, may I have a word?'

'Of course, Naomi.'

'I've been watching you.'

'Have you, Naomi?'

'Yes. And you really are coming on well.'

'Oh! Thank you!'

'In fact I might ask Miss Brock to give you a shot in the team. How does that strike you?'

'That would be *tremendous*, Naomi. Thanks most awfully.'

After this tumultuous exchange Naomi strode off smartly, her cloak wrapped around her, in a hurry for her tea, leaving Adeline quite *bouleversée* in the middle of the path.

There was nothing that Adeline recognized as sensual in her devotion to Naomi. She experienced none of the confused and conflicting emotions that assailed her in the presence of Simon. Indeed, when Adeline received her first letter from him, enclosing a photograph, she was the talk of the school for a day or two and her elation knew no bounds. But when she had composed and sent off her reply the following Sunday (via Elizabeth, letters to young men not in the family were not allowed), the elation seeped away, and Naomi was still there.

Of course, there wasn't a girl at St Agatha's who had not got a father, or brother, or uncle, or cousin at the Front, and the soft-voiced summons to Miss Daniels private drawing room, denoting news of the worst possible kind, became a regular and melancholy occurrence.

Naomi Keating was among the first to receive this summons, and poor Adeline, all unaware, was the first to encounter her afterwards. She was on her way to the studio, and met Naomi in the narrow passage known as 'Lower Long' which ran parallel with the main hall, and linked the dormitories with the rest of the school. Naomi was striding along with her head down, as she often did.

'Good evening, Naomi,' said Adeline politely. And at once Naomi, as if she had been struck, or subjected to the cruellest treatment, burst into tears. Adeline was shocked, mortified, aghast. This was no ordinary crying. Naomi leaned against the wall, her face contorted, her shoulders heaving, her fists kneading her eyes.

'Naomi – I'm sorry – what's the matter?'

The recognized and universal response to this question, at St Agatha's, was 'Nothing'. But Naomi was not even sufficiently composed to utter this one word. Her weeping just became more intense, she turned away and put her arms over her head. Adeline, at a loss, stepped forward and put her hand on Naomi's shoulder.

'Cheer up, old thing,' she said, boldly and encouragingly. 'Can't you tell me about it? Then you're bound to feel all right.'

In another few weeks she would have known better than to make this suggestion. Naomi lifted a face contorted not just by grief, but by fury and contempt.

'Don't be so stupid, you – you silly little girl! What do

you know about it? You don't know *anything*! Go away!
Get away from me!'

But it was Naomi herself who fled, with none of her
usual grace and athleticism.

Her brother, Alan, had been killed in action. By the
time Adeline and her classmates reached 'Stodge Hour',
the period just before supper set aside for reading, this fact
was common knowledge.

They were being supervised by a prefect, or 'topper'
as the Aggies had it, named Frances Pennington, whose
responsibility it was to ensure silence and encourage concentration. But on this occasion the charm of being in
possession of certain salient details was too much for her,
and she entered into conversation with her charges,
though not without a token demur.

It was Adeline who raised her hand and asked: 'Please,
Frances, will Naomi be going home?'

Frances looked up from her book with a fairly good
pretence of someone startled out of a reverie.

'I beg your pardon, Adeline?'

'I'm sorry to disturb you, I just wondered – will Naomi
be going home?'

'I really don't know, Adeline, and this isn't the time to
discuss it. Get on with your reading, please.'

Everyone looked down again, but in response to
repeated nudges and mouthed exhortations from her best
friend, Mary Younge, Adeline raised her hand once more.

'Excuse me. Frances!'

Frances again looked up, with studied patience.

'Yes, Adeline, what is it this time?'

'It's just that I met Naomi and she was so terribly
unhappy. I just wondered if she was all right, or – how
she was,' she finished lamely.

But she had achieved her objective. Frances closed her
book and sat gazing down almost reverently at the cover
for a second or two. The younger girls watched her in a
trance of virtuous expectation.

Frances was grave and restrained. 'I presume from your
question that you know what has happened.' They nod-

ded. 'I don't think that under the circumstances Miss Daniels would object to my speaking to you for a moment on the subject. Poor Naomi, we must keep her in our thoughts,' she went on piously. 'Her brother was only twenty. I've met him on one or two occasions. The Keatings are a very close family and this is a terrible blow for all of them. In answer to your question, Adeline, I believe that Naomi's mother will be coming to take her home for a while tomorrow, and till then we must all try to understand how she must be feeling, and to treat her with special kindness and sympathy.'

The girls murmured their agreement, though Mary whispered to Adeline, 'If we're too sympathetic it'll only make it worse. You found that out!'

When the bell went for the end of Stodge Hour, Mary said to Adeline: 'It won't last, the war, surely, will it? It'll be over by summer.'

'I don't know,' replied Adeline. 'Plenty of people thought it would be over by Christmas.'

Mary stared at her friend's face, trying to find some crumbs of comfort there, but Adeline looked uncharacteristically grim.

'Your Simon doesn't say it's too bad,' offered Mary.

'People don't necessarily write what they know in letters, they write what they think other people want to hear.' Adeline was in a mood to prepare not just Mary, but herself, for the worst. She had seen with her own eyes and at close quarters the first, devastating effects of bereavement: the crumbling of the personality before it, the loss of pride, the hostility to all others not connected with the lost loved one. Her earlier feelings towards Naomi, feelings of breathless admiration and humility, had been swept away; they had been simple irrelevancies when real comfort had been needed. She felt most keenly her own inadequacy in the matter, and wished she had known what to say or do that would not have appeared either intrusive or silly. After all, she thought, it was not when people were in the ascendancy that they needed you, but when they were brought low.

She confided this to Mary after lights out.

'I felt such a chump, but I had no idea what had happened.'

'Of course you didn't, how could you have? She won't hold it against you, anyway. I bet when she comes back she'll go on being extra nice to you –'

'But I don't *want* her to!' Adeline's voice rose in exasperation, to be greeted by a chorus of 'Shushes'. She lowered it to a ferocious whisper. 'Don't you see that?'

'Not really.' Poor Mary felt that the rug had been pulled out from beneath her feet. She tried one last tack. 'Perhaps she won't come back to school.'

'Perhaps.' Adeline rolled over, pulling the bedclothes tight round her shoulders. 'Perhaps that would be best.'

They saw Naomi once more. The next day, just before lunch, Mrs Keating arrived by taxi from the station to take her daughter home. She was a little, fat, distracted-looking woman, even more frayed at the edges by grief. The table at which Adeline sat in the dining room was near the window that overlooked the drive, and after Mrs Keating had spent some time with Miss Daniels in the drawing room she saw her, and Naomi, emerge and climb back into the cab. Seeing her with her mother Adeline had a sudden, clear picture of exactly how Naomi would look in middle age: no longer a god-like being tearing up the wing, but a dumpy, inarticulate person with few social graces to ease her path through life. Her last sight of the two of them was as they huddled together on the back seat, a study in misery.

The incident shocked all the girls at St Agatha's, but more because of its effect on Naomi than because of its wider implications. To the younger girls the war was still something distant, faintly glamorous, not real. As it escalated, the fateful summons to the drawing room, the emergence of the broken and tear-drenched recipient of bad news, and the daily scanning of *The Times* casualty list which

Miss Daniels pinned to the board, brought it closer. In an attempt to put it all into some geographical context Miss Daniels also put up a large map, highlighting the main theatres of war, and regularly indicated, with coloured pencils (and advantages) how things were going for the British troops.

At home in the Easter holidays Richard returned for a few days' leave, and Adeline's mood of grim, self-inflicted pessimism lifted in spite of herself. Everything, under his auspices, seemed more relaxed and normal. Elizabeth let her meetings go hang, people came to visit, there was drinking and laughter and Adeline was allowed to stay up until ten o'clock each night.

He didn't talk about the war much, explaining that now he was here it was the last thing he wanted to discuss, but on the occasions when he did allow himself to be drawn he painted a picture of chaps getting on with the job in hand, not always in very comfortable conditions, but in good spirits and with moderate success. He had seen Frank, and had news of Simon, and both were well apart from the everyday afflictions of coughs and colds and trench foot which he made sound almost funny. Both the boys, he promised, would be due for leave before too long so they'd be able to see for themselves.

The most obvious alteration that Adeline could see was in her father's relationship with Bob. No matter how hard he tried to evince an intelligent interest in Bob's studies, no matter how civilly he listened nor how encouraging his comments, nothing could hide the gulf in experience which now divided them. Added to which Bob was developing a Bolshy tendency which seeped like smoke through the chinks in his careful restraint. One evening at supper Richard began to expound on some not very firmly held theory of his concerning farm management, in which area he was, like most other gentlemen farmers, generally paternalistic. Chris Dance was there, the atmosphere was genial and relaxed, and Richard went on, and on, apparently unaware that Bob was beginning to twist and fidget in his seat and to look crosser and crosser. For Adeline,

who was all too keenly aware of it, it was like watching
one of those summer storms get up, when lowering navy-
blue clouds mass on what was a calm horizon, and a sharp,
irritable breeze swirls through the branches, rattling them
and tearing off the leaves, and making doors and windows
bang. The squall was coming but only she could see it.
Elizabeth and Chris smiled and agreed and were happy,
for to them this was a conversation of the most everyday
and peaceable nature.

Adeline caught Bob's eye and decided, in an attempt to
divert him, to strike up a parallel conversation.

'I'm supposed to do a portrait this holidays,' she began.
'I wonder – '

'Excuse me.' Bob put down his spoon alongside his
untouched castle pudding (Richard's favourite, made specially by Miss Purgavey). 'D'you mind if I leave the table?'

Richard, in mid-sentence, looked vaguely and smilingly
down the table at him.

'What's that, old boy?'

'I'd like to leave the table, if you don't mind.'

No offence would have been given or taken if he had
left it at that since Richard, in the manner of those who
are in an outstandingly affable mood, could detect no rancour in others.

'Are you quite all right?'

'Perfectly, thank you.' Bob laid down his napkin and
headed for the door, adding in a voice just too audible to
be dismissed as an undertone: 'I just can't stand listening
to any more of this.'

That was all. Nobody picked him up on it, and in the
very brief pause which followed the door closed behind
him.

Richard looked from Elizabeth to Chris, and back again.

'Did he say what I think he said?'

Elizabeth got up. 'He most certainly did. I'll go and
fetch him.'

Richard put a hand on her arm and drew her gently
down again. 'No, no, Lizzie, don't let's have a fuss for
goodness' sake. I don't suppose he meant anything by it.'

'Perhaps not, but he could at least have stayed and argued his point with you.'

'I dare say he didn't want a fuss either,' pointed out Chris Dance, 'and just didn't go the right way about it.'

'Absolutely,' said Richard, relieved as always to be presented with a reason for leaving things as they were.

'It was very rude of him,' persisted Elizabeth, 'and there's no excuse for rudeness.'

'Oh, gauche rather than rude,' said Richard, adding in a different tone of voice: 'I say, Addy, you and I might finish up that pudding between us, we don't want Old Purgatory to think us unappreciative.'

After supper, when Elizabeth and Chris, in one of those curious reshuffling of roles which had taken place since the start of the war, began discussing some current estate matters, Richard said to Adeline: 'Shall we take a turn in the garden, madam? What do you say?'

It wasn't summer, nor anything like it, but it was a still, clear evening, rapidly darkening. Richard put on one of the wide-brimmed straw hats he wore when painting out of doors and whistled up Trigger and Mark. The hat gave him a distinctly quixotic look which Adeline adored. She was unconditionally happy in his presence, and to be having this little while alone with him when they could recreate their easy, unchanging relationship with one another.

'So tell me, my darling,' he said, as they strolled along the terrace arm in arm. 'How is school? Is the boisterous Miss Daniels living up to expectation?'

'School's marvellous, and the boisterous Miss Daniels is a very good egg.'

He pulled a delighted face, as she knew he would. 'A good egg, is she? Do you have many more funny expressions like that?'

'Oh hundreds, there's practically a whole language.'

'I want to know the lot, so I can use them when I get back and baffle my friends.'

'I'll write them down if you like.'

'Do that. And what about work? Do you do any?'

'Of course! Masses and masses of it, in fact it's positively hectic. I'm ahead in English and French and miles behind in science and maths and about average in everything else. The only thing I really hate is domestic economy – '

'Domestic economy? What's that when it's at home?'

'Running a house. Working out budgets and menus for the week and that kind of thing. We only have it once a week but I'm completely useless at it.'

Richard laughed contentedly. 'Obviously you're going to have to be the sort of woman who doesn't need to bother with all that.'

'Well . . .' She hesitated, remembering Dorothy's strictures on the connection between darning and independence. 'I don't know about that . . . but I can learn those things *any* time. I'm good at lax – '

'Lax?'

'Lacrosse, I was in the team once, and I'm doing a lot of painting and drawing. In fact, that's what I'd really like to do – go to art school.'

Richard stroked her hair, then gave it a gentle tug. 'Don't hurry too fast, there's plenty of time.'

They reached the side of the house, with the stableyard and garage to their left, and the walled kitchen garden beyond. An enormous white, dappled moon hung low in the sky and in the distance the lonely black ridges of Dartmoor were visible against the soft night-blue of the sky. Daffodils and narcissi, white in the moonlight like ghost-flowers, lit up the long grass at the side of the path. From the open kitchen window they could hear voices. Women's voices, Miss Purgavey and Mabel, and Mrs Trodd who, with her husband, had come to replace Bryer and Black. Trigger and Mark were hunting rabbits in the woods bordering the garden.

'Addy, what did I say to make Bob so angry?'

It was quite unlike Richard to enter into speculation about guilt or motive, as he found it so much simpler and more comfortable to take people at their face value. The mere fact of his having asked the question made Adeline realize how carefully worded her answer must be.

But it was difficult, and she fell back on the Aggies' all purpose, 'Oh – nothing.'

Richard sighed.

'It's not fair to ask you. It's just that he's so clever – too clever for me, I'm afraid – and I dare say he finds your mother and me a pretty uninteresting pair these days. Uninteresting and reactionary.'

'That's not true, he doesn't!'

'Well I hope he doesn't hold it against us, not seriously.'

'He thinks the working men should have more say in how things are run,' she said, all in a rush. 'And at supper you were talking to Chris about the tied cottages and the wages in kind and everything, and it made him see red!'

The unconscious aptness of this last expression made Richard chuckle. He was easily mollified, especially if the explanation of an event accorded with his view of the world.

'Ah, I see! Yes, I expect he did well to leave the room before he exploded, and it did mean extra pudding for us, so it's an ill wind . . . I'll be sure to tread very carefully for the rest of my time here, and by the time I come back again he'll have grown out of it, if I know anything.'

Adeline was by no means so certain about this, but she was glad to see Richard happy again.

'Come on,' he said. 'It's getting chilly.'

Two days after that Richard returned to France, and for the remaining week of her holidays Bob was especially nice to Adeline, going out of his way to spend time with her, even accompanying her when she went out on Beau, bumping and rattling alongside on his bicycle. Elizabeth returned to her meetings and societies and Adeline realized that she missed the society of Mary and the other Aggies more than she would have thought possible. She even confessed this to Bob, explaining that she felt rather guilty about it.

'I don't see why,' he said in his dry way. 'Anything would be preferable to this place at the moment.'

They were sitting by the river, on the grey-white trunk

of a willow which leaned out almost parallel to the water, trailing its green sleeve on the surface. On the Island opposite the swans had built their enormous nest and the female was sitting, her long neck erect as a bullrush among the reeds while the cob glided watchfully back and forth.

'That's an awful thing to say,' exclaimed Adeline. 'If you hate it so much why on earth do you come? Why don't you stay in Oxford instead of coming here and complaining?'

Bob began to break little pieces off a stick, dropping them in the river to be snatched and borne off by the current.

'I come back,' he said, 'to see Mother, who's on her own here now, and to see you, though God knows why I bother. Filial duty. What a joke.'

'Sorry.'

'Don't bother. I quite see I'm a fish out of water. The fact is I don't really fit in anywhere at the moment. You know what I think it is – ?' He became suddenly more animated, threw away what remained of the stick and leaned forward. 'I think I have no talent for youth. It's not my time, I don't suit it and it doesn't suit me. I don't want to have fun and games and larks, fun to me is working, or talking to people I find interesting – who seem to be horribly rare – or poking about in libraries and museums. You take Frank, now, he was born to be young, to be carefree and dashing – to have *fun*.' He pronounced the words as if it were the name of some abstruse religious rite. 'I haven't the slightest doubt he'll cover himself with glory in this bloody silly war, and good luck to him. I admire him. I envy him a little, just at the moment, not for being out there – the army doesn't want me any more than I want the army – but I envy him for being what he is. If I didn't think my time would come I'd be pretty much at my wits' end. As it is I've decided it's just a waiting game.'

Adeline had listened to a good many self-examinations by her clever, discontented brother over the years, but this struck her as the most rational to date, and therefore cause for cautious optimism.

'You're absolutely right,' she said. 'Every dog has his day.'

'Oh God . . .' Bob put his hand to his brow, 'I hear Nanny talking. A blunted epigram for every occasion. I wonder how she's doing these days?'

On the way back they fell into a comfortable exchange of memories. Adeline didn't realize that her brother's mind had still been running on their earlier conversation until he suddenly said, in the hall:

'I think when you reach your time, you stop.'

'I don't understand.'

He was immediately impatient. 'I mean when you get to the age you were always meant to be, you stay there, You feel comfortable, so you stay.'

'I hope to goodness I'll know when I get to mine,' said Adeline.

Bob seemed not to have heard her. 'You take Father, for instance,' he said. 'He's never grown up. The irony is – if he had, he'd be at home now. He just couldn't bear to be left out.'

Not long after the start of the summer term, Frank and Simon turned up at St Agatha's to visit Adeline. Their arrival, in uniform, and driving a motorcar of stupendous dilapidation, caused a major stir. Going off the school premises under these highly unorthodox conditions was quite out of the question, even allowing for the fact that one of these young men was Adeline's brother. Instead, all three of them were entertained to tea in the drawing room and then allowed to walk round the garden for three quarters of an hour. They took this exercise like inmates in a prison yard, under the gaze of dozens of pairs of eyes watching enviously or suspiciously, according to age, from most of the downstairs windows.

For Adeline it was like being with not one, but two pairs of people. One of these pairs comprised the people she knew, her brother, Frank, and his boyhood friend, Simon.

The other two were creatures from another world, strange and foreign, emissaries of the War which provided the lurid backdrop for every activity.

The visit came and went in a flash, leaving only a bright, intense memory that dimmed gradually over the following weeks. She couldn't remember what they'd talked about, it had all been very frivolous and teasing and silly and enjoyable: but she carried away one impression that did not fade, which in fact grew stronger as the visit receded into the past, as if it were the only real thing about it. This was that Frank and Simon shared some secret, something so private and well-buried that it was not even a matter for discussion between themselves. Though both were cheerful and high-spirited at the start of a week's leave, Frank was quieter than she might have expected, Simon more febrile. It was Simon who finished jokes, who elaborated on stories, who roared with laughter at her descriptions of St Agatha's, while Frank smiled and watched. These differences were not sufficiently marked to warrant enquiries, but there they were, worming away at her memory of the visit and somehow tarnishing it.

Not that the Aggies were permitted much time for morbid reflection. Rose Daniels, though in the vanguard of girl's education in many ways, still adhered to the notion that girls should be kept too busy for what was referred to as 'silly talk'. The idea of 'girlhood' as a pure, free state, untrammelled by the sordid preoccupations of maturity, was a sacred tenet of the new girl's schools, as it had been of the old, and the characteristic product of St Agatha's was honourable, forthright, sensible, energetic, and curiously asexual. It was as well for Adeline that she had spent most of her life till now with her brothers for company, for otherwise she might have emerged from school with a rather odd and one-sided idea of a woman's role in society – that of a cheerful, well-educated captain of games.

As it was, she was among the heretical few who were

prone to fits of giggles when the Aggies raised their collective voice in the school song:

Fortis qui se vincit is our motto, speak it bold!
And never let the wearer flinch who wears the Green and
  Gold;
In classroom and on playing field be this our constant aim:
Oh let your heart not seek the prize but glory in the game!
Green and Gold! Gold and Green! St Agatha's for aye!
And every failure bravely met secures a place on high!

The promise contained in the final line was always sung with special fervour by the not-so-bright, especially since its validity could not be proved either way until it was too late. But somehow the frequent use of the exclamation mark in the school song typified the bracing, energetic, no-nonsense approach to life of Miss Daniels herself. As she had indicated to Richard and Adeline on their first visit to the school, an endless round of exercise, both mental and physical, ensured that the Aggies had little time for introspection during the day, and slept the sleep of the utterly exhausted at night.

So the oddly disturbing memory of Frank's and Simon's visit was unusual in its persistence. But otherwise Adeline was happy. She had many friends, she had a range of activities almost all of which she enjoyed and at some of which she excelled, she had people to respect, and others to lead. It was the period in her life during which she was perhaps the most content, but her contentment was short-lived.

When Adeline was an old lady she could still recall with absolute clarity a certain early July day during her second term at St Agatha's. There was the scent of newly mown and rolled tennis courts, the soft ringing sound of racquet on ball, the sound of voices calling the score in brilliant afternoon sunshine. Through the open windows of the hall drifted the shrill exhortations of a psalm, as the choir practised for Speech Day: 'Praise Him on the lute and harp! Praise Him upon the loud organ . . .' She could recall that a group of junior girls were weeding the round herbaceous border on the top lawn between the courts and the main school building – practical tasks were character forming. She could recall that she and Mary Younge had won the first game of the second set, and the four of them were changing ends. As she walked back to serve she saw the window of Miss Daniels' drawing room open, and saw the headmistress summon one of the juniors. She turned her back to serve, and hit the ball into the net. Before she could serve again the junior, pink and perspiring, was at the side of the court.

'Adeline!'

'Yes?'

'Please, Adeline, Miss Daniels says can you go and see her in the drawing room, please.'

It was as though everything – the sun, the singing, the three other girls on the court – had dissolved, leaving her on her own. Her body felt leaden, her vision darkened, she felt, for the first time in her life, as if she might be going to faint. But conditioning prevented her. She walked to the net and leaned her racquet against the post, picked up her green cardigan and pulled it on, smoothed back her hair with her palms.

Mary was beside her, full of concern. 'Would you like me to come, Adeline?'

'No, it's all right. You carry on.'

She left the court and headed for the school. She felt the group of younger girls watching her as she passed. Miss Daniels stood in the window of the drawing room, her hands cupped on either side of her eyes, shielding them from the light. Adeline went to the downstairs cloakroom and splashed her face with cold water. Catching sight of herself in the mirror, she was surprised that she looked no different. But as she walked down Lower Long, to the front of the school, she was seized by an acute nervous trembling so that she had to clench her teeth and her fists in an attempt to control it. Her hand, when she knocked on the drawing room door, made a rattling sound.

'Come in. Ah, Adeline . . .'

Rose Daniels opened the door herself and led Adeline gently by the arm into the room. It was warm and drowsy, with sunshine pouring through the open window on to tables covered with books and magazines, a neat desk with a pile of exercise books, and walls crowded with paintings. In the hearth stood a white jug filled with pink and blue hydrangeas.

'Come and sit down.'

Miss Daniels led her to the window seat, and sat down next to her. The sun was hot on their backs, and a tortoise-shell butterfly flittered in through the open window from the flower bed outside and settled for a moment on the corner of the desk.

Miss Daniels sat so close to Adeline that their knees touched, but she kept her hands folded in her lap. Adeline, to contain the shivering, had folded her arms, something usually not allowed, but she was not reprimanded.

'It is my very sad task,' said Miss Daniels, 'to be so often the bearer of bad news. Just now I received a telephone call from your mother, in which she told me that your father has died.'

For some reason the last word was not what Adeline had been expecting to hear.

'Died?'

'Your mother says he caught an infection and developed pneumonia.'

The trembling had stopped. Adeline felt nothing now except a cold, sharply focused desire to establish the facts. Dying did not happen in a war. Dying happened at home, it happened to the old and the sick, it was expected.

'I think – I believe from what she told me – that she knew your father was ill. But the complications set in suddenly and the end was very quick. Tomorrow she will be coming to see you, and you may go home for a while if you'd like.'

'Thank you.'

'Praise Him upon the loud cymbals!' sang the choir. Adeline stared fixedly at the many small interlocking Vs that formed the weave of Miss Daniels' skirt. There was a cry of 'Double fault!' from the courts outside.

'Adeline.' Miss Daniels put her hand over Adeline's clenched ones. 'Adeline, I'm so very sorry.'

'Thank you,' said Adeline again. Still she felt nothing, except that she was becoming uncomfortably hot.

'Can I offer you something? Would you like a cup of tea?'

'No, thank you.' She got up. 'I'd better get back to my game.'

Miss Daniels was bewildered. 'Your game?'

'My game of tennis.'

'Well my dear . . . you must do whatever you feel best. Shall I call Mary Younge to keep you company?'

'There's no need.'

'As you wish.' Miss Daniels accompanied her to the door. 'But please remember my door is always open for you. Don't hesitate to come and see me at any time, and the same goes for any member of my staff. These are tragic times we are living through, Adeline, and we're all touched by them in some way.'

'Yes.'

Adeline went back along Lower Long, and out to the tennis courts. The choir had moved on to a Purcell anthem, very brisk and spirited. At the side of the court, with Mary and the other two girls, stood Miss Brock, the games mistress.

'Adeline,' she said, striding towards her. 'Did you have bad news?'

'Yes, Miss Brock,' replied Adeline. 'My father has died.' She felt nothing. Beyond Miss Brock she saw the appalled reaction of the other girls, their exchange of horrified looks.

Poor Miss Brock was not cut out for delicate emotional exchanges but she was having to learn, and now she did her best.

'Would you like Mary to accompany you on a walk? Or would you like her to take you to the dormitory?' she asked, with a hint of desperation in her voice.

'No, thank you. We might as well get on with the game,' said Adeline, going to the net for her racquet.

They finished the game. Adeline and Mary won, despite Adeline being a little slower on her feet than usual. Afterwards, rebuffed by her apparent self-possession, and perhaps a little relieved by it too, the others made no mention of her father. There was the usual undignified scrummage to get upstairs and change before tea. Tender-hearted Mary considered saying something when they were upstairs, but before she could sufficiently collect her thoughts Adeline had whisked shut the blue cretonne curtains around her bed, cutting herself off.

Adeline took her green and white striped linen afternoon dress from the narrow wardrobe and hung it on the curtain rail. She poured water into the enamel bowl on the washstand. On the far side of the curtain the voices of the other girls were subdued, she felt, in her honour, and yet she herself was as blank and tearless as a clockwork doll.

But as she moved to fetch clean stockings from the drawer of her locker, her attention was suddenly caught by the framed photograph of her parents which stood on top of it. The effect was like that of a sharp and unexpected blow. Sensation returned with terrible acuteness, she was suddenly flayed raw by shock. For there he stood, the person she loved most, her eternal ally and friend, in one of his silly wide-brimmed hats, leaning cross-legged against his walking stick with Trigger and Mark sitting grinning at his feet.

No more. The utter finality of his death washed over her, snatching away her breath so that she had to sit down on the edge of the hard bed. Her father just wouldn't be there any more, ever again. She remembered that she had never sent him the promised list of slang, nor had she even written to him as often as she had to Simon, and now he was gone. The Snug would have no purpose, the dogs would have no master; there would be no-one to drink whisky with Chris Dance, nor to josh her mother and call her Lizzie; no further use for the battered hats and the much-patched 'walking jacket' that hung in the hall.

Whatever would they do without him, those that were left? She stared in anguish at the photograph. In her memory everyone was more distinct than him, more highly coloured and sharply defined, and yet she saw now that it was her father around whom the family had centred, and that much of their happiness as children had sprung from knowing that he was there, with his amiable contentment and capacity for simple pleasure, a man with a small store of vanity but almost no conceit.

And now, taking the photograph from its place and clasping it to her, she cried, sobbing and gasping until first Mary, then the dormitory prefect and finally Miss Daniels herself came to try and calm her. She didn't really notice them, but at last they persuaded her to go and lie down in the greater privacy of the sanatorium where she cried herself to sleep, still clutching the photograph. When they tried to wake her later in the evening for something to eat, they couldn't. It was as if all the doors of consciousness were closed for the moment, not just against these well-meaning women but against the reality of the present. In the small hours of the morning she awoke suddenly and with a sense of horror, not knowing where she was or, for a split second, what had happened. She was astonished to find that she had been changed into her nightdress, her clothes were folded neatly over a chair – all this had happened and she'd known nothing. She began to cry once more, quietly, and Matron came in and soothed her, and made her a hot drink which this time she accepted gratefully. When she was alone again, with the light out, she felt calmer, but she still could not encompass the completeness of her loss. Instead her mind ran over and over the past like a mouse on a wheel, as if by sheer repetition and rehearsal of past events she could bring Richard back to life. She began to shiver again, her shoulders hunched with tension and her teeth chattering. The windows showed grey and the first birds were singing when she fell asleep again.

Matron roused her at midday and she washed, got dressed and went down to lunch. She felt exhausted, and fragile. She hoped no-one would say anything too kind or sympathetic, because she knew she would burst into tears. She tried hard to put her grief into some kind of common perspective, but it was no good, she could not identify with the other sufferers. She felt that even to mention Richard, if she had been able to bring herself to do so, would have been a betrayal, and a denial of his uniqueness. All through lunch, conscious of the sympathetic and curious eyes turned her way, and with Mary allowed to leave her own table to sit next to her, she tried to keep her thoughts on small, manageable, everyday matters, and to listen to what was being said. But she dared not speak, for fear she'd cry.

As she filed out of the dining room after lunch, Miss Daniels called her aside.

'Adeline, your mother's here. Why don't you come to the drawing room and then I'll leave you to talk in peace.'

Elizabeth was standing in the middle of the room, with her back to the door. She looked completely out of place, and at a loss. It was another fine, hot day but she was wearing a thick grey suit, and gloves. She didn't seem to hear when the door opened.

'Here's Adeline,' said Miss Daniels.

Adeline heard the door close behind her, and as Elizabeth turned she went straight to her and hugged her, the tears coming again at the sight of this one other person to whom both she and Richard had been close, and who would be feeling as wretched as herself.

But when she drew back and saw her mother's face she knew that things were not as she had expected. There was all the evidence of distress, but the puffy and shadowed eyes held no comfort for Adeline. On the contrary, Elizabeth looked untypically forbidding, and set her daughter aside by the shoulders before she spoke as if to put a real as well as an emotional distance between them.

Adeline fought for control, but it was beyond her. She wanted not to cry if Elizabeth wanted her not to, but it was hopeless. Feeling foolish and helpless she stood there shuddering and sobbing.

'Come along, Addy. Please try, there's a good girl.'

'But Mother . . . what shall we do? What are we going to do without him?'

'We shall manage, I dare say. We shall have to.' Elizabeth sat down heavily.

'Will they bring him back?'

'It's possible, but I said no. He'll be buried over there.'

Adeline sat down opposite her mother but Elizabeth avoided her eye, removing her gloves and smoothing them, over and over again, on her lap. Adeline suddenly realized that she had always been a little nervous of her mother, and that it was Richard's affectionate ease with her which had helped dispel the nervousness. Now it suddenly resurfaced, ambushing her when she least wanted it to.

'Wouldn't he have wanted to come home?' she asked.

'It can hardly matter to him, now that he's dead.'

'But we won't know where he is.'

'Of course we will. He's in the military cemetery – Addy, this is a pointless, painful discussion!'

'I'm sorry.'

Elizabeth's voice became a little gentler. 'We have to be practical. I came to see how you were, and to find out if you would like to come home for a few days. The headmistress says you may, if that's what you want.'

It was not an invitation, but an offer thrown down on the table. There was no warmth in it.

'Do you want to?'

'I don't know. Is anyone else there?'

'Bob is with me for a few days.'

'Then you've got company. You don't want me around the place, and it's only two or three weeks till the end of term. I might as well stay here.'

'Very well,' There was no mistaking the note of relief. 'There are so many things that need doing, it is probably best if you're here with your friends, darling.' The endearment, like an echo from a happier time, hung in the air. Adeline, knowing that she had said and done the right thing, pursued her advantage. She wanted to know more, and she had a feeling that if she did not elicit what information she could from her mother now, she might not have another opportunity.

Elizabeth told her what she knew, which wasn't much: a bleak little litany of facts. Only once did she seem to weaken.

'It's so silly, in a way . . . Dick was always so healthy. He hardly ever had even a cold. And then he goes away to war and catches the 'flu . . .'' She turned her head away, biting her lip, and her hand stroked and stroked the gloves. But she quickly took hold of herself. 'At least he was whole, not torn to pieces or horribly wounded, I'm glad about that.'

Adeline thought of her father, on their last walk together, his arm through hers, and was grateful too.

They talked a little more, about school. Elizabeth explained that she would not be coming to Speech Day, and Adeline said she didn't mind, which was true.

'But when you come home,' said Elizabeth, 'perhaps you and I might take ourselves off to London for a week or two. It would do me good to get away and we could do some shopping, go to the theatre.'

Adeline could not imagine a world where shopping and the theatre meant happiness, and dreaded such a trip.

'Will we stay at Brown's?' she asked, for something to say. When she and her mother went alone to London, they always stayed at Brown's. When they had gone as a family, or with Richard, they stayed at the Cavendish.

'No, the Charterises have very kindly asked us to stay with them. We can go when we like as long as we give a little notice. It would be so much less effort to be with friends . . . under the circumstances.'

Adeline was appalled. She had forgotten the existence of Howard and Cynthia, and that her mother should contemplate staying with them, now, was beyond her comprehension. But before she could demur Miss Daniels entered, explaining that she had asked for coffee to be brought, and the time for questions was past.

For another half an hour Adeline sat politely, sipping coffee, which she loathed, and listening to the carefully

elaborate exchange of adult expressions of grief and con-
dolence. She despised it. She knew her mother suffered,
so how was it possible to conceal it so well, to discuss
ways and means and plans for the future with this woman
who was, after all, a stranger to her?

At about three the taxi returned, and Adeline went into
the outer hall with her mother to say goodbye. It was a
soulless, no-man's-land of an area, furnished only with a
hard chair and a small table upon which lay the visitors'
book.

'Goodbye, Addy,' said Elizabeth, taking her hands and
kissing her on one cheek and then the other. 'Take good
care of yourself, and I'll see you very soon. We'll have a
little holiday, it's what Dick would have wanted.'

Adeline knew this had been said to mollify her, but its
effect was just the opposite. The mention of her father's
name in the same breath as that of a holiday with Howard
Charteris was like a red rag to a bull. Only anger prevented
her from starting to cry once more.

'Why hasn't Howard gone to the war?' she asked.

'He has a reserved occupation. Why?'

'What does he do that's so special?'

'He's in shipping, Addy, and we need ships. Now stop
this.'

'Mother – I really don't *want* to stay with them.'

'You'll feel differently when the time comes. It's too
soon to think about it. In another month or two it'll all
look different.'

'It won't.'

'Please, Addy – '

'I *hate* him! I couldn't bear to stay in his house!'

'Darling, calm down.' Elizabeth put her hands on Adeline's shoulders. 'We don't need to decide now, in fact it
would be absolutely wrong to decide anything, and we
won't. Let's talk about it again when you come home.'

They went out to the taxi. Just before Elizabeth got in
she said to Adeline:

'You mustn't hate Howard because of what's happened.
One life isn't traded for another, you know. We're lucky

to have such good friends, it's a comfort to me, if not to you.' Then she kissed her again, and left.

That night, back in the dormitory, Adeline took Howard's sovereign from beneath the layers of clean underclothes in her locker.

'What's that?' whispered Mary.

'A coin. A kind of memento.'

'Oh . . .' Mary squinted in the darkness, trying to see her friend's face. 'Something to do with your father?'

'No,' said Adeline. 'It's to remind me of why I hate someone.'

CHAPTER SIX

1917

'Does it hurt awfully?' asked Adeline.

Simon said: 'I don't want to talk about it. I'd so much rather talk about you, you're like a breath of spring in this frightful place.'

Adeline looked around them at the ward. It had come as a shock to her to realize that she had never been inside a hospital before, that she had led, both at Fording Place and at St Agatha's, what is known as 'a sheltered life'. But all that was coming to an end, she could feel it.

'Is it so frightful?'

'Not really, I suppose. It's the regimentation . . . the straight lines . . . worse than the trenches!' He laughed gaily. He looked astonishingly well. 'Everyone begin lunch on the count of three, at twelve hundred hours precisely! By the right – eat! Everyone chew each mouthful thirty-two times! Everyone down forks at twelve-thirty!'

A nurse, rustling down the centre of the ward, caught some of this spirited imitation, and came over to Simon's bedside.

'What are you saying to this young lady about us, Lieutenant Charteris? I hope you're not making fun of the way we do things at St Bede's.' She smiled, first at Simon, but then including Adeline as well. It was plain she thought the world of him and Adeline basked in reflected glory.

'Oh, nurse, how could you think such a thing?' Simon was saying. 'You're angels of mercy, every one of you, and I promise faithfully I shall eat up whatever you put in front of me this evening. Even mince and rice.'

'I believe that's what it is. With carrots.'

'Then especially mince and rice!'

'I don't know . . . we'll be glad to get rid of you,' said the nurse, with an expression of fond indulgence, and rustled away.

'She seems nice,' said Adeline.

'They're all nice. But not half as nice as you. Honestly, Addy, you're a sight for sore eyes. And you've grown up! Shall I tell you something?'

'Yes.'

'The very first thing I'm going to do when I get out of here is to take you out for a slap-up dinner somewhere smart.'

Adeline was enchanted. As he spoke he had taken hold of her hand, and now he lifted it to his lips and gave it a quick kiss. The man in the next bed grinned at Adeline.

'Is that man bothering you, miss? You've only got to say.'

She blushed scarlet. 'Oh no! Not at all.'

'Stop it, Bullman,' said Simon, 'can't you see you're embarrassing her?'

'If I am I'm not the only one!' Bullman, who was big and balding, with a gap between his front teeth, chuckled wheezily to himself.

'Take no notice,' said Simon, 'he's just jealous. Now let's think where we might go to turn all the other fellows green with envy . . .'

Adeline could have sat there all night, listening to him, her hand in his, her eyes on his face. He seemed a changed

person, a hero. The gaiety that had seemed a little feverish
and exaggerated when he had visited her at school was
now utterly charming. And he *would* not, he would *not*
talk about the terrible thing that had happened to his leg.
Elizabeth, who had had it from his parents, had told her
he was coming to St Bede's, and she had said, too, that
his leg had been amputated below the knee because of a
wound that had developed gas gangrene. Adeline had been
horrified and shocked. She had actually dreaded coming
to visit him, and had not known what she should say or
how she should behave. But incredibly he had simply
swept her along, not giving her time to feel awkward or
self-conscious. It had almost been possible to forget that
he was terribly injured and maimed. Her gratitude and
admiration knew no bounds, and the trembling little flame
she had somehow nursed and kept alive even in the bracing, bustling winds of St Agatha's leapt up again, brighter
and warmer and steadier than it had ever been because
now, as Simon said, she had grown up.

She knew she looked nice today, because she had made
an effort, in a hat that Cynthia had bought for her. It was
a curly-brimmed felt, in tawny brown ('to go with your
eyes,' Cynthia had enthused, a trifle fancifully in Adeline's
opinion). It had a wide, green ribbon round the crown
stitched into a bow at the back, with the ends just long
enough to flutter behind her when she walked. With her
hair up she knew she looked smart and jaunty and hoped
she looked more than seventeen. She didn't, because luckily no amount of titivation could outshine the bounce and
brightness of youth. If St Agatha's had to accept responsibility for the striding, energetic walk and rather louder-
than-ladylike laugh, they could also take credit for Adeline's handsome, upright figure and healthy vibrancy
which emanated from her and made her (though she
hadn't believed it when Simon said it) the focus of nearly
every man's attention in the ward. Yes, she knew she
looked nice, but she did not realize that excitement had
given her hawkish face a softening glow of near-beauty.

'We might go dancing,' Simon said. 'They'll fit me up

with a peg leg in no time and I intend to be absolutely proficient. Not so hot for ragtime perhaps, but I'll be a champion waltzer. Three-four time's perfect for dot-and-carry-one.'

She couldn't believe that he could make a joke about it. All afternoon she had kept her eyes away from the blanketed tent that concealed the horror, the stump. Now she stole a quick, scared glance at it and was mortified to discover that he had noticed.

'It's all right, you know, Addy,' he said more gently, making the tears prickle behind her eyes. 'I'm over the worst of it. I'm not just fooling around and putting on a show. But there is something jolly important I want to ask you.'

She nodded. Anything, anything.

'Did they teach you to dance the man's part at that school of yours? Because I shall expect to be led.'

They both collapsed into laughter which, in Adeline's case, was perilously close to crying. Under cover of it she was able to take a handkerchief from her bag and mop at her eyes and nose.

'That's better,' said Simon. 'That's my best girl.'

He began telling her about the fearsome matron who came round in the evenings, 'to inspect us,' he said, 'and she's twice as terrifying as the average RSM!' And on he went, as merry, apparently, as a cricket.

Adeline laughed appreciatively as he talked, but a good deal of her attention was focused not on his words but on his appearance. How could he, with all that had happened, contrive to look so cheerful? Of course, the past two and a half years had taken their toll, he was thinner, than he had been, his hair which had been golden seemed darker, he was a man and not a youth. But his good looks had always been of the poetic kind, quite unlike the robust Gundry appearance as typified by Frank. He had always been so gentle, so easily discomforted, she remembered how she had wanted, and tried, to be his champion, but now the memory made her wince with embarrassment. For he had changed: the Simon whose bed she sat beside this afternoon was in manner far more like the burning-eyed overmastering lover of her youthful imaginings than she could ever have believed possible. Adeline was socially inexperienced, but she knew when she was being wooed and flirted with, and it was delightful. This Simon was more at ease, more confident, more *cheerful* than the old one had ever been. And the slight stammer had gone.

'. . . rattling on, and what I really want to know about is you,' he was saying.

'What shall I tell you?'

'Everything. You're so different, Addy, I feel a lot has happened that I don't know about.

'You're different, too. But then – you've been through so much.'

'Have you left school? I suppose you must have done or you wouldn't be here.'

'No, I haven't actually. But it's a half-term holiday so Mother and I came up to London. She comes quite often these days since – well, she likes the change of scene.'

'Mother wrote that she'd been to stay with them several times. I'm so sorry about your father, Addy, that was a damned tragedy. I know what he meant to you.'

'Well, we do miss him. But we've got used to missing him. Sometimes, especially when I'm at home, I wake up in the night and I still can't believe it's true, but that happens less all the time. It's quite frightening, really, how in the end you accept things, terrible things, that you once thought you could never accept.'

'But that's only right, Addy. I bet your father wouldn't have wanted you to be sad for too long, he was such a grand chap. I know the parents were awfully cut up about it at the time.'

She couldn't raise a reply to this, and he went on: 'So when will you be leaving school?'

'At Christmas!' she was glad of the opportunity to discuss a less painful subject.

'And then what?'

'I'm going to work on my portfolio, and try to get a place at the Slade for next autumn.'

'The Slade? Art school?'

'Yes, if I can. Miss Lake, who teaches me at St Agatha's, says I should be able to get in just on my drawing, but I've got a lot of work to do on watercolours. I thought Mother might not like the idea very much but she's been wonderful about it.'

Simon smiled at her so kindly, so warmly, that she knew she was blushing again.

'That would be a dream come true for you, wouldn't it, Addy?' he said.

'Yes – oh, yes!' she replied. But even as she said it she realized that that particular dream had been usurped, utterly, by another.

Since the awful day when Elizabeth had come to see her just after Richard's death, Adeline had kept her faith with regard to Howard. She and Elizabeth had, with tolerable success, shored up the damage done by that strange and painful encounter, as people must who share the same boat in uncertain conditions. But nothing would persuade her to stay at the Charterises' London house even though Elizabeth did so quite often in her absence. Of course, to abjure his company altogether would have been virtually impossible since he and Cynthia were regular guests at Fording Place, and in London he acted as their patron and host even when they were staying at Brown's. Theatre tickets would be left for them, flowers sent, cabs would arrive as if by magic, dinners would be arranged. These Adeline would suffer with only that politeness necessary to prevent hostilities breaking out. Often, he was away: he had a branch of the business and a house in Dublin, and the increased demands of the war kept him occupied. When he was present it was sometimes quite hard to remember how much she hated him, and why, for whether it was to do with Adeline maturing or with Howard mellowing, he seemed these days to be a great deal more human. There was no outward change, he still grinned and glowered and shouted and slapped, but that was just his way, and there had been no Simon around for him to victimize. If Adeline had feared him it had generally been for his influence rather than his behaviour, and she had always been able to trade blow for conversational blow with him. And oddly, these days, he very often took her part, and appeared to understand her on occasions even better than Elizabeth did. Not that Adeline allowed him the satisfaction of knowing this. On the contrary, she would remain grim and haughty and would rush to her room afterwards to stare at the Judas money and try and whip up some of the old, fine fury.

There had been no repetition of the disturbing scene she had glimpsed in the Snug, and it began to take on the aspect of a dream. If it hadn't been for the Judas money she might by now have dismissed it altogether from her memory. It had been such a fleeting, momentary thing and at the time more confusing than horrifying. Now, as her own awareness of such matters grew, she saw it for what it was but could find no echo of it in either Howard's or Elizabeth's present behaviour. From time to time her vengefulness felt a little foolish, even to her.

She longed to talk about it to someone, but who? Too much water had passed under the bridge for her to raise the subject with Elizabeth; Howard himself was out of the question; Frank, when he was home on leave, was a friendly, manly stranger with whom any kind of intimate discussion was now unthinkable. There remained Bob. And it was to Bob that she finally mentioned the incident. Elizabeth and Adeline had gone to visit him in Oxford, and one fine afternoon they had taken a punt up the river. After their picnic they left Elizabeth sitting under a chestnut tree complaining about the gnats, and walked along the bank.

The hot, hazy, shimmering afternoon made them at ease with one another, so, 'May I tell you something?' said Adeline.

'Anything you like.'

'It's something that happened ages ago, and I don't quite know what to make of it.'

They reached a stile, beyond which sleek cows drifted like clouds. Bob leaned on it, hands in pockets.

'Go on.'

She told him, trying not to colour the story with the confused and painful feelings that had accompanied it at the time. When she'd finished she stared anxiously at her brother.

'Am I just being silly?'

'Silly? No. A bit over-dramatic perhaps.'

At once she felt slighted. 'So you think that what I saw, the two of them, doing that, was all perfectly in order, that there was nothing wrong in it?'

He shrugged. 'Depends what you mean by wrong. They weren't hurting anyone. It was perfectly discreet. The worst thing about it was that you saw.'

'But what about *Father*?' This was what she couldn't bear, and saying it made her feel again, like a re-opened wound, the pain she had felt then.

'Steady on, Addy. Father knew.'

'He can't have done!'

'Of course he did, or he had a pretty fair idea. Most people knew Howard was sweet on Mother, he has been for years, probably still is. I agree it's not very comfortable to be confronted with the evidence like that when you were the one person who wasn't aware of it, but as I say they were discreet, and when you think how long it had been carrying on for one slip-up isn't bad going.'

She was stunned. Rebuffed by his starkly practical response, she could think of nothing more to say.

'Shall we go on a bit?' asked Bob.

'All right.'

They climbed over the stile and walked on. The cows lifted their heads and stared, munching. Suddenly and uncharacteristically Bob gave Adeline's shoulder a squeeze.

'Look, I'm sorry. That was a bit brutal and I didn't mean it to be.'

'I know.'

'I'm not condoning what went on, it wouldn't make

much difference whether I did nor not anyway. It was just a fact.'

'But Bob – how did you *know*? How did you find out?'

'I didn't so much find out as gradually absorb it. It may sound odd but I honestly can't remember a time when I didn't know. I mean for God's sake, Addy, you only have to look at Howard when he's in the same room as Mother – he simply can't see anyone else.'

'Yes, but – ' She frowned, kicking the grass as she walked, struggling to express herself. 'But actually touching her – kissing her – how did he dare? And in Father's house!'

Bob gave a short, barking laugh and clapped his hand to his brow. 'Addy! Come off it, what would you have preferred them to do? Run away together? Sheets knotted out of the bedroom window, the note pinned to the pillow? They were both far too comfortable and worldly for that. And besides, you're overlooking the most important thing.'

'What?'

Bob stopped, and caught her arm to turn her towards him. 'Mother loved Father. She'd never have left him for anyone.'

'But now that he's gone – ' The possibility was so terrible that she could not utter it. Bob linked his arm through hers and they started back the way they'd come.

'Now that he's gone,' said Bob, 'it's over. I'm sure of it.'

'I don't see how you can be. She's always going to stay there, and they come down to us, too.'

'Of course, they were good friends, the four of them. But I'm prepared to bet that since Father died, that's all they are. Otherwise it'd be like kicking a man when he's down, which isn't Mother's style.'

Now they were back at the stile and could see Elizabeth again. She had become bored with the shade, and the gnats, and with sitting down, and was walking towards them, using her furled parasol like a walking stick.

'Hallo you two!' she called. 'You didn't go far! Who's for a proper walk?'

Adeline, her view of her mother coloured by Bob's reassuring words, felt a sudden rush of affection for her. She jumped down off the stile and ran along the towpath to meet her, while Bob, with his lurching walk, followed more slowly.

That had been just over a year ago. In the light of Bob's opinion, Adeline harboured fewer suspicions about the present relationship between Elizabeth and Howard, but she still would not unbend towards Howard himself. It was not simply a question of losing face. He would never have given her the money had he not felt guilty about what she had seen. She trusted in both his reaction, and hers. What was more it was plain to see that while Elizabeth might be unwilling to betray Richard's memory, Howard had no such scruples. Otherwise, why the flowers, the treats, the delicious dinners, and more-than-friendly attentiveness? No, she told herself, she was right not to forgive.

Of course, now that Simon was back all that was pushed into the background along with everything else. In him she saw reflected an entirely new, and pleasing, image of herself. No longer the hoydenish little sister, the awkward, unfledged admirer, the gauche and giggling schoolgirl, but a young woman with every right to his attention. She visited him in hospital every day of the five they were in London, keeping to the afternoons because Howard and Cynthia tended to go in the evenings and she couldn't bear to share Simon with anyone, least of all his father. On her last visit before returning to school, Howard arrived just before she was due to leave, and Elizabeth was with him.

He looked completely out of place in the ward – too big, too dark, too vigorous, and, Adeline thought, too robustly civilian in his dark suit and waistcoat, with a yellow rose in his lapel. She wondered how he managed to care so little about the impression he created in this place that was full of broken bodies and ruined lives. His confidence astonished and appalled her.

Elizabeth came to the bedside first, and took Simon's hand in hers.

'How are you, my dear?'

'Better for seeing you.'

'Enough – I only came to collect my daughter. She and I are joining Cynthia for tea.'

'And I,' said Howard, coming forward and dropping his thick blue coat and his black hat over the rail at the end of the bed, 'am catching the boat-train to Dublin tonight in order to avoid the fixture altogether.'

He reached out his hand as if he might be going to touch Simon's head, but then withdrew it and smoothed his moustache. 'I wanted to say goodbye before I went.'

There was a pause, an incipient awkwardness which Elizabeth nipped in the bud.

'I've been out riding!' she announced. 'I hired a nag and went out in Hyde Park. It's not in the least like hacking in Devon but the autumn trees were quite, quite glorious, it did me the world of good.'

'The trouble with you,' said Howard, 'is that as soon as you get away from those blasted parochial activities of yours you miss them.' He glared at her. 'Isn't that so?'

'Not at all.' Elizabeth exchanged a smile with Simon. Howard directed the glare across the bed at Adeline.

'And how are you, young lady? I must say you're looking far too pretty these days to be incarcerated in a dame school.'

Adeline ignored the compliment and flew to the defence of St Agatha's.

'I'm not incarcerated, and it's not a dame school.'

'No, it most certainly is not,' agreed Elizabeth, 'and anyway she only has another term there. By this time next year she'll be a paint-stained art student with broken nails, won't you darling?'

This was said with perfect amiability and Adeline replied: 'I certainly hope so,' though it was an automatic response, lacking its usual conviction. Howard snorted with laughter.

'Well,' said Elizabeth, 'come along. I'm sure you've talked enough for about a dozen visitors and Cynthia's expecting us.' She bent and kissed Simon on the forehead. 'She'll be along this evening as usual, and sent her love. Perhaps next time we see you you'll be up and about.'

'I think I will be – I've started some exercises and it's healing well, so they should be able to start measuring me up for a peg leg fairly soon. I can't wait.'

'And so say all of us!'

Adeline saw that she was going to be dragged away with no opportunity for the tender, intimate farewells which she had envisaged. Her mother was already at the end of the bed, giving a little wave. The prospect of school no longer held any charms, but looked ominously like the incarceration Howard had mentioned.

'Goodbye then,' she said stiffly.

'Cheerio, Addy,' he said. 'And don't forget our arrangement.'

'What – ?' She couldn't think what that was.

'About the dinner – and dancing.'

'Oh! No, of *course* I shan't forget.'

'Aha!' said Howard. 'A tryst. Well, doesn't the fella get a kiss?'

Badly flustered, knowing that the eyes of Howard, Elizabeth, Bullman and half the rest of the ward were on her, she brushed Simon's cool cheek with her hot one, felt his hands touch her waist lightly, and his hair soft as feathers on her face. Apart from when he had kissed her hand on that first occasion it was the first kiss of this, their new relationship, and for it to be so public and so formal was a bitter disappointment to Adeline. She longed to throw her arms round Simon's neck, but already Elizabeth was saying 'Come along Addy' and she had to go, adjusting her hat and pulling on her gloves, anything to disguise her wretchedness.

In the cab on the way to Leinster Gardens, Elizabeth

said: 'I expect you're bored to death with St Agatha's, Addy. You must be longing for Christmas.'

'Oh, I am!'

'I'm very proud of all my children,' added Elizabeth unexpectedly. 'All so different and all so clever – and I know your father would have been proud, too.'

'I hope so. I wish . . .'

Elizabeth patted Adeline's knee. 'I know, and I wish too. I find this time of year so terribly nostalgic. And Christmas – but we shall celebrate the end of school and drink to the future!'

Seeing that Elizabeth was in this hectic frame of mind, Adeline said: 'Howard must be proud of Simon, too, don't you think? He is being utterly splendid about everything. Sometimes when I'm sitting there and he's rattling on and making me laugh I forget what's happened to him. That's real courage, I think, not to draw attention to yourself at all but to be able to set other people at ease. Do you know he's never said how it happened, or anything? Howard used always to be so beastly to him before the war, but now he's a hero – '

'There are a great many heroes just now, Addy,' said Elizabeth in quite a different sort of voice, looking out of the window. 'This war is turning them out by the dozen.'

'Don't say that! It's an awful thing to say!'

Elizabeth tucked some hair under her hat with her gloved hand. 'Why?'

'You sounded so hard and unfeeling, and you're not like that.'

'No. But Addy, just because someone has been terribly injured doesn't make him a hero.'

'I know that, but Simon's so wonderful about it, so cheerful, and uncomplaining and – '

'Don't imagine you're in love with him, Addy.'

For a split second Adeline wasn't sure she'd heard her mother correctly. When the words had sunk in she opened her mouth to answer, but Elizabeth spoke first.

'Don't tell me whether you are or not. I'm not prying, I'm just giving you the very best advice I can. You're very young, and talented and lovely and the world will be your oyster, believe me. So fall just a little in love with Simon if it makes you happy, but don't mistake it for anything it's not. Don't mistake *him* for anything he's not – oh, here we are!'

Elizabeth's speech was cut short by their arrival outside 15, Leinster Gardens, and she alighted from the cab quickly, as if relieved not to have to continue.

Once inside, it was exactly as if some capricious Fate had been eavesdropping on their conversation, and was now hell-bent on sabotaging Elizabeth's advice. Cynthia, away from the dominating presence of her husband, blossomed.

'My dears,' she cried, hurrying across the hall to meet them, and pressing her soft, scented cheek to each of theirs in turn, 'how lovely that you could pop round so I could see Addy once more before she goes – I'd have been so sorry not to say *au revoir* . . .'

She led the way upstairs to the first floor room at the front of the house which she was pleased to call her 'study' but which was actually a charming miniature drawing room, providing for Cynthia, no doubt, what the Snug had once provided for Richard. The main drawing room bore the stamp of Howard's taste, running to dark velvet curtains, and leather armchairs, and the strange modern paintings he admired so much and collected, rather to his wife's embarrassment. Cynthia's study was sprigged and swagged and goffered and flounced – sweetly pretty, a city woman's dream of what life might be like in a thatched cottage.

Tea, when it was brought, was as dainty and delectable as one might expect in such surroundings, consisting mainly of items which could be picked up between finger and thumb and popped into the mouth whole – a tea which one could not imagine being eaten by men.

'This is so nice,' said Cynthia in her gentle, cooing voice, 'so civilized. Adeline, another sandwich . . . Tell me, how was my boy?'

'Wonderfully cheerful as usual. He seems better every

day and he's even talking about walking soon – and dancing. He asked me if I'd go dancing with him as soon as he's able!' Adeline's eager outburst came to an abrupt halt as she caught sight of her mother's expression, but Cynthia chimed in at once.

'He *is* remarkable, isn't he? But my dear, you must take a good deal of the credit for his high spirits. I can't tell you how much your visits this week have meant to him, he talks about you so much, and so warmly – *entre nous* I think he's more than a little smitten!' She gave a delighted little laugh, and went on: 'I can't think of anything that would give me more pleasure than to see the two of you together.'

Elizabeth put down her cup with a loud clinking sound. 'What on earth do you mean, Cynthia?'

'You know what I mean! Our two families . . . Simon and Adeline . . . one doesn't have to be a matchmaker like me to see how lovely it would be.'

'I've never heard anything so ridiculous,' said Elizabeth, fiercely, sweeping invisible crumbs from her lap. 'Simon has to learn a completely different way of life, and Addy's only seventeen, for goodness' sake.'

'Perhaps, perhaps,' said Cynthia, giving Adeline a conspiratorial smile, 'but she certainly doesn't look it. She's a young lady, nearly as tall as you.'

'That has nothing to do with it.' Elizabeth's voice was cold and severe as it had been on that occasion after Richard's death: Adeline shrank from it. 'She's spent most of the last three years at a boarding school, and she has her future to think of.'

'Now then, I know, you're one of the new women, Elizabeth,' said Cynthia, 'but I'm quite sure even you would admit that the future for most attractive girls includes marriage to a nice young man.'

Adeline, by now in an agony of embarrassment, felt the time had come to put a stop to this exchange.

'Please,' she said, 'I do wish you'd stop talking about me as if I wasn't here!'

'Yes, it's most unfair,' agreed Cynthia. 'I was only being

meddlesome. After tea, Adeline, I want you to come down and tell me what you think of Howard's most recent acquisition.'

'Another painting?'

'Another painting. I think it's absolutely ghastly but I shall bow to your superior judgement, and we can all say just what we think now that the old bear has left for Dublin.'

From the corner of her eye Adeline saw her mother made a small, convulsive movement of irritation. There was no doubt that the clear waters of Cynthia's little tea party were irretrievably muddied, and only Cynthia herself seemed unconcerned.

If Elizabeth and Cynthia had not chosen to take the lines they did, Adeline's love for Simon might have petered out in time. But young and sheltered though she was, she was also extremely strong-willed, and they had all unwittingly turned her youthful passion into a *cause célèbre*. She returned to St Agatha's for the remaining weeks of term knowing herself to be the focus of a great deal of attention. With the end of Aggy-dom in sight she could not concentrate at all on her work, and even Miss Lake had cause to criticize her lack of application.

'You must work on your painting portfolio,' she said, 'or you stand no chance with the Slade.'

'Oh, I know, and I shall, honestly,' said Adeline, while in her head she was already composing the letter she would write to Simon.

Poor Mary Younge, reduced to playing a peripheral role in her friend's life, tried to involve herself in the project.

'What are you going to say?' she asked eagerly. 'Are you going to declare yourself?'

'I want him to know that I'm thinking about him, all the time, and willing him to get better,' said Adeline, though she knew the purpose of the letter was, in effect, to declare herself.

'My cousin has an artificial leg,' volunteered Mary. 'He

was in the RAFC and he crashed. He said the worst thing when they first put it on you is the itching.'

'Really . . .?' Adeline was not in the mood for confronting stern practicalities, but Mary, having discovered a toe-hold in the situation, struggled to climb higher.

'Yes, the thing is you sweat a lot and your skin gets all sore and chafed and itchy, so you have to put powder on the, you know, the stump, and – '

'Look, Mary, do you mind leaving me on my own for a little while?'

'Oh! Yes. Sorry.'

Left in peace in her cubicle – 'toppers' were allowed an hour's free time before bed – Adeline spent a few moments re-creating the right mood, and then began to write. It wasn't hard. In fact the words positively poured on to the page. It was only the opening which gave her pause. She would have liked to put 'Dearest' or 'My Darling' but when she actually wrote the words they looked too portentous, even for her. He must be the first to use them, and she must show, by the strength of her feelings, that she was worthy of them.

She settled for 'My dearest Simon' and then continued:

Since coming back here I have not been able to stop thinking about you, and how you are. I can't tell you what the last week has meant to me, seeing you each day. I lived from each visit to the next – did you do the same? I dare say that in the past you've looked on me as a rowdy little girl and a bit of a pest – though of course you were too polite and kind to show it – but I feel that we've both changed a lot since we last met, and become so much closer. May I say something? You have behaved so splendidly about your leg, *everyone* thinks so, but there must be times when you're alone when you feel wretched and desperate. I want you always to remember that you need never be alone, because I'm with you in spirit and want nothing more than to share whatever happens to you. I miss you, and our lovely talks, terribly, and I don't know how I shall get through the next few weeks. Please, please do write and tell me I'm not being foolish, and let me know all that's happening about your leg. Anything I can do, anything at all, is yours for the asking.

She was pleased with that, and felt encouraged to conclude with a fine flourish: 'You are in my mind and heart always – ever your 'best girl' – Adeline.'

She had decided against 'Addy' because, though she didn't mind Simon calling her by the diminutive, to refer to herself in this way reminded her of the sort of shallow person she had once been, and was no more.

Toppers were allowed to write one letter a week besides that which they sent home, provided that letter was to a relative or close family friend. When Adeline told Miss Daniels about Simon, the headmistress at once agreed that it was perfectly in order for her to write to him. She might not have been so content had she actually read the letter, which would almost certainly have come under the heading of 'silliness'.

In only a few days a letter arrived for Adeline, post-marked London.

'Is it from him? It must be!' cried Mary.

'Yes – yes it is.' said Adeline. But that was as much information as she was willing to give. She was in a hoarding frame of mind, and went at once to her cubicle.

The letter was all she could have hoped for, and more. At first she skimmed through it, taking in its substance with mounting excitement. Then she went back and read it slowly, savouring every word.

My own dear Addy [he began]. Thank you for your enchanting letter, which would be the very thing to cheer up any miserable chap languishing in hospital. But especially so for me, because it was from the person who means most to me in all the world. Having you beside me day after day has made me realize just how important you are to me, and always have been. You write that I must have thought of you as a pest, or some such rubbish, and it's not true – when I look back on those days I only remember what a wonderful friend you've always been to me, and how you've always been on my side, even when no-one else was. Now I would like to think that you and I have become much more than friends. I miss you horribly, and am in serious danger of turning into a cranky, crotchety cripple without you. And when Mother comes in, she talks about you in such glowing terms your ears should be burning! Surely the answer must be that we're meant to be together . . .

The doctor has told me that I can start to get about on crutches, and I've been taken down in a wheelchair to the place where I'll be measured up for a leg over the next couple of weeks. I'm awfully weak and wobbly and feel rather a fool, but it's a little easier each time. So roll on the day when we can arm it down the street together!

I suppose what I'm trying to say, Addy, is that I've fallen in love with you. And now that I've written down those words I feel so happy about it that I think it must be true! Write again soon, my dearest – all my love – Simon.

Adeline read and re-read until she felt quite drunk with the words. Intoxicated, she began at once to write another letter, this time pages and pages of it, the thoughts and feelings falling over one another on to the paper. It was just as though she'd kept her love stored away in some cupboard in her heart, and now the door was opened after so long it just rushed out, higgledy-piggledy, chaotic and disordered, at Simon's feet.

It didn't occur to her for one moment to wonder why Simon, a young man of twenty-two with three years' experience of the trenches, should write a letter so exactly mirroring her own, a schoolgirl of seventeen. In spite of the outward badge of his suffering, and the changes in her own outlook and appearance, Adeline still saw their relationship to each other in the same terms as before.

Hero he might be, but he was crippled, he would need her more than ever, and the need to be needed was strong in Adeline.

From the time of that first letter her course was set. She was hurtling, out of control, down the gentle slope that would end in marriage to Simon. Naturally, she did not calculate it in quite these terms. She did not calculate it at all. For her it was simply an exhilarating, wonderful, headlong rush into the arms of her love.

Christmas didn't help. For at Christmas, apart from Richard's absence, it was like old times at Fording Place. Howard, Cynthia and Simon (now quite nippy on crutches) came to stay, Bob was home, and Frank on leave.

But if Adeline had been expecting to tell Frank about the thrilling new developments in her life, and that as her benign elder brother and Simon's friend he would be pleased and proud, she was quite wrong. From the moment that she and Bob met him at the station she saw that he was changed, and that to tell him anything for the moment at least would be quite inappropriate.

It was two days before Christmas, the evening before the Charterises were due to arrive. The weather had been blustery and wet, but tonight it had settled and hardened into a clear and breathless frost. Standing on the platform, alone except for the elderly stationmaster coughing in his office, they could look up at the stars and pick out almost every constellation as clear and sharp as if they were in a planetarium, and beyond those constellations others, further away and further, faint dustings and sprinklings of stars unimaginably distant. When they heard the train whistle as it entered the tunnel before Tarrford the shrill wistful sound seemed to make the stars tremble.

Or so Adeline thought. Bob, stamping his feet and blowing smoky breath before his face, was more prosaic.

'Thank God, I'm half frozen.'

'But it's so beautiful, so Christmassy.'

'It's bally Arctic!'

They walked to the end of the platform and back to

keep warm, and as they returned they saw the stationmaster come out of his office, well wrapped-up, and the train rounding the shoulder of the hill, with a bonnet of flying steam and occasional flurries of scarlet sparks spurting from its wheels in the dark. Three people got off, and when the train moved out and the steam cleared, only Frank was left standing here, looking around for them.

'Frank! Frank, we're here!' Adeline rushed up to him and put her arms round his neck, dragging his face down to hers and planting a kiss on it. 'Oh, I say, what have you done?' She pulled back and took in his appearance. 'You've grown a moustache!'

'Yes, a bit less face to shave. Hallo, Bob.'

'Frank . . .'

Adeline watched her brothers shake hands in the guarded, reflective way that men did, and then walked between them through the station and out to the motor-car. He held the door for her to get into the front seat, and then climbed into the back, tossing his kitbag and case in before him. Bob, hauling himself awkwardly in behind the wheel, asked: 'Sure you wouldn't like to drive?'

Frank shook his head. 'I'd like to do absolutely nothing.'

'Fair enough. You'll have to excuse a few bumps.'

Frank smiled – a small smile that got no further than his lips. As they moved off Adeline half turned in her seat and put out her hand to touch his knee. But whether he actually moved away or she simply imagined it, she could not reach him. His face in the darkness, and further obscured by the peak of his cap, was turned in half-profile towards her and though she could not make out its exact expression it seemed distant and preoccupied, as immovable as the face of a corpse.

When they got home he submitted himself leadenly to Elizabeth's excited embrace, and at her prompting went clumping down to be welcomed by Miss Purgavey. Then Bob and Adeline saw him up to his old room and Bob, having set down the suitcase at the foot of the bed, left. Adeline remained for a moment, wanting something more, though she wasn't sure what.

'It's so lovely that you're home,' she said. 'Mother dreads Christmas without Father, and all of us being here makes such a difference to her – '

She stopped. Frank flung himself heavily down on the bed with a great heaving, grunting sigh that was nothing like his real voice. Adeline realized she had been talking to herself.

'Frank?'

But he was already asleep. She went to the side of the bed and looked down at him, and was again reminded of the expression 'the sleep of the dead'. Though he had survived the war so far with only the most minor injuries, he might have been ten years older than Simon. His face was scored and etched with tiredness.

Feeling she should do something, Adeline went to where his right leg still trailed over the side of the bed, and began to tug off the boot. It resisted, but Frank only shifted a little and didn't wake, so she tugged harder and at last it came off in a rush. She removed the other one too, and this time the sock came off as well and she was confronted by the shocking spectacle of his foot, all covered in blisters and callouses and abrasions, inflamed and broken between the toes. It looked, thought Adeline, standing there and staring down at it in dismay, like the foot of an old, poor person.

Quickly she folded the bedspread over him, loosened his tie, and left the room, closing the door softly behind her.

Frank slept round the clock. So it was after tea the next day, when the Charterises had already arrived, that he made his appearance and encountered Simon and Adeline in the hall. It had been difficult, with everyone about, and all the greeting and talking and so on, for them to recapture the wonderful intimacy they had had in the hospital ward. Even Bullman's leery looks, and those of the other patients, had not seemed too intrusive – at least they had seemed to collude with them, to regard them as lovers. Over the last few weeks their letters had grown more and more feverish and now here they were, together, but with no opportunity to be alone. And Simon's impaired mobility – though he did wonderfully well, as everyone said – meant that it was difficult to escape from the gathering with any degree of spontaneity. The least move on his part gave rise to a flurry of helpful manoeuvres which made it scarcely worth the bother.

But now, during the cosy, soporific interval between tea and changing for dinner, Simon had asked if he might look at Adeline's drawings and they had effected an escape. But at the moment the drawing room door closed behind them and they turned to one another, shining-faced, a voice said: 'Hallo Simon,' and they looked up to see Frank coming down the stairs.

He looked better, having had a bath and changed into his own clothes, but Adeline still sensed the difference in him.

At the foot of the stairs he clasped Simon's hand and pressed his shoulder.

'I'm so sorry about that,' he said, glancing down at the stump in its neatly shortened and pinned trouser leg. 'How are you coping?'

Simon grinned, with a kind of eagerness. 'Not too bad, not too bad at all.'

'You must have been through absolute hell.'

'Well . . . it could have been worse. One simply has to put up with it.'

'I suppose so.' Frank's eyes were on Simon's face, he looked thoughtful. 'So what now?'

'Family firm for me. It's what I would have done anyway, this just brings it a bit closer. And of course I've got to get the hang of walking again with the new leg when I get it. Quite exciting in a way – a whole new start.'

It seemed to Adeline that Simon's remarkable cheerfulness had suddenly, in the last few moments, taken on the excitable, unstable quality she had noticed on his first leave, when he and Frank had come to the school.

'I'm glad you're managing to be so optimistic about it

all,' said Frank. 'I don't know how many would be, in your place.'

'How have you been?' asked Adeline.

Frank gave a grin that made him, for a second, his old self, and put his arm round her shoulders. 'I'm a lot better than I deserve to be, all things considered little sister. And I really believe we've got them on the run at last, so the whole damned show may be over soon.'

'Oh good, good!' She kissed his cheek.

'By the way,' he said, 'I'm sorry I flaked out on you last night. I'd never have done it intentionally, but I could hardly see straight.'

'I know, and it doesn't matter at all. You're home for Christmas, that's the main thing.'

'Yes, and I must go and say hallo to the others. You two look as if you're on some urgent business, anyway. Don't let me keep you.'

He went, leaving Adeline with the sense of having been belittled in some way she couldn't quite define.

To save Simon the long and painful journey up the stairs, she ran up and collected her portfolio and brought it down to the library. The room was drab, with no fire, but Adeline turned on the lights and drew the curtains and came to sit on the sofa by Simon, with the portfolio on the rug in front of them.

She had taken out only the third drawing when he took her by the shoulders and kissed her. It was the kiss she had been waiting for, the kiss she had been dreaming of for six long weeks, and yet as his lips touched hers she found herself starting back stiffly.

'Addy . . . Addy I love you. I've been thinking of you all the time, I've lived for your letters . . . kiss me, Addy . . .'

His cheeks were pink, his eyes downcast, watching her mouth as if it were in some way separate from the rest of her. Though his balance was still poor, and it was awkward for him to turn sideways on the sofa, he had developed surprising strength in his upper body, and she felt herself firmly held. This is it, she told herself, he is claiming you, he loves you – and you love him, she added, more than life itself.

Desperately, determinedly, she put her arms about his neck and returned his kiss. This action wrought several changes in Simon: he seemed to become both more pliant and more urgent, he made a small sound in his throat, his eyes closed his fingers dug into her shoulders and back, his breath came shallow and quick.

'Oh Addy . . . you're so beautiful . . . so lovely and strong . . . I love you . . .

'And I love you,' she replied, holding him as tight as she dared, frightened by the strength of the response she had provoked, but pleased by it, too.

But when he suddenly took her right hand and tried to press it to his half-leg she swiftly and involuntarily snatched it away.

'Please,' he moaned into the side of her face, 'please . . .' And took hold of her hand again. 'Show me you don't mind.'

But she did mind.

'No, Simon, no!' She pulled away from him, shocked and flustered. For a split second she saw him as she had left him – his face loose with frustrated passion, his tie awry, his mouth gaping in disappointment – and she looked away.

'I'm sorry,' she said weakly, meaning it with her whole heart. 'I'm afraid I might hurt you.'

She heard him pulling himself upright and composing himself, clearing his throat. For his sake she wouldn't look at him again until he reclaimed her hand – gently this time – and said in his normal voice:

'Poor Addy, I'm sorry. I was a brute to frighten you.'

'No, *I'm* sorry.' She was nearly in tears. The moment which should have been ecstasy had been spoiled, and by her. Tremulously she turned her head and met his eyes. He smiled his most charming, loving smile and pulled her gently on to his shoulder, kissing her hair. Her heart began to slow and steady, she let her arm rest lightly across his chest.

'We have all the time in the world,' he said. He moved his head so that he could look down at her. 'Don't we?'

'Yes, we do.' She nodded, happy now. 'And I love you.'

Christmas took its predictable course, dipping into troughs, rising into peaks, settling from time to time into flat, arid plateaux of boredom. But this year all of it, even Elizabeth's by now traditional children's tea party, was illuminated for Adeline by the secret she shared with Simon. For it was still a secret, in spite of Cynthia's fond, knowing looks, and Elizabeth's determination not to notice them. Howard, to be sure, offered his usual fierce compliments on her looks and remarked that were he twenty years younger he'd need no second bidding – but that was just his way. Frank appeared gradually more relaxed, but he was still preoccupied and there was unmistakably a cooling in the friendship between him and Simon. Bob stalked and prowled the perimeters of the house party in his usual cross but dutiful way, but obligatory festive gatherings had never been popular with him and he joined in only as much as was demanded by common politeness.

Simon and Adeline stole a few more kisses, but they were very fleeting, decorous affairs which even had they been discovered by the others would have scarcely raised an eyebrow. For the rest it was simply fun to be in a room together, with other people around them, and to exchange covert looks and smiles and silent messages. It was very innocent stuff, but Adeline was enchanted with it. When she thought of all the times when, as a girl, she had exhausted herself in the attempt to get one solitary flattering word, one smile, out of Simon – and now she was the whole focus of his attention, his love! More than anything she wanted to show him that she was not a silly, squeamish thing who couldn't face the realities of his injury. She helped him up and down stairs, she fetched his crutches, she made her shoulder available when he needed someone to lean on – it was her pleasure to do it.

On New Year's Eve the Hyde-Latimers gave a small party to which they were all invited, and there was dancing. Adeline, who adored dancing, took a perverse and exquisite pleasure in refusing every invitation to take the floor, so that she could sit on the arm of Simon's chair and keep him company. It was, she thought, rather like being a royal consort, for as they sat there all sorts of people came over to make commiserating remarks, and to add how well he seemed to be taking it all. One of them was Louise Vale.

'Simon – !' she cried. 'I've only just heard about this ghastly thing – hallo, Adeline – please, you must tell me how you *really* are.' And she crouched down before him, nodding, wide-eyed as he talked. Adeline was sore afflicted. On the one hand she wanted Simon to be admired and paid attention to. On the other she was consumed by jealousy. She need not have worried in any case. She was secure in Simon's affections, and Louise was no longer interested in Simon other than as a friend. She was a bright, beautiful, sophisticated young woman, but far too basically kind and well brought up not to do the right thing in these painful circumstances. Her devotedly attentive manner was an acquired skill which had become second nature to her, it meant very little. She had literally dozens of eager young men dipping in and out of her life as they came home on leave, and had not yet told any of them that she was as good as engaged to a newspaper proprietor more than twice her age.

But Adeline knew none of this and by the time Louise had popped a kiss on Simon's cheek, and on hers, and told them to take care of themselves, she was quite rigid with resentment. However, some legacy from St Agatha's prompted her to say: 'She's marvellously pretty, isn't she?'

'Yes, she is,' replied Simon, and then took her hand, adding: 'But not half as pretty as you.'

This was patently untrue, and Adeline knew it, and yet she also recognized it for the declaration it undoubtedly was. That was probably the moment when her sense of the inevitability of their union became complete. The compliment may have been the merest flattery, but the feeling behind it was the truth.

Next day the Charterises left and Adeline, in a haze of emotion, experienced the sweet sorrow of parting. Only she, surely, had ever felt this exquisite melancholy. In the hall Simon kissed her very properly on the cheek, but squeezed her hand and murmured in her ear: 'I love you always.'

Elizabeth was taking them to the station, and as the car moved round the curve of the drive and disappeared from view, Bob and Frank moved away, hands in pockets, with that pleasant listlessness that accompanies a release from social obligations. Adeline remained standing there by the front door for a full two minutes after they had gone, her view of the empty drive shimmering with unshed tears. When at last she too turned and went back into the house her listlessness was not in the least pleasant. Not only was she utterly miserable, but also quite unable to focus her attention on anything but her own misery. She began a letter to Simon, but with his real, thrilling presence so fresh in her memory this seemed a poor project, and she couldn't sustain it.

To make matters worse, no-one paid the least attention to her. The next day Frank went out with Chris Dance, acquainting himself with various estate matters; Bob took the train to Exeter to buy books and Elizabeth was a mere blur of organized activity. She alone was bereft, and bored. She became more and more depressed, a glum and ghostly presence at meals (though sadly she could not manage a convincing loss of appetite) and not prepared so much as to take a walk with anyone else for the rest of the time.

When this state of affairs persisted into a second day Elizabeth, who had been exercising superhuman patience in the matter, rashly intervened. They were sitting down to lunch and Adeline had barely spoken for half an hour.

'Well, Addy,' said Elizabeth, 'I suppose now you'll be wanting to get down to some painting in earnest. I was thinking it would be best if we could make a room available to you – a sort of studio, what do you think?'

'I don't mind,' replied Adeline.

'It's a good idea,' said Frank. 'What about the nursery?'

'Yes,' agreed Bob, 'artists are supposed to operate in attics.'

'It has good windows and a north light,' reflected Elizabeth. 'That might be just the thing. What do you say, Addy? We could all get up there and convert it for you –'

'Count me out,' said Bob.

'Those of us who want to, I mean – it could be fun. Hm?'

'If you like.'

Elizabeth's encouraging smile hardened a touch. 'No, if *you* like.'

'You don't understand, Mother,' said Adeline. 'I don't *care*!'

'That,' said Frank, 'is an incredibly rude and stupid remark, Addy.'

'It wasn't meant to be rude. But I'm really not sure that I'm interested in all this art business any more. And I wouldn't want to put you to any unnecessary trouble.'

Bob folded his napkin and pushed it through its ring with the finality of someone shooting the last bolt on the Bastille. 'Allow me to diagnose this state. Temporary loss of interest in the entire world, due to calf love.'

This shaft had the desired effect, that of shocking Adeline out of her assumed languor. Unfortunately, it had hit home a little too hard. She stood, scarlet-faced, picked up her glass of water and hurled the contents over her brother.

'How can you say that? How can you be so cruel, you nasty, sarcastic *beast*?'

'I have a talent for it,' said Bob equably. 'Excuse me while I go and get dry.'

Frank folded his arms with the air of someone settling

down to watch a cricket match. Elizabeth, too, had shot to her feet.

'Addy! What in God's name is the matter with you? I am sick, *sick* of this behaviour of yours. If you want to be thought of as a young woman – then behave like one!'

Unfortunately all Adeline needed was this final evidence that the world was a harsh, evil place expressly designed to torture her. With tears streaming down her cheeks she rounded on her mother.

'But I *am* a woman!' she shouted. 'And none of you will treat me like one! I don't want a studio, I don't want to be petted and pacified and told to get on with my work! I love Simon! I want him! I want to marry him!'

Frank's expression changed. Elizabeth's face was white and pinched. Her voice when she spoke was a thin, brittle icicle of a whisper.

'Don't be ridiculous, Adeline. You are going to the Slade.'

'I'm not! I'm going to be with Simon – he needs me!'

'He may very well need someone but it is not you. And you are not going to marry him, or anyone else in the foreseeable future. You're lucky to have a talent, you must make use of it.'

'I love Simon! You ought to understand – I thought you loved Father – '

'Addy!' Frank stood and put a restraining hand on her arm but she wrenched away from him and ran to the door. With her usual feeling for a dramatic exit she turned and yelled defiantly at both of them, at the whole world:

'I wish he was here! Father would have wanted me to be happy!'

CHAPTER SEVEN

1918

ALITTLE UNDER A year later, on 10 December 1918, Adeline married Simon in the parish church of St Mark's, Tarrford. About sixty family, friends and staff attended the ceremony, and the reception afterwards at Fording Place.

The bride, who was given away by her elder brother, looked very striking in ivory satin, with the Gundry family veil of six yards of Honiton lace held in place by a coronet of hot-house gardenias and peach-coloured rose-buds. She carried an enormous bouquet – being tall and statuesque she could carry it off – composed of more roses, both white and peach-coloured, white lilies and long strands of greenery which brushed the hem of her dress.

If Elizabeth had deliberately set out to send her head-strong daughter careering into an early and ill-advised marriage she could not have gone about it with a surer touch. Adeline was already predisposed towards the idea and her mother's apparently unjustified disapproval of it simply confirmed her picture of herself as someone holding out for love in a cold and uncaring world. This picture was slightly marred by the unexpected emergence of Howard as an ally. He, like Cynthia, was entirely for the union, and against all her instincts she felt obliged to accept invitations to Leinster Gardens, on her own, in order to visit Simon. As a result of this she half-expected a rift to develop between the Charterises and Elizabeth, but curiously it did not happen. In spite of her mother's frequently expressed dismay over the whole thing, she seemed loth to bring it to a head.

If, in the face of repeated advice along more-in-sorrow-than-in-anger lines, Adeline lost her temper, Elizabeth would retreat, literally. That is to say she would neither retaliate nor retract, but simply stalk from the room. Her line was always the same – that Adeline was too young, that what she felt was pity and not love, that she had no idea what she was taking on: that by withdrawing her application to the Slade, and entering instead upon this marriage, she was simply throwing away the chance to use those gifts she was fortunate enough to possess. The only one of these arguments which carried the slightest weight with Adeline was the last, and even that was as nothing beside her determination to be Simon's wife. She was quite prepared to concede that she felt pity as well as love and strove sedulously to show that her pity could be translated into action. She won the heartfelt admiration of the nurses, the consultant and the physiotherapist for the way she helped Simon through the difficult period of learning to use his artificial leg. She showed herself spirited, unsqueamish, persistent and cheerful. The consultant expressed his opinion to Howard, who confessed himself not in the least surprised and relayed the information to Elizabeth.

'You'd be mad to stand in their way,' is what he said, over the telephone. 'She's the best thing that's ever happened to Simon. She's obviously absolutely devoted to him, and frankly I doubt whether he could do without her, now.'

'But Adeline is not a nurse!' shrieked Elizabeth with that

rising note of hysteria which Howard so often heard in her voice these days. 'Being a brick in a crisis is no basis for marriage!'

'I agree, but anyone can see that they love each other. And that *is*.'

'Oh – !' There was a breathless, exasperated silence and then a sound almost like a sob from Elizabeth, most un-weepy of women. 'Damn you all!'

So Adeline had support from the most important quarter, though her brothers would not align themselves with either side. Bob had joined the staff of a left-wing Fleet Street newspaper, the *Courier*, and might as well have been on another planet. Frank wrote his sister one letter alluding to the subject, and it expressed no direct opinion:

> Mother appears to be thoroughly worked up about all this, and you are still young, so I do advise you to think very, very carefully before taking any decisions. Simon is an old friend and I wish him all the luck in the world, but one must face the fact that he is crippled. He is cheerful now but there are almost certainly some bad times ahead for him, and for you if you marry him. I don't mean to sound disloyal, but you must appreciate what it is you are taking on. Mother's anxiety is quite well justified, and no-one will think any the worse of you if you back out now. With that said, of course I wouldn't want to stand in the way of your happiness . . .

And a little more in that moderate and sensible vein. It was a kind and careful letter and Adeline took it in the spirit in which it had been written, but it did nothing to change her mind. She was happy, in spite of the conflict that rumbled on in the background, or perhaps even because of it: it helped to focus and drive her energies, and like her mother – with whom she had much in common – she liked to be purposeful.

In fact in many ways 1918 marked the happiest time in her relationship with Simon. The challenges – mental, physical and emotional – which they had to overcome in order to maintain it, brought out the best in both of them, and a general lack of privacy meant that any potential awkwardness, such as that encountered in the Gundry's library at Christmas, was avoided. Simon proposed to her in August, in Regent's Park, during his first outing with the new leg.

They sat on a bench in warm, grey weather, admiring the handsome houses along Prince Albert Road.

'I wouldn't mind living in a house like that,' said Simon. He held Adeline's hand in both of his.

'I don't know about London,' she admitted. 'I'm a hayseed at heart.'

'On the other hand,' he went on musingly, not looking at her, 'I could live anywhere so long as it was with you.'

'And me.' She rested her chin on his shoulder and kissed his cheek. She felt quite weak with love and pride.

'So are you going to marry me? Then I shan't give a hang where I live.'

'Yes. Of course I am.'

They embraced, a little awkwardly, and her hat fell off. Passers-by smiled indulgently at their ardour, noticed the walking stick propped against the seat and wished the hero well. They were so young, so handsome, so much in love – who would have the heart to deny them anything?

Together they had travelled down to Fording Place to confront Elizabeth. Adeline was fully prepared for a set to, and had warned Simon of squalls ahead.

'The very last thing I want is a fight with your mother,' he said. 'I'm quite sure we can win her round. I've always got on rather well with her.'

Adeline shook her head. 'That doesn't make any difference. She simply doesn't want me to marry you – or anyone.'

But Elizabeth deprived Adeline of her scrap, and in doing so gave her daughter her first real chill of doubt.

In spite of glorious high summer sunshine they were in the library, whither Elizabeth had retreated now that she was on her own most of the time. Mark had died, but

Trigger lay near the door as he always did these days, in order to be first to greet Richard if he should magically reappear.

Elizabeth sat on the upright chair at her writing desk, but facing them. She had lost a good deal of weight and Adeline suddenly saw the changes that had taken place over five years as if they had happened overnight. Elizabeth was now a gaunt, angular, middle-aged woman, still good-looking but no longer concerned with her appearance, and with an expression of tired defiance.

Adeline sat on the edge of the sofa. Simon stood to one side of the fireplace, leaning on his stick, his false leg resting at the slightly unnatural outward angle which gave it away.

'I love Adeline very much,' he said. 'I've asked her to marry me and she has said yes. We do so hope you will give us your consent and your blessing.'

Elizabeth, who had been staring at her lap, lifted her eyes and looked at Adeline. There was a silence of perhaps five seconds, which seemed to Adeline like five hours. Then she said:

'I've said everything I have to say about this, and it's made no difference. Tell me, Addy, is there anything I could say at this stage that would make you change your mind?'

'No. But Mother, we want – '

'Then go ahead.' Elizabeth rose. 'Get married.' She went to each of them and kissed them on the cheek, a kiss, Adeline thought, that was like a farewell.

'And now we should have a drink,' she said, and rang for Mrs Trodd.

Adeline went to her mother, and took her hand.

'Mother, please don't be like this, please understand – we want your blessing!'

'You have my permission, Addy. And I hope you'll be happy, that's all I've ever wanted.'

Adeline, with the sensitivity of guilt, caught the allusion. 'I'm sorry – I'm sorry I said that about Father.'

Elizabeth gave her head a dismissive shake and looked past her daughter to Simon.

'Simon, my dear, do your parents know about this?'

'I think they've got a pretty shrewd idea – but not officially, no. We naturally wanted to speak to you first.'

'Oh – naturally.'

Mrs Trodd appeared, and champagne was summoned. Adeline went to stand by Simon and he put his arm round her shoulders and kissed her cheek with a smile. But she had the sensation of having won a hollow victory.

The sensation didn't persist, for the Charterises were so wholeheartedly pleased, and all their friends so enthusiastic, that any residual doubts were simply swept away in the torrent of good will. The date was set, the invitations sent out, the dress decided upon and its making initiated, the vicar primed, the banns read, the menu for the wedding breakfast chosen. All this Elizabeth handled with her customary *élan* which managed, with most people, to pass for enthusiasm. Only Adeline was aware of her lack of warmth – that her mother was going through the motions with no enlivening current of happiness. In spite of her exuberance Elizabeth had never been especially demonstrative towards her children – that had been Richard's province – but now there was a marked holding back. Thrown together with Adeline in all those pleasant processes of assessment, selection and acquisition in which mothers and daughters are usually at their most companionable, she contrived to maintain a small, cold, unbridgeable gap between them. She touched her as little as possible, managed to smile amiably enough while never catching her eye, and let her have her own way in most things. It was this last which perturbed Adeline most, for she knew that it meant her mother washed her hands of her. Financing the wedding was not a problem, because Howard was paying for most of it. Adeline could have wished otherwise, but realized that it would be both churlish and unrealistic to object.

The ending of the war, and Armistice Day, coming as

they did only a few weeks before the wedding, seemed to enhance it, to bathe the whole day in a warm glow of general as well as personal happiness. It was, as many of the guests said, so *suitable* somehow to be wishing these two attractive young persons well on their shared life together after the long, bleak years.

Chris Dance met Dorothy Sugden in the church porch on the way in, and this time had no hesitation in complimenting her on her hat.

'You look as smart as paint, Nanny,' he said. 'I suppose I shouldn't be calling you that now.'

Dorothy beamed at him, more at ease with him now that she had moved on. 'Once a nanny always a nanny,' she said, 'But Dorothy will do very nicely.'

'A very happy occasion,' he remarked as he escorted her to a pew.

'Yes, but it's just the start, of course,' she said, rather more tartly than she had intended. 'They've got a long way to go.'

'Absolutely right, Nanny,' said Chris, but when she glanced at him and saw that he was teasing, he added: 'Dorothy.'

In church, Anne Hyde-Latimer tapped Bob on the shoulder.

'Hallo – you're quite a stranger these days.'

'Anne! I didn't see you there.'

'What's it like being Scoop Gundry of the *Courier*?'

'Hardly Scoop. I make a lot of tea and telephone calls and cover the occasional story that's beneath everyone else's dignity. I take orders like a man.'

'I have the greatest difficulty in imagining that,' said Anne. 'I mean the taking of orders. Don't they have any sense of self-preservation?'

Bob grinned and nudged her arm off the back of the seat. He liked Anne, who was bright and sensible but no bluestocking, and reasonable enough looking without being as terrifyingly lovely as Louise Vale. Speaking of whom . . . there she was, Bob noted, with short hair, and a little hat, and diamonds round her neck, accompanied by a large, florid man who looked as if he might use a ten pound note to blow his nose.

Louise noticed that Bob Gundry's hair was receding slightly and that, oddly enough, it rather suited him. The effect of a widow's peak above his thin, intelligent, severe face was quite distinguished. She touched her husband's arm and pointed discreetly with her scented, grey-gloved hand.

'That's the younger brother, darling,' she whispered, 'the one who's joined the *Courier*. He's awfully clever.'

'So what's he doing working on that rag?' was Edward Maybury's reply, but delivered in a perfectly good-humoured tone.

'Ssh! Ted!' Louise was reproving. 'Just because you don't like Carlton's politics . . . you know he's regarded as one of the really brilliant editors. You'd poach him if you possibly could.'

'Nonsense, wouldn't touch him with a barge pole.' Edward gazed about him, bored with waiting, met the eye of someone he knew, equally bored, and raised a hand.

'Who did you see?' asked Cynthia.

'Ted Maybury. Our paths cross from time to time. We went to dinner there about a year ago.'

'Oh yes, the newspaper man.'

'The newspaper man. Exactly.' Howard grinned at his wife, pleased with this description of Maybury. Cynthia, pleased that he was pleased, glanced at Simon, sitting in the pew in front. He looked so handsome, he and Adeline were so right for each other . . . Cynthia looked forward to this marriage as a new beginning . . . such a delightful couple, so much admired, and there would be grandchildren, of course. Cynthia suspected that she would make rather a good grandmother, fond, feminine, indulgent. Elizabeth had become, poor thing, somewhat formidable and intimidating in recent years, through no fault of her own – she was not really a small children's person.

The best man – another old school chum of Simon's; he didn't seem to have made many friends in his army days – looked over his shoulder, gave her a nervous smile, and nudged Simon. The organ paused, as if drawing a deep breath, and then launched with all its wheezy strength, into 'The Arrival of the Queen of Sheba'.

'She's coming!' whispered Cynthia excitedly to Howard, but he was already half turned and looking down the aisle.

Elizabeth, doing the same on the other side of the aisle, could not help catching his eye for a second. They neither of them smiled but she felt, for that fleeting, unguarded moment, as if they were alone together. Quickly she looked away, trying to arrange her face into an expression of proud maternal welcome for Adeline. Here she was, looking beautiful and a little defiant, her strong chin noticeably lifted beneath her veil. Elizabeth's eyes smarted dangerously. She knew Cynthia would notice, and think that she was overcome with tender emotion at the poignancy of it all. But she wasn't going to cry. And the emotion she felt was horror.

They had found a picture-book cottage on the edge of Dartmoor for their two-week honeymoon. In the new year they were bound for a small, smart flat in Lancaster Gate while Simon acquainted himself with the Charteris business, but for now that seemed light years away. The cottage was on the outer perimeter of the land owned by Elizabeth's parents, and the tenant farmer's wife, Mrs Meredith was more than willing to be the young couple's housekeeper, to keep them supplied with groceries, to clean the cottage and cook a homely, nourishing supper when required – which was frequently, since Adeline still couldn't cook.

Though the village was only two miles away, the cottage's great charm was its air of secrecy and seclusion. It was not even visible from the village road, and it was only if you knew the mossy cart track that wound down through the woods that you came upon the cottage, pressed up against the side of the hill, the trees clustering protectively at its back, its pretty, unkempt garden bordered by a stream, the hillside beyond rising through waist-high bracken, then tussocky grass, then heather, studded with grey, licheny rocks – the beginnings of the moor.

Howard had given them a motorcar, for although Simon would not be able to drive for the foreseeable future, Adeline had persuaded Elizabeth to teach her during the summer and autumn. It wasn't possible to take the car right down the track, but they drove it for the first thirty yards and then Adeline parked it among the trees and they covered it with tarpaulin. When they walked nearby and saw it, standing there incongruously in the woods under its shroud, Simon christened it Old Dobbin.

Not that they did very much walking, for all sorts of reasons. It was mid-winter and, though dry, it was bitterly cold, with a scudding, snapping wind off the moor. And Simon still couldn't manage any sort of rough going with his leg, though he did better all the time. And most of all, they simply didn't want to go out. The cottage, with its thick walls and low ceilings, its wood fires that roared and crackled in open stone grates, its one heavy door which could be closed against the world – the cottage was where they wanted to be.

Mrs Meredith was the very soul of discretion, coming in the afternoon to do the cooking and cleaning, and always whistling or singing a little as she approached. But she need not have worried, because for five days and nights there was precious little of an intimate nature to disturb. In spite of their mutually professed desire, it wasn't easy at first. Adeline wanted love, she longed for it, she craved it body and soul. But though the heart and spirit were more than willing, the flesh proved strangely unresponsive. Sitting curled in Simon's arms on the bumpy, sagging sofa before the fire, full of Mrs Meredith's rib-sticking brown stew, and dreaming pleasantly of the future, she was as relaxed and content as a well cared-for tabby cat. But upstairs, between the cold, slightly harsh, lemon-smelling linen sheets, her well-being drained away to be replaced by a paralysing anxiety that was close to panic.

Adeline had grown used to the sight and the feel of Simon's amputated leg. It no longer disgusted or frightened her. She had come to terms with its smoothness, and its peculiar completeness, as if it had simply grown to that length and stopped growing. She had conscientiously learnt about its problems, about the artificial limb and how it was strapped on, and how Simon had to use it, with a kind of whip-crack, flicking motion from the hip. She could touch it and examine it and help to put talcum powder on the stump when it was chafed and sore. But when, suddenly, it became a part of her naked, panting lover, when it nudged blindly against her or, worse still, when he guided her hand to it as if asking for some kind of absolution or forgiveness, then her flesh would shrink and her head turn away in a powerful involuntary spasm of distaste. Worse, she couldn't explain how she felt, so when he asked, desperately, urgently, 'What's the matter?' she said 'Nothing' just as the Aggies used to, hoping that would be enough and knowing it wasn't. He was not persistent. His ready acceptance of her rejection made things even worse. On the first two nights as she lay rigidly on her side, her eyes wide open, with slow, silent tears trickling across her face on to the pillow, he must have assumed she was asleep, for she was conscious of quick, furtive movements against her back, his voice stifled to a thread of sound, a stickiness on her skin and on the sheet. But on the third night he simply heaved a great sigh and said, 'Don't worry . . . never mind . . .' and rolled away from her and went to sleep.

Each day, in the morning, they managed to banish the horrors of the night by playing house. Adeline would get up early and make tea and burn bacon and cut large uneven slices of bread. They would huddle by the ugly, crouching, black, iron range in the kitchen and feel the warmth and life creeping back into them. Then they would light the fire in the tiny sitting room, and perhaps Adeline would bring in some more logs from the pile at the back, and they would write some thank you letters for their innumerable wonderful wedding presents, and talk about how kind everyone had been, and the wedding itself, what a lovely, memorable occasion. They read, sometimes aloud to each other, and played cards and pencil and paper games like two convalescents in a school sanatorium. When Mrs Meredith came, after lunch, they'd chat to her, drawing more comfort than she could possibly have known from her practical, country motherliness. Then sometimes they went out for a while, arm in arm through the black, silent winter wood to check on Old Dobbin, or over the plank bridge and up the hill a little way, with the stark breath of the open moor on their faces. After that they often pressed Mrs Meredith to stay and have a cup of tea with them, and when she'd gone there was the long, cosy evening with good food and the dreamy, lapping firelight. It was quite easy to believe in their own and others' picture of themselves as star–struck young lovers in a romantic hideaway, until the moment when bed could be postponed no longer and Adeline would find, yet again, that she could not go through with it.

Curiously, it was a remark of Mrs Meredith's which put things right. On their sixth day at the cottage she encountered Adeline crank-starting the car in the woods. Simon's leg was troubling him and he had fallen asleep on the sofa, so Adeline had decided to run the motor to the village garage and fill up the petrol tank. In spite of a leaden cold that promised snow, her face was scarlet and her breath fumed, dragon–like, before her face with each twist of the crank handle. 'Oh, damn the wretched thing!' she snapped, and stood up, blowing on her frozen fingers. 'Mrs Meredith, hallo. I'm sorry but I can't get the thing going.'

'Don't mind me, sorry I can't help,' said Mrs Meredith, beaming. 'You'd do quicker to walk.'

'Yes, but it needs starting, and I thought I could go into the village . . .'

'Is Mr Charteris about down there?'

'His leg's sore today, he's having a rest.'

'Honeymooning's hard work,' opined Mrs Meredith.

Adeline pushed her hands into the pockets of her coat. 'It is in a way.'

'Oh yes, not enough of each other and then too much. Men need a lot of humouring and yours more than most I wouldn't be surprised, with his poor leg and all.'

Adeline smiled. She wasn't put out by Mrs Meredith's forthrightness: it was just her way, and it reminded her rather of Dorothy. On the other hand she didn't want Simon characterized as a petulant and demanding invalid.

'He's marvellous. He never complains,' she said.

'Just the same, it's a lot for a young girl like you, taking on a man full time,' persisted Mrs Meredith, as if talking about some singularly unrewarding job of work. 'I was married with a baby on the way at about your age. My husband's a good man, but I'd rather mind six children than go through those early days again. A child you can teach a few manners, but not a man.'

At this point Adeline felt she had heard as much as she wanted to, and prepared to address herself once more to the crank handle.

'Good luck to you, then,' said Mrs Meredith, continuing down the track. 'Let's hope you're not still here when I come back!'

But shortly after that Old Dobbin coughed and honked and shuddered into life and Adeline was able to drive into the village. Bowling along the road her spirits rose, partly (though she wouldn't admit it even to herself) because she was completely alone for the first time in days. And also because Mrs Meredith's good-natured scepticism had put her nocturnal problems into some kind of perspective. Of course it wasn't the end of the world. It was a difficult period, a period of adjustment, marriage had to be learned and worked at like anything else. She smiled to herself. She was part of the great sisterhood of wives. Even her beloved Simon, her gentle hero, had to be catered for, and it was up to her to comply with all the understanding at her disposal. She was young and healthy and her husband adored her, theirs was undoubtedly a marriage made in heaven and with one or two small concessions, a very little effort on her part, they would scale the heights together.

In the village, determined if a little self-conscious, she bought a bottle of brandy, the only one in the shop and dusty from having stood on the shelf so long. That night after supper she poured them both a nightcap, and two hours later their marriage was consummated, Adeline was no longer a virgin and they fell asleep facing one another, for the first time. The euphoria they both felt from this point onwards was quite unjustified by the act itself, which had been quick and severely to the point. But with the obligatory part of the honeymoon out of the way they relaxed, and became like two children with a new toy. Every night, and sometimes in the early morning too, they did it and Adeline was bathed in the glow of well-being that accompanies a duty honourably discharged.

It snowed, and the cottage was half buried in muffling white drifts. Flakes continued to drift down, sometimes singly, sometimes in whirling profusion, and an eerie metallic light turned the day to perpetual evening and even the darkest nights into hours of cold, moonlit beauty. There was nothing and no-one to draw the curtains for, and they'd lie huddled up against the bolster in the old brass bed and watch the black shapes of half-starved animals on the hill opposite, drawn down from the high tors to the houses by the weather – shaggy ponies, a watchful fox, the occasional deer. Once a huge barn owl swooped across the garden, outlined for a moment against the black trees around the stream and then disappearing again, like a bird made of snow.

They were willing enough prisoners, but the Merediths, having assumed responsibility for them, were diligent in carrying out the rescue. Half a dozen farm labourers, with little else to do at that time of year and with the bad weather, cleared the cart track and dug out the car – just like seven maids with seven mops, as Adeline said, and every bit as futile, for the snow kept falling.

'I reckon you'll be here for Christmas, like it or not,' observed Mr Meredith cheerily, when he and his men had breached the drifts and were enjoying a well-earned cup of tea in the kitchen.

'No, no, we shall be on our way soon,' said Simon.

'I wouldn't be so sure. Tez unseasonal this.'

'All the more reason for it to thaw within a week!'

Mr Meredith shook his head. 'Doesn't follow.'

'Anyway, we couldn't impose.'

Adeline caught his arm. 'Simon – why don't we stay for Christmas? I mean, why don't we stay anyway? No-one's going to mind.'

'No-one'll mind,' echoed Mr Meredith. 'My wife's enjoyed having you two to do for and the cottage is empty till spring. Do it good to be kept warm,'

'Well . . . we'll see,' said Simon.

Later, in bed, he added: 'What about your mother?'

'She'll be fine! Frank's there now, remember.'

'I'm not sure . . .'

'Simon! Darling!' She bent over him, folding her arms on his chest and resting her chin on them. 'We're us, now, a married couple – Mr and Mrs Simon Charteris.' She outlined their visiting card in the air. 'If we want one more week to ourselves why shouldn't we have it?'

He threaded his fingers in her hair and pulled her head down for a kiss.

'No reason.'

'Good – then I'll walk up to the village tomorrow and telephone Mother.'

Perversely, the sun came out the next day, and the snow began to thaw. Adeline moved through a landscape that sparkled and shone with a false spring. The drab browns, and blacks and tawny greens seemed vibrant after the snowbound monochrome of the past few days, and the sky beyond the black lattice of bare branches, was brilliant blue. Though it was beautiful, Adeline also found it unsettling, as if some spell had been broken and the world was closing in.

She walked to the post office and telephoned Fording Place.

'Good God,' said Frank, 'had enough already? Here's Mother.'

'Hallo?' said Elizabeth, in her overloud telephone voice. And then said, when Adeline had explained: 'If that's what you want, my dear, stay on by all means. Will you both be all right? Are you being looked after?'

'We're being looked after beautifully.'

'You wouldn't like me to tell the Pater you're going to be there a bit longer?'

She referred to her elderly and redoutable father. Adeline was appalled.

'Oh Mother, *no*, they'll only fuss and ask us up to the house on Christmas Day which is exactly what we want to get away from – ! I'm sorry, I didn't mean it in quite that way.'

'That's all right, I understand,' said Elizabeth drily. 'If they should ask I can always say you were snowed up.'

'Till today we have been, more or less. Look, I mustn't be long – '

'Addy. How are you?'

'We're fine!'

'I mean, are you happy?'

'Of course! Sublimely happy! It's our *honeymoon*, Mother.'

'Yes, of course.'

'And you're not terribly hurt that we're not joining you for Christmas?'

'My dear, you're Mrs Charteris now,' said Elizabeth. She said those words over and over to herself in bed at night to make them come more easily, but she still tripped on them. 'You're Simon's wife – ' She bit on that word, too. 'Whether you spend Christmas with your ageing mother is neither here nor there now. I'll come and visit you in London in the spring.'

'Yes.' Adeline could not picture London, nor spring, least of all Elizabeth paying them a visit. She found talking to her mother unsettling, she wanted to end the conversation. 'Yes you *must* do that,' she said, and shortly afterwards rang off.

In effect, though, their idyll had ended, and they were left with their extra week like an unwelcome and ill-chosen present that they didn't know what to do with. The weather turned mild and wet, and there was mud everywhere which meant Simon could scarcely walk at all out of doors, it was so treacherous, and Adeline caught a cold and felt wretched.

Their new toy, so hard-won and so much played with, lost much of its charm under these conditions, but on the other hand they settled into a pattern of mutual comforting and petting which was, Adeline reflected over strong sweet tea laced with brandy, just how it was with proper married couples.

They began to look forward to London, and to getting on with real life.

CHAPTER EIGHT

1918–1920

AT FIRST, REAL life came well up to expectation. The flat in Lancaster Gate was elegant and well appointed, and Cynthia had engaged a cook-housekeeper for them, Marjory, who lived in. Nonetheless Adeline threw herself into the business of being a wife with her usual wholeheartedness, and took on much of the everyday cooking herself. After a predictable procession of burnt offerings and collapsed puddings, she not only got the hang of it but discovered that she enjoyed it and became quite adventurous. After a minor triumph with rack of lamb (a speciality of Miss Purgavey's) she even felt moved to write to Dorothy Sugden on the subject. 'I simply had to tell you that I've learnt to cook – and I'm not half bad! So all your gloomy predictions about my future were quite unfounded!' Dorothy, on reading the letter, was not so sure, and rather wished she had not placed such emphasis on the domestic arts, but duly wrote back in time offering heartfelt congratulations.

Adeline had meant it that afternoon in Regent's Park

when she had said she didn't want to live in London, but now that she was here she found she adapted quite readily. Cynthia assiduously fostered their social life, introducing them to several well-to-do and pleasant (if a trifle dull) young couples; Mary Younge was in London, doing a typing and stenography course in Kensington, and of course there was Bob in his cluttered, scruffy, but curiously inviting rooms off the Holloway Road. For a wedding present he had given them an odd little statue, of stone and about three feet high, of a girl in a cloak, looking over her shoulder.

The stone dryad glancing forever backward gave the impression that she was keeping an eye on them, perhaps on someone else's behalf, and sure enough only two weeks after they arrived in London Bob telephoned and invited Adeline to lunch.

He took her to a noisy, smoky restaurant near Ludgate Circus, not far from the offices of the *Courier* and obviously frequented by many of the more junior staff, for Bob's sleeve was plucked and his name called all the way from the door to their table. It was clear he was no longer a loner, and he was on the way up, getting bylines and earning more. The face, form and manner which had made him something of a misfit at Fording Place were perfectly suited to these surroundings, and made him appear not just quite at home, but even rather distinguished. Adeline, in a blue suit and high-necked blouse which Simon liked, felt that she looked prissy and overdressed. There were perhaps half a dozen other women in the restaurant and their clothes, though undeniably cheaper and older than Adeline's, seemed to sit on them with easy, comfortable grace, like a second skin. It was the people you noticed here, not the clothes. Everyone was either talking animatedly or listening intently. Adeline liked everything about the place.

'We'll have the hotpot, it's cheap and cheerful,' announced Bob in his slightly ungracious manner. He placed their order for this and a bottle of red wine, with the elderly waitress. Then he folded his arms and stared at Adeline. She felt uncomfortable.

'What are you staring at? Have I got a smudge on my nose or something?'

'Far from it, Pretty as a bandbox and neat as a new pin.' Bob managed to make both these observations sound deeply disparaging. Adeline was stung.

'I'm sorry if I don't suit, but I'd no idea where we'd be going.'

'You might have deduced it wouldn't be the Ritz,' he said drily, but then smiled and added: 'You look fine. One of these days you and Simon must come and see me at my digs and do some real slumming.'

'We'd like to.'

'Would you?'

'Yes! Bob, stop this!'

'What?'

'I don't know – !' She stopped in mid-sentence as the waitress brought a carafe of wine, then continued in a fierce whisper as Bob poured two glasses: 'Stop pretending I've got too big for my boots, and you're some sort of penniless bohemian!'

'That's more like it,' said Bob. He took a packet of cigarettes from his jacket pocket, opened it and held it out to her. 'Want one?'

'Why not?' replied Adeline defiantly, who had never smoked before in her life.

Bob lit the cigarette for her and leaned back in his chair, watching expressionlessly as she struggled for breath.

'I apologize,' he said, 'if I seemed rude. You just didn't seem like yourself.'

'And I do now?' Adeline coughed and wiped her eyes.

'You will do, if you survive that cigarette.'

'Thank heavens for that – oh, this is a horrible thing!'

'There's the ash tray. And anyway, here's lunch.'

Over the hotpot their conversation was confined to safe topics such as Bob's work, and Frank's decision to remain at Fording Place and run the farm. But when the coffee came, Bob asked:

'So, how's married life?'

'Wonderful,' she replied, as she always did.

'What on earth do you find to do with yourself all day?'

'Lots of things, There's the flat to run, and I go riding, I see quite a bit of Cynthia. She's introduced us to some nice people, we entertain – '

'Do you draw at all, or sketch?'

'Not much. Well, not at all really. I've rather outgrown all that.'

'Outgrown it!' Bob accompanied this exclamation with a look of scornful disbelief. 'What rot.'

'It isn't rot, it's the truth!' Adeline's anger was in direct proportion to her discomfiture. 'My life's taken a different turn. I've so many other things to think of now. I expect I shall do it again some day, as a hobby – '

'Hobby?' again the sarcastic incredulity. 'You see yourself perched on a little stool by the Serpentine, do you, painting vapid watercolours?' His eyebrows rose, he cocked his head on one side. She turned hers away, scarlet with embarrassment, but he caught her chin and made her look at him.

'Come on, Addy, aren't you bored stiff?'

'Of course not! I told you, I'm busy the whole – '

'Yes, yes, *busy*.' Bob waved a hand, scattering ash. 'But isn't it tedious?'

'No!' She felt badly flustered, could hear the note of rising agitation in her own voice. She hated Bob at that moment – Bob, the eternal spoiler. Bringing her voice under control, she said, 'I've honestly never been happier. I say, do you think I could try another cigarette now?'

It was true that she was not bored: she was working much too hard at being a good wife for that. On only one or two occasions over the next few months did she experience a slight twinge of discontent, as she saw Mary Younge blossom and change, and tell Adeline about the sort of work she'd like to do. And then there were suppers at Bob's digs, where his friends brought food, and he provided the drink and everyone sat where they could amidst the clutter. She and Simon enjoyed these evenings, becoming slightly drunk and listening spellbound to all the talk of politics and deadlines and scandals and who was doing what with whom. But afterwards they would fall into a kind of awkward silence, in which each of them was preoccupied by what had gone before, and somehow unable to talk to the other. Often, this lasted right through until the next day, until they had re-established their own pattern and their own way of doing things, and then the effect of the evening would fade and eventually disappear.

But no, she wasn't bored. Her life centred around her husband, and his happiness was hers. She drove him to the office in Blackfriars each day, and collected him at five. It was her pleasure to do so. Simon used to joke about it – being chauffeured around by his pretty young wife to a job that was more a paid holiday than proper work. When Adeline tentatively ventured the opinion that he might prefer to be more challengingly employed, he teased her gently for being a little puritan at heart.

A slight, though perfectly supportable, distance developed between them as it must, thought Adeline, with all married couples. It was, she considered, part of the natural process of maturing, and of fulfilling their separate roles within the marriage. The physical side of their relationship had settled into an agreeable pattern: she knew what made Simon happy, and it made her happy to be the means of providing it. She was cheerfully acquiescent. Afterwards as she lay in the curve of his arm, with her head on his shoulder, he would kiss the top of her head and say: 'Still my best girl?' And she'd answer: 'Of course', glowing with pride that he depended on her still, and couldn't do without her.

Then, in November 1919, they went to Ireland.

At Kenarvon, the country house outside Dublin which Howard had rented for them, Adeline was most definitely bored. Bored, and miserable and frozen. The house, besides being much too large for them, was dank, draughty and spartan. Adeline, effectively alone in it for three quarters of each day (apart from a secretive crew of servants) was simply never warm. Her whole being, body and mind, seemed to slip into some lower order of existence, like hibernation, in order to cope with the awful chill.

She had never expected married life to be lonely, but here in Kenarvon it was. She was not shy, nor retiring, nor, she thought, hard to get along with, but she had reckoned without the mistrustful reserve of the servants, or the sheer distance of her neighbours – the nearest was five miles away. In this great, dismal isolated house, they were both deprived of those little domestic enterprises and games with which, in London, they had so successfully distracted themselves from the inadequacies of their relationship. The kitchen, the garden, even the motorcar – each was the exclusive and jealously guarded preserve of one or other of the staff. And Adeline was too young, and too eager, still, to fall in with what she took to be Simon's wishes, to barge in where she was not wanted. With no social life nor any domestic responsibilities to speak of she had nothing to give a framework to the day, and when she did take long walks over the sodden Irish countryside her solitude made the exercise seem pointless.

The house was set in a moist, green hollow, and was itself so damp that Adeline sometimes felt she might be turning into a water creature herself – voiceless, deaf, slippery, and cold-blooded. The central core of the building dated from the seventeenth century, but annexes, wings and additions had been tacked on over the years so that now it had very little character of its own and was a shambling mixture of styles and architectural persuasions. The lush dairy farming land, of which it had once been the centre, had been sold off and now there was only a walled kitchen garden, some stables and outbuildings a dank and gloomy shrubbery, and six acres of ill-kempt grass which squelched beneath the feet.

Inside, where one might at least have expected to find space and gracious proportions, it was curiously huddled and pokey. The fires, when lit, provided tiny, futile islands of warmth as though some well-intentioned fairy were shaking her fist at a gigantic and implacable monster of cold. Getting up and going to bed in the main bedroom was an exercise in allowing as little as possible of the surface of the body to be exposed to the air at any one time. Adeline wore almost as many clothes at night as she did during the day, and the bed itself seemed always to be chill and clammy. When the maid, Eileen, applied the warming pan to the sheets they hissed and gave off steam.

Nor was the chill confined to the fabric of the house. Like a stealthy, unseen virus it infected the occupants, too. To begin with, Adeline and Simon clung together for warmth, tried to laugh about it and tell themselves it wasn't for ever and, anyway, they had each other. But little by little they stopped, first the clinging, then the laughing, then the protestations of love. Adeline, even in the face of her growing fears, might have soldiered on in the hope of restoring the situation by sheer tenacity and willpower. But with every day Simon seemed to move further away from her, not just in body but in spirit, as though a silent horde of fears, kept at bay by the bustle of life in London, had now seized their opportunity to move in and claim him. He was agitated and anxious, and yet unwilling to accept comfort or to offer an explanation. He was preoccupied, and unable to settle. In bed at night he fell instantly into a dead sleep, his back to Adeline – and yet if she put out her hand in the small hours of the morning, he was not there.

When intimacy was quite out of the question – taking meals under Eileen's watchful eye, or on outings to Dublin – he was more his old self, kind and diffident, and somehow apologetic, as though he admitted his shortcomings and begged indulgence for them. He did not need to beg, he had Adeline's forgiveness and she would have done whatever was necessary to comfort him, had she only been allowed to. She, too, was lonely and unhappy and longed for closeness, however lacking in passion. But just over a year into her marriage, Adeline had come full circle, and lay each night staring wide-eyed into the darkness, feeling more isolated than ever before in her life.

She tried to make friends with the servants – remembering with profound nostalgia her conversations with Dorothy, and even her subtle sparring with Bryer – but they seemed to see her only as a signer of chits and handler of cash. Her anxious amiability robbed her of what little natural authority she had possessed and they began to exercise a subtle tyranny over her. She started to conduct her life for their benefit, taking solitary luncheons in the gloomy dining room so that nothing should be wasted, and stodgy teas in the drawing room which she neither wanted nor enjoyed.

Kenarvon was furnished, but that was all. There was about it no hint of affection, nor of a fond personal taste being exercised. There were chairs to sit on, tables to eat off, beds to sleep in and a picture for each wall, but not one of these items bespoke even the tiniest shred of pleasure in its acquisition. For the past thirty years the house had been in the hands of a Dublin agent, and lived in by a dozen sets of tenants. As fixtures and fittings had worn out or got broken they had been conscientiously replaced, but it was so long since the house had been a proper home it had forgotten how to be.

And Adeline felt that she too had been set down here in the same spirit, as that necessary adjunct to a large country house – a wife.

Only she was no wife. She was not allowed to be. At four-thirty each afternoon, as she sat by the small fire in the sombre drawing room, eating Mrs Donaghue's salty scofa bread, and plum jam full of skins, she would determine that evening to make things right again, to take Simon in her arms and show him that she was still his best girl. Given the chance she knew she could melt the barrier of reserve and anxiety that separated them.

But the chance never came. Each evening when he came back, and they were forced to greet each other under Eileen's opaque black gaze, and then to sit on opposite sides of the fireplace because there was no sofa and that was how the chairs were arranged, the feeling was stifled in her.

For the first time she feared she might have made a terrible mistake. Frank had warned her there might be troubled times ahead for Simon. She had been prepared for them, but had also expected that her husband would turn to her for comfort. Instead, he was drifting away from her and drinking, too, rather more than in the past. And there were other things, things she had always half known but thought she could change: his nervousness, his susceptibility, his occasional small outbursts of foolhardiness (usually followed, like the ill-advised drinking, by periods of genuine remorse).

His role in Dublin was to maintain the Charteris presence at the Irish end of Howard's shipping business. Each day Donaghue, husband of the cook, drove him into the city, and returned him on the dot of six-thirty, and each day Adeline, as she watched his tall, slim figure bend almost double and disappear into the dark interior of the car, was overwhelmed by the wrongness of it all. He was so utterly unsuited to the driving, power hungry, interior world of commerce. She thought how admirably he would have fulfilled the kind of role her father had played at Fording Place, that of genial, leisured supervisor. In that role Simon would have been popular and admired. In this he was a fish out of water. He no longer joked about being paid a hefty salary to do nothing, and she no longer had the confidence to mention it. That, like everything else, had become a taboo subject.

In the March of 1920 Adeline bought herself a lurcher puppy, Clancey, a quaking, bounding, panting bundle of unconditional adoration. Though he could hardly have been expected to appreciate it, Clancey had entered a canine paradise – never was a dog so lavishly loved, nor expected to provide so much. Without Clancey Adeline often felt she would wither and die from neglect.

'How is the pup, sir?' enquired Donaghue in his soft, slightly prissy Irish brogue. He was driving Simon home one evening in late January, making conversation. His shoulders and head remained erect and motionless behind the wheel, but his moist brown eyes reflected back at Simon from the rearview mirror.

'Coming along. Pretty uncontrollable,' replied Simon.

'They need a firm hand, sir,' agreed Donaghue. 'My cousin has always kept the lurchers, and they're good dogs, but they need telling.'

'My wife's very soft with him, I don't know why.'

'The ladies are soft, sir!' said Donaghue. 'Myself, I wouldn't trust a woman with no dog of mine.'

'It's not mine, Donaghue, it's hers.'

'Ah – !' Donaghue did not actually say 'the more fool you' but the whole phrase was there in his voice.

Simon was appallingly discomforted by Donaghue. The man's manners were exemplary (perhaps a little too exemplary, they bordered on the satirical) and he was punctilious in the execution of his duties. And yet Simon felt that Donaghue despised him. The politer, the more obsequious he became, the greater the humiliation.

The glistening brown eyes once more focused on him.

'Did you have a good day, sir?'

'Yes thank you,' said Simon, 'not bad.' He shifted in his seat in an attempt to move out of Donaghue's range of vision.

'Is the leg troubling you, sir?'

'Just a little.'

''Tis the wet and damp I dare say.'

'Very possibly.'

'A spot of good whiskey always helps with stiffness in the joints.'

'Yes.'

Simon took the *Irish Times* from his case as an excuse not to converse any further. He stared at the print, but did not read. It was a lie, what he had just said: his days were always bad, and he was not equipped to make them otherwise. His secretary, motherly Miss Coltrayne, had long since seen through the charming helplessness he used to gain her support. Now she firmly steered him through the daily minefield of correspondence, meetings and business lunches, only too well aware that he could not cope without her.

The lunches, at first a high trial from which he would emerge doubled up with acute nervous indigestion, were now not quite so bad. After all, a few drinks were not only acceptable but proper on such occasions, and with a bit of Dutch courage he could at least be relaxed and amusing. He was sure the visiting businessmen whom he entertained could never have guessed at his incompetence, and with his unlimited expenses the head waiters at the Gresham and the Shelbourne greeted him with gratifying civility as a valued customer. Indeed, the lunches had taken on an inflated importance in his life. He made it one of his first tasks in the morning to check that there was such a lunch in the diary, and if not to instruct Miss Coltrayne to arrange one. In this way the hours from ten till one could be sweetened by anticipation, and those from three till five dulled by whiskey, rich food, claret and liqueurs. But over the last half hour, after Miss Coltrayne put her head round the door and enquired 'All right if I go now, Mr Charteris? All straight my end,' (it never varied), his head would start to ache, and to clear, and he would grow once more despondent at the prospect of the evening ahead at Kenarvon, with Adeline.

The car began to leave the city and to travel more swiftly along the open road. Simon sighed and pinched his temples. He gave up the pretence of reading the paper and let it lie on his knee as he gazed out of the window. He loathed Ireland. It was more foreign than he had expected. He hated its air of atavistic catholic secrecy, its huge divide of bloated wealth and sly poverty, the loud, extravagant horseflesh barons in the bars of the big hotels, and the whining beggars crouched in all weathers against the balustrade of O'Connell Bridge.

He hated it most of all because it had plunged him brutally into the welter of fear and shame that he thought he had escaped. The humiliations of his work, that awful house, the look on Adeline's face – they were mere flea bites compared to the depression that hovered over him like a great black bird.

'. . . for a few minutes, sir?'

The car had stopped, and Donaghue was asking something over his shoulder.

'I'm sorry?'

'Will you want to stop for a few minutes, sir?' repeated Donaghue. They were pulled up at a pub, the Pear Tree, on the open road between Kenarvon and its nearest hamlet, Kilmainham. Simon had got into the habit of breaking the homeward journey at the Pear Tree, and taking a fortifying stout with a whiskey chaser at the bar. Until now Donaghue, though slowing down slightly as they approached the pub, had always awaited instructions. His failure to do so this evening stirred Simon into exercising his small authority over his driver.

'Not this evening. Please, drive on,' he said.

'As you wish, sir,' said Donaghue in a voice so soft and sibilant that only the consonants could be heard as the car moved forward once more.

Simon leaned his head back on the seat and closed his eyes, sweating with embarrassment and irritation. His father, of course, would not have been put out by Donaghue. Good Lord, Howard did nearly everything to excess, and was admired for it: mistresses (and not always of a very high-class type), gourmandizing, gambling, a Havana permanently jutting from his face, expensive tie-pins and cufflinks glittering on his chest and wrists. A little matter of taking a drink on the way home from work would simply have been the subject of a man-to-man joke between him and his chauffeur, if it was discussed at all, and any presumption would have been quelled peremptorily and forgotten the next day. Whereas Simon felt guilty about his stop at the Pear Tree because he knew – and knew that Donaghue knew – that he didn't just want the drink, he needed it.

The war had been the most terrible experience, for Simon more than most. He had never discovered that camaraderie in the face of common danger which helped many young men come to terms with their situation. He was simply mesmerized by the danger itself, and the terrifying suffering all around him.

The deprivation, discomfort and disease of the trenches were bad enough, but they simply set the scene for slaughter on a scale he had never in his worst nightmares imagined – though now in nightmares he saw it over and over again. Towards the end he had felt that every time he took a step he was walking on a spongy turf of rotting bodies. The parapets themselves were bolstered up with corpses and severed limbs, swollen and wet so they were barely distinguishable from the sandbags that surrounded them. Simon was astonished by the courage he saw displayed on every hand by men – and women – who could have been no better prepared for these horrors than him. How did they do it? Where did they find it? He knew the adage that to be brave is to experience and overcome fear but he could not believe that so many ordinary people could be so brave. How did those young men find it in them to swarm over the top, revolvers lifted, shouting exhortations to those who followed, into a storm of shelling and machine-gun fire? How? From what reserves of character and breeding which, it appeared, he did not possess?

It was not just that they faced the likelihood of death every day. Death was the kindest of the options. Far, far worse was the *pain* – the revolting mutilations for which there was no help, the bellies and heads crushed, cracked and ripped open by shrapnel, the protracted and ghastly torture by poison gas, the excruciating indignities of dysentery, the smell of pain, and the noise of it, the sight of men in an extreme of agony which Simon knew he could never endure.

He had lived in abject terror. And unlike those, Frank among them, who managed to draw energy from their fear and to use it to fuel displays of courage which won them the adoration of their men, Simon had succumbed, utterly.

For two years, his own energy had been entirely taken

up with the avoidance of danger. Impossible, one might
have thought, under the circumstances, except that like
any deceiver he became astonishingly adroit at the deceit,
to the point where he almost convinced himself. He
became expert at hanging back, always on some apparently excellent pretext. He sprained an ankle. He had so
impressed his commanding officer with his grasp of tactics
that he had been put on liaison, from which it had been a
relatively short step to the comfort and security of Staff
HQ. He had been well liked by his superiors, tolerated by
his peers, and disdained by his subordinates.

Of course a certain number of calculated risks had been
necessary to maintain the fiction of keenness. He had been
sent out one day to deliver a message to a company commander near Vimy, leaving early in the morning on his
motorbike while things were relatively quiet during the
breakfast stand-to. Humming happily along the country
roads in fine weather, he was suddenly menaced from an
unexpected quarter. From out of a clear blue sky a couple
of German planes appeared. The pilots apparently in a
mood for sport, began toying with him, buzzing over the
summery fields, skimming the trees which lined the paved
road, spraying the area with random fire. Panic-stricken,
Simon had veered sharply off the road and wound up in a
ditch, weeping with terror, as the planes, with a final swallow dive like a mocking salute, climbed back into the blue
and disappeared.

Simon never delivered the message. He simply waited,
cowering and trembling, in the ditch for a reasonable
length of time, and then set off back to HQ at a hectic
pace. On his return, his spattering of cuts and bruises lent
credence to his observation that it had been 'pretty busy
out there', and only one or two were curious as to why
a platoon from 'F' Company should have advanced so
perilously close to a German gun emplacement at Vergès
Farm, not twelve hours after receiving information about
its location. The platoon was, of course, wiped out.

When Simon was sent back up the line in the early
autumn of 1917, his fear – which he now recognized as

cowardice, pure and simple – grew unmanageable. He had grown afraid of the fear itself, and it was becoming harder and harder to dissemble. On 2 October as he ran, choking and stumbling, across no-man's-land under fire, he fell into a shell crater. He lay there, curled up, his arms around his head, for a full two minutes before looking up and seeing that there was another man in the crater with him – a German soldier, very dead. With the curious lucidity that very often accompanied his worst terrors, he conceived a plan. It would involve pain, but his fear of pain was now as nothing beside his dread of this war of attrition on his nerves. He was close to a breakdown. Very soon, he knew, he would be able to bear it no longer and he would turn and run away from the line – run and run until he was caught, and court martialled and publicly shamed. Shot, probably. What he needed was an escape that was quick, complete and which carried with it some semblance of honour. And at this moment he was presented with an opportunity which he must grasp with both hands. He crawled over to the German, wrested from him his fixed bayonet, with its characteristic jagged blade, and plunged it into his own right leg not once but twice, between knee and ankle. Then in an ecstasy of pain he restored the bayonet to its owner and fainted.

It had all worked out. He had come round at the field hospital and had discovered that now, in the face of the pain, and the gas gangrene that followed, and the trauma of amputation, he had it in him to behave like a hero. The knowledge that he was safe, and cared for, and would never again have to go up the line acted upon him like a powerful analgesic. All the nurses admired him, he could see it in their eyes. They had seen fortitude in plenty at the field hospital, but his uncomplaining cheerfulness was exceptional.

Only Frank had looked at him in a different way. They had been thrown together a good deal in the days before Simon had been put on Staff, and even then Simon realized that Frank knew him too well to be fooled. The war had not only changed people, it had showed them in their true colours, and there was a thoughtfulness about Frank these days which was unsettling. Between them they shared the knowledge, always unspoken, that Frank had risen to the occasion and Simon had not. Simon was plagued by the idea that his friend might guess at what he had done. Wounds in the foot and lower leg were often self-inflicted, but he had used the distinctive German bayonet, he had even been discovered not two yards from the German soldier who had carried it . . . would that be enough? He had hoped against hope that it would be and yet, when he had encountered Frank again that time at Fording Place, the air of quiet scepticism had still hung about him and made Simon cringe with shame.

'Nearly there, sir,' said Donaghue. 'And here comes the rain.'

He wound the wheel of the car into the sharp left turn that took them through the gates of Kenarvon. Simon stared out of the window at the trees flinching and bending before thin whips of sleet. He tried to brace himself for the evening ahead. It was a bitter irony that Adeline's warm, open, enquiring nature, the heroic streak in her which had so attracted him and upon which he had so often depended – it was this very quality which now demoralized him, for she seemed to ask so much more of him than he could provide. The extraordinary euphoria that had buoyed him up for over two years had drained away from him since they had come to Ireland. He was depressed and fearful, he had difficulty sleeping and, when he did sleep, it was to pass through a landscape of horrific recurring night-mares. He had begun to wonder seriously if he were not a little mad.

'Home sweet home,' said Donaghue. 'Nothing like it, eh sir, after a long day?'

'No,' said Simon. Kenarvon loomed frowningly through the rain.

The car drew up before the front door and Donaghue got out and opened the rear door for Simon with that perfect, smooth civility which Simon knew mocked his own inadequacies. He was a little awkward climbing out, and Donaghue caught his elbow and helped him upright. He did it easily: he was a big man, and very strong.

'Thank you.'

'I'll see you in the morning, sir.'

'Yes. Goodnight, Donaghue.'

'Good night to you, sir.'

The chauffeur climbed back into the car and drove round to the side of the house. Simon stood alone in the dark before the front door. He clutched his attaché case and umbrella like amulets, to see him through the perils and dangers of a night at home with his wife.

Adeline, sitting in the chair to the right of the fire in the drawing room, saw the lights of the car arriving, and heard the brief, unvarying exchange between Simon and Donaghue. As the car drew away again she rose, stubbing out her cigarette, and saw, through the not-quite-drawn curtains, her husband standing motionless in front of the house. He wore his dark winter coat, and his face looked very white. But most of all she was struck by his air of utter desolation. He was unaware that he could be seen so this, then, was the truth, and she shrank before it. What was there she could do in the face of such dread, such terrible unhappiness? She knew neither the cause of it, nor the means by which it might be overcome. Slowly and heavily she went into the hall to greet her husband.

Eileen was there first, as always, marching to the front door with a curt 'I'll see to it madam' so that she felt she had been put in her place, whatever that might be. So she just stood there with her head held high, and felt the cold damp air rush against her face as the door was opened.

Simon was greeted by the usual tableau: Eileen's square, red face at the side of the door, and beyond her Adeline, standing near the mirror so that he could see her straight, stiff back as well as her welcoming smile.

'Thank you.' He handed Eileen his case and umbrella, and shrugged off his coat into her waiting hands. 'Hallo, Addy.'

'Hallo, darling.'

He walked what seemed a mile to his wife and kissed her. She put her hand up to his neck but he was already moving away from her into the drawing room.

'Let's have a drink,' he said.

'Yes, pour me one, please,' said Adeline. Eileen hovered. 'Yes, Eileen?'

'Shall I let the dog in now, madam?'

Faintly, Adeline could hear Clancey barking and barking in the kitchen. She steeled herself.

'After dinner perhaps . . . he's so boisterous.'

'As you wish, madam.'

Adeline did not wish, but she could not bear the contrast between the exuberant affection of her dog and the cold unhappiness of her husband.

Simon poured two glasses of sherry and Adeline lit herself another cigarette and the two of them sat down in their usual chairs. At this point Simon usually said how pleasant it was to be home, but tonight there was no such pretence: he sat on the edge of his seat, his glass cradled in his hands, taking occasional snatches at the sherry as though it were unpalatable medicine.

'You look tired,' she said.

'I am rather.' He swigged what was left in the glass and rose to refill it.

'Top me up too, will you?'

He did so. His hand shook and the heavy lip of the decanter clinked on the edge of the glass.

'Do you know,' she said, as lightly as she could. 'I wouldn't blame you if you didn't look forward at all to seeing me in the evening. I have an idea I'm becoming a bore.'

'That's not true, that could never be true,' he said abruptly, brushing aside her attempt to focus his attention away from himself. His depression was almost palpable, she could sense it in the room, blundering blindly about like an animal in a trap, seeking release in expression but always failing.

'At any rate,' she went on, 'we should have a holiday in

the spring. Just tell Howard you need to be released from your duties for –'

'Oh, for heaven's sake . . .!' Simon sounded more wretched than angry. 'You know as well as I do, Addy, that I have no duties. It doesn't make a jot of difference whether I'm in that office or not. It runs itself. The job's a damned sinecure.'

'Then it wouldn't matter if you went away for a fortnight,' retaliated Adeline spiritedly. 'And I think that's what we should both do – in late April or early May. We could go to Fording Place for a while, and then perhaps to Paris. I've never been there. What do you think?'

'I don't know. Perhaps.'

Characteristically, having made one outburst Simon relapsed into silence. Sitting slumped in his chair, his face averted, he looked a picture of abject despondency.

'Did you bring home a newspaper?' she asked.

'I'll fetch it.' He went out into the hall to get the paper from his case. Over recent months the debonair grace had left his step and he had developed a slight stoop.

'Here you are.'

Adeline opened the paper and scanned it. The eerie bark of a vixen outside emphasized the heavy silence of the room where they sat. Adeline thought of the kitchen downstairs where Mr and Mrs Donaghue and Eileen would doubtless be keeping warm and drinking stout – perhaps amusing themselves by talking about their employers. She pictured Clancey, consigned to his basket. But there was no sound. The heavy doors which stood at the entrance to the back of the house were closed. The two worlds were firmly separated.

'There's the bloodstock sales coming up soon,' said Adeline. 'I think I might try and buy myself a decent horse. Cullen would come along and help me. What do you think?'

'By all means, if you want to.'

'This is hunting country. It would give me something to talk about with our neighbours. We'd be in with all those terrible people!'

'That's true.'

'Then I shall embark on a concentrated programme of entertaining,' said Adeline. 'We've been dull for too long. I am going to take our social life in hand –' She looked across at Simon. He had not been listening. His head was in profile to her, leaning against the back of the chair. She felt a surge of misery, but spiced with enough youthful resentment to make her blurt out: 'I wish you'd tell me what's the matter!'

He didn't look at her. 'Nothing's the matter.'

'Something must be!'

'Do stop all this –'

'What's gone wrong? Is it me? Have I done something wrong? How can I possibly make it right if I don't know?'

In her anguished frustration her voice rose sharply. His, when he cut across it, was dull and heavy, a blunt instrument.

'For heaven's sake, Addy, don't be so self-centred. Stop imagining everything begins and ends with you. It doesn't.'

That hurt so much that for a moment she was speechless with pain. But she was not going to let him brush her aside. She rallied.

'I don't think that, and I never did. But if it's not me, then what? Why won't you tell me?'

'I'm just a bit tired. Things are rather on top of me at the moment.' He threw these sentences to her as though he knew them for the hollow excuses they were. And by doing so he implied, unmistakably, that she merited nothing more.

She tried again, from a different and more dangerous angle. 'I only want to help,' she said. 'I love you.' With a shock she realized for the first time that this assertion was, or had become, a lie. That she could even recognize it as such dismayed her. So eager was she to undo the lie that she repeated it.

'I love you, and I can't bear to see you so unhappy.'

'Then I'm afraid that's your bad luck, Addy. This is real life, you know, not fairyland. Uncomfortable though it may be for you, you can't be surrounded the whole time with cheerful, smiling faces and bright sunshine.'

'That's not fair!' She shouted it, because it was true. And as if to compound the injustice, she heard at once how petulant the truth sounded. Simon reached across and took the paper from her.

Adeline knew, instinctively, that in essence she was right, and he was wrong. But she also saw, in his bowed head and the grey newsprint, that no matter how often this scene or others like it were played out, she was not going to win.

The drawing room door swung open and there stood Eileen, her opaque black eyes bold and accusing as she announced: 'Dinner is ready, madam.'

That night in bed Adeline raised herself on one elbow and put her face close to Simon's. He was deeply asleep, though she could see the small movements of his eyes beneath his lids as he dreamed, and now and then his shoulder twitched convulsively like a dog that hunts rabbits in its sleep.

She fell back on the pillow. She wondered at herself, at both of them. Not much more than two years ago she had been a child, enjoying the eternal girlhood of St Agatha's, playing lacrosse and tennis, acting in plays, improving her drawing and dreaming her dreams. Then all things had seemed possible. Now, suddenly, she was confronted by the possibility that this could be the rest of her life – this emptiness and loneliness and loveless desolation. Decades of it stretched before her, with no hope of relief without admitting failure. Her pride, and the remnants of her love for Simon, would keep her as securely imprisoned as bars and a padlock. What was worse, the same pride would not allow her to turn to anyone in the hope of a sympathetic hearing. She had made her bed and she must lie on it, that was what Dorothy would have said.

She turned on her side, her back to Simon's, and closed her eyes, overlaying one darkness with another.

Simon knew that he was dreaming. But the knowledge did nothing to allay the terror brought on by the dream.

He was in an empty, barren landscape, an undulating plain studded with dwarfed and blighted trees. Across the plain scurried an icy wind that stirred his hair and the bare stumps of branches, and carried with it a faint sound which always, to begin with, he could not identify. It was a distant yelping, something like the cry of hounds picking up a scent. He sensed that he was the quarry, and began to run, slowly at first, then faster and faster, slipping and slithering over the wet ground, becoming covered in foul-smelling mud, his breath labouring painfully. And all the time the wind, gaining in strength, would boom and blunder round him, impeding his progress, and bringing with it that plaintive, baying sound, drawing nearer all the time. But as his desire for flight grew more urgent, his strength grew less. His legs, heavy with wet clothing and mud, became leaden, his lungs burned, his arms flayed the air wildly. The dreadful sound was closer, almost upon him now, and he began to cry with fear and panic, until at the very last moment, when he knew he could run no more, he looked over his shoulder and saw not hounds, but men. The men were almost upon him, but they were not running. They could not run. Instead they crawled and swayed and lurched towards him, accusing him with mouths that gaped redly, reaching out their maimed and mutilated limbs towards him, sighing and slithering through the mud. Exhausted, he fell and they swarmed over him. His nostrils filled with their smell, and his mouth with the bitter taste of bile. Their cold, sticky hands laid hold of him and pressed him down into the mud until he began to choke –

And then he awoke. His eyes snapped open, but for a second the dense darkness of the bedroom persuaded him that he hadn't woken at all but was still in the dream, suffocating and drowning in the black mud. Then gradually, as his heart slowed and his eyes grew accustomed to the dark, he could see the familiar features of the room, and hear Adeline's even breathing. He rarely disturbed her, for he never screamed. The habit of concealment was strong, even in sleep.

He was damp with sweat. When he blinked it got into his eyes and made them sting. He was so tense that his shoulders and head trembled slightly. The fear still swirled inside him, he was possessed by it, it was the purest and most intense feeling he had ever experienced.

Shivering convulsively, he pulled aside the covers and lowered his good leg to the ground. The rug beside the bed felt chill and damp. Feeling for his sticks he banged the bedside table and it rocked perilously; he only just prevented the lamp from crashing to the floor. He caught his breath and froze in case he had woken Adeline, but she only shifted a little and made a small sighing sound. Clancey, in the corner of the room, raised his head and stared at him. He slipped into his dressing gown and lurched awkwardly towards the door. It was heavy and the handle was stiff, but he had learnt that by pressing the door itself as he turned the handle he could ease it open silently.

Out of the bedroom, the place of nightmare, he felt a little better and his shivering began to subside. As he made his way down the stairs with both hands on the banisters, the grandfather clock rumbled and launched into its sonorous chime: half past twelve.

Simon stood still in the wake of the chime for a moment, until the silence closed seamlessly around him again.

He went into the drawing room and turned on the light. In the hearth the fire was still just alive, the grey rubble of dead coals glowing red in places. He took the brass poker and shifted some of the ash, and then took a few pieces of coal from the scuttle by hand, and placed them carefully on top. He was panting fiercely with the effort. He poured himself a whiskey, two-thirds filling the tumbler, and then lowered himself heavily to the floor near the fire, his dressing gown drawn tight around him. The coals began to catch, one or two pale, darting flames flickered in the hearth. Simon took a long draught of the whiskey and felt the warmth, inside him and on his face, beginning to work its cure. Gradually the horrors withdrew, like the ebbing of a cold tide, and were replaced by an exhaustion so complete that he could not stir even as far as a chair. He managed a few more mouthfuls of whiskey before his eyelids drooped and his fingers encircling the glass went limp. The glass fell into the hearth, shattering and spilling what was left of its contents. Simon sank down on the rug and slept, like the dead.

Adeline was awakened by the faint, distant chink of the breaking glass. Rolling on to her side she saw that Simon wasn't there. It was a familiar pattern. She did not usually go after him, since her attempts at comfort were unwelcome and useless. But the broken glass convinced her that this time she should go down. She couldn't leave him to be found by the sharp-eyed, knowing Eileen in the morning. She got out of bed, and at once Clancey rose and padded to her, wagging his tail. Pulling on a cardigan and a dressing gown, and carpet slippers over the woollen socks she wore in bed, she went downstairs and into the drawing room, guided by the light beneath the door.

Simon lay curled, fast asleep, on the hearth rug like a dog, his sticks beside him. There was an overpowering smell of malt whiskey. The fire burned merrily. Suddenly frightened, Adeline ran to him and kneeled down, shaking his shoulder. Clancey sat, and whined. Simon didn't wake, but his face was tranquil and his body felt limp and warm. She heaved a great sigh of sadness and relief. For a moment she could not summon the energy to rouse him and guide him back to bed. She picked up the pieces of glass and put them in the wastepaper basket, and sprinkled a shovelful of ash over the spilt whiskey. Then she went to the bookcase and took down a collection of metaphysical poetry. For an hour or so she sat, with her husband at her feet and her dog beside her, waiting for the moment when she might escort him back to bed to avoid embarrassment before the servants, and reading, with curiosity, about love in all its motley and intoxicating variety.

When she finally woke Simon, at a quarter to two, he was stiff and disorientated.

'Oh God, Addy, I'm so sorry . . . you don't know how sorry . . .' he kept mumbling as she steered him up the stairs.

'It's all right, don't worry,' she replied. But she fancied that she heard in his muddled apologies, the echo of a sorrow other than mere domestic guilt. A pining, perhaps, for what they had lost. Or for what they had never had, and allowed to evade them.

CHAPTER NINE

1920

THANKS TO ADELINE's determined organization, they did take a holiday in April. They went first to London, to stay with Cynthia and Howard for a few days, and then to Paris, for a second honeymoon. This was far better than the first, because Adeline, who had never been abroad before, was captivated by the place, and there was so much to do and see they hadn't time to dwell on themselves. Indeed, Adeline decided that she had been a victim of *accidie*, that things were not nearly as bad as she'd imagined. They had been going through a bad patch, a thing most married couples did as far as she could see, and hadn't they solemnly promised to see it through for better or worse?

It was even possible to feel quite romantic, what with fine spring weather and the food and the wine and the flower sellers on the banks of the Seine, and the fact that the French unquestioningly accepted them as young lovers. Everywhere they went little treats were pressed upon Adeline, a rose for her buttonhole, a chocolate, a whoosh of delicious scent in a dress shop, a pretty compliment accompanied by a smile and a wink for Simon – she would have had to be made of stone for all this not to work on her. And Simon, away from the anxiety at work, and the chilly gloom of Kenarvon, brightened and was more his old self, even managing to express some hopes for the future.

'We shan't be in that place forever,' he said one night, as they walked arm in arm near their hotel. 'I should think I'll be back in head office in a few years, and we can get ourselves a nice little place just out of town.'

'But we must make the best of Kenarvon while we're there,' she replied. 'We must at least try.'

He smiled at her and kissed her cheek, much as he used to do when he called her his 'best girl'. But he did not reply. Under the influence of Paris, Adeline was able to contemplate Kenarvon and marriage with far greater equanimity. It seemed that Simon felt the same.

At night he would kiss her and sometimes even put his arm round her, and then fall deeply asleep. She didn't mind. The act itself didn't mean very much to her, she had decided, and if Simon no longer wanted to do it, then that was fine. She assumed that this was all quite normal and customary, a part of the everyday process of marriage. She was always awake after he slept, but quite contentedly, knowing that for the first time in months he was sleeping deeply and soundly and would do so till morning. But in a little restaurant a few doors down the street there was a woman singer with a husky, lilting, suggestive voice, and each night Adeline would fall asleep with that voice in her ears, not fully understanding why she felt so sad.

Once back at Kenarvon at the beginning of May, Adeline had no trouble in maintaining the improvement begun in Paris. Before leaving she had purchased a six-year-old dark bay gelding, Sholto, who had been left in the care of the groom and was now wild-eyed and fresh, ripe to be ridden. The weather bloomed into spring, a little later and more tentative than in Paris, but spring nonetheless, with a respectable complement of daffodils and crocuses, and a froth of sparkling new green on the austere trees on either side of the drive. Kenarvon itself would never be a beautiful house, but the lush green of its setting in the kindly light of the sun showed it off to advantage. It wasn't such a bad place, Adeline decided, but like its occupants it needed cheering up.

As she had rightly surmised, she was living in a part of the world where a good horse constituted a passport to society. After only a few weeks of riding out on Sholto, with Clancey bounding and leaping behind, she had made the further acquaintance of their two nearest neighbours (their association with whom had so far extended to no more than a few glasses of sherry on a Sunday morning), and had invited them to dinner. Mrs Donaghue was set quite by the ears, as she explained to Eileen, because not only was the dinner party sprung on her and a certain menu requested, but the young madam had declared that she would prepare the soup herself! Just as if she, an experienced cook, was not competent!

But the dinner party was accounted a success, and Adeline and Simon were invited back, and when she expressed her intention to hunt that winter they were asked to help form a party for the hunt ball. Adeline found these occasions, and the hard-riding, hard-drinking set who frequented them, rather hard work, but her morale was raised by the knowledge of a challenge well met.

Having scandalized Mrs Donaghue, she swiftly brought Donaghue into line by turning her attention to the garden, or lack of it. 'There's far too much of this dreary, poor quality grass, and nowhere to sit,' she announced. 'I'd like some nice flowering shrubs, and perhaps an arbour – a rose arbour.'

Donaghue expressed, in his smoothly courteous way, his doubts about the general cost and viability of the project, but she swept them aside, paid a visit to the market garden, where she bought up half the stock, and began at once to dig, weed and plant like a thing possessed until Donaghue was shamed into co-operating.

So Adeline was busy once more, and in better spirits. But she was not a fool, and she recognized that within a few days of their return Simon was withdrawing into his unhappy private world of nameless anxiety. He charmed the people they met socially, because on those occasions he was well fortified with drink. They had heard, of course, about his having lost his leg in the war and Adeline, looking on proudly, could almost see the old battleaxes' eyes become dewy as they talked to him, and the weather-beaten faces of their husbands, from the MFH downwards, mellow and assume approving expressions.

But that was in company. Alone with her his depression stood always in the background, like a beggar with its face pressed to the glass. With no response to make she did her best to ignore it, in the hope that it would simply go away.

There were, too, more concrete causes for concern. Adeline, in spite of what she read in the newspaper, had tried to dismiss them as having nothing to do with her until the day that an elderly officer of the Garda bicycled up to the house, scarlet and perspiring, expressly to warn her against going out in the jaunting car on her own. She was in the habit of using the car, pulled by a trim Connemara mare, for going back and forth to Kilmainham.

'But it's so much nicer than the motor in this weather,' she cried. 'I'll miss it terribly.'

The policeman mopped his glistening forehead and took another long draught of lemon barley.

'I'm sorry, Mrs Charteris, but it would not be safe just now.'

'Really? Surely out here, nobody – '

'I'm told to tell you it would not be safe, Mrs Charteris. We can't say what will happen.'

The poor man looked so hot and bothered that Adeline didn't argue any further. Privately, she considered the danger grossly exaggerated. She even thought she might welcome a little excitement.

For Simon, the Troubles had become an almost daily and terrifying reality. 1920 was a year in which violence seethed and bubbled in Dublin, and hardly a day went by when there wasn't some kind of incident involving de Valera's followers and the police. Journeys around the city were now ordeals for Simon, to be borne as best he could, in a state of flinching, sweating anxiety. One afternoon as he travelled by taxi down Parkgate Street there was a sudden stutter of small arms fire, terribly loud and close, and two men ran from a side street, shouting, one of them carrying a revolver. Mothers snatched at children, a news stand was overturned. The taxi in which Simon was travelling was caught in a stream of traffic, and was standing, engine idling, nearest the pavement. Simon was suddenly sure that the men would rush the taxi, perhaps hijack it, and they were armed. He panicked, banging on the partition and yelling at the cab driver: 'Drive on! Move, can't you? For God's sake drive on!'

'There's nothing I can do, sir,' replied the man phlegmatically. 'Not a thing.'

In fact, the men were gone in seconds, running pell-mell down the pavement, scattering people on either side. And the Garda, emerging from the side street only seconds later, were confronted by Parkgate Street looking much as it usually did, and a large number of potential witnesses declaring unhelpfully that it had all happened too quickly for them to notice anything about the men.

As the taxi moved off again the driver looked over his shoulder at Simon and grinned cheerfully.

'Not to worry, sir! 'Tis not your battle!'

This was no comfort to Simon, who felt, with some justification, that all his life he had been caught up in battles that were not of his choosing or his making, and now it looked as if it might be going to happen all over again here. And no matter how blameless he was, he was still undeniably and unmistakably English, a representative of the oppressors, whether he liked it or not.

All through the summer he struggled to keep his terror in check. At home, Adeline was in the habit of pooh-poohing it all. In deference to the kindly constable she had abandoned the jaunting car for a while, but in August the weather turned fine and hot once more and she took to it again. If any rebel sniper had been looking for a target he could certainly have found no more obvious one than Adeline, in her enormous straw hat, with Clancey sitting panting beside her as if riding shot gun. To advertise herself still more she very often sang as she drove, and the strains of 'Poor Butterfly' and 'The Grand Old Duke of York' rang round the lanes over the Connemara's spanking trot. But she never encountered any danger, either there or on her infrequent trips to town.

In early September, though, the Troubles did brush them with their wing tip. It was a calm, lovely evening and after they'd had supper Adeline and Simon went for a walk in the garden. Since Paris, and without any conscious decision on her part, she had evolved a different attitude to her husband, a different way of dealing with him. If he would not allow her to be close to him, if he would not confide in her nor admit any need, she would simply treat him as another of her challenges. She no longer wasted energy on trying to understand, she simply hardened her resolve and swept him along with her. She refused to take no for an answer, she went about her business and did as she pleased and dragged him with her. She stopped wearing the kind of clothes she supposed he liked, and wore instead those which provided her with a comfortable disguise. She retreated behind a style of dress whose hallmark was practical eccentricity. She concealed her figure in capacious, comfortable skirts, and even trousers, and hid her hair under enveloping hats with sweeping brims that kept the weather out. If Simon was no longer attracted by her, she would cease to try and look attractive. Since suiting her husband seemed to be out of the question, suiting herself became the order of the day. On the rare occasions when they went out together she abandoned the disguise and dressed like a lady. The rest of the time she looked like a rather imposing gypsy. Simon did not appear to notice. This approach had the advantage of keeping her reasonably cheerful but it also, as it was intended to, prevented her from noticing changes in her husband's state of mind. Because she was contriving to keep on an even

keel, she persuaded herself that he was doing the same.
There was no longer any attempt at intimacy or tenderness
between them. She treated him with a terse, corrective
kindliness very reminiscent of the way Dorothy Sugden
had treated her.

Now she wanted to show him the last of the roses, and
those places where she had put in bulbs for next spring.
She put her arm firmly through his and walked and talked
and elicited his comments.

'You've done wonderfully well,' he said, a little wistfully.

'I have, haven't I? When everything's had a year or two
to mature it's going to be a picture.'

'And we shall be gone.' He gave a dry little laugh. He
often said this, and she, being in a positive frame of mind,
always ignored it.

'I thought we might plant some nut trees. A nut grove
– wouldn't that be nice?'

'And where would you put it?'

'I'll show you.'

She led him round the side of the kitchen garden to the
south wall. And it was here that they found the young
man.

He was half sitting, half lying up against the wall, his
head turned away from them, one leg bent beneath him.
His coarse striped shirt, wet with perspiration, clung to
him, his dark hair was slicked to his skull.

'Who is it?' Adeline at once ran forward.

'Addy – have a care!'

But she was already at his side, leaning over him. She
touched his shoulder.

'Are you all right?'

'Addy!' Simon came over. 'We should call the police.'

The young man rolled his head towards them. The
right side of his face and neck were covered with a
glistening slick of blood from a shallow wound on his
temple. His eyes were mere slits, flicking from Adeline to
Simon, desperately trying to make sense of them.

'Oh God! The poor thing! What can we do?' Adeline

was shocked, appalled. She began dabbing at the blood on the man's face with the corner of her jacket.

'I'm going to ring the Garda,' said Simon, turning away.

'Don't, sir!'

It was Eileen, coming round the corner with Donaghue. She carried a pail of water and a clean cloth. Donaghue had a china cup with something in it.

'Eileen, do you know this man?' asked Simon.

'He's my brother, sir. He won't be here no more than a moment, I promise you. Please say nothing and he'll be gone in a jiffy.'

The normally stolid and impassive Eileen knelt down beside the young man and shook him roughly.

'Don't do that!' said Adeline. 'Can't we take him into the house and do something for him?'

'There's no question of it, Addy,' said Simon in a quiet, shaken voice. He was very pale. With her arm through his and her shoulder beneath his armpit, Eileen hauled her brother into a more upright position and began cleaning his face with the cloth. He groaned petulantly.

Donaghue said: 'Much better not, madam, he needs to be away from here double quick.'

'He shouldn't be here at all!' Simon's voice was sharp with anxiety.

'God knows I know it,' muttered Eileen, mopping and dabbing. The water in the pail turned a rusty red. 'Can you not just make out you never saw him?'

'Of course we will, Eileen,' said Adeline. 'Simon, we will, won't we?'

'I don't know . . . it isn't right . . .'

'Simon – !' Adeline gripped his arm tightly, pulling him away. 'We know nothing about it, do you understand?'

'That would be best, sir,' agreed Donaghue. He kneeled down and offered the young man the cup. He took a swallow, spluttered, and wiped his mouth with the back of his wrist. For the first time he looked at Adeline and Simon and seemed to focus on them.

He said, in a low voice, but quite distinctly: 'I don't need any favours from you.'

'Be quiet, you bloody little idiot!' Eileen smacked the side of his head hard, and he yelped. Donaghue left the cup on the grass and stood up.

'Don't you think it would be best to go and say no more about it?'

'I'm sure it would.' Adeline turned away. 'Come on.'

Simon followed more slowly. At the end of the wall he cast a last fearful glance over his shoulder to find that the man on the ground was staring after them, sneering.

On Saturday, 20 November, Adeline went hunting. The meet was at the Dun Cow, a few miles to the east of Kilmainham. It was at half past ten, but Adeline intended to leave Kenarvon at about nine, and ride quietly and unhurriedly to her destination, savouring the peace and freedom of her journey, knowing that she could take her time and still be among the first.

She woke with a silent shock of anticipation soon after six. It was cold and dark, and the knowledge that she didn't have to get up for at least an hour and a half kept her curled close and snug as a fist against Simon's warm back. When she did clamber out, shivering, in the late, dank dawn it was bleak, the first day of real winter after the mellow glory of a mild autumn. The walls and floors of the house seemed to resonate with the chill.

Adeline's riding clothes, laid out the night before, were stiff and unyielding, cleaned, pressed and starched till they were more like armour than clothing. As she put them on she felt herself undergoing a metamorphosis. The shape and texture of the clothes, the feel of her legs in tight breeches and her feet in clean, shining boots, her head neat and defined with her hair in a net, her chin lifted by the starched stock, her body trim in the dark blue jacket with its velvet collar – all these worked on her as she imagined a proud uniform must on a soldier. She felt keen, and strong, and competent.

In the bed Simon still lay exactly as she had left him,

sleeping like a child with one hand beneath his cheek, and his mouth open. She knew he had had another disturbed night: she had found the light on on the landing, and his sticks lay discarded untidily on the bedside rug. Before leaving the bedroom she propped the sticks against the foot of the bed, and tucked in the bedclothes on her side so that he shouldn't feel a draught on his back. As always on leaving him she felt affectionate, solicitious – understanding, even.

But as soon as she had closed the door behind her her excitement swelled, and she ran down the stairs two at a time. Clancey overtook her and ran across the hall to the door, where he stood with his thin whip of a tail waving, jaws gaping in an expectant grin.

'No, good dog – not your turn today,' she said.

Catching something from her tone, but still hopeful, he followed her into the dining room and watched as she filled a small flask with brandy and put it in the inner breast pocket of her jacket.

Adeline then went down to the kitchen, with Clancey trailing even less optimistically in her wake. Mrs Donaghue did not start work till mid-morning at weekends, but on the table was a covered plate of ham sandwiches, put out the night before, and the big brown teapot stood next to the kettle on the range. Adeline ate half the sandwiches as she waited for the kettle to boil, wrapped the remainder in greaseproof paper and put them in her pocket. She shot back the heavy bolts on the back door and let Clancey out for a few minutes, standing in the doorway and sipping her strong, sweet tea as she waited for him. The morning was light now, a grey and grudging light, but imbued with that special early-morning stillness when the stars are extinguished, the fading moon loiters, and the horizon begins to breathe. The air was sharp and brackish and the grass was silvered with a thick, cold dew.

She called Clancey back into the house, closed the door, rinsed her cup at the stone sink and went back up to the hall. Standing before the mirror she put on her bowler and gloves and subjected herself to a final inspection. She scarcely recognized herself. She looked so sleek and trim, so controlled, with not a hair out of place. Her appearance, she decided, was the outward and visible sign of her new approach. She had taken charge – of herself, of her marriage, of her life. Chaos and turmoil, she thought, had been subdued, and order restored. Feeling quite pleased with herself, she said good-bye to the disconsolate Clancey, and left the house.

Outside the landscape was damp, withdrawn. The crunch of her solitary footsteps on the gravel was an intrusion. The white scut of a rabbit darted and jinked away from her and then disappeared as if snuffed out.

In the stableyard there was a lantern still lit: Cullen had risen early to begin work. Now Sholto was tied up outside his box while the groom gave him a final polish with a hay wisp.

Cora, the driving pony, put her head over the stable door and reached out rubbery lips, cadging for a titbit, but on this occasion received only a pat.

'Good morning, Cullen.'

'Morning . . .' The groom nodded to her and stood back from his handiwork.

'He looks splendid. Thank you.'

Sholto's coat shone like warm wood. When Adeline went to his head and stroked his nose he greeted her with a sound between a grunt and a whinny. His eyes, close to hers, were dark and calm. Adeline breathed in his beauty and strength. She gave him the sugar lumps she'd brought. Little flags of stream arose from the horse's lips as he munched, and from Cullen as he blew between his teeth, wielding the hay wisp.

'That's him then,' he said now. He was a plain, heavy set young man of few words, whom it would have been easy to dismiss as simple were it not for his preternatural affinity with horses.

Between them they tacked up Sholto, buckling straps with cold, clumsy fingers, taking silent satisfaction in their shared task. The leather was spotless, gleaming and supple, the stirrups shone. When Adeline mounted she felt like a queen. And looked like one, Cullen thought. His slow heart beat faster for a second as he watched the horse respond, and appear to collect and lift himself under her touch. He himself could not ride, but he understood horses well enough to appreciate anyone who could.

'Thanks again,' she said. 'We'll see you later.'

Cullen lifted his hand in farewell, and watched as she rode out of the yard. For a full minute after she'd gone he stood there, until the sound of Cora bumping and whinnying in her box reminded him that he had other jobs to do.

It was a good day, a day when nothing could go wrong for Adeline. She might have been out of her body, flying above the other riders, seeing everything more clearly, able to take the right decisions, to judge every jump to a nicety, to ride at once faster and more safely than anyone else. And Sholto was in tune with her, eager and full of running but sensitive to her commands. They were well to the front of the field all the time. Once, on a bank, Sholto slipped, his back legs shooting crazily beneath him, scrabbling for a foothold to prevent himself crashing back on to his hocks on the take-off side. With a sort of God-given, once-in-a-lifetime confidence she sat still and gave him his head until he had regained his balance, and then, with a great bound, he was off the bank and on his way, as the rest of the field poured over, a torrent of plummeting hooves and sweat-darkened flesh. Galloping across the field with hounds giving tongue not two hundred yards in front, Adeline felt her heart hammer not with fear, or relief, but with exaltation.

From the meet, they had covered some seven or eight miles in a wide circle, and were heading south once more in the general direction of Kenarvon. But now, at a dry stone wall, the hounds lost the scent and the huntsman, having cast them again with no result, called them off. They went to draw again at a black, tangled wood about a mile from the Kilmainham Road.

Sholto stood quiet, and Adeline let the reins lie. She was

struck by the severe beauty of the scene – the dark, sharp-edged wood, the bleak sky the colour of watered milk, the riders bunched together, an elegant group in blacks, browns and whites, seen through a fine mist of steam and smoking breath. The scarlet of the hunt servants' coats showed like gouts of blood against this austere background.

Deep in the covert hounds began to bell, and in a moment the horn sounded the thrilling, urgent call: 'Gone away!'

Suddenly Adeline, who was a little apart from the rest, saw the fox – a lean, dark arrow streaking across the plough in the direction of the road. As always, she felt a stab of sympathy for their quarry. But now the huntsman's horn was bright and keen, and the hounds were in full cry, and there was no ambivalence in her response as she urged Sholto forward. She wished the fox well, but she wanted too the thrill of a good hunt which only he with his well-tuned instinct for survival could provide. As they poured across the field she forgot about the small, clever animal who, having frantically criss-crossed the road, now lay with jaws gaping and flanks heaving in the lea of the hedge, planning his next move.

By the time the hunt reached the road the fox had moved on and was loping wearily, tongue lolling, through the trees on the edge of Kenarvon land. Hounds were temporarily baffled by the zig-zagging overlay of scent and this gave him a little more time to put distance between himself and them. At the edge of the wood he paused and gazed ahead with fierce, staring eyes before moving on, too tired to seek cover, a brown moving target threading the rough grass, mask and brush carried low, ears laid back.

In the house, Eileen had just made the bed in her employers' room, and removed the untouched tea tray which she'd left outside the door hours earlier. Hearing the hunt, she went to the landing window and looked out. Not two hundred yards from the house the fox was trotting across the grass, then over the drive and round the corner in the direction of the outhouses and stables.

Eileen sucked in her breath through pursed lips. 'They'll get you, you thievin' devil!' she whispered to herself. She came from a farming family, and had no scruples about destroying pests. She only wondered why they didn't shoot the creatures instead of going to all this song and dance.

As if to endorse her prediction the horn whooped and sang, and downstairs Clancey began to bark. Eileen sighed gustily. She supposed she'd have to shut the dog down in the kitchen if the hunt was coming this way. She wished Mr Charteris would take some interest in the animal. As it was, he'd gone off somewhere early and it would fall to her, as usual, to mind the dog until Mr Charteris got back.

As she turned to go down the stairs the pack leaders emerged from the trees and the excited cry of hounds and horn sounded in her ears.

Adeline was close behind the Master, Johnnie Durrent, as they burst out of the wood. As they crossed the drive and skirted the trees on the far side she glanced at the house, wondering if Simon might be watching from a window. But in winter Kenarvon reverted to type and presented a dour, closed appearance.

They were going to kill here, on their land. The hunts-man and whippers-in could be heard urging hounds on as they blundered about near the outbuildings at the back of the stables.

Durrent wheeled to come alongside her. 'Any objec-tion, Mrs Charteris?'

'None at all.'

'Then I think we've got this feller.'

In the stableyard Cullen emerged phlegmatically from the tackroom where he'd been cleaning the driving harness. All hell was breaking out. Hounds were in the big barn at the back which they used as a hay store, and where the jaunting cart was kept. They were exciting Cora, who whinnied and fretted, turning round and round in the limited space of her loose box. It wasn't the first time the hunt had been this way, and it wouldn't be the last, but they had never before been so close to the house.

Cullen didn't care for the hunt, it bothered and upset him. Not wanting to be drawn in he just stood quietly minding his own business, rubbing the harness with a piece of saddle-soaped rag. He wasn't going to react unless or until he was invited to.

He didn't have long to wait. A big fellow on a heavy grey appeared in the archway.

'You seen him, man?'

Cullen shook his head.

'We think he's holed up in this big barn of yours. Can you lend a hand with the door?'

With slow deliberation, Cullen returned the harness to the tack room. When he emerged, the man was stood there waiting impatiently, the grey fussing and sweating. Cullen went through the arch and round to the barn entrance. The door stood open about a foot, but it was huge and heavy, warped by the weather. Hounds had gone in and were yelping and snapping inside like nobody's business. Cullen was not versed in hunting lore, but he knew there was always a potential for embarrassment when the pack was on private land. Let them sweat, he wouldn't hurry for them. He spotted Mrs Charteris – the gelding still looked good. He gave her a little nod before turning his attention to the door.

The moment it was drawn far enough back the huntsman rode into the barn. The horses outside stirred and snorted as his whip cracked, bringing the pack to order. Cullen didn't care – let them sort themselves out. He went up to Sholto and patted his neck.

'How's he been?'

'Wonderful!' Adeline was elated. 'A hero.'

The huntsman emerged, whipping half the pack before him, yelling at the other hunt servants to take charge of the remaining hounds who were still busy with something inside. There was a harsh shrillness in his voice, and his face looked sickly and drained beneath its weatherbeaten flush. He rode his big grey alongside Johnnie Durrent, standing head to tail, his back to Adeline as he whispered something to the Master.

Durrent whispered something, his eyes on Adeline's face. She caught only the words '. . . Holy Mary'. Then he rode over to her as the huntsman returned to the barn, his horse disappearing like a great, white ghost in the darkness. Durrent cleared his throat.

'They've found something, Mrs Charteris,' he said. 'But I'm afraid it's no fox.'

'Oh?' She didn't understand what he was saying to her. His face, normally so ruddy and beaming, appeared blank and collapsed. Something dreadful occured to her.

'Not Clancey . . . oh, no!' She dismounted and passed the reins to Cullen. The other riders whispered to one another. Excitement had ebbed away and been replaced by foreboding. She moved in the direction of the barn.

'Mrs Charteris! Adeline!'

It was the use of her christian name that made Adeline look up. That, and the fact that the Master had laid the heel of his whip on her shoulder, restraining her.

'What? What is is?'

He dismounted and came and stood very close to her so that she could see the tiny blood vessels in his pale blue eyes, and could smell his sweat. On horseback, Johnnie Durrent was a centaur. Off it, he was a short, rotund, unsophisticated man with a high colour.

Now he cleared his throat and said again: 'Adeline.' And then, 'My dear – I'm not sure you should go in.'

'Why not?' She glared down at him, both frightened and angry. When he didn't immediately answer she brushed past him. 'Don't be ridiculous, of course I must.'

Inside, the whippers-in were having trouble with the few remaining hounds, who were playful and relaxed, as hounds will be when diverted. Those who had been successfully whipped off milled about with their sterns waving, tongues lolling. One or two were still worrying the body, pulling cloth and growling at one another. As Adeline appeared, with the Master, on foot, behind her, the whippers-in redoubled their efforts and cleared the barn with a tremendous shouting and cracking of whips.

'I'm sorry,' said Johnnie Durrent. He sounded utterly broken. 'I'm so sorry.'

By the look of him, Simon had not been dead all that long. His limbs were not stiff, they had moved eerily as hounds tugged at his clothes. His artificial leg, cruelly exposed, lay at a crazy, sickening angle. He had found a length of worn old rope with which to hang himself. It had bitten deep into his neck below the point of the jaw. A fuzz of frayed ends protruded from the knot.

The hounds had pulled him down: a piece of rope was still attached to the crossbeam above the jaunting car. He must have clambered on to the tailboard, and then jumped. A bitter smell arose from the dark matter released by his sphincter, which stained his trousers. His face wore an ugly, grinning expression. He had undoubtedly had the last laugh.

For so long Adeline had wished she might be closer to her husband, but now she found she could not take so much as another step towards him. This was his final repulsion of her. This was how much he wanted to escape.

Straightbacked and trembling, almost blinded with shock, she walked past Johnnie Durrent and out of the barn. Faces swam in front of her, hands reached out, some touched her, voices expressed concern and distress, but her little hell of horror enclosed her utterly and she did not respond.

When she was clear of the stables she began to run, stumbling and tripping, until she was back at the house. She was only dimly conscious of someone running after her, gasping for breath . . . of Eileen's startled, staring face in the doorway . . . of voices, Eileen's and Durrent's, urgently whispering in the hall as she blundered up the stairs.

In the bedroom she lay down on her side, staring out

into the room as she had so often done before. When Mrs Donaghue brought her a toddy and advised that she change out of her wet muddy things and get under the covers, she drank up gratefully and did as she was told. Under the comforting influence of the hot drink and warm blankets she began to cry, and sobbed and sobbed for an hour or more until she slept. A good thing, people said, a good thing that she could cry, and let all her feelings out. She was so young, after all, and tears were a healthy, normal reaction and a great healer. Let her cry it out.

They were right, of course. But what none of them, not even Elizabeth, nor Simon's parents, could know, was just how many of those healing tears were tears of sheer relief.

Part Two

CHAPTER TEN

1921

IT SURPRISED ADELINE when Howard offered to pay her fees for the Slade. She still kept, as a reminder, the Judas money, and was not above wondering if this far greater sum – nearly thirty pounds per annum – was to be given in the same spirit. But it was only the idlest curiosity, and ultimately she had no difficulty in accepting. Indeed she was touched by Howard's fierce determination that she should make good use of her talent, after the grief and shame of his son's death. Cynthia had, predictably and understandably, gone to pieces. All her fond fancies and hopes had been brutally dispelled, not just by Simon's death, but by all that it implied – the fear, the misery, the corrosive, secret despair.

Howard suffered in silence. That he did suffer was plain to see: every line on his face was scored deeper, and he seemed overnight to have become greyer and older. There was a new and different intensity in his manner as if he suddenly realized there was not enough time left for all he wanted to do.

Adeline struggled to come to terms with her own reaction to her widowhood. Could she really be this heartless, this unfeeling? Was she some kind of cripple, an emotional freak? When Cynthia wanted to talk about him, Adeline couldn't. No matter what they all asked of her, the door was closing, inexorably, on his memory. Only Elizabeth seemed to understand, and said to her quietly: 'It's over, my darling. It's all over,' which was exactly what she needed to hear.

Later in her life she was able to look back and see all too clearly the causes of her confusion. At the time of Simon's suicide she was only twenty, and had experienced neither the excitement of pursuing her own ambition, nor the ecstasy of passion, nor even the happiness of a contented, companionable marriage. She had abandoned everything and run headlong to embrace a romantic ideal which had turned to empty air in her arms. Her years with Simon had been years of painful attrition, of lessons learned the hard way: alone. For all that time she had been too proud to let slip a murmur of complaint or self-pity to anyone. She emerged from her marriage in an unbalanced state, two people in one skin. In some ways she was old for her age. She had learned control, and sublimation, and the ability to cope. She had learned the most pernicious kind of deceit, that of herself. She had acquired a capacity she was never to lose, a capacity for taking simple, concentrated pleasure from ordinary things while her emotional life was in turmoil and uproar. As her marriage and her husband had deteriorated before her eyes she had contrived to enjoy her riding, her gardening, the company of her dog. She had learned to create happiness for herself.

Kenarvon was placed once more in the hands of the agents. She left it without regret. The volatility of the political situation was the least of her reasons. The house had been the setting for a chapter in her life that she was glad to close. She sold Sholto to Johnnie Durrent, but Clancey she took with her. When she looked at the work she had done in the garden she acknowledged to herself that in a very short while it would be overtaken again by weeds and grass, particularly if the house stood empty through the summer, but she didn't care. The work had been an end in itself.

Among the staff, as they were disbanded, it was only Cullen for whom she felt any sadness on saying goodbye. She would have liked to tell Eileen to rot in hell, but was instead at her most ladylike and dignified, and gave both her and the Donaghues references which spoke of competence and hinted at insubordination. But Cullen had shared her love of horses, and shared too that terrible moment when they had found Simon. When she shook his hand he was as speechless as ever, but his cheeks were pink and his eyes moist. On her recommendation he had been given a job nearby, looking after carriage horses, and Cora would be going with him.

By Christmas she was back at Fording Place, among the same people and facing the same decisions that she had spurned beneath her heel three years before. It was as though her marriage had been a mere aberration, as if she had stepped side-ways from her pre-ordained course, and had now rejoined it at the same point. Except that she herself was not the same. She had acquired a store of thorny and instructive experience.

With the shock of Simon's death behind her she felt, unmistakably, the soft breeze of freedom blowing on her face. But a sensitivity to the feelings of others, notably Simon's parents, kept her silent on the subject of future plans. Ironically it was Howard who broke this silence, on a visit toFording Place in January 1921. One night after dinner, when Elizabeth had gone to one of her village meetings, he said bluntly: 'You'll be wanting to go to art school no doubt.'

Adeline glanced at Cynthia, but she was smiling her wan little smile, her eyes vague, her mind elsewhere. She was already in the early stages of the premature senility which would overtake her in the next few years.

For her sake, Adeline said: 'I don't really know . . . .'

'You should. I'm sure you ought to.' Howard relit his

cigar with a spill from the fireplace. He sucked on the cigar, then prodded the air at Adeline.

'You've been neglecting that side of things.'

Clancey rested his head on Adeline's lap and she stroked him busily.

'I just haven't been interested, not for – oh, ages. I don't know why. Perhaps in time –'

'No time like the present,' said Howard.

'The trouble is –' She could feel the eagerness creeping into her voice. 'I don't have anything recent to show. And hardly any painting.'

Howard waved the cigar again, dismissively. 'You can remedy that, if you want to. The point is, I think you should re-apply to the Slade.'

She smiled at his presumption on her behalf. 'They won't remember me.'

'They will if you remind them! Look, Adeline.' Howard leaned forward, staring intently and urgently into her face. They might have been alone in the room. 'You don't want to go through the rest of your life feeling that you missed this opportunity.'

'No,' she conceded, 'I don't.'

'Right.' Howard slapped his knees as if the matter were decided. 'I know your mother agrees with me,' he added. Adeline glanced at him with a small shock. It was the first time he had mentioned Elizabeth in her presence since the evening of the Judas money. She took it to be a challenge, a test of what he perceived to be a new relationship.

'It's what she always wanted,' she agreed quietly.

'It is! It is.'

Adeline turned to Cynthia. 'What do you think, Cynthia?'

Cynthia moved her head a little in Howard's direction. Her lips began to move, but only a few words could be heard. 'Such a clever girl,' she murmured.

'She should go to art school,' declared Howard.

'Of course, if that's what she wants . . . all the young women nowadays seem to want to do something . . . Adeline was always so talented . . .' Cynthia directed her pale, distracted gaze at her daughter-in-law and smiled a smile of piercing sweetness, exactly like Simon's.

'You just write to old Tonks and re-apply,' said Howard. 'You could be there in the autumn.'

Afterwards, Adeline remembered that Howard had known the name of the formidable principal of the Slade, as if the notion had been at the base of his mind for some time. She reassembled her portfolio, attempted some watercolours, which she loathed, and wrote her letter of application. She was curiously optimistic and her optimism proved justified. Tonks liked 'the dashing young widow' as he privately called her. He thought highly of her draughtsmanship and found her style, both in drawing and in dress, highly entertaining. Since the Slade, under his auspices, put drawing above everything, he was not bothered about the paintings which, he agreed, were 'insipid, uninspired, and generally frightful'.

'I tell you something else,' he said to her as he held up portraits of her family for inspection in the Professor's Room. 'Your gift is quite commercial.' He cast her a sharp glance, reminiscent of Howard. 'There's unlimited scope for improvement, but this facility is handy – nice and handy.'

'Thank you,' said Adeline. 'For what?'

'For making money, Mrs Charteris.'

'You really think so?'

Tonks disdained to answer this.

'Good,' said Adeline. 'I'm glad.'

Her robust response to what many of his students would have seen as an accusation also endeared her to Tonks. He told her she could start in October, to keep drawing, and to forget altogether about painting until further notice.

'I look forward to seeing you again,' he said, showing her out.

Adeline paused and thrust out her hand. 'Thank you, sir,' she said, shaking his hand firmly. 'I look forward to seeing you, too.'

As she left the building, via the dingy hall, the two sets of chipped and peeling doors, and crossed the quad with its bare winter lime trees, Adeline could not resist a leap of sheer elation. Her hat fell off and she scooped it up and went marching on her way, arms swinging, portfolio in one hand and hat in the other, a broad and delighted grin on her face.

Professor Tonks, watching her go from his window, smiled too. He had seen so many hundreds of students come and go and he considered himself well qualified to assess their potential and their character. The young widow, though, was like a collection of highly coloured jigsaw pieces, each different and distinct and quite separate, from which a most unusual and interesting pattern might one day be formed. He was getting hard to surprise in his old age, but she had succeeded in surprising him. He had had many more talented students than her but few more interesting.

' "Look forward to seeing you, too," ' he said to himself. 'Ha!'

Accepting Howard's offer of the fees was Adeline's only concession to the past. She was determined that in all other respects this should be a completely fresh beginning, a new life in which she would make her way independently, accepting help from no-one and taking responsibility for her own decisions. After the war, at Howard's prompting, Simon had made a will, of which she was the sole beneficiary, and there was some money left to her in trust by Richard, to which she had access on her majority. In fact, had she not been in a position to pay the fees herself she would, perversely, have refused Howard. But allowing him to pay was very different from needing him to do so. She also declined politely, Cynthia's offer of the flat in Lancaster Gate, and her subsequent well-meant suggestion that she should stay with them in Leinster Gardens. Adeline explained that it was too far away, and that she needed somewhere where she could work.

At the end of September, a full three weeks before the beginning of the Slade term, she went up to London and moved in as a lodger with Bob. This proved unsuccessful, even as a temporary arrangement. Though Bob had declared her extremely welcome, and had not demurred over Clancey, whom she was determined to accustom to city life, it was plain he found their presence something of a trial. He was moving on, his workload was increasing all the time and his surroundings were arranged to suit himself.

Adeline, on the other hand, was unaccustomed to a life bounded by employers, salaries and deadlines, and had recently lived only in spacious accommodation with servants, no matter how disagreeable, to keep it in order. Though not by nature lazy, she was, left to her own devices, hideously untidy, a failing against which she was to struggle all her life. In the close confines of her brother's room she wrought havoc by default. Where Adeline had just been, there were most of her possessions to be found, forming drifts and dunes on every available surface. Determined not to be a burden she cooked large and wonderful meals, but left the tiny slot of a kitchen in chaos and uproar. She would not allow Bob to vacate the bedroom for her, and slept on the sofa in the living room, but after a while had so invaded and occupied the surrounding area that Bob insisted, in the bluntest possible terms, that she use his bed.

Then there was the question of the dog. Clancey was an attractive animal and eager to please, as Bob was ready to concede, but his attempts to gain favour were ill-judged and misdirected. The disembowelling of marauding cushions, the worrying to death of socks and ties, the removal of stray eatables from the kitchen table, and the defence of the flat against all comers were major sources of irritation to his landlord. He seemed more like an elephant than a dog. Even when he was at his most ingratiating, his long, whiskery whip of a tail swept books, papers and ashtrays to the floor, and when he was exuberant he filled the room, havoc made flesh.

Adeline was endlessly apologetic, but where Clancey was concerned she could hardly have been said to be impartial. In the face of his growing catalogue of crimes she remained loyal to, and amused by, him.

'London is no place for a dog,' said Bob. 'It's hopeless. It's ridiculous. Why don't you leave him with Frank and Mother at home? They'd probably be delighted to have him.'

'That's not the point!' she replied spiritedly. 'He's my dog and I want him with me. He'd pine if I left him with other people – *I'd* pine. He'll adjust to London in time.'

Bob clapped his hands to his face, lowered them slowly. 'The landlady doesn't exist who'll put up with him.'

'Yours does.'

'As a favour to me, and on the understanding that it's only for a short while. You have to take him for walks all the time –'

'It does me good.'

'– and he's just too large. There's too much of him. Really Addy, he's a nice enough dog but you're mad to have him up here.'

In spite of Bob's gloomy prognosis, Clancey was actually instrumental in securing digs for Adeline. Following up an advertisement in the London evening paper she went to call on a Mrs Fairyhouse at 114 Gower Street, a mere stone's throw from the Slade. On the telephone Mrs Fairyhouse was discouraging about the possibilities of the room still being free. She had had several applicants already, she said, it was the time of year for it, but she couldn't prevent Adeline from making what might well be a wasted journey if she was set on it. Adeline was set on it. Clancey had knocked a tea tray off the table in the kitchen that morning, causing what seemed an ocean of Assam to run in every direction and breaking two cups and the teapot. Bob had left for the *Courier* hard-eyed and tight-lipped. What with this and the fact that the beginning of term was less than a week away, the need for a move had become urgent.

They travelled by bus to Gower Street and walked in the gentle autumn sunshine to 114. Passing the gates of University College Adeline felt a thrill of excitement and optimism. Her life was beginning to take on a new shape, step by step she was making her way along a new road of her own choosing.

Luckily the Fairyhouses were disposed in her favour on two counts. Firstly, and most importantly, Mrs Fairyhouse was a crashing snob who knew breeding when she saw it, and whose natural caginess evaporated like dew in the sunshine in the presence of a well-spoken and financially solvent widow.

'Three or four have expressed an interest,' she confided to Adeline in the dim hallway with its stuffed animal heads, 'but none of them's been back to me yet, so you might just as well take a look. Oh, may I introduce my husband?'

Adeline shook hands with Mr Fairyhouse, but his eyes were already on Clancey.

'What a nice boy,' he said, patting Clancey on the head. 'What a handsome boy. Lurcher?'

'That's right. I bought him in Ireland. I should say right away that I do want to keep him with me if I possibly can.'

A look of consternation appeared fleetingly on Mrs Fairyhouse's face, but by now her husband was crouching down and scratching Clancey's chest enthusiastically.

'I don't see that's any problem if you take responsibility for him,' he said, without either looking up or referring to his wife. 'He's a fine chap, aren't you, eh? Yes, you are . . .' He rose, as if tearing himself away, and revealed the second reason for Adeline's popularity. 'I'm a taxidermist,' he explained cheerfully. 'I can appreciate a good animal.'

Adeline held tight to the lead and glanced a little apprehensively over her shoulder as Mrs Fairyhouse led the way to the first floor landing.

'We have several young women from the art school here,' said Mrs Fairyhouse, unlocking a door, 'so you'd be among friends.'

'I'm only just starting. It was something I was going to do before I got married, and then since my husband died I decided to try again.'

'Such a wicked tragedy . . .' Mrs Fairyhouse sucked her
teeth and held the door open for Adeline. 'And so young.'

It was just one room, with a kitchen area at the back,
overlooking a narrow strip of dusty garden. But its lofty
dimensions at once commended it to Adeline after the
constraints of living with Bob. At the front of the room
two tall, narrow sash windows looked out on Gower
Street. The ceiling was high, with a strip of elaborate
moulding at its junction with the walls, and an enormous
boss of the same at its centre, from which depended a
length of brown electric cord and a single bulb with a
parchment-coloured shade.

Adeline walked into the centre of the room and turned
this way and that, getting the feel of it. A once-grand
chipped marble hearth housed a gas fire, with a squat black
coin meter crouching alongside and a woolly rug depicting
the Good Shepherd lying before it. When Adeline dropped
the lead Clancey at once went and flopped down on the
rug, causing Mrs Fairyhouse to remark: 'Well, he's made
himself at home!'

Adeline moved around, touching things. The faded
striped curtains were pulled right back on the wall on
either side of the windows and sunlight streamed in on
furniture culled from second-hand marts and junk shops,
furniture which had seen better days but was now down
on its luck: two slightly greasy looking brown wing-
backed chairs; a threadbare chintz fireside settle; a divan
bed pushed up against the wall, with one small cushion
lying on the seersucker counterpane; a square table of dark
wood, patterned with innumerable circular stains, a hideous green glass vase in the centre, two spindly hard chairs
on either side. On the wall over the divan hung a freckled
oblong mirror, tilting on its wire. Adeline felt that
another, larger mirror was needed, over the fireplace and
opposite the door, and as she thought this she realized she
had already decided to take the room.

'. . . bath and WC are shared,' Mrs Fairyhouse was
pointing out, 'and you have to check the pilot light on the

geyser in the bathroom, but the water's good and hot, isn't that right, Miss Simpson?'

She addressed a small, neat young woman who had emerged from a door opposite, coat on, and was heading for the stairs.

'Isn't what right?'

'The water's always hot.'

'Oh yes, the water's hot enough,' said Miss Simpson, giving Adeline a quick smile before pattering down the stairs at high speed.

'Miss Simpson's at the art school,' explained Mrs Fairyhouse, 'just starting her second year.' This surprised Adeline, who had taken the young woman for an efficient secretary or businesswoman.

She picked up Clancey's lead. 'I'll take it,' she said.

Over a cup of tea in the Fairyhouses' flat on the ground floor, Mrs Fairyhouse supplied Adeline with the answers to all the questions she should have asked. She told her that the rent was five shillings a week, that the meter took pennies and threepenny bits, that gentleman callers must be out by ten, that she was an easy-going soul who had never been blessed with children herself and who liked to see her lodgers (there were four) as a surrogate family. She encouraged them, she said, to call in on her and Mr Fairyhouse whenever they felt inclined, to share any worries they might have, or just to have a cup of tea. Mr Fairyhouse, feeding garibaldi biscuits to the dog, said, without looking up, that they didn't usually take her up on that, but his wife said still, the offer was there and her door was always open, and Adeline said it all sounded absolutely what she'd been after and she'd like to move in right away. Mrs Fairyhouse added that she had never been asked about dogs before, but that this one seemed well enough behaved. She had, however, to emphasize that if there was trouble of any sort she would have to ask him to leave. Adeline entertained a fleeting picture of Clancey being handed his notice by the landlady, and docilely departing. She assured Mrs Fairyhouse that she perfectly understood, and the bargain was sealed with a second cup of tea.

Bob, helping his sister to move in the following evening, stared in dismay at the snarling foxes, otters, stoats and badgers who appeared to have thrust their heads through the wall next to the stairs.

'Please understand, Addy,' he said, 'I never wished that dog of yours any ill.'

Adeline looked at Clancey, who lay on the fireside rug as if he'd been there all his life.

'Don't worry about it,' she replied. 'He likes it here.'

Bob came in and lowered a box of books heavily to the ground. 'Each to his own. It would give me nightmares.'

'We're not so sensitive.'

Later, as they stood amongst the cases and boxes drinking wine which Bob had brought to celebrate the move, Miss Simpson came up the stairs and crossed the landing to her door.

'Hallo!' said Adeline.

'Oh –' Miss Simpson turned. 'Hallo. You're in then.'

'Just about. Sort of.' Adeline waved her glass at the clutter. 'Would you like to join us? We're wetting the baby's head.'

Miss Simpson came in and took a glass of wine from Adeline. Clancey, not yet sure of his territory, didn't bark, but did bounce at her in amiable greeting, and she shrieked.

'Oh my God! Help! What is it?'

Adeline grabbed Clancey's collar and pulled him away. Miss Simpson's face was chalk-white; it was plain to see she was genuinely scared.

'I'm awfully sorry, he is rather large.'

'Oh –!' Miss Simpson sank down on the nearest wing-backed chair and took a large mouthful of her wine. 'I'm afraid I'm not used to dogs. He was absolutely the last thing I expected to see.'

'Perfectly understandable,' said Bob. He set his glass down on the table. 'I must go. Nice to meet you.' He shook Miss Simpson's hand without meeting her eyes, and headed for the door. He was still decidedly ill at ease in the company of most women.

Adeline went with him to the head of the stairs. 'Bless you for everything,' she said, kissing him warmly. 'You must come over and have supper when I'm organized.'

Bob raised his hand. 'All in good time. Good luck.' He glanced at the wall.

'Look after the mutt. I don't want to see him staring down at me next time I come.'

'I will.'

Adeline watched Bob go down the stairs and out of the front door and then returned to her guest, who was sitting more upright and looking a better colour.

'My brother Bob,' she explained. 'He's been helping me move in.'

'You've got a lot of stuff.'

Adeline looked around and saw that it was so. 'Yes. Well . . . one tends to accumulate things . . .' she said, a little embarrassed.

'I'm the opposite, always throwing things away,' said Miss Simpson.

'Lucky you.' Adeline pushed a box of cups and saucers aside with her foot, and sat down in the other chair. She was suddenly tired, and a little forlorn. 'By the way,' she said, 'my name's Adeline Charteris.'

'Antonia Simpson. My parents used to call me Toni.'

'What about your friends?'

'Whichever they like.'

'Toni's easier.'

'Fine.'

They sized one another up. Adeline observed a small, thin, well-turned-out girl, wearing a dark coat with a high collar which she had not undone. Above the collar her face was pale and pointed with a long nose and a thin, precise mouth. Only her hands, each nail rimmed with a fine dark line of paint, gave her away as an art student. Her black shoes weren't new, but they were highly polished. She spoke with a London accent. She might have appeared rather severe, except for the hint of contained humour about her, as if she were seeing the funny side of things rather against her better judgement.

Toni Simpson, at nineteen the eldest of five children from Leytonstone in east London, saw a young woman older than herself, but from the kind of background which kept people young for longer. Black haired, she was built along imposing lines, with a booming, resonant voice, a wonderfully exotic face, and an attractively unguarded manner to which it was impossible not to respond. Toni was not a gregarious girl, she was at the Slade to work and she deliberately resisted friendships. Now she told herself that the last thing she wanted was a popping-in relationship with a student living in the same house.

'I mustn't stop,' she said. 'Things to do.'

'What about me?' Adeline reached for the bottle. 'We might as well kill this.'

Toni covered her glass with her hand. 'No really, it goes to my head.'

'That's the idea.' Adeline sloshed some more into her own glass. 'Come on, just a drop. I need a friend.'

This bald declaration of precisely the contingency Toni was trying to avoid disconcerted her. Meekly she allowed her glass to be refilled, and watched as the empty bottle was stuffed into a cardboard box. Clancey rose and moved to his mistress's side, laying his head on the arm of her chair. Toni tucked her feet tightly under her seat.

'I shall have to take him out soon,' said Adeline. 'Can you recommend anywhere nearby?'

'You want grass, do you?' asked Toni doubtfully.

'Ideally.'

'There's a little square, second left, a few hundred yards, with a garden in the middle.'

'Is it private?'

'Not that I know of. No, I don't think so, I've seen people eating sandwiches in there at lunchtime.'

'Then that's where we shall go,' said Adeline to Clancey, putting her face close to his and rubbing his wiry scalp. 'In a minute. Now go and lie down, you're making Toni nervous.'

Toni realized she was being referred to in a manner that

bordered on the proprietary, but it did not put her out as much as she expected.

'Is *he* going to be living here?' she asked.

Afterwards, Adeline was glad that her first impressions of the Slade were gained through Toni's eyes. For like her, Toni was something of an oddity, and an outsider, who saw school, staff and students with a clear and impartial eye. That her standpoint was the polar opposite of Adeline's did not matter; it was her separateness Adeline valued.

It was true that wine went to her head. Having been persuaded to the second glass and pressed into talking she became a good deal more animated, and her thin, sallow cheeks took on a very slight, but becoming flush.

Toni Simpson was a second year student, who had paid for the first year by working as a waitress at the ABC restaurant in Holborn, full time in the holidays and part time in the term. This year, she said, in a matter of fact way, she had a scholarship, but had decided to get a room near college instead of travelling back and forth from Leytonstone each day. To pay for the room she continued to work at the ABC. She didn't find it particularly tiring, it was all a question of organization, and if she hadn't been fortunate enough to get into art school she would have been working far longer and more gruelling hours at some job she couldn't stand. She wasn't particularly interested in socializing, she added.

For Adeline, Toni had all the fascination of a being from another world. Instead of the practical, ambitious, dedicated working–class girl she undoubtedly was, Adeline saw a foreign and exotic creature as unlike herself as it was possible to be.

'What about college?' she asked. 'What's it like?'

Toni gave her close smile. 'There's plenty of silver spoons about,' she said. 'You'll fit in a treat.'

In fact Adeline did not fit in in quite the way Toni meant. She was considerably older than the others in her year, and she had retained the 'Mrs' in front of her name out of loyalty to Simon. Both of these factors made her conspicuous, and added to them was the dash she unconsciously cut. The loose swaggering clothes which had both protected and disguised her in Ireland had now become her style. Where before they had concealed her they now proclaimed her individuality and her new-found freedom. She *liked* cloaks that swirled, and hats with dashingly down-turned brims, and laced-up boots that were good for walking. On the other hand she was acquiring a taste for jewellery, and added to her small store of good family pieces anything she saw that took her fancy and that she could afford. She wore the cheap and the valuable together, and in profusion, using hatpins as brooches and brooches on hats, and threading rings on to necklaces if she felt like it. She also began experimenting with make-up and found it wholly delightful to enhance her already theatrical appearance with colour and shading. In short she was emerging from the grey chrysalis of marriage into a large, bright and exotic butterfly. She had become an arresting sight. It was hardly surprising that she turned heads on her first morning at the Slade and continued to do so for several weeks thereafter. Art students, then as now, were a conventional crowd, keen to appear as much like one another as possible in order to be unlike everyone else. Mrs Charteris resembled no-one in particular. She stood out amongst the pale, dreamy-eyed, droopily-smocked girls in the approved Gwen John mould much as Rex Whistler, in his dark suit and tie, did amongst the men in their baggy corduroys and moleskins. She arrived that grey and drizzly morning in October wearing an ankle-length black serge skirt with black rubber-soled laced boots, an enveloping bottle-green mackintosh riding cape, black gauntlets and a tweed fishing hat – discarded by Frank – adorned with fishing flies and assorted colourful brooches. Beneath the brim of the hat her face, with its glossy vermilion mouth, green and violet shadowed eyes and luxuriant upswept lashes, was quite startling. Her black hair, bobbed to jaw length, tended to curl in the wet, and stuck out from under the hat like a stiff petticoat escaping from a dull skirt. Clancey, still adjusting to city life, had chewed through his lead, and was consequently being led on a piece of washing-line rope provided by Mrs Fairyhouse. Special permission had been requested from Tonks to bring the dog into college, and granted on the understanding that no-one should know a dog was present.

'The first time I hear someone say "There's a mutt in the school",' he told Adeline, 'is the last time he attends. I want to hear no more about it.'

In the pale, chilly atmosphere of the Antiques Room Adeline struggled to make a young lurcher invisible and silent. It was no easy task persuading him to lie down by the wooden 'donkey' on which she herself was to sit, and her efforts to do so got her very hot and bothered. She began to feel too large, too disorganized, too inappropriate, but the operation gained her a generally sympathetic audience, to whom she kept up a staccato commentary, knowing that she probably sounded a fool, but feeling nonetheless that affability was the best policy.

'Sit! Lie down! Sorry about this . . . I assure you he'll soon get the hang of things – down! Whoops – I say I am sorry, was that your – Clancey, stop that. Lie down. Good dog . . . no! Stay. Yes. Good dog. I really do beg your indulgence, it won't be like this every morning, it's just that he's used to the wide open spaces of – *no*, no down – I haven't been in London that long. Good dog. Right. There now!' She looked up triumphantly at the slightly dazed students around her. Someone sitting next to her said, 'Well done!' and began to clap and a few others joined in before the Professor arrived and class began.

The Slade believed in drawing, and draughtsmanship, and then more of the same. At least a year had to be spent in the Antiques Room, copying frigid, white, blank-eyed plaster busts, before drawing from life (strictly segregated) was allowed. As regards painting and the use of colour, the clutch was let out very, very slowly, if at all, and was supervised every inch of the way. Every student was taken on his or her ability to draw, but it was made quite clear that this ability was only the starting point for the attaining of the required Slade standard. Henry Tonks, a former Fellow of the Royal College of Surgeons, held that his students' taste and style should be purified by the study and copying of Graeco-Roman sculpture in the Antiques Room. There was no appeal. The Slade motto was 'Drawing is an explanation of the form', and intelligent, detailed understanding of line and anatomical construction was demanded from everyone, with no exceptions.

To ensure that his ideas were put into practice at the earliest possible opportunity, the Professor himself presided over the Antiques Room. His was an imposing presence. He was enormously tall, aquiline and gaunt, with an air of sharp perceptiveness, and a tongue to match. Women students outnumbered men by three to one at the Slade in 1921, a fact made all the more curious by the Professor's style of criticism, which left many of the young ladies shattered and weeping. The harshness was often unintentional. When he asked a girl whether her spectacles were effective, it was in a spirit of genuine inquiry, and not intended to be sarcastic. When he asked exactly what it *was* a student was drawing, it was in the same spirit. He was a perfectionist, and he was direct, and he liked to see these qualities in those he taught.

Only after serving this rigorous apprenticeship were students allowed to go downstairs to work in the Life Room, and then initially for short, twenty or thirty minute sessions. Tonks rationed the good things of art as if they were rich food. The palates of the young had to be trained to accommodate them, and their stomachs filled with plenty of plain, nourishing bread and butter to counteract greed.

But though Tonks was a stickler, the regime of the Slade was more like that of a club than a college. Students must sign in as they arrived in the morning, but thereafter there was no means by which their movements could be checked, and neither did anyone try. Though socializing between the sexes was vaguely discouraged within the

building ('This is an art school, not a marriage bureau',
Tonks had thundered in his early days), nothing could
stop close and even intimate friendships forming where all
had such an absorbing interest in common.

On that first morning Adeline considered herself fortunate
to have made at least one friend. The initially reluctant
Toni had accompanied her as she strode across the quad,
rather as a tugboat escorts an ocean liner into harbour.
Once inside, nannying was neither asked for nor offered,
and Toni had simply pointed her charge in the direction
of the Antiques Room, and hurried to her Life Class with
a slightly shameful feeling of relief.

It appeared she had a second friend when the morning
session ended and her neighbour in class – the same who
had applauded her efforts with Clancey – leaned across.

'I say,' he said, 'I do think your dog is absolutely splendid.'

'He has been good, hasn't he? I simply must take him
out now.'

'Mind if I come? I could do with some fresh air.'

'By all means. I brought sandwiches.'

'And me.'

They went out into the quad. It had stopped raining and
when they had walked Clancey round the perimeter they
sat on a low wall to eat their sandwiches. The young man,
whose name was Peter Marchant, was affability itself and
immensely talkative. Nothing was required of Adeline but
that she listen. He explained that he had been at Harrow,
and that his arrival at art school followed a protracted
though polite battle with his parents who had wanted him
to go into the army.

'I have great expectations,' he said merrily, throwing a
crust to Clancey, 'about which I don't give a hang. It's the
most frightful bore. My sister now, my sister Fenella,
would be perfectly suited to the role of chatelaine. In fact
in the area of inheritance I'm all for female emancipation.
She wants nothing more than to be an ornament to society
and spend money in all manner of tasteful ways.'

'And you? What do you want to do?'

He gave her a collusive smile. 'Who knows? I don't suppose I shall be an artist, whatever that is, but at least I'm attending the Great School of Life, and not Sandhurst. I intend to enjoy every minute.'

Adeline laughed. He was such a jovial, outgoing, straightforward sort of boy – she thought of him as a boy though he could not have been much younger than her – and there was something about him which reminded her of how Frank had been, before the war. Not that Peter Marchant had Frank's looks. He was the sort of young man in whom the middle-aged one – stout, benign and balding, with a high colour and an exuberant manner – could plainly be seen waiting to get out. She was sure that whatever path he eventually chose, he would follow it with confidence and be rewarded with success.

On the way back to the building they encountered Toni, carrying a bag of shopping, and Adeline introduced her to Peter.

'I say!' he said, with a loud, cheerful laugh. 'This is my lucky day! Scarcely started my career as a roué and I've met two beautiful girls!'

Adeline glanced at Toni and was amused, though not surprised, to see that her face was a study.

Adeline made many friends during the four years, but the closest and dearest, the friends who were to last her all her life, were made in that first week. And they were all, in their different ways, misfits, individuals who were congenitally unable to conform to the general pattern of Slade students. They weren't rebels, in the accepted sense of the word; they didn't have to try to be different – it was in the nature of the beast. To the outside observer Peter Marchant would have appeared more at home in the Guards Club; Toni Simpson was like an efficient typist, managing well on a modest salary; Adeline Charteris would have looked odd in any milieu one cared to name. It would have been hard to imagine a more ill-assorted trio. Until Duncan and Joel made it a quintet.

Adeline's small and unhappy store of sexual experience was not out of place at the Slade, where the preponderance of women and the predominantly public-school backgrounds of the men made sex a subject more for discussion than for experiment, at least in the first year. So perhaps it wasn't surprising that the first time she was confronted by a deep and active sexual relationship between two unmarried people of about her own age, it was a relationship between men. Joel Briggs was a first-year student, a small, pale, sensitive-looking youth of eighteen, from Newcastle Upon Tyne. Duncan Colley was a heavy-set, hirsute, choleric man who had fought in the war and then worked as a representative for a cigarette company before deciding to follow his inclinations and risk applying for art school. They were an unlikely enough pair of exquisite lovers, but their overwhelming attraction for one another was obvious, though perfectly discreet. Adeline was stunned by them, attracted by their passion as only those who have never known passion can be. She watched them with fascination and admired with all her heart both their self-possession and their mutual devotion.

Perhaps it was simply expedient to be faithful – they were lucky, in the circumstances, to have one another – and yet Adeline was touched to find Duncan lying on the pavement by the main gate, his hands and arms spattered with oil, changing the chain on Joel's bicycle; or to see the sunrise of pride break on Joel's face when Duncan, who was uncompromisingly modern in his work, received rare praise.

Duncan, she recognized, was the type of man whom other men (she found herself thinking of Howard) referred to as a 'pansy' or a 'nancy', and yet she adored him unreservedly. There was no-one who could make her laugh so much. She found his over-sized affectations, his off-colour jokes, his flouncey caricatures of himself painfully funny. All of it was a defence, an I'll-say-it-before-you-do deflection of potential slights. Quite often there were tears in her eyes, and not tears of laughter, as she listened to his outrageous stories, peppered with 'dear boys' and 'fancys' and 'poppets'.

Joel, on the other hand, had at first seemed so shy and reserved that she despaired of ever getting to know him. Everything about him, from his fine, straight, mouse-coloured hair to the tips of his delicate, bony fingers, seemed terribly vulnerable. Even his skin was as white and fine as a child's so that the tracery of blue veins showed through at the temples and on the inside of his arms, and on his chest when he wore an open shirt. And yet, as Adeline discovered, the waiflike appearance masked a stoical and resourceful nature. Joel did not need to put on the motley to protect himself. When she mentioned this to Duncan he simply said: 'Ah yes. Jo has composure of the heart.'

This phrase stuck in Adeline's memory, not least because she intuited that such composure would never be hers.

When Toni told her that they were almost certainly lovers she was shocked almost as much by the oddness of the match as by the match itself.

Toni was amused at her astonishment. 'You've led a very sheltered life I can see that, Mrs Charteris.'

'It would seem I have,' admitted Adeline humbly. The day was still far off when she would be able to tell anyone here about Simon's suicide and the humiliation and despair which had preceded it. 'They're so different,' she said. 'And it's not as if either of them is the sort to find life easy.'

'It's their decision.' Toni's life had been tough, and she coped with it. She expected others to do the same.

But for some months Adeline regarded the two men as one might a pair of unicorns – as strange, wonderful, and incomprehensible.

Nonetheless, she looked on her life and saw that it was good. She loved the Slade with its dingy corridors that gave magically on to cool, light, echoing rooms. She loved to be in a place where so many others were concentrating on the same pursuit of excellence, and where each person's view of a single subject could be so utterly, perfectly, different. She loved her big, untidy barn of a room which was gradually adapting to her needs as Clancey was adapting to it, and to London. She loved Clancey, the fool. More than anything she loved her wonderful, diverse, funny, loyal and loving friends.

Perhaps there was one thing missing, one element which could complete her happiness. But there again, she thought, maybe this is all I need – art, freedom and friendship.

CHAPTER ELEVEN

1924

FOR A FULL three years the magical trinity sufficed, and more than sufficed. Adeline was certainly happier than she'd been for some time, her soul seemed to unfurl and breathe in a way it hadn't done before, not least because she was doing something she enjoyed. She had no illusions about the extent of her talent. When she looked at the work of Toni, or Duncan, or any of half a dozen others, she realized she couldn't hope to compete. On the other hand she had, as Tonks had remarked at her interview, a facility which might prove to be a commercial asset. At the end-of-year exhibitions her pictures attracted attention: people were amused by them, they peered and pointed before passing on; her work was entertaining and Adeline had the good sense to see that this was a strength upon which to capitalize.

Inevitably, she grew bored with the tyranny of the Antiques Room, and her habit of embellishing her draw-ings of the haughty classical heads with elaborate hats of her own design led to one or two run-ins with the Professor. Being a wily old fox in the field of student psychology, he confined his criticisms to the quality of the draughtsmanship, refusing to comment on the rights or wrongs of the hats' existence. On one occasion he tapped her shoulder, indicated that she should move, and himself took her place on the wooden donkey. Clancey, trained to move with his mistress, stood up, tail wagging. Tonks ignored him. Around the margins of Adeline's drawing he drew two or three sketches of the hat worn by her version of the Discobolus. The hat was gigantic, its curly brim boiling over with flowers and plumes and grapes, the kind of hat worn by elegant society beauties in the portraits by Gainsborough and Reynolds. Adeline watched as Tonks drew the hat from different angles – from above, from the side, from the back. All were perfect, the textures differentiated, the proportions accurate. You could have taken the hat from the page and worn it.

Having made his point, Tonks handed back her charcoal, vacated the donkey, gave Adeline a courtly but ironic little bow, and moved on.

It wasn't the Professor's intention to curb any student's individuality, nor to crush this particular student's urge to entertain. He simply wished what was done to be done well, and Adeline accepted the criticism in the same spirit in which it was offered. Even when she had progressed to the Life Room she could not resist turning what was simply an exercise into an event. Having laboured over a model who was very often not in the first flush of youth and beauty, she would begin to add details – socks, and sock suspenders, a lorgnette, earrings, a row of medals adhering to a naked breast. Very often she introduced a second figure into the drawing, a wild-haired woman with a distracted look, wearing an artist's smock.

Tonks was a less frequent visitor to the Life Class, but when he did choose to make his rounds he could hardly fail to notice Adeline's additions.

'And who is this?' he asked one day, leaning over her drawing board. 'Who is this madwoman in the corner?'

'That's just a student sir,' replied Adeline, 'seeking inspiration.'

'Alas,' said Tonks, 'she has not yet found it.' But to hhis colleague Wilson Steer he later remarked:"She need never worry where her next meal will come from. There's money to be made from cartoons.'

The friendships forged in Adeline's first weeks at the Slade continued and strengthened. The five of them – Adeline, Toni, Peter, Duncan and Joel – took enormous pleasure in each other's company. Though Adeline and Peter might have had access to money, the pastimes of all of them were geared to a student's pocket. They went to endless galleries and exhibitions, and occasionally to the cinema. They walked in the parks and round the street markets, they travelled by bus south to Greenwich and north to Hampstead, and had picnics. Occasionally, in a mood of fresh extravagance, they would go to the ABC where Toni worked in the evening, and share two pots of tea and a plate of bread and butter, sabotaging Toni's natural efficiency and leaving a disproportionately large tip.

But their chief entertainment consisted in simply getting together and talking. They found themselves – their tastes, their backgrounds, their dreams and aspirations – a subject of consuming fascination. They would forgather in Adeline's room, or in the umbrageous basement flat rented by Duncan and Joel in Passmore Gardens off the Euston Road. Peter's rooms – comfortable and well-appointed, a young gentleman's rooms – were in St John's Wood, near Lord's Cricket Ground, a little too distantt for casual getting-together, and Toni quite simply never invited them. In all the time she lived in Gower Street Adeline was never admitted to her friend's room. It wasn't that Toni was mean – at least twice a week she would bring food across the landing to Adeline's kitchen and they'd cook it together. She frequently signed Adeline in when she was late, she automatically tidied up her possessions, she even overcame her nervousness with Clancey and took him for walks. But she guarded her privacy with stern single-mindedness. Adeline was piqued by her friend's ability not to feel obligated by other people's hospitality. Toni's resolve remained immutable.

'You like your place full of people,' she'd say, 'and that's your privilege. I like my place to myself. That's mine. I can't help it if I seem rude, it's the way I like it.'

The truth, which Adeline came to appreciate in time, was that the modest room (it was only half the size of Adeline's) on the first floor of Mrs Fairyhouse's establishment was the first that Toni had ever had to herself, or to call her own. All her life she had been hemmed in by other people, their needs, their requests and requirements, a second mother to her brothers and sisters, a reliable lieutenant to her hard-pressed parents. Her room in London was a haven and a sanctuary, the reward for her diligently fostered and husbanded talent, and a great deal of hard work.

Every so often Peter invited them all for something he chose to call 'an indoor picnic' but which was in fact a feast of smoked salmon, and gulls' eggs, and ripe stilton, washed down with champagne. On these occasions they ate and drank gluttonously. The first time Duncan had teased Peter unmercifully.

'You're an absolute fraud, Pedro,' he shouted, mopping delicious juices from his chin. 'You're just a bloated capitalist pretending to be a student.' Peter obligingly roared with laughter. It was impossible to embarrass him. 'Oh, I'm a bloated capitalist, all right, and I'm not pretending to be anything else. One of these days I shall take you all down to our family place and then you'll see just how bloated I really am!'

In these surroundings, the group fell naturally into two sections. The more extrovert members – Adeline, Duncan and Peter – sat round the table, hooting with laughter, smoking and drinking and throwing unsuitable titbits to the dog. After supper Peter put on gramophone records and he and Adeline danced, with Duncan supplying extra rhythm with his knife and fork.

Joel and Toni retreated to the sidelines, sitting quietly

together on the floor in the corner, their backs to the wall, watching the others and occasionally conversing confidentially.

'They're being disapproving! They want nothing to do with us!' Duncan bellowed scattering ash from his cigarette. 'What's the matter with you two, why are you being so bloody old-fashioned?'

'Just leave us alone, Duncan,' Joel said in his soft Geordie accent, 'we're not stopping you enjoying yourselves.'

'But you are, you make me feel guilty!'

'That's your problem.'

Later on Duncan, remorseful and awash with wine and tender sentiment, took Toni's place by Joel's side, his arm across his shoulders, and Toni tactfully joined the other two to drink coffee and talk until the last bus.

It took only a few months for Peter to fall in love with Adeline. He first proposed to her on the annual Slade picnic in Epping Forest in the summer that ended their first year. Two charabancs had taken the students out of town on a day when the tarmac wavered in the heat and the horizon was lost in a trembling haze. After lunch they went for a walk, arm in arm, companionably as Adeline thought, in and out of the dappled green shadows and puddles of sunlight. They came to a dew pond and sat down on the grass, their backs against a tree. Distantly, from among the trees, came the voices of the more energetic picnickers larking about. Clancey went to the pond and drank noisily and long.

'This is the life,' said Peter.

'You sound like my father.'

'Oh? Is that a compliment? What sort of a chap is he, your father?'

'He's dead now, but he was the loveliest man imaginable.'

'Good. I was a little afraid you might be likening me to some pompous old windbag that you couldn't stand the sight of.'

'No.'

'Tell me now, would you consider marrying a man who was like your father?'

'I'm not considering getting married at all.'

'But if you were?'

She shrugged. They both had their eyes closed, their faces lifted to the sun. It was a pleasant, meandering conversation, the idlest speculation.

'If I were,' said Adeline, 'I'm not sure I'd want to marry the sort of man who'd have me.'

She felt Peter's shoulder shudder as he laughed.

'What about me? I'd have you.'

'Is that a proposal?'

'Yes.'

It was Adeline's turn to laugh, now.

'No, honestly,' said Peter, 'don't laugh. I'm asking you to marry me.'

'When? I can't make next Saturday.'

'Whenever you like.'

Adeline opened her eyes and rolled her head sideways to look at him. He was staring at her with his habitually cheerful, optimistic expression.

'Well?'

'No! Of course not! It's preposterous!'

'Why?'

'Because we're friends!'

'Can't a married couple be friends? Besides, I'm in love with you.'

'Oh, *Peter* . . .' Adeline lowered her forehead on his shoulder. 'You are a fool.'

'I suspect you're right. On the other hand I know what I like.'

Adeline kneeled up and prepared to address herself to the issue more seriously. Unfortunately for Peter she was looking her handsomest, in a loose navy blue cotton dress with a blue and red patchwork jacket and an enormous cartwheel straw hat with a red scarf tied round it. On the other hand he was sanguine of ultimate success, no matter what her reaction now. Peter had enjoyed good fortune all his life and he had no reason to suppose his luck would suddenly run out.

'Listen,' she said, 'I've been married once. It wasn't a success. I'm older than you. Most of all I'm not in love with you.'

'Fair enough. The first two don't concern me but you're right, the third is something of a stumbling block.'

'It is. So can we just leave the subject of marriage?'

'Certainly.'

'You're not very persistent, it can't possibly have been serious.'

'It is deadly serious, and I'm horribly persistent. I agree we should let the matter drop for now, but I reserve the right to propose at regular intervals over the next two years until you come round to my way of thinking.'

Adeline got up and hurled a stick into the pond, watching as Clancey bounded to retrieve it in an explosion of spray.

'You can do what you like,' she said, 'if it'll make you happy, but it won't make the slightest difference.'

This curious conversation, coming as it did quite out of the blue as far as Adeline was concerned, was treated by both of them as if it had never been. Because Peter himself was so ebullient and unflappable it was hard to believe that he suffered as a result of her rejection. But he was as good as his word and offers of marriage, in one guise or another, came at regular intervals. It became a joke in the group, that Peter was Adeline's swain, her courtier, her 'would-be gentleman of the bedchamber' as Duncan put it, a joke that Peter accepted with perfect equanimity, and even encouraged. It was impossible to ruffle his composure or disturb his good humour. From time to time Adeline told herself that it might be better for both of them if she stopped having anything to do with him, but that seemed like cutting off her nose to spite her face, for she was so fond of him and he was such delightful company. When eventually they became lovers it felt like a natural and comfortable progression from the affectionate friendship they'd enjoyed for so long.

And comfortable was what their affair was. During lazy afternoons and evenings at his flat, Peter made love to Adeline with robust delight and dozed contentedly afterwards with his arms around her. There was none of the anguish and uncertainty of those troubled nights with Simon. Neither was there ecstasy, but then Adeline had no past ecstasy by which to measure her experience. There was, however, warmth, affection, intimacy and release. Peter's open and enthusiastic enjoyment of her body made a gift of Adeline to herself, and she was happy, and grateful.

The sheer relief that she was not, as she had once feared, someone incapable of love was aphrodisiac enough. She also took a sneaking pleasure in knowing that she now qualified as the rather 'fast' woman that the other Slade students had always, erroneously, believed her to be. But she continued to reject his offers of marriage. It was impossible, unthinkable. Even her friends did not know that she still from time to time awoke with a start in the night, bathed in sweat and not knowing where she was, the image of Simon as she'd last seen him staring at her out of the darkness. She had succeeded in shutting away everything but that, and it haunted her. Peter's arms kept the past at bay. For all his money and breeding, he was a homely man, and his aura of comfortable well-being spread to those around him and especially to Adeline. She suspected that he was good for her, and that he was good himself, a good man – honest and loyal and lacking in vanity and malice. But his goodness and sureness disconcerted her, and she was afraid of making another mistake. The only way that she knew of repaying his honesty and love was to be honest in return, so that when he said 'I love you' she would smile, and kiss and cuddle him, but would not reply. She knew that they could not truly be called lovers, because he persisted in seeing her as his future wife, and she in seeing him as her best friend.

Married was the last thing Adeline wanted to be. Her life had moved on, she could not go back. She felt as though, after a long, wearisome, gruelling and often disheartening climb she found herself on the crest of a hill, commanding a view of a new and undreamt-of landscape, full of thrilling possibilities. To be married, even to someone as charming and understanding as Peter, would be to retrace her steps and sink once more into the vistaless undergrowth on the hillside.

She knew that she had changed, and was still changing, that there was something different about her. She saw the difference reflected back at her in the eyes of her family. Particularly in those of Frank. Each time they met now she felt her new experience of life surrounding her like an aura. Sometimes she actually saw his eyes narrow, as though he were trying to make out the sister he remembered behind the dazzle of difference and recent change. And because she saw this, and understood it, she appreciated all the more the quiet, plain politeness with which he treated her, a respect almost, an acknowledgement of the strides she had made.

'You're happy now, aren't you?' Frank asked, when she was down at Fording Place in the spring of her second year at the Slade. 'You're really happy.'

'Yes, I am.' She glanced at him. 'I'm sorry.'

'Why sorry?'

'It seems wrong to be so happy after what happened.'

'Far from it, I'm glad that you are.'

They were sitting up late in front of the library fire. Elizabeth had gone to bed: her days tired her more than they used to, though she didn't sleep heavily and Adeline often heard her moving about in the small hours. At their feet lay the dogs, Frank's black labrador bitch, Tosca, and Clancey, flat out with his head on the fender. He had to become, to all intents and purposes, a city dog. On fine days in Gower Street he would lie on the front step at Mrs Fairyhouse's and watch the traffic go by, and never wander, only rising if Adeline called him, or if she left to go out, and clicked her fingers for him to accompany her. Indulged by Mr Fairyhouse and by the students, he had become a dog for all seasons and settings, a patient and adaptable presence, able to curl up and sleep in the smallest and most unpropitious corners, and to emerge and lay his chin soulfully on the knee of whoever seemed the softest touch. But on visits to Fording Place he relived his half-forgotten earlier life as a bold and buccaneering country dog, racing and barking through the park, swimming in the river at a safe distance from the swans, and hunting rabbits and hares in the fields. In the evening, as now, he fell into a deep and blissful sleep that was like a little death.

Adeline lit a cigarette and stretched out her legs, ankles crossed.

'I made an awful mistake, didn't I?'

'I think you did. But we're all entitled to some of those.'

'Mother was right. She never wanted us to marry. Neither did you.'

'I didn't feel that strongly, but I had my reservations, certainly.'

'What were they?'

'Look, Addy, let's not rake it all over, Let's just leave it be.'

'But I want to know!' She leaned forward and stared hotly at her brother in a way that reminded him of someone though he couldn't think who. 'I want to know why you were so damn right, and I was so hopelessly wrong.'

Frank wouldn't be hurried. He's ageing, thought Adeline, watching him as he bent to stroke Tosca with maddening slowness. He's twenty-eight years old and he's beginning to be middle-aged. Since taking over at Fording Place he was more solid, both in form and manner; he had developed a countryman's deliberateness. Given the right setting he could still summon the old gaiety and dash but it was no longer his natural style. She had a sudden vision of Duncan, who was the same age as her brother, and who had fought in the same war, and she wondered what they would make of one another.

'It's not a question of who was right,' he said now. 'I was just concerned for both of you. Simon suffered a lot more as a result of the war than just that wooden leg of his, you know.'

'I know. He was so depressed. And he had dreams. He seemed to get worse and worse and I couldn't help him.'

'He was scared of you.'

'Scared of *me*?' Adeline half laughed in amazement. 'How could he have been?'

'Very easily. You were always so confident, you always took charge. When he was feeling up, he liked that. But when he got the horrors I don't suppose he could face telling you why. Addy, the plain fact was that Simon was scared stiff all through the war, and almost as scared of telling you. I wasn't surprised to hear what he'd done. I expect he felt trapped.'

'But all I wanted to do was *help*,' cried Adeline. 'I couldn't imagine what he'd been through, I wanted to be told so that I could share it, or comfort him, or something – anything. Instead of which he just withdrew from me, and treated me as if I were a leper. I don't understand. Surely everyone was scared, and wretched? I remember when you came on leave how different you were – '

'Addy. Yes, we were all scared. We were all terrified. But we were not all cowards.'

'You mean . . .' She met Frank's steady, serious stare for a moment and then dropped her own eyes and stubbed out her cigarette. 'You mean Simon was.'

'Yes.'

'You can't possibly know that.'

'I'm as certain as it's possible to be. You get to know the type, to spot the signs. He was very good at avoidance, and yet he was the sort of chap the senior staff officers thought the world of. He worked himself into all the right jobs. He only made one mistake and a dozen men died as a result of it. A battle zone's a chaotic place, Addy. It's surprisingly easy for someone to hide. But poor Simon was in a blue funk the whole time. He was a case, he'd have cracked up completely and done something really stupid if he hadn't done that to his leg first.'

Adeline was about to say that at least he had borne the suffering bravely, and gone out with honour, but there was something in Frank's expression and his voice which warned her not to take the discussion any further. She thought, for a moment, the unthinkable, and felt quite ill with shock. If it were true, and Simon had done that to himself, it was almost too sad to bear. She did not want to hear it in this room where they had so often been happy and where she had still idolized him.

'For what it's worth,' said Frank, 'I think he was set on his course. You've got nothing to reproach yourself with.'

'Except marrying him in the first place.'

'Well . . . as I say . . . but you had your reasons. And at least you lived up to his idea of you. You helped him feel like a hero. He'd have been the loneliest devil on earth if it hadn't been for you, Addy.'

'Oh, Frank.'

Adeline buried her face in her hands and wept, with loud, racking sobs, while Frank laid a quiet, patient hand on her shoulder. The door she had so firmly closed on Simon had been forced open and memories rushed clamorously back at her, not to be denied. And yet it was the first time that she had truly grieved for him. From that day on she had no more nightmares.

In London Adeline had fallen into the habit of having lunch with Howard about once a month. The arrangement was never referred to as a regular one, he would simply ring her up on the communal telephone which stood in Mrs Fairyhouse's hall, beside the outstretched arms of a North American Black Bear, and invite her to join him, usually at Boulestin's in Covent Garden.

She enjoyed these lunches. Howard was a good host, attentive and interested, more especially because he himself was experiencing some difficulties at the moment. Cynthia's decline had accelerated to the point where she was more or less housebound and Howard had to employ a nurse to look after her.

Though he didn't talk much about the business, he told her that he had closed down the Dublin end of the operation because of labour problems following on the Troubles. He worried about who was to take over from him; he was preoccupied. But he made no secret of his pleasure in seeing Adeline, and his willingness to hear talk about the Slade, and her work. He plied her with food and drink and ate little himself, and watched her face as she talked. She would feel herself becoming increasingly flushed and garrulous but he never did anything to suggest he found her overpowering, nor did he seem bored. Sometimes he would put out his hand and touch one of her many brooches, or necklaces, and give a short little laugh, an abbreviated version of the loud bark she remembered so well. She remembered, too, how as a child she had used to picture him as a great noisy fiery wind bursting into the house and disturbing everything and everyone, and how she'd hated him for it. Now the positions were reversed, and it saddened her. She liked to think that their lunches gave him pleasure and that that was why she always accepted, but the fact was they gave her pleasure too. She looked forward to them eagerly and left with a sense of well-being.

Their talk was of the present and the future – Adeline's – hardly ever of the past. Never of Simon.

Once he asked, suddenly and without preamble, 'Tell me how your mother is.'

'She's well. Very busy, very hectic, full of good works. Frank's been there with her, of course, which I'm glad of now that Bob and I are in London all the time. At least she's not lonely.'

'Being lonely has nothing to do with whether or not you've got people round you.'

'I know that.' He was still able to make her bridle. 'But Frank isn't people, he's her son.'

'And you think he's a comfort to her?' There was unmistakable irony in his voice.

'I'm sure she must be glad he's there. Apart from which he's managing things and generally – '

'We don't seem to see her these days,' he said. It was plain he hadn't been listening to her answer. 'With things as they are it's difficult to ask her to stay with us in London, and I wouldn't want to leave Cynthia . . .' His voice tailed away and for an instant his face took on an uncharacteristically introspective expression. Then he glanced up at her with his fierce, scowling grin and said: 'We'd better go before they throw us out. Drink up.'

Only Bob was able to move in and out of her present life at will and without awkwardness. He would turn up at Gower Street with a bottle in his hand and spend the evening with her, eating a Spanish omelette and talking. If the others were there he wasn't in the least put out, but simply mucked in, listened more and talked less. Adeline recollected the evenings she and Simon had spent with the crowd from the *Courier* at Bob's flat, how strange and shy and awkward they must have seemed, what an exalted group of beings the others had appeared to them!

Bob had once spoken of having no talent for youth, and this theory was borne out by the fact that he seemed more at ease with himself each time she saw him. As children she had always felt that she had more in common with bold, daring Captain Frank than with taciturn, limping, bookish Bob. Now, like so many things, it was the other way about. Her world at the Slade was much closer, both geographically and in spirit, to Bob's than to the distant, rural, family world of Fording Place.

She observed with delight Bob's interest in Toni. His attentions were so dry and oblique, and Toni herself was so practical and private that Adeline despaired of there being any real communication between the two. But gradually, perceptibly, over a period of some eighteen months during which Bob visited perhaps once a week, he grew bolder and she more responsive. Now, if they were all together, it was more often Bob, not Joel, who sat to one side with Toni and talked earnestly into her ear as she sat staring ahead like some slightly prim out-of-work actress in her inexpensive, well-cared-for clothes.

Peter was delighted. 'Perhaps he'll be the first person she invites into her room,' he said.

Duncan disagreed. 'Don't be silly, Pedro. That door across the landing represents Antonia's hymen. The day a man breaches that he can say goodbye to freedom. You won't catch me cadging an invitation!' He shuddered and rolled his eyes.

'She wouldn't want you,' said Joel, 'you're far too messy.'

'Nag, nag, nag,' moaned Duncan.

Adeline drew a picture of Bob and Toni in the pose of Rodin's 'The Kiss', with Toni in her ABC pinny, and Bob with a pencil behind his ear.

'That'll be the day,' said Peter.

At the end of Adeline's third summer at the Slade, Toni completed her course, *summa cum laude,* and left. To the dismay of Joel and Peter and the amusement of Adeline and Duncan, she went to work in an advertising agency, Cutler, Barr and Waring. She remained at Mrs Fairyhouse's, but she gave up the ABC and her clothes became noticeably more expensive.

'I ask you,' said Peter to Adeline as they lay on the grass in Regent's Park with Clancey panting beside them, 'what hope is there for the rest of us if someone with her talent sells her soul to a ruddy ad agency?'

'Every hope! You are a snob, dear. She didn't go to CBW because it was all she could get, she went because it was what she wanted to do.'

'Incomprehensible.'

'Not to me. Anyone can see Toni's not interested in starving in a garret, or suffering for her art. She's done all that, and now she wants to see a return on her investment.'

'But think of the things she'll be asked to do, Addy! Jars of jam, proprietary worm powders, cleaning fluids and worse.'

'She won't necessarily do it for ever.'

'I couldn't do it for even one week.'

'That's because you don't need the money.'

'No-one needs it that much.'

'That just goes to show how little you know.'

Peter stretched out his hand and took hers. 'Would you work in an ad agency?'

'Of course. I'd much rather do that than hang about feeling superior and not having any fun.'

He lifted her hand to his lips and kissed it. 'I believe you would, too. And not by any stretch of the imagination do you need the cash.'

'It's better to do something than nothing, for me anyway. A job's what you care to make it.'

'*God* – !' Peter covered his eyes with his free hand. 'Spare me the homely philosophy.'

'Don't tell me what to do – '

Clancey, anticipating a game, got up and stood over them, wagging his tail and licking Peter's face.

'Aah! Get that animal away from me!'

Adeline cackled with laughter. 'You deal with him. Kill, Clancey, kill!'

The prostitution of her gifts notwithstanding, Toni gave every appearance of thriving at Cutler, Barr and Waring. The dark shadows disappeared from under her eyes, there was a spring in her step, she was prettier and more carefree. Conservative creature that she was, she still spent many evenings with her friends from the Slade. When Peter twitted her about drawing jars of jam she smiled and refused to rise to the bait.

'It's not that different to Tonks's Antiques Room,' she said, 'and what's more, I earn money doing it.'

Adeline wasn't sure if Bob was still playing court. His career at the *Courier* had taken another step forward and he was in features now, often working on ideas that he himself initiated, and away for days at a time. During the summer he and Adeline went to Tuscany together, renting a dilapidated farmhouse in the hills near Siena for four weeks.

The heavenly, sun-baked, aromatic indolence of those weeks loosened both their tongues. Adeline told her brother about Peter, and his proposals.

'You could do a great deal worse,' was his observation. Adeline, who had expected to be laughed at, was taken aback.

'But it's completely out of the question!'

He shrugged. 'You raised the subject.'

'What about Toni?' she fired back.

Bob mopped busily at the olive oil on his plate with a heel of bread. 'I like Toni.'

'Only that?'

'No, not only that. She's – attractive. Unpretentious. Different. Also she's not at all flirtatious, which is agreeable. You know me, I can't manage endless banter, playful exchanges, that sort of thing.'

'What *does* she say to you?' asked Adeline curiously.

'What does she say to me . . .?' Bob, replete, leaned back in his chair with his hands behind his head. He had put on weight, and his skin was tanned. With his black hair worn rather long on his neck and brushed straight back off his brow, he could have passed for an Italian himself. How times have changed, thought Adeline.

'. . . She doesn't say all that much, but she's a good listener, an intelligent listener. She doesn't seem shy – just not particularly interested in talking. Though when we go into an art gallery she makes it an education.'

'Are you in love with her?' asked Adeline. She could not imagine another context in which she would have asked so sensitive a question in such a direct way. But this was, after all, Italy, with the golden-bronze hills slumberous in the heat, and a hawk quivering in the blue-white sky, and wine still in their glasses here in the cool of the crumbling, vine-canopied terrace.

'In love . . . I don't know. I don't know how being in love feels. You tell me.'

Adeline leaned her chin on her hands. 'I don't know either.'

'I see.' Bob felt in his pocket for cigarettes, offered her one and lit both with a match struck from the corner of the table. 'What a pair of romantics we are.'

'I think,' she said reflectively, 'that if you don't know, then you've not experienced it. That's what I'm hoping.'

'I suspect you're right.'

'And?'

'And?'

'What about Toni?'

'We enjoy a nice, sensible, undemanding rapport, that's all. Not love.'

But Adeline wasn't so sure. She was even less sure when, as she left for college one crisp morning in October, she encountered Toni in the hall with her arms full of yellow roses and Mrs Fairyhouse in close attendance.

'Just look at this!' called Mrs Fairyhouse as Adeline and Clancey came down the stairs. 'Flowers for the birthday girl!'

'Is it your birthday? Many happy returns!' Adeline kissed her friend's glowing face above the flowers. 'I say, aren't they absolutely beautiful? Who are they from? An unknown admirer?'

'No – no, they're from Bob . . .' Toni looked almost radiant as she closed her eyes and breathed in the scent of the bouquet.

Mrs Fairyhouse beamed indulgently. 'You must pop in this evening and have a glass of sherry with us dear, promise me that?'

'Yes, thank you . . .'

When Mrs Fairyhouse had withdrawn, Toni looked up at Adeline with shining eyes. Her normally pale face was pink with pleasure.

'Oh, Adeline, I never had such a gorgeous present, and so *extravagant*! Isn't that a lovely thing to do?'

'They are lovely. I never knew the old stick had it in him.'

'I must dash and put them in water before I go,' said Toni, dropping her bag and umbrella on the floor and beginning to run up the stairs, clasping the roses in both arms like a child. On the landing she turned and called to Adeline:

'He's one in a million, your brother!' before dashing into her room.

As she walked up Gower Street, Adeline reflected that

only one emotion could effect that transformation, and it looked astonishingly like love.

Adeline had not been entirely accurate when she said to Bob that she did not know what love felt like. She had not as yet known a grand passion, but seeing Toni so enchanted and enchanting reminded her of those weeks when Simon was first back from France and when she had visited him in hospital each day. Fool's gold it may have been, but Toni and her roses brought back to her the intoxicating happiness, the sense of being beautiful, which had accompanied that time. It also made her more certain than ever that she did not love Peter.

That night Duncan cooked supper for them at the flat in Passmore Gardens. Toni had gone to the theatre with Bob, and Joel had a terrible cold. They were all a little subdued as they sat around on the floor eating Duncan's Welsh rarebit, in which ale figured more prominently than cheese, long viscous strings of the stuff trailing from their forks and clinging to their chins.

'If Antonia had consented to stay with us,' remarked Duncan, 'instead of painting the town red with that chap from the *Courier*, we'd have had an excuse for a party. It's too bad of her, in my view.'

Joel stifled a sneeze and foraged for his handkerchief. 'I'm in no fit state for a party.'

'Misery. Go and put your feet in a mustard bath or something.'

Peter put his plate down on the floor next to him. 'My parents are having a party for my sister's twenty-first. If any of you would like to come I could make sure you get invitations.'

Adeline, who had already been told about the party, could hardly believe her ears. A society twenty-first, a phenomenon of which she had some experience, was hardly the milieu most likely to welcome a couple of Duncan and Joel's proclivities.

'Addy's coming, of course,' said Peter, putting his arm round her shoulders.

For the first time, she felt a little uncomfortable at his touch, and annoyed by his assumption of some claim on her.

Duncan clapped his hands. 'Won–der–ful. I've been dying to see the family seat for ages. But are sure that's all right? What about the mater and pater? Won't they mind?'

'Of course not,' said Peter. 'The upper classes are known for their broadmindedness, or hadn't you heard?'

'I promise we shan't tango together.'

'I thought I'd ask Toni, and Bob too, I shall have to perform a few fraternal duties, but nothing that will prevent my enjoying myself. It'll be a very respectable bash, good band and as much champagne as you can hold, though, with one or two exceptions, I can't vouch for the rest of the company – that's why I need you.'

Duncan whooped. 'Summoned to the aid of the party! I love it! Count us *in*, absolutely, Pedro.'

Joel sniffed. 'We'll have to hire evening clothes. I've got nothing suitable stowed away in mothballs.'

'We shall sally forth to Moss Bros,' said Duncan, 'and do the thing in style.'

Adeline, irritated by Duncan's euphoria, asked: 'What about your sister? She doesn't even know us.'

Peter waved a hand airily. 'Fenella will think it's frightfully smart to have some artistic types about. She doesn't count me. Anyway there will be simply hundreds of people milling about and most of them won't know each other. You'll be lost in the mêlée.'

'I don't think it's for me,' said Joel. 'Thanks all the same, Peter.'

'Nonsense,' said Duncan, standing up and beginning to collect the dirty plates. 'We shall both be coming. I don't get so many invitations from the squirearchy I can afford to turn them down, and I'm not going without rain-in-the-face here. We'll *all* be coming!'

As Peter walked her back to Gower Street afterwards, he asked: 'You will come, won't you?'

'Oh – I don't know . . .'

'You're cross with me.'

'No. Just cross.'

'You must come.' He was holding her arm and now he stopped her, pulling her round to face him. 'I want you to be there. Everyone'll be bowled over by you.'

'I doubt it.'

'I know it.'

'Peter – '

'Please, Addy. For me.'

He smiled at her, his cheeks dimpling, and she smiled back in spite of her huff. There was no denying that the air he carried with him of coming from a world she knew, even if she had abandoned it, was pleasant. It was as if beneath the new language that they both now spoke there was another, native language running like a submerged current, binding them together. It was difficult to deny him anything, for he wasn't used to being denied, and demurs tended simply to bounce back off the resilient surface of his breezy cheerfulness.

He put his hands on her waist. He was a little shorter than her but it didn't concern him. His stocky, open-shouldered figure, with its tendency to corpulence, was as familiar to her now as her own; his round, eager face that had never lost a certain out-of-town ruddiness was the face of a friend she was loth to lose, even if it was not that of the man she wished to marry.

'Don't worry,' she said. 'I'll come. I'd love to.'

'That's the ticket!'

'Now let's get on, I'm tired.'

When he had kissed her quickly on the doorstep and she had gone upstairs to her room – noticing as she did so that Toni was not yet back – she looked down into the street and saw him hailing a cab. Duncan was right. Peter was, if not a fraud, then certainly a dual personality. She watched him get into the cab and then drew the curtains. Clancey, whom she had left behind this evening, stretched and yawned cavernously, with a yelping sound. She didn't turn the light on, but sat down on the edge of the divan, stroking the dog's head as he sat beside her. Thinking of

Toni, and her happiness, she felt rather lonely, as she hadn't done in months. Perhaps she was displaced, a fish out of water; perhaps she was just playing at being a different sort of person.

She remembered once, early on, meeting Peter as he left the college to join his father for lunch at White's. Usually he was indistinguishable from his fellow students, in the cord trousers, threadbare pullover and five o'clock shadow of the serious artist, but on this occasion the transformation was so complete she hardly recognized him.

'My, ain't you the toff!' she'd exclaimed, admiring the immaculate pin-striped suit, the gleaming white shirt disciplined by starch, studs and links, the silk tie with a gold pin, the cheeks smooth and fragrant as a baby's, the hair glossy and brushed close, the patent leather shoes gleaming fit to break a debutante's heart.

'Like it?' he asked, flicking a speck of dust from his lapel.

'Like it? I adore it. You're good enough to eat.'

'And every bit as greasy. I just hope I don't meet Duncan.'

It was these occasional forays into the uplands of toffishness which had endeared Peter to Mrs Fairyhouse. Catching sight of him in his finery one evening, she had waited till the front door closed behind him and then emerged from her parlour to engage Adeline in a brisk bout of soupy adulation.

'Now that, in my opinion, is how a young gentleman should look when he goes out on the town – don't you agree, Mrs Charteris? Breeding and class – they're beyond price, and you have them too. I notice these things.'

'Thank you, Mrs Fairyhouse.'

'How are you getting on over there, anyway?' Mrs Fairyhouse had continued, anxious now to talk. 'Do you find you're getting along with them all right, what with you being from such a different background and so on?'

'Oh yes,' Adeline had said, beginning to edge her way up the stairs. 'I get along with them famously.'

Now, sitting in the dark with Clancey's eyes fixed mournfully on her face, she felt suddenly old, and uncertain. Her judgement so far had proved anything but sound. She wanted to go it alone, but was she equipped to do so?

Had Adeline been religious in any conventional sense she would have asked for a sign. Instead she first took Clancey out and then went to bed. She lay awake with her hand on his back, until she heard Toni come in, and then she fell asleep.

CHAPTER TWELVE

1924

FENELLA MARCHANT'S BIRTHDAY party served to remind Adeline of what she had missed by marrying so young. Having moved straight from Fording Place, where she had scarcely entered society, such as it was, to the brief time in London and then the isolation of Kenarvon, and thence to the highly idiosyncratic milieu of the Slade she had not fully realized what was going on in that other world of dinner gongs and white ties and sports cars and dance crazes.

Bob had declined the invitation. He was going north, he said, on a story, but Adeline knew he could never have borne such an occasion. Toni had consequently been loth to attend, but they had besought her piteously. Duncan's argument had finally carried the day, with its unashamed self-interest.

'My darling, you simply have to come to give myself and the lad here a spurious air of respectability. Two boys, two girls – what could be more suitable? Antonia, it's your duty to be there!'

Peter went down to Hartfield House, near Lewes in Sussex, the night before the dance to hold, as he put it, his mother's hand. There was a house party to which Adeline had been invited, but she had refused, preferring to spend the night at the North Star pub in Snipe Green with the others. Peter had, however, insisted on paying their bill.

'It's absolutely the least we can do,' he said. 'The parents would go mad if they thought you'd come all this way and weren't being properly looked after.'

'They sound positive paragons,' observed Duncan as they travelled down by train, in a compartment they had claimed to themselves. 'If I were Peter's mother I'd make sure that people like us weren't allowed within a stuffed olive's throw of my daughter's party.'

'If you were Peter's mother,' said Joel in his quiet way, 'it would be a miracle.'

'I shall ignore that. As a matter of fact,' went on Duncan, 'I've been in a taking about what to wear.'

'I thought you had descended on Moss Bros like the wolf on the fold,' said Adeline.

'Well, we did in the end,' admitted Duncan, 'but I confess I was strongly tempted to cut a dash and dress down for the occasion. Then I decided it wouldn't be fair to embarrass Pedro in front of half the county. Antonia, tell us what you're wearing, you're so clever with clothes.'

Toni, who had not considered it worthwhile to buy an expensive dress for this one, singular occasion, began to outline what she had done to a perfectly ordinary little frock to make it suitably glamorous.

Adeline glanced at Joel. He sat in silence, his forehead leaning against the window as he stared out at the grey November landscape. She touched him on the wrist and he started slightly.

'Sorry, I was miles away.'

'Not looking forward to the party?'

'It's not that. I don't like parties much anyway. I've scarcely been to any, to be honest. I know I'll be very silent and dull, which is tiresome for Duncan.'

His eyes rested for a moment on Duncan, who was

roaring with laughter at some remark of his own, and Adeline saw there, not for the first time, the look of love in all its vulnerable, uncompromising nakedness.

'I shouldn't worry about that,' she said. 'Does he look like someone who wants competition?'

Joel smiled. 'Perhaps not.'

'Just look on it as a lark, I'm going to.'

'But you know the rules.'

'I don't, not really, not any more. I've been at great pains to unlearn them over the past couple of years.'

Joel looked away again. 'We shouldn't be here,' he said.

'Nonsense, you heard what Peter said. We're very welcome, all of us.'

Joel shook his head. Toni handed round a bag of boiled sweets and Duncan, in exceptionally good form, asked: 'What have you done with the pooch?'

'The Fairyhouses are minding him for me. Mr F. enjoys it.'

Duncan pulled a face. 'I'm sure he does! Aren't you taking a bit of a risk, dear, leaving your pet in the hands of a necrophile?'

He entertained them for the rest of the journey. It was impossible not to be infected by his high spirits though Adeline found herself wondering, as Dorothy Sugden might have done, if it would all end in tears.

It was getting dark when the train hissed and trundled into the tiny rural halt of Snipe Green, but they could make out Peter on the platform, a large many-coloured golfing umbrella keeping off the cold autumn rain. The station-master, having blown his whistle and waved his flag to send the train on its way, disappeared for a moment and re-appeared with a trolley for their bags.

'My God, where are we?' enquired Duncan, peering into the gloom. 'It must be the edge of the known universe at the very least!'

Toni put her arm through Adeline's. 'The country gives me the jitters.'

Peter went ahead of them into the puddle-filled ruts of

the lane beyond the station building, and opened the boot of his car.

'Hurry up!' he called. 'I'll have you in the bright lights of civilization in no time, O ye of little faith!'

'Down from Town, are you?' The stationmaster asked as he and Peter loaded the cases into the boot.

'How can you tell?' murmured Duncan.

'They been arriving all day,' said the stationmaster, a shade accusingly.

Adeline pulled off her hat and turned her face up into the rain. A thick mulch of fallen leaves squelched beneath their feet as they climbed into the car.

'Help, my shoes!' wailed Toni. She, Duncan and Joel went in the back and Adeline, as the person with the longest legs, sat in the front. Peter smiled at her, eyebrows raised.

'I take it you're all right?'

'I'm enjoying myself. Home from home.'

'Attagirl!'

'I say,' asked Duncan, leaning forward between them as the car moved off, 'is this the family barouche?'

'Good Lord no, she's my old crate,' said Peter. 'I've had her ages. She's in need of a complete overhaul, poor old girl.'

'You could have fooled me. Why don't you have it in London?'

'Oh, I don't feel the need of a car in Town.'

'And what about the rest of us, pray? You could run us around all over the place, take us to nice country pubs on a Sunday and heaven knows what. I think it's a downright scandal you have a perfectly good car and leaving it down here in the sticks!'

'Now then, where are we?' asked Toni, rubbing the steamed-up glass with her gloved hand. 'Isn't there supposed to be a village, or something, or one or two houses?'

'There is,' replied Peter. 'Or there will be in a minute. Patience.'

'I think I shall have a large gin when I arrive,' said Duncan. 'And then very possibly a second.'

Peter glanced over his shoulder. 'That's up to you, but I recommend a cup of tea if you want to survive the torrents of champagne tonight.'

'Oh!' Duncan put his arm round Joel's shoulders and squeezed them. 'Pinch me, Jo, I must be dreaming.'

Cosy red and amber squares of lighted windows began to appear in the dusk.

'Here we are,' announced Peter. 'Snipe Green. And here –' He wound the wheel to the right and drew up at the kerb. 'Is the North Star, where at the last count you could get a clean bed and a hot supper for five bob.'

He hauled on the brake with a grinding sound.

Toni peered at it. 'It looks ever so old,' she said doubtfully.

Peter jumped out and opened the door. 'It's even older than old. Innumerable monarchs and their floozies are supposed to have slept here. Or stayed here, anyway.'

Adeline threw the door open on her side and got out, slapping her hat back on her head and clutching her cloak around her with folded arms.

'Well I think it's marvellous. And I'm going to organize you bunch of snivelling townies. We shall sit by a roaring fire and have a proper tea, with toasted Sally Lunn and chocolate cake if they've got it, and then when we've all got our glad rags on we'll reassemble for a stiffener before our chauffeur returns to collect us.'

She picked up her case and pushed open the door of the pub, looking for a moment, as she was outlined against the light, a large figure in wide-brimmed hat and long cloak, rather like the female *doppelganger* of Augustus John. The others followed more diffidently.

'Isn't she masterful . . .?' breathed Duncan. 'What a woman!'

Reg Dyson, proprietor of the North Star, saw the 'two boys, two girls' of Duncan's proposition, but only the presence of Mr Marchant, whom Reg had known since boyhood, made them appear even remotely 'suitable'.

The young woman who entered first seemed to fill the

hall on her own, and had to duck to avoid striking her head on the central cross beam. She was dressed like – Reg didn't quite know what, but it was neither smart, pretty nor ladylike, and yet her face, with its wide mouth, prominent, slightly hooked nose and thick black brows was startlingly made up. His fears were only allayed, just, by the appearance of Mr Marchant carrying two cases, and by her voice which had the carrying power of someone from a good background.

'Hallo!' she cried. 'I think you have rooms booked for us!'

She was followed by a smart little thing, trimly turned out in a blue wool coat and a matching hat, but whose speech, lamentably lacking in Hs and Ts, betrayed her as a cockney. Reg knew the bill was being settled by the Marchants, but he had a countryman's suspicion of native Londoners.

As these two signed in, the two men entered and filled Reg with still greater foreboding. Oh dear, oh dear, there weren't many of *those* to the pound in Snipe Green, thank the Lord.

'It's lovely and cosy, anyway,' said Toni, looking round at the small, dark-beamed hall with its threadbare red carpet, its smell of cinders and polish and roasting meat, its coal fire, its respectable magazines on a low table.

'Talk about another world,' agreed Joel. 'Listen.'

They listened. A clock ticked stolidly and the coals rustled.

Toni cocked her head. 'I don't hear a thing.'

'That's right,' said Reg, heading for the stairs with a case under each arm and another in each hand. 'No bright lights and noisy motor cars here, sir. Will you come this way?'

Duncan raised his eyebrows, caught Joel's eye and mouthed: 'So there!'

Peter caught Adeline's hand as she went up the stairs.

'Addy – thanks for coming. I'm so glad you're here.'

'So am I, and I intend to enjoy myself.'

'I love you.'

She smiled and shook her head. 'Get along with you.'

They had declined the Marchants' invitation to dinner beforehand. Peter had pointed out, to Adeline in particular, that her non-attendance, and the sacred responsibility of his mother to ensure equal numbers, might result in him being 'stuck with some dull, giggling local girl', but Adeline stood firm. They, too, had appearances to think of, and were a foursome. They'd have something to eat at the hotel, and see him afterwards.

When Peter had gone, with promises to return at nine, they unpacked their bags and then went down for the tea. The room which Reg Dyson called 'the Residents' Lounge' was a small, snug, front parlour leading off the hall on the opposite side from the bar. There were three people already there, an elderly couple who gathered themselves together and left at their approach, and a solitary middle-aged woman who was knitting, and at the same time reading from a book on a small lectern that stood on the table next to her. She glanced at them once only and thereafter seemed entirely absorbed in what she was doing.

Here there was a bigger fire, of logs, round which they sat to have their tea. It was almost as Adeline had predicted, except for lardy cake instead of Sally Lunn, and fruit cake instead of chocolate. When they'd eaten, the spell of being in a different atmosphere and place made them suddenly quiet. Duncan was no longer excitable but drowsy and reflective, staring into the flames with his chin sunk on his broad chest. Joel turned the pages of an out of date *Country Life*. Toni, who usually perched rather than sat, had kicked off her shoes and was curled sideways in her chair, with her eyes closed.

Adeline thought that this moment was almost perfect. She could imagine going her whole life and not finding for a second time this exact blend of harmony and warmth and peace and contentment. She was glad that Peter was not here for her, nor Bob for Toni: that kind of love, one's

own and other people's, seemed always to be accompanied
by anxiety. But this, this encircling cocoon of friendship,
built as it was on trust and freedom and the acceptance
of one another's faults and differences, this was precious
indeed, and she gave herself up to it, loth to move or talk
or break the spell.

The clock which they had heard in the hall stood in the
corner of this room, its tick like a resonant heartbeat. The
door to the hall was not quite shut and from time to time,
with the small comings and goings of the pub, a draught
scurried across the floor, lifting the fringe on the edge of
the rug and moving the fine grey wood-ash on the edge of
the hearth. Once a cat stalked in, long-haired and yellow-
eyed, and pressed for a moment against Adeline's legs,
surveying them all appraisingly. It detached itself from
her, and sat down and washed itself, its tongue making a
small rasping sound as it did so. Then it stalked off.

Duncan stretched out his legs and crossed his ankles.
The soles of his shoes were nearly worn through in two
half-crown-sized patches, the left rather more than the
right. His socks were yellow, perhaps to match the yellow
and red paisley handkerchief which sprouted like a robust
flower from his breast pocket. His jacket was velvet, his
pullover Fairisle, his shirt cuffs frayed. His bushy, curly
hair needed a cut . . . Adeline found that he was looking
at her, perhaps sensing her scrutiny. He smiled, but for
once was silent.

Toni had fallen asleep, her head resting sideways on her
hand. She looked very small and young, and her breath
came in little puffs from her half-open mouth. Joel had
taken a notepad and pencil from his pocket and was drawing, with absolute concentration, one of his elaborate
doodles, a fantasy of squares, circles, spirals, curlicues and
delicate cross-hatching, always beginning at the top left-
hand corner and creeping across the page like a lacemaker
covering her cushion. His tongue protruded childishly
from his lips as he worked, the only spot of colour in his
white face.

Suddenly the woman in the corner stopped knitting,

pushed her wool on to the ends of her needles, collected
up her book and lectern and left, as if obeying some inner
summons.

The tick of the clock stuttered, to be followed by a
whirring and then the first of six high-pitched chimes.

Duncan stretched, arching his back, the threadbare cuffs
falling back from his large, hairy wrists as he raised his
hands above his head.

'Oh –! Someone carry me upstairs – Adeline, my dear,
you could manage it? I must find a bathroom and mon-
opolize it for at least three quarters of an hour.'

'Me too.' Toni stood up and slipped her feet back into
her shoes, emerging from sleep with catlike ease. 'I'm off,
and I'm not carrying anyone, either.'

'Heartless Jezebel.' Duncan hauled himself upright with
a great yawn. 'Beat you to the bathroom!'

In a sudden burst of energy the two of them raced across
the room and out into the hall.

Adeline and Joel followed, more desultorily. As they
left the room the cat re-entered it. The spell was broken.

The dress Adeline wore that night was one that had been
made in Ireland, for a ball they had attended. It was no
longer fashionable, and it was also a little tight for her
these days, but when she put it on and looked at herself in
the narrow wardrobe mirror she saw a person she recognized and felt at home with, and who was, if not beautiful,
certainly striking.

It was black velvet, trimmed at the shoulder with red
satin roses. At the front the hem was ankle-length and the
neckline just skimmed her collar bones, but at the back the
skirt fanned out into a fish-tail train and the bodice was
bare almost to the waist. It was a dress designed to show
off the good points of a tall, dark-haired woman with a
long neck, an imposing bust, a fine set of shoulders and
the back of a valkyrie. With it Adeline wore her reddest
lipstick, her most dramatic eye-shadow and her palest,
most luminous powder. Realizing that she already looked
as if she were wearing fancy dress, she added garnet and

jet earrings like miniature chandeliers, and two long rope necklaces of the same which she let hang down against her bare back. Her hair was still bobbed but she brushed it back vigorously so that it stood away from her face in a dark halo. Her high heels took her to well over six foot, but she had towered over people for as long as she could remember, and like many a tall daughter of a tall mother, didn't care.

Well, she said to herself, looking at her reflection one last time before turning off the light and going downstairs. They'll love you or loathe you but they'll be hard put to ignore you.

There was no doubt which camp Peter belonged to.

'Ravishing!' he exclaimed as she came down the stairs with her cloak over her arm. 'You're going to knock 'em dead!'

She raised her eyebrows. 'What about the dull local girl . . .?'

'Ah –' he winked at her. 'Mother came up trumps and broke the rule of a lifetime.'

'Odd numbers at dinner?'

'I was the spare man.'

'Well, good for her!'

Peter, in great good humour, turned his attention to the rest of the party. 'I say! Can this really be my familiar little band of struggling artists?'

'What did he expect?' Duncan asked the others. 'Paint-stained smocks and berets?'

Joel looked down at himself sheepishly. 'I feel a fraud.'

'You are a fraud!' said Duncan. 'But who else is to know? Chin up and look good.'

During the drive to Hartfield House the rain grew steadily heavier. By the time they turned in between graceful iron gates and began to ascend a gently rising drive it was thundering on the roof of the car and almost obscuring the great banks of carefully tended shrubs on either side. The house itself, brightly lit, white, pillared and porticoed like a sumptuous wedding cake, appeared shimmering through the downpour.

'Bloody hell,' said Joel. 'Is that it?'

Peter chuckled. 'I told you I was even more bloated than you took me for.'

'It's beautiful,' said Toni. 'Someone tell me what I'm doing here . . .'

A shaft of golden light, carrying with it the sound of laughter, and talking, and a distant band, spilled down a curved sweep of shallow steps and gleamed wetly on a queue of expensive motor cars waiting to disgorge their passengers at the door. A footman with a giant umbrella opened the doors of the cars and escorted each couple up the steps until they were safely under cover.

When it was their turn he beckoned Peter to pull up as close as possible to the bottom step, indicating the huge lake which had formed on the drive. Then he came round to Peter's window, his pleasant, reddened face glistening with rain.

'Hallo again, sir. Would you like Canter to park this for you? There aren't too many spaces near the house now and your father asked for some of the older people's motors to be put in the garage.'

'Thanks, that's a good idea, Aldous. Can you just see my guests in first?'

'My pleasure, sir.'

Even in the short distance from the car to the wide pillared porch Adeline felt the hem of her dress become heavy with water, and rain streamed from the spokes of the umbrella, like a swinging bead curtain around them as they ran. When they were safely deposited at the door Aldous shook the umbrella vigorously.

'What a night! And I can remember the day Miss Fenella was born: beautiful sunshine it was! We're going to have trouble with the fireworks. Still, I hope you enjoy the party, madam . . .'

'He remembers the night the young mistress came into the world!' parodied Duncan. 'My God, how feudal.'

Peter ran up the steps two at a time. 'Sorry about the

blasted rain! I'm afraid the weather's one thing even my
mother can't organize! Come on, come and be introduced.'

In the hall, which was a bower of pink, cream and white
flowers representing a small fortune in mid-November,
lit by glittering electroliers apparently suspended in space,
their humble coats, hats and scarves were whisked away
by two Italian maids, and Adeline and Toni were directed
upstairs to a suite of rooms where several other girls were
titivating before a long dressing table, flounced and
swagged in grey silk.

'And what exactly do we do in here?' Toni whispered.

'Finishing touches,' Adeline whispered back. Two girls
of sylphlike slenderness and languor murmured, ' 'Scuse
us' and wafted past them as if borne on the back of a
zephyr. Another rose from her stool at the dressing table
and turned this way and that, checking the hem of her
dress, which came only halfway between knee and ankle.

They stood aside as she, too, left. Toni put her hand to
her cheek.

'How can an ordinary working girl hope to compete
with that?'

'By not competing!' declared Adeline. She took her friend's hand and led her to the centre of the room so that
their twin reflections looked back at them from the arched
sections of the mirror. 'What do you see?'

'You and me.'

'Exactly. And each of us absolutely unique. Did you
notice they all looked the same? To think I might have
been just like them!' Enthusiastically she pushed her fingers into her damp, slightly curling hair and fluffed it out.
Seeing that Toni looked doubtful she took her by the
shoulders and addressed her directly. 'Yes?'

Toni smiled a little ruefully. 'Yes.' She glanced once
more at her reflection. The pretty, understated rose-pink
dress she had so artfully revamped, did it just look cheap
and ordinary now . . .? Her frown returned. 'Adeline,
you don't think –'

'No,' said Adeline. 'I don't. Come on, they'll be waiting for us.'

Downstairs they joined Duncan and Joel at the end of a reception line.

'I must leave you,' said Peter, *en passant*. 'I'll see you anon. Are you all right?'

Duncan caught his sleeve. 'What are we queuing up for? Drinks?'

'I can assure you that drinks will be pressed on you the minute you get in there, more than you can possibly hold.'

'Don't bet on it.'

'This is just to say hallo to my mother and father and Fenella. The birthday girl.'

Though Sir Stanley and Lady Marchant were a charming and distinguished couple who made well-bred noises of welcome, there was no indication as to where their daughter had come by her looks. Adeline even heard an appreciative intake of breath from Duncan and caught, in Toni's slightly too refined 'How do you do, and many happy returns' the guarded admiration of the average for the superlative. As they paused in the drawing room to accept champagne from a loaded salver it was Joel who put their reaction into words.

'Isn't she the loveliest creature you ever saw?'

Toni sighed. 'Peter's a swine. He should have warned us.'

'My dear,' said Duncan, cheerfully, 'it makes one feel like a fairy that's seen too many Christmasses. But look – bright young things galore, and music and dancing. What are we all standing around here for?'

Adeline followed, but not before she had stolen another look at Fenella Marchant. She was dressed in white – stark, matt, parchment white, against which her unusually pale skin took on a warm, honeyed glow. Her ensemble was as up to date as it was possible to be, and yet she was as unlike the dead-eyed girls whom Adeline had disparaged upstairs as Adeline herself. In Fenella, fashion and nature seemed to have found a perfect, dazzling synthesis. Her slender, faun-like figure might have been created for the simple, daringly short Grecian sheath she wore, and her sleek red hair for the urchin cut which, on another woman, would have been harsh. Her small, uptilted face was like a flower on its slender stalk of a neck. Her eyes were pale, her mouth uncertain, a child's mouth. A difficult face to paint, thought Adeline, and realized how much she wanted to paint it.

A hand appeared and waved up and down before her eyes.

'Hey,' said Toni. 'Come on, we thought we'd lost you. We've got our own table, the works.'

'She's extraordinary,' said Adeline as they walked through together. 'And it all looks natural.'

'Hm.' A rich heritage of working-class scepticism was in Toni's voice. 'I very much doubt that.'

The dais for the band and the dance floor had been assembled in a huge conservatory. High above, rain beat furiously on the glass roof, and lightning flashed in a black sky, but between the roof and the dancers great baskets of flowers hung like pink and white nimbus clouds trailing trembling ringlets of fragile greenery. The band seemed adrift on a raft of flowers, the tables, shrouded in sweeping white cloths, swagged in pink silk and with posies of pink and white flowers on them, were set against a backdrop of tall ferns and palms and arrangements of lilies and gladioli that were as broad and high as the spread tails of peacocks. People were already dancing, the men like elegant black reeds amongst the whirling, flowing light-coloured dresses of the girls.

'They've really gone to town, haven't they?' said Toni. 'It's not like being in a room. They've changed it into something quite different.'

Duncan and Joel were sitting at a table to the right of the dance floor, about halfway between the door and the band. Duncan had his chair tilted back, the ankle of one leg resting on the knee of the other, his hands thrust into his pockets, a cigarette between his lips, his face a study in fascinated delight. His white bow tie was listing slightly. In contrast, Joel looked shy and awkward, leaning forward with his elbows on the table, his fingers nervously dismembering a white carnation from the posy in the centre. A half-full bottle of Mumm's stood between them, with two glasses, Joel's untouched, Duncan's almost empty.

'Ladies! Please –' Duncan, enjoying himself hugely, leapt to his feet and pulled out two of the spindly white and gold chairs. 'Sit down. What's your pleasure? Bubbly? Champers? Or the fizz is very acceptable.'

Adeline laughed. 'I think I'll have the bubbly, kind sir, and no half measures!' She could feel a silly, wayward excitement building inside her, something she'd scarcely felt since peering through the banisters to watch the guests arrive at Fording Place. The music was up-tempo now, the saxophones singing gaily, the piano and drums beating out a prancing rhythm. The young men and girls danced madly, coat tails and necklaces flying, skirts swirling, mouths laughing, feet skimming the polished floor. Beneath the table Adeline's foot tapped, the champagne sparkled and exploded like fireworks on her tongue. This was like a drug she had craved, without knowing it, for years.

Duncan leaned across the table with a conspiratorial air. 'Do you realize our crust will be *breakfast*, at two a.m.? I'm going to wish I'd brought some of that cake from the pub in a paper bag!'

'Stop thinking about your stomach,' said Toni, 'and get up and dance with me while you still can.'

'The pleasure, dear lady, is all mine.' Duncan rose, only a shade unsteadily, swept Toni into his arms with a flourish and danced her away to the 'Maple Leaf Rag'.

Adeline tried not to watch them enviously. She sipped her champagne and looked instead at Joel. He was white and tense, his fingers moving among the white petals of the carnation, shredding each one into tiny flakes.

She tried to catch his eye. 'Cheer up. It may never happen, and if it does, do we really care?'

'He's going to be paralytic two hours from now. He'll need pouring into a flask and carrying out.'

'You must stop behaving like his keeper. Don't worry about him, he can take care of himself.'

'You think so?'

'I do. And even if he can't, it's not the end of the world. Let's worry about it when it happens. Why don't we dance?'

He gave her a surprised smile. 'What, me? With you?'

'Of course,' he laughed. 'Since Toni and I are supposed to be providing you with a front of respectability we might as well take advantage of it.'

'Where's Peter?'

'I don't know – doing the rounds, playing the host, who cares? We have each other and the night is yet young –'

'You're bigger than me.'

'Tush!' Adeline pushed back her chair. 'Everyone's bigger than you, and most people are smaller than me. We must both learn to live with it. Come on.'

They rose from the table. The ragtime had given way to a sweet, romantic waltz as Adeline and Joel began to dance. He felt light and spare, taut as a spring, the top of his head was about level with her eyebrows, but his lead was surprisingly firm. Adeline hummed happily. The air on the dance floor was humid and fragrant with the scents of the flowers and of the girls. Far, far away the walls of black glass were streaked with angry rain, but in here all was warmth and perfume and colour and music.

'Where did you learn to dance?' asked Adeline. 'You're awfully good.'

'My mother taught me. She was keen, but my father could just about walk from here to there without falling over, so she latched on to me. I was a right little mummy's boy. We used to waltz and two-step and tango around the front room. This was in broad daylight in a terraced house in Newcastle, mark you. Can you wonder . . .' He spun Adeline around.

'Can I wonder what?'

'That I'm – the way I am.'

'No. Your mother has a lot to be proud of.'

Joel smiled, the first time he'd looked happy all evening. 'They make a handsome couple, don't they?' he said. 'Duncan and Toni?'

'They do. Unlike us, we make an eccentric one. But don't we dance well together?'

'And under certain grave natural disadvantages.'

'If we don't make the grade as painters we could open an exclusive ballroom dancing school. In Newcastle per- haps.'

'Or Wolverhampton. Or Bradford, or Bristol. Good class provincial.'

As the evening went on, the tenor of the birthday party grew more hectic. During the supper interval a honey- voiced black pianist serenaded them, and when the band returned, in fresh suits of white with gold piping (like naval officers, as Duncan remarked), they went into the new, lilting and seductive foxtrot.

Joel, emboldened by his sortie with Adeline, invited Toni on to the floor and they glided away. Duncan, look- ing very flushed and hot, pulled a fresh bottle of cham- pagne from its frosted bucket.

'They think of everything, don't they? More?'

Adeline pushed her glass towards him.

'Just fancy what all this must have set old Marchant back,' he said. 'It boggles the imagination. But I suppose it's nothing new to you, dear, coming as you do from the stirrup-cup and hunting-horn set.'

'Stop provoking. My parents would never have gone in for all this even if they could have afforded it, and in Ireland Simon and I lived like a couple of hermits.'

'One of these days you are going to have to tell me the story of your life, really and truly. I feel there are a lot of salient details to which I am not privy.'

Suddenly Peter arrived at their table, with Fenella on one side of him and a strange, dark young man on the other.

'Addy, I brought Fenella over to say hallo to you all properly.'

Duncan stood up, the fingers of his left hand spread on the table to brace himself.

'The birthday girl, how nice.'

'And this,' said Peter, 'is an old school friend of mine, Nicholas Eyre.'

Adeline shook a hand that was cold and dry and which did not properly grip hers.

'May we join you for a moment?' asked Fenella, sitting down in Joel's place and crossing slim, rounded legs that would not have disgraced Mistinguette. Nicholas sat down next to Adeline, and without looking at her, his head turned towards the dance floor as if he were rather bored. Peter touched Adeline's shoulder, and left.

'Are you all having a lovely time?' asked Fenella.

'Oh, a *gorgeous* time,' replied Duncan. He was quite drunk now, and Adeline caught the unmistakable note of parody in his voice. It was, however, lost on Fenella.

'I'm so glad. One never knows when it's one's own party.'

'It's sweet of you to include us in your celebrations,' said Adeline, 'when you don't know us at all.'

'We could have been absolutely *anybody*,' agreed Duncan.

Fenella tipped back her exquisite little head and gave a peal of affected, musical laughter. 'Peter gave you all impeccable references!' She looked at Adeline, as if eliciting a sensible answer from the only dependable source. 'And you've been well looked after, you've had plenty to eat and drink?'

'It's marvellous.'

'Our every whim has been indulged,' said Duncan. 'Or almost.'

Fenella giggled again. 'You must tell me what it is that we haven't provided.'

'Good Lord!' Duncan rolled his eyes and put his hand to his breast. 'In mixed company?'

Adeline heard Nicholas Eyre give a little sigh.

'Where are the others?' asked Fenella.

'They're dancing,' said Adeline. 'It's a wonderful band.'

'Yes, they are fun, aren't they?' Fenella's gaze came to rest on Nicholas for a moment. She tipped her head a little to one side and her pretty, childish mouth seemed about to frame a question, but the object of her scrutiny remained entirely impassive and preoccupied, staring at the dancers. Assuming once more her bright, sparkly air she turned back to Duncan. '*I'd* adore to dance,' she said.

They went, leaving Adeline alone with the saturnine Mr Eyre. She felt a little resentful. It was a bit much of Peter simply to swan off and leave her with this uncommunicative stranger.

Abruptly, he turned and said: 'So. Down from the smoke for the weekend?'

'That's right. Peter probably told you, we're all at the Slade together. Except for Toni, who's with CBW, the advertising people –'

'Yes, I have heard of them. Cigarette?'

'Thank you.'

'You're not in the house party?'

'No . . . I was invited, but we thought – well, we're complete outsiders.'

'And we outsiders must stick together.'

She didn't know what he meant by that, and didn't answer.

'You know,' he went on, 'if you had asked me at Harrow which of my contemporaries was likely to go to art school, old Peter would have been last on the list. He's just about the most conformist devil I know.'

'He has talent, though. He wouldn't be at the Slade if he didn't,' said Adeline, quite sharply.

Nicholas Eyre blew smoke over his shoulder as if dismissing the idea. 'He's messing about. Playing around.' He smiled at her, a quick, cold little smile. 'As are we all, Adeline.'

She found that she didn't care to hear him use her name. She was rattled.

'Speak for yourself,' she said.

'Oh, but of course I do.. I do.' He laid his outspread hand on his gleaming white shirt front. 'He's awfully stuck on you, isn't he.'

This was the last course Adeline wished the conversation to take. She pretended she hadn't heard, and asked instead:

'What exactly is it you do?'

Again the small, chilly smile. 'I go to parties and strike up conversations with interesting women.'

She did not return the smile. 'I mean apart from that.'

'I play the piano.' He allowed a pause to develop, his eyes on her face, so that in the end she was forced to ask: 'Oh? I mean in what way? Where?'

'In a club.'

'A nightclub?'

'Yes. How do you think the stuffy old Marchants got hold of Rich Parker for the cabaret? Their contacts in the world of jazz are hardly legion.'

Adeline would not admit that she had never heard of Rich Parker before tonight.

'That was through you, was it?'

'All my own work. Though of course he's a star and I'm a mere toiler in the vineyard.'

'What are you aiming for?' asked Adeline, knowing she sounded censorious.

'You are assuming that I'm not perfectly content to play popular ditties in a club for the rest of my days. Which I am. I don't have the application for concert work, and I'm not good enough to be a Rich Parker, I can't stand the thought of teaching and I haven't enough imagination to compose. So –' He shrugged. 'I play for my supper, and for friends. And during the day I work as a waiter at the Waldorf.'

'What a waste.'

'Not at all. Actually I'm a rather better waiter than I am a pianist. I have a natural aptitude for it. It takes grace, diplomacy, a retentive memory, a smart appearance, and a limitless capacity for self-ingratiation.'

'It doesn't require modesty.'

'No. Self-effacement, but then that's not the same thing.'

'Obviously not.'

She was openly sparring with him, but he didn't in the least appear to mind. On the contrary she had the annoying impression that she was reacting exactly as he had intended.

'Tell me, Adeline,' he said, 'do you have many friends in Town? I mean, outside the charcoal and turpentine brigade?'

'I have the friends I want, both in number and kind.'

'I only ask,' he went on, as if she hadn't spoken, 'because I know some rather interesting people that I think you might like to meet. And I know they'd be interested in you.'

'Really?'

'Oh yes.'

'What makes you think I'd like to meet them, or vice versa?'

'My instinct in these matters is quite reliable. Looking at you –' He did so. 'I'd say you needed to be dragged away from all these daubers and doodlers and introduced to some properly creative people. Grown-ups,' he added with slight, offensive emphasis as Joel and Toni came back to the table, flushed and elated from their exertions on the dance floor.

'Did you see us?' asked Toni. 'We were showing them how it's done where we come from.'

Duncan and Fenella returned, and Nicholas stood up, stubbing out his cigarette and stretching slightly as if he had been kept waiting.

'Ah, there you are,' he said.

Duncan mopped his face with his handkerchief. 'I'm a broken man!'

Nicholas leaned towards Adeline. 'Nice talking to you. See you anon.'

He strolled away and Fenella, with a little wave, followed.

Duncan refilled their glasses, and raised his. 'Here's to gracious living!'

Toni giggled. 'I'll drink to that.'

'Duncan,' said Joel. 'Steady on. Don't you think you've had enough?'

'Nowhere near enough!'

Adeline, seeing again on Joel's face that unmistakable tender watchfulness, felt a stab of envy.

Shortly after that, when she had danced with Duncan, who propelled her round the perimeter of the floor, leaning heavily, Peter joined them, and asked her to dance.

'I'm sorry I've not been with you. Circulating and all.'

'Of course. I understand.'

'Did I tell you that you look absolutely splendid?'

'You did, and thank you.'

'My father's quite smitten with you. You're what he'd call a well set-up woman.'

'That makes me sound like a shire horse.'

'Well it's high praise coming from him. And I know just what he means by it.' Peter pressed his cheek to hers for a moment. 'Tell me, what did you make of Nick?'

She could not, for a second, connect the friendly diminutive with anyone she'd met. When she did, she asked carefully: 'Is he a good friend of yours?'

'Not really, these days. We were close at school. I used to idolize him. He was very clever, and musical, and also something of a rebel, which was awfully seductive to a stick-in-the-mud like me. He had a quite awe-inspiring line in talking back to masters. For a while I was his obedient henchman, but then we were both rusticated for half a term for drinking, I had the fear of God put into me by my old man and returned to the safety of the straight and narrow. Soon after that he left. I think he did a year or two at the Academy – he's a gifted pianist – but he didn't finish and now he lives on his wits. Peculiar chap, in many ways. But I reckon if it hadn't been for his influence I might have been languishing in the army, so I have that to thank him for, indirectly.'

'You don't see much of him now?'

'No. He and Fenella go about together quite a bit. I suspect she finds him madly glamorous, though what he sees in her God alone knows.'

'Peter! She's beautiful – enchanting.'

'Plenty of pretty girls about.'

Adeline knew enough about the attitude of brothers towards their sisters to realize that she would be wasting her time to defend Fenella any further.

'No,' Peter went on, 'we're not great oppos these days, but I still have the dull boy's sneaking admiration for a rake. I thought he might amuse you – you haven't answered my question.'

'I didn't like him.'

'Oh?' Peter leaned away from her to look into her face. 'Why's that?'

'I don't think I'm being touchy, but he struck me as rude and patronizing.'

'The blighter!' Peter exclaimed admiringly. 'What did he say?'

She tried to remember what he had said which had so incensed and outraged her.

'It was more how he said it.'

'Oh, you don't want to mind that, it's just his manner.'

'He was disparaging about the Slade, about all of us – about you, for heaven's sake. He said you were the last person he'd have expected to go to art school, that sort of thing.'

Peter chuckled. 'Perfectly correct.'

'He implied that we were like children, playing at being artists. He told me there were some people he wanted me to meet who were "properly creative" as he put it, and "grown-up". I could have smacked his smug face!'

'You should have done! That would have livened us all up no end and Nick, I'm sure, would have taken it in good part. He enjoys a good drama.'

'In that case, thank heavens I didn't give him the satisfaction.'

'I say, he really did rub you up the wrong way, didn't he?'

'Yes. Yes, he did.'

'Let's wander for a moment.'

Peter led her by the hand back to the side of the dance floor and thence past the tables into the relative cool and quiet of the drawing room where they'd been received. Groups of guests sat and stood around, talking and drinking, but they found a comfortable chintz sofa in the corner of the room and sat down.

'Can I get you another drink?'

'No thank you.'

'Cigarette?' He proffered his case. She shook her head and he took and lit one for himself. 'Honestly, Addy,' he went on in his warm, affectionate way, 'you mustn't let him rattle you. It isn't worth spoiling your evening over. I'm only sorry I introduced him to you.'

'No –' She shook her head again and put her hand for a moment to her forehead. 'No, it's me that should be sorry. I don't know why I reacted as I did, it's all too silly.'

'It's certainly not like you.'

It struck Adeline that a good many people were presuming what was and was not like her this evening, to the extent that she hardly knew what she was like herself.

'I'll have that cigarette now, please,' she said.

As Peter held his lighter for her he remarked, 'I tell you one thing: I shouldn't let Nick force any of his friends on you, he mixes with some very odd types.'

'How do you mean? What sort of odd?'

'I don't know . . . eccentric, not to say mildly potty . . . free thinking. I know one shouldn't hold any of that against them, but I met a couple of them once and frankly they were a thoroughgoing pain in the neck. It was impossible to conduct any normal sort of conversation with them. Most self-centred characters I've ever met.'

'But who were they? What do they do?'

'Couple name of Elverstone. They're both writers, though she's rather more of a lion than him –'

'Marian Elverstone?'

'Yes, I think so.'

'They say her novels are wonderful.'

'I don't say they're not, I just didn't care for her, or her husband. But Nick's well in there. They treat him like a kind of mascot, or a court favourite or something, and he seems to suffer from an uncontrollable urge to expose people to them. It's as though meeting the ruddy Elverstones is a kind of test, for what purpose I haven't the remotest idea and which I signally failed.'

Adeline smiled and laid her hand on his. 'I can see you're broken hearted about it.'

'Desolate. Better?'

She nodded. As they rose to leave the drawing room she caught sight of a painting which hung immediately over the sofa where they'd been sitting. It was of Fenella, sitting in a grey chair, wearing a white dress, and with a book on her lap. The book was open but her hands lay listlessly folded on the pages. As a likeness it was accurate, as a painting it was skilful. And yet it seemed to Adeline that the artist had captured nothing of the essence of Fenella, the piquant blend of poise and uncertainty.

'Not bad is it?' asked Peter. 'Makes her look quite presentable.'

'It's all right,' said Adeline, 'as far as it goes.'

'Ah! Do I detect a note – Good God in heaven, what was that?'

A deafening crash resounded from the direction of the conservatory, followed by a split second of silence as the band stopped playing, then a hubbub. The guests in the drawing room looked at one another and began to move in the direction of the noise, but Peter was there first, edging his way politely through the throng with Adeline in his wake. The band, troupers to a man, had struck up once more, but they had lost their audience. Loud, angry voices rose above the music and the clash and scrape of tables and chairs being ungently moved was clearly audible.

'Oh Lord,' said Peter, and then added confirmation of what Adeline already feared: 'It's Duncan.'

When they reached the edge of the dance floor it was

quite clear that the small scene which confronted them contained within it the seeds of a considerably larger one, seeds which were already beginning to germinate.

It was not hard to work out what had happened. Two of the waiters were righting the table, which had fallen on its side. The ice bucket had spewed most of its contents on to the red carpeting. Ashtrays and glasses, some broken, were scattered about, and one or two of the girls and young men were engaged in picking up minute pieces from the floor. Toni, tight-lipped, eyes cast down, was setting the chairs back in place. The tattered shreds of the white carnations which Joel had dismembered were strewn about like snow.

Joel himself stood there looking, thought Adeline, like a man who would prefer to face a firing squad than the consequences of this particular blunder. His face was a blueish white, his eyes blinked constantly, nervously. One hand was in his pocket, the other pressed his hair back, over and over again. Duncan, on the other hand, was almost purple with rage. He looked swollen and inflamed with it, might even have looked comical had it not been for the obvious violence of his wrath. The object of his anger was a tall, roman-nosed young man with slightly bulging eyes that lent him a startled expression.

'. . . don't you look where you're going, you great ape?' Duncan was snarling. 'And I didn't hear a word of apology –'

'I said I was sorry, old boy –'

'Don't old boy me.'

'I apologized, but you didn't hear me. Not surprisingly.' The young man allowed himself a small smile at his own cleverness.

'And what's that supposed to mean?' Duncan took a step forward. Peter did the same, his arm outstretched, some conciliatory remark on his lips, but Duncan batted him aside. A girl giggled nervously.

'Nothing. Nothing at all, let's forget it,' said the young man.

'Yes, you'd like that, wouldn't you, you clumsy, super-cilious halfwit!'

'Look here, I'll withdraw the apology if you go on being so damned offensive.'

'If this goes on a moment longer,' said Peter, standing between them, 'you'll both owe one to your host and hostess.'

'I know. Peter, I'm sorry about this –'

'Do you know what you are?' asked Duncan. 'You're a prize pig –'

'And you're drunk.'

'Yes, and I'm drunk, drunk as a lord but with rather better manners. Christ, I detest people like you with your plummy voices and your condescending attitude. You hurt my friend here. Look!' Duncan dragged Joel's stiffly resisting hand out of his pocket to reveal a cut across the inside of the fingers, about two inches long and bleeding freely. 'See that? You did it! But it's all a bloody great joke to you, isn't it?'

'No, not at all, and I'm sorry, but it was only an accident.'

'Of course it was,' said Joel in a voice that was the merest, choked breath of sound. 'Really. It's nothing, and it doesn't matter. Duncan, please.'

Fenella took Joel's arm and led him away. People parted sympathetically to let them through. Some, on the far side of the room, began to dance again, others to talk and drift away from the argument. Peter smiled encouragingly and laid a hand on Duncan's shoulder.

'Panic over. Come on, let's calm down, no harm intended and none done. Here comes another bottle. Look, both of you, why not shake hands. Duncan? Hugh?'

Hugh, with the air of someone who has found something unpleasant clogging the plughole, extended his hand.

'No hard feelings.'

Duncan made an ugly, sneering face that made Adeline despair, and caused her heart to sink.

'You honestly think I'm going to shake hands like a little gentleman?'

Peter turned so that his head was fully averted from Hugh, and he faced Duncan.

'Come on,' he said quietly, 'just for me.'

'For you, Pedro, and only for you,' said Duncan, and passed his palm across the other man's in the most perfunctory and slighting way possible. Then he sat down with a grunt and pushed his fingers into his hair. Peter gave his shoulder a brief squeeze and moved off, smiling affably, spreading good humour where there had been consternation.

As Adeline and Toni resumed their seats on either side of Duncan, Adeline was conscious of two things: one was the phrase 'drunken pansy' spoken just loudly enough to be audible above the other noises around them. The other was the figure of Nicholas Eyre, standing nearby, part of a group of two or three young men. Defiantly she glared at him, and he returned her glare with a light incline of the head and a quizzical, smiling look as if to say: Well? And what now?

'Hell's bells,' breathed Toni under her breath, and reached for the bottle. 'I don't mind if I do. You?'

'Thanks, yes.'

The band, whether by coincidence or some inspired sense of irony, began to play 'Stormy Weather'.

'Hell's bells,' said Toni again.

Adeline gazed over her glass at the now utterly deflated and dejected Duncan, and nudged his foot with hers.

'Hey. Cheer up.'

He bowed his forehead on to the table, clasping his big hands behind his neck. His voice was muffled.

'The bloody, bloody bastard . . .'

'You weren't exactly Sir Galahad yourself, you know.'

Duncan muttered something she was glad not to hear, and then looked up with reddened eyes and asked: 'Where's Jo?'

'Our hostess took him away to minister to him. I'm sure she'll bring him back again,'

'Oh –!' He let his forehead drop again with a bump. 'I feel like death.'

'You richly deserve to.'

'Doesn't he just?' said Toni.

'Come on, troublemaker,' said Adeline. 'Dance with me.'

He rolled his head from side to side. 'Can't . . . possibly.'

'Yes you can, and you're going to.' She stood up, hauling on his arm. 'You'll feel better for the exercise. Come on, man, pull yourself together.'

She dragged him, moaning and shuffling, on to the dance floor, put his nerveless arm about her waist, took his other hand in hers and began propelling him firmly in front of her until instinctively, grudgingly, his feet began to move in time to the music.

'That's better.'

The saxophonist put down his instrument and began to sing. He was portly and middle-aged but his voice was soulful and sweet, caressing the wistful cadences of the song, relishing its bluesy languor. Adeline saw Duncan's eyes brim with maudlin tears, and leaned her cheek briefly against his.

'Your own fault, you know. You realize that.'

'I know, I know . . . but that god-awful fellow, all these god-awful people with their palsied respectability . . .'

'Not two hours ago you were having the time of your life. Hypocrite.'

Duncan executed a sudden, violent turn. 'What about poor Pedro? Will he ever forgive me?'

'He shouldn't, but I dare say he will.'

'Friends.' Duncan looked into Adeline's face and for the first time she glimpsed a return of the old, mocking swagger. 'Wonderful friends – what would life be without them?'

'Indeed,' said Adeline. 'A very poor thing.'

Not long after that a birthday cake of stupendous size and grandeur was wheeled in on a white-robed trolley. Sir

Stanley Marchant made a fond speech, and Fenella's health was proposed by her equally distinguished godfather. After the cake they all clustered at the side of the conservatory – it was too wet to go out, though the rain had abated – while Aldous, Canter and assorted other helpers did what they could with the fireworks. Then more dancing, then scrambled egg with smoked salmon, and buck's fizz and coffee . . . the incident of the upset table seemed light years ago, the moment when they had run up the steps in the rain, another world, another life.

When at last they were leaving, Nicholas Eyre came up to Adeline in the hall. 'You enjoyed yourself, I hope?' he asked, almost as if he had been the host.

'Very much.'

'And your friends – they've regained their composure?'

'I believe so.'

'I'm staying here. I just wanted to say *au revoir*.'

'Goodbye.'

'Would you have any objection to my getting in touch once we're all back in London?'

Adeline had every objection, but all she wanted now was to get away from him, and to get to bed, and to sleep.

'It's up to you.'

'Good.' She half expected him to ask for her address, but he did not. 'I'll do that then,' he said, and walked away.

The rain had quite gone, now. It was three-thirty in the morning, and the air was clear and cold, the stars like splinters of glass, the puddles freezing over and the road treacherous. Peter drove slowly, and they were silent. When Mr Dyson admitted them, in his dressing gown and slippers, they refused the tea he offered and went straight to bed. Even Peter didn't linger, but simply lifted Adeline's hand to his lips, and then left.

In her narrow bed with its clean, slightly harsh sheets that smelt of lavender Adeline had a sudden sense of each of them alone in their rooms, perhaps doing the same, lying and thinking, trying to make sense of things, to see a pattern. And she felt as she had not done before how alone every one of them was, horribly free to make or mar their lives. The last face she saw before falling into an exhausted sleep was that of Nicholas Eyre, and she realized with a sense of shock that the strong feeling he had aroused in her her was not anger, nor even hatred, but fear.

CHAPTER THIRTEEN

1924

NICHOLAS EYRE, ON his way to visit the Elverstones, crossed the Euston Road, turned left down Malet Street and entered the thoughtful grey canyons behind the British Museum. Here the yellow light from the street lamps fell, ignored, upon warmly curtained windows that concealed a secret, interior world whose natives were entirely self-absorbed.

He had never been invited to Allerton Square. That was not the way they did things. 'Nick!' they would say, from the depths of their armchairs and sofas or, in the summer, from the green distances of the walled garden. 'There you are . . .' and he would simply slip into the niche he had worn for himself in the elaborate warp and weft of their lives. He liked that. It pleased him to know, as he walked to and from his spartan little flat in King's Cross, that they had as little interest in knowing where he lived as he had in telling them. For them, especially for Marian, their friends existed like characters in fiction, who had life only when it was breathed into them by their creator, and who could be picked up or set aside with equal ease.

He entered Allerton Square, ran briskly up the steps of Number Twelve, and pulled the bell rope. As usual, the ring was answered by Consett, the Elverstones' housekeeper, a pale, dour woman in whom the capacity for surprise had long since been stifled by excess.

'Oh Mr Eyre, come in.' She closed the door behind him and took his hat and scarf. 'Shall I tell them you're here?'

'No, no, I'll take myself in there.'

'As you like.'

Nicholas crossed the dark, high-ceilinged hall and opened the drawing room door. As usual, the room was severely underlit, but the curtains on the french windows overlooking the garden were still not drawn. A pall of cigarette smoke added to the crepuscular haze. The half dozen or so people in the room lay sprawled about amidst the cushions and shawls and ferns and palms like a pride of lions relaxing round the remains of a kill – the corpse of someone's artistic reputation, Nicholas had no doubt. The contrapuntal burble of two separate conversations only slowed for a second as he entered, and Marian's voice, not in the least raised, but always audible, said: 'Here's Nicholas,' as if they'd been expecting him. He could make out the pale frond of her arm, half raised in salute, and made his way towards it.

He sat down next to her on the velvet sofa, the outlines of which were blurred by piles of cushions of various shapes and sizes.

'You'll be staying for supper, won't you?' said Marian, her hand brushing Nicholas' arm, pausing for a second as if blown up by the wind.

'What is it?'

'Don't be foolish.'

'I'll have to see.'

Marian's husband, Neville, came and stood over them. 'Nick – drink?'

'Thank you.'

Neville went to the corner of the room furthest from

the window, where a single lamp had been lit to illuminate the drinks table. There was no choice. At this time of day they drank Scotch whisky. Neville lifted the water jug and, in response to Nicholas's nod, added some to his glass. As he handed it to Nicholas he said: 'Terence was telling us about the new book, and the battle he's been having with that swinish crew at Gillow and Mayne.'

'Is that so?' said Nicholas, glancing across at Terence, an author of small but burnished reputation. He wasn't in the same league as the rest of them, and he was ponderous. Nicholas could only assume they tolerated him because he amused them. 'What are they trying to do to you?' he enquired.

Terence heaved awkwardly round in his chair, re-crossing his long legs with their huge and heavily shod feet and folding his arms with shoulders hunched, so that his badly cut Norfolk jacket stood up proud of his neck.

'They want me to alter the emphasis, make the "I" figure into an active participant. All totally wrong. The depressing thing is that they seem not to have understood the idea behind the book, not to have understood it at all. They speak of enhancing the underlying theme when it's painfully obvious they haven't grasped the theme themselves.'

'Depressing,' agreed Nicholas.

Others took up the cry and Nicholas resumed the role of observer. He had been acknowledged, named and furnished with a drink – he had taken his place amongst them. A little later he and Neville might have some time to themselves, but for the moment nothing more was required of him.

He wondered idly, as he often did, how any of these people managed to produce the novels, poems, essays and critiques upon which their reputations rested. How did they find the time, given the Byzantine complexity of their private lives, and the interminable talk, and the lack of any apparent organization? And how did their constitutions bear up under the onslaught of so much alcohol? Each time he visited, Nicholas was impressed afresh by their consumption of drink, and its apparent failure to have the least effect on them. He had been to pubs in the Kilburn High Road where less whisky was downed in the space of an hour, and where the patrons were largely incapable.

His eyes were now accustomed to the twilight and he could see who else was in the room. Beyond Neville and Terence, who sat on a battered chesterfield to the right of the velvet sofa, were two enormous shapeless armchairs, rendered even more shapeless by the addition of oriental printed draperies which swamped them and trailed on the floor on either side. Here sat the sculptress, Ida Rabone, and a theatre critic whom Nicholas had not encountered here before but whom he recognized as Paul Hudson of the *Courier*. By narrowing his eyes he could make out the small movements of their heads and hands which showed they were confiding in each other. It was curious, he thought, that no matter how small, exclusive and intro-verted any given group of people might be, there was still room for it to split and subdivide like some tiny fluid organism viewed under the microscope. There was always something happening in Allerton Square, and it would generally have scandalized any decent British working man. Nicholas liked everything about the place and its occupants, but for one thing: he was a person who pre-ferred on the whole to manipulate relationships rather than be absorbed in them, and here he was amongst people whose talent for manipulation equalled and outstripped his own. To avoid a case of the biter bit he had to be on his guard the whole time.

'. . .at the Primavera in Charlotte Street,' Ida Rabone was saying, in tones of the utmost pique. 'The fool of a head waiter hadn't a clue who we were, we had to tell him, and then –'

'Oh?' asked Marian. 'And who were you?'

Nicholas admired that sort of thing. He smiled at Marian but her round light brown eyes were fixed on Ida in an expression of scientific enquiry.

'Unfair, Marian, I was referring to Gustav,' said Ida

reprovingly. 'It was embarrassing for him. You know very well I don't give a damn about that sort of thing.'

'It won't have done Gustav any harm,' said Terence, combing his fuzzy beard with his fingers. Nicholas hated beards. 'I'm afraid I think he's suffering from a severe case of galloping lionization. His stuff is all style, all surface, it has no real content, no decent ideas rigorously pursued. It's overrated fluff. If I sound waspish I'm sorry, it's only my opinion.'

'I suspect,' said Neville in his good-humoured way, 'that it suffers in translation. It reads immeasurably better in German.'

'That's because one doesn't understand it! Almost anything sounds more important couched in those fearful polysyllables, smothered in umlauts and contiguous consonants.'

'This is all very unworthy,' put in Marian. 'Ida was only pointing out how waiters have gone to the dogs and here we are demolishing poor Gustav.'

'Let no blame attach to me,' said Paul Hudson, raising well-manicured hands, palm outwards. 'I haven't even heard of the wretched fellow.'

Neville laughed delightedly. 'Well spoken, Paul!'

Nicholas felt irritated. He wished that Hudson, with his head of glossy, wavy, prematurely grey hair, was elsewhere. He was being set up, it was one of Marian's and Neville's little scenarios and he resented being part of it.

Neville turned to him. 'Nick – play us something.'

'Very well.' Either refuse point blank or agree without demur, that was the thing, thought Nicholas as he went to the piano. Any kind of prevarication was invariably taken at its face value, no-one would bother to draw you out and you were left looking petulant and foolish. He felt more soothed as he sat down and adjusted the piano stool. They couldn't catch him out.

He began to play, instinctively choosing something as contrary as possible to the present mood of the gathering, a bouncy little Chopin mazurka which he took at a breathless pace, knowing no-one would stop him. The bright, loud avalanche of notes seemed to crowd the darkening room like birds, to fill it with intrusive, uncaring noise and excitement. He finished with a tremendous flourish, a run of the whole keyboard, and then rose immediately and went to replenish his glass.

'Bravo!' cried Paul Hudson. 'Very rousing.'

'Just what was needed,' agreed Ida. Terence appeared to have gone to sleep, his long, grasshopper limbs bunched around him. Neville and Marian made no comment, but then they never did. As Nicholas returned to his seat, Marian said: 'Turn a light on, Nick, would you? It's like a bag in here.'

He did so, and sat down. Neville began discussing some new play with Paul, with Ida listening attentively. There was no fire in the room and it was becoming increasingly cold. Nicholas felt a spasm of annoyance with their indifference to creature comforts. Putting his glass down he got up again and went to draw the curtains. No-one took the slightest notice, but as he returned Marian said, without looking at him: 'Is it cold in here? I suppose it is.'

'It's absolutely freezing.'

'Oh dear . . .'

Nicholas refused to give her the satisfaction of arguing the point any further. He took large, angry gulps of his whisky and felt it gradually beginning to take effect. A slightly lecherous torpor descended on the room. It began to be quite pleasant sitting there, listening to his stomach rumble, and to the various unspoken currents of affection, censure, suggestion and aggravation which trickled about the room with the cigarette smoke. The whole pack of them were sex-mad, he reflected, it was their saving grace.

He looked at Marian. She had leaned her head back, and her eyes were closed. Beneath her fragile, blue-veined lids her eyes moved, watching her thoughts. Everything about Marian was thin, and fine and delicate-seeming, from her wispy brown hair to her long, bony feet. Her face had a consumptive pallor and melancholy, yet her wit was razor-sharp: her body was willowy, it gave the impression of drooping under the effort of everyday life, and yet she was as strong as an ox. She was a woman in whom every weakness seemed a strength, and where she was weakest of all, Nicholas reflected sourly, she wielded absolute power.

He didn't admire many people, but he admired Marian. Neville's easy-going affections were infinitely more desirable because of the cool and careless hold she exercised upon them. She was a worthy adversary. She also exuded, as she lay back on the sofa cushions, her glass tilting in one hand, the stub of her cigarette just caught between long, dangling, brown-stained fingers, a powerful and unforced sensuality. She seemed always to be waiting for someone to rouse her. Nicholas thought at once of robust, powerful, richly coloured Adeline Charteris – the very antithesis of Marian Elverstone and yet, he was sure, eager and untried, looking for someone upon whom to lavish her first passion.

He sighed, then felt a hand on his arm and turned to find Neville leaning across to him with his sweetest, kindest, most confidential smile.

'Nick . . . what have you been doing with yourself? We've missed you.'

Nicholas began to describe what he had been doing with himself, knowing very well that not a word of it would be retained beyond the time it took to tell.

'Madam. Dinner is on the table.'

Marian looked round at Consett with the air of someone startled from a pleasant dream, and still not entirely free of its influence.

'Good. Thank you, Consett. Come along everyone and let's eat.'

Everyone followed Marian's lead, and began to move from the room. Nicholas sat still and waited till last, not out of deference but because he liked watching them group, and regroup and rearrange their faces and bodies to suit different circumstances. They were brilliantly good at it, the most accomplished players of social and sexual games he had ever come across. To hell with their books, their paintings, their pensées, their eternal bloody conversation: the skill in which they were most proficient was one they were long since largely unaware of practising: that of seduction.

Ida Rabone, last but one to leave the room, drew alongside the sofa like a punt nudging a riverbank, as if she hadn't really meant to, but now that she found herself here she might as well pause for a moment.

'Nick, I'm having an exhibition next month at the Sedley. You will come, won't you?'

Nicholas got up, stubbing out his cigarette in Marian's large, hand-painted pottery ashtray. 'Yes, Ida, I'll come. How's business by the way?' Ida had a line in tastefully idealized busts of the young scions of monied families, the profits from which, she claimed, enabled her to do her more experimental work. 'Still selling like hot cakes?' asked Nicholas.

'Now don't take that attitude,' she said, playful but nonetheless nettled. 'I refuse to apologize for being successful.'

'I should think not indeed.'

'And what about you? Off to play with that beastly little combo at the Music Box?'

'Of course.'

Ida tut-tutted at him. 'You ought to be ashamed of yourself.'

'Why? I refuse to apologize for being successful.'

'You're so rude,' said Ida. 'It's childish. Only children think there's something clever and important about being rude.'

'Your knowledge of children is, of course, encyclopaedic.'

'If I had my way,' responded Ida in a silky undertone, 'you'd never have set foot over the front door step of this house. It's only because Neville is so ridiculously soft that you're here.'

'Quite so,' said Nicholas, smiling blandly at her. This particular exchange was following a familiar pattern. Ida liked to think of herself as a self-made woman, who supported herself comfortably by her own efforts and initiative, and she became thoroughly rattled by what she saw as Nicholas's lack of both talent and industry. Her irritation was not helped by the fact that he seemed to fit in at Allerton Square rather better than she did; he had a natural feel for the way things were done here, and she was sufficiently perceptive to see that she did not.

'Excuse me,' she said. With something which Nicholas considered perilously close to a flounce she narrowed her eyes, turned away her head, and walked her prancing walk to join the others. She had a round, heavy body and her face had a fleshy Latinate beauty which would, in ten years, be swallowed up in its own fat. Nicholas always suspected that Ida frequented Allerton Square in order to vaunt her smart, made-up looks and her hard-won commercial success, to show these drab bluestockings what a woman of the world she was. And yet she was a baby next to them, a pouting, red-lipped, fashionable moppet.

He crossed the hall and went into the long, narrow, rather gloomy dining room. They sat round an oblong table made of maple wood – Nicholas would not have had any idea what it was made of, but Neville was proud of the table and had told him on his first visit.

'Made for us by Donald Moncaster,' he'd said. 'Do you know his stuff at all?' Nicholas didn't, of course, and so Neville had described it to him exhaustively.

Now, a variety of foods was set out on it. Neville stood to slice a huge, floury loaf, Marian dished out pickled red cabbage with a tarnished silver spoon. There were cheeses on a china plate, celery in a tankard, cold meats, Bath Olivers, pickles, and a bowl of russet apples. It looked like food in a naive painting, laid out according to colour and texture, placed in whatever assorted containers took the artist's fancy. Nicholas enjoyed the food-as-fuel attitude that informed the Elverstones' catering. No sort of ceremony was made over either its preparation or its consumption, and certainly no apologies for its plainness. There was always plenty of it, and the long wait that invariably preceded its arrival ensured that it was welcome.

As they trooped in, Consett stood at the door, as if she

were counting heads like a teacher with a batch of unruly schoolchildren. When they were all seated she retired, grimly, closing the door behind her.

Neville sat at the foot of the table, with Nicholas on his left and Ida on his right. On the floor between Neville and Nicholas sat Neville's dog, Bloomer, a shaggy wire-haired mongrel, his bright eyes fixed on his master's face, his thoughts centred on the slices of rare roast beef on the table. Every so often his tongue would dart out and he would shift his weight from paw to paw and emit a squeaky sound of contained impatience, followed by a huge yelping yawn and a shake of the ears. Marian didn't care for domestic pets and chose to behave as if Bloomer didn't exist, and this was one area in which Nicholas was entirely in sympathy with her.

Paul Hudson was next to Nicholas, on Marian's right, with Terence opposite him. It was now time to move on from whisky to rough red wine, several bottles of which stood in the centre of the table next to a sheaf of bronze chrysanthemums in an unglazed earthenware jug. Neville opened one of the bottles and poured the contents into the assorted glasses which were clustered nearby, running the stream of wine continuously from glass to glass and splashing the maple wood a good deal in the process. Everyone helped themselves to the wine, and the food, and ate and drank enthusiastically.

'Delicious,' said Marian, who entertained no artificial scruples about liking her own food. 'For once Consett did not incinerate the beef.'

'What might be called a rare oversight,' said her husband, chuckling at his weak joke. But the others, with the exception of Marian, laughed too because it was hard to deny Neville anything. As the conversation moved on, Nicholas stopped listening and observed his lover appreciatively.

Neville Elverstone was a charmingly handsome man – six foot tall and broad shouldered without being beefy, with thick, curling auburn hair. He was well into his forties, but his boyish manner and slightly distrait air of well-being made him seem far younger. His skin was smooth, his brown eyes shone, his rather soft, drooping mouth was given a hint of danger by a moustache, darker than his eyes, which he allowed to grow long at the corners. He was very vain, but because his vanity was about artlessness only those who knew him best could tell. From his untidy hair to his wrinkled socks Neville was aware of his appeal and exercised it to the full. When Neville smiled at someone, that person was instantly put in his debt.

Nicholas watched as Neville picked up a long piece of fat from his plate and dangled it in front of Bloomer's nose: it was snatched and wolfed down with indecent haste, in case something better should be missed.

His eyes were still on the dog, as he said: 'What about you, Nick?'

'I'm sorry, I wasn't paying attention.'

'We were talking about Cornwall,' said Paul Hudson. 'Marian's trying to persuade me to go down and stay with them there next year.'

'Is she?' said Nicholas. 'That doesn't sound like her.'

'We've almost given up on Nick,' said Neville amiably.

'You might as well complete the process then. I'm simply not attracted by weeks of listening to the wind howl on some blighted cliff top.'

Marian, her eyes on her plate, smiled to herself but Ida intervened heatedly: 'It isn't a bit like that! It's quite delightful. Of course it depends how wedded you are to the dubious delights of city life,' she added. 'Personally it does me all the good in the world to escape from them for a while. Down there I can almost feel the cobwebs being blown out of my brain.'

'Thank you, Ida,' said Neville, laughing.

'I don't mind the country,' said Terence. 'I was brought up there after all, but I can't stand it when it becomes *obligatory*, when one's constantly being urged to get outside and do something strenuous and uncomfortable for one's own good.'

'Oh, the Pink House isn't a bit like that,' Neville assured him. 'Everyone does as they please. Marian's generally engaged in herculean labours in the garden, so she sometimes commandeers some help with that, but I myself do a great deal of serious lying around and snoozing, that sort of thing.'

Marian waved the spoon once more over the red cabbage. 'More, anyone?'

As Terence passed his plate, she said: 'I don't know why you're bothering to advertise the place. We like it. If anyone else wants to join us they're perfectly welcome. If not, what does it matter?'

Paul Hudson gave Nicholas an 'isn't-she-a-character?' look, to which Nicholas did not respond, and said: 'Come, come, Marian, you were being positively pressing a moment ago.'

Nicholas watched with pleasure as Marian's round, pale eyes widened slightly and she tucked a wisp of hair behind her ear. he could have told the idiotic Hudson that that was not the way to go about things.

'Pressing? Was I? Surely not . . . I was simply conveying how nice it is, suggesting how much you – or anyone – would like it. I don't count Nicholas, he's simply brutish about the place.'

Nicholas grinned. ' 'Fraid so. Put me a mile beyond Hampstead and I go all to pieces with the ghastly tranquillity of it.'

'It's pure affectation,' said Neville. 'You just don't care to be seen to like things that other people like. Cutting off your nose to spite your face, my boy.'

There was a grain of truth in this observation but Nicholas was unperturbed by it, since he knew that his continued welcome at Allerton Square depended to some extent on a show of resistance. He might not be as clever as the Elverstones, but he could be easily as devious. It was his greatest weapon in the quiet war which passed, with them, for friendship.

The Monday after Fenella Marchant's party Adeline, having slept only lightly, woke early and with a sense of restless urgency. Taking advantage of her mood she braved the freezing bathroom before Toni. Like some intrepid female explorer she sat huddled on the white-painted wooden chair, swathed in both dressing gown and cloak, her feet in thick socks and slippers. The Arctic air of the bathroom caused the hot water to give off clouds of encouraging steam, but also had the effect of cooling it within minutes, so that one was obliged to get in at once with feet like lobsters and shoulders covered in goose pimples, and wash at high speed before the inexorable chill took a hold. The bath itself was long, narrow and high-sided with taps and plug that looked like accoutrements from the boiler room of an ocean liner. Running from just below the taps to about two-thirds of its length was a black mark, rimmed with grey, where the enamel had been worn away by the pressure of running water and countless supine bodies. The black mark resembled a map of some strange deserted island, a Pacific atoll or half-submerged reef, or sometimes, as now, the uneven back of a monster rising through the swirling mist of a Scottish loch.

As she returned to her room, one of the girls from the top floor came down the stairs.

'Marvellous! I can get in next. What's it like?'

'Perishing.'

'Is the pilot light still on?'

'As far as I know.' The lighting and maintenance, once lit, of the pilot light was a vital but sensitive operation, the failure of which could lead to a weakening of morale throughout the house. The tiny blue and yellow spark fluttering in the dark recess of the geyser had to be tended like the Olympic flame if the hot water of which Mrs Fairyhouse was so proud was not to run out.

'Hooray,' said the girl from upstairs and scampered for the bathroom door, the ends of her thick woollen scarf flapping.

Back in her room, Adeline knelt by the fireplace and fed the meter with threepenny bits from her store in an old tea tin. Then she turned up the gas, struck a match and held it to the blackened honeycomb of the fire. It caught with a soft whoosh, and the row of blue jets shivered and grew, gradually turning to a warm, pulsing orange. The sound of the fire being lit was Clancey's cue to leave his rug beneath the window, stretch languorously, shake vigorously, and join his mistress. For a moment, the beautiful warmth on her face, arms and legs was such bliss that she couldn't bring herself to move, and she sat there, her arm round the dog, like a lizard that must lie in the sun in order to store the energy to scuttle away. She heard Toni come out, try the bathroom door and mutter 'Damn!' before returning to her own room. The thought that the meticulous Toni might be late for work, while she, chaotic Adeline, would be early for the very first time, galvanized her into action. She assembled her clothes before the fire and tugged them on, adding an eclectic mix of chains, bangles and brooches from the jumble on the mantelpiece. She then hoisted the last of the butcher's scraps in off the windowsill, where they spent the night tethered by string to the catch, mixed them with the dry crusts which were always in plentiful supply, and gave Clancey his breakfast. While he gobbled down the meal as though it were his last, and then gulped water like a dog dying of thirst, Adeline stood over him, consuming strong tea and slightly charred toast. When they'd both finished she put her plate and cup in the sink, turned off the fire and leaned across its fading warmth to peer in the mirror and paint her face. She didn't regard this exercise as a covering-up or disguising of herself – though not vain, she was quite at home with her appearance – but more as a sort of celebration of the start of the day and the fun of dressing up. Highly decorated comfort was the keynote of her toilette, the decorations being part of the comfort. When she felt ready she picked up her portfolio and the battered brown Gladstone bag in which she carried the rest of life's essentials, put Clancey on his lead, and left. Down in the hall the black bear by the telephone wore a chequered wool headscarf, knotted beneath the chin, like a facetious metaphor for Mother Russia.

Adeline took Clancey to his usual square and stood just inside the gate as he nosed about in the drifts of frosty leaves and along the cinder paths. It was bitingly cold, dank and raw and she was conscious of London spreading around her in a chill grey maze. A milk cart clattered at the far end of the square. She could hear the long, smoking snort of the horse as he pulled up at the kerb and the chirpy voice of the milkman talking to him . . . a car went by . . . two young men on bicycles, perhaps students like herself, with caps pulled down and scarfs pulled up over their mouths like visors . . . Adeline watched them pedal past, and then turned back towards the gritty garden to recall Clancey. It was then she heard the sound which shocked her to the core, and which only seconds afterwards did she recognize as a scream.

It came from further down the street, and from above street level, perhaps from an upstairs window, a gasping, barking sound as though someone were fighting off a terrible attacker. In fact Adeline's instinct was to clutch at Clancey's collar, half expecting to be attacked herself, her skin crawling with fear and with something more complicated, too, a kind of dread as though she herself had made the sound. In the bitter early morning air pinpricks of perspiration dotted her back.

She clipped the lead back on Clancey and stepped out into the road, closing the small iron gate behind her. About twenty yards down the square was the milk cart, the milkman standing on the pavement with his back to her, looking in the same direction.

'What on earth was that?' she called, crossing over to him, disproportionately glad that he was there.

He glanced over his shoulder at her, then back the other way, shaking his head slowly. 'I dunno, miss. Give me the shudders.'

'And me. You didn't see anything?'

'Not a thing.'

Adeline was about to add something when they both heard the sound again, but no more than the edge of it before the sharp bang of a sash window being slammed down cut it off. The horse stamped and nodded his head up and down. Clancey sat with ears pricked. But now there was absolute silence again. The milkman gave Adeline a quizzical look.

'Funny thing eh?'

'It was a person, wasn't it? I mean, not an animal?'

'Someone in a bad way, a real bad way . . . mind you, that house . . . nothing would surprise me,' he added, with the return of a certain glum cockney assurance.

'Why?'

'There's all sorts going on there, all hours from what I can see. I been round here earlier than this some mornings and there's been music playing, people just leaving. And the worse for drink.'

He intended this dissertation to be sinister but in fact the implied puritanism behind it made Adeline smile.

'Well,' she said, 'that explains it. Someone obviously had a richly deserved fit of the horrors.'

Just the same, as she walked away, that strange sound resonated in her head, and she felt compelled to glance over her shoulder in the direction from which it had come as she turned out of Allerton Square.

She was so early at the Slade that she had to drag the porter away from his tea and sandwiches to let her in.

'Got the urge this morning?' he asked roguishly.

'I woke up early, that's all.'

'Ah – sign of an unquiet mind,' he saïd, in a bizarre unconscious reference to what she had just heard.

She went downstairs to the empty Life Room and sat down, taking a sketchpad and pencil from the Gladstone bag. Clancey stood for a moment, tongue lolling, waiting for the hordes of people to arrive. When, in about a minute, they had not materialized, he lay down, his chin on the ground between splayed paws. Adeline scribbled, her pencil making a small whisper of sound in the stillness. The white walls, the emptiness, the clear still chilly air gave her the curious sensation of being out of doors in some secret, snowbound landscape. The room was so silent that the faint whisper of her pencil on the paper seemed loud. She could hear Clancey's even, grunting breaths as he dropped off to sleep. Idly, with no particular subject in mind, she drew the figure of a young girl, exaggeratedly slender, with long, faun-like limbs and a tiny, large-eyed head on a wand of neck. Having done the figure once, she drew it again and again, superimposing one drawing on another so that the girl seemed to be whirling in a wild dance. On the right-hand side of the paper she sketched in a second female figure, tall and more heavily built, her legs concealed by a long skirt. The contrast appealed to her, more especially because she now realized who it was she was drawing. She took a fresh piece of paper and repeated the sketch, with the figures in different attitudes. She became entirely absorbed.

In time, in the hallways and corridors of the Slade, the other students began to arrive, their chatter and bustle like circulation being restored to a chilled body. Doors opened and closed, voices called, footsteps clattered up and down stairs.

Peter arrived, with Joel and stood behind her.

'What's all this then?'

'I didn't sleep well, so I got in early.'

'Let's have a look.' He leaned over, his cheek close to hers. 'It's not half bad of Fenella. I swear if she gets any thinner or has her hair cut any shorter I'll be able to pass her off as my kid brother.'

A middle-aged Italian woman carrying a large shopping bag arrived and glared at the two young men.

'Model's here,' said Joel out of the side of his mouth. 'Time we were gone.'

'Yes.' Peter looked down at Adeline. 'We'll see you at lunchtime?

'I should think so.'

'By the way, who's the other woman?'

'Her? Oh, I think that's me.'

'It's not very flattering.'

'It's not meant to be.'

As Joel and Peter left, someone out in the corridor gave a shrill shriek of laughter and she felt her skin jump with shock, reminded of that terrible earlier scream.

Dorothy Sugden saved her letter until she was sitting in her usual seat on the promenade at Sidmouth. Hardened by years of walking her charges out and stoutly dressed in thick, long underwear, uniform blouse, skirt and cardigan, black wool stockings and grey flannel coat and hat, she was impervious to the stiff on-shore breeze that scudded up the shingle beach and stirred the fringe on the pale blue pram blanket. It was late November, and the seaside town had turned its back on the frivolities of summer, closed its shutters and cleared the last vestiges of colour from the parks and gardens which abutted the seafront. Only serious walkers or those with a reason to walk, like herself, were here today. In spite of the wind and the occasional handful of salty spray in her face, she felt more private and at ease here than in her own room. Here, no-one could knock on the door and ask her to do this or that, there was no mending or tidying she should be attending to, she was discharging her responsibilities simply by being here.

She patted her pocket with her gloved hand, and felt the letter sitting snugly in there, waiting to be read. If she stopped to think about it she felt rather ashamed of herself, getting so excited about a letter – was she becoming as spinsterish as all that? – on the other hand she didn't receive many, so one from Adeline was something of an event. She appreciated these letters enormously, far more than her laboriously written and formal-sounding replies managed to convey. They came sporadically, no more than two or three times a year, pages and pages of galloping black handwriting which Dorothy sometimes took days to decipher, but the substance of which was always fascinating and foreign, and delivered in precisely the way that Adeline spoke. Dorothy doubted that she would recognize her now. She hadn't seen her since the wedding, and in fact the letters had only started up again since the tragedy (which Dorothy was inclined to see as a merciful release), as though during her marriage Adeline had been separated from friends and family by more than just the Irish Sea.

Dorothy took the letter out, but before opening it she

leaned forward to make sure that three-month old Bertie Shelmadine still slept soundly. His small, pink, snub-nosed face, almost obscured by the frill of his crocheted bonnet and his mittened fist, was tranquil. He was a good, placid baby, and bore the easy yoke of Dorothy's nursery routine with the utmost equanimity. So Dorothy was grateful to him on two counts; for his good humour and for his presence of mind in being born just when his brother Harry had started prep school and it looked as if she might have become redundant once again. As it was she had an easy time of it at the moment, with only Bertie to look after for much of the time.

She opened the envelope neatly, along its top edge, took out the letter and replaced the envelope in her pocket so that it shouldn't get snatched away by the wind. There were five scrawling pages, and these she held firmly, in both hands, quite close to her face. She was becoming a little short-sighted but hadn't the least intention of resorting to spectacles before it was strictly necessary.

The writing was always quite legible to begin with.

Dear Nanny, How are you? I can't remember when I last wrote, but I've just written one letter so I may as well write another.

Dorothy smiled to herself, it was just like Adeline not to realize how that might sound.

The other letter, I may as well tell you, is to someone whose portrait I'm hoping to paint. I've suddenly realized that this time next year I shall no longer be a carefree student struggling to learn my craft, but out in the world and attempting to make a living from it, so I thought I'd take the bull by the horns and see if I could obtain a few commissions *now*. I've been told by all and sundry that I'm hopelessly unrealistic in wanting to do portraits, but it's painting people that interests me, and I'm determined not to give up without having tried.

Quite right, thought Dorothy, who knew nothing about the world of fine art but who held firm opinions about aiming high, opinions which grew firmer as her own escape from nannying grew less and less likely. She read on.

The person I have approached is one of those society belles you used to be so fond of telling me about at Fording Place. You may even have seen her photograph if you ever get hold of *Tatler* or *Country Life*. Her name is Fenella Marchant. [It meant nothing to Dorothy.] You'll remember my telling you about Peter Marchant, who is in my year at the Slade? Well, she is Peter's sister. I met her when we all went down . . .

Here the letter went on to describe some dance that Adeline had been to, and the writing became considerably more hectic. Dorothy skimmed the page, picking up a word here and there and promising herself to return to it later. The mention of Peter Marchant was good news, though. Without having met him, Dorothy had formed a favourable impression of this young man, who was well-bred and well-to-do, but obviously no mere debs' delight or he wouldn't have been at art school. He sounded most promising. While bearing Simon Charteris no ill will, Dorothy could have foretold that that particular liaison would end in tears. Young Adeline needed a man who could give her a run for her money.

Of course, Fenella has been painted before, she is absolutely beautiful and filthy rich, but I have some ideas of my own about how it should be done. [Dorothy's knowing nod was trumped immediately.] Such arrogance! I know. But I'm no Joshua Reynolds, and all I have is my originality so I may as well make use of it. And since I intend to be a journeyman artist, earning my living by my trade, I have to have something unique to sell, and customers with the money to *pay* for it!

Dorothy smiled, and put the top page to the bottom. On the second page the writing improved again, thank heavens.

> I've bought myself a bicycle because I decided I was getting fat and lazy in London. Clancey wasn't too sure about it at first, I think he thought it was some kind of mechanical pet which might usurp his place in my affections [Dorothy struggled with some of this] but now he's got the idea, and trots along beside me through the traffic as to the manner born. As for me, I've developed quite a passion for what Peter refers to as my tin horse, and go off all over the place on it, as free as air. I still see Mr Charteris for lunch quite regularly, and when I can summon the resolve I go and see Mrs Charteris, but she's very bad now, senile really, and hardly knows me, so it's a bit of a strain just sitting there and listening to her ramble on.
>
> Bob and I meet up from time to time, because he's not far away, and is still going great guns with my dear friend Toni (Antonia), who I think I've told you about. You'd hardly recognize him, Nanny, he's become really rather formidable and handsome in his funny, beaky way. Isn't it odd how things turn out? There's Bob, one of the *Courier*'s star writers (do you ever see it, by the way? If not I'll send you a copy) and with an attractive girl on his arm, while Frank is down at Fording Place, rapidly becoming a solid gentleman of the land. He's still an absolute dear, of course, but he *has* changed, no doubt about it. And Mother tears about in the background, full of good works and bad driving. They make the funniest pair. . . .

Dorothy laid the letter down on her knee, her fingers crumpling the edges of the paper, her eyes closed. Frank. Just the sight of his name was like a blow to the heart. Inside her many layers of thick, serviceable clothing her body seemed to flare for a moment, making her conscious of its weight, shape and texture, reminding her painfully that she was not some separate species, a nanny, custodian of other people's children, but a woman who longed to know what passionate love was like. She had not been without admirers; she had, for instance, always known that if she'd given Chris Dance the least encouragement she might have had him: but her love was reserved, wholly and hopelessly, for Frank. And here – she looked down again, through tears, at the letter – Adeline was telling her – what? That Frank had become dull, a fuddy-duddy? That he was now outshone by plain, grumpy Bob? That he had buried himself in the country with his mother? That he was no longer the golden, laughing, longed-for boy she remembered . . . ?'

She couldn't bear it. The waste, the separation . . . res- olutely, she turned the page and read to the end.

Life seems suddenly to be racing by and I feel I hardly have time to catch hold of it, I get quite panic-stricken with the speed of it all. However, I don't suppose I'd want it any different, so I shouldn't complain. I really must come and visit you some time, Nanny, so we can have one of our talks. I often think of our times together at Fording Place, me with my interminable questions and you with your dependable answers. I'd love to know if you're still so *sure* about everything. I hope so, or the earth will stop turning! I seem to feel less and less sure as I go along – Lord alone knows what I'll be like when I'm an old lady. In a permanent dither I expect.

Do write back if you get the chance. [Dorothy shook her head. When didn't she get the chance?] and tell me how you are and what you're up to. Apologies for the handwriting, I know it doesn't get any better – love always – Adeline.

Dorothy put the pages in order, folded them and slipped them neatly back into the envelope, which she replaced in her pocket. She sat staring out to sea, the wind and the spray spattering on her face as if on a pane of glass. Already, at half past three, dusk was falling, the hardy walkers were turning for home with their collars turned up. In the deep recesses of his pram Bertie grew red, and grimaced, and scrabbled with his woolly fist on the viyella sheet, emitting little grunts of hunger and impatience.

Attuned as she was to these first stirrings, Dorothy recalled herself to the present and stood up, letting off the brake of the pram and setting off at a brisk pace for the house of Mr and Mrs Shelmadine. It was fortunate for her that Bertie depended on her for his every need, otherwise she might at that moment have felt somewhat unhappy and alone.

Adeline was both surprised and gratified when before the week was out she received a reply from Fenella Marchant, acceding to her request, saying what fun it would be and enquiring when they would start. The letter was written in a curling, childish hand on thick, parchment-like note-paper, with the Marchants' address engraved in black on the top right-hand corner.

When she showed Peter the letter, however, he was sceptical. 'Typical,' he said. ''She hasn't a clue what's involved – '

'She's had her portrait painted before, though.'

'That was entirely different. It was that society fellow who does all the debs. One sitting in his flat in Belgravia and he does most of the rest from a decent photograph. Nella knows precisely nothing about the agony and the ecstasy of putting paint on canvas.'

'Well come to that, neither do I. Agony and ecstasy are not in my line.'

'Don't run yourself down, Addy. You're an artist.'

'Would-be. Would-be artist. Your sister's doing me a considerable favour, remember.'

'Hm. You could have found yourself a more interesting subject. Can you really see yourself trailing down there every few days, spending half your time being civil to the aged Ps and the other half flattering Nella and listening to her prattle on? She does prattle on, you know.'

'I don't care. I want to paint her. And as for trailing

down to your run-down little shack in Sussex, of course I should loathe it if that was what I was going to do. But I'm not. I'm going to invite Fenella here.'

'Tell you what,' said Peter, putting his hands on her shoulders, his thumbs stroking her neck. 'How about marrying me? Then you can forget about this earning-a-living nonsense.'

He said this to annoy, knowing they knew each other well enough for it to fail. And she replied 'No', knowing that he would be astonished if she did otherwise.

That same evening, undeterred, she rang Fenella and arranged a date in the new year for her first sitting. As she put the phone down, the front door bell rang. At once Mrs Fairyhouse's hurrying step was to be heard, and her door opened.

'Don't worry,' called Adeline. 'I'll answer it.'

On the front step stood Nicholas Eyre, in overcoat and hat, smiling as if he had expected to see her.

'Good evening! I hope you don't mind my dropping in like this?'

'Hallo – no, I suppose not.' She could hear the combination of alarm and distaste in her own voice, but apparently they were lost on Nicholas, who stepped inside, saying: 'Mind if I come in? It's perfectly frightful out there.'

She was obliged to close the door behind him, and Mrs Fairyhouse now came forward with an enquiring smile on her face.

'Who is our visitor?' she asked.

'This is Nicholas Eyre. Nicholas, this is my landlady, Mrs Fairyhouse.'

'How do you do,' said Nicholas, removing his hat and shaking Mrs Fairyhouse's hand.

'Would you like a cup of tea, Mr Eyre?'

'That's most kind, but I only wanted a quick word with Mrs Charteris.'

'We're not allowed male visitors after ten,' said Adeline firmly. Her landlady's smile widened, it looked ominously as if she might revoke the rule in the face of Nicholas's urbane charm, but he said at once:

'Oh good heavens, I'm not stopping. I just wanted to pass on an invitation from a friend and then I'll be on my way.'

'I'll leave you to it then,' said Mrs Fairyhouse and retreated into her lair, leaving the door fractionally ajar.

Nicholas turned to Adeline, his eyes wide and bright beneath slightly raised brows. 'I come bearing a summons,' he said, 'from a couple of friends of mine, Neville and Marian Elverstone.'

'Summons?'

'They're delightful people, very hospitable. They're keen to meet you.'

'Why on earth should they be?'

'I told them about you. Marian in particular likes to surround herself with clever, attractive people – of whom you are most definitely one. I'm sure you'd like each other. And before you resist any further,' he added, catching her belligerent look, 'let me point out that they could be useful to you as well. In fact I said as much to Peter, and being the decent fellow he is, he at once agreed to let you off the leash for the evening to further your interests.'

Adeline bridled. 'There is no leash!'

'A joke, merely.'

'Why can't Peter come too?'

Nicholas raised an eyebrow. 'Because he isn't invited. Manners maketh Marchant. Besides, he can't stand the Elverstones. No, if you can bear the thought of an evening spent away from your chevalier . . .'

Adeline felt herself scrabbling for a foothold on the slippery scree of a conversation from which she could not hope to emerge with honour.

'I'm going down to Devon for Christmas, to stay with my mother and brother,' she said lamely.

'Then you'll be dying for some civilized company. By the way, I understand Fenella's going to sit for you.'

'Yes. In the new year.'

'All the more reason why you should come along to the

Elverstones' party on New Year's Eve. They have more interesting paintings per square yard in their house than I've seen in most galleries.'

'I shan't know a soul there. Will it be a huge party?'

'I've no idea. One never knows what to expect. It certainly won't be like Fenella's do, if that's what's worrying you. Come as you are. Absolutely.' He looked her up and down with that mocking look of his. She knew she looked terrible, her face smudged, her hair tangled and flopping over one eye, her jumper streaked with paint and her skirt shiny and bagged with age. She wanted to be rid of Nicholas, and the simplest way to do it was to agree. Plenty of time between now and then to find an excuse.

'All right,' she said, 'I'll come. If you're sure I won't bore them to death,' she added ungraciously.

'I'm sure you can if you try,' said Nicholas, not to be outdone in gracelessness. Seething with annoyance, she opened the front door for him, and he replaced his hat. 'I'll pick you up about half past eight on New Year's Eve, then.'

'Yes.'

'Happy Christmas.'

'Yes. Goodbye.'

When he had gone she bounded back up the stairs two at a time before Mrs Fairyhouse could subject her to a fascinated interrogation about her caller.

In her room she felt trapped, for the first time. Her mood of cheerful purposefulness was destroyed. She felt like a foolish child who, by its capricious behaviour, is its own worst enemy. And what, in God's name, did one wear when summoned by intellectuals to attend their pretentious party?

CHAPTER FOURTEEN

1924

SHE TRAVELLED DOWN to Tarrford by train the day before Christmas Eve. For most of the five-hour journey she couldn't settle because she had been unable to find a seat close to the guard's van, where the disconsolate Clancey was billeted. But after the first change of trains at Salisbury, and the second at Tayton St Mary, they were travelling in a small, non-corridor train, and the friendly Devonian guard allowed Adeline to have the dog with her, provided it was in a third-class compartment, and caused no inconvenience to other passengers.

Virtuous with gratitude, Clancey sat leaning up against her legs, panting gently. For a couple of stops they were on their own, and Adeline began to wonder, guiltily, if Clancey's large presence might not be keeping people out. Then at one of the country halts a plump, friendly woman with a little boy of perhaps six got in, and at once began admiring him.

'What a beautiful dog, eh Colin? Isn't he just beautiful!'

Clancey, knowing he was being discussed, panted

harder and thumped his tail obligingly. Colin, big-eyed, looked from Clancey to Adeline.

'Do 'e mind petting, miss?'

'No, not at all, he loves to be made a fuss of,' said Adeline, ruffling Clancey's ears to prove it.

'Can I give 'un a pat, Mum?'

'You must ask the lady.'

'Do, please,' said Adeline. 'There's nothing he'd like more.'

'There you are then,' said Colin's mum.

Both women watched indulgently as the boy kneeled on the swaying floor of the compartment and fondled Clancey adoringly. Looking up, their eyes met and Adeline felt obliged to say something.

'He's obviously very fond of dogs, your son.'

'Oh my word, 'e do go on about nothing else, but we got no room for pets with three children in our little house. And my husband's a cowman, he says dogs are for doin' a job of work, not lying around cluttering the place up.' She blushed and laughed abruptly, a little embarrassed. Adeline could picture a whole life of domestic trials stoically born. She smiled back at the woman.

'I think your husband's right, really. I was brought up in the country and our dogs were always kept for a purpose. But now that I'm in London I still like to have a dog about the place, and the result is that this old reprobate is a hopeless softie.'

They both focused once more on boy and dog. It occurred to Adeline that her fellow passenger was scarcely any older than her, and yet their situations could not have been more different. Here was a married woman of some years' standing, with three children and a cantankerous husband to cope with, a woman used to managing and making do, to denying both herself and the rest of her family for their own good. A woman whose serviceable coat, unflattering hat and much-mended laced shoes had been come by rather than selected, and retained for the purpose of decency and warmth and no more. Adeline was not given to self-consciousness, but she felt a little

self-conscious now, because everything about her denoted
the vigorous exercise of free choice, especially her large
and unnecessary dog who probably consumed as much
meat in a day as the small boy did in a week.

She opened her Gladstone bag and took out a bar of
chocolate.

'I'm afraid this is a weakness of mine,' she said. 'Would
you like some?'

She snapped off two squares and offered them to the
young woman, who shook her head.

'No, thanks very much.'

'Colin?'

'Thanks.'

Colin took the chocolate, broke it in half and put one
piece in his own mouth, the other in Clancey's. Adeline
gazed out of the window. The lights had been turned on
in the train and her own emphatic and slightly exotic
reflection looked challengingly back at her, with the other
woman no more than a drab, ill-defined figure in the background. She realized yet again, with a kind of honest,
respectful relief, that only tragedy had rescued her from
the consequences of a terrible mistake. A mistake she
swore silently never, never, to repeat.

Frank was there to meet her at Tarrford station, and they
drove back to the house through a landscape as familiar to
her as the palm of her own hand. And yet its very familiarity, its unchanging sameness, made it as foreign to her
as another country, for the relatively short amount of time
and space which divided her life here from that which
she now led in London represented, for her, a shift of
experience so complete that she felt like a different person.

Frank drove slowly, and in the middle of the road, as
one who is accustomed to moving about his own domain
in a supervisory capacity. He was nearly thirty now,
Adeline realized with that little shock peculiar to those
who are still on the right side of twenty-five. But in spite
of his enormous age he looked well, his face was ruddy
and he had filled out: the boy was now quite absorbed in

the man, and it suited him. On the platform the only sign
of the slight awkwardness between them was that he
greeted Clancey first, before embracing his sister warmly
and chuckling, lips pursed, at the cockaded hat and the
gauntlets. Once in the car, having asked how she was, at
first he didn't seem disposed to talk but occasionally, as
he drove, he would glance at Adeline and give her a crin-
kly-eyed, affectionate smile.

'How's Mother?' she asked after a while.

'In good form!' he replied, as if the realization of this
fact rather surprised him. 'I just let her get on with it –
being a pillar of the community. I think she's happy. In
fact I sometimes wonder if she didn't waste a good brain
marrying Father and riding to hounds. Still, common
enough phenomenon, I suppose . . .' He cleared his
throat. 'Howard and Cynthia are with us, by the way.'

Adeline felt a sharp, momentary dismay. 'But why?'

Frank gave her a sideways look. 'Mother invited them.
You know she likes people about her at Christmas, and
Bob wasn't to be coaxed away from London. Anyway,
it's not so dreadful, surely.'

'No, of course not, I didn't mean to sound as if it was.
But isn't Cynthia – I mean, how is she?'

'You know how she is, the poor thing. Very vague
and confused, not quite all there. But it varies apparently.
Some days are better than others. She's in good health
otherwise. Frankly it's Howard I feel sorry for, he's astonishingly patient with her and it's not as if he's a chap to
whom patience comes naturally.'

'No.' It was funny, but down here, knowing that
Howard was at Fording Place, she felt a resurgence of her
old antipathy towards him. She did not want him in her
home, occupying the place that had been Richard's.

'Is the nurse with them?' she asked.

'No, she has Christmas off. But Anne's come over to
help.'

'Anne Hyde-Latimer?' He nodded. 'That's very kind of
her.'

'It is, but then she is very kind. And to be fair I think

she wanted to come and the sense of being useful prevents her from getting the ridiculous idea that she's a burden or a nuisance of whatever. She's not one of nature's guests.'

There was food for thought in all this and they drove in silence for a little while until suddenly Frank pulled up, not bothering to draw into the side of the road. Adeline, used to weaving along busy London streets, instinctively looked over her shoulder, but Frank was pointing through the dusk to the indistinct outline of a low building at right-angles to the road.

'Remember those cottages, Addy? They're all empty now, except one, and it's costing me an arm and a leg to keep unoccupied premises maintained.'

Adeline studied not the cottages, but her brother's face. 'You're every inch the landowner, old thing, aren't you?'

He took one hand from the wheel in a gesture of acceptance. 'And proud of it. Father just wanted to preside and let things take their course, and before the war he could afford to do that. I actually want to make my mark. I'll have to, there simply isn't the manpower now. A lot of the young chaps want to be in the towns, working regular hours and earning more money. A tied cottage in the middle of nowhere doesn't appeal to them.' He started the car up again. 'Things move on.' He sounded matter of fact rather than disconsolate.

'You still have Chris Dance, though,' said Adeline.

'Good Lord yes, don't know what I'd do without him. He's an absolute tower of strength.'

They turned in at the drive. Adeline knew which trees would still wear a ragged covering of leaves, which windows would be lit, at exactly which juncture the dog would bark. Clancey whined and fidgeted, ears cocked, in the back seat.

As the tyres crackled on the gravel sweep – revealed by the headlamps as mossy and unraked now – the front door opened and Elizabeth stood silhouetted against the light. Tosca hustled over the front step to greet them. Clancey became almost hysterical with excitement.

Stepping out into the boisterous tumult of canine welcome, leaving Frank to cope with the additional furore caused by Clancey's arrival, Adeline went to her mother, tugging off her hat and enveloping Elizabeth in a hug so that the two of them were wrapped together in her cloak.

'Darling Mother, so lovely to see you.' She pushed her away. 'Now, how are you?'

'I'm well. I'm so glad you could come down, Addy, and help to make it a real family party.'

'You couldn't have kept me away!'

'You know Howard – '

'Frank told me, that's splendid.'

'He's upstairs with Cynthia at the moment. Just come and say hallo to Anne.'

As Frank struggled in with her Gladstone bag and suit-case, surrounded by scuffling dogs, and pushing the front door shut behind him with his heel, Anne appeared from the direction of the library. She looked just the same, thought Adeline, except that she had now given up the unequal struggle to appear pretty and smart and was simply her intelligent, straightforward, pleasant-looking self. She wore plain, good quality countrywoman's clothes with flat shoes, her hair was caught in a bun on the nape of her neck and she carried in one hand a pair of spectacles, as if she had just taken them off. Her face was wreathed in smiles.

'Addy!'

Adeline enfolded her in a second giant hug. 'What a surprise you being here! And Frank tells me you're being an absolute brick!'

'Does he?' Anne gave Frank, who had appeared beside them, an amused look. 'That's very decent of him. I'm just much happier if I'm making myself useful, as he very well knows.'

Frank made some sort of non-committal grunt, and Elizabeth put her head on Adeline's shoulder.

'Now come on, you get along upstairs and do whatever needs doing and then come down for a drink. What about this creature of yours, does he need anything?'

Anne bent over, hands on knees, and gazed at Clancey,

who at once rolled on to his back, invited her to scratch him. 'I'll take him to the kitchen and find him something after his horrid long journey.'

'The girl's a wonder,' said Adeline.

Adeline encountered Howard as he emerged from one of the guest bedrooms. It was a moment before he saw her, and in that moment she noticed that he was greyer than before, and that his face was drawn into lines of irritable stress. Beyond him as the door closed she caught sight of Cynthia, beautifully dressed, sitting in a chair with something on a tray on a table before her.

He shut the door and turned to cross the landing, catching sight of Adeline as she reached the top of the stairs.

'My dear girl!' His pleasure at seeing her was so obviously genuine, and his embrace so warm, that Adeline felt a stab of guilt over her earlier feeling of resentment.

'How's Cynthia?' she asked.

'Pretty distrait this evening. She's having her supper up here.'

'Should I go in and say hallo?'

He shook his head. 'Complete waste of time at the moment. She's perfectly happy in her way. Young Anne's been marvellous with her, she's got the patience of a saint – the infirm are not my forte, I'm afraid.'

'Nor mine,' said Adeline, to cheer him up.

'I seem to remember a rather different story with my son.'

'Well – ' " She was temporarily discomforted. 'That was different.'

'Really? Ah.' He began to go down the stairs. 'I'll see you below.'

As Adeline passed the closed door of the guest bedroom she heard the faintest, fluttering thread of sound: Cynthia, talking to herself.

When, just ten minutes later, she entered the drawing room, the first thing she noticed was the difference in Howard.

Anne sat on one side of the fireplace, her glass raised to be recharged by Frank, who was circulating with the decanter. Howard and Elizabeth sat on the sofa on the other side, facing Anne, but talking together. As Adeline came in it was to the sound of her mother's shouting peal of laughter. She sat with glass in one hand, cigarette in the other, her head tipped back, the very picture of whole-hearted amusement. Howard was on the edge of his seat, elbows on knees, his eyes on Elizabeth's face. He was grinning broadly, conceitedly, pleased with whatever joke he had told that had so tickled her. There was something unmistakably intimate in their respective attitudes.

He looked up at Adeline, the grin still on his face. She felt like an intruder.

'Ah, there's the girl!' he cried. 'What'll you have to drink?'

He got up, but Elizabeth was still laughing, pressing her glass to her brow as if to cool herself and her laughter infected him so that he chuckled too, looking down at her.

Frank handed her a drink and she sat on a footstool by Anne, who began asking about London and the Slade. Adeline answered, but was conscious all the time of her mother and Howard, the sound of their conversation, the angle of their heads, the movement of their hands. Bob had said that whatever it had been, it was over, and until this moment she had been satisfied with this view, and soothed by it. Her lunches with Howard in London had seemed to confirm it. Elizabeth's busy, parochial life was perfectly consistent with that of a woman who had come to terms with loyal widowhood.

But now . . . Adeline was not so sure. The contrast between Howard as she had seen him upstairs, taut and stooped and strained, and as he was now, flaring and ebullient, was too marked to ignore. It was impossible, too, not to be aware of the gulf that divided that almost silent first floor room where Cynthia sat, elegant and unmoving before her untouched food, murmuring to herself, and the atmosphere of a private party which these two had created about themselves. There might well be nothing of a sexual nature going on at present, but without a shadow of a doubt both spirit and flesh were willing, and ready. They were – she tried to find another phrase, but none sprang to mind that was half so apt – they were merely waiting.

Elizabeth's parents were now too ancient, too set in their ways, and 'too bloody awkward' (Frank's words) even to be invited to Christmas lunch, a contingency which gave cause for considerable unconcealed relief on all sides.

'We're generally a far jollier party without them,' declared Elizabeth, drinking buck's fizz from a tankard in the library just before they left for church, and then added, perfunctorily, 'Bless them.'

It had been made clear over breakfast that church attendance was not obligatory but that Elizabeth herself would be going because, as she put it, she was 'like that' with the rector. Frank referred to it as church parade, and would never have considered not going, Anne went because she liked to. Howard had never made any secret of his dislike of, and boredom with, organized religion but this morning Cynthia was much better, and enthused at the prospect of going out in a new hat, even if it was only to St Mark's, so Howard felt obligated to accompany her.

'No,' said Adeline, 'I shan't come, the pew's going to look gratifyingly full without me. I'm going for a walk.'

She put on an old skirt and sweater, her cloak, gauntlets and tweed fishing hat, rummaged in the infamous scullery cupboard for a pair of boots that fitted her, and set off with the ecstatic Clancey executing great arcs and loops about her as she walked.

She went first down the lane by the Dower House, where there was plentiful evidence of new occupancy, and of Frank's determination to make his mark. The hedge so beloved of Beau had been replaced by a post and rail fence, and the house had been repainted a fresh white, with the window frames picked out in black. The area of scrubby grass at the side of the house had been transformed by the hardworking Mr Prothero into a vegetable patch and now contained neat rows of leeks and brussel sprouts.

Leaving the lane she turned through the woods and walked along the path by the Tarr. It hadn't changed, except here and there the shoreline of the river had altered slightly, eroded in some places, banked up in others. A big old willow tree whose roots had once arched into the water from the bank like the hooked claws of a bird, had now lost its grip on terra firma altogether and lay in the water, smooth and pale as a skeleton, its bare branches stirred only slightly by the bustling current. The swans on their island squelched about with ungainly strides among the frosty osiers and bullrushes, and the cob launched into the water and accompanied her for a while, challenging her intrusion.

She went right through the woods to the point where she could rejoin the Tarrford road, and walked for a mile and a half along it, around the side of the hill to the picnicking spot where they'd gone on that fine spring day before the war. A few trees had been felled, and the trunks lay in a neat pile near the road. It was a still, crisp winter's morning but up here there always seemed to be a slight wind . . . she remembered how they'd talked of ghosts, and how the sighing of the branches had changed their mood and made them feel suddenly cold.

She whistled to Clancey and strode purposefully upwards, through the crater of the old fort to the lookout place, not stopping until she had reached the tower itself. Here, while the dog trotted and nosed about, she leaned her back against a tree and rested for a moment. There was little colour today. The sky was pale and heavy, the trees black, the grass sparse and bleached with cold. Only the ploughed fields on the hillside opposite showed warm, bright red where the rich Devon soil had been turned, as though the blood of the countryside had seeped from below and stained its surface. A lone seagull, an immigrant from Tarrmouth, fifteen miles away, swooped across the face of the hill, a gliding white speck, now dull, now bright as it turned in the air. This piece of countryside, this familiar view, with its immeasurable age and its enduring sameness, seemed to mock and belittle the changes she had herself experienced. Was it really so many years ago that she'd stood here, breathless with Simon's arm across her shoulders, never dreaming she would be his wife? So many years ago that Richard had discomforted poor Bryer with his talk of shrotted pimps, and that she had drawn two hats in conversation, Sarah's and Cynthia's? Three of those people were now dead, others gone, others changed out of all recognition, and yet this place was utterly, uncaringly the same.

Suddenly chilled to the marrow, her hands and feet aching with cold, she called Clancey and began running back through the trees towards the road, her footsteps making no sound on the dark, cold mulch of fallen leaves.

At lunch she chatted to Chris Dance. As he responded to her questions about the estate and its administration she observed that he had changed. Instead of the immensely capable and self-possessed manager that she remembered, a man generally acknowledged to be running the show under the amiable auspices of the unbusinesslike Richard, she saw a middle-aged man beginning to display the signs of unwelcome bachelordom: a man a little unsure of himself socially, a little stiff and awkward in mixed company, dressed in dated, over-careful clothes. It occurred to her that no matter how great Frank's debt to Chris Dance, the change of management at Fording Place had subtly altered his status, and his view of the future.

'. . . breaking even, but I expect we'll have to sell off some more before we're through,' he concluded, laying his knife and fork together. 'Not that any of this is very interesting to you, Mrs Charteris.'

'Nonsense. This is my home, still, remember. I'm very interested in what happens to it.'

There was a brief pause, during which Chris Dance cleared his throat, and smoothed his napkin over his knees with large, weatherbeaten hands.

'Tell me,' he asked, 'do you ever hear anything of Miss Sugden – Nanny, that was?'

Adeline rounded on him with what she did not realize

was a somewhat over-zealous expression of delighted interest.

'How strange you should ask that! I only had a letter from her a few weeks ago! We have kept in touch, though I'm a horrifically sporadic correspondent. Whenever I do write I get an answer straight away. It puts me to shame!'

Chris nodded and smiled. 'And how is she – down in Sidmouth, isn't it?'

'Yes. She seems well, and happy. In fact,' said Adeline, formulating the plan as she spoke, 'I think I might go and visit her while I'm here, I've been meaning to for simply ages. I wonder if Frank would lend me the car?'

'I'm sure he would,' said Chris. 'And if you do go, would you be kind enough to give her my regards?'

As she parked the car outside 3, Victoria Villas, Sidmouth, Adeline felt a sudden shudder of apprehension. The ease and speed with which the arrangements had been made had taken her by surprise and it was, after all, six years since she had seen Dorothy. Perhaps the whole idea of this meeting was ill-judged, as Elizabeth had indicated. But the pleasant-sounding Mrs Shelmadine had been cooperation itself on the telephone yesterday – 'Oh but you must come, Nanny has a day off tomorrow and I'm sure she'd be thrilled to see you, we've all heard about you of course!' – and here she was.

She rang the bell, looking about her. Here was a very different environment to that of Fording Place. This was a Victorian villa by name and by nature, solid, neat, well-maintained, windows netted, hedge trimmed, knocker polished. An opulent Christmas tree was visible in the room to the left of the front door.

The door now opened and there stood a smart, attractive woman in her thirties, smiling welcomingly. A small boy of about nine stood just behind her, staring at Adeline with open curiosity.

'Hallo, Mrs Shelmadine? I'm Adeline Charteris. How do you do?'

'Mrs Charteris, come in. I feel almost as if I know you!

Harry, run upstairs and tell Nanny her visitor's here.' The boy dashed away, thundering up the stairs two at a time. Mrs Shelmadine closed the door and clasped her hands together, beaming with satisfaction. 'I do hope you don't mind my saying, but you're exactly as I pictured you – here, let me take your things.' She relieved Adeline of her cloak and hat. The latter, with its sweeping pheasant feathers, perched on the hatstand like some exotic bird of passage pausing on its flight to sunnier climes.

'This is awfully good of you,' said Adeline. 'I hope my coming hasn't put you out at all.'

'No, no, no!' Mrs Shelmadine grew quite pink with emphasis. 'As I said, we always give nanny a day off on the day after Boxing Day – she's earned it after the pandemonium of the festive season! Ah, here she is – Nanny, here is Mrs Charteris!'

'Hallo, Nanny.' Not pausing to think, nor even really to look, Adeline stepped forward and kissed Dorothy warmly on the cheek.

'Hallo, Adeline.'

'Now,' said Mrs Shelmadine, 'you make yourself at home upstairs, and your tea will come up in about half an hour. If you want to go out, please do Do whatever you like.'

'Would you like to come up?' said Dorothy.

'Yes, lovely. Thank you.'

Adeline, following Dorothy up the stairs, realized that Mrs Shelmadine was treating them as Nanny and child. In fact, that was how she felt. She heard a hasty, muted exchange as Harry asked if he could accompany them, and was refused. Then the drawing room door closed.

Dorothy was not in uniform and yet, thought Adeline, she had presented herself rather as if she were, as if the habit of dressing in a certain way had now become so ingrained that it was second nature. She wore a dark blue, long-sleeved dress with a grey cardigan and sturdy black shoes. The dress was enlivened at the neck by a small garnet and paste brooch in the shape of a Tudor rose which Adeline recognized – it had been Dorothy's mother's. The only real concession to vanity was a pair of flesh coloured silk stockings which showed off the small area of her calves that was visible to advantage.

'Come along in and sit down, Adeline.'

Here, Dorothy had a bedsitting room separate from the nursery. It was bright and well appointed, but very small, and the furniture was proportionately tiny. Adeline felt like a giant. She wondered again whether she should have come. The atmosphere at present was very strained. On the dressing table and mantelpiece were framed photographs of herself and her brothers, those that Elizabeth had given Dorothy when she left. There on the pillow was Dorothy's quilted nightdress case, and in front of the mirror her fearsome Mason Pearson hairbrush. The room was fiercely tidy, a nanny's room.

'How are – ?'

'Did you – ?'

They both began to speak at once, and laughed, but it was Adeline who continued. 'I was going to ask if you have any friends down here. It must be much nicer for you being in a town instead of stuck in the middle of nowhere as you were with us.'

'To be honest I haven't made any friends, outside the family. But when you're with little ones all day you enjoy your own company.'

Adeline had been placed in the only easy chair while Dorothy sat in an upright one at the card table, covered with a cloth, which awaited the arrival of tea. This inequality in their positions gave her the curious illusion that she was interviewing Dorothy.

'Excuse me,' she said, 'do you mind if I join you?' she took the second chair at the table and leaned forward on her elbows. 'That's better!'

At once they were more comfortable with one another. For the first time Dorothy smiled knowingly at Adeline as she used to do, and Adeline grinned back. She picked up her bread and butter knife and began fiddling with it, tempting Dorothy to tell her not to fidget.

'Same as ever, I see,' remarked Dorothy.

'And you. You haven't changed a bit, Nanny. You're ageless.'

'Oh no. It's just that nannies are never young.'

Adeline filed this comment, but chose not to take it up. Instead, she said:

'Everyone sends their regards – Mother, and Frank. Bob's not there this Christmas – he has a lady friend in London, believe it or not! Chris Dance especially wanted to be remembered to you, by the way.'

'Oh yes . . . well, you must give him my best.' Dorothy touched her hair, which was cut short now, but caught back in two combs on either side of her face. 'How's Frank getting on?' she asked, and then added, all in a rush: 'I didn't like the look of him at your wedding, he didn't seem himself at all. He had the cares of the world on his shoulders.'

Adeline cast her mind back, and found she could remember almost nothing about her wedding, though she did recollect the night when he had come home on leave and she had found him fast asleep on the bed.

'It was just after the war, Nanny,' she said. 'Although he wasn't wounded he was exhausted. He's right back on form now, running the show at Fording Place, far more efficiently than darling Father.'

'Young ladies, I suppose,' said Dorothy a shade disapprovingly, smoothing the tablecloth with her slim, tapering hands. She has the hands of the artist, thought Adeline, and I have those of the nanny.

She said: 'No, as a matter of fact. I think he's too busy for much socializing. Mind you – ' She leaned forward confidingly, knowing Dorothy liked to gossip. 'Anne Hyde-Latimer's staying at the moment, so perhaps there's something going on there.'

'Anne?' Dorothy raised her eyebrows. 'That homely one? A very nice girl, but no dress sense?'

'That's the one.'

Dorothy laughed happily. 'Well! There's no accounting for taste!'

After that, the process of mutual adjustment seemed complete, and the next two hours passed quickly and enjoyably, fuelled by a splendiferous tea. Dorothy interrogated Adeline, and Adeline responded by telling her all – or almost all – about her life in London, and the Slade, and her friends. She even allowed Dorothy to indicate, from her position of confident ignorance, that Peter Marchant was the very man for her. In other words, they conducted their conversation pretty much as they always had done, though when it was time for Adeline to go and they stood together in the hall, with the sitting room door discreetly closed beyond them, Adeline said:

'How would it be if I stopped calling you "Nanny"?' She saw the look of alarm dawning on Dorothy's face and to spare her blushes turned away to adjust her hat in the mirror. 'I mean,' she said, 'I'd really rather feel like your friend, now.' She straightened up, hat in place, and subjected Dorothy to the bright, direct, slightly intimidating look that was typical of her. 'We are friends, aren't we?'

'Oh yes,' said Dorothy.

'Well then?'

Dorothy stepped forward and gave the front of Adeline's cloak a little brush with her hand, afterwards rubbing her fingers together to rid them of some invisible dust. In that one small gesture she made her position perfectly clear.

'We'll see,' she said.

In spite of the comparative success of her visit, Adeline was troubled as she drove home. She was haunted by images of a restricted and solitary life – the small, neat bedroom, the framed photographs, the card table with its seersucker cloth. She could understand all too readily why a woman who lived like that would be unwilling, perhaps even unable, to step forth into the real, untidy, unpredictable world. But Adeline remembered Dorothy as she had been – pretty, voluble, romantic, waiting for something to come up. Now it appeared that she had given up waiting: or just given up.

Adeline accelerated ferociously up a steep hill. It

wouldn't do. She wouldn't allow Dorothy to settle into timid, sterile nannyhood. For goodness' sake, it was Dorothy who'd encouraged her to make something of herself, to have ambition, to aspire – she owed her something in return.

One of these days an opportunity would present itself, and she would grab it. She recalled the silk stockings and smiled to herself. All was not lost.

It wasn't until she was back in her room in Gower Street, burning pounds' worth of coins in an attempt to warm it up after a week's absence, that she remembered she was supposed to be going to the Elverstones' party with Nicholas Eyre the following night. The urgent desire to be rid of Nicholas and her subsequent mild curiosity about the event had delayed the concoction of an excuse, and now it would be too late.

'Damn and blast!' She felt cold, and cross and out of sorts. She could picture all too clearly a roomful of self-consciously 'artistic' people, middle-aged bohemians with no sense of humour, who would probably patronize an unsuspecting newcomer to death. Worse still, she was going to have to submit to the patronage of Nicholas himself who, as her sponsor for the evening, would certainly make the most of every opportunity to discomfort her.

In a mood to rub salt in the self-inflicted wound, she pulled open the door of her rickety wardrope with such force that the cupboard itself nearly fell on top of her, and surveyed the contents. There was nothing there that struck her as remotely suitable. Her interest in clothes did not run to the purchasing of those expensive, well-made, understated garments which would, as the pundits put it, 'take you anywhere'. In vain and in anger she rummaged through the clothes looking for something to fit the bill, but even had there been such an item there she was in no mood to spot it. What would they all be wearing? She despised herself for giving the matter a second thought, but the prospect of arriving, in Nicholas's company, in something jarringly inappropriate, appalled her. Where was the svelte frock, alluring but clever, in which she would blend effortlessly into her surroundings?

Blending, however, was not nor ever had been, Adeline's strong suit. In the end she dragged the long velvet evening dress, that which she had worn to Fenella's party, from its hanger, and held it against her, scowling challengingly at herself in the mirror. 'To hell with it, she muttered. 'It'll just have to do.'

The following evening her toilette was fraught with minor setbacks. The geyser would not light, and as she stormed down to inform Mrs Fairyhouse she turned her ankle over painfully on the stairs. When she was applying her make-up in the mirror above the fire she almost singed the front of her dress, withdrew sharply to prevent further damage and trod on the hem at the back with a rending sound. Fortunately Toni arrived back from Leytonstone, and hearing her wails and expletives, appeared with tea, sympathy and needle and thread to repair the hem, but it was too late to restore her morale, which had reach rock bottom by the time Nicholas arrived to collect her.

But despite, or perhaps because of, her grim look he was gallantry itself.

'That is a magnificent dress.'

'You've seen it before,' she reminded him curtly as they climbed into the waiting taxi.

'I find I'm able to put up with that.'

She stared out of the window as they pulled away from the kerb. 'Where are we going?'

'Scarcely any distance, but too far to walk in this weather.'

It had turned cold. Fresh flakes of snow darted and spun on the night air, careering crazily in and out of the lamplight and making the streets appear strange and remote, so that she did not at first realize where they were, until they were at the foot of the steps that led to the front door.

'Isn't this Allerton Square?'

'That's right, you know it?'

'I walk the dog in the gardens.' Looking about her she

saw that they were in that part of the square from which she had heard the scream that early morning in November. She thought of how she might have been with Peter, or even at home with Toni, sitting by the gas fire and talking cosily. She shivered.

They stood for some time on the doorstep waiting for their ring to be answered. The hall beyond the glass fan-light was only dimly lit, but from the curtained window to the left of the door came a hubbub of voices and music, a sudden burst of laughter. Adeline had the childish and irrational feeling that it was she herself who was being laughed at.

The door opened and Consett appeared, her face wear-ing its usual expression of implacable scepticism.

'They're all in there,' she said as she hung up Adeline's cloak on top of several others. The hall was full of outdoor paraphernalia – coats, capes, shawls, mackintoshes, hats, scarves and umbrellas, some of which had been opened to allow the melted snow to run off and form large damp patches on the carpet.

'We'll fend for ourselves,' said Nicholas, quite unnecessarily, since Consett was already heading in the direction of the back stairs. Adeline conjectured that his exaggerated civility and her extreme brusqueness were part of an established pattern.

'Come along in,' said Nicholas, walking ahead of her and opening the door on to the party.

The large room was only slightly less dimly lit than the hall, and it was very warm, due more to the crush of humanity than the very small coal fire which could be glimpsed on the far side of the room like a solitary light in a jungle. Nicholas said, in her ear, 'I'll fetch you a drink,' and disappeard.

Though it was only half past eight, the other party-goers seemed to have been there for some time. The air was thick with smoke and the sort of dense conversation which is laid down layer upon layer over a considerable period. Full ashtrays, empty and half-empty glasses, and plates with remnants of food thronged various surfaces.

A record was on the phonograph and people were dancing – rather well, Adeline observed, and with a sort of careless, idiosyncratic abandon – and as they danced they talked. She received a blurred general impression of her fellow guests as being in the main older than her. Animation hovered and flickered over the throng like the holy ghost, but it was not the same animation which had informed the proceedings at Fenella's party. Here were people, she sensed, with a prickle of trepidation, who spent their time locking intellectual horns. She caught odd bits of conversation: 'Don't be bloody silly, how can you say that?' . . . 'There's no depth in any of his work, it's simply a trick of the light' . . . 'When I wrote that I was a different person' . . . 'Excuse me, but are you someone I should know?'

She snapped out of her reverie to find standing next to her a tousle-haired engaging-looking man, staring into her face with an enquiring smile.

'I haven't the remotest idea,' she replied with asperity, feeling that she must assert herself and not realizing that her face, form and demeanour were quite emphatic enough in their unasserted state. 'And who are you?'

'I believe,' said the man, continuing to smile, but furrowing his brow as if in thought, 'that I'm your host, Neville Elverstone.'

'Oh God, I'm sorry!' snapped Adeline. She held out her hand. 'I'm Adeline Charteris, and you don't know me. I came with Nicholas Eyre.'

'Good,' replied Neville happily. 'Now, do you have a drink? No, I see you don't. Shall we do something about that?'

'It's all right, Nicholas has gone to get me one – here he is.'

'Nick!' Neville swung round and embraced Nicholas warmly, still holding in one hand a glass of whisky and water which tilted dangerously. 'So glad you were able to come, and to bring Adeline here with you.'

He referred to her, Adeline thought, both as if he had known her all his life and yet knew her not at all. She felt herself noted, absorbed and set aside all in a moment. The usual early stages of acquaintanceship, the mutual questioning and assessment, had either been dispensed with or had been contracted into so short a time that she had failed altogether to notice them.

'Pleasure,' said Nicholas, handing Adeline a glass of red wine but addressing Neville. 'You do remember I said she'd be coming along?'

Neville beamed and shrugged. 'You know me.' He turned the beam towards Adeline. 'But this way it's a pleasant surprise.' Adeline realized she had not been invited.

'I haven't the remotest idea why I'm here,' she said, rudely.

'Neither has any of us!' replied Neville, as if amazed and delighted by the coincidence of it all. 'Is it somebody's birthday?'

Both men laughed, Neville uproariously, Nicholas merely to oblige. Adeline gulped at her wine, which made up in vigour what it lacked in finesse, at a rather more than judicious rate. She wished to get drunk as soon as possible in order to feel less out of things.

'You two had better dance,' suggested Neville. 'You do dance, Adeline?'

'Indifferently, when asked.'

'When asked, of course. Mind you, there are females present tonight who will drag a partner on to the floor or, failing that, take to it by themselves. Isn't that so, Nick?'

Nicholas had been looking around, not listening. 'Where's Marian?'

'Oh . . .' Neville peered vaguely over the heads of his guests. 'I couldn't say. Somewhere in there making some poor wretch feel uncomfortable. Why? Do you want her?'

'Me? No,' said Nicholas in a manner, and with an emphasis, which prompted Neville to turn to Adeline.

'Adeline, I'm going to try and find my wife for you, I know she'd like to meet you.'

'I don't see why,' said Adeline though not, this time,

in order to be rude, but because a certain brusqueness seemed to be going down quite well.

'She likes new people . . .' said Neville vaguely and simply, still peering.

Adeline drained her glass and shrugged. 'I'm in your hands.'

'Let me get you another,' said Nicholas, and disappeared with her glass. Neville linked his arm through hers, leaning on her slightly, and she realized he was quite drunk. She wondered, as he led her through the crush into the centre of the room, how old he was. She had been expecting someone ascetic, greying, perhaps eccentric in some way, but Neville, with his thick, unruly hair, full mouth and bright, snapping brown eyes, was boyish. It was, she realized ruefully, impossible to dislike him.

'Now then,' he murmured, turning round and round, his arm still through hers so that she was obliged to turn too, like a ballerina on a musical box, 'Where can she be?'

'Who are you looking for?' asked a woman close to them, turning away from the man she'd been talking to and looking with thinly veiled curiosity at Adeline. 'Ida,' said Neville, 'Let me introduce Adeline. Now would you excuse me while I go in search of Marian . . .?' He moved off, no longer focusing on them.

'How do you know the Elverstones?' asked Ida.

'I don't,' said Adeline. 'I'm an interloper. I can't even claim the most casual acquaintance.'

'So how did you come to be here?'

'Nicholas Eyre invited me.'

'Oh . . .?' Was Adeline mistaken or did Ida seem intrigued by this information?

'Before you ask,' she added, 'I barely know him, either.'

The phonograph had stopped and someone – Nicholas, presumably – began to play the piano with considerable verve. The couples around them danced with renewed vigour, many of them with glasses still in their hands and cigarettes between their lips.

Ida inclined her head in Adeline's direction. 'Shall we go and sit down before we get trampled to death?'

An elegant but threadbare chesterfield was pushed back against the streaky velvet curtains, and Ida sat down and patted the seat next to her.

'That's better. Cigarette?'

'Thanks.'

'You haven't got a drink.'

'I think Nicholas got diverted. Tell me,' went on Adeline, realizing that she had at her disposal a ready source of information, 'when did the party start?'

'Do you know, I've no idea?' replied Ida. 'I've been here at least an hour and there was quite a crowd when I arrived. One tends to turn up when one feels like it in Allerton Square. The door's always open. Marian and Neville like nothing better than to be surrounded by people. It's meat and drink to them.'

'But she's a novelist – I mean, I've heard of her – when does she work?'

'When she wants to write she goes up to her bolthole on the top floor and locks the door, irrespective of who's here. Liberty Hall it may be, but one doesn't expect Marian to play the hostess; she's a law unto herself. As a matter of fact – ' Ida turned her head in an imitation of someone scanning the room. 'I haven't seen her all evening. Which is a pity.' She glanced almost coquettishly at Adeline. 'Because I know she'd like to meet you.'

'So people keep telling me.'

'What do you think of Nicholas?'

Since plain speaking was the order of the day, Adeline answered: 'I don't care for him.'

'My dear, who does? Unfortunately he would hate to be liked. Being a little bastard gives him a certain distinction.'

For the first time that evening Adeline was conscious of enjoying herself. 'Tell me more.'

'There's precious little to tell. Nicholas is a very ordinary young man with a modest musical talent and an exaggerated notion of his own importance in the scheme of things. And he is absolutely besotted with the Elverstones.' She lifted one plump, beautifully manicured hand. '*C'est tout.*'

'They – well, Neville at any rate certainly seems to like him.'

'Neville likes everyone. But he's Neville's little darling, of course. Such a waste of that charm, and those looks . . . really it makes me impatient.'

Adeline was saved from having to find a response to this by the arrival of Neville himself, an open bottle in one hand, glass and cigarette in the other. He flopped down on the chesterfield next to her with a comically despondent air.

'Couldn't find her,' he said. 'She must have gone to ground. Still, Ida's looking after you.'

'She is, yes.'

Neville's face was filmed with sweat, his forelock was damp with it: he had been dancing. Now he jerked his head in the general direction of the piano.

'What d'you think of Nick? Plays a treat, doesn't he?'

'I don't know much about it.'

Neville tapped his foot. 'He can turn his hand to anything on the old joanna.'

'A perfect jack of all trades,' murmured Ida sarcastically on Adeline's other side.

Abruptly Neville stubbed out his cigarette and put the bottle and glass on the floor.

'Like to dance?'

Having led her on to the floor and clasped her to his shirt front, Neville did not seem disposed to talk, and Adeline was quite happy to be led by him and the rhythm of the music, and to watch the other couples moving around them. As they jigged past the piano Nicholas gave her a little wave which she pretended not to see. In a moment she noticed that Ida was dancing too, with a tall, gawky, bearded man who held her at arm's length and talked earnestly. All going round in circles, thought Adeline. Her one glass of wine had been enough to remind her that she hadn't eaten since midday, but in spite of the plates she saw no food laid out, and no-one had directed her to any. Her stomach rumbled against the warm expanse of Neville's shirt, but he seemed not to notice as he hummed tunelessly into her ear. She sensed once more his amiable but complete lack of interest in her, but this no longer irritated her. Instead she found the freedom from another's expectations rather exhilarating. She remembered the last time she'd danced – with Peter, with Joel, and with poor, enraged Duncan. A scene of the kind she had witnessed that evening was inconceivable here, though she had not yet been able to analyse why this should be so.

She saw that the walls of the room were covered with pictures, by no means all of them framed: pen and ink drawings, watercolours, photographs, pencil and charcoal sketches on sheets torn from a sketch pad, newspaper cuttings and paintings of every description hung cheek by jowl, sometimes overlapping each other and sometimes, as in the case of the sketches and cuttings, pinned one on top of another as the old had been superseded by the new in the Elverstones' esteem.

She remarked, into Neville's ear: 'You have an enormous number of pictures.'

'Yes, we like them. Marian and I like to acquire pictures and books lavishly and not too discriminately. These things shouldn't be over-revered. Throw 'em all on the wall, let them vie for attention – survival of the fittest, that's our policy.'

'Yes.' Adeline looked again at the giddying mass of material. 'I like that.'

'If you want to be serious,' he went on, 'and you take the view that art offers a perspective on life, you should expose yourself to masses of it and not be too pernickety.'

'Do you paint?'

'Only for my own amusement. Marian earns our crust. She it is who buys things and tricks us and this place out in the manner to which we've become accustomed.'

'So what *is* it you do exactly?' continued Adeline, much emboldened by this atmosphere of untouchy tolerance.

'You wonder how on earth I fill my time? Well, I espouse causes in an unenergetic kind of way, and I pen articles for various papers and magazines. And I nurture

Marian. She has the real talent, so I tend the flame.' Adeline
felt a little resentful of this omnipotent, cherished, but
absent hostess to whom everyone paid so much verbal
court. 'Have you read her stuff?' asked Neville.

'No.'

'I haven't either,' he said reflectively, as if in the process
of deciding whether to do so. 'I'm told they're rather
remarkable.'

'I've heard of her, of course.'

'Of course.'

Nicholas finished playing and got up from the piano, to
a smattering of applause. Somebody put another record
on. Neville released Adeline and said: 'Another drink?'

'No thank you. But I'd love something to eat.'

'Right.' Neville led her to the door and opened it. 'Over
there's the dining room, just help yourself.'

'Thank you.'

'And do feel free to wander about, take a look at things.
Nothing's private. If it's pictures you like there are some
quite amusing ones on the first floor landing.'

With that he withdrew once more into the warm, sim-
mering stew of the party, leaving Adeline in the odd, not-
quite solitude that goes with being shut out of a room
where much is going on.

She crossed the hall and went into the dining room. It
was a big, high room, nearly as large as the one she'd
just left and, with only a single standard lamp on, equally
poorly illuminated. To Adeline's left, at the opposite end
from the window, two men sat on hard chairs by the unlit
fire, talking quietly and earnestly, and they looked up only
briefly as she walked in. After the heat of the party the air
struck cold and refreshing on her burning cheeks.

There was plenty of food, and Adeline was ravenous.
On a chipped willow-pattern plate she piled bread, salad,
cheese and two slices of a dark, fiery-looking Italian saus-
age and sat down at the end of the table to eat. At the
sound of her knife and fork a shaggy dog emerged from
beneath the table and cadged shamelessly for scraps. She
threw him a piece of cheese which he caught with practised

ease, and chewed gluttonously, his pink tongue darting round his moustache afterwards to pick up stray crumbs.

On the wall behind the huge oak sideboard (on which piles of papers and magazines lay in uneven, sliding heaps) someone – perhaps Neville – had painted a mural. It was in the style of *Déjeuner Sur l'Herbe*, two couples picnicking in sunlight at the edge of a wood. It was not an elaborate piece, but there was a sort of luminosity about it, the pale sunshine seemed to be reflected off the grass, the silvery green leaves and some distant, grey-blue water. The faces of the two men and two women were almond-shaped and all rather similar, with inscrutable opaque eyes and closed, serious mouths. They appeared deliberately secretive. It occurred to Adeline that one of them might be Marian, and when she'd finished eating she rose, brushing crumbs from her lap, and went to take a closer look. But all that was revealed was the cracked plaster beneath, and the dry streaks where the brush itself had been insufficiently loaded with paint.

Feeling much better for the food, Adeline went out once again into the hall. The dog nosed his way through the half-open door behind her and stood at her side, gazing up at her with bright, dark eyes.

'What are you after now?' she asked aloud, thinking herself alone.

'He's a pest,' said a sharp female voice. It was Consett, shaking and closing an umbrella. The hotch-potch of discarded outdoor clothes bore witness to her ministrations. Her mouth was a tight line of disapproval which Adeline, having met the occupants of the house, now felt she could understand.

'Whose dog is he?' she asked appeasingly, stooping to pat the animal's head.

'It's his. And he spoils it.'

Adeline smiled. 'I'm afraid I've been guilty of that, too. He's very appealing.'

'That's a matter of opinion.'

Adeline placed her foot on the stairs, and felt the housekeeper's gimlet eye upon her.

'I'm going for a wander round – Mr Elverstone said I might.'

'Go where you like,' said Consett, with a don't-blame-me air.

Adeline went up the stairs, lifting the hem of her dress in front of her. The dog went with her. The first floor landing was in complete darkness, but she found the switch and pressed it, to turn on a single bulb in a red tasselled shade in the middle of the ceiling. The promised 'quite amusing' pictures turned out to be erotica, assorted eastern lithographs and line drawings, sinuous, elegant and explicit. She found herself wondering, as she studied them, how often Neville, his wife, and perhaps Nicholas, paused to look at the pictures as they passed. In amongst them she came across a cluster of framed sepia photographs, stained and spotted with age, and it was as she peered at these to distinguish and perhaps identify faces, that she heard the weeping.

It came from above, and quite near by, a soft, desperate, insistent sound. Its softness seemed to come not from being muffled, but from being utterly unforced. Adeline thought that if tears themselves could make a sound as they flowed, this would be it. Reaching her quite unexpectedly as she stood alone on the wide landing with its dim island of light, the sound of the party no more than a distant hubbub below, it was shocking. She stood completely still, breath held, her skin crawling with apprehension.

Downstairs the drawing room door opened, emitting a blast of sound. A voice shouted: 'No, no, I've had enough of all this! I'm going to satisfy the inner man!' Then there was a burst of laughter, a woman's voice, an exchange of a teasing, scuffling sort, and the door closed again. Consett had gone from the hall. Adeline was suspended between two worlds. The weeping was still there, anguished and private, somewhere near. She looked around. In the twilight around the edge of the landing, doors stood open or half open on deeper darkness. She was disorientated now, the crying seemed all around her, vibrating in the cold, enclosed air. Tentatively she went to the nearest door and felt about the wall just inside for the light switch. Revealed was a large bedroom in a state of such extravagant untidiness that it might just have been ransacked by thieves. On the massive carved wooden bed, a tangle of sheets and blankets lay piled on the mattress, a patchwork quilt trailed on the ground. The other furniture – dressing table, stool, chairs, desk – was cluttered with books, and clothing, and papers and brushes and bottles and flowers, many of them not just dead, but dried out, standing in waterless vases. The curtains were half drawn. A large and beautiful chamber pot decorated with pink and guilt roses was visible beneath the bed. The room smelt, not altogether unpleasantly, of recent habitation. 'Nothing's private,' Neville had said, and yet so powerful was the sense of occupancy, of feverish secrecy, about this room that Adeline felt like an intruder and quickly turned off the light once more.

As she turned back she saw that the dog had crept a little way up the next flight of stairs and was standing, ears pricked, looking upwards. The crying continued and the dog whined in sympathy. Taking the animal's collar Adeline went up the stairs, which rounded a corner at a small half landing, after which they became steeper and narrower, leading to the top floor of the house. Here the ceiling was lower and the floor area had the drab, threadbare look that attends little-used parts of any house. It was dark and there appeared to be no overhead light, but from beneath a closed door to the right a thin line of light was visible. It was from behind this door that the crying came. It was possible now to hear the sharp, broken breathing that accompanied it.

The dog put his nose to the base of the door and blew, his head tilted on one side. Not to be put off, Adeline knocked.

The crying stopped abruptly, leaving behind it a dense and muffling silence. To break the eerie spell Adeline knocked again, more firmly. There was no response and she grasped the handle and tried it.

'Is everything all right? May I come in?'

Her face was so close to the door that when, with the rattle of a bolt it flew open, she nearly fell forward. This room at least was brightly, even harshly lit, and as she stumbled she received a swift, sharp impression of the person who occupied it – a thin, pale woman whose outline seemed to tremble with a curious, painful energy like a flame caught in a capricious draught. The face was gaunt and smudged with crying, but illuminated by huge pale eyes that held an expression of angry defensive fear that reminded Adeline of a cornered animal. The gasping sound she made recalled another sound which had haunted Adeline for almost two months, though she could not immediately place it. By the time she had righted herself the woman had retreated and was sitting in a narrow upright chair at a desk, her back to Adeline.

A voice, low and quiet but surprisingly clear, said: 'I don't know who you are.'

It seemed neither accusation nor query, but an expression of agonized bafflement.

'No,' Adeline stepped into the room and the dog, too, crept in past her ankles.

'I don't want that in here,' said the woman, without turning.

Knowing at once that she meant the dog Adeline complied with the request and the invitation to herself that it implied, gently pushing the dog out and closing the door.

'I'm so sorry if I'm intruding,' she said, her voice loud in the reclusive hush of the room, 'but I was looking at the pictures on the floor below and I heard you crying.' There seemed no point in pretending it might have been anyone else. There was no reply. Marian Elverstone sat, feet together, head bowed, hands in lap. The nape of her neck, beneath wispy, loosely coiled hair, and her shoulder blades, where they pushed the fabric of her unseasonal cotton dress, looked childishly thin. The dress itself was blue, with a bleached pattern of lighter blue flowers. On the floor beside the desk lay a black, fringed shawl. As Adeline watched she saw the narrow shoulders tighten and shiver convulsively, and acting on instinct she went to pick up the shawl and place it round them. Marian's hands did not rise from her lap and she said nothing.

Adeline stepped back. 'If there's nothing I can do, or no-one I can fetch for you, I'll leave you in peace,' she aid.

She paused, hoping perhaps to be detained, and then turned to leave, but as she did so Marian said: 'I have no peace.'

The terrible plainness of this remark stopped Adeline in her tracks. She looked round to see that Marian had stretched out one hand, fingers extended, palm to the ground. Her face was still averted but the outstretched hand was enough for Adeline. She clasped it in both hers – it felt smooth and cold – and crouched beside Marian's chair.

'What is it? What's the matter? Please tell me. There must be some way I can help. Would you like Neville to come?'

'Who are you?' said Marian, again as if she were talking to herself, but Adeline was now determined to open at least one line of real communication between them.

'I'm Adeline. I came to the party downstairs, but we've never met before.' She chafed the cold hand between hers and repeated, 'I'm Adeline.'

'Oh yes, the party . . .'

'Everyone's having a wonderful time, but they miss you.'

Very gently, with a movement so light and graceful that it contained no hint of rejection, Marian took her hand from Adeline's and began to pin up some stray strands of hair. The loose, elbow length sleeves of the dress fell back and the blue tributaries of veins on the inside of her arms seemed barely concealed by the white, transparent skin. As she pushed at the hair pins, and adjusted the fringed shawl about her shoulders she appeared to be simultaneously regaining some degree of mental composure. Adeline remained crouching on the floor, watching her face. It was an oval face, with a high forehead and a curving, rounded chin. The deep indentation between chin and mouth was emphasized by a tendency of the full lower lip to droop, and both lips were reddened and dry like those of a child with a fever. The large, light eyes were rather protruberant, the cheeks sunken and boneless-seeming, the left one marked by two moles. Because of the extreme paleness of the face, the marks that weeping had left upon it were exaggerated. Adeline was fascinated and stirred by it. She was overcome by the pathos of this woman crying all alone in an upstairs room while her guests drank and danced and talked about her.

'I wonder,' she said, feeling she must maintain the small improvement that was taking place, 'would you like a drink? A whisky or something can help if you're feeling low.'

'No drink, thank you.' Marian's voice was firmer now. 'But could you pass me my cigarettes? They're on the shelf behind you.' Adeline got to her feet and found the packet on the lowest of three bookshelves. On the desk, she noticed some white carnations in a glass jug, their frilled edges turning brown.

Adeline would dearly have liked a cigarette herself, but it was not offered. Instead Marian took a box of matches from a drawer in the desk and lit her own, inhaling deeply with a breath that Adeline heard with a pang still shook slightly. 'You've been enjoying the party,' said Marian in a curious way that was neither enquiry nor observation, but speculation. The remark invited no reply, but Adeline answered eagerly anyway.

'Oh yes. I came with Nicholas Eyre.'

'Nicholas brings a lot of people to see us, some we like, some not so much.'

She might have been referring to food, or clothes. She sat back in her chair, one hand holding the edges of the shawl together the other with the cigarette, her eyes resting appraisingly on Adeline as if seeing her for the first time. Adeline found that she did not object to being stared at and assessed by Marian Elverstone.

'And now he's brought you,' added Marian. 'Miss

Adeline,' she said, with a mocking echo of the Deep
South.

For the first time that evening Adeline did not feel compelled to sweep aside her connection with Nicholas Eyre.
Spoken by Marian his name took on a different quality.
She conferred upon it a certain status while herself remaining aloof and ironic. Her eyes as they scrutinized Adeline
had lost their terror-stricken look and shone with a mild
but flattering curiosity.

Adeline, who had been standing since passing the cigarettes, made to crouch once more on the floor, but Marian
shook her head.

'No, no, you mustn't do that in that beautiful dress.
Take the chair.'

The only other chair in the room was a carved wooden
one with a barred back and curving arms, such as one sees
in a farmhouse kitchen. Adeline pulled it up to the desk
and sat down. As she did so she observed for the first time
that Marian Elverstone was barefoot, her feet a bluey-
white on the bare boards.

'Aren't you cold?' she asked. Marian shook her head. 'It
was snowing when we arrived, quite hard.' She stood,
leaned across and drew aside the curtain covering the small
window beyond the desk. The black air flickered with
dancing flakes. 'Yes, look! It might be a white New Year's
Day.'

She stared out, transfixed by the silent, rushing beauty
of the snow and the sense of privileged secrecy that it lent
to the attic room.

'Close that, would you?'

She let the curtain drop and sat down again. It was clear
that Marian had not been interested in the snow, but now
she looked up again at Adeline with the suggestion of a
smile on her tremulous, drooping mouth.

'I suppose they sent you to spy on me,' she said.

Adeline was shocked. 'No-one knows I'm here.'

'I'm quite safe up here, I suppose . . . that's what I like
to think. It's probably foolish of me. Nowhere is really
safe, but here – ' She looked up at the sloping ceiling,

turning her head to scan it. 'Here there's no-one above me, and only that door, which I can keep locked.' She pointed to it with a sort of pride.

Adeline felt a cold surge of anxiety.

'I should say you were perfectly safe,' she said. 'Is this where you write?'

'Write?'

'Were you writing – I mean, have you been writing, earlier this evening?'

'No. Oh no.' Marian shook her head again. 'I have to be so careful.' She seemed to have forgotten that she still held a lighted cigarette, a long tube of hot ash fell on to her lap and singed her dress as she let it lie there.

'Here, let me.' Adeline brushed it off, feeling the cool, narrow thighs beneath the skirt, conscious suddenly of her own strength, and warmth and energy. She would have liked to take Marian in her arms and comfort her, but the desire to do so startled and embarrassed her.

'What are you working on at the moment?' she said. 'I'm afraid I haven't read any of your books, or not yet, but they're always marvellously reviewed.' She was babbling foolishly but couldn't seem able to stop. 'And now I shall read them with special attention because I've seen the place where they're written – '

'No, no, you shouldn't be in here . . .' Marian got up, letting the shawl slide to the ground and dropping the cigarette end which Adeline retrieved from the floor and threw into the fireplace. The grate was choked with burned paper like thin black leaves. Marian began to touch and sift through the things on the desk as if looking for something, but her movements became increasingly uncontrolled. Pencils rattled to the floor, the inkwell over-turned and a glossy black lake bloomed over the note-books and loose sheets of paper, all of which, Adeline now realized, were blank. She swept the vase of carnations off and they lay amidst the pieces of shattered vase in a small pool of rusty, dank-smelling water. She seemed frantic now with anxiety, her eyes darting here and there, endlessly searching, her hands flying blindly amongst the ink-soaked papers, her breathing quick and shallow.

Her panic infected Adeline. 'Please, don't!' she cried, rising so quickly that the heavy wooden chair crashed backwards. 'What are you looking for? You must let me help!'

'There's nothing here,' Marian whispered, 'someone's taken it, someone's been here . . .'

'What's missing? If you don't tell me I can't do anything – ' Adeline reached out and grasped Marian's wrists, hoping to contain the destructive gale of energy that threatened to destroy the room.

What happened next took her utterly by surprise. Though Marian's wrists felt as thin and brittle as twigs in her hands, both arms forced upwards with an explosive, jerking movement and were free. In the second that it took Adeline to recover, Marian's left hand, bunched into a fist, came down to deal her a hard blow on the side of the face. The attack was so unexpected and so powerful that Adeline staggered back, catching her heavy skirt on the legs of the upended chair and falling. Her cheekbone smarted and throbbed, she could feel the warm crawl of blood over an incipient swelling as she struggled to her feet, but already Marian seemed to have forgotten her and was continuing with her ransacking of the desk. She was muttering fiercely, her face contorting into a series of grimaces as she conducted some terrifying internal battle. Small sobs broke from her at intervals.

Adeline was afraid – afraid of the other woman's unpredictability, afraid of her fear, and the unknown thing she feared. But neither did she want to leave her.

'I'll fetch your husband,' she said loudly knowing that her presence was forgotten and her voice could not be heard.

Out on the landing the dog sat near the top of the stairs, but as Adeline emerged he ran away with his tail between his legs as if expecting to be struck. She shut the door firmly and followed him down the two flights of stairs to the hall. The drawing room door stood open, warmth, smoke and noise tumbled from it like the contents of an over-full cupboard. As Adeline, breathless, reached the last stair Neville emerged and picked up the hurtling dog in his arms.

'Bloomer old son, where've you been? Consett'll scrag you if she finds out you were here all the time . . . my dear child, what have you done to your face?'

Adeline wiped the blood from her cheek with the back of her hand. 'It's nothing, I fell over – '

'But it looks ghastly. You must – '

'No, no!' In her agitation she felt tears welling in her eyes. 'It's your wife – I heard her crying and went to talk to her. I don't think she's at all well . . . she might hurt herself.'

'God in heaven!' A changed man, grimmer, older, he released the dog and dashed past her, disappearing up the stairs two at a time.

Nicholas and Ida appeared in the doorway. When Nicholas saw her he closed the door behind him. Ida gasped.

'Adeline, there's blood on your face.'

'Scrapping again,' said Nicholas.

'I went upstairs to look at some pictures and tripped in the dark. It's this long skirt, and I'm such a clumsy great fool . . .' She wondered why her instinct prompted her to lie to them. Nicholas stood with his hands in his pockets, the trace of a maddening smile on his face.

Ida bustled forward. 'Well, however you did it we must clean it up. You poor thing, come with me and we'll find a basin and some water.'

They went to a large cloakroom at the back of the house, with a black and white tiled floor. Like everywhere else it was cluttered: with garden tools, easels, brushes standing in cans of turps, boots and shoes, tennis racquets broken and unbroken, desiccated plants over-wintering in pots. There was a large, cracked stone sink, and Ida soaked her lace handkerchief in cold water and applied it with small, dabbing strokes to Adeline's face.

'I don't know . . . the oddest things happen in this house. Does this hurt?' Adeline shook her head, wincing.

'I blame the wine they serve. I always have a terrible hangover afterwards. I should stick to whisky.'

'But I only had one glass!'

'Of course!' Ida gave her a shrewd glance. 'You've been exploring. I suppose Neville told you to go where you liked.'

'He did, actually.'

Without it having been said in so many words, Adeline inferred from Ida's remarks that she had some idea of the truth.

'Look at yourself,' said Ida, holding up a small mirror from her evening bag.

'Oh hell . . . ! What a sight!' Adeline noted with horror a rapidly closing eye, a large and inflamed contusion crowned with a congealing blob of blood, hair in wild disarray, and a generally febrile and over-excited air that contrasted oddly with the velvet dress.

'You're right,' she said. 'I'll need a good story.'

Nicholas was waiting in the hall.

'Want to dance?' he asked, and for once she was glad of his coldness, his inability to express concern of any sort.

'Aren't you playing?'

'They've resorted to the phonograph.'

'I will dance then, in a moment. It's just – I think I left something upstairs.'

She saw from his face that he was about to advise against it, so she quickly left his side, gathered up her skirt in one hand and ran quickly and quietly up the stairs.

She heard some murmured remark of Ida's, and the door swung to behind them, stifling the sound of the party.

In the large bedroom, the light was on. The door was half open and Adeline could see both Neville Elverstone and his wife. She stood like a penitent as he undressed her. Her head was bowed passively, her long elegant hands hung at her sides. She looked almost as if she were asleep on her feet. Neville removed the blue dress, unbuttoning it at the front and slipping it down over her shoulders to the ground, tapping her thin white legs one at a time to make her step out of it. Beneath it was a white cotton petticoat that bore the small brown mark of the hot ash Marian had let fall on her lap. Neville removed the petticoat in the same way, so that for a moment his wife's arms were pinned to her sides by the narrow straps. At this precise moment he kissed her on her bare, angular shoulder. Adeline caught her breath.

When she was naked Neville moved out of sight for a moment, leaving her standing there. Her body was willowy and fragile, sensuous and yet ambiguous, reminding Adeline of the Saint Sebastian of mediaeval paintings. The breasts were as slight as those of a budding young girl, but with the slight droop of an older woman, the flesh of the stomach swelled just perceptibly outward towards the triangle of dark hair at the top of the legs. Her body looked the very essence of female vulnerability, and yet – Adeline put her hand to her mouth. She experienced a violent throb of desire.

Neville returned with a long, white nightdress which he slipped over Marian's head, lifting her arms one by one and coaxing her hands into the sleeves and through the smocked cuffs, tying a length of ribbon at the neck. He was as tender and solicitous as a mother now, the ardour of the stolen kiss was gone. He moved away again briefly, perhaps to rearrange the bed, and it was now that Marian looked up. Her large, frightened eyes were vague and unseeing, and then seemed suddenly to focus on Adeline. Her eyebrows drew together as if she were struggling to recollect where she had seen this face before. One hand closed and opened convulsively. Adeline put her finger to her lips and then turned and ran, her heart racing, back down the stairs.

CHAPTER FIFTEEN

1925

ON THE MORNING of New Year's Day, 1925, Consett set about the awesome task of clearing up after the party at 12 Allerton Square. She consoled herself with the thought that she was the only person of the six remaining in the house who felt well. At ten o'clock the Elverstones had still not emerged from their room. Three of the guests who had slept the night – Ida, Nicholas and Paul Hudson – were collected palely about the dining-room table drinking coffee and picking at dry toast. When she drew the curtains in the drawing room, another – Terence – was revealed, deeply asleep on the sofa, the long-drawn-out vibrato of his snores making his wispy beard tremble. She gave his shoulder a far-from-respectful shake, but he only snorted and moaned and curled up with his back to her, like a child. Crossly she cleared up round him, stumping about the room, clattering glasses and ashtrays and crashing furniture. The place stank of stale smoke and drink, and those unfinished scraps of food which the perishing dog had been unable to reach and which had consequently lain out on plates all night. She flung open the windows at the front and back of the room, her face pinched with disgust. Outside the snow of the night before had given way to a raw grey chill. Some patches of white prettified the garden in the centre of the square, otherwise whatever snow had lain had become speckled grey crusts of frozen slush along the gutters and in the lee of walls.

Unfortunately Consett knew that the mess in the drawing room would be the least of her worries. Once she had found a hypodermic syringe in the bathroom, whose purpose she could only guess at darkly. And the Elverstones' friends with a few drinks inside them were not as careful as they might be when using the lavatory. More sinister still, on this occasion she had come across traces of blood in the cloakroom sink. And then there was upstairs . . . she shook her head and blew out her cheeks as she contemplated the bedrooms. Consett had a friend who was by way of being a dressmaker, and who was continually advising her to hand in her notice rather than submit to further indignities, but though Consett agreed that it was scandalous what she had to put up with, she could never quite get round to leaving. Life was certainly not dull in Allerton Square, she was never short of something to talk about, and she was well paid. Besides, who else would they find to do their dirty work?

The doorbell rang. It was a delivery from Moyses Stevens, the florist: a sheaf of white roses offset against some dark green trailing foliage, a touch funereal in Consett's opinion.

'Bouquet for Mrs Elverstone,' said the man. 'There's a card with it.'

'Very nice,' said Consett. 'She's not up, but I'll see she gets it. Not much of a day, is it? Do you want a cup of tea?'

'Thanks all the same but I've got to get going.' The man looked beyond her and grinned as Terence staggered across the hall, yawning and scratching. 'Looks like you got a houseful, anyway.'

'Hm.' Consett gave Terence's receding back view a

glare of pure scorn. 'They can look after themselves, but if you can't stop you can't stop.'

Disappointed, she closed the door after him. She would have liked the opportunity for a cup of tea and a chat with a civilized human being.

Ida and Paul Hudson emerged from the dining room and began putting on coats.

'Oh, Consett, aren't they heavenly! Who are they for?' asked Ida, advancing to take a closer look, but Consett was too quick for her.

'Mrs Elverstone,' she said from halfway up the stairs.

On the landing her own curiosity got the better of her and when she was sure she could not be seen from below she took the card from its thick white envelope and studied it. Whoever it was had such large writing that they had not only scrawled across the address of the florist but covered both sides of the card as well.

The sender had begun by putting 'Dear Marian' and then added 'and Neville' as an afterthought, obviously, for the two words hovered above the rest of the line. 'Thank you for a memorable evening.' Consett smiled grimly at this. 'I hope Marian will soon feel better – Yours, Adeline Charteris.'

'Soon feel better' was it? Consett replaced the card in the envelope. So she was not herself. That would explain a good deal of the ructions which had grumbled and spat in the background for the past couple of months. Temper tantrums over nothing, things wilfully broken, shouting matches at all hours of the day and night. And in between, nice as pie and perfectly normal, or what passed for normal in this house. And weeks of it still to come, she had no doubt . . .

Gathering herself together, she pounded on the bedroom door. When there was no response she called. 'Sir? Madam? Flowers for Mrs Elverstone.'

There was a creak of bedsprings and footsteps padded across the room. The door was opened by Mr Elverstone, obviously just aroused from sleep, but still dressed in shirt and trousers.

'Oh . . . Consett.' He thrust his hands into his hair and pushed it back from his face, which was red-eyed and unshaven. He looked, thought Consett, like death warmed up. He stared blearily and uncomprehendingly at the bouquet. 'What's this?'

'Bouquet arrived for Mrs Elverstone.'

'Deal with it, would you?'

'Very well.' She was about to go when he seemed to change his mind and held out his hand for the flowers.

'On second thoughts I'll show it to her. She's not feeling too good today – might cheer her up. Just stay there a second.' He disappeared with the bouquet and returned carrying Bloomer. For a moment Consett thought he was going to hand her the dog to hold in the same way. She bristled with indignation but, after giving it a kiss, he set the animal on the ground. 'Take Bloomer back down with you and let him out in the garden. She'll be upset if she wakes up and finds him in the room.'

This was one matter in which Consett was in complete accord with Mrs Elverstone. She dragged the unwilling dog across the landing by his collar and sent him summarily down the stairs. As she followed she could have sworn she heard – though her suspicious imagination may have supplied the image – the rustle of the roses being dropped on the floor. She sucked her teeth. They didn't know how lucky they were to have even one guest with the manners and consideration to thank them and send flowers. Most of them, she considered, were just so much lah-di-dah riff-raff.

Adeline had been unable to sleep for the remainder of the night after the party. She had stayed until after midnight, not because she wished to see the new year in but in the vain hope that Neville might reappear with news of Marian. None of the other guests seemed either surprised or put out by the absence of their hosts and because she herself felt in some way privileged to know a little of what had gone on upstairs she did not discuss it. The few who enquired about the injury to her face were easily satisfied

with the explanation of a fall. Only Nicholas looked at her
in a way which suggested that he knew more than he let
on, smiling with a secretive, arrogant awareness which
infuriated her. When, at half past twelve, there was no
sign of Neville she announced that she was going and
Nicholas did not try to detain her. In the hall he leaned
against the wall watching her as she searched for her cloak
and put it on. She realized, with a mixture of relief and
indignation, that he was not going to offer to accompany
her, though he did ask discouragingly if she wanted him
to call a taxi, and she refused, for once glad of his rudeness.

'So have you enjoyed yourself?' he asked as she was
about to go.

Even had she wished to she could not have begun to
describe to Nicholas the turmoil of confused, new
emotions engendered by that evening.

'It was very interesting,' was all she said. She supposed
she ought to thank him. 'Thank you.' He shrugged.
Something occurred to her. 'I'm surprised Fenella wasn't
here.'

'Fenella?' His eyebrows rose. 'This is no place for Fenella.'

Suddenly she was exhausted, tried beyond endurance
by his lack of directness. Her face hurt. She felt the strain
of the evening like a physical pull on all her muscles. She
wanted more than anything to be alone with her thoughts
which at present, with Nicholas there, she could not take
out and examine.

'I have to be going,' she said. 'Goodbye.'

He didn't answer, but lifted one hand, palm outwards,
like a red indian. Outside she found that she felt no trepidation about walking home alone in the small hours. The
snow had stopped falling and this was the brief period
when it lay, pure and secret and unmarked, on the ground.
Her footsteps were the first, and the last, to be printed on
it. She drifted, her tiredness gone, and the sounds of other
parties behind warmly curtained windows made her feel
solitary but not alone. She was lifted and carried by an
elation she'd never experienced before, compounded of

delight and longing and sadness, and a certainty that she would see Marian Elverstone again.

Back at Gower Street she undressed and got into bed, but instead of sleeping she rehearsed over and over again the events of the evening, certain scenes and images which were fixed in her memory so that she could replay them at will in perfect detail, like a magic lantern show. Of these, three were clearer than all the others: her very first impression of Marian, resonating with wild, angry fear; Marian's stooped, seated back view, arm outstretched to implore help from her, a total stranger, and the words 'I have no peace'; and then that brief, piercing moment when their eyes had met, across the black divide of Marian's distress and there had seemed for a second to be a fine thread of communication between them. Adeline did not think she was deluding herself in believing that the thread was still there, strong and resilient in spite of its fineness, and that it would not easily snap.

In the early morning, lightheaded from lack of sleep, she put Clancey on his lead and walked all the way to Moyses Stevens in Victoria, arriving before the doors opened. Her bruised face, her urgently commanding manner and her large dog assured her of the shop's best attentions if only in order to get rid of her, and she handed over what she knew was a ludicrous sum on the understanding that the flowers would be delivered at once. Exhausted, she caught a taxi back. When on her return she found Peter on the doorstep, come to collect her for a day in the country about which she had entirely forgotten, she did not at first even recognize him. Or at least he was like a person in a dream whom one knows to be familiar, but not how, or why, or from where. She actually stopped at the foot of the steps and stared at him, trying to collect her thoughts.

'Morning!' he called, running down the steps and approaching her in his cheerful, open way, spreading his arms for her. 'Happy New Year! Hangover?'

She shook her head, confused, smiling in his boisterous

embrace but feeling that her heart would break with disappointment.

He drew back to look at her. 'I hope you won.'

'I'm sorry . . .?' He touched the cut on her face. 'Oh, I fell over.'

'Are you all right?'

'I'm fine.'

'Where've you been at this hour, and the morning after the night before, too?'

'Oh, just out for a walk . . . you know what it is when you don't get to bed till the small hours. You don't sleep well.'

'We're going out though? I've got the jalopy in town specially.'

'Just let me get ready.'

'You don't need to – you look wonderful to me as you are.'

She could only allow herself to be carried along by his happy, dependable, unwavering devotion, and try to feel fortunate. But both the day out and Peter himself seemed entirely unreal. She expressed pleasure and gratitude as best she could because the last thing on earth she wanted to do was hurt Peter, but the expressions were hollow. The true, feeling part of her was shut away, jealously guarding ripe, raw longings like an animal with a fresh kill. He was no fool. On the way back from Maidenhead in the dark, humming intimacy of the car he said, his eyes on the road, 'So how was it at the Elverstones' last night?'

Now she was touched. Her eyes smarted with sudden tears. She could not discuss it with him.

'It wasn't too bad.' She felt him glance at her. 'I see what you mean about them.'

'Nick being civil?' She nodded. 'Good, because I sat about all evening thinking about you and wondering why on earth I let you go.'

'Then why did you?' Her voice, which she had meant to be teasing, sounded a little desperate, even to her.

But he misunderstood her. 'You know why, they're the centre of a high-powered artistic world. Silly to ignore it.

And bad manners apart, I knew you wouldn't come to any harm with Nick – his interest lies in other directions as you may have gathered.'

She realized he meant Fenella, and seized the opportunity to change the subject. When they reached Gower Street she pleaded tiredness and escaped, her mood changing the moment the front door closed behind her. Here, there was always the possibility that they might summon her, and all her energies, which returned as she flew up the stairs, could be poured into awaiting that summons, and being ready for it.

The next day came, and went, and the next, and several after that. There was no summons. As the interminable hours of waiting shuffled by, Adeline could not rid herself of those images of Marian. They grew sharper and clearer as the rest of the evening began to fade, and she polished and examined them and tried to interpret their meaning as an explorer might with the strange mysterious treasures of some remote tribe.

She walked about in a kind of trance, unable to concentrate on even the simplest domestic task, let alone any painting or drawing. When from time to time she caught sight of her reflection it was a shock to find that she still had that solid, corporeal existence, that shock of dark hair, those fiercely bright eyes. She felt herself to be a vaporous, insubstantial being without identity or definition, a hollow vessel waiting to be filled. Waiting.

Each bitterly cold morning with Clancey she walked past the house in Allerton Square, hoping for some happy accident – a chance meeting, an invitation to go inside, simply a glimpse of Marian through one of the long windows. But the only person she saw was the surly Consett, shaking a duster, flapping a rug, collecting milk from the cart. Otherwise the house presented an aspect so closed, contained and secretive that had it not been for those vivid mental pictures she could scarcely believe she'd ever been there. On New Year's Eve it had seemed the most vital place in the world. Now it was as stiff and cold as a death mask. The realization that she – like so many others, apparently – had come under the spell of the house's occupants, and especially of Marian, did not make her rebellious. She submitted to the spell willingly, she longed to be consumed in it. She alternated between elation at what might happen, and despair at what might not. She lived in dreams. The flowers that she had sent took on in her imagination the role of hostages to fate. She pictured Marian arranging them lovingly, placing some, perhaps, on her desk so that they were by her as she wrote, leaving them there until they withered and died. While the white roses were inside that closed house she would not be forgotten.

In the Elverstones' bedroom the roses lay abandoned on the floor where Neville had dropped them, the crisp, half-open hothouse heads turning brown and rotten, the glossy foliage first withering and then becoming as grey and desiccated as ash, so that the draughts from the doorway caught and scattered it across the room. On the dressing table, as often as not, was a tray of untouched food, prepared by Consett, brought by Neville at appropriate times and removed an hour later. There was no time in the room. The curtains were drawn, so it was always dusk. Marian walked up and down, up and down, her arms clasped tightly about her, until she was too tired to walk further, and collapsed on the bed to sleep a dead and leaden sleep. Her inward-looking terror was pitiful. Only Neville could come near her. She did not recognize him but at least she seemed to sense his familiarity and concern, as a blind and injured dog will with a master it trusts. Nothing could be moved: though she seemed not to notice her surroundings, the tiniest change in them caused her to panic and rage. Who had been here? Why had they touched her things? What were they trying to do to her? Nothing could persuade her to leave the bedroom, either. It was both her prison and her sanctuary. Neville brought warm water, face flannel, towel, clean clothes and she submitted to his ministrations with a vacant, doll-like stiffness. When she slept he changed the pillowcases, put the bundle of dirty washing outside the door, emptied the chamber pot. He was patient and tireless. He would brook no partisan sympathy from Consett, and he asked for no help because it was impossible for anyone to give it.

From time to time as Marian walked to and fro she would step on the stalks of the roses and the thorns would scratch her bare feet. When they had been dead for some days Neville threw them away to save her from further injury. The moment she awoke she saw what he had done and attacked him, a clawing, flailing uncontainable dervish, her very brittleness making her impossible to withstand. He clasped his arms over his head and waited until she was exhausted. When, burned out, she slept again, he let Bloomer into the room and they lay together, dog and man, on the carpet, and slept with her.

The day after this had happened, a week into the New Year, Neville went down into the hall in his stockinged feet to talk to Nicholas Eyre. Weary and dishevelled, but pleased to see him, he put one arm around Nicholas' neck and kissed him.

'Dear Nick . . . I can't be long. If she wakes up and finds she's alone there'll be hell to pay.' He sat down heavily on the bottom stair and rubbed his hands back and forth over his head. Nicholas sat by him and took out a packet of cigarettes. He lit one and handed it to Neville, lit another for himself.

'It looks as if there has been already,' he said.

'What?'

'Hell to pay.'

Neville glanced down ruefully at the backs of his hands, covered with scratches and bruises where he had fended off his wife's blows. 'You know how it is.'

'Not really. Is she very bad this time?'

'Yes. I knew she would be. It's been brewing for such a long time. It's pathetic to see her –' He looked away, drawing on his cigarette but failing to disguise the trembling of his mouth. 'I'm just so tired, Nick, so bloody tired.'

'Have you had the doctor?'

'Well I have, I always do, but it's a waste of time. She abuses him shockingly, and he can only advise that she be sedated and taken into some heinous institution or other which she would never survive and I'll never allow. No, it simply has to be ridden out. It's not as if I don't know that, but I'm getting older, I don't have the stamina I used to.'

'I think you should let her go somewhere – just for the duration of the illness. I don't suppose for a moment she knows where she is. She'd be expertly looked after and you'd get a rest.'

'Bugger expert help. No, sorry Nick. I know what you're saying but it would be absolutely impossible. She does know where she is. Not consciously perhaps, but if there's the slightest change she's aware of it. If she woke up from a doped stupor and found herself in a hospital room I dread to think what she might do to herself, or other people. She went beserk because I took away some dead roses. Oh, by the way, I think they were sent by that woman you brought to the party, that big fierce girl with the – ' His hands executed a sweeping downward gesture indicative of a long skirt.

'Yes. Adeline Charteris.'

'That's it. I thought it was her when I saw the card. Well she sent these roses the morning after, which was rather sweet of her. If you see her would you be kind enough to thank her?'

'Of course.'

'Thank you.' Neville laid his hand briefly against Nicholas's cheek. 'Look, I'd better go. Thanks for coming.' They both rose.

'I'll be back.' said Nicholas.

'Do, any time. Just don't expect too much of me.'

Nicholas watched Neville as he trudged back up the stairs. Back to his self-inflicted purgatory, he thought. Back to his bloody self-indulgent penal servitude. Still, he reflected, smiling to himself as he left the house, things were progressing satisfactorily. Once Marian pulled herself together he confidently expected to occupy Neville's whole attention.

The currents of her everyday life – friends, meetings, work, family – flowed round and past Adeline as she clung tenaciously but with increasing desperation to her memories of the party. By the third week in January it was no longer possible to avoid her commitments. This was the week of Fenella Marchant's first sitting, and soon term would start, but her spirit was elsewhere. Her friends knew her well enough to see the difference in her, but she brushed aside their tactful oblique enquiries. The clue to the exact nature of her feelings was to be found in her reaction to Peter. She discovered that she could no longer bear his stubborn, determined love, far less his touch which embarrassed and appalled her as though it were the manifestation of some sordid personal weakness. Not wanting to hurt him, she simply said that she wanted to concentrate on her work and the portrait of Fenella. That was all right with him, he said, he understood, she must have time to herself. His very niceness sickened her, as did the implication that he would bide his time until she recovered, for she had no wish to recover. It was Marian Elverstone's embrace she craved. It took Bob who, in the way of brothers, was not hampered by concerns of delicacy or tact, to exclaim bluntly: 'Good God, Addy, you look awful!'

He and Toni were about to go out to dinner and had called in to see her first, as they generally did. Toni, who privately agreed with him, came to Adeline's defence.

'She does not. She's just lost some weight, which is more than most of us have managed to do over Christmas.' She glanced first down at herself, then at Adeline, and smiled. Bob took his sister by the shoulders and made her face the mirror, looking over her shoulder accusingly.

'Lost some weight? Look at yourself, you're a cadaver.'

She shrugged free, not caring for that burned-up, ghostly creature she had become. 'I ride my bicycle all over the place.'

Bob made an impatient gesture like waving away a fly.
'Forget I said it.'

The conversation became general, about a play they had
seen, about work, about Bob's visit to Toni's family over
Christmas. Adeline sat with her features arranged in an
expression of affectionate interest, longing for them to be
gone. When they finally did move off, Bob said: 'By the
way, did you know Howard had been ill?'

'No. I saw him at Christmas. He seemed fine then.'

'He had a heart attack. Nothing much, I gather, just a
twinge. He's getting on for sixty after all, and he doesn't
exactly lead a healthy outdoor life. You ought to go and
shine the light of your countenance on him, Addy, he's
always liked you.'

'Yes, well . . . I might.'

As she saw them out she reflected that never in a million
years could she face Howard, even a debilitated Howard,
at the moment. How could she expose the woman Bob
had showed her in the mirror to that dark, direct glare?
No, she would write him a letter and stay away.

Fenella Marchant came on 18 January. She arrived in
Gower Street driving herself in a white sports car which
she parked two and half feet from the kerb and at a sharp
angle. She wore a black and white hounds-tooth check
suit with a long, loose jacket and pleated skirt, a tiny,
close-fitting black hat, a pillar-box red scarf at her neck.
Adeline, having watched her arrival from the window,
went down to open the door before Mrs Fairyhouse could
lay claim to this vision of wealth and elegance.

'Heavens, how *priceless*!' carolled Fenella of the stuffed
animals as they went up the stairs and then, as Adeline
showed her in, 'What an *interesting* room, you don't know
how I envy you your independence!'

But she went to the window and stood looking out as
if reminding herself that escape was always possible.

The impulse which had prompted Adeline to write to
Fenella now seemed so strange and distant that she experienced a bafflement with the situation which bordered on

panic. What had she been thinking of? Why was this woman, with whom she had nothing in common, here at all?

'Do you want to take off your jacket?' she asked frostily.

'Yes, it's so beautifully warm in here,' said Fenella, unable to keep the note of surprise out of her voice. As she handed her things to Adeline she caught sight of Clancey who had been standing just behind her, waving his tail, waiting patiently to be greeted. 'Oh, aren't you a poppet!' she exclaimed and sank to her knees to make a fuss of him. Adeline realized that she was not the only one who felt awkward with the situation, and that as its initiator she must take responsibility for its success.

'I thought we might have some lunch here,' she said, 'and get to know each other a bit this time. I'll make some sketches while we talk.'

'Do whatever you like, I'm in your hands. But you shouldn't have bothered about lunch.'

'It's only some bread and cheese and things.'

'*Anything* – I hardly eat.'

'And some beer. Would you like some?'

'I've never had it, but I'd love to try.' Fenella returned to the fire and stood before it, studying the sketches that were pinned along the rim of the mantelpiece.

'Are these yours? They're so amusing. You are lucky to have a talent, and clever to be able to use it. I can't do anything.'

She made this last remark with a self-conscious laugh. Adeline warmed to her, and was struck again by the ambivalence, the curious contradictions in her guest which were, of course, the reason she had wished to paint her. She handed Fenella a mug and a bottle of beer.

'I'm sure that isn't true. For a start, anyone who dresses so beautifully as you do must have a good deal of artistic sense.'

'Oh, clothes!' Fenella gave another laugh, this time scornful. 'Anyone can dress nicely if they have the money. Oh dear –' She poured the beer inexpertly and it foamed over the edge of the mug. 'I'm so sorry!'

'It doesn't matter,' said Adeline, 'Clancey'll lick it up, it's his favourite tipple.'

'Nicholas always tells me I'm a duffer with my hands. He plays the piano quite wonderfully, you know, but as a child I never even got past 'Twinkle, Twinkle Little Star'. My fingers simply wouldn't do it.' She spread her left hand and surveyed it in consternation. Adeline noticed for the first time that the long, fine-boned fingers were stub-ended: Fenella bit her nails.

'You met Nicholas, didn't you?' she went on.

'Yes.'

Fenella sighed and sat down gracefully, and with an admirable lack of caution, on one of Adelhne's lumpy junk-shop chairs. 'He keeps me up to the mark.'

'Is that necessary?'

'Oh, *yes*! I'm very spoilt and sheltered.' Again the little laugh. 'I simply adore Nicholas. I do so admire anyone who can strike out on their own the way he has done, not just do what everyone expects of them. Don't you?' she asked abruptly, as if feeling she'd talked for too long and must draw Adeline into the conversation. But then before Adeline could answer she added: 'But of course you're like that. A free spirit. I'd like to be, but I'm afraid it's just not in me.'

Adeline was quite glad to have been spared the necessity of making any comment on Nicholas's supposedly admirable qualities. She was certain Fenella knew nothing of the Elverstones, or the events of New Year's Eve. Nicholas Eyre kept his life in watertight compartments.

She said: 'You could do whatever you liked, I'm sure.'

'Well I could afford to, I know –'

'I didn't mean that.'

'– but my life's mapped out for me, really. Everyone seems to know that I shall marry some very suitable person, and have children, and entertain smartly in a house in the country and a flat in Belgravia.'

'And what about you? Do you think they're right?'

'I'm sure they are. The only thing I might do to surprise them is marry someone not quite so suitable.' She gave

Adeline a mischievous smile, the first glint of real confidence she had displayed since arriving. Taking a gold case from her handbag she offered a cigarette to Adeline, placed one in a gold and ivory holder for herself and leaned forward as Adeline lit them both with a spill from the gas fire. 'Now then,' she said, 'tell me. What must I do? Must I sit stock still and not talk?'

'On the contrary, you must talk as much as you can. I want to get to know you as well as possible in a short time, so that I can decide exactly how I'm going to paint you.'

Fenella pulled a face. 'Don't expect too much. I'm not at all a deep or interesting person, as everyone will tell you.'

As Adeline had suspected, once she had gone to the kitchen to fetch food, Fenella began to talk more freely. There were no revelations, it was the cheerful stream of chatter of someone used to making small talk and to concealing any worries and weaknesses beneath a girlish vivacity. People and events were described as being either 'tremendous fun' or 'the most frightful bore'. The picture that emerged was of a conventional, privileged upbringing, coloured by the well-meaning callousness of the English aristocracy. A childhood busy with improving and often strenuous activity, most of which Fenella had disliked, but accepted in good part as being the way things were done. Her parents emerged as 'darlings', though distant, and Peter as a kindly and protective brother who 'put up with' her and her lack of competence to a quite unlooked-for extent. So the young Fenella had learnt poise, if not composure, in the exacting school of dances, house parties, tennis teas and theatre suppers. She was a sparkling, brittle artifice of acquired skills without an ounce of real self-esteem to support it.

Adeline took the tray of bread and cheese and put it on the settle between their chairs. Clancey advanced to a judicious distance and lay down, his head on his paws, staring soulfully at the food.

'Just look at him,' said Fenella. She cut off a knob of cheese. 'Is he allowed?'

'Not really.'

'Just this once.' She threw the cheese to the dog.

'Don't stand on ceremony,' said Adeline, 'help yourself.'

'Thank you.' Fenella continued to smoke, and watch. She had drunk none of the beer.

After a moment or two of watching Adeline eat, she stubbed out the cigarette, laid the holder carefully across the ashtray, and took a very small piece of cheese and a stalk of celery at which she nibbled tentatively. When Adeline neither commented on her lack of appetite nor pressed her to take more, she cut herself some bread and began to eat more hungrily, sitting with her plate on her lap, knees together, feet apart.

'I was hungrier than I thought,' she said. 'Isn't it funny?'

'I know,' said Adeline. 'If you were an animal, which would you like to be? You first.'

'Women usually want to be cats, don't they, because cats are so glamorous and elegant, but I think it would be nice to be something homelier than that. When I was very little I had a sweet shaggy pony called Tinker. Actually I hated riding him, but he was the most adorable animal, I can't tell you. His life must have been absolute bliss because everyone loved him – I loved him more than I loved anything, including Mummy and Daddy. He didn't have to *do* anything for me to love him, just be himself. So that's me – a lovely shaggy pony belonging to a little girl like I was.'

'It does sound nice.'

'And what about you?'

Adeline put her plate down on the floor and, folding her arms, gazed up at the ceiling. 'I'd like to be . . . a bird, I think, something proud and predatory, living on rocky crags, a bird with a seven-foot wingspan and yellow eyes.'

'Yes, you could very easily be that,' agreed Fenella.

Adeline rubbed the bridge of her nose. 'I certainly have the beak for it. And the other part of the question is what you actually are. Which animal you yourself most resemble. I have a nasty suspicion that instead of an eagle

I'm a noisy, bossy, highly coloured parrot with far too much to say.'

But if she'd hoped to coax Fenella further from her shell, she failed. 'I don't know what I am,' she said, and then added with unexpected candour, 'that's my whole trouble.'

The afternoon wore on. Adeline sketched, and their conversation grew more desultory, but the silences were companionable. Fenella came into the minute kitchen alcove and helped to dry up plates in a vague, unpractised sort of way. Having done no work to speak of for more than a month, and having roused herself from the trance she had been in since the turn of the year, Adeline suddenly found that she was exhausted.

'I must take my dog out,' she said bluntly. 'Do you mind?'

'No, no, not at all! May I come too?'

Adeline could only agree, though in fact she longed to be alone. She felt treacherous, as though she had betrayed a trust by so wholeheartedly giving up these hours to Fenella and to the pursuit of an objective which in no way included Marian Elverstone. Every afternoon at this time the realization was forced upon her that yet one more day had gone by, and she had heard nothing.

Today, as the two of them left the house, it was still and grey and dank. The squares and terraces of Bloomsbury were like a materialization of the weather. Guessing rightly that it would mean nothing to Fenella, Adeline took her usual route through Allerton Square. As they walked slowly up the south side she could not resist saying: 'I know the people who live at Number Twelve. I was there on New Year's Eve.'

'Oh? Good party?'

Adeline realized that the gulf between Fenella's picture of a New Year's Eve party and the reality of that night was too great to bridge.

'Yes,' she said. 'It was quite.'

They were crossing the top of the square and Adeline had recalled Clancey from the garden and was putting on his lead, when Fenella, who was feeling the cold and stamping her feet, said: 'Look, are those your friends?'

Adeline looked up. Marian and Neville were dressed in outdoor clothes, Neville in a loose checked overcoat and soft hat, Marian in a green plaid cape which she held tightly swathed about her. She had a shawl over her head – the same black, fringed shawl that Adeline had placed round her shoulders in the attic room. Only her face was visible as they came down the steps together, a small, staring white disc. Even at this distance Adeline could distinguish the eyes, large and clear and slightly protruberant, shadowed by illness.

Fenella blew on her fingers in their black chamois gloves. 'Do you want to go and speak to them? Please do, don't mind me.'

'No. No, I shan't bother. She hasn't been well.' Even as she said it she wondered why, when she saw Marian now after the so much anxious waiting, she could not go up to her as any casual, friendly acquaintance might, and enquire after her health? And yet it was impossible. Everything about the two of them indicated that it would be a gross and insensitive invasion of privacy to do so. Neville was escorting his wife down the steps with one arm clasped about her shoulders. Marian stared straight ahead, apparently trusting him entirely to prevent her from falling. He looked from the ground to her face, and back again, solicitously.

'Oh dear,' said Fenella, 'she does look awfully frail.'

The Elverstones reached the pavement. Neville asked her something and slipped his arm through hers as if inviting her to walk. She took a step or two then stopped abruptly. He spoke to her, clasped her hands together in his, spoke again more urgently. But she shook her head, pulled her hands free and covered her face.

Fenella said something that Adeline did not hear. A hundred yards away Neville bent his head to Marian's, whispering, enquiring, cajoling. It was agony to Adeline to observe their intimacy, and not to be able to hear what passed between them. Marian moved her hands to the sides of her head as though shutting out what was being said to her. Neville, with a dispirited air of resignation, escorted his wife back up the steps, his arm round her shoulders as before, and into the house. Not once did Marian look up. Her narrow figure, swathed in shawl and cloak, head bowed, might have been that of an old woman.

Suddenly and cruelly, Adeline wished to be rid of Fenella.

'Let's go home,' she said. When, as they left the square, she glanced over her shoulder in the gathering darkness at the house, it was as closed and impassive as ever, and no window showed a light.

Somehow, she couldn't remember how, she said her farewells to Fenella and stood on the pavement waving as the sports car swung away from the kerb, pushing a funnel of yellow light in front of it. They had made an arrangement for a full sitting a week from today. So that she had time to reflect on the sketches, she had said, but in truth it was simply to get rid of Fenella. Her store of friendliness had been running low. The sight of Marian had dispelled it utterly. And Neville's loving kindness had been too much to bear. She was now sure of what she had only feared before, that she had been the merest casual visitor to their house, swiftly acknowledged and as swiftly forgotten. The circle was complete and she was not, nor ever could be, part of it.

Five days later she received a note from Marian Elverstone, delivered, apparently, by hand, for the handsome envelope bore only the words 'Adeline Charteris'. Inside, the note itself was written on a sheet of lined foolscap paper – the same paper, Adeline realized, that she had seen lying on Marian's desk. Trembling with excitement she read the note so quickly that she almost distilled its substance from its form at a single glance.

My dear unknown lady [Marian had written]. I believe

you sent some beautiful flowers, in spite of having seen me at my lowest and worst. I am not known for my organizational abilities, but should you care to come round to 12 Allerton Square at any time I should have an opportunity to express my gratitude and to further the friendship begun so inauspiciously.

I look forward with the keenest pleasure to our meeting again. Your unorthodox hostess, Marian Elverstone.

It was late afternoon on 23 January, and the letter was dated the same day. Adeline read the note through several times, in ecstasy. Coldness, tiredness, dullness left her, she was flooded with a warm and blissful energy. Every other consideration was swept aside to make way for this single, marvellous truth. She had not been forgotten. The summons had come.

CHAPTER SIXTEEN

1925

MARIAN ELVERSTONE WROTE. Her hand was stiff, and her shoulders tight and tense from concentration, and yet she was at ease. Body and mind were of one accord, bent to the task in hand, the activity at which they excelled. Everything was clear to her, both her surroundings and her thoughts. She wrote continuously, her imagination dictating the pages to her. She was completely immersed.

It wasn't always like this, of course. Marian was not one of those fortunate journeyman novelists who could write at will. For this reason she had long ago trained herself to take advantage of the creative mood, no matter what hour of the day or night it occurred and irrespective of who was in the house. This particular good spell was that which generally followed on a period of madness – she called it that because that was what it was. Marian did not care for euphemisms. And besides, madness was the only word which truly conveyed the horror and excitement she experienced.

Each time there were several clearly delineated stages, varying in length. After the nerviness and bad temper came confusion, immediately followed by the terror of madness itself, and oblivion. She would emerge from this in an exhausted and apathetic state, sure that she would never move, or speak, or initiate the smallest decision ever again, let alone write. Then suddenly, as yesterday, daylight would pierce the fog. Her body, weakened by weeks of abuse, would take longer to recover but her mind would open and flower and grow in strength by the hour as if it had fed on its own suffering.

The initial apathy was due in part to boredom. When she was ill everything centred on her. She felt herself to be the focus of the entire world. She was self-obsessed in a way that was impossible, afterwards, to convey to others, even to Neville. For the duration of the madness she inhabited a wild, exotic, dangerous and unpredictable landscape inside herself, a fearsome internal world in which she wandered alone and unprotected, prey to every horror and irrational fear that she encountered. Marian had spent most of her forty-two years devising and perfecting a style of living and behaving which rendered her as nearly emotionally invulnerable as it was possible to be. Madness stripped her utterly of that and left her as vulnerable, and yet as curiously protected, as an infant in a storm.

But no matter how terrifying this inner world, it was not dull. Everything in it was brighter, sharper, louder, more violent and more awesome than anything to be found in real life. When she was in it there was no energy to spare for the everyday processes that supported, like a skeleton, the limp fabric of a more normal existence. She could not eat – or only those mouthfuls which could be coaxed down her by her beloved Neville – and now, as she wrote, her blouse and skirt hung on her like the clothes of another person, and she could see the long bones fanning out on the back of her hand.

The world of madness had receded now to a distant, half-remembered clamour. The real world was back in focus, and she welcomed it. The transition from the one to the other had begun with the realization that she could hear what was being said to her, retain, interpret and respond to it. Then she had found that she could formulate small decisions for herself, and act upon them. If she wished to change her dress, she could do so. If she wanted something that was in another part of the house, she could ask for it and Neville would fetch it. The simple, satisfying patterns of cause and effect enchanted her.

Physical emergence from the cocoon of her room was more difficult. Her newly discovered lucidity seemed to depend on her being surrounded by familiar objects, and she felt that if she were to venture out into the strange and unfamiliar territory beyond her door she would panic, and once more spiral, helplessly, into insanity. It took all Neville's patience and persistence to persuade her to step first on to the landing, then to descend, falteringly, the stairs, finally to venture out of doors where the light, the air, the noise and the vastness almost stunned her.

Once the reclamation of her immediate surroundings was complete, her confidence returned in full. The simplest things, the domestic minutiae of life at 12 Allerton Square, gave her pleasure. Food, not just its taste but its appearance, smell and texture, was so wonderful that she couldn't get enough of it. She would go to the kitchen between meals in order to construct delicious savoury snacks for herself, much to Consett's fury.

Then there was the house, and everything in it. Neither of the Elverstones was much concerned with decor or interior decoration, preferring to allow their habitat to evolve and accumulate round them, layer upon layer, like vegetation in a rain forest. Piles of paper and periodicals, hundreds of paintings, sketches, cartoons, photographs and cuttings, *objets trouvés* of every description, stones, pieces of driftwood, pottery, curious and often vulgar bric-à-brac bought on holiday, rugs, shawls, hangings, plants, musical instruments – and people. Marian liked to gather them round her and absorb their variety. Now, after the weeks of exile, she gazed on her possessions with the delight of a blind person restored to sight. Was this entrancing and unusual carving really hers? Where had she found these shells? Had she read every one of these hundreds of books, row upon uneven row of separate worlds? The house was an Aladdin's cave of discovery and recognition.

The garden, even at this time of year, was her special province, the kingdom where Marian reigned supreme and unchallenged. Not for her ladylike ministrations with gloves, garden kneeler, trowel and trug. She would disappear into its narrow, high-walled depths and become part of it, hauling up weeds, setting new plants and tending established ones preferably not with tools, but by hand, losing all sense of time and emerging after hours soothed and content, her hands scratched and stained with earth. At the end of January there was little she could do in the garden, but she derived intense enjoyment from re-acquainting herself with it, simply walking round it, touching the plants and trees, seeing where the first snow-drops had sprouted and making plans for the spring. Near the house was a paved terrace where she and Neville sat in summer, but even this was in danger of being overtaken by encroaching undergrowth from the tubs, pots, urns and baskets placed around its edge.

Marian passionately loved flowers, but she would no sooner have picked them from her garden than commit murder. Cut flowers, in her opinion, were under sentence of death, and she consequently saw it as an act of mercy to buy them from stalls and barrows in the street. It was then her custom to keep them until they were dead, for she liked to think that in her care the poor things could at least live out their allotted span as naturally as possible instead of being trimmed, refreshed and then discarded the moment they began to wilt. The result of this whimsical notion, as Consett was quick to point out to anyone who would listen, was that the house was permanently full of dead and dying flora.

Marian had not, as Neville supposed, been entirely unaware of the bouquet which arrived on New Year's

Day. She had been conscious of it lying on the floor of the bedroom, a spray of white flowers against dark green leaves, eerily like flowers laid on a grave. In her imagination that was what they had become, flowers on her own grave, an appropriate remembrance from those who cared about her. When they disappeared she had felt furious, neglected and abandoned. It had been her blackest moment.

By the time she was better all that remained of the bouquet was the card which had accompanied it, which Neville had tucked into the corner of her dressing table mirror.

'What's this?' she'd asked one morning as she sat brushing her long, fine hair – another of those perfectly ordinary and necessary tasks which gave her pleasure during her convalescence.

Neville, standing behind her, rested his chin on the top of her head and slid his hands from her shoulders to where they covered, easily, her small, pointed breasts. She gazed with her large, cool eyes at his reflected face.

'It's from a young woman,' he said, teasing her nipples with his thumbs. 'A young woman who sent you flowers.' He kissed her hair. 'A young woman whom you've obviously enslaved, but about whom I suspect you remember nothing.'

Ignoring her husband's embrace she leant forward and removed the card from the mirror. As she read it she began once again to brush her hair with slow, idle strokes, and Neville, dismissed, leaned against the edge of the dressing table with his hands in his pockets.

Marian smiled. 'I see that you were an afterthought.'

'Nothing new in that.'

'A memorable evening . . . God in heaven . . . yours, Adeline Charteris. When was this?'

'She was at the party on New Year's Eve. Nick brought her. She was the one who found you.'

'Was I a brute to her?'

'You struck her in the face.'

'Poor little thing.' Marian's voice was amused rather than concerned. Neville laughed out loud.

'Little she was not. She was a great big woman, built like an opera singer, with a roman nose and beetling brows. Handsome if you like that sort of thing. But she'd make three of you, Mary-Anne,' he said, using the pet name that was the only means by which he reminded her of her need for him.

She put the card down, laid her hairbrush forgetfully on top of it and began coiling her hair at the back of her head. Neville's unflattering description of the young woman had connected with some half-formed memory.

'I'm off now,' he said. 'I've got a lunch at the Garrick. Will you be all right?'

'Of course.' She gave him one of the hooded ironic looks that disconcerted so many people. 'Don't worry, I shan't talk to any funny old country folk or bite any apples.'

When he'd gone she read the card again. No, this was not the handwriting of a poor little thing. It was huge, black and swift, whole words were written without the pen having been lifted from the paper. Marian was something of a student of calligraphy, and as she studied the writing the memory for which she had been blindly fumbling sprang abruptly into focus. She saw in her mind's eye the face of a woman, young and handsome, but too dark and emphatic for beauty. The woman was staring back at her with an expression so passionately intent that it could almost be felt, like a touch. Marian could not place this image in a context, either visual or spacial, and yet it was so vivid that she knew it for the distillation of a real encounter. It must be – she reached for the card again and glanced at it – Adeline Charteris.

It was an image that remained with her and this morning, out of curiosity rather than courtesy, she had written a note to Adeline Charteris. Having no idea of the address, she had given the envelope to Nicholas, when he called in on his way from the Waldorf, and asked him to deliver it.

In the days between her reading of the card and the

sending of the note the novel on her desk, begun in the autumn and sadly neglected, had spluttered and smouldered and finally burst into life, fanned by her renewed vision and energy. Now it positively blazed, and she felt compelled to tend it for hours each day, fuelling it and feeling its warmth rushing back to her, a constant cycle of regeneration. Having sent the note she thought no more about it. She was quite confident that her invitation would be accepted, either sooner or later.

The house in Allerton Square, its heart pumping again, had resumed its habitual pace. People came and went, music played, Bloomer barked and ran up and down the stairs, glasses and ashtrays accumulated on the downstairs furniture and the clumps of luminous snowdrops stood like sylphides in the brown and tangled winter garden. But Marian heeded none of it: she wrote. A fire had been lit in the grate, but she had since neglected it and now it was no more than a dwindling pile of grey rubble, veined with red. She did not, however, feel cold. When she was writing her face burned, and she often discarded her cardigan and her shoes. Then, when she finally pushed back her chair and stretched, she would feel the chill, and shiver, and wrap up and run down the stairs to pour herself a whisky aand to seek out Neville who knew how to hug and chafe her circulation back into life.

It was now five o'clock and the window in front of her desk, still uncurtained, was dark. The dull rattle of the doorbell sounded distantly, two floors below. She had heard it several times during the day and had identified, the voices of Ida, Terence and others. She had not been in the least inclined to go down and mix with them: Neville, whose concentration was at best a delicate plant, would be only too glad to do that.

She looked down at the page before her. Her fine, spidery, backward-leaning writing covered it like lace. Completed pages formed an untidy pile on the left of the desk, the smooth block of unused paper was on the right. Marian thought of the clean paper as a mountain which had to be dispersed, as it were, with a teaspoon, like the prince's challenge in the fairy story. The removal of one sheet made no visible difference to the pile and yet gradually, imperceptibly, it diminished. The satisfaction she gleaned from the task was incomparable. She picked up her pencil again, saw that it was worn to a stub, and took another from the tin. When all of them were blunted Neville would sharpen them with a penknife.

'Mrs Elverstone! Can you hear me?'

Marian could tell by the tone of Consett's voice that it was not the first time she had knocked on the door.

'Yes?'

'You have a visitor.'

'I don't. I don't have visitors, Consett.' She heard the exasperated sigh.

'As you wish, madam.'

'Who?'

'A Mrs Charteris. I'll say you're busy.'

Consett's footsteps receded across the landing. Marian pushed her chair back, went to the door and unlocked it.

'Consett!' The housekeeper turned, with a put-upon expression. 'I think perhaps I do want to see Mrs Charteris. Would you show her up?'

Consett made a point of rarely being surprised, but now she was ambushed by astonishment. 'What?' she exclaimed. 'Up here?'

'Certainly up here.'

Typical, grumbled Consett to herself as she made her way downstairs, typical of her to break the habit and rule of a lifetime and then behave as if other people were stupid for being surprised. But then what could you expect of a lunatic?

Before Consett could finish, Adeline said, 'I know my way,' and brushed past her, impervious to the look of pure vitriol she received for doing so. In the drawing room, Bloomer barked and a voice – Neville's – said, 'Wonder who that is?' but she didn't stop until she reached the second floor landing.

The door of Marian's study stood slightly ajar. Marian

herself was kneeling by the grate, rekindling the fire. She blew on the embers, put on some pieces of coal with her hand, and brushed aside a wisp of hair leaving a smudge on her forehead. Then she rose, and turning away from the door said in a calm voice devoid of the slightest agitation or excitement:

'Adeline, there you are!'

Adeline felt as though a harsh and heavy burden beneath which she had been labouring was suddenly lifted from her. Her body lightened, her head was clear, she felt as pliant and happy as a child who is at last in the very place it has always wanted to be. The weeks that had passed since she was last in this room seemed to contract and evaporate.

Still standing in the doorway, she said: 'You remember me.' It was an expression of wonder.

Marian sat down by her desk, but with her back to it. 'Of course. Come on in.'

Adeline entered and closed the door after her.

'Oh – I bolt it.'

Adeline did so. The secrecy of this action, and the implied privilege which it conferred on her, enthralled her.

She had remembered every detail of this room and it was almost exactly as she remembered it. Except that before, the room and its occupant had been in conflict: now they were in harmony. The desk was tidy; the work, she observed, was in progress; the fire glowed. Marian wore a long, loose dress in a print of reds and browns. Over the back of the chair she sat in hung a thick knitted cardigan, and beneath the desk lay a pair of scuffed, flat-heeled brown shoes. Her face was still pale, she was still thin, and her hair was untidy. But now the large, round eyes, instead of being a window on to that terrifying inner world, were calm and outward-looking as she smiled at Adeline.

'You must have come at once,' she said.

'Yes.' Adeline shrugged off her cloak and went to sit down, instinctively pulling the chair closer to Marian's like someone drawing up to a fire. 'I've been wanting so

much to see you and to know how you were. I've thought
of nothing else.'

Perfect directness seemed the best and most natural
thing here, and she did not even consider for one moment
the possibility of caution, or reticence. Indeed, such
behaviour she sensed would not only have been out of
place but wrong. Herself was all that she had, and she
offered it unreservedly.

'You must be better,' she went on. 'I see that you're
writing.'

'As much as I possibly can. I have to strike while the
iron is hot.'

'Am I disturbing you? You would say, wouldn't you?'

Marian nodded, eyebrows raised. 'When you've known
me longer you'll know better than to ask that.' The vision
of a shared future rose before Adeline. 'Tell me,' said
Marian, 'do I owe you an apology?'

'No, of course not.'

'But Neville tells me I hit you.'

'You weren't yourself. I understood. And anyway, it
was nothing.'

Involuntarily, as she spoke, she had put up her hand to
her cheek and Marian at once reached out and moved the
hand aside, turning Adeline's face and touching, with
cool, exploratory fingers the small scar that remained.

'Well, well,' she said, reflectively rather than repent-
antly. 'I wonder what possessed me to do such a thing.'

'You were very upset, you thought you'd lost something. When you began turning everything upside down
I was afraid you'd hurt yourself and I tried to stop you by
holding you still – '

'So instead I hurt you.'

'Not very much. I was surprised at how strong you
were, though.'

Marian laughed and gave Adeline's chin a little push as
she released it. 'Mad people are always strong.'

'I've heard that.'

Marian laughed again. Adeline felt like a child who has

unintentionally behaved in the right way and receives praise for it.

'It's a curious thing, you know, but I remembered you,
your face, looking at me. When Neville showed me that
card that came with the flowers I was sure it was you who
sent them.'

'But in your letter you called me "unknown lady".'

'I didn't know you. I still don't, that's why I asked you
to come here, so that could be remedied. It was simply
that you made an impression on me – no easy task when
you consider the state I was in. I suppose that what I am
trying to say is that some link was forged when we first
met, and it has survived the events of recent weeks against
all the odds. It seems to have been inevitable that we
should meet.'

It was so exactly how Adeline had felt that she could
not prevent herself from crying out, 'Yes! Oh yes, I felt
the same! I don't know how I managed to stay away all
this time – '

'Then why did you? People don't usually wait to be
invited here, you know.'

'I didn't want to intrude.'

'My dear,' said Marian a shade tartly, 'you couldn't have
intruded if you wanted to. No-one would have made the
slightest effort on your behalf, I because I wasn't capable,
and Neville because his time and energy were entirely
taken up with looking after me.'

'He must be a remarkable man.'

'Oh, he is. I know full well that all sorts of well-meaning
people, including the doctor, advise him to bundle me off
into an institution for the deranged and feeble-minded,
but it would kill me, and he knows it. I trust him absolutely. Yes, in spite of everything I have London's most
uxorious husband.'

To banish the intrusive presence of the loyal, devoted
and adoring Neville, which for some reason she found
disturbing, Adeline asked: 'Do you know when you're
going to be ill?'

'Oh yes. When you're only mad from time to time, as

I am, the approach of madness is absolutely recognizable. And inevitable. You can't imagine, Adeline, how terrible it is to be slithering gradually into a dark pit, losing your footing inch by inch, screaming for help and yet knowing with absolute certainty that you'll fall anyway. It's not pleasant.' During the course of this speech she had been first coolly objective, then passionate, finally ironic. She was like a stretch of water whose colour and texture changes according to hidden currents and unseen breezes. And now she changed again, leaning forward and placing her hand once more against Adeline's face, cupping the curve of her jaw and gazing at her with an expression of fascinated and benign curiosity. 'You know, you are wonderful to look at . . . so strong and vivid. We must be together often.'

Before she could withdraw her hand Adeline caught and clasped it in both hers.

'That's what I want. You don't know how much.'

'Then let's do it, my dear girl.' Marian let her hand lie quite still until Adeline released it. She then shrugged on her cardigan, slipped her feet into her shoes and stretched her arms above her head, yawning. The sleeves of the cardigan slipped back to reveal her arms, thin and white. Adeline looked away.

'What is your book about?' she asked, her eyes on the desk.

'What is it about?' echoed Marian, as if considering the question for the first time. 'My publisher asks that. I generally tell him it will be about two hundred pages.'

Adeline glanced back at her, and laughed. The mood had changed again. 'You must get tired of being asked the same tedious question – but I am genuinely interested.'

'Of that I haven't the least doubt, and I should genuinely like to tell you. But not now because I'm gasping for a drink. So let's go downstairs and see if we can prevail on Neville to pour us both one.'

She was suddenly brisk and energetic, putting a fire-guard in place, pushing her chair up to the desk, straightening papers, unbolting the door. Adeline rose obediently.

She did not wish to leave this room or to seek out Neville. She had the sense, unusual for her, of being the passive object of another's more powerful will.

She followed Marian down the flights of stairs, past the open bedroom door and the mocking erotic drawings. Marian called as she walked: 'Neville, are you there? I've got someone for you to meet!'

The flattened cushions in the drawing room indicated that others, or at least one other, had been there, but had only recently left. First Neville, then Bloomer came to greet them, but before the dog could reach them Neville took it by the collar and led it from the room, closing the door behind it. He then beamed at Adeline.

'Hallo! I wondered who'd been admitted to the inner sanctum. We've met before, haven't we?'

'She sent me flowers,' said Marian as though it were she, not he, who had first known this.

'And now you'd like a drink – and you, Mary-Anne.'

He offered no choice but went to the drinks table. Marian sank bonelessly into a large armchair, and took a cigarette from the box, saying, 'Help yourself if you'd like one.'

Adeline did so and sat down on the sofa which still bore the imprint of Neville's supine body. In the clinking silence as he poured drinks she could hear the hiss and tick of a record on the phonograph, the music finished but the needle not yet removed. The room that had been a dense forest of people on New Year's Eve was now a great twilit cave, its far corners in darkness. It breathed, exuding an atmosphere and a presence which all her life Adeline sought in vain in other rooms, in other houses.

Having furnished everyone with whisky, Neville sat down by Adeline on the sofa, his arm along the back. He wore a threadbare jumper and down-at-heel slippers, Bloomer's long, wiry hairs dusted his trouser legs. There was something in his air of amiable slovenliness that reminded Adeline of Richard.

'So you've been stopping her working,' he said. 'Not

many people can do that, you know. You should feel flattered.'

'I hope I wasn't doing any such thing,' said Adeline, her
self-esteem at a rather higher level with Neville than it had
been with Marian. 'I'd hate to think I'd been the means of
preventing a Marian Elverstone novel from being written.'

'Will you stay to supper?' asked Marian suddenly, as if
the matter had been preoccupying her for some time.

'I'd love to.'

'Pot luck,' explained Neville. 'We have no idea what
Consett will present us with.'

'Shush, you'll put the girl off,' said Marian.

Adeline opened her mouth to say that she could eat
anything, but Neville spoke first.

'It'll be cosy,' he said, 'with just the three of us.'

The pot turned out to contain Irish stew with dumplings
over which Marian and Neville, rather surprisingly
Adeline thought, cried out in ecstasy. Not that it wasn't
delicious – she herself had two helpings – but that she had
somehow expected something less homely. One or two
scraps of fat and bone were left on the plates and she looked
around in vain for Bloomer who had, apparently, been
banished. Talk flowed across and around the table continuously, sometimes eddying and swirling, sometimes
idling and meandering. In the main, though Adeline was
taken account of, she was not included. It was not so much
that the Elverstones talked only about themselves, but
that, like empire builders, they seemed to claim and
occupy each subject as it arose so that it was well nigh
impossible for an outsider to gain a toehold.

Adeline, happy simply to be there, and still somewhat
dazzled by her hosts, was perfectly content on this
occasion to listen and observe. She saw how detached they
were. Even when they became animated in discussion of
politics, they remained curiously uninvolved, as though
the great struggle of national politics was merely a side-
show and had nothing to do with them. When they talked

of other people – most of whom Adeline did not know –
they were as casually cruel as children dismembering
insects. Ida Rabone, whose kindness she remembered, got
short shrift.

'Ida asked again if we'd be going to her exhibition,'
Neville said.

'I can't think why. She knows I won't go. I can't bear
that sentimental stuff of hers.'

'I think I might. It'll be full of the most ludicrous
people.'

'Well it's you she wants. She hopes you'll write a piece
on her.'

'I could well do but I doubt if she'll thank me for it. I
wonder why she persists in the idea that deep down we
really admire her work.'

'Because,' said Marian, looking suddenly and with a
little smile at Adeline as if inviting her complicity, 'she is
a silly, vulgar little woman.'

Adeline, dumbstruck, concentrated on her plate. She
scarcely knew Ida so she was in no position to defend her
against an allegation which, though it may well have been
the truth, could not possibly be the whole truth. An unfair
challenge had been issued, a challenge which she could not
possibly take up. She found herself wondering – as she
suspected they meant her to – what they would say about
her when they were alone together.

And yet what opinion could they have formed? For – in
spite of Marian's declared intention that they should get
to know each other better – they seemed wholly uncurious
about her. They did not ask her even the dull, polite questions which people use socially to establish their relation
to one another, and the result was she felt diffident about
volunteering information. It was as though her existence
outside these walls had neither relevance nor reality for
them, that by their calm denial of it they could ensure that
she came to life only within their ambit.

And yet she found them irresistible. This was hardly
surprising in the case of Neville, who was not only good-
looking, but possessed enough amiable, easy-going charm

for ten men. But it was Marian who held the most powerful and ineluctable fascination for her – Marian who made
no apparent attempt to charm or attract, who made no
claim to beauty or elegance, and whose manner from time
to time was deliberately calculated to repel. She seemed to
imply by her behaviour that only the bravest and the most
discerning could both perceive her allure and deserve her
attention. So absolute was the fealty she exacted that
Adeline would have been unable to withhold it, even if
she had wished to. Some distant, as yet uninvolved, part
of her brain told her that if someone were simply to
describe to her a character like Marian Elverstone, she
would find that character cold and unlikable, even abhor-
rent. And yet here, at her table, watching her and listening
to her, she was in thrall.

After supper Marian threw open the french windows in
the drawing room and walked out into the bitterly cold
night. With her hands in her pockets she flapped the sides
of her cardigan, like wings, and leapt and twirled on the
terrace like a strange bird.

'The woman's mad,' said Neville, sitting down
comfortably on the sofa and lighting himself a cigarette.
He seemed to find nothing indelicate in the use of that
word.

'Come and see my garden!' called Marian.

'She can't see it, Mary-Anne, it's as black as Egypt out
there!'

'It won't be, away from the house . . .'

As if to prove her point she moved away down some
steps, the blurred grey of her outline melting into the dark,
a tantalizing half-seen flicker.

Adeline turned to Neville and found he was looking
up at her with an expression that was different from his
habitual open-faced affability. His eyes were narrowed
above the cigarette which was held between his lips, his
hands were linked behind his head. The look was a cool
one, of appraisal and anticipation.

'I'd like to see,' said Adeline, and he blinked once,
slowly, like a nod. As she closed the french window she

caught sight of him again, and he was still watching her. She was glad to escape.

Once away from the steps, and the light from the house, the darkness was less opaque. There was a three-quarter moon, and an infinity of clear sky crowded with flinty stars.

She walked slowly forward. 'Marian . . .?'

The faint echo of light behind her was doused abruptly as the curtains were drawn. Adeline felt that it was she, rather than the room she had just left, that was being enclosed.

There were trees in the garden, and she moved between them, touching their dank trunks with her hands as she passed, as if fending off a group of silent, importunate people. She didn't feel the cold.

Beyond the trees the garden opened out again. Adeline could see the dark mass of a high wall, and some way beyond it the rooftop of another house. Clumps of snow-drops showed here and there, luminous in the dark. The beginnings of frost made her footsteps sound purposeful. She stopped.

'Marian . . . are you there?'

'Here.' Marian appeared, materializing from the black lee of the wall and walking out on to the grey grass, her face tilted upward to the sky. 'Isn't it beautiful?'

'Yes. Lovely. So clear.'

She looked up, their two faces united, as it were, by the distant beam of the stars. She felt dizzied and cleansed by their numbers and remoteness, stars on stars leading away to where neither the eye nor the imagination could reach. When Marian took her hand, the gesture, dwarfed by their surroundings, seemed small and simple. Marian lifted her hand in both of hers, as though she were going to drink from it, and kissed the soft inner fold of the palm with an open mouth, her eyes on Adeline's face. Adeline felt all sensation drawn to a thread by that enclosed and secret joining.

She said: 'I don't know what to think . . . I feel so strange.' And her voice, awestruck, came from far away.

Marian dropped Adeline's hand and placed her own on either side of Adeline's face and ran them slowly and lightly over her cheeks, down her neck, and along her shoulders. As she did so she watched with a quiet concentration as though she were re-creating, for herself and in her own way, the body beneath her hands. In the same detached and deliberate way she moulded back, stomach, breasts and thighs to her will. Adeline, weak with desire, knew herself to be possessed.

'Stop . . . please stop.'

'Yes. We have all the time in the world.'

'I want to be yours.'

'You shall be. You are.'

'But you must show me how. I'm scared of the way I feel . . . of how *much* I feel.'

'There's nothing to be frightened of.' Marian put her arm about Adeline's waist and began walkiing back in the direction of the house. 'We shall make each other happy. Happy and glorious!' she added mockingly. Her shift of mood, so quick, complete and unexpected, while Adeline still resonated to her touch, seemed calculated to display her power.

'But what we're doing is wrong!' Adeline cried, not from conviction but out of a desperate need to restore some more general perspective on a course of events that was threatening to sweep her utterly away.

'Wrong?' Marian stopped and confronted her with an expression of the most scathing incredulity. 'What can you mean?'

'In the eyes of most people. Unnatural.'

'What most people think is of no concern or interest to me. If it is to you, then go. I shan't stop you.'

'You know I won't go – I can't!'

'It's a matter of indifference to me. If the world's opinion is something by which you set store, then you and I have no basis for a friendship.'

'It isn't the world's opinion, as you put it, don't you see?' Adeline clasped Marian's wrists as she had done at their first meeting, but this time there was no resistance.

'It's my opinion of myself. I'm a stranger to myself when I'm with you, there's so much I don't understand.'

'You're hurting me, Adeline.'

'I'm sorry.'

'You worry too much about understanding. There is no plot, Adeline, no grand Machiavellian scheme that is making us behave as we do. We have followed what the prayer book would call the devices and desires of our own hearts. It's not complicated, it's simple and clear. Whether you continue to follow them is up to you, your own affair, but if you do, I beg of you not to bring all this cringing guilt and lay it at my door. I want no part of it. It's neither use nor ornament.'

Adeline was stung. 'I was not cringing. I was hoping for your help!'

'I've given it to you. There it lies, in your eye.'

'You've deliberately belittled me!'

'In that case you are too ready to feel belittled. You must have a poor opinion of yourself. Be careful you don't infect others with it.'

Hands in pockets she walked away towards the house. Her voice, light and unemphatic, floated back to Adeline. 'I'm cold, suddenly. Let's go back to Neville . . .'

Adeline was cold, too. She could not believe that Marian would leave her now, expose her to Neville's smiling scrutiny with the blood, as it were, still fresh on her wounds. She felt destroyed, wretched.

In the house, which she reached only seconds after Marian, it was as though they had been together in there all this time and only she, alone, had been in the garden. Seamlessly the two of them, man and wife, had closed ranks. Neville was at his most charming.

'Adeline, dear girl, a whisky, quick. You look positively starved with cold.'

He ushered her to a chair, and busied himself at the drinks table. Marian stood by the piano, smoking a cigarette, picking out a broken little tune on the black notes. 'You know,' went on Neville, 'I live in the serious expectation of finding the bleached bones of some unfortunate

guest who has been led out into the impenetrable undergrowth, lost, and left to die.'

'You are ridiculous, Neville,' said Marian, closing the
piano lid and touching his cheek as he passed with Adeline's drink. 'It's not even a very big garden.'

'Speaking as one who abhors horticulture in all its
forms, I find it a great deal too big. Sitting on the terrace
on a fine summer's day, with a jug of something cold to
hand, and a quality newspaper with which to cover one's
face – that's the way to enjoy gardens.'

Adeline took great gulps of the whisky and felt some
small degree of self-respect creeping back with its reviving
warmth.

'Yes,' she said, 'I miss having a garden.'

'You don't have one where you are?' asked Neville.
Adeline was conscious of Marian moving about the room
beyond them, her arms folded, restless yet self-possessed.

'Oh no, it's just a rented room, in Gower Street,' She
realized that this was her first opportunity to tell them
something about herself and her life. 'I've been there the
whole time that I've been at the Slade, that's more than
three years now, and it suits me very well. Before my
husband died – ' She had never used this phrase to them
before and at once regretted it. 'We lived in Ireland. We
had a rented house with masses of land.' She could now
feel her every word sounding more and more ridiculous,
though she spoke nothing but the plain truth. 'I like to feel
that there's some space outside my four walls.'

She felt breathless with humiliation. Neville's face wore
an attentive little smile, but she knew he wasn't listening.
Marian stood in a corner, flicking through a book she had
taken from the shelf. Adeline was conscious of having
prepared an elaborate and clumsy dish for people who
were not in the least interested in food. They would not
taste it, nor even take it from her, she did not know what
to do with its ridiculous, dead weight.

She put down her glass and stood up. 'I should go, it's
late.'

'It is quite.' Neville glanced at his watch. 'How will you go? Do you want to call a cab?'

'No, it's not far. I'll walk.'

No-one demurred. Marian began to move towards them, though slowly, and still gazing down at the book.

'Oh – I left my cloak upstairs. You don't mind if I go and get it?'

'Of course not.'

As she ran up the stairs and fetched the cloak from the dark, empty study she heard the sound of their voices, muffled by doors and walls. And a laugh. She recalled her first visit and the feeling she had had that a burst of laughter at the party had been occasioned by her.

They were waiting for her in the hall. Neville held Bloomer in his arms. He kissed the dog's face extravagantly, looking over its head at Adeline.

'Drop by any time,' he said, 'any time at all. Everyone does. We don't promise to entertain you.'

'Thank you.' She thought: Everyone does. She had been put in her place. 'And thank you for the supper.'

Neville disappeared through the drawing room door, murmuring to his dog. Marian looked at her as if awaiting the answer to a question.

'Shall I come again?' asked Adeline. 'Do you want me to?'

'Come whenever you like, Adeline. Freely, openly. I asked you to come here once, I shan't again, because it's not necessary. If you want to be with me, come. It's your decision now.'

Bitterly, Adeline reflected on her walk home: Marian spoke of freedom and of openness, but the freedom was to be a willing slave, and the openness led to an enclosed and secret world. More than anything she wished to be that slave, and to inhabit that world.

CHAPTER SEVENTEEN

1925

HOWARD RETURNED FROM his club in a rage of boredom. His hated, hidden weakness was like an incubus, infecting his spirit. He felt well, vigorous even, and yet he was marked by infirmity and old age. When his chauffeur opened the door for him the gesture seemed to contain a new solicitude. He noticed for the first time that Parker was a younger, fitter man than he, and it irked him. His broad shoulders convulsed in a twitch of irritation as he let himself into the house in Leinster Gardens. The enforced inactivity of convalescence seemed to him a hollow sham. What good could it possibly be doing him to be so dull and idle? States of unaccountable depression – what the young people called 'the blues' – were foreign to Howard's nature. When he was out of sorts he had always, till now that is, simply increased the amount of work he did, and the pace at which he did it. He had been justly proud, damn it, of his physical powers.

He went up to visit his wife and encountered the

nurse, a rosy-faced Scots girl, on the landing. She put her finger to her lips.

'She's having a wee nap, sir. I'd leave her be.'

Howard was only too glad to oblige, but lingered for a moment, not from concern for Cynthia so much as a desire to savour the company of the comely nurse.

'How has she been today?'

'Quite well and happy. But she was no' so good last night. We had some ups and downs, that's why she's tired now.'

Howard nodded and raised a hand, palm outwards, to show that he would not dream of intruding. Cynthia was increasingly incontinent and she also, in the manner of those whose lives have become static, took little account of the difference between day and night. He thanked God for people like Nurse Munro who were prepared to do his dirty work for him. She was worth her weight in gold.

'And you're all right, Mr Charteris? Did you have an enjoyable lunch?'

'Never better, to the first. Tedious beyond belief, to the second.'

'Oh dear . . .' Her voice and face expressed genuine disappointment. Howard felt he had been too brusque.

'No, no it was perfectly pleasant.'

'It'll have done you good to get out, sir, at any rate.'

Downstairs, Howard stood gazing out of the window, his hands in his pockets. He found the girl's enquiries saddening more than anything else. She thought of him, no doubt, as a poor, crusty old stick who needed a bit of fun in his life. How right she was. But how wrong to presume that the male fastnesses of the Travellers' Club could provide it. She was a nice, healthy, well brought up girl, and she'd be shocked if she knew how clearly he could picture the warm bounce of her breasts beneath the stiff and shapeless uniform.

He closed his eyes.

Adeline saw Howard standing in his window, and waved to him without realizing that he could not see her. In the grey winter afternoon light and with the front garden separating them she could only discern that he stood there alone and that there was a certain bleakness about him which she put down to ill health. When he failed to respond to her wave she reminded herself that her purpose in visiting was to share, and ameliorate by sharing, his troubles rather than her own.

'But you're a tonic, Adeline, the best damn thing that's happened in weeks!'

He said this in the face of her muttered apology for coming unannounced. 'And you're still my daughter-in-law. You don't need an appointment.'

They sat down in the big leather armchairs in his comfortable but curiously impersonal drawing room. She commented on a new painting over the fireplace, a dark-eyed young woman with her arms folded, her lips curved in an ironic smile.

'Yes, you should like it,' he said. 'It's a Gwen John. Only keeping the place warm till I can hang one of yours there, though. If I can afford one,' he added, glaring teasingly at her. His obvious pleasure at her arrival shamed her. Tell him something, she thought, tell him what you've been doing. Behave like his daughter-in-law, fill the space, talk.

For over an hour she did talk, with only the smallest prompting from Howard. She described Fenella, and how she planned to paint her, she displayed a little of the allowable vanity in which Howard delighted.

'But will the young woman like it?' he asked, grinning.

'That doesn't matter. It's what I see in her that counts, and whether I can put it on the canvas.'

'You sound just like your mother.'

She pretended not to hear this, and changed the subject, telling him how well Bob seemed to be doing, and about Toni and how they were quite a pair. Anything, anything, so long as he didn't ask questions. The reality of her life since Christmas, its feverish and obsessional nature, she kept close and, she hoped, well hidden. Not apparently well hidden enough, for at one point he abruptly leaned forward, fixed her with his most penetrating and brilliant stare, and interrupted her with:

'Adeline – are you quite well?'

'I'm fine, absolutely. Why on earth do you ask?'

'Because you don't look it.' He scowled. 'I'm suppose to be the one with the vapours, but I flatter myself I look in rude health compared with you.'

'I'm just a bit tired, that's all. Really!' she insisted, as his expression did not change. 'This is too ridiculous . . .' She fumbled in her bag for a cigarette to hide the fact that her mouth trembled and her eyes were suddenly brimming with tears.

'I see.' His voice was gentler. 'You aren't by any chance in love?'

'Good Lord, no!'

'I shouldn't be offended, you know, if you were.'

'Well I'm not!'

He did not pursue it any further, though she suspected that he took her agitation as answer enough. He was saying something about Bob.

'. . . funny you should mention him. I was lunching with Ted Maybury – newspaper publisher, he married your friend Louise . . . and he's launching a new paper. It appears Bob's acquired a bit of a name for himself and Maybury's interested in hiring him. I don't read the *Courier* myself, not my politics. Still, it's nice to hear of the family doing well.'

This gave Adeline a chance to regain her composure and she agreed, with a creditable display of enthusiasm, that it was gratifying.

Not long afterwards, she left. Howard kissed her hand, as always, a gesture which contrived to be both more and less intimate than the traditional family bumping of cheeks.

'Thank you for coming,' he said. 'You don't know how much good it does me to hear you talk. I'm bored to death at present.'

'I'm only sorry I didn't come before.'

'I'm not. Flowers and sympathy aren't in your line, or mine. Good luck, Adeline,' he added.

She wondered, as she walked down Leinster Gardens in the direction of the park, why he had said that. And concluded that he knew her, had always known her, much too well.

The following day was the one appointed for Fenella's first full sitting. Adeline welcomed it only as an opportunity to fill her time, to occupy hours when she might otherwise have been drawn towards Allerton Square.

Away from them her pride, which had been transcended and forgotten in their company, reasserted itself. She would go back, she could not otherwise, but she determined that this time she would return with some achievement of her own to sustain her self-esteem. No matter how hard and painful it might be, she would finish the portrait before seeing Marian again.

It was a grey, wet day. Grimy London rain streaked the window and poured mercilessly on Adeline and Clancey as they walked round Passmore Gardens. On the way back she stopped at the small Italian grocery shop to buy supplies for lunch. Mr di Angeli, her friend, said: 'You paint me some Italian weather, maybe?' and she said she would try. She wished she could paint for herself a new day, a new outlook, a new life. She was shocked by the power that one, absent person was able to exercise over her, but the shock was at one remove, it had no power to change her.

Fenella was due to arrive at eleven o'clock from the Marchants' house in The Boltons, but she was late. At twelve-thirty Adeline, by now sunk into the angry melancholy occasioned by waiting, stood at her window looking out for the little white car. But it was a cab that eventually drew up, and as Fenella, obviously flustered, ran up to the front door, she caught sight of the figure of Nicholas Eyre in the back seat.

'I'm so *sorry* that I'm so dreadfully late!' said Fenella, divesting herself of her hat and coat and going at once to kneel by the fire. 'I couldn't help it.'

Her whole manner was so childlike that rancorous resentment died in Adeline.

'That's all right,' she said. And then, realizing that after all it was true: 'It's good of you to come at all.'

'We're really going to start today?' Fenella looked at the easel set up near the window, a dustsheet spread on the ground beneath it, the table drawn up alongside it, covered with an oilskin cloth and set out with Adeline's paints and brushes.

'Yes, we are.' Adeline noticed that in Fenella's mind the portrait had become a joint enterprise, undertaken by both of them equally.

'Is what I'm wearing all right?'

'It's fine.'

'If you want to drape me in a curtain or something, do say. But I warn you I have very bony shoulders!' She laughed nervously.

'No, I like you as you are.'

Fenella was dressed in a style that was in direct contrast to her manner. She wore immaculate, country-lady clothes: a soft russet tweed skirt, a cashmere twinset the colour of brown egg shells, brown punched-leather court shoes with tasselled laces. The only sign of a more whimsical taste at work was a necklace of tiny coral beads, such as Adeline could remember wearing to parties as a child. The tension between the lady Fenella was affecting to be, and the child-woman she was – that was what Adeline wanted to capture on the canvas.

She had invested in a bottle of Mr di Angeli's red wine for the occasion, and she poured them both a glass.

'Come and sit down.'

She had drawn up one of the wing chairs facing the easel, and thrown a plain white sheet over it. The effect when Fenella sat in it was, as she had hoped, one of impermanence, of someone in an empty house, where the furniture was kept beneath dust sheets. It emphasized a lost quality in Fenella, and the white background threw her face and figure into relief.

'Don't feel you must sit still, just be comfortable,' she said.

She had prepared the canvas beforehand and now she began to sketch a faint outline. As she made the marks, confidence drained from her. The sense of occasion, the importance of this picture, the responsibility she shouldered, rose up and threatened to choke her. Her hand, holding the charcoal, felt as heavy and insensitive as a club, the marks she was making were meaningless. Perhaps Fenella sensed this ebbing of confidence, for she was silent and fidgety, lighting a cigarette and snatching at it nervously, drinking her wine rather fast, crossing and uncrossing her legs.

After three quarters of an hour, during which the canvas steadfastly refused to yield up its secrets, Fenella asked:

'How's it going? Am I allowed to have a look?'

Adeline sighed. 'There's nothing to see, I'm afraid. Let's have something to eat.'

'Oh dear – am I a bad subject?' Fenella rose and followed her to the kitchen. 'Is there anything I can do to help?'

'No. No, you're a marvellous subject and there's nothing you can do. It's just that – ' She looked at Fenella's anxious face, trying to decide whether to confide in her would be to injure or improve their carefully balanced relationship. The decision made, she went on: 'It's just that this portrait is so important, to me if not to anyone else. I want to paint you just the way I see you, to get it exactly right – and now that we're ready to start I suppose I have a kind of stage fright.'

Fenella nodded seriously. 'I do understand.'

'Let's have another glass of wine and something to eat. Perhaps when the body's refreshed the spirit will be too.'

Over lunch, Fenella said again: 'I'm sorry I was late. Nicholas came round.'

'I saw him in the taxi. I was quite surprised he didn't come up.'

'Oh no, he was off to call on some people he knows

who live near here. Sometimes I feel – it's silly I know – '
She gave her breathless little laugh – ' that I'm a bit of an
ass with him. He takes an awful lot for granted and I put
up with it. I know any number of men who are far, far,
nicer to me than Nicholas is, who spoil me and buy me
the most beautiful things, but I always drop everything
for him – perhaps it's because he *expects* it of me. What do
you think?'

'I think,' said Adeline, 'that has a lot to do with it.'

'And, of course, I adore him.'

'What do your parents make of him?'

'They like him. They're so amused by him. He's always
perfectly charming with them. He can be extremely
charming when he wants to be, you know,' she added,
as if explaining her infatuation for her own rather than
Adeline's benefit.

She looked helpless and disconsolate. Adeline realized
that if she had anything in common with Fenella Marchant
it was vested in the sardonic, self-satisfied and manipulative person of Nicholas Eyre.

A little afterwards they began work again, and the portrait of Fenella began to take shape.

From now on, she worked with absolute concentration.
Completion of the portrait had taken on a superstitious
importance in her life. It represented the barrier through
which she must pass in order to see Marian again, and
she closed her mind to everything else. In doing so she
discovered a fact about herself which was to stand her in
good stead professionally, while forever closing the gates
to critical acclaim – she was a fast worker. The hardest
labour for her would always be in deciding how she
wanted to represent her subject. Once that was achieved
she flew at the canvas with ferocious single-mindedness,
all her energies focused on capturing and expressing the
idea before she lost it. Her absorption in the painting for
the short time she was involved with it was complete.

For nine days she scarcely left her room except to walk
Clancey and purchase essentials. The new term had long

since begun at the Slade, but she did not go to college. Emissaries came. Duncan, as usual, was the most frank.

'We all know you're painting Peter's heavenly sister, but aren't the rest of us *ever* going to see you again?'

'When I've finished.'

'Tonks takes a dim view of students taking commissions before they've finished the course, you know.'

'This isn't a commission. It's a speculation.'

'May one take a peep?'

'One may not. Goodbye Duncan.'

It rained. Oh how it rained, driving against the window day and night, smudging the outlines of people and traffic in Gower Street with long, slanting strokes, splashing from guttering and rushing and gurgling down drains. Though it wasn't necessary, Fenella, fascinated, came each day, often bringing delicious and expensive contributions towards lunch reminiscent of Peter's indoor picnics in St John's Wood. During those grey, lamplit days, with the imprisoning rain streaming down the window pane, Fenella and Adeline drew closer. Though their lives now could not have been nore different, their background were not dissimilar, and as the portrait progressed Adeline felt that their separate worlds were emerging like volcanic islands from the surrounding sea and revealing, as they did so, a common base. As they became more at ease with one another, little nuggets of information were vouch-safed by Fenella and filed away for future reference by Adeline.

'None of us really knows what Peter's doing at the Slade,' said Fenella one day, sitting curled up on the dustsheet, her arms hugging her knees. 'It's not where he's meant to be. He should be an officer in the Guards by now. That's what Father wanted, you know . . . there was quite a horrid atmosphere about it for months. It's not that Peter's a rebel or anything. He seems so easy and accommodating, but he gets these great *enthusiasms*, and once he's on to something he's awfully hard to shake. He's unbelievably stubborn, but because he's never cross or rude he gets away with it.' Adeline detected a distinct note of sisterly rancour in this remark. She could picture the two of them, the nervy little girl and the confident, smiling little boy, she could hear a reproving mother saying, 'Take a leaf out of Peter's book, he's never cross or rude . . .'

'Actually,' Fenella went on, 'I think Nick may have had something to do with it. He always pretends to be surprised about Peter doing art, but he really *is* a rebel and I think he encouraged Peter to kick over the traces. He once said to me that he likes to alter the course of people's lives. He said it's fun to make people do what you want without their noticing – or something like that – '

'I expect that's right . . .'

'Anyway, we're sure Peter will tire of it. He's already getting a bit disheartened. I suppose he can see how much better the rest of you are than him, but even if he does give it up it'll all happen again in a year or so with something else. It was the same when we were small. He'd have a wonderful idea and I had to be the dog's-body. One summer he wanted to produce a children's newspaper. He was the editor, of course, writing articles and going to interview people, and I was secretary, with all the dull jobs. Just when I was beginning to enjoy it he told me I was welcome to be editor if I wanted to, because he was more interested in natural history. He couldn't see it was no fun at all being editor with no-one to give orders to.'

Adeline smiled as she painted. She wondered, with detachment, if Peter's feelings towards herself could be dismissed as a fleeting 'enthusiasm'. But Fenella supplied the answer to her unasked question.

'We always know,' she said, 'when Peter's serious about something because he hardly talks about it. When it's a craze he goes on and on and on.'

'I see,' said Adeline. 'I . . have to bear that in mind.' But her heart sank.

'Lor!' Fenella put her hand to her cheek. 'Do I look like that?'

Adeline was cleaning her brushes. 'You are like that, or I think so.'

'Heavens . . .' Fenella leaned forward and peered at the canvas, as though she might have missed something essential. 'And it's completely finished?'

'I don't want to do any more to it.' Adeline laid the brushes down and rubbed her hands over her face. She was exhausted. 'I've completed a picture that no-one wants and that I have no idea what to do with.'

'Oh, we'll think of something!' cried Fenella. 'It's terribly unusual.'

Adeline wished she would go. Fenella seemed to have drawn comfort and energy from the portrait's completion while she herself felt only numb, and strangely let down as though a longed-for treat had been, in the end, a disappointment. Fenella would go and forget her now leaving her with the distinctly uncertain fruits of her labours.

She sat down and watched dully as Fenella powdered her nose and did her hair in the mirror, then put on her fur coat, picked up her gloves and handbag and turned to leave, head high and eyes sparkling, presenting a face as different as was humanly possible from that which Adeline had committed to canvas.

'It's all so exciting!' she said, as she left.

When she had gone, Adeline sank down on the bed, kicking her shoes off and closing her eyes. Her head, and every joint in her body, ached. Her eyes were sore. It was painful to swallow. Clancey came to sit by her, with a little whining sound, asking to be taken out, but she hadn't the energy. She only knew that if she slept now, long and deep, tomorrow she would see Marian, and come alive again. She put out her hand to soothe the dog but she'd no sooner touched him than her hand slid to the floor and he was forgotten.

Standing quietly near the window in the half-darkness, was Adeline's portrait of Fenella Marchant. It showed a thin, pale, awkward girl, at ease neither with herself nor the rest of the world. She sat on a dustsheet-covered chair against an indistinct background. This impermanence of her surroundings underlined the sitter's own uncertainty.

She sat leaning forward, shoulders hunched, her arms resting, wrists together as if handcuffed, on her knees. Her
long legs, without shoes, splayed outwards like a young
giraffe's. A half-smoked cigarette rested between childish fingers. The face, open-lipped and large-eyed, wore an
expression of frowning anxiety.

The picture was no perfect likeness. Nor did it do justice
to its subject's famous beauty. But it was instantly and
affectingly recognizable.

The next day Adeline felt worse, much worse. When Toni
knocked on the door, early, wanting to tell her some news
about Bob, she saw at once how things were.

'You poor thing – I knew you were sickening for something.'

'Toni, would you be an angel and take Clancey out for
me? I just can't . . .'

'You can't and you mustn't. Of course I will. Shall I ask
the Fairyhouses to have him with them for a while?'

'No, I like him here. But perhaps when you get back –
'

'Don't worry, I'll see to him. Get back into bed, for
heaven's sake. Come on, boy.'

'Oh, and Toni . . .'

'What?'

'I don't want Mrs F. making a fuss and coming in and
out. I'll be fine if I'm left alone.'

Toni did not reply to this request, and though Mrs Fairyhouse exercised the utmost forbearance she did appear
in the middle of the day, clucking and sighing and bearing
hot honey and lemon, for which Adeline was grateful. She
also, on Adeline's murmured instructions, fed Clancey,
and promised to bring back more butcher's scraps. Before
leaving she pressed a large, dry hand to Adeline's brow.

'You're running a high temperature – I'm not at all sure
I shouldn't get a doctor in.'

'No Mrs Fairyhouse, *please* . . . it isn't necessary.'

Mrs Fairyhouse tutted at this, glanced at the covered
easel and the surrounding paraphernalia and tutted again.

She would like to have set to and made things nice, but she had a healthy respect for Mrs Charteris who even now, from her pillow, exercised a certain natural authority.

'As you wish,' she said. And, with a sigh, left.

The next day was Saturday. Adeline felt no better. She had passed a bad night, beset by both discomfort and bad dreams. When Toni came at eleven o'clock to walk Clancey, she said:

'I've got a visitor for you. Mrs F. says she has no objection even though you are in bed, because you're obviously too ill to be compromised.'

'But Toni, I don't want to see anyone . . .'

'Hallo, Addy.'

It was Peter, coming in as Toni and the dog went out. Adeline groaned. 'Please go away!'

'Don't worry, I will. You must admit I've been as good as gold for weeks. I haven't claimed even the tiniest kiss.' He stood looking down at her, his hands in his pockets, and she turned her face away. 'But now that you've finished the portrait I thought I'd pop round and remind you that you still have a devoted follower. Mind you,' he chuckled, 'I'm not surprised you feel dicky after a couple of weeks of Nella's company. May I take a look?'

He took the cover from the easel, scrutinized the painting in silence, covered it again and came back to the bedside.

'Clever, aren't you? It's brilliant, Addy. Anyone who can make my flighty sister look interesting gets my vote.'

'Thanks.'

'My pleasure. And now,' he announced, 'I'm going to do a spot of shopping. I'll be back anon with one or two of those little things that make life worth living.' He must have caught her look of dismay, for he added: 'Don't try and stop me, I feel unstoppable this morning.'

When he had gone she turned on her side and lay quaking and throbbing and swallowing, painfully, salt tears of self-pity. But no sooner had the front door closed behind him than footsteps on the stairs and a brisk knock heralded the arrival of Mrs Fairyhouse carrying a tray of tea and toast, and a letter.

'I brought you these,' she said. She was a shade censorious this morning. She glanced round the room and handed Adeline her cardigan from the back of the chair. 'You'd best put this on. I told Mr Marchant he could come back with a few things. I shall be down below,' she added darkly.

Adeline sipped the tea and lifted, as if it were a huge weight, the letter. The envelope had no stamp. The writing, blurred, swam into focus. Suddenly everything was clear and sharp, she forgot her illness and tore open the envelope. There was no address, date nor preamble to the letter.

> I wonder [Marian had written] what you have decided to do. Are you ever going to come back and see me again, or have you decided that the shame would be too great? Or perhaps some wild beast carried you off as you were returning to your flat? Our doorbell rings incessantly but it is never you. I confess I'm curious. Don't disappoint me – Marian E.

Adeline pushed back the covers, got up and dressed. Mind had risen high above matter. Her face in the mirror was flushed, the eyes red-rimmed, her scalp flinched with each touch of the brush, but she felt swift and light. She checked her purse – she had just about enough money for a taxi. Outside, for the first time in days, the sun shone from a clear sky, and there was foretaste of spring in the air.

Peter, getting back with his purchases, saw Toni on the landing with Clancey.

'Peter – she's not there.'

'Having a bath, perhaps?'

'No, her bag and outdoor things are gone. She must have gone out.'

Peter reached the top of the stairs and peered in at the

rumpled bed, the obviously empty room, the untouched tray on the floor.

'Why on earth would she do a thing like that? She had the flu. She was expecting both of us back.'

Mrs Fairyhouse appeared, swollen with her contribution to the mystery.

'I brought her a tray and a letter that arrived for her, just after you went, Mr Marchant,' she said. 'Five minutes after that she was off out the door with her war paint on.' She walked into the room and pointed at the tray in a Holmesian manner. 'The letter's not there now, so she must have read it.'

'But where was she going?' asked Toni.

'There wasn't time to ask, she was in such a hurry. I don't suppose she'll be long. She cares about that dog even if the rest of us don't count. If you ask me,' she added grimly, squaring her shoulders, 'she's not herself. Hasn't been for weeks.'

The house in Allerton Square presented a quiet aspect, and there was no barking from Bloomer when Adeline rang the bell. For a moment the silence was so complete that she thought no-one was there, and tears of sick disappointment stung her eyes. She rang again, and this time the door was opened, by Marian herself.

'Well, at last. Come on in, I'm all alone.'

Adeline left her things in the hall and followed Marian into the drawing room. The french windows stood open and the clear February sunshine poured in. It was cold. Marian wore baggy, threadbare corduroy trousers and a grey jumper with a good many loose threads hanging from it. On her feet were thick speckled socks and a pair of once-white plimsolls. Her hands were black with soil.

'You can see what I'm doing,' she said. 'Come and keep me company.' She made no reference to either their past conversation or her letter. Adeline might have been the most casual of everyday callers.

They went out on to the terrace. Spread on the ground was yesterday's *Courier*, the sheets separated to give a greater area, and on the paper stood a great many seed packets, seed trays and flower pots.

'So many decisions . . .' murmured Marian. 'Sit down, do.'

She herself kneeled down by the seed packets and began studying them with great concentration. Adeline looked round for a seat, but there was none, so she perched on the low stone parapet that surrounded the terrace. It was cold and uncomfortable but she scarcely noticed. Now that she was here she felt as malleable, docile and content as a child who has been forgiven. Willingly, she surrendered all initiative and waited for what would happen.

Beyond them in the garden a bird sang a jubilant, misguided paeon to spring. In the sunshine the garden itself appeared smaller and less mysterious, put in its place by the tall houses around it. The trees that had seemed to crowd and delay her as she searched for Marian that night were no longer sinister. Happiness seeped through her like sap.

'Where's Neville?' she asked.

'Mm . . .?' Marian was busy with soil and seeds. 'He's going to a beastly loud lunch party down in Chiswick, given by some editor or other. It will be full of second-rate writers and their put-upon spouses. I wanted no part of it. I've told him to plead madness on my behalf. Do you want to help with this?'

'I'll try.'

Adeline kneeled beside Marian. On her instructions she began to fill the trays with potting soil. Marian explained that she was creating a rockery, she wanted a waterfall of colour, did Adeline know anything about Alpine plants? Adeline confessed that she didn't. Marian poured some seeds into her hand and told her to set them in one of the filled trays. As Adeline peered at the tiny seeds her head throbbed. She couldn't see properly, and she was shuddering feverishly so that it was impossible to separate one seed from its companions. She moaned in frustration, and Marian looked at her sharply.

'What's the matter?'

'I'm sorry, I'm being clumsy. I've had the flu. I'll just go and fetch my cloak.'

'You're cold?'

'I am rather.'

She struggled, stiffly, to rise, and her head swam. Marian, rising with her, said:

'You still have the flu.'

'I don't think so, not really . . . I've been working very hard.'

Marian smiled. 'Come with me.'

'But – please . . . I don't – '

'I'm going to look after you.'

Quickly, purposefully, Marian led her into the house and motioned her to wait while she washed her hands. Then she escorted her up the stairs and opened a door next to that of the main bedroom.

'The bed's made up,' she said. 'We're always ready for guests.'

Despite this declaration, the room had the quiet, undisturbed chill of a space seldom used. The window looked out on to the square. The walls were papered in a dark red and the bedspread was white. On the chest of drawers, in front of an arched mirror, stood a large willow pattern bowl filled with dried lavender. There were some shelves containing books but otherwise the walls were bare, the only walls in the house that were not covered by pictures. The room was as neutral and expectant as a blank page.

Marian turned back the bedspread. 'Get undressed and I'll fetch you something to wear.'

Unable to manage even the politest token protest, Adeline began to peel off her clothes. When she was in her petticoat Marian reappeared, suddenly and silently and without knocking.

'Here, it's something of Neville's.'

'Will that be – ?'

'Put it on. I got it from his drawer, it's clean.'

Adeline hesitated. It was obvious Marian was not going to leave the room, but neither did she watch her. Instead she went to the fireplace and, moving aside the fire screen and guard, kneeled down. The fire was laid, a conical pile of sticks and coals propped on newspaper, grey with dust. Marian struck a match and held it to the outer edges of the pile. Her face, watching the match, was calm and intent.

Shivering, Adeline removed her petticoat and slipped into Neville's nightshirt. It was of pale blue silk, with his initials on the breast pocket, an expensive, dandyish garment, exquisitely comfortable. Gratefully she slipped into the bed and pulled the bedclothes up round her shoulders.

Marian rose, said, 'I'll be back,' and left the room, drawing the door to behind her.

Adeline closed her eyes. This was the shady side of the house, and the room was dim. The square outside the window was quiet. The only sound was that of the fire crackling as the sticks began to catch. Her shivering began to subside as she gave herself up to the pervading sense of seclusion and secrecy. She entertained a fleeting mental picture of her own room in Gower Street, the easel by the window, the meter empty, the bed cold and stale. Then she slept.

She woke up with a nervous start, hot and disorientated. The room was dark now. She could hear voices muffled, in some other part of the house.

Remembering where she was she fumbled for the switch on the bedside lamp, turned it on and looked at her watch: it was three o'clock in the afternoon. Someone had been in the room while she slept, for the curtains were drawn and a book, open and face down, lay on the chair beside the fireplace.

Her throat was still sore, but she was sweating and she felt a little better. Rolling on to her back she felt the slithering caress of the silk nightshirt. Her body, lethargic from illness and sleep, felt rich and heavy. She felt herself a willing and protected prisoner. Her debility had become a sensuous thing, lapping and lulling her . . . she slept again.

She awoke the second time to find the room in firelit darkness. Marian was sitting in the fireside chair, the book open on her lap, watching her.

'Adeline . . .?'

'Yes?'

'Ah, you're awake.' She came to sit on the edge of the bed. She had changed into a black skirt and a white crepe de Chine blouse with a wide Quaker collar. For the first time that Adeline could remember she had on a little scent. Her hair looked soft, as though it had just been washed, and fine strands of it, caught in the red glow from the fire, formed an aureole about her head. But with her back to the only source of light her face remained shadowed and unreadable.

'How are you feeling?' she asked.

'Better. It's so wonderful just to be here.'

'You'll stay with me for a while now.' It was a statement.

'Yes. You're so kind.'

'Oh no.' Marian laid the curved back of her hand against Adeline's hot cheek and stroked. 'That's one thing I am not. Do you know,' she said, 'that I have never before asked twice for anyone to come here? And I'd never have asked a third time, never. So it's just as well you came when you did.'

'You don't understand. There's nowhere else I want to be, and no-one else I want to be with but here, with you. But after last time I thought you despised me, I had to do something, achieve something of my own before I could face you again. I would have come sooner, but I've been ill – '

'Ssh. I know . . . I know.'

Marian leaned forward and kissed Adeline lightly, first on the cheek, then on the lips.

'My beautiful girl,' she said, and there was both wonder and triumph in her voice. 'My most beautiful girl. I never really doubted you.'

In a single easy movement she was lying beside Adeline, her head on the pillow next to hers, her hand resting on her throat in a way that was both indolent and possessive. In the warm, dark room Adeline could feel only Marian's hand, and see only her wide and dreaming eyes.

A little while later, in another world, a door opened downstairs. Adeline gasped but Marian said:

'It's only Neville.'

'But what if he comes up here?'

'He won't just yet. He's saying goodbye to Nicholas.' She kissed Adeline lightly and repeatedly on the face and neck, little tantalizing, bird's wing kisses. 'You mustn't worry. Everything's fine.' She drew back, her hands on Adeline's shoulders. 'Are you happy?'

Adeline's whispered answer was drowned in their embrace.

'And now,' said Marian, standing and smoothing her hair. 'I'm going down to get us some tea. Stay exactly where you are.'

'What time is it?'

'About six o'clock.'

Before leaving she smoothed the bedclothes and put some more coal on the fire. She seemed to Adeline to have undergone another of those swift and baffling changes at which she excelled. Now she was neither intense, nor manipulative, nor passionate but warm and wifely, a sprightly, charming chatelaine. Adeline could hear her bidding farewell to Nicholas down in the hall, laughing at some inaudible remark of his, closing the door, then saying to Neville:

'I'm going to take a tea tray up to the invalid.'

A murmur of assent, then: 'Would she mind a visitor . . .?'

'You must ask her yourself!' Something in Marian's voice, and the tiny interval before her footsteps moved away towards the back stairs, told Adeline that she had kissed him. This made her feel not jealous and affronted, but safe. She seemed, like an infant in the womb, to be suspended, warmly and sensuously in a secure and secret element.

She switched on the lamp and lay tranquilly listening as Neville came up the stairs, tapped lightly on the door.

'It's Neville – may I come in?'

'Of course.'

He entered, and stood at a respectable distance, smiling at her. He was smarter than usual, in a shirt and tie and green velvet jacket. Adeline remembered the lunch party.

'So,' he said, 'it's poor old you.'

'Isn't it foolish? I'm sorry, I don't normally collapse on people like this.'

He shrugged. 'Collapse away. I like sick rooms. Visiting the sick is the next best thing to being ill oneself. There's nothing half so nice in my considered opinion as loafing about in bed with a good book and hot drink, and the door open just enough – ' He demonstrated – 'so that one can hear everyone else going about their business and thank God one's not part of it. Unfortunately,' he sighed, 'I suffer from rude health, so I have to take my perverted pleasures vicariously.'

He approached the bed and peered at her. 'I say, is that my nightshirt?'

'I'm afraid it is.' Adeline's hand flew to the monogrammed pocket. 'Marian gave it to me.'

'Quite right. And you look so much nicer in it than I do.' Briefly, he fingered the sleeve of the nightshirt as if testing the quality of the material. Adeline wondered that he couldn't sense where Marian's hands had touched. She lay perfectly still, and burning, veiled in a sweat that was not just feverish until he moved away again.

Moving Marian's book he sat down in the chair by the fire, legs crossed, hand linked behind his head.

'Yes,' he said, 'it's nice having someone in this room, it gives one somewhere to escape to.'

'Do you need that – in such a big house?'

'The place is always swarming with people. Which is fine, that's the way we like it, but one needs a bolthole. Marian has her eyrie, but I do my lesser scribblings where the mood takes me. Now that you're here I shall have somewhere to go.'

His assumption that she would not have the least objection to his coming and going at will was quite overshadowed by the far greater one that her stay at Allerton Square would be of indefinite duration. She did not question either of them.

Marian came in, carrying a tray with tea things, and a loaf of bread with butter and jam. She put the tray on the ground and took from it a brass toasting fork which she handed to her husband.

'Here – make yourself useful.'

'Of course.'

Neville cut an uneven slice of bread and stuck it on the fork as Marian set out cups. Their two figures made a pretty domestic tableau around the fire as they went about their tasks without reference to Adeline, almost as if they'd forgotten she was in the room. When they spoke, their voices had the easy, quiet neutrality of people who talk together often, and alone. Though Adeline was no more than three yards away from them their conversational manner ensured that she felt like an eavesdropper.

'Tell me,' asked Neville, turning the toast, 'why did you give her one of my nightshirts and not one of your nightdresses?'

'Nothing of mine would have fitted her.'

'Ah . . . not that I mind, Mary-Anne. She's welcome . . . Is this done? What do you think? Another minute or so?'

'You should hold it to the red coals, not the flame, or it'll be burnt.'

'Is that a fact?'

And so on. They seemed unusually placid, like two children in a play house. When Neville had spread the slice of toast with butter and jam he carried it over to Adeline, the plate resting on poised fingers.

'Madam. Anything else Madam requires?'

'Yes,' said Marian, 'she'd like her tea,' and she held it out for him to place on the bedside table.

A little eddy of anxiety from some forgotten backwater nudged at Adeline. 'Neville – '

'Madam?' He maintained his waiter's manner, head tilted obsequiously.

'Would you – could you let my landlady know that I'm here? I left without telling anyone.'

'Of course, of course. Don't worry. I've deputed Nick to call round.'

'Thank you.' She could have wished the messenger to be anyone but Nicholas, but it was done. She sank back on the pillows, her tiny twinge of conscience soothed. Neville returned to his place by the fire and began to talk, to Marian mainly, about the party at lunchtime. His description was vivid, gossipy, and disparaging. Marian listened, gazing into the fire. From time to time she punctuated his remarks with a few brief words of her own, or a high, incredulous little laugh. As before, they seemed both to accept Adeline's presence and to negate it. She found this soothing: she was where she wanted to be, and nothing was asked of her. She was enfolded in an exquisite tranquillity. When she closed her eyes it seemed to her that it was now Marian that was talking, and that she heard her own name spoken low, like a password.

She fell asleep again, and dreamed, not knowing that they watched her.

When she woke again she was alone in the room. The fire had died down and the guard was in front of the red embers. Marian's book had gone, and the tea things had been removed, but the faint, nursery whiff of burnt toast hung nostalgically in the air.

Her throat ached, but her body felt light, taut and buoyant, inflated with remembered, dreamed-of ecstasy. A tall glass of water had been placed on the bedside table and she dipped her fingertips in it and brushed them over her forehead and temples. She wondered if Marian was up above in her study, and if this were so whether she herself could creep up and be there with her. She pictured the house all around her, silent just now and mostly dark, but containing like her own body the silent processes and currents of life, its many different chambers, its channels and passages and cells all made unique by Marian . . . It was so quiet that when she laid her head to one side she could hear the stalking footfall of her heart against the pillow. She touched herself beneath the silk nightshirt and felt her skin rush to meet her hand. She longed, she yearned, for Marian to return, but knew she could only wait, as the house waited, transfixed by this potent enchantment.

She turned on to her other side, pushing the covers away impatiently. She was no longer sleepy, but she had no book, nothing with which to beguile the silent hours. Facing this way she saw the bookshelves. Her eye drifted uncuriously along the uneven rows until it came to three volumes of near identical height and width. On the spine the name 'Marian Elverstone'.

Unsteadily she climbed out of bed and took the volumes from the shelf. Back in bed she adjusted the pillow behind her back and studied the cover of the first book. On the fly-leaf was a photograph of Marian. Her heavy-lidded, unsmiling, somewhat haughty face gazed back at Adeline with an expression of intellectual weariness. Her hair, neater than usual, was swept back in two smooth wings from a centre parting. She wore a severe dark blouse, buttoned to the neck, and a cameo brooch. She looked, as she had doubtless intended to, like a formidable and somewhat humourless lady of letters obliged to submit to these indignities for the benefit of the common reader. Adeline found herself pitying the photographer. The title of the book was *Another Life*. On an impulse she turned the page and read the dedication. It was brief: 'For Neville'.

She picked up the second book and did the same: 'For Ida'. She felt a pang of disquiet. The dedication of the third book was simply 'To N.E.'.

She began to read the book entitled *Letters From a Stranger* but had scarcely begun when she realized with a shock that the last dedication might be as for Nicholas.

She read for a while until Consett brought her some

supper. As the evening drew on she was feeling quite ill again, and scarcely ate. By the time Consett returned for the tray she had set aside the book, and was dozing again. When Consett was gone she switched off the lamp. She slept, lightly and uncomfortably. The dark seemed stifling and the hours interminable, the night began to take on the aspect of a difficult and hostile landscape through which she was obliged to travel, wretchedly and alone.

Very late, she didn't know when, Marian came back, dressed in a long white nightdress and with her fine, straight hair loose on her shoulders, and lay down with Adeline. She was a different Marian again, gently whispering and soothing, stroking Adeline's hair and her back and remaining with her until she fell deeply asleep.

She woke next day feeling considerably better. The room was cold, but the curtains were outlined in a sharp, white rim of sunlight. A handful of snowdrops had been placed in the glass of water on the bedside table. Adeline got out of bed and drew the curtains. A long sword of early morning sunshine cut between the roofs of the houses on the far side of the square and struck brilliantly on her face. Not far along the road a couple in evening dress alighted from a cab, the woman yawned and leaned on the man's arm as they walked to their front door. Church bells pealed in the middle distance. The black winter trees glowed warmly. She had to get up.

Wrapping herself in the bedspread she went out on to the landing. The door of the main bedroom was closed, and outside sat Bloomer. He rose and wagged his tail as she appeared, enlisting her friendship.

'Good dog – ssh,' she whispered, and he lay down again with an air of weary resignation.

She located the bathroom at the back of the house at the head of a short passage. It was large, grand and cold with a forbidding, high-sided bath on a platform, and a tall, drooping palm in a china urn. But there was soap, an assortment of untidily draped towels and the water, after some preparatory spurts and splutters, ran hot. She washed at the basin, combed her fingers through her tangled hair, and returned, swathed like a squaw to her room.

She felt a little shaky after this expedition and was glad to see that someone had been into the room during her short absence, to straighten the bed and leave a breakfast tray with a boiled egg. Whoever had been had simply melted away, for the house was still utterly quiet.

She got back into bed, ate some of the breakfast and read more of Marian's novel. It could have been written by no-one else, she thought: Marian's voice could be heard in every clear, precise sentence, especially in the descriptions of the central character, a woman separated from her beloved husband by the demands of his job who finds her love dying under the strain of absence. The mixture of passion and analytical detachment in this woman were Marian's. And as Adeline had once suspected she might, she found the character unsympathetic. She read on and on, hoping to be won over, to be able to feel as well as see the connection between the woman on the page, and the woman who had aroused her, loved her, and soothed her to sleep.

About mid-morning, to her intense relief, she heard someone moving about downstairs. She put on her clothes, which felt heavy and strange after the silk nightshirt, and went downstairs, noticing as she did so that Bloomer was no longer on the landing. Consett was in the hall, dressed to go out and pulling on some gloves. She cast Adeline the briefest and most uncurious of glances.

'Good morning.'

'Could you tell me – are Mrs and Mrs Elverstone up yet?'

'He's not. She's been out in the garden for hours.'

'I see, thank you.'

'I'm off to church,' said Consett, as though somebody had to maintain a link with the Almighty and it had fallen to her to do so.

Adeline went out on to the the terrace. The seeds and trays had gone and there was no sign of Marian. The sun had not yet come over the roof and only the far end of the garden was in sunlight. The terrace was shady and cold, thickly dusted with frost.

She fetched her cloak from the hall and went over the terrace, down the three mossy, shallow stone steps and across the lawn, a rose bed on one side, a herbaceous border on the other. She walked between the trees and out into the area at the end, made more theatrical by the sudden brightness. Now, in the daylight, she could see a lily pond with a stone dolphin leaping from its centre, the brown sticks of clematis and honeysuckle, which in summer would shroud the walls in colour and sweetness, the first green spikes of crocuses pushing through the lawn. To her right, with her back to her, was Marian, wearing the same threadbare skirt and jumper as before, working on her rockery.

In spite of her thin and delicate-seeming frame, she was surprisingly strong, energetically lifting and pushing a large slab of stone into place, packing soil around it. She wore no gloves, and when she stood back to inspect her work she pushed strands of hair off her face with her bare wrist.

'Can I help?' asked Adeline.

'Of course not, you're a convalescent.' Without turning Marian held out her hand to her as she had done at their first meeting, but this time drew her into the curve of her arm. She was warm from her work, and Adeline felt a current of heat and energy from that encircling arm. She was also in enthusiastic good humour, her attention entirely focused on the task in hand.

'It's taking shape, isn't it?' she said. 'What do you think?'

'I don't know how you've managed all that by yourself. It's wonderful.'

'Oh, I'm addicted to heavy labour. When you come with us to Cornwall you'll see I've hewn a garden from the cliff with only the smallest assistance from Neville. I told you before, the mad are preternaturally strong.'

She gave Adeline a sudden, delightful, almost playful smile, a look so unlike anything that had preceded it that it was like an unexpected gift. Impulsively Adeline embraced her and they stood tightly clasped for a moment, their compact sealed. Adeline had the sense, both exhilarating and frightening, of having taken an irrevocable step into an unknown land, from which there could be no going back: the journey must be undertaken. There were no landmarks and no guide. She was alone, trapped in a terrifying freedom.

Mrs Fairyhouse took the lead from Toni, closed the door and sat down. The dog wouldn't sit, though she tried to make it. It was tense and wretched, in a state of permanent watchfulness.

Mrs Fairyhouse stared with an expression of baffled disbelief as her husband took a biscuit from his plate and offered it to the animal. When Clancey sniffed and rejected it, gazing sad-eyed at the door, her expression changed to one of indignation and she left the room.

'You think you know people, then you find you don't,' Mr Fairyhouse called after her, but when she failed to reply his attention returned to the dog.

'Poor old boy,' he said. 'What's she up to, eh? Where's she gone? It's a shame.'

He fondled Clancey's ears with a gentle, almost an apologetic movement, the dog moved its head in order to maintain its vigil on the door through which, at any moment, Adeline might reappear.

Tonks accosted Peter as he left the painting class.

'Mr Marchant! A word.'

'Yes?'

'Mrs Charteris seems not to have been among us this term. Would you happen to know why that is?'

'She hasn't been well, I know that.'

'On the mend now, I hope?'

'I'm not sure . . . I'll make a point of finding out.'

'I think that would be a good idea.'

Fenella had persuaded Nicholas to join her and her parents for dinner at the house in The Boltons before going on to the Music Box. She considered it important to show that he could be as solidly respectable as the next man.

Over the chicken à la king she attempted to describe the portrait which Adeline had done of her.

'It actually makes me look awfully pale and interesting!' she cried. 'She's very gifted – I wish you could see it.'

'I agree,' said Sir Stanley. 'She'd better bring it round her so we can take a look. She's rather a handsome girl if my memory serves me.'

'Still just a student, though,' said his wife, rather more cautiously.

'But you must just see it,' insisted Fenella.

'Um – ' Nicholas leaned forward. 'You'll have to wait for a while. I don't think she's there at the moment.'

'Where is she then?' Fenella was unused to other people not being present when she needed them.

'No-one has the remotest idea,' said Nicholas. 'Isn't it mysterious?'

Bob had spent an hour in Ted Maybury's office, resisting the blandishments of both Maybury and the putative editor of his new newspaper, when Louise Maybury was shown in by the secretary. She caught Bob's eye and lifted her hand in a little 'don't-mind-me-I'm-not-really-here' gesture before sitting down on the sofa against the wall and lighting a cigarette.

'Look,' said Maybury, 'I have to go. Let me just say this. You have reservations about my politics. Well don't. I want to publish a paper that's not for stuffed shirts, something to set them by the ears. Michael here – ' He slapped the editor on the shoulder, ' – will have absolute autonomy. He wants you and I want him to have the best team he can get.'

'We're just asking you to think about it,' said the editor. 'But not for too long.'

The meeting adjourned, and Maybury moved the group affably but firmly towards the door. Louise rose, was motioned over, greeted and presented.

'I believe you know my wife,' said Maybury to Bob.

They agreed that they knew each other, shook hands, exchanged a couple of pleasantries. Maybury opened the door.

'Ring Michael tomorrow,' he said, 'and let him know. We'll expect the answer yes.'

As he walked blindly across the outer office and along the corridor to the lift, Bob, dazzled and intoxicated by Louise, contemplated such an answer for the first time.

'My dears,' said Elizabeth. 'How perfectly lovely. Anne –' She kissed her future daughter-in-law. 'I couldn't be more pleased.'

Certainly, Frank had never looked happier. He was quite flushed with pride and delight. And Anne was – well, Anne was never going to be radiant, but she was laughing, as if the whole thing were a rather splendid and amazing prank.

'We thought perhaps the end of April,' she said, 'when the weather's better.'

'Of course,' agreed Elizabeth. 'Everyone will want to come.'

'No fuss, Mother, please,' said Frank, 'we want to be very quiet.'

'Well, of course it must all be just the way you want it.'

Elizabeth must have appeared crestfallen, though they mistook her reasons for being so, for Anne, her hand in Frank's, said:

'Let's be honest, I'm not exactly the white lace and organdie type, am I?'

Frank lifted Anne's hand to his lips and kissed it in a gestured so gallant and fond that Elizabeth blurted something about wanting to spread the news, and left the room.

In fact, she wanted more than anything to speak to Adeline. But when she sat down by the telephone she was too dispirited to lift the receiver.

She was glad they were happy – especially glad that Frank was, for he'd seemed so careworn at times in recent years. It was just that – she struggled to identify her feelings – that nothing was turning out as she'd expected.

Elizabeth was reasonably honest with herself, and had always striven not to be a match-making mama. But she could not disguise the fact that she'd entertained great hopes of Frank, the eldest child born out of the best years of her marriage. He was the one, with his looks and his style, that she had expected to go far, and do great things, and make a glittering marriage to some lovely, gifted girl. Instead of which – and Elizabeth was ashamed to be entertaining such thoughts – he was dutifully overseeing the family acres and was going to marry plain, jolly, home-grown Anne.

And since the old Hyde-Latimers had died it had been a foregone conclusion that 'all the fun of organizing things' as Frank had jovially put it, would fall to her.

Elizabeth knew she couldn't have managed without Frank at Fording Place and she knew, too, that Anne was the nicest woman in the world. But nothing could prevent her from feeling, deeply, treacherously, disappointed.

Duncan and Joel, arriving at the gates of the Slade on Thursday morning, saw a familiar figure crossing the quadrangle in front of them.

'Good God,' said Duncan. 'It's her. Addy!'

They ran to catch up with her, Joel easily, Duncan puffing, clutching his hat.

'Addy! Wait!'

She stopped and turned, smiling. The dog bounded and fussed round the three of them as they greeted each other. In response to their anxious and slightly accusing questions she was serenely pleasant.

'I don't know what all the fuss is about. I had the flu, I was with some friends, and they persuaded me to stay for a few nights. That's all.'

'But Addy – ' Duncan looked comically aggrieved. 'We're your friends, we've been distracted with worry. Pedro says you vanished into thin air and he, poor man, is looking quite wan and wasted. Unlike you, one is bound to say.' He looked her up and down. 'Whatever you've been up to it certainly agrees with you.'

'Yes, I'm quite recovered now.' She beamed. 'I'm glad everyone's missing me.'

They continued into college, Duncan expostulating, Adeline laughing at him, refusing to explain. Joel followed more quietly. There was no doubt that Adeline looked wonderful, and yet for the first time she was holding out on them. The charmed circle was no longer charmed. She had a secret.

He found himself feeling unaccountably sorry for Peter.

CHAPTER EIGHTEEN

1925

ADELINE TOLD NO-ONE what had happened to her during those five lost days, nor where she had been. She knew that to do so would be to rupture the delicate caul of understanding that wrapped her relationship with Marian Elverstone. That part of her life was not so much secret as separate, lived in what seemed increasingly to be another dimension.

During the months that followed she learnt to preserve the distance between the one life and the other, and the learning was an instinctive rather than a conscious process. Since her preoccupations and achievements were of little or no interest to the occupants of Allerton Square, she realized that no matter how sedulously she prosecuted them on the outside, they must be left on the doorstep when she went to visit Marian. With Marian the present was all that mattered, and each time they were together it had to be created afresh, without colour or shading from the past.

Which was hard at first, for things were going well for

Adeline. To her delight and astonishment the Marchants
liked her portrait of Fenella and offered to purchase it for
what seemed to her to be a ludicrously large sum. 'It's
very much how she used to look, wouldn't you say, Stanley?' was Lady Marchant's response. 'Before she became
a flapper.' This last word was pronounced complete with
inverted commas. The word spread fast. Here, said debutantes to their mothers and fathers and to each other, was
someone who could make you appear quite shockingly
and daringly different, while still recognizably yourself. If
Adeline Charteris could do *that* with Fenella Marchant of
all people, and get away with it, what might she not do
with the rest of them? The desire to be flattered and ideal-
ised was suddenly old hat, dull and *passé*. Bright young
things whose bright young faces concealed only brightness and youth wanted nothing more than to be shown as
they *really were*. Besides which Fenella herself turned out
to be a gifted natural publicist, whose high-spirited gossip
concerning Adeline did nothing to harm her commercial
standing. Why, the artist herself was so young, still a student, for heaven's sake, and a widow, how absolutely fascinating! And the *on dit* was that she was a little eccentric
and had a dog that went simply everywhere with her, too
killing. There was no doubt about it, Adeline was new. A
craze was beginning.

It was impossible not to enjoy it. Adeline loved to be
busy, she loved to paint, she had no qualms about making
money from art. Her only problem was that of being certain that her subjects interested her. There had to be something there that was not just beauty, nor the desire to be
immortalized, nor the cash to pay. She made a point of
finding it.

About a month after the portrait of Fenella had been
framed and delivered to the Marchants' London house,
she received a letter from the mother of nineteen-year-old
twins, the Honourable Diana and the Honourable Isobel
Carteret, to the effect that she knew the Marchants, and
that both she and her girls had been 'very taken' with the

interesting portrait of Fenella . . . Adeline had received her first commission.

The twins were not at first sight promising material, being identically plump-faced and thick-legged, with difficult, frizzy hair. On the other hand they were nice, eager, enthusiastic girls who laughed a lot, and who thought Clancey was quite the sweetest thing they'd ever met in their entire lives. If told to sit down and relax they turned into two pudding-faced effigies, but with the dog they were as boisterous and natural as children. Adeline painted them with Clancey between them, occupying the centre of the canvas. By making a lot of sketches on their first meeting she managed to give the painting an unposed, photographic quality, with the Honourable Diana leaning forward as if talking to the dog, and the Honourable Isobel leaning back, in fits of laughter. The result was amusing and charming. No-one could have made the twins look beautiful but they did look lively and fun. Clancey appeared dignified and benign. After a brief, nail-biting interval during which the girls had winked and made reassuring faces, their mother had turned to Adeline and declared herself 'enchanted'.

So she could paint the lovely and the not-so-lovely and make both appear interesting, the society mamas murmured to each other over buffets and bridge tables – and oddly enough she was 'one of us', one of the Devonshire Gundrys, did you realize . . .?

After the twins there began a steady trickle of commissions. Not enough to make her wealthy, for she only charged just enough to make her customers feel it was worth paying. And she did not, yet, become famous, simply *recherché* among a small section of the already small number of people who were able and disposed to purchase portraits. Outside that restricted and rarified market she was either completely unknown, or ignored. Adeline was well aware of this. She knew that the smart and well-to-do were more interested in vying with one another than in owning a work of art. Some of them were frankly dismayed by her work, but paid up anyway to avoid the ignominy of appearing old-fashioned. Some of her more knowledgeable customers thought her naturalistic style sentimental and considered that, though she succeeded in capturing a likeness, her means of doing so was suspect. She was clever, she had a facility, but her talent was like that of the mimic as compared with that of the serious actor. By all means buy one of her paintings, these people said to their acquaintances, but don't expect it to be any kind of serious investment: she won't last.

But though Adeline knew this, her confidence remained undented. If she had entertained an inflated notion of her own worth, she might have worried, but she had always been a realist. What she had always wanted and been able to do, was to convey with beguiling immediacy a particular aspect of her chosen subject. There was an element of theatricality in her work; she sought to entertain and surprise.

Not that much of this was a conscious process. In spite of what many people thought, and usually said, she did not tailor her paintings for a specific and lucrative market. She would pursue an idea for her own enjoyment, and presumed that the more she enjoyed it the more successful the outcome would be. She knew how extremely lucky she was to be an artist whose modest but peculiar gift had happened to find its time.

Her college work suffered, of course, and since she was in her final year this caused sufficient concern to warrant a summons from Tonks himself.

'I'm sorry if that's how it looks,' she said, 'but if people want my portraits, I can hardly turn them down. I could actually earn my living by doing what I most enjoy.' She almost shouted at the august professor in her amazement at her own good fortune. He raised both hands as if to fend off this tidal wave of unstoppable enthusiasm.

'Mrs Charteris – sit down, do – it's none of my business what you do in your own time. But you are here, after all, to gain a qualification in Fine Art, and I suggest that if you fail to gain that qualification your commercial standing at some later date may be jeopardized.' Tonks knew his subject and observed, with satisfaction, that her expression became more thoughtful. He continued: 'Until now your attendance has been good and your work interesting. It's certainly well up to scratch. I think I mentioned at the outset that I had no doubt you'd be able to make money from your work, and it's gratifying to see that apparently I was right. I would just warn against taking on too much, too soon.'

His practical approach commended itself to Adeline. 'I do understand. And I will pay more attention to the course.'

'I'm sure you will.' Tonks rose to dismiss her. 'By the way, Mr Marchant told me you were ill at the beginning of this term. Nothing serious, I hope?'

'No. Only the flu. I went to stay with some friends.'

'Good, good . . .' Tonks surveyed her reflectively. She was not someone whom it was easy to influence. 'Quite recovered now?'

'Oh, perfectly.'

As the door closed behind her Adeline knew this was only partly true. She was in perfect health, but the cure itself had begun an addiction so fierce and overwhelming that she could not imagine, and could scarcely remember, life without it.

Though she could hardly have said as much to Tonks, she was obliged to work on her commissions during the week, because her weekends were spent at Allerton Square. Only the most hectic activity and the most iron self-control prevented her from being there at every spare moment. Her life was geared to filling two-thirds of her time as intensively as was humanly possible, in order that the remaining third might be light and free as air.

She had come to accept the unwritten rules of Allerton Square as the price she must willingly pay for Marian's love. That the price was also exacted from her family and friends was something of which, in her bewitched state, she was not really aware.

When Toni, to whom self-pity and complaining were anathema, called specially one evening to ask whether she

had seen or heard anything of Bob, she replied cheerfully
that she had not. She failed to read (as she would have
done in the past) the sub-text of the question, or to see
the unhappiness in her friend's face or, later, to hear her
weeping (for only the second time in her life) in her room.
Her emotional antennae were directed towards one person, and one person only.

In the same way, when she decided that she could no
longer allow Peter to harbour any hopes concerning her,
she told him so with an abruptness that would, until
recently, have been uncharacteristic of her. She chose to
tell him in the casual hubbub of the Slade refectory, out of
some quite unfounded notion that he might make a scene,
and it would be harder for him to do so here.

'I see,' he said, pushing aside his untouched plate. 'So
you're banishing me.'

'I'm not. We'll still see each other.'

'I mean from your affections, Addy.'

'Not entirely. We can go on being friends – '

'We were more than that.'

'You thought so. But I don't know that we were.'

She realized that in denying all that time when she had
been warmly grateful for Peter's loyal love and his protective, reliable embrace, she was behaving just as Marian
would have done. He looked away, as if trying to regroup
his forces, and then back at her, searchingly.

'Where do you go, Addy? What are you up to? It isn't
just me, because I love you. We've all noticed it. We've
lost you.'

He had struck a nerve, and she was piqued. 'You hav-
en't. I'm here, aren't I?'

'Well – in body, yes. You know very well what I mean.
It's not those damn Elverstones, is it?'

'Oh for heaven's sake!' He was moving too close to her
other world, and she lost her temper. 'You don't own me,
any of you! I happen to have made some friends outside
the Slade, that's all. Can you wonder when you behave
like this that I want to escape from time to time?' Her voice

had risen, heads turned, she lowered it to a fierce whisper.
'I won't be interrogated!'

Peter smiled, because for that moment she had seemed
so much more like herself.

'May I ask you a favour, then?'

'I suppose so.'

'May I wait till you come back?'

She was exasperated. 'Peter – '

'No strings.'

'I shan't come back. Not in the way you mean.'

'But you might. And I want to be there if you do.'

'You'll be wasting your time.'

'I'll be the judge of that.'

'Then you're more stubborn and conceited than I
thought!'

Oddly enough it was this final, furious insult, hurled
down at him from a great height as she left the table, that
persuaded Peter it might be worth not entirely abandoning
hope. But still he had no stomach for either food or work
that afternoon, and went instead for a long walk in the soft
spring air that seemed designed for lovers.

Because of the altered perspective of her life, Adeline had
not been astonished as she might have been by the news,
delivered by her mother over the telephone, that Frank
and Anne were to marry. She was no longer sufficiently
interested to reflect on how unlikely a union this would
have seemed in pre-war days.

But when the invitation itself arrived, accompanied by
a friendly handwritten note from Anne, it was forced
unwillingly upon her attention. Saturday 21 April. Damn,
she would have to go. It wasn't even term time, and she
had no excuse to offer that would possibly justify the non-
attendance of her elder brother's wedding. And yet it
would mean the whole weekend, two or even three days
that she would otherwise have spent with Marian. She
bitterly resented her family's quiet and confident claim
upon her.

The situation was made worse by Marian's refusal to

acknowledge her excuses, let alone admit their validity. She was not interested.

'So you'll be going to this family gathering,' she said, her head resting on the back of the sofa, eyes closed.

'I must, I'm afraid. I'd so much rather be here, but – '

'Don't worry about us, we shall amuse ourselves famously.' Thus did Marian touch unerringly the raw nerve of jealousy that Adeline tried to keep hidden. She opened her eyes and caught Adeline's expression. At once she was graceful in victory, her voice was tender when she spoke.

'Come here. Come here, by me.'

Adeline moved close to her, and Marian drew her head down on to her shoulder.

'Don't say any more about it. You're here now, and that's all that matters.'

The day of the wedding was clear, sunny, tremulously fresh, a day for hope and new beginnings if ever there was one. There was only a handful of people in the church, and Adeline, taking her place in the pew just behind Frank and Chris Dance, could not help being struck by the contrast between her own wedding – how many aeons ago? – and this. She felt again, rather than remembered, her shining, impatient optimism, the satin dress, the rich scent of the hothouse bouquet, the rows of indulgently smiling faces turning towards her as she walked up the aisle, reflecting her youth and happiness. There had been just one face, Elizabeth's, that for a fleeting moment had displayed a bleak and helpless prescience. And outside the grey winter's day had pressed against the windows of the church so that the lamps had to be lit.

Today the spring sunshine gave its blessing to what, on the face of it, was a much less likely marriage. The proceedings were imbued with a quiet and sensible confidence which Adeline found both touching and faintly oppressive. The church, the people in it and the ceremony itself proclaimed a permanence that unsettled her. Frank, standing in profile to her, his right hand clasping tightly his left wrist, his face gravely handsome, seemed the very epitome of certainty. While Anne, coming up the aisle on the arm of her uncle, for her father had died, was smiling broadly, almost chuckling with delight. It was clear the rest of them were mere onlookers, that these two needed no-one's approval. Adeline felt that she was witnessing a rite that was now foreign to her, impressive yet incomprehensible. She glanced at Elizabeth, but there was nothing to be read from her expression.

Afterwards there was a lunch party. Adeline noticed how easily and naturally Anne slipped into the role of hostess at Fording Place, as if she had always been there, Her rightness for the job was manifest, and Elizabeth had sidestepped into the part of dowager with surprising grace. She and Howard, who had come to the wedding alone and was returning the same evening, seemed pre-occupied with some shared concern. Even when they were separated Adeline sensed the lines of communication humming between them. Over champagne in the drawing room she sought out Dorothy, who was listening to Chris Dance explain some arcane agricultural matter with the practised air of absorption learned from years of listening to children.

'Dorothy, Chris! May I butt in? How lovely to see you again.'

Chris retired outnumbered by women and Adeline and Dorothy went through to the library to admire the wedding presents.

'She's certainly got some beautiful things,' remarked Dorothy, touching silver and glass, peering at cards. 'She's a very lucky young woman.'

There was no denying the implication and Adeline knew Dorothy too well to let it pass.

'Oh, Dorothy, Frank was always your favourite, wasn't he? Does all this make you sad?' Adeline realised that she had not said 'Nanny' – and had not been reproved.

'Sad? Heavens above no! A wedding's always a happy occasion,' replied Dorothy briskly, removing and replacing the lid of a teapot to see if it fitted.

'But you think he could have done better, is that it?'

'He's a grown man and he's made a very sensible choice. These cups'll let the tea go cold.'

As they returned to the other guests and Chris Dance appeared to reclaim his position at Dorothy's side, Adeline reflected that wooing Dorothy must be akin to one of the labours of Hercules: a near-impossible task requiring superhuman spirit and determination. Only when Frank and Anne stopped to talk to them on their peregrinations around the room did Dorothy's face light up, so that it sounded quite strange to hear her brother refer to this vivacious, handsome woman as 'Nanny'.

After lunch Anne went upstairs to change from her simple, unremarkable dress into an equally unremarkable suit, and invited Adeline to keep her company. Following her up the stairs Adeline found herself frankly dreading any womanly confidences that might ensue, but was a little taken aback to find Anne's attention turned on her.

'I'm getting fat,' said Anne, looking at herself in the mirror. 'Unlike you, Addy, you've lost weight. If you're not careful you'll become positively elegant. Brooch or not?' Adeline shook her head. 'No, you're right. But you seem different, not your usual bouncing self. Are you worried about anything?'

'No. Well – ' Adeline decided to offer some plausible excuse. 'This is my last year at the Slade, so there's the future to consider.'

'But Bob tells me you've been getting commissions – that you're quite sought after!'

Adeline was nettled. 'He seems to know a great deal considering I haven't seen him for months.'

'But journalists are supposed to know things, aren't they?' said Anne placidly, donning an ill-judged fussy hat. 'I must say I was pretty astonished to hear he'd decided to go and work for Edward Maybury. It's quite cheering in its way to know that even Bob had his price.'

As Adeline digested this, Anne turned from the mirror, picked up her handbag and flapped her arms at her sides, presenting herself. 'How's that?'

'Nice. Very smart.' Adeline rose from the bed, forcing a smile, her polite, affectionate compliment soured by the spectre of what Marian would have said. Anne tugged at her jacket. 'Once more unto the breach, then. We agreed away by three-thirty no matter what.'

Just before they left the room she paused and looked at Adeline, her shrewd, humorous face at odds with the silly hat.

'Happy?' she asked.

'Yes.'

'Good!'

It was only as Adeline watched her descend the stairs at Frank's side, calling cheerfully to the people gathered in the hall, that she realized it was she who should have asked Anne that.

After Anne and Frank had left, Howard was the next to go, and then Chris Dance ran Dorothy to the station, and the other guests trickled away. Adeline and Bob, feeling their filial responsibilities, had agreed to return to London together the following day since Elizabeth was bound to feel rather glum. But in the flat, anticlimactic wastes of the late afternoon, without the shared focus of Anne and Frank to bind them together, they separated and drifted awkwardly, unable to relax together but feeling that they should not be apart.

In the end Elizabeth went to the library to begin putting away the presents and compiling a list of their senders, declaring firmly, even forbiddingly, that she did not require any help. Bob and Adeline faced each other across the drawing room hearth while Clancey, released from purdah in the kitchen, lay at full stretch on the rug.

'So you've sold out to Ted Maybury,' said Adeline. She felt fractious and combative.

'I'm working on his new paper, yes. Michael O'Dell, the editor, is a good bloke. I like him, and Maybury doesn't seem to interfere.'

'And the money's good.'

'Yes. Look, Addy – ' Bob threw his cigarette end in the

fire with a gesture of impatience. 'I don't know what you're trying to imply but it's infernally annoying.'

'I'm not implying anything, just that you always said the *Courier* was the only paper you could respect. The only paper with any integrity, you called it.'

'Well I'm hoping the *Recorder* will be another. And quite honestly I didn't know that you had such a tender concern for my politics.'

She was ensnared in her ill-humour. Bob lit another cigarette and added: 'Besides, I'm a professional journalist, not a politician, and this is a much better job, with pay to match.'

She allowed a pause, conceding him that, and then said: 'They didn't come today, the Mayburys. Weren't they invited?'

'I expect so. I believe so.' He leaned forward to pat Clancey, his face hidden. 'They're madly busy, the way the rich are – places to go, people to see . . . probably just as well.' His voice dropped and became muffled, and Adeline only thought she heard him add: 'We couldn't both have been here . . .'

And then Elizabeth was in the room holding aloft a green glass lamp and asking whether they didn't think it was quite the most ghastly thing they'd ever seen, and they all had a drink, and agreed that it was.

Throughout that spring and early summer the circle of friendship between Adeline, Toni, Peter, Duncan and Joel, which had been displaying signs of wear and tear since Christmas, slowly disintegrated. This was due at least partly to practical considerations. Toni moved out of the house in Gower Street to a little top floor flat off the Edgware Road. Adeline was either not there, or absorbed in her work. Peter's enthusiasm for the artistic life had waned and he was discussing a business venture with Nicholas Eyre. Duncan and Joel were preoccupied with the increasingly vital question of how to make ends meet. By the time college ended they had effectively already flown the nest, their respective results were of only the most fleeting and distant interest. Adeline scraped through with an undistinguished pass mark, and Duncan did the same; Peter failed – his enthusiasm, they realized must have died long before they knew – and Joel emerged, like Toni before him, with the laurel wreath. As reward for his excellence he was offered a contract to paint landscapes for the Shell country calendar, and accepted with alacrity. Duncan, protesting a little too often that he wasn't fussy what he did so long as someone would pay him for it, came to rest in a large magazine publishing company, drawing clean-limbed upper-class heroes for a boys' weekly comic.

The class of '21 had moved on.

In July Adeline finished a portrait of young Lady Violet Burgoyne and her two pale, gingery children, paid Mrs Fairyhouse two months rent in advance, and left for Cornwall with the Elverstones. The weather was fine, the future spread before her, full of delightful possibilities, and Neville and Marian were at their most beguiling.

Like a child relieved of all cares and responsibilities, she sat in the back seat with the dogs watching the countryside move past the window and listening to the Elverstones as they sang. They possessed a huge repertoire of songs, ranging from famous arias and cod recitative – to which they had grafted obscene lyrics of their own – to popular songs of the moment, with in between a whole range of ditties, rounds, lays and laments. In song, the Elverstones changed places – Marian droned in a lower register, Neville in a light, melodious tenor. No matter how grand, how banal, or how downright vulgar the words, they delivered their renditions with a pseudo-serious musicality, conducting themselves, hunching their shoulders and narrowing their eyes for pianissimo, scowling portentously for the final rallentando, spitting out their Ts and Rs like a couple of prima donna assolutas in the front of the dark blue Austin Seven.

Adeline was almost delirious with laughter, which she kept under control only so as not to break the spell. This was another of those periods, quite divorced from the demands and surroundings of everyday life, which was so perfect that Adeline would have liked it to continue ad infinitum.

She had been worried about Marian's reaction to Clancey, for she had had no intention of leaving him with the Fairyhouses, and had decided in the end to play Marian at her own game and simply bring him along. It was affection for Clancey, not rebelliousness towards Marian, that had prompted her action. She accepted, absolutely, Marian's power over her. Their lovemaking was such a powerful drug, it took her to such dizzy heights and left her so weak with the desire for more, that she was hopelessly addicted. Nothing in her life before had prepared her for this: she was her body's slave. She wanted Marian all the time, so that if Marian should touch her, however casually, it was like a match being laid to dry grass and she came alight. And because her lover was a woman she learnt narcissism. Their lovemaking was like a perfect and continuous circle, or a stream running through their lives, sometimes surfacing and sometimes hidden, but always there. It dominated and outweighed all other considerations – Marian's aloofness, her arrogance, her perversity and presumption. At last sex had entered Adeline's life and taken it by storm. And Marian's rejection of all things past had one advantage – it protected Adeline from the knowledge of how many there had been before.

They arrived at the Pink House at eight o'clock in the evening, when the brilliance and heat of the day had stilled and quietened and taken on a soft, enchanted bloom. They had been on the road all day, they were tired and stiff, the dogs were curled on the seat in attitudes of lolling gloom. Marian had taken over the driving.

They wound down into the narrow creek of Port Prynne, and when they'd gone perhaps a mile up the hill beyond it they turned off the road, which was only a narrow lane anyway, and began bumping along a flinty cartrack over the cliffs. The westering sun struck across the austere landscape and the few grey cottages of Port Prynne were hidden in the fold of the cliffs. They might have been the only people on earth, or chieftains claiming new territory for themselves. Before them was the sea, turning to violet in the evening light, and as calm and still as the air itself.

The cart track began to descend towards the sea now, and the bare flat turf gave way to longer grass full of wild flowers, and then to bracken, and gorse and broom, and great ramparts of brambles covered in new, green berries. Marian stopped the car. After the rattling and bumping and the uneven roar of the engine the stillness was beautiful, a benison. The dogs lifted their heads. They could hear a curlew crying and, soft but insistent and distinct, the wash and whisper of the sea. Above them in the enormous, secret sky a hawk trembled.

'The Pink House,' said Marian.

Whatever Adeline had expected, it wasn't this. Her ideas about country houses were based on the mellow and orderly beauty of Fording Place. The Pink House was an elaborate Victorian folly, a pale pink miniature castle complete with fairytale conical towers, castellated balconies and an arched wooden door in the style of a portcullis. It was both whimsical and vulgar, but there was a impudent charm in its unexpectedness, and the loveliness of its position showed that the cotton king who'd built it had known what he was doing. It stood on the shoulder of the cliff. To the west it commanded, like a fort, a view of the wild and tumbling Cornish coast, butting and punching at the sea, away to a distant horizon. To the east, below the house, the densely packed bushes, huddled in the lee of the hills concealed a narrow path, hardly more than a goat track, which led down to the beach.

Neville turned in his seat to look at Adeline.

'What do you think?' he asked, his smile mischievous.

She shrugged helplessly, happily. 'It's not what I imagined.'

'The locals,' said Marian complacently, 'loathe it.'

She started up the engine once more and drove down

to the house. The dogs, sensing their imminent arrival, sat up and panted, quivering with longing.

The Pink House had two acres of land to call its own, some of it tamed and brought to order, most of it reclaimed by the wild since the days of the cotton king. When Marian spoke of having hewn a garden from the cliff, it was no more than the truth. At the side of the house, overlooking the sea, was a terrace, a lawn (in dire need of mowing, but a lawn for all that) and borders crammed with shrubs and flowers and soft fruit, rising in steps like paddy fields. The ground was enclosed by a dry stone wall, patched with lichen and moss and adorned at this time of year by shocks of pink thrift and spears of mauve and white foxgloves. They entered through a gap in the wall – there was no gate – and wound down a sandy track to the house.

They climbed stiffly from the car, stretching and yawning. The soft evening sunshine striking across the face of the house seemed to have singled them out, to be shining exclusively on them. The dogs trotted away, sniffing greedily at a feast of new, untried smells.

'Come along,' said Neville, 'let's see what Mrs Playle's left us.'

He unlocked the door and went inside. Marian had wandered away over the lawn, head up, arms folded, and was standing quite still facing into the sun. Adeline guessed that her eyes were closed. She hesitated, wanting to go to her, but Neville called: 'Adeline? Come on, let me show you around.' And she went in.

The inside of the house was as strange and elaborate as one might have expected, as romantically fanciful as Allerton Square was austere. Though it was only a large house, and certainly no castle, the cotton king had given free rein to his imagination. The floors were flagged, the doors were timber with black iron work, the windows were narrow, pointed arches, deeply recessed into the thick walls. Steps and stairs were everywhere, little runs and flurries of them at the end of passages, in and out of rooms, up and down from galleries. Spiral staircases

climbed up each of the towers at the front corners of the
house, leading to a gallery off which were the bedrooms,
and from the centre of which the main staircase descended
to the hall. Enormous beams traversed the ceilings and
framed the open fireplaces which must, Adeline thought,
have been essential, for many of the walls were plain, bare
stone.

The place was clean and scrubbed, their footsteps echoed loudly in the emptiness and the dogs, when they
rushed in to explore, skidded and skittered on the flags
and the polished wooden staircases. Adeline saw that here
the Elverstones had made no attempt to impose themselves or their taste upon the house, but allowed it its
faintly potty idiosyncracy. There were some books, but
few pictures; the furniture was comfortable but plain; the
rugs and carpets well worn.

'Hey!' shouted Neville. 'Who's for supper?'

She followed his voice to the kitchen, which was large
and, because it was at the back of the house, beginning to
be cool in the deepening shadow. But the range had been
lit, and the larder was fully stocked, with bread in a crock,
a cooked ham, enormous pasties bursting with mutton
and potatoes, cheese, fruit eggs and milk.

'Good, good,' said Neville. 'Now first things first.' He
put the pasties into the oven to heat and took from the
meat safe some hefty butcher's scraps for the dogs.

'It's like magic,' said Adeline. 'How did all this food get
here?'

'The saintly Mrs Playle,' said Neville, taking a note
from the table and handing it to her.

It was written in a round, laborious hand. 'Dear Mr E.
– ' So Neville had made the arrangements. 'I been and
cleaned all round and put food in I'll see you Friday Yours
E. Playle'

So some village woman had trekked all this way to make
things ready for them. Adeline thought how spoiled they
were, in many ways more spoiled than the society girls
she painted, who had at least been brought up on the prin-
ciple of noblesse oblige. Marian and Neville seemed

simply not to realize how much dull and trivial work took place so that they could float, untrammelled, in their special element. When Neville referred to Mrs Playle as saintly it was the merest token appreciation.

Now he went out to collect the luggage from the Austin. She followed him and walked over to where Marian was inspecting her terraced garden.

'It's wonderful!' she called, her hand shading her eyes from the dazzle of the low sun. 'Incredible! I love it!'

Marian came down to join her, and kissed her with her hands laid flat on Adeline's breasts. She appeared to seduce and to bid her wait at the same time. Adeline tried to embrace her but she slipped away and walked towards the house.

'Let's eat,' she said, over her shoulder. 'There's a lot to do.'

At Allerton Square the Elverstones created another world. In Cornwall there was no need. They were cut off by inclination, by distance and by circumstance. Even the coast path, beloved of hikers, was treacherous and was interrupted between their bay and the neighbouring one of Port Prynne so only the occasional hardy and expert walker passed by. As Marian had rightly observed, the villagers disliked the Pink House and, by association, anyone who owned or cared to live in it. Only Edna Playle came, once a week, and, so far from being the apple-cheeked motherly farmer's wife of Adeline's imagination, she was a thin, hard-eyed young woman, deserted by her husband for reasons that were not difficult to guess at, and with 'no better than she ought to be' hanging round her like the cloud of 'Tropic Breeze' she wore. Saintly she was not, but Neville took a mischievous delight in treating her as if she were, crying, 'What would we do without you?' and 'You're really too good to us, Mrs P!' in a way that Adeline would have found offensive if it hadn't reduced her to waves of uncontrollable laughter. Some provisions Edna brought in her bicycle basket, others were delivered for collection from a box at the top of the cart track:

occasionally they took the car to Polzeath, or Roc, and
went shopping, most especially for drink and cigarettes.
When they made these forays the Elverstones would
behave as badly as unsupervised children on a day out,
revelling in their anonymity and their presumed superiority to the holiday-making families with their golf clubs
and shrimping nets. Adeline was awed and elated by their
cavalier attitude not just to the proprieties, but to the law.
In cafés and restaurants they would order enormous meals
and then pretend, at great and elaborate length, that they
had no cash. Only when they were sure that all the patrons
and most of the staff were watching them with scandalized
fascination did they 'find' the necessary money – only just
enough – and hand it over, coin by agonizing coin.

Another of their specialities was what Marian referred to
as 'hanging out the washing'. For this exercise, anywhere
would do provided there were a reasonable number of
people going quietly about their business. The Elverstone
would begin to argue, at first in whispers, then sotto voce,
finally at full belt, the bone of contention being the bizarre
sexual proclivities of one or the other, or both. It was both
a divine parody and plain reality. When they considered
the show at an end, or when some irate and courageous
local worthy had told them to take their squalid problems
elsewhere and not offend the hearing of decent upstanding
people any longer, then they would walk away, arm in
arm, a picture of harmony, leaving their audience thunderstruck.

They stole, just for the fun of it, sometimes picking up
an item on the way into a shop only to replace it on the way
out. Anything that was lying about – a hat, an umbrella,
an apple, a tin bucket and spade – they would take, and
generally discard within minutes, the excitement over.

Adeline watched their antics, horror struck, but
admiring their style even while she deplored their callousness. She dreaded being commandeered as a participant,
but – for the moment – they seemed content to let her be
a spectator.

But still, these expeditions were infrequent, and their

wild activity only served to underline the very different
tenor of life at the Pink House. In their castle, at the heart
of their cliff-top kingdom, they enjoyed perfect freedom.
They could gaze in all directions to a far horizon, but could
not themselves be seen. The weather was hot and golden,
and their bouts of industry were followed by long periods
of hazy indolence. They went about naked, and for the
first time Adeline made sketches of Neville and Marian:
Neville in a deckchair, holding a glass and a cigarette, and
wearing only a straw hat . . . Marian asleep on a rug,
her only covering a forgotten book lying open on her
stomach . . . The two of them playing croquet, their
fierce concentration at odds with their vulnerable bare
bodies . . . Neville, the day his shoulders got burnt, sitting at the table on the terrace with a towel round his neck,
staring at a hand of cards . . . The dogs resting in a tangled
heap in the shade of the wall. They took no notice of her
drawing, and never asked to see what she had done, but
she was quite pleased with the sketches and amassed a large
number which she squirreled away in her portfolio.

Every day they swam, taking ten minutes to go down
to the beach along the narrow track, and almost half an
hour to get back. But they had the tiny cove to themselves
and here too they went naked, from the crisp, cold breakers to the warm sand and the hot rocks. They would collect things – shells, and weed and pieces of driftwood,
and starfish – and then halfway back they'd get tired of
carrying them and discard them at the side of the path.
The tides were very sharp, and sometimes they'd misjudge
them and arrive to find the waves lapping the rocks at the
base of the cliff. Then they'd simply dive in, looking down
through the clear water, beyond their pale, waving legs,
at the places where only the day before they'd sunbathed
and read and ate.

Neville was lazy, but Marian had finished her book and
had a surfeit of energy. She did immense amounts of heavy
work in the garden, clearing and digging the wild ground,
gradually pushing back the boundaries of her territory.
Because she scarcely slept she was always up long before

the others, and Adeline liked to wake and hear her, knowing that all she had to do was walk out of the house and be with her. She changed before Adeline's eyes from the pale and slender intellectual of Allerton Square to a wiry brown gypsy. They walked for miles along the cliffs, leaving Neville dozing in the garden and often, on the secluded slope of some headland or the sand of a deserted beach, they made love.

Though from the start Neville had condoned and approved their affair implicitly, as Marian approved his with Nicholas, they maintained, even in the Pink House, the outward appearance of a conventional domestic ménage. Marian would never touch or use endearments to Adeline in Neville's presence. At night they slept in separate rooms, Marian and Neville, the married couple, in one of the round tower bedrooms at the back of the house, Adeline in the other. In dozens of small ways she was reminded that their union came first, and was the fertile soil in which others were permitted to flourish. Adeline did not resent this. Accustomed now to accept them unquestioningly, she was unaware that the roots of their marriage were gradually, almost imperceptibly, loosening, and that she herself was the cause.

It was in mid-August, when Neville returned to London for a week, that they began to dress up. They'd driven him to the station in Bude and returned to the Pink House at midday. It was one of the few days when the weather was less than perfect, the air was close and heavy and purple thunderheads towered on the western horizon.

Adeline lay with Marian in the bed that still bore the marks of her last night's lovemaking with her husband. His smell was on the pillows, his striped bathing towel was draped over the sill of the open window. The sky they could see from the window, above the inland shoulder of the cliff, was blue, but distant thunder rattled far out to sea.

The two women lay perfectly still in the aftermath of sex. Marian was half propped on the pillows, one arm behind her head as she gazed out of the window, the other hand touching Adeline's mass of black hair. Adeline lay sprawled across the bed, her cheek resting on Marian's stomach, her arms clasping her about the waist. There was a difference, however, between Adeline's face, shut-eyed and content, and Marian's, wide-awake and thoughtful.

'Adeline?'

'Mm?'

'It's going to rain. What shall we do?'

'Hm . . .? I don't know . . . stay here.' Eyes still closed, Adeline pressed her face into Marian's stomach, nuzzling and kissing the smooth skin that tasted of sun and salt. Marian's fingers closed on a handful of her hair and gave it a sharp tug so she was obliged to look up.

'Ouch. Why did you do that?'

'To wake you up. I want to show you something.'

Adeline kneeled up and leaned forward to take Marian in her arms, but Marian swung her feet to the ground and stood up.

'Stay there.'

She left the room and closed the door behind her. Adeline stacked all four pillows against the bedhead and leaned against them with her legs curled to the side. She still felt swollen with desire, her body seemed to float heavily in her own imagination, she pulled the sheet up so that it covered, lightly, the tensile weight of her breasts, aching for Marian's hands. Her breathing, her heartbeat, the very flow of her blood seemed to slow to the merest tick of life as she watched the door waiting for Marian's return.

But it was not Marian who returned. It was a slim young man in a snap-brimmed hat, a suit and a plum-coloured waistcoat.

'Well, what do you think?'

Adeline was astonished. 'Marian! You're unrecognizable! Whose clothes are they?'

'Mine.'

'Yours?'

'I keep them here. I like them, it's fun to be someone

else.' She took Adeline's hand and pulled her to her feet.
'Come and see.'

Suddenly demure in the presence of this fully and
smartly dressed person, Adeline swathed herself in the
sheet and followed Marian into the small next-door bedroom always referred to as Neville's dressing room.
About a third of the space was taken up by a wardrobe.
The door was open, revealing a collection of suits, blazers,
shirts and trousers, half a dozen ties over a rail, a couple
of pairs of shoes on the ground and some hats on the shelf
above.

'These are all yours? Not Neville's?'

Marian tipped her head back in a monosyllabic, mocking laugh. 'Neville's? Hardly. You know he dresses like a
tramp.'

'Except in bed – that beautiful nightshirt.'

'A present from Nicholas.' Marian was dismissive, rif-
fling through the hangers stopping here and there to
inspect some items and display others. 'But I have some
wonderful things. Look at this – ' She took out a blue
velvet smoking jacket and held it against herself. 'And this
– ' it was a suit in Prince of Wales checks. 'And this, for
instance – ' she exchanged the snap-brimmed hat for a
boater with a red and green band. 'Aren't they dashing?
Aren't I the last word in dandification?'

Adeline expressed her agreement and admiration. She
found it curiously touching that this lady of letters, whose
clothes generally tended towards the droopy and drab,
should harbour fantasies of being an Edwardian beau. The
clothes were indeed beautiful, but they were period pieces,
a music-hall impresario's idea of what an Edwardian man
about town should look like. Here was yet another
Marian, and Adeline fell in love with her all over again as
she posed before the wardrobe mirror.

She caught, too, the mood of excitement. 'But what
shall *I* wear?' she asked.

'You,' said Marian, 'must be a lady, of course, but not
a perfect one. Look.'

She took a small suitcase from alongside the hats, laid it

on the chair and opened it. It was full of costume jewellery of the cheapest and most outrageous sort, a Pandora's box of execrable taste. Adeline, laughing plunged her hands in and lifted a heavy mass of gilt, paste and beads, letting them pour back into the case like water. 'I shan't know where to start!'

'Yes, you will,' said Marian. 'After all it's not that different from what you usually wear.'

Adeline opened the sheet and wrapped them both tight in it. 'How dare you? Say sorry!' and they struggled and laughed until they sank into a kiss. Only then did Adeline realize with a rush of tenderness that this was the first time Marian had teased her.

So it began. That first evening they stayed in in their finery, eating at the oak refectory table in the pretend-Gothic dining room, and getting drunk on wine and hilarity while the thunderstorm at first prowled round, then roared and sprang, mauling the house with ineffectual fury. The dogs, forgotten, whined and cringed under the beds upstairs.

After that, they took to going out. After an early supper they would go up to the dressing room and set about transforming themselves into Mr and Mrs Goodbody of Lyme Regis, a couple conceived as monsters but for whom, as they became more and more real, they developed a real affection. Mrs Goodbody – they decided her christian name was Irene – was a booming, bourgeois nymphomaniac whose fearsome pseudo-gentility masked a craving for anything in trousers. But it was Marian's Mr Goodbody who was a triumph of subtle characterization. With her hair cut short, and wearing the natty but slightly bizarre clothes, she looked every inch the perky, vain, but hag-ridden husband of the ghastly Irene. Her performance, for one who displayed little interest or sympathy for those less gifted than herself, was full of details and nuances which left Adeline breathless with admiration.

Their assumption of these characters gave them, as Marian had promised, a sort of freedom. They were brazen, and became increasingly so as time went on. Their

modus operandi was this: having decided on a venue, a
pub or a hotel with a public bar, they would arrive with a
flurry, Adeline in the van, Marian scurrying in her wake.
They would order cocktails, often fabricating outlandish
names and setting the unfortunate barman to rack his
brains and experience for the possible constituents.

'I'm in the mood for a Stingray!' Adeline would declare
con brio, shaking her bangles in anticipation.

Marian would be pathetically gallant. 'Then that's what
you shall have, my love . . . and I'll settle for a Tio Pepe
–'

'No, no, where's your spirit of adventure? You'll have
no such thing. Barman, he'll have a – let me see –' She
would look Marian up and down as if assessing her
measurements. 'He'll have an Ace in the Hole tonight.'

Adeline always spoke loudly enough to ensure that
everyone in the room could hear her, so that when the
wretched object of her attentions – very often the barman,
who would only just have recovered from the humiliation
of the cocktails – was trying politely to deflect her
advances, he was assured of an audience. Marian's role
while this was going on was to act as devil's advocate,
explaining to anyone who would listen that Mrs Goodbody was an actress by profession who had been torn from
a promising career by her passion for him.

'She craves gaiety and company, it's meat and drink to
her,' Marian would explain to some startled brigadier and
his lady, down for a spot of golf and some walking. 'If it
wasn't for me she'd be a glittering star in the musical comedy firmament by now. I love to see her enjoying herself . . .'

The refusal of 'Mr Goodbody' to be in the least put
out by his wife's behaviour made it doubly difficult for
Adeline's victim to repel her advances. Confused and desperately embarrassed, he would have to submit to knee-
pressings, cheek-pattings and whispered confidences of an
intimate nature with reasonably good grace. Very
occasionally he would turn out to be made of sterner stuff
and would display a reciprocal interest, and this was the

cue for Adeline's call to retreat: 'Mr Goodbody! It's time
you took me home!' She would then sweep out, jangling
with agitation, with Marian falling in at the rear, smiling
apologetically at the assembled company and murmuring
something about the artistic temperament.

By the end of the week the Goodbodys were no longer
childless, but had a son, Mervin, who (being artistic) was
a difficult boy whom no-one, least of all his admiring
parents, could understand. Mervin was at a minor public
school in Sussex. One of Adeline's most successful conversational gambits was that which dealt with the agonizing and emotionally lacerating time she had suffered in
childbirth. Having told her listener a great deal more than
he wished to know about the protracted labour and the
damaging effects on her libido from which she was only
just recovering, she would proclaim that Mervin was their
'whole world' now, and that in him was vested the sacred
responsibility of gladdening his mother's heart by playing
the great Shakespearean roles . . . Oh, she was an apalling
woman – vulgar, insinuating, familiar, mawkish and
insensitive, and Adeline took a fiendish delight in adding,
each night, new ornaments and flourishes to her dreadful-
ness, knowing that Marian would assimilate and act upon
them as soon as they were invented.

When Neville returned from London, Adeline expected
the Goodbody outings to cease. But to her surprise Marian
told him about them at once, describing with great self-
satisfaction the discomfiture of their victims and their own
cleverness, while Neville laughed indulgently. It was
obvious that what Adeline had already guessed was true –
this game had been played many times before.

They continued with it, though more intermittently,
until the end of the month. They could not in any case have
carried on indefinitely for it would have been impossible to
visit the same place twice, and they were obliged to venture further and further afield for their sport. Also, with
Neville's return and his blessing on the outings, much of
the spice of danger had left them. Adeline felt like a child
who has been scrumping apples from a neighbour's

garden, only to find that the neighbour has been watching benignly all along.

It was nearly September. They would have to return to London within the next fortnight, but could not summon the energy or resolve to set a date. It was dark at eight o'clock now, and the light had sharpened in anticipation of autumn. The year was at the turn. Their idyll was ending.

Marian and Adeline had decided to give the Goodbodys one last outing. They would go to the Clarence Hotel in Truro, which held *thé dansants* every weekday afternoon. The dancing, they agreed, would supply a much-needed new dimension to this, their final fling. They planned what they would wear and looked forward to the trip with the somewhat mixed feelings that generally accompany the closing of any chapter.

The night before, Marian and Neville had an argument. More than an argument, a bitter, savage row. There had been no inkling of it over supper, nor in the drowsy, slightly bored hours between supper and bed. But Adeline was wakened between one and two by the sound of Neville's voice, furiously raised, and Marian's muted and intense. She lay rigid in her bed in the round tower room, staring at nothing, trying to understand, cold with shocked apprehension. She had never heard Neville angry before. The harsh, staccato fire of his voice was dismaying, terrifying, as if his face had been suddenly revealed as a mask covering the hideous reality. The voice crescendoed to a snarl, broke, fell back like a wave, began to rise again, was momentarily interrupted by Marian's, which it cast furiously aside as it thundered on. Clancey, asleep by her bed, raised his head and tilted it, ears cocked. He got up and stalked to the door, scratching and whining to be let out to investigate.

'Clancey – come here, good dog.' He returned to her and she lay with one hand on his collar, waiting for it to finish. As with the laughter on her first visit to Allerton Square, she had a terrible sense of being the cause of it all. After half an hour a door opened and she heard footsteps run along the gallery and down the stairs, and across the hall, followed by the rattle of the front door opening, and the dull, heavy bang as it closed. Neville's voice called, sharp with a mixture of anger and anxiety: 'Marian? Marian –!' And then the bedroom door closed, too, and she heard him make some muffled, inarticulate sound between a sob and a shout.

In silent panic she got out of bed and left the room, Clancey padding beside her. She went round the gallery to the first of the narrow, diamond-paned windows that overlooked the front door. It was an overcast night, with little moon. The sea was no more than a stirring darkness flecked with occasional white, the sky was dense with cloud. She could just make out, flittering in and out of the bushes like a will-o'-the-wisp as she made her way down the cliff path, the figure of Marian.

She knew better than to follow, to admit by her action that she had heard anything. But as she turned to go back she looked across the dark vault of the hall at Neville, standing in his doorway, his face a grey blank in the darkness. He neither spoke nor acknowledged her in any way and almost at once he stepped back, and the door closed.

The following day there was nothing to show that this disturbing little drama had ever taken place. Neville, though yawning and complaining of more-than-average lethargy, was as cheerful as ever, and Marian was composed, studying a survey map for the best route to Truro. Neville announced his intention of taking the dogs out for the day, and having lunch in a pub in Polzeath, and left the house long before they did, plodding leisurely up the brow of the cliff, whistling as he went.

'Right,' said Marian. 'Hold on to your hats, Truro, the Goodbodys are coming.'

They enjoyed their day, though not in the way they had expected. The Wednesday *thé dansant* at the Clarence Hotel was poorly attended, and its few patrons were either mild, elderly people whom it would have been cruel to bait, or serious dancers who glided and spun across the floor like clockwork figures, and were just as unapproachable.

'Well, Irene Goodbody,' said Marian, putting down her cup and rising to her feet. 'May I have the pleasure of this dance?'

'Charmed,' said Adeline. 'I thought you'd never ask.'

From three until half past five they danced together, and ate little sandwiches and cakes off thick white china, and poured strong tea from a speckled silver plate teapot. They did the waltz, the foxtrot, the rumba, the quickstep, and the tango, after a fashion. They even attempted the wild novelty of the charleston. Used by now to their costumes, they did not notice the looks of frozen consternation on the faces of the other dancers. For that one afternoon, fantasy and reality blended and became one. In public, and with some semblance of propriety, they thought, in this most respectable of settings, they held one another, gazed into one another's eyes, learnt new and delightful things about each other's bodies. When the orchestra played 'God Save the King' at half past five, and the people drifted away, and the musicians began to fold their music stands and glance at them for the first time with undisguised civilian distaste, it was like a douche of cold water.

They passed the long journey home in silence except that Marian said as they began to descend the cart track to the Pink House: 'I shall be glad to go back to London,' and Adeline understood what she meant.

As they approached the house they could see Neville, sitting on the grass in the last of the evening sunshine, his forearms resting on his upbent knees. The dogs heard the car first, bursting from the front door and hurtling towards them up the unmade drive. Neville, alerted by them, turned his head and raised one arm in a lazy salute.

Marian pressed her horn, but Clancey was already level with the car, leaping up at the passenger window to greet Adeline.

'I'll let him in the back seat —'

'No! Damn dogs.'

Neville rose heavily and began ambling towards them,

hands in pockets. Marian stopped and rolled down her window.

'Neville! Do get these dogs out of the way before there's an accident.'

He drew his head back a little, you could see he was laughing. Then he cupped his hands round his mouth and called:

'Calm down, Mary-Anne. Just drive slowly and they'll stay out of your way.'

It happened in seconds, less than seconds. Marian's face turned white and wild with anger. Her foot went down on the accelerator and the car sprang forward, their heads snapped back beneath the force of its speed, Neville suddenly ran, raised his arms, his mouth a black hole in his face, and then there was a bang, a sickening and explosive impact that stopped them dead. Marian's feet slipped from the pedals and her hands from the wheel. She sat in her seat limp and expressionless as a doll. Neville appeared in the wide frame of the windscreen, his face dragged by horror. A dog whined.

Clancey was not quite dead when Adeline fell on her knees beside him. He was perfectly still, his hindquarters and back legs pinned beneath the wheels of the Austin. Bloomer lay at a distance, shrunken and trembling, bearing for all of them, the guilt for the tragedy. For a moment as she stroked his head Clancey's eyes rolled towards her, small windows of uncomprehending panic in his pain-locked body. Then they fogged, and closed, and he had gone.

Neville crouched down by her. 'Poor, poor old boy . . .' he said, and she could hear that he was almost in tears. She could only keep stroking, couldn't trust herself to move or speak. The driver's door clicked open and Marian walked round and stood at a slightly oblique angle to them as if unable or unwilling to confront what had happened. Her hands were in her jacket pockets, her mouth was tight. She looked thin and hard as a blade.

Her voice was coldly furious. 'I'm sorry. I'm sorry, I'm sorry.'

Neville stood up. 'So you should be. What the hell were you playing at? You killed him!'

The tears poured down Adeline's face. 'Please . . . don't. It's all right. It was an accident. Just don't . . .'

But her broken-backed attempts at conciliation had the opposite effect from that which she'd intended. Marian advanced on them sharply, as if she were going to attack them, and screamed:

'What are you? Why are you being so stupid? Why are you crying and snivelling as if something dreadful had happened? It was only a bloody dog!'

And she walked away from them with stiff, snapping strides, towards the pink sugar castle which glowed in the setting sun.

CHAPTER NINETEEN

1925–1926

FOR THE REMAINDER of that nightmare evening Marian kept to her room. In spite of her mourning for Clancey, Adeline was worried about her.

'Will she be all right?' she asked Neville. 'The responsibility – she must be going through hell.'

'Let's hope so,' was all Neville would say.

Together, they buried Clancey on the edge of the rough ground. Adeline scratched a 'C' and the date on a lump of rock and they embedded it firmly at the head of the grave.

Adeline fought, and failed, to control tears. She was glad that Marian was not with them to witness the extravagance of her grief, quite disproportionate (Marian would have said) to her loss. What Marian had shouted in anger and self-reproach was true: this was only a dog. And yet she felt that a part of herself had died and was buried with him. Clancey had come into her life for the express purpose of alleviating the loneliness of her loveless marriage and willingly, exuberantly, he had fulfilled that purpose. For so many years he had been her familiar, adapting uncomplaining to her changing circumstances and the vagaries of her emotions. She remembered with remorse how she had abandoned him without a second thought to go to Marian, and saw the cruel irony in the manner of his death. Wanting there to be a reason, but unable to accuse Marian, she blamed herself. She should never have brought him here, where she had known he was unwelcome. By doing so she had wilfully created the conditions in which such an accident could happen. It was all her fault.

Having expressed, in the sincerest possible way, his own sadness, Neville became calm and detached, neither commenting on nor attempting to soothe her tears but allowing her distress to run its course. She was grateful, and acknowledged again what she had almost forgotten – the strength which lay beneath the easy-going exterior, and on which Marian depended, literally, for her sanity. Mindful of this, she did not go to Marian, much as she wanted to. Neville went up once, to ask if she wanted anything to eat, and she refused, through the closed door. At ten o'clock they went to bed, going their separate ways along the gallery, hurrying the awful day to its close.

Adeline lay in the darkness, missing her dog, and conscious of the bleak silence from the other bedroom, more disturbing in its way than the raised voices of the night before.

Some time later she was wakened by Marian, slipping into bed beside her. She was cold to the touch, and shivering convulsively, her eyes and mouth closed as if she could only communicate on this most primitive level. Adeline put her arms round her and they lay like effigies in a mute and sexless embrace until dawn.

Though they put this incident behind them, agreeing that it was a sad accident but no more than that, they each knew that a turning point had been reached. There was no longer any reluctance to go back to London and they returned two days later, Adeline to a life that no longer embraced and absorbed her as it had done before, but seemed to challenge her with its emptiness. She realized how much she had taken for granted the Slade, and the welcome of the friends she knew she would find there. She had deliberately begun to cut herself off, and now the process had been completed for her. Toni's room was occupied by a fearsome middle-aged ward sister from University College Hospital, who went to church twice on a Sunday and showed not the slightest interest in cultivating an acquaintance with her fellow tenants. There had been a brief letter from Peter, saying, 'Don't know when you'll be back, but I'm in Scotland until end of Sept., hatching a plot with Nick. Still quite happy awaiting developments, Undying love, Peter.' She was uncertain, as he had intended her to be, whether the developments he awaited were of a business or a emotional nature, but she had to admit it was comforting to hear from him. There was a letter from Anne, full of village goings-on – 'news from the front' as she put it – which made it plain she was settled in as Mrs Gundry, mistress of Fording Place. Adeline wished her every joy of it: the mere contemplation of all those fêtes and bazaars and Dorcas parties and church flowers was enough to bring on shortness of breath, though she applauded anyone with the energy and enthusiasm to arrange them. She couldn't help wondering, too, how Elizabeth was coping with this vigorous and well-intentioned challenge to her previously unassailed position as chatelaine and organizing genius.

Two other letters contained enquiries about portraits, and these she replied to at once. She needed to work for reasons that were emotional as well as severely practical, and it was also increasingly apparent that she would have to find somewhere else to live. Though Mrs Fairyhouse was only too delighted have society coming and going over her threshold, the conditions were less than satisfactory for Adeline, who had continually to order her living space to the requirements of the sittings. She longed for a separate studio, no matter how modest and decided that this was the first substantial investment she must make with the money she was earning.

In the week immediately after her return from Cornwall she tried twice to contact Bob, but he wasn't there. She supposed his absence was due to the demands of his new job on the *Recorder*. At least, she did so until she went round to Passmore Gardens to visit Duncan and Joel. When they had caught up on each other's situations, with Duncan at his most outrageous on the subject of Harry Hardacre, Undercover Agent, she asked if they'd ever seen Toni. Duncan rolled his eyes warningly.

'Yes, I have,' said Joel, 'I bumped into her in Piccadilly a few weeks ago. She was the same as ever, you know. She doesn't give much away. She sent you her love.'

'Oh you're impossible!' cried Duncan. 'Don't say you were actually going to leave out the interesting bit, the *only* bit Adeline wants to know?'

Adeline turned to him. 'What's that, Duncan?'

'Your fascinating brother has done the dirty on her. Yes!' he declared, seeing her expression of disbelief. 'He has! Gave her to understand his intentions were long-term and honourable and then simply left her flat!'

'People go their separate ways. It's not unusual. So Bob changed his mind – I don't see that that makes him a villain.'

'Well of course on its own it *wouldn't*,' said Duncan, 'but wait till – '

'I'm not sure,' Joel broke in, quietly but incisively, 'that telling Adeline this serves any useful purpose.'

'It probably doesn't,' said Adeline, 'but you've started now.'

When they told her it did not come as a surprise. They had been walking up the Haymarket and had seen Bob and a beautiful dark woman coming out of the theatre together. As they waited for a taxi, Duncan said, they were 'obviously madly enamoured'. They both felt very sorry for Toni, up against such a formidable rival, but it wasn't until Joel went to the dentist two days later and saw the woman's photograph in the *Tatler*, that they realized she was Louise Maybury.

'And isn't he working on one of Maybury's newspapers

now?' asked Duncan. 'He's going to have to be a lot more discreet than *that* if he wants to keep his job!'

Adeline's affair with Marian Elverstone continued through the remainder of that year and well into the next, but its character had subtly altered. The peculiar conditions in which it had taken root and flourished no longer pertained. Though nothing was said, Adeline knew instinctively that Neville's approval of their liaison had been withdrawn, but for what reason she wasn't sure. He seemed more often to be with them, with his uxorious manner and his 'Mary-Anne', and the balance between himself and his wife seemed to have shifted subtly in his favour.

Marian seemed to be more tender and more distant. For the first time, as winter gave way to spring, Adeline felt that she had secured a place in Marian's heart as well as her imagination, and that she was needed. And yet she was aware of Marian withdrawing, or perhaps being pulled away from her by forces which she could not control. Their sexual encounters, though less frequent, grew still more feverishly intense, as though they both knew they were snatching what they could from the jaws of impending disaster. Whenever they were together, in no matter what circumstances, their mutual desire reverberated in the air they breathed. They were like two violins on which a single long, high note was being played. The sad and confused ending to their stay in Cornwall had never been referred to again and yet its implications hovered over the house in Allerton Square, like a hawk awaiting its moment.

The usual people came and went, as they had always done, and now that she was more assured Adeline began making sketches of them as they sat about and smoked and drank and argued and danced and seduced one another. She was able to take a more objective pleasure in their company, for she had learned how to do so from Neville and Marian. As for Ida, Paul, Terence and the rest they were far too self-obsessed and vain to have the slightest objection to being sketched by her. Only Marian was suddenly unwilling, and if she was sitting near Adeline and suspected she was being drawn, she would reach across and place her hand over the paper and shake her head warningly.

Still, it was a measure of the greater consideration she accorded Adeline's work that she offered her the use of a room on the top floor of the house as a studio. She had seemed genuinely dismayed at the idea of Adeline moving from Gower Street.

'But supposing you're further away? What then?' Again the new note of concern which both touched and disturbed Adeline.

'I shouldn't take anything very much further away. But it's so difficult to work where I am – it's only one room, and was never intended as a studio.'

'Then why not work here? Neville, Adeline must have the top room. It only needs clearing out.' She turned from one to the other of them, eliciting their agreement. 'And you'll be near me when I'm writing.'

Adeline looked across at Neville, but his face gave nothing away. 'By all means,' he said, 'if you can find somewhere to put all that lumber.'

With Consett's glum assistance the lumber was disposed of, though of course when Marian actually saw it she was loth to part with most of it, and it was dispersed around the house. It consisted mainly of clothes, hats and shoes, and a greater volume of paper than Adeline had seen before in her life: books, files, notebooks, loose sheets, magazines, newspapers and photographs, mostly jammed into boxes where they had become compressed into damp blocks which had to be dismantled layer by layer, to sighs and groans of recognition. Some of the clothes were in split and tattered suitcases, others in great straggling piles, spotted with mildew and nibbled by moth.

Adeline did not enjoy the clearing-out process. She found the lumber eerie, and Marian's childlike rediscovery of it uncharacteristic. Neville apparently shared this view, for once he came up to the top floor landing and, finding his wife on her knees, immersed in the musty rubbish, took her quite fiercely by the shoulders.

'Mary-Anne! For heaven's sake – you don't want this junk. That's why it was put in here in the first place, remember? Let's for God's sake burn the lot!'

Marian was unruffled, limp and unresponsive in his grasp, so that he was obliged to let her go and, muttering, 'Oh, what the hell . . . keep it if it makes you happy,' went away again.

The room when cleared, however, was ideal. It was at least twice the size of Marian's study, and stretched from the front to the back of the house with dormer windows on either side and a skylight on the northern slope of the roof. When Adeline and Neville had moved her painting gear over from Gower Street in the Austin, she felt as if she'd worked there all her life and her current sitters, a couple of Eton schoolboys, found the house in Allerton Square quite terrific, and its endlessly shifting tide of occupants a source of fascinated speculation.

Nicholas Eyre, however, was no longer one of the visitors to the house. Adeline had seen him only once since their return from Cornwall, and she took his defection as yet another ill-omen. She did not, however, know the reason for it until the end of April, when she went to The Boltons to attend a cocktail party given by the Marchants. It was a gathering in which she enjoyed some celebrity, for her painting of Fenella hung over the fireplace and the guest-list contained several past customers and numerous potential ones. Being conspicious, both by virtue of her height and her spectacular black and gold shift, sparkling with jet beads, the hem adorned with a six-inch black silk fringe, she had little to do but remain in one place and wait for the world to come to her.

'Can a chap crave an audience?' It was Peter. He had put on weight since she'd last seen him and looked at his most confident and well-heeled, immaculate in evening dress. 'I suppose I can't persuade you to come slumming with us afterwards? Dinner and dancing, bourgeois things of that nature?'

'Who's 'us'?' she asked.

'Oh, just a group of us having a bit of a celebration.'

'What is there to celebrate?'

'Damn, I forget how out of touch you are, Addy. Nick and I are opening a club, and this week we've bought what are going to be the most elegant and exclusive premises in London, due to open at the end of the year. Superb food, wonderful band, top-notch clientele – you know the sort of thing.'

Adeline threw her head back and laughed the clear, ringing laugh that was so like her mother's.

'Peter, you're incorrigible. What ever happened to art?'

'It gave me up, if you remember. I don't care to be reminded of it. Anyway this is far more my line of country. With my cash and contacts and Nick's low cunning, I don't see how we can fail. Talk of the devil – Nick!'

Nicholas and Fenella joined them, Fenella sprite-like in leaf-green chiffon. She cut through the greetings of the two men and fell on Adeline's neck.

'Adeline! I've got so much to tell – look!' She fluttered her childish hand on which sat an enormous dowager's diamond. Adeline thought it obscenely ugly and inappropriate but said, obligingly:

'Fenella, congratulations. Who?'

'Nick of course!' She put her arm through his and stared raptly into his face as he continued to talk to Peter. Adeline tried to arrange her features into an expression of warm delight, but failed, and settled instead for one of what she hoped was benign neutrality.

'You're obviously very happy. I'm glad.'

Nick turned to her, his hand covering Fenella's, and spoke as if he'd seen her only yesterday.

'Yes, I've decided to become entirely respectable. It's the only thing. Fenella's parents are being more than generous, and when the Fulbourne Club takes off I expect to be able to keep my wife in the considerable state to which she's accustomed.'

'Silly . . .' said Fenella. Adeline was appalled. Peter intervened.

'Come on, you two. I've been deputed to make sure you circulate, and besides, people are queueing up to touch the hem of Adeline's dress.'

'Go on, darling,' said Nicholas, 'it's you and the ring they want to see. I just want a brief word with Adeline.'

When they'd gone veneer of genial sophistication disappeared with them. The Nicholas that confronted Adeline now as the one she remembered all too well: cold and mocking.

'You see now what you've done?' he said. She knew he meant Marian.

'I don't know what you mean.'

'She fell for you, and that's not allowed. I certainly never foresaw it. It isn't what I planned at all.'

'I'm heartbroken,' said Adeline icily.

'You should be. I never thought I'd live to see Neville jealous, but he is – jealous as any common little suburban husband.' His voice was harsh with a mean, sneering anger, but his face was impassive. 'My idols had feet of clay after all. Such a disappointment. So you see I had absolutely no alternative but to marry money.'

Adeline felt a sick shock. 'I don't want to hear this. Go away.'

'Oh I shall, I shall. Tonight I'm the fiancé, on parade to persuade these stuffed shirts that Fenella hasn't thrown herself away.'

'Which she has,' said Adeline.

'Not entirely. I shall look after her, you'd be surprised. I'm careful with my possessions. You're the one who needs to take care, Adeline, with your little *ménage à trois*. I dare say you think you're pretty clever, winning the heart of the infamous ice-maiden, but I warn you – it'll all end in tears.'

A fat woman in blue brocade hovered near, smiling beguilingly, and Nicholas turned to her with a courtly smile.

'Mrs Brammell, good evening! Now you want to talk

to Adeline, I've no doubt, so I'll make myself scarce.
Adeline, you'll be joining us for dinner?'

'No.'

'Pity. Never mind, another time. Bye for now – and
prenez garde!'

By the time Adeline realized the extent of Marian's mental
upheaval it was already well advanced, and she had been
sucked into its powerful vortex. Looking back, she felt
that she should have been able to see the signs – the row
with Neville, the furious outburst after Clancey's death,
the sudden air of vulnerability since their return – and
yet she had come to accept Marian's every shift of mood
without question.

   Not that the illness had yet reached the stage at which
Adeline had encountered it before. Marian had simply
become entirely unpredictable. Adeline was glad she had
completed the portrait of the two schoolboys, for heaven
knows what they would have made of her furious rages,
sometimes directed at the hapless Consett, sometimes at
her unfortunate publisher, over the telephone; and of her
equally abrupt and irrational shift to sunny and affectionate good humour. For the moment Adeline was working
on a large canvas, a sort of group portrait of the Elverstones and their friends in the drawing room. All of them
were there, their forms and attitudes culled from her enormous stock of sketches, but in this case it was not individual likenesses she aspired to so much as an evocation of
the room's atmosphere, the haze of contention and
seduction, of criticism, flattery and analysis that hung over
its occupants along with the cigarette smoke. For the first
time she worked slowly and thoughtfully, not sure of herself, feeling her way. Loyally, she depicted Marian only
from the back, a thin, dark figure, head bowed, picking
out a tune on the piano keys with one finger.

   There was no way for her to keep the painting a secret,
for Marian, so jealous of her own privacy, liked to wander
in and out of the studio at will. Her new novel was due to

be published in July and she had lost interest in writing. Her restlessness filled the house like a breeze.

'What's this?' she said when she first saw the picture. 'Is this us?'

'It's your room. The people in it aren't necessarily supposed to be recognizable, but I'd like anyone who sees the picture almost to be able to hear what's being said – if you can understand that.'

'Yes, I can understand. I just don't care to see my own face staring back at me.'

'I know that. I've been careful only to show your back view. But you're so vital to this house, and its whole atmosphere, you had to be there somewhere even if only I knew it.' She shook Marian's hands – they were cold – and asked, 'You don't object?'

'I object to you working all the time. Let's go out tonight.'

'I'd like to.'

They quite often went out in the evenings, always without Neville, but never again dressing up as they had in Cornwall. It was inconceivable that Marian could play the plucky and dandified Mr Goodbody in her present state. She would never have been able to sustain the deception. Her attention span was now so short that if they went to the theatre she would want to leave before the play was half over. Sometimes she would say she wanted to have dinner somewhere and her eyes would light up as she made a long and careful selection from the menu, but within minutes of the food arriving she would want to leave. It was almost as though she didn't see it, and she certainly didn't appear to be hungry. She seemed not so much bored as over-excited, like a child waiting for some unspecified treat or outing, unable to concentrate on anything in the meantime. Adeline, helplessly ensnared, could only indulge her, while feeling that Neville observed them, and waited.

She became more and more certain that what Nicholas had said to her was true. It made sense of so much that had happened, a pattern of perfect symmetry and logic was now visible. All unwittingly she had suceeded where others had failed and by doing so she had destroyed the delicate balance that had existed before. Her natural openness disposed her to confront Neville, to try and establish the two of them as allies in their love for Marian, but each time she seriously considered this she realized how impossible it was. They had spun around themselves this delicate web of understanding and tact and trust, which for more than a year had kept Adeline suspended in an erotic paradise. But now the web had trapped them. They could neither draw closer nor escape, but must watch each other suffer.

That evening Marian wanted only to walk. They took a taxi to Leicester Square and moved through the crowds in the early summer evening, Marian always a little ahead as if searching for someone or something. They moved in the direction of Soho. At one point, as they turned into Shaftesbury Avenue, they were no more than a hundred yards from Edward and Louise Maybury as they alighted from their taxi and entered the Café Royal, nor from Toni, who was in Piccadilly underground station. They felt themselves to be alone in the crowd, and in one sense they were. They were observers, explorers, isolated by inclination and design. Their affair had become to them their world. The shrill, gay, novelty-mad and experience-hungry London society of 1926 they regarded both with wonder and with a certain superiority. Adeline admired and aspired to commercial success, but her admiration was tempered by Marian, who had that success and yet appeared to despise it.

As they walked it was Marian who gazed about her and Adeline who had eyes only for her lover, following where she went, pausing when she did, sometimes obliged to catch her arm to prevent her crossing a road in the path of the busy motor traffic.

Their wanderings ended, as they invariably did, in the Parnassus, a drinking club in Greek Street. It was just before they went down the narrow stone stairs that scurried from the dirty pavement to the peeling door of the club that Adeline saw Bryer. She knew at once that it was him, with the sure instinct of childhood memory. It was in the split second after recognition that she took in the eerily emphasized features and the awful dull chestnut wig. For one brief and shocking moment as he passed, his measured butler's stride just tainted by a swagger, their eyes met, and they exchanged an unspoken message of great complexity which was perfectly understood by both of them. Then he was gone, and Adeline was going down the stairs after Marian. She was shaken by the incident, more profoundly shaken than she could have believed possible. Had it, then, come to this? She remembered her profound dislike of Bryer, based on a formless, atavistic revulsion. Now, all was clear, and she felt only a squeamish pity. Loneliness and desperation were ugly, to be confronted by them as she had just been was to open a door in one's own life and to look down a bleak, unlit corridor. It did not occur to her for one moment to link Bryer with Duncan, or Joel, least of all Neville. It was not his sexual preferences which dismayed her, but the terrifying lovelessness which had informed that grotesque face with its expression of anxious defiance. Quickly and boldly, before Marian could knock on the door, she kissed her. She knew that almost everyone she knew, and whose good opinion she cared about, would have been appalled if they could see her now, in this depressing dive, the lover of this eccentric and demanding woman. But she also knew, with relief, as if it were a kind of revelation vouchsafed her, that it was love that redeemed her, that could redeem almost anything.

At nine o'clock the Parnassus had barely begun to tick over. Its clientèle was divided into two distinct tribes, the early and the late. The early tribe came straight from work, or as a preliminary to 'going on' somewhere else; the late tribe were the true habitués, the motley, the exotic and the frankly disreputable, who arrived in the hour before midnight and remained until three or four in the morning. Though most of them would have liked to be called 'artistic' they were only artistic in the sense of not being anything else. In their way they were as timid and conventional as the dark-suited businessman on the eight-thirty from Esher. They needed to cluster together in order to assure themselves of their own eccentricity. They shone only when drawing energy from one another. However, no such accusations could have been leveled at the club's owner, Vasha Hoffman. Vasha was a fat, exuberant woman in her fifties, German by birth but English by choice, who was so fond of booze and parties that the club had started as a means of satisfying these two addictions. Vasha had spent virtually nothing on its decor: it was a dim, drab basement room with the bar along one wall and a sprinkling of strictly utilitarian tables and chairs around the edges. Vasha was a night owl who cared little for the daylight and slept through most of it, so even on the finest summer evenings the Parnassus was heavily curtained and illuminated by artificial light only. It had no pretensions to be anything but what it was: a place where anyone could meet anyone else, and talk and drink till all hours.

The raffish and Bohemian reputation on which it capitalized so successfully was Vasha's chief – indeed her only – contribution to the club's ambience. She was a lesbian of operatic extravagance, always dressed in a dark, heavy suit and a tie, her red hair cut short, brushed flat and pomaded, her hands, when not occupied with a pink gin and a cigar, thrust into her pockets, her voice deep and booming. Yet beneath these disconcerting trappings, which Adeline had found frankly repellent at first, there beat a warm and generous heart and a genuine interest in her fellow man and woman. She attracted people to her cramped subterranean premises by sheer personal magnetism. She was one of those people, as Adeline remembered her mother to have been in her way, who made the place where she was seem like the best place to be.

At nine o'clock the Parnassus was quiet, in the interval between the departure of one tribe and the arrival of the next. Vasha was pleased to see them.

'My dears – you're so welcome!' Coming between them and linking her arms through theirs she led them to the bar. 'First one's on me. What's it to be?'

She regarded it as her sacred duty to entertain the customers. As their drinks were poured she began telling them about the fall from grace of Posy Urquhart, one of Nancy Cunard's set.

'She's the nicest girl,' growled Vasha, 'pretty as a picture and up to all kinds of stunts. I wish her no ill whatever. But the mother, apparently, a disgusting scraggy old crow dripping with diamonds, doesn't approve. Thinks little Posy goes too far. Said it would all end in one of three things – drink, dope or niggers – none of which sounds too bad a way to go, but there. At any rate, she hadn't even considered the worst end of all – another woman! Now, dears, you and I know that nothing could be nicer, but Lady Urquhart is having a seizure. Listen, Posy comes here a few weeks ago with one or two of the boys from that Freddie Lonsdale piece round the corner. I introduced her to Thelma Wheeler – bang, instant fireworks. They've taken off to France together, happy as you like. All rather romantic in my opinion, but of course the Urquhart escutcheon is blotted good and proper. Scandal! Despond! Tearing of the hair . . .' She rumbled on for a few minutes, highly delighted with herself for this bit of matchmaking, and then turned her big, questing head in Adeline's direction.

'See the Marchant girl's marrying beneath her.'

Adeline approved this sentiment so heartily she had to smile. 'Nicholas Eyre, yes.'

'He played the piano here for a while. Couldn't stand him. Absolute snake, wanted his bread buttered on both sides. Don't suppose Marchant *mère et père* are any too tickled about that, either.'

'They seem to like him. He can be quite charming. Besides which he's entering some business venture with Fenella's brother, so he obviously hopes to become rich and respectable.'

'Snake. Bastard. Why are you acting devil's advocate, anyway?'

'I'm not. It's just that like most snakes he's got me mesmerized.'

'Very good, very good. 'Nother of those?'

Vasha went to get more drinks from the latest in a long succession of 'strornily pretty girls' behind the bar. Adeline looked at Marian.

'You're very quiet.'

'It's Vasha, she talks so.'

'Yes. What my nanny would have called a rattle. But good value just the same.'

Marian shrugged. 'If you like scurrilous gossip served up *molto con brio, presto furioso.*''

There was more than a glint of the old steel in this remark, which comforted Adeline.

'Do you want to go?'

'No, I want to watch the people. Where are they all? It's like the grave in here tonight.'

'It'll soon warm up!' Vasha said, returning with their drinks, her thick fingers bunched round the stems of the glasses. 'Theatre crowd'll be out soon, all the usual riff raff will be jostling for attention.'

In less than an hour the Parnassus was packed, the heat and the noise were only just bearable and the air was humid with perspiration and alcohol fumes and clogged with smoke. Vasha literally in her element, was swallowed up in the crowd, traceable only by her booming voice and her great, coughing laugh, like the roar of a lion. Marian, too, was happier now, recognized by this one and that, swept away to other groups, not saying a great deal but bestowing her slightly diffuse attention on other conversations. Occasionally with her eyes she would seek out Adeline, where she sat at the table in the corner and, having re-established the link, look away again. Neither of these forms of behaviour, not the movement from group to group, nor the anxious searching, would have been in the least typical of the Marian of a year ago.

By remaining at the table Adeline ensured that she

would not have to talk to anyone. Tonight she wanted no part of the clamour of excited and exciting discourse. She was unhappy. Tonight she found the club not just uncomfortable, but peculiarly threatening. If Marian had not so obviously been happy she would have suggested again that they leave. She thought of the contempt and the dry, withering sarcasm with which the old Marian would have treated these people. Now she seemed almost pathetically eager to be with and of them. Adeline thought of Neville, alone in the house in Allerton Square, and considered how perfectly at home he would have been in this company.

The heat was stifling, her drink was warm, and perspiration crept down her back and between her breasts. She closed her eyes for a moment and pressed her glass to her forehead, but it was warm and smeary. She longed to be out in the cool evening air, but knew she could not leave Marian. Her mind drifted back to Bryer, an outsider, a grotesque, touting for affection, and experienced again that shudder of empathy. There, but for the grace of God, went she. She had love, though she knew that even now it was a poor, unequal thing, and she'd paid dear for it. For the privilege – and she saw it as a privilege – of being with Marian in this place she disliked, hemmed in by people who bored and appalled her, for this privilege she had turned her back on her family, her friends, and a man who still, unaccountably, loved her. With each day that passed now she felt that a door closed behind her, as she followed Marian to whatever strange and terrifying place she was impelled.

A chair was pulled up next to her and the scent of hair lotion sweetened the musky air.

'Adeline – all alone?'

It was Paul Hudson, not a habitué of the Parnassus, and looking to Adeline almost as uncomfortable as she felt.

'No, actually. I came with Marian. You?'

'By myself. I must say I'm a little surprised to find you in this ghastly place, though I've learned to expect anything of Marian. It wouldn't be my choice of watering hole. I prefer a bit of comfort and elegance.'

'Then why are you here?'

'I badly needed a drink before composing the obituary of the worst musical comedy I'm ever likely to see. This was the nearest place to hand when thirst struck. But listen, Adeline, what game does your brother think he's playing?'

'I've no idea what you mean,' said Adeline. She wished Paul Hudson a million miles away. She was certainly not going to give him the satisfaction of gossiping with her. But he wasn't in the least put out.

'You must be the only person in London who hasn't, then. Come along Adeline, tell all. He either has the most incredible nerve, or he's stupid or he's blinded by his passion. They're the only reasons I can think of for being so horribly indiscreet with the wife of one of the richest men in London.'

'You mean Louise.'

'Does he think Ted Maybury's a fool? It's only through other people's tact and sense of decency that he hasn't yet realized what's going on, or at least with whom, but it can only be a question of time. Bob seems actually to make a point of being seen about with her.'

'It's his business. I haven't seen him for ages.'

'No, of course not.' Paul surveyed her thoughtfully. 'I just thought a sisterly word in the right place might pay dividends. We on the *Courier* watch his progress with interest. We regard him as our *protégé*, you see.'

'That's very touching.'

'Silly of us, I know . . .' Paul stared about him at the throng. 'God, what a hole! Where is Marian, by the way?'

'She's with some people – I don't know . . . she's in a rather more sociable mood than me, anyway.'

'Say no more, I can take a hint.' Paul's voice held more than a trace of genuine offence.

She knew she had been rude but had neither the will nor the energy to apologize.

'Good night, Adeline. Give my best to Marian and Neville.'

'Good night.'

It was about half an hour later, when Vasha drew alongside the table like an ocean liner nudging a jetty, that she was shocked out of her depression.

'Marian's not with you, then?'

'No.'

'Wonder where she's got to. She's in particularly good form.'

This comment, the very opposite of the truth, prompted Adeline to get up from the table and go in search of Marian. Pushing, elbowing and edging her way through the crush, she felt panic begin to beat and clamour inside her. 'Excuse me . . . excuse me . . .' she kept saying, her anxiety like a drawstring that made her voice thin and shrill, her face a creased mask.

People said they'd seen her of course, they'd had a word, she was more relaxed that they'd seen her for ages, but then she'd just sort of . . . They'd seen her with so-and-so, why not try him? But all the time the certainty grew in Adeline that Marian was no longer there.

Vasha called to her as she ran up the stairs: 'My dear, what's the hurry? Stay and enjoy yourself, she'll be back . . .'

The well-intentioned callous words echoed in Adeline's head like an accusation as she flew down the street. Everything transcended by her fear – the darkness, her aloneness, the uneasy, insinuating threat of people who brushed past, or spoke to her, or watched, uncurious, from half-lit doorways. She was conscious of nothing, could feel nothing but this awful dread.

Not knowing where to look, and too distraught to rationalize her search, she looked everywhere, fanning her panic to a blaze. It was a quarter to twelve, the pubs were shut, the theatres empty, the smart set had gone to their restaurants and nightclubs, the population of the streets had changed, but Adeline feared no-one. Her fear surrounded her and buffeted the people she approached, protecting her. One or two of them tried to detain her, to ask more, to be more of a help, but when their faces changed and she saw the 'no', the 'sorry' forming behind their eyes, she was already gone, focused on the next corner, the next person. Every alternate moment she was punched by hope, then despair.

More tired than she knew, she suddenly tripped and fell, crashing down on her knees. The shock and the pain broke the spell and she began to weep, there on all fours, her shoulders shaking helplessly, her head hanging.

Large, firm hands took her by the shoulders and steered her to her feet.

'Bad luck, miss, you came a cropper. No bones broken?' asked the policeman. He kept one steadying hand beneath her elbow, and held her handbag in the other. His face was kind, grave, a shade disapproving.

'All right then?' he asked, passing the handbag.

'I'm sorry . . . I tripped . . . I'm looking for someone, and I'm so worried . . .' She began to cry again, weakly. A couple walked past, their faces turned first towards her, then to one another. She struggled to control herself, to elicit some help from the constable who stood there patiently, as if waiting to take her statement.

'I've lost a friend,' she said. 'She disappeared from the club where we were, and she's not well, not properly responsible – ' Her voice broke.

'I'm sure there's no call to worry, miss,' said the policeman. 'When was this, that she – disappeared, you say?'

'Oh, I don't know – an hour and a half . . .'

'Well then, there you are.' He seemed enormously comforted by his information. 'That's no time at all. You say she's poorly. She's probably gone home.'

Since the studio, Adeline had her own key, but tonight she felt like a thief as she turned it in the lock.

The hall and downstairs rooms were silent and dark. The dog had been locked away in the kitchen; she could hear his faint, plaintive bark as she entered. Only on the first floor landing was there the merest suggestion of light.

At the foot of the stairs, gleaming black like a slick of oil, lay Marian's silk shawl. Adeline picked it up and buried her face in it, breathing in the very faint, light scent that Marian sometimes wore. Drained and faint with relief she sank down on the bottom stair, the shawl spread over her knees, her cheek resting on it.

'Yes, she's here. She's here and she's safe, no thanks to you.'

Neville stood at the top of the stairs, his darker mass just visible against what Adeline now divined to be the light from the half-open bedroom door. She rose, clutching the shawl in her arms like an infant.

'Neville, I'm so sorry – '

'Don't come up here.' His voice was sharp.

'Neville, please, I won't stay. I just want to see her before I go, to let her know I haven't forgotten about her. Please – '

'No, Adeline.'

He came down the stairs, sinking into the deeper darkness, but walking straight past her. She felt, rather than saw, his implacable contempt.

He went to the door and turned on the light. It was like an assault, that sudden, brilliant illumination of her exhausted, swollen face streaked with tears, the blood on her skirt and on her legs where she'd fallen.

'Is she all right?' Her voice was a whisper.

'She didn't come to any harm, if that's what you mean. God protects drunks, and little children. And the insane, I shouldn't be surprised.'

'Did she – has she mentioned me . . . ?' She was humiliated by her love.

Neville sank down on a chair, as if suddenly exhausted. 'No. She hasn't. And I doubt whether she will, for some time. I'm the only one she wants now.'

He scrubbed at his face savagely with his hands, 'I've seen this coming for months. I should have put a stop to it long ago.'

She didn't dare ask him what. She had begun to shiver with a kind of delayed shock.

'I'm sorry . . . I'll go.'

She moved towards the door, not realizing she still held the shawl. He put out his hand and took hold of it, exerting no pressure, but saying: 'I'll have that.'

Now utterly bereft, she asked: 'May I come tomorrow? My painting – '

He shrugged. His disdain and indifference were his cruellest weapons. 'Do what you like, you have a key. We've never told anyone to stay away and I shan't start now. But please don't attempt to see Marian. It'll do no good and it could do a great deal of harm.' Heavily, he rose and walked back towards the stairs. 'Let yourself out. If she wakes and I'm not there there'll be hell to pay.'

The next day Adeline did not go to Allerton Square. She could not go there simply to paint, to close her studio door and ignore what was going on, to behave like a stranger, and Neville must have known that she could not. His permission, or at least his refusal to debar her, placed her in an agonizing position. She needed time to collect herself, to gather together what was left of her pride, to try and distance herself a little from these events which threatened to engulf her. But she was wretched, plagued by Marian's imagined journey home, tortured by her own failure to help in any way, her inability to avert the disaster that had now overtaken her. Still she could not, would not, believe that what Neville said was true – that she was no longer wanted, or needed – and yet she was powerless to disprove the assertion since he would not allow her near Marian.

She never felt so alone. It was a beautiful early summer's day, a gash of brilliant blue sky showed between the rooftops of Gower Street, and dusty sunshine poured into her neglected room, mocking her miserable isolation. She did not want to go out, there was no-one she could turn to, there was nothing she wanted to do. She sat, like an old woman, her back to the window, her hands holding the arms of the chair, petrified by unhappiness. When in the middle of the afternoon the doorbell rang, and there were muted women's voices down in the hall, she didn't recognize them, and only the second knock on her own door aroused her.

'Ah,' said Mrs Fairyhouse, 'she is there, I thought so. I'll leave you to it.'

'Addy darling, may I come in?'

There was something shocking in seeing Elizabeth here, where she had never been before, and where so much that was secret had happened to Adeline. She felt, as she accepted her mother's kiss and watched her walk to the window – why was it people did that, as if to assure themselves they were not trapped? – that her confusion, and deception, and pain must rise from the fabric of the room like a mist, that Elizabeth must surely sense it.

And yet she did not, and she seemed preoccupied, full of her own separate tidings.

'Mother, can I get you something, some tea, or – '

'No, Addy, no.' Elizabeth rummaged, with a kind of desperation for her cigarettes, and lit one. She stood stiffly, with her back still to the room, one arm held tightly across her waist, the other hand holding her cigarette to her lips. Adeline realized that her mother did not want her to see her face – the position, the stance, the cigarette, were a kind of armour. She approached a little way, trying to adjust her focus, to open herself to Elizabeth. It was hard, like using muscles wasted through neglect.

'Mother – what is it?'

'Howard died.' Elizabeth's voice was matter-of-fact but tight and strained.

'Last night. That's why I'm here, I came up to Leinster Gardens to help organize things. Howard is dead,' she said again, as if forcing herself to acknowledge it. 'He had a massive heart attack.' She bit off the end of the sentence, and caught her breath. 'The funeral will be the day after tomorrow, I thought you'd want to be there.'

'Oh, Mother – poor, poor Mother . . .' Adeline went to embrace Elizabeth but she moved away averting her face.

'I'm sorry. I don't want to start crying, I may never stop. No sympathy.'

Adeline spread her arms helplessly, then let them fall to her sides. She sat down, slumped in the chair where she had sat all day. She felt the shock of Howard's death like the boom of a distant explosion, the effects of which had not as yet quite reached her. More immediate was her pity for her mother whose happiness, she knew, was destroyed.

Elizabeth cleared her throat. 'I dare say you knew – that you realized – about Howard and I.'

'Yes. Years ago.'

'Did it upset you badly? I know how fond you were of Richard.'

'It did at first, but not any more. And Howard's been good to me.'

'Yes . . .' Elizabeth drew a deep breath as if about to add something, then exhaled again, and said quietly,' I loved Richard too, you know. We had a good marriage.'

'I know that.'

'I never wanted to hurt him, and I don't believe I ever did. But I couldn't help myself. Richard and I had a wonderful, loving friendship and a great deal of happiness. But with Howard . . . I couldn't help myself.'

'I understand.' Adeline thought that Elizabeth would never know how much.

'No-one realized how unhappy Howard was,' Elizabeth said with a spark of anger. 'Cynthia is a cold, silly woman. But he stuck by her. Now he's dead and she'll probably go on for years,' she added, with dreadful bitterness.

'You couldn't have kept him alive, Mother.'

'No, but I could have made him happy.'

'What, by marrying him after he divorced Cynthia, a poor, pathetic mental case? Think what people would have said about him, and about you, and Father.'

'Howard is your father.'

The words were so few, so quickly and quietly spoken that their effect on Adeline was delayed. She could not believe she had heard them, and had mustered no response when Elizabeth swung round, unleashing upon her the full force of her anger and grief.

'*Was* your father, I should have said. Was. It's all in the past now, isn't it, so we can all afford to be civilized about it.'

A rapid series of memories, some of them buried for years until now, but appearing bright and new-minted, took Adeline by storm. Howard, bellowing with laughter when he believed it was she who had broken the car window . . . Howard at the picnic, fiery hot and fidgeting . . . framed in the door of the Snug, his black head bent over Elizabeth's white shoulder . . . Howard pressing the Judas money into her hand, daring her to betray him . . . Howard asking gently, knowing her too well, 'You're not by any chance in love?' . . . Howard, her father, now dead.

'Why didn't you tell me?' Her voice surprised her with its firmness and volume.

'There seemed no point. I didn't tell anyone, not even Howard. He may have suspected something, I don't know – you were always his favourite, even when you were at your most rude and impossible. And Simon – Simon was such a disappointment.'

Simon. Adeline was suddenly, violently angry. 'You let us do it, Mother! You knew, and you let us do it!'

'You wouldn't have been very easy to stop. Yes, yes, I should have said something, but it would have meant everyone knowing – can you begin to imagine what that would have meant? As it was, it was only me that suffered, my God how I suffered! And in the end, well perhaps it was all – '

'Don't!' Adeline sprang to her feet. 'Don't say in the end it didn't matter, don't! Mother – you should have told me!'

Elizabeth crumpled. It was as though her spine had suddenly become soft. For the first time since entering the room she seemed beaten by grief. She did not weep, but her face looked flaccid, wasted, the face of an old woman. When she spoke, her voice was passionless.

'Yes Addy, I should have done. And I'm sorry. If you remember I did try to tell you . . . I knew it was a mistake, but the whole world disagreed with me. I haven't often been weak in my life, but I was weak then. And Addy, you're young, with everything before you, all the chances and the dreams, you can afford to forgive me, because I miss him so much . . .!' Her face seemed to split and smear into ugly tears of fury and loss, uncontrolled, unchecked, unhidden. And now she allowed Adeline to put her arms round her, to rock and soothe her as she wept. Adeline knew at that moment that she had changed, that the fibres and tissues and cells of which she was composed had moved to form a different pattern and could never move back. As she stood there, comforting her mother, and unable herself to be comforted, she realized that all her life till now had not been the truth, and that by admitting the deception Elizabeth had unwittingly denied her the release of confessing her own. She bore the weight of a double sadness, and alone.

She pushed Elizabeth back and kissed her face. 'We'll all come to the funeral,' she said. 'And you must look magnificent, the way he'd have wanted you to.'

Elizabeth did look magnificent, but the funeral service, and the burial in a cemetery in north London, were bleak. This was the end of a man who had focused his passion, his mind and his energy, all of them considerable, on his work, and on a very few people; and as he had sown, so did he reap. There were barely a dozen mourners in the echoing church, which was cold even on a fine day. The vicar delivered his splendid, sonorous cadences in a lofty and impersonal moan. The singing was thin. In the silences you could hear a faint, twittering thread of sound – Cynthia, addressing herself in her own happy, infantile world. The Mayburys were there, and Bob, who arrived late and sat right at the back, like a casual passer-by. Frank and Anne, painfully up-from-the-country in clothes that were stiff and too heavy. After the burial they went back to Leinster Gardens for tea, but it was a soulless, miserable occasion that bore no relation to the man whose passing it marked. They drifted on their separate ways after no more than half an hour. Elizabeth was to stay another night at the house, but was going that evening to dine with Frank and Anne at their hotel. Arrangements were being made for Cynthia to go into a private nursing home.

Adeline hated all of it. The vicar's piety, the dark clothes, the grim faces, the dreary tea and the muted voices. When she had pressed her cheek to Elizabeth's and to Cynthia's for the last time, and left the house, she pulled off her hat and broke into a run, running until her heart pounded and her lungs heaved, and sweat trickled down her face. On the corner of the Bayswater Road she saw Bob crossing over to enter the park. His tie was loosened and his jacket hung over one shoulder, a man about to take a stroll in the sun before returning to work. But his face, when it was turned briefly in her direction as he checked the traffic, was scowling, furious. She walked quickly away.

Curiously, the dreadful funeral gave her a kind of strength. Howard had so disliked church services, she had almost felt his restless, irritable presence at her side as she sat through it. She had taken a certain pride in what she now recognized as her likeness to him. Confronted with her present dilemma she found herself wondering what he would have done, and the answer was simple.

Back at her room she changed out of her funeral clothes and put on a cotton skirt and blouse, and sandals. She washed her face clean of make-up, because she wished to feel, and to appear, absolutely and directly herself. Her confidence had returned, and her resolve was firm: she wanted to see Marian and to be what comfort she could, and no-one would prevent her.

It was a lazy, golden evening, and some children were playing in the centre of the square where she'd so often walked with Clancey. People were returning from work, preparing to go out, windows stood open to the sunshine. It was impossible not to believe in the victory of normality. She wondered why she had allowed herself to be the victim for so long of confusion and havoc. Now that she knew the truth about herself, everything else was becoming clear. She approached Number Twelve buoyed up by this clarity.

Consett opened the door and Bloomer was in the hall to greet her. The door of the drawing room was closed and beyond it she could hear voices.

'He's with the doctor,' said Consett. 'You know she's not well again.'

'Yes.'

'You've come to work, I take it.'

'No, I came to see Mr and Mrs Elverstone, but I'll go up to the studio until the doctor's gone.'

'She's asleep, thank heavens,' said Consett. 'And she's not to see anyone but him. I'm sorry,' she added, with an unprecedented hint of friendliness.

Adeline went up to the top floor. The house was quiet and orderly, and gentle sounds of the square trickled in through the open windows. Outside the Elverstones' bedroom lay an untouched tea tray. She did not even look into the room; she owed it to Neville to speak to him first.

On the top floor landing the door of the studio stood ajar. A single piece of paper, like part of a trail, lay on the floor. She picked it up. It was a piece of one of her sketches.

She pushed open the door. The studio was full of sunshine. She was momentarily dazzled by reflected light from the blizzard of torn paper that covered the floor. Every sketch, every drawing and painting in the studio had been systematically destroyed. On the long trestle by the easel her oil paints were crushed and smeared like the relics of violent death. her brushes were snapped in half.

She moved with a dreamlike slowness through the drift of paper. It was like walking through snow, or leaves, there was a perverse beauty in this scene of wild destruction bathed in the quiet evening sun. The windows on both sides were open, and a butterfly bobbed and fluttered in the air.

She confronted the easel. Her painting, almost finished,

had been cut with a knife. Not slashed, but carefully and meticulously defaced with intersecting lines that formed a star. The knife had been blunt, and you could see where it had been forced through the canvas at the top of each stroke. The task had needed considerable strength.

Adeline closed her eyes. It was quiet and warm, a red glow beat on her eyelids. She felt her strength and serenity increase in proportion to the injury she had sustained.

When she opened her eyes, Neville was in the doorway, his face white.

'My God,' he whispered. 'I had no idea . . . when can she have done this?'

'I don't know. I suppose I should have foreseen it.'

'I'll make it up to you – financially – of course.' He came a little way into the room, and breathed again: 'My God.'

'There's no need,' said Adeline. 'I don't care.' At that moment it was the truth.

She walked past him to the door.

'Where are you going?'

'Away. I just want to see Marian first.'

'She's asleep now. The doctor gave her something.'

'I know that.'

She went down the stairs and into the bedroom. Marian looked tranquil and content. She lay on her stomach, with her head turned to the side, her arms and legs stretched out, like a sunbather. Adeline had seen her lie like that often in Cornwall. She seemed both vulnerable and protected. The knife from her tea tray, its round blade messy with paint and fibres of canvas, lay on the floor where it had dropped from her hand. She must have used it immediately after the doctor had left her.

Adeline leaned over and kissed her goodbye. It was like kissing a photograph, a memory. There was not a flicker of response. Marian remained sealed away, the suggestion of a smile on her lips, a strand of hair that lay across her face trembling as she breathed.

Adeline left the house. Neville may have spoken her name; Consett, in the hall, may have asked her something, she didn't know. She wanted only to be free of them. Out in the square she began walking with long strides, drawing great, deep, even breaths. She was a blank slate, an empty glass, a bare stage. She must begin again.

With the bleak, clear vision of humility she knew how desperately she needed, now, her long-neglected friends.

Part Three

CHAPTER TWENTY

1937

ADELINE GUNDRY DROVE west along the winding road that clung like a white ribbon to the Cote d'Azur. She adored her car, a scarlet Alvis convertible – wickedly fast and completely unsuitable for a woman in Frank's opinion – and she adored this particular stretch of road, so she was driving at high speed. The top of the car was down. The sun, not quite at its height, beat steadily on her shoulders and arms, and on her hands on the wheel, all already deeply tanned. When she'd left the villa half an hour ago she had bowed to Fenella's insistence that she wear a scarf to protect her hair, but she had discarded it as soon as she'd reached the open road, and to hell with the destructive effects of heat and dust.

To her left the aromatic wooded cliff fell steeply away to a hidden shore. Beyond the trees lay the electric blue Med, empty here except for a single white motor yacht, like a wedding cake, far out to sea. On the right of the road the cut face of the cliff rose sheer for about sixty feet, with tenacious bushes and small trees clinging to its baked

and inhospitable surface like people leaning out of windows as she zoomed by.

As she drove, she sang, with gusto, an up-tempo version of Hoagy Carmichael's 'Lazybones'. She knew most
of the words, and where a few went unaccountably missing she lah-lahed with equal brio. She was in high good
spirits. The Alvis swept round the steep bends at speed,
trailing a plume of dust that swirled and then diffused,
hanging in the hot air like a shock wave.

Adeline had been told what to look for, and did not
expect to come across it yet. And in fact she had travelled
some thirty miles, and the road was beginning gradually
to descend towards the sea again, when she saw the small
black car parked on the opposite side and at a rather
uncomfortable angle.

This, she thought, must be it, but of its owner, whom
she wouldn't have recognized anyway, there was no sign.

She pulled across the road and as far on to the treacherous verge as she dared and got out. Without the movement
of the air on her face the heat settled round her like a skin.

Glinting in the sunlight, and at a distance of some yards,
the car looked perfectly serviceable, but now that she'd
approached it she saw that its condition was ramshackle.
Patches of rust spotted the bodywork, the windows were
rimmed with dirt and greyish fungus and the front bumper
had sustained a dent.

She peered in at the windows. The brown leather
upholstery was scratched and split; she could smell it bak-
ing in the sun. On the back seat lay a battered suitcase
covered in peeling labels, and held shut by a length of
grubby rope. There was a copy of *Le Monde*, one of yesterday's *Courier*, a paper bag full of apples, a half-eaten
baguette, a straw hat and a crumpled blue linen jacket. A
pair of sunglasses, the hinge of one arm reinforced with
sticking plaster, rested on the dashboard.

Adeline circled the car once, half expecting to trip over
the owner's recumbent form protruding from beneath it.
But there was no-one there, and the air of recent derelic-

tion that hung about the dilapidated vehicle caused her a frisson of anxiety.

She gazed about her, temporarily nonplussed. At this point on the road the trees had given way to a dry, rustling green scrub beyond which was a short vertical drop to a snaggle of sharp rocks. She and the car were on the apex of a long bend in the road, which coiled about the foot of the hill, reappearing more hazily about a mile and a half further on. In the distance, blurred by heat, the red and white domed bell-tower of the church of Cipriane was just visible. It was so still that she could hear the chitter of insects in the bushes below. A buzzard floated across the cliff face opposite, trailing his stunted midday shadow like the tail of a kite.

The distant hum of an engine swelled and drew closer, like the sound of the heat itself, and a green Citroën rounded the bend from the direction of the town. Seeing a large, glamorous and lost-looking woman standing between two cars at the side of the road, the driver very properly pulled over and wound down his window.

'*Madame, qu'est ce qui se passe? Pourrais-je vous aider?*'

'*Non, merci.*' Adeline was not sure whether she needed help or not, or if she did what form it should take. She smiled politely. '*J'attends quelqu'un.*'

'Aaah . . .' The driver looked around at the empty landscape with delicate Gallic irony. '*D'accord.*' He nodded in the direction of the black car. '*Il n'y a personne dans là dedans?*'

No need for sarcasm, though Adeline, especially since her French did not allow for a rejoinder in the same vein. Her polite smile broadened to crocodile-like proportions. '*Il viendra bientôt, j'espère.*'

'*Oui, je comprends.*' The young man, smooth, dark and plump, raised a hand to signify his complete understanding. '*Eh bien – bonjour, madame.*'

'*Au revoir.*'

The Citroën disappeared, and Adeline realized what it was that its driver had so suddenly and incomprehensibly understood. Of course, all she had to do was wait.

She returned to the Alvis and, kicking off her shoes, sat down in the passenger seat, with her crossed ankles resting on the top of the opposite door.

Waiting she could manage. The climate, the view, the atmosphere . . . all seemed ideally suited to the business of waiting. What was a holiday if not an endless series of waits – waiting to drink, waiting to eat, waiting to swim, waiting to go out, and to come back? She who was always so feverishly, chaotically, busy had almost forgotten what it was to work . . .!

Mind you – she smiled to herself – she didn't suppose that her hosts, the Eyres, were enjoying the wait so much. In their exquisite villa in the hills behind Cannes, Nicholas would be frozen with annoyance, and Fenella would be pale and tense with ignoring him. Peter – her ex-husband, being the only person not to care a fig for Nicholas's uncertain temper – would be attempting to josh them out of it.

Adeline tipped her head back, and laughed out loud. She was well out of it. Sooner or later the late arrival would show up, but she didn't much care when.

The sun beat down. She had acquired a deep tan and a few extra pounds in weight, and felt sleek, dark and fleshy like one of the wonderful local fruits they ate each day – an aubergine, or a fig. For the past week she'd been in a state of powerfully sensuous well-being. She suspected the rest of the house party at the Villa Clemency would have been shocked if they'd known how strongly she craved a sexual encounter . . . her body was glossy and ripe, aching to be consumed . . . She shifted in the seat and stretched her arms before letting them fall heavily into her lap.

Her stomach was quite rounded – her daughter, Dora, with a nine-year-old's ruthless grasp of essentials, would have said she was getting fat. Adeline sucked her stomach in, and released it, watching it thoughtfully as though she were lying alone in her bath, in England. She wondered what Dora was doing now. As all the legacies of Adeline's first marriage had been sad, so all those of her second had been happy, and the happiest was Dora. Even here, with nothing to do but laze and luxuriate, she missed her company. She took pleasure from the fact that Dora, running wild at Fording Place, eating her head off, staying up late and shamelessly indulged by her grandmother, aunt and uncle, would miss her only fleetingly, at bedtime, before falling asleep.

Adeline wanted only Dora's happiness. From the moment her writhing, sprawling eight-and-a-half pound daughter had been dumped in her arms she had been helplessly in thrall to her. No painting, no love affair, had ever provided this thrill of pride, this ecstasy of creative achievement, this fiercely sensual empathy. Her adoration was only enhanced by her keen sense of her own inadequacy as a parent. Having moved through pregnancy like a warrior queen, and given birth like a peasant, Adeline had entered upon motherhood like a Dresden shepherdess. Would she drop the baby? Starve her? Overfeed her? Drown her? Suffocate her? Dorothy had been contacted, and recalled, but the more she and Peter told her to relax and do what came naturally, the less Adeline knew what the natural thing was. When Dora yelled, tears sprang to Adeline's eyes. If she slept long and deep Adeline leant anxiously over her, convinced she had died. She wore herself out with worry until Peter, exasperated, put his foot down. He pointed out that Dorothy had been employed to look after Dora, was more than competent to do so, and must be allowed to get on with it. He removed his wife, under protest, to Italy where she spent four weeks glaring at the majesty of Rome through a haze of frustration.

And yet Dora had grown sturdily through all this maternal turbulence and had emerged as level-headed and lovable a child as one could wish to meet. She was tall like her mother, round-faced and blue-eyed like her father, her brown hair worn these days in two long, thick plaits. To Adeline's distress she was short-sighted and had to wear glasses – would this depress, upset, embarrass her? It did none of these things. Dora accepted what life had to offer with equanimity. Which was just as well. It was the four-year-old Dora whom Adeline had most dreaded telling about her parents' separation. And yet it was Dora who had understood, tearfully, the explanation: 'I don't love Daddy enough.'

Adeline was not proud of having made a second mistake in marriage, but at least she knew she had done the right thing in extricating herself. Now, five years later, when she looked about her she saw the justification for her decision, the evidence that she had been right. For her close and loving friendship with Peter, though submerged for a while in the sadness and confusion of divorce, *had* survived, and Peter had married again. His wife was with him at the Villa Clemency and Adeline had taken pleasure in their company. The only stain on this pleasure was that she knew she still occupied an unassailable position in Peter's heart. The responsibility was awesome. She recognized, without vanity, that it was within her power to spoil his new life. So she must always be beyond reproach, her attitude so finely tuned that she never by so much as a glance or a gesture appeared to recall him to her. It was the very least she owed him.

After the horror of her parting from Marian, she had sunk back into Peter's arms like a storm-battered traveller sinking into a warm, familiar bed. He had asked her no questions, demanded no explanation, offered no advice: he had simply welcomed her back. His unselfish fidelity provided the antidote to Marian's capricious self-obsession. Adeline had wrapped herself in it. And utterly exhausted, blinded by relief, deafened by gratitude, she had accepted his inevitable proposal. The tiny, distant, voice of warning had been swamped by the hubbub of general approval that had broken out on all sides.

It took time for the full extent of her mistake to dawn on her, and when she could ignore it no longer she was effectively trapped. She had a small daughter whom she worshipped, a devoted and universally well-liked husband and an enviably comfortable life. But Adeline felt like a caged lynx, pacing back and forth, back and forth, staring

out at a world she might have inhabited. It had taken all
her strength and resolve to free herself. Late one evening
she'd told him, feeling like a thief or a murderer inflicting
pain on him under the cover of darkness. They'd been
sitting over coffee at the table, but at once he rose and
stood with his back to her.

'There's someone else, is there – that you'd rather be
with?'

'No, no-one else.'

'There must be. We've been so happy.'

'I could never be unhappy with you, Peter.'

'Then may I ask why? I don't understand.'

She could no longer avoid the shameful, pitiful truth.
'Peter . . . you remember at college – how you were
always asking me to marry you? And I always refused.
Well I was right then, and I should never have changed
my mind. It's all my fault, believe me I know that, but
my guilt's no basis for us carrying on –'

'But I love you, Addy!' His control cracked and she
heard the desperation in his voice.

'I don't deserve it,' she said.

'You don't have to!' He turned to face her. 'It's unconditional, Addy.' That was when she'd almost weakened,
and knew she mustn't.

'I know that – that's why I also know I don't love you
as I should. And that's not good enough for me, or for
you. Please understand.'

'I can't.' She realized he was telling the truth. Then he
added: 'And I never will.'

That was the moment she knew that he would let her
go, not as her husband but as her friend. She went over to
him and took his hand, and kissed it.

'You can do so much better than me,' she said, meaning
it.

'I doubt it,' he replied. 'But if there's one thing I'll never
do it's hang on to you against your will, Addy.'

And so she had broken free. And in time Peter had, as
she'd predicted, found the perfect wife. He was a naturally
affectionate, uxorious man and seemed blissfully happy.

Whereas she – she had succeeded, through a mixture of industry and good fortune, in welding together the disparate elements of her somewhat ramshackle independent life. Through her portraits she had money and a small portion of fame – some would have called it notoriety. She had had several enjoyable affairs, and retained the friendship of people she truly cared about. And she had Dora.

In her bad moments, Adeline despaired of herself. In her good moments – and this summer was made up of many such – she considered herself the luckiest woman alive.

Mind you – she slipped her feet back into her shoes and got out of the car – the late arrival of this one man ('a lame duck of Nella's' was how Nicholas had described him) had introduced, by his mere absence, a note of mild contentiousness into the holiday.

Charles Farrell was driving down through France, and had been expected some days ago. Day after day his arrival was anticipated, and day after day reverse-charge calls were received from various points along his erratic route, explaining that he had been delayed, had trouble with the car, got talking in some bar or café. Adeline had been amused by the spectacle of the usually sardonic and imperturbable Nicholas becoming positively rattled by this cheerful, disorganized off-stage presence, and when at breakfast this morning yet another call had come through, saying that the car had packed up altogether, Nicholas had actually lost his temper. No, he bloody well wouldn't drive halfway round France to pick up some idiot who scarcely knew the time of day, and God alone knew why he'd taken the fellow on, he must have been mad. Adeline, seeing Fenella's face assume that stiff, blank whiteness which denoted rebellion, had stepped into the breach, and said she didn't in the least mind going for a spin along the coast road to collect the lame duck.

The message was that Charles Farrell, having walked back to Cipriane the previous night and found the natives more than friendly, had enough remaining funds (just) to take the local taxi from town to be reunited with his motor, and would wait there for the cavalry (his word) to arrive.

Adeline glanced at her watch. She'd been here for a full twenty minutes now and was beginning to feel both impatient and ridiculous. Flies hummed greedily over the broken baguette and the apples, which smelt slightly alcoholic. Adeline scanned the unhelpful green scrub.

'Mr Farrell? Are you there?'

Her voice sounded small and cautious, lost in the great vibrating bowl of heat.

She walked to a new position, a little further down the hill, behind the black car, and shouted more vigorously. Instantly she was alerted by a small answering movement amongst the green. The movement, a glint of white shirt, brought into focus the body of a man in the undergrowth about twenty yards below where she was standing.

'Oh my God,' she muttered in horror. 'Oh no . . .'

She called again. 'Mr Farrell, is that you?' And when there was no response added: 'Just my rotten luck.'

She looked down at herself. She was wearing a cotton blouse and trousers and flat sandals. She swung her leg over the low rail that separated the road from the scree and began to go down sideways digging her feet into the gravelly soil to keep her balance. When she reached the bushes progress was easier. She could grab the branches for support, and the knobbly half-exposed roots gave her a foothold. Just the same she was hot, bothered and scratched when she finally reached the man, and the realization that he was neither dead nor injured but comfortably asleep did nothing to improve her humour. He lay on his side, his outstretched legs pointing down the hill. The back of his left hand cushioned his right cheek, the other arm loosely encircled his waist.

Irritation gave way once more to relief. Adeline scrutinized him with the indecent thoroughness of the unobserved. He was in his mid-twenties, stocky and dark haired, lightly tanned. There was a gold signet ring on the little finger of his left hand but this was the only outward sign of gentility. The lower part of his face was shadowed with stubble, his shirt was dirty, and one of his battered shoes was without laces. From the pocket of his trousers peeped a dog-eared cigarette packet and a French bank note. His chest rose and fell gently, his face was peaceful – too peaceful, thought Adeline, for someone asleep on the side of a cliff.

He was waking up. He did this as though greeting the new day in the most luxurious of feather beds. He stretched, he yawned, he rolled on to his back, and then opened his eyes – very bright, brown eyes – and smiled at Adeline.

'Oh miss, have I died and gone to heaven? Are you an angel, miss?'

'I'm Adeline Gundry. Are you Charles Farrell?'

'I am, yes!' He sat up, brushing the dust off his sleeves. 'I say, I'm sorry. Have you been wondering where the hell I was?'

'Yes.' She saw no point in beating about the bush, especially since he showed not the least sign of repentance. 'Are you all right?'

'Do you know, I just had the best kip I've had in days,' he said, as if expecting her to be as delighted as he was. 'Cigarette?'

'I think we ought to get going.'

'Really? No, nonsense, take the weight off your feet for a moment.' He pulled the cigarette packet out of his pocket, bringing the note out with it.

Adeline captured it and handed it back. She sat down awkwardly.

'Thanks. What the hell? It's only money.' He lit their cigarettes with a match which he struck on his thumbnail, a trick Adeline had only ever seen practised on the cinema screen. He caught her admiring look.

'Clever, isn't it? It's little things like that that keep the boys in awe of me.'

Adeline, though she found herself liking him, could imagine no one less awe-inspiring. 'Boys?'

'I'm a schoolmaster.' He waved his cigarette at her.
'And you're the cavalry?'

'Yes.'

'Name again?'

'Adeline Gundry.'

'I know it . . . I have a feeling I'm making a more-than-average fool of myself. Are you an actress or something?'

His straightforwardness commended itself to her and she laughed. 'A painter.'

'That's right. Good for you,' he added. 'Had you been waiting around up there for long?'

'About twenty minutes.'

'Oh, no time at all, that's all right then. It was so ruddy hot that quite honestly this seemed the most sensible thing to do.' He smiled at her, the voice of sweet reason, so that it seemed churlish to deny him an answering smile. 'Right,' he said, as though he had been waiting for her, 'shall we push off?'

They struggled back up the scree, which was hard work for each step slid back on itself. He reached the rail well before her, and held out his hand to pull her up. Adeline leant, gasping, against the Alvis.

'What are we going to do about your motor?' she asked. 'Just abandon it?'

Charles Farrell looked from one to the other. 'I should think so. Is this yours? What a little darling . . .' He caressed one of the silver headlamps. 'No, the old chap from the petrol station in town – he runs the cab, too; I got to know him over a game of cards last night – is coming out to tow her away later on. Though I rather doubt there'll be much he can do but administer the last rites. She's been a grand old girl –' He gave the bonnet of the black car a friendly slap – 'but this trip was her swan song. I only paid a few quid for her so she's more than repaid the investment. And anyway I'm here,' he concluded, as if this were all that mattered.

He collected his effects from the black car and threw them on to the back seat of the Alvis. He then got into the passenger seat with obvious delight.

'Home, James, and don't spare the horse-power.'

Liking her car to be liked, and anyway quite unable to resist a challenge regarding speed, Adeline performed a brisk three-point turn in the middle of the road to an accompaniment of squealing tyres. As they begun the homeward journey she asked:

'You've been here before?'

'Last summer. I help young Miles keep his head above the academic water.' He referred to the Eyres' eight-year-old son. 'I could do more in that direction if Nicholas would let me.'

'He doesn't like you.'

'You've noticed.'

'I shouldn't worry, the world's crowded with people Nicholas doesn't like,' said Adeline. She glanced encouragingly at her passenger, but he had fallen asleep.

Three quarters of an hour later she turned the Alvis in between the wrought-iron gates of the Villa Clemency and Charles Farrell awoke and sat up straight as though some sixth sense had informed him of their imminent arrival.

'Lunch, wonderful lunch,' he said.

Adeline pulled up before the door as Fléance, in his brilliant white jacket, appeared to greet them. She said, in a spirit more of assistance than criticism:

'You'll want to go and change.'

'Of course.' He chuckled. 'Don't worry.'

As Fléance opened the door for her, Farrell jumped out, all energy now, put on his jacket and hat and retrieved the rest of his possessions from the back seat. Fléance's normal expression of grave restraint gave way to one of delight.

'Monsieur Farrell – welcome!'

'Hallo Fléance. It's good to be here.' They shook hands warmly. 'Now if you could show me where I'm billeted, I ought to have a wash and brush up.'

He turned to Adeline. 'Tell them I'll be there in two ticks, not to wait lunch any longer or anything.'

Adeline shrugged. 'I want a drink before lunch.'

She watched him disappear into the house, a quixotic and untidy figure next to the manservant's neat, elegant one. She followed slowly, savouring her passage from the buzzing, scented heat into the cool twilight. Ahead of her was the verandah door beyond which Nicholas, Fenella and their house guests sat sipping pre-prandial drinks in dappled shade, framed by the laden vine which wreathed the south side of the house. They did not appear impatient but relaxed in this extension of the happy hour. A face turned, and a hand lifted lazily. Someone said, 'Here's Adeline. They're back.'

A small, dark figure tugged open the door and ran to meet her. It was Miles, who almost cannoned into her in the sudden darkness.

'Where's Charlie?'

'He went to change, he'll be down in a minute.'

'Can't I go up?'

'He'll be quicker if he has five minutes to himself,' suggested Adeline, who had cast herself in the role of peacemaker on this holiday, and who could readily imagine what would be Nicholas's view of small boys pestering adults in their rooms.

'Can I just go up and say hallo – through the door?'

His agonized impatience was too much for her. 'Well, I suppose so –' He was off, and she called softly after him, 'But don't badger him!'

She went out on to the verandah and was greeted with the lazy gratitude of those who have recognized that a dull chore must be done by someone, but who are awfully glad that on this occasion it wasn't them. They were seven. Apart from Nicholas and Fenella there was Peter Marchant and his wife Pru, hugely pregnant, and Paul Hudson. A little to one side, perched on the verandah wall with a glass of orange juice, sat Miles's nanny. She was a sensible, highly qualified girl not usually uncertain of herself, who nonetheless seemed uneasy about her status at the villa. She was caught on the cusp between Fenella's insistence that, because this was a holiday, she should be 'one of the family', and Nicholas's belief that children and all their works should be kept separate from the adult world. So Deirdre Martin was with them but not of them. As Adeline went to sit down in the remaining basket chair, a large gin and tonic in her hand, she murmured:

'Don't worry, my dear, he's being good as gold. My responsibility.'

'Where is he?' asked Nicholas. 'Didn't you bring him?'

'Of course I brought him. He went to get cleaned up.'

'I say Addy!' Peter waved his cigar at her. 'We knew he wouldn't dare stand you up!' Everyone except Nicholas smiled. Fenella said:

'Thank you so much for going, Adeline, we do appreciate it.'

'My pleasure. Mm . . . that's good. . . .'

Adeline turned her chair to face the sun, ignoring the small tensions which drew taut the social fabric of this group. Over recent years, since her divorce from Peter, she had learned detachment. She was not her brother's keeper, nor her friends'. Not without difficulty, she retained her neutrality.

Beyond the verandah the white-paved terrace glared brilliantly in the sun. Dotted about on it were great stone urns boiling over with flowering plants. A hummingbird hovered like a tiny firework near the trumpet of a huge, red lily. At the foot of a shallow, fan-shaped flight of steps the swimming pool burned like a sheet of bright blue glass, and on the far side of the pool a stretch of lawn, baked and cracked in the August heat, gave way to a hillside misty with lavender. A row of sentinel cypresses marked the valley road, a mile away, that led down into Cannes. The city's rooftops could just be seen to the south east, romantic and alluring in the shimmering haze.

The verandah door slammed open.

'Charlie's here!'

There was a scraping of chairs, a chorus of greetings, the chink of glass. Adeline looked over her shoulder, smiling. Charles Farrell, clean and changed, was accepting a drink from Nicholas, apologizing disarmingly for being such a nuisance . . . but the greatest transformation was in Miles.

He was a thin, pale, uncoordinated child, rather over-pol-
ite and anxious as a rule. But now, looking up at this new
arrival he brightened with pleasure. Along the verandah
Fléance and Toinette, the cook-maid, began to turn over
the wine glasses on the pale pink cloth, to set out bread
and bowls of salad. Adeline closed her eyes. She sipped
her ice-cold drink felt the sun beat redly on her lids, smelt
the lavender.

'. . . dead to the world,' Farrell was saying. 'Then I
opened my eyes to find this rather out-of-sorts angel of
mercy hovering over me. It brought me round like a whiff
of salts.'

'Hear that, Addy?' called Peter. 'He's calling you an
angel!'

Adeline lifted her shoulders to show she had heard but
was too lazy to answer.

'She's a sweetie,' said Pru, of whom the same might
have been said. 'She likes to make out she's a bit fierce but
we all know different.'

'I don't know,' said Paul. 'Have you ever driven with
her?'

'Good point,' agreed Peter. 'Looks like an angel when
she wants to, drives like a bloody maniac.'

They were teasing her, trying to make her turn and
defend herself, but she wouldn't oblige them. Instead she
laughed and said:

'I can't be that bad. Ask Mr Farrell, he slept all the way
here.'

'Guilty,' said Farrell. His voice was closer, he was sitting
on the verandah step beside her.

'That's nothing to go by.' Fenella's scent drifted by as
she moved towards the table. 'He leads a life of dissipation
and debauch. Lunch everyone.'

Adeline put down her glass and rose. The others made
their way along the verandah, giving way to Pru's ripe,
swaying fecundity.

'Is that true?' Adeline asked him. 'About the dissipation
and debauch?'

'It is when I can get it.' He grinned at her. He had merry

eyes, and there was something openly flirtatious in his manner that Adeline found most agreeable. She was attracted.

'But you're a teacher – '

'Schoolmaster.'

'The same thing, surely.'

'Not at all.'

'You have to set an example.'

'Damn, I never thought of that.'

She laughed. Miles caught his wrist. 'Can I sit by you?'

'Of course.'

'Now, Miles,' began Deirdre, but Farrell shook his head. 'He can sit between you and me, Nanny. After all, we have to discuss our timetable, yes?'

They went to sit down and as they did so he said to Adeline: 'By the way, my mother calls me Charles and the headmaster calls me Farrell. Everyone else calls me Charlie.'

It struck her that this was a pet name. It was on the tip of her tongue to ask him when he would discard it, but for some reason she didn't wish to sound sharp.

'All right, Charlie it is,' she said.

At the lunch table she was separated from him, because Nicholas preferred Miles and Deirdre to sit at the far end of the long table, at a slight distance from the rest of them, and Charlie, Adeline saw with amusement, chose to align himself with them.

'I'll go below the salt if you don't mind,' he said. 'Important matters to discuss.'

Adeline noted that discussion of the timetable involved a good deal of hilarity and mirth, and rather wished she could have joined them. The improvement in Miles was still most marked, and Deirdre lost her air of conscientious politeness and grew quite pink and giggly. Somewhat reluctantly Adeline recalled her attention to her more immediate neighbours.

Paul was in his usual ecstasy about the food, rhapsodizing about Toinette's cold turbot with chive sauce.

'I simply don't know how I'll adjust to gravy and potatoes when I go back,' he was saying.

'Very readily, I should think,' commented Nicholas in his chilly way, 'since I've never seen you eat gravy and potatoes in your life.'

Everyone was a little tired of Paul, who seemed to have been taken up by Nicholas to occupy the position in his life once held by Neville. Adeline didn't know on what level the relationship was conducted, but she suspected that Nicholas was bored with it. Paul Hudson was handsome and intelligent enough, but he had none of Neville's charm, none of the mystery and allure that the Elverstones had exuded so effortlessly. She caught Fenella's eye and they exchanged a smile. Adeline was sure that Fenella was not happy, and yet at the same time she seemed to be making the best of her strange marriage. She even displayed a certain stubborn spirit, refusing to be demoralized by her husband's coldness, or his impertinently time-consuming 'friendships' with other men. She worked on the rest of her life – Miles, and her houses, and her entertaining – and polished and improved them to the level of an art form. She was an excellent, beautiful and amusing hostess, a devoted mother, a charmin g companion. She never complained, nor these days did she gossip about others and this alone would have been enough to win her society's respect and admiration. Only a very few, Adeline included, knew how often the King and Wallis Simpson had been to dine at the Eyres' house in Cheyne Walk, and that they'd eaten at this same table, looked at this view, slept in this house while the world had gasped in thrilled amazement over their holiday aboard the *Nahlin*. Along with her brother, she had been brought up to shoulder heavy responsibilities in a debonair manner. Peter's boisterous, fruity laugh rang out.

'Eating for two, that's it,' he said in response to some remark of his wife's, 'or is it three?'

Pru placidly took more fish. 'I've no idea, but this is absolutely lovely and I'm famished.'

'You do very well, darling.' He patted the taut protruberance of her belly beneath its covering of navy and white spotted silk. 'By Jove there's some activity in there today.'

Nicholas looked faintly disgusted. Adeline said: 'Don't you find this heat exhausting, Pru?'

'It would be if I did anything,' Pru replied, her pink moist face wearing its usual expression of pleased surprise, 'but all I do is lie about in the shade and eat and drink.'

Peter squeezed his wife's shoulders as she guided a fork-ful of turbot towards her mouth. He was as pleased with her pregnancy as a boy with a train set.

'She's a wonderful woman,' he declared. He topped up his glass and raised it in Adeline's direction. 'I wouldn't marry any other sort.'

Pru swallowed and giggled. 'Peter, really – !'

Adeline thought how ideally suited they were. Pru was only twenty-three, a full thirteen years younger than her husband, but it was as though she had been in training all her young life for this marriage, this childbearing, these trips to Harrods for Marmot prams and layettes of stagger-ing ornateness. She had the placid, kindly, thoughtless likeability of those born to comfort and who recognize no other world. She laughed a lot at nothing very much, had the knack of accepting the attentions of others with good grace, and would be fat in middle age. Contentment sur-rounded her jolly, burgeoning bulk as unhappiness hung about the lovely, thin Fenella.

It was Peter's apparently painless transition from herself to Pru, following their divorce, which had confirmed Adeline in her opinion that she had done the right thing. It had been hard, hard to have to hurt Peter who had been so kind, such an ever-present help, such a tower of strength when she'd not known where else to turn; and hard to disappoint all those who had seen it as an ideal match. Everyone had loved Peter, he had fitted in at For-ding Place just as she'd always known he would: Elizabeth had been completely won over, Anne thought him the nicest man she'd ever met and Frank had at last found someone with whom he could share the odd joke and talk farming without feeling he was being dull.

Only Bob had had reservations, which she had chosen to ignore. His affair with Louise Maybury had been a famous scandal, and when Louise had walked out on Ted Maybury and her two enchanting children it had made front-page news. No-one could deny that they loved each other, but they had had to weather bad times together, they'd been ostracized and isolated by all but their closest friends for nearly two years and there was a sadness about them. Bob had had to leave the *Recorder*, and everything he'd worked for, and go freelance in a professional world where his name had become poison. Only relatively recently – and then, like Caesar, after three refusals – had he accepted the *Courier*'s invitation to return to the fold. He was battle-hardened. As now Adeline was too.

Peter, she observed, was one of those people possessed of a limitless fund of love, and who could attract it just as readily. If one channel were closed off, his affections would redirect themselves. He and Pru, with their amiable, unquestioning acceptance of themselves and of other people, were ideally suited. Peter's numerous business ventures, no more orthodox than his flirtation with art, and no more popular with his ageing parents, flourished. He was, in his own words 'filthy rich', congenitally idle and generous to a fault. His energy and acumen went into setting things up and launching things. Once they were up and running he relapsed into indolence for a while until some new project took his fancy. So Fenella's analysis, delivered to Adeline in the room in Gower Street as the rain streamed down the windows, had been entirely accurate. And in appearance he was just as she herself had forseen all those years ago (when Pru, she reflected, had been just a schoolgirl). Peter was stout, his hair was receding, his face flushed with enthusiastic good living, his voice guttural with cigar smoke.

The remains of the turbot and salad were removed, the cheese and fruit arrived. Beyond the verandah the countryside began to take on the drugged, whitened look of siesta time. The hummingbirds and butterflies had gone, the pool glared blindingly, the flowers stretched parched gaping faces into the unforgiving heat.

Miles took a peach and was escorted away by Deirdre for his afternoon rest.

'See you later,' said Charlie, 'for some intensive measuring of the swimming pool.'

'Ripping!'

Charlie moved up to sit next to Peter, and opposite Adeline. Fenella leaned across in his direction.

'I'm glad you're here, Charlie. Miles is always so happy when you're around. He worships you.'

'I do hope not.'

'No, really. Even if he doesn't learn a thing he'll have gained some confidence, which is every bit as important.'

'What will you be doing with him?' asked Adeline. She was aware of Nicholas's cool, hostile stare from the top of the table.

Charlie began twisting the stem off a yellow apple. 'We shall be addressing ourselves to all sorts of grave problems, such as – if it takes one man five minutes to do six lengths, how long will it take one man and one boy to do the same? And there again, if a boy can eat three double-glaces fraises in an afternoon, how many can he eat in a day – ?'

Fenella shrieked with laughter. 'You won't be able to fill him full of ice-cream this time, Charlie. You don't have a car.'

'Nor I do. Darn it.'

'Just as well,' said Nicholas, with cold annoyance. 'He needs some fairly intensive coaching, particularly in Latin and Maths, if he's not to fall disastrously behind.'

'I understand, of course,' said Charlie, adjusting his manner to suit Nicholas's, 'but you mustn't regard it as a disaster if he does fall a little behind.'

'No, Nick,' said Fenella. 'He's so young.'

'Anyway, you're a fine one to talk,' put in Peter with hair-raising directness. 'You did precious little but smoke and drink when you were at school. Conjugate a Latin verb for me, go on, let's hear you do it! – there you are

you see? No idea. Let him that can conjugate cast the first
stone – !'

Nicholas smiled frostily. 'Just because I had a misspent
youth doesn't mean I want Miles to do the same.'

'Doing well at school isn't always a recipe for success in
life,' said Paul.

The discussion continued on more general lines.
Adeline leaned across to Charlie.

'Tell me the difference between a teacher and a schoolmaster.'

'A teacher is someone with a vocation, a schoolmaster's
just vaguely enthusiastic.'

'Vaguely?'

'Not in your lexicon, I'm sure.' He grinned. 'You
know, I was rather bright at school myself. I went up to
Oxford to read English. I spent three idyllic years picnicking and playing poker and falling in and out of love, and
then failed my degree. Cast adrift, I realized I liked places
of learning, I wasn't entirely without brains, and I got
along well with my fellow man – there had to be a niche for
me somewhere, and there was. At St Luke's prep school.'

'But what exactly is your role at this school?' Charlie
was exposed to the bright, somewhat intimidating beam
of Adeline Gundry's curiosity. 'Prep school masters
always seem to be amiable duffers. Or else bright young
things waiting for something better to come up.'

Charlie spread his hands in a gesture of helpless acquiescence.

'All my life I've been training to be an amiable duffer,'
he said. 'And I think I may be on the verge of qualifying.'

'Come on,' urged Adeline, 'defend yourself. Surely you
can't be planning to spend the rest of your life in some
educational backwater?'

'Well, put like that . . . no, the fact is I don't make plans.
I like it at St Luke's. I like the duffers and the eccentrics,
and I like the boys.' He shrugged. 'For the moment, it
suits me down to the ground.'

Adeline lowered her voice a shade. 'Miles is at your
school?'

He shook his head.

'Then how do you know them?'

'I answered an advertisement.' He must have read something in her expression for he added, 'I suspect I make a rather better interviewee than I do a tutor.'

Toinette began removing plates and Fléance brought coffee for Fenella to pour. Adeline accepted one of the strong, cheap cigarettes from Charlie's battered packet. When he'd lit it for her, she said: 'You didn't do your trick.'

'Not the right company.'

'So what subjects do you – get enthusiastic about? Maths and Latin, obviously.'

'Yes, and Eng. and hist. and geog, and scrip. – oh yes – not to mention games and singing.'

'You sing?'

'I didn't say that.' She laughed. 'At prep school level one has to be a jack of all trades, that's one of the many things I like about it.'

'So you're happy in your work,' she observed.

'Absolutely. Just like you.'

Fenella suggested they take their coffee to more comfortable chairs. As they did so, Adeline reflected that if she and Charlie Farrell were alike in enjoying their work, it was the only way in which they did resemble each other.

When they'd finished their coffee the hypnotic torpor of early afternoon descended on the occupants of the Villa Clemency. Pru and Fenella retired to their rooms for a nap. Paul sat in the drawing room, reading a two-day old copy of *The Times*. Peter, Nicholas, Charlie and Adeline remained on the verandah. Charlie and Peter slept, Nicholas read: Adeline sketched the three men, each so different in repose. Peter sat with his hands laced over his stomach, head sagging, knees dropped apart. Occasionally he would jerk forward and emit a snort of surprise before righting himself with a contented snuffle.

Nicholas was reading a novel of Marian Elverstone's that Adeline herself had just finished. *A Friend of a Friend* had disturbed her terribly. It was a dark, confused story, the writing had great power but seemed uncontrolled, and some mystery at the core of the plot was never resolved. Many years, and marriage, and not a few lovers had come and gone since Adeline's time with Marian, and yet its echo still resounded in the back of her mind and the deeps of her heart. That Marian had loved her, if only briefly and unwillingly, bestowed upon her, she felt, a kind of responsibility that she did not know how to discharge. The novel, Marian's latest though three years old, had been like a coded message which she was unable to decipher but whose significance she recognized.

Nicholas, however, was reading it as one might a foreign phrase book. He scanned each page quickly and expressionlessly. As he read, he smoked, occasionally tapping the cigarette over the side of his chair, allowing the ash to fall on the floor. There was something dismissive in the gesture, as though he found what he read predictable and unremarkable. Adeline wished she could snatch the book away from him.

She glanced at Charlie. He, on the other hand, was a picture of youthful relaxation. His frayed straw hat covered his eyes. His arms were loosely folded on his chest, shoulders pushed up in an arrested shrug of peaceful insouciance. His crossed ankles rested on the verandah rail. Adeline liked the look of him, a hammock-shaped, smile-shaped young man. Drawing him was easy, she found, a few sweeping lines captured his attitude precisely.

The verandah door opened slowly and quietly and Miles appeared. The black wool waistband of his swimming trunks showed above his tan shorts and he carried a towel rolled beneath his arm. Only she had seen him. She smiled, and blinked her eyes slowly as if to say 'hallo'. He did the same. He looked exactly like his mother, but in him the sum of the parts did not amount to Fenella's beauty. He was skinny and sallow and big-eyed. His dark hair, on Nicholas's insistence, was cut so unflatteringly short that it was no more than a stubble on the back of his neck and above his ears.

Deirdre came out, also ready to swim but wrapped in a chaste towelling robe. Nicholas closed the book and dropped it with a dull, slapping sound, on the floor.

'Going for a dip?'

Deirdre said: 'Is that all right? It's earlier than we usually go, only I thought that now Mr Farrell's here Miles might be doing other things later – '

'It's fine. It's what it's there for,' said Nicholas.

'Come on then,' said Deirdre to her charge, sounding pretty much like a child herself in her anxiety to exchange the restraints of the villa for the cool, blue freedom of the pool. She went ahead over the terrace and down the steps. Miles, passing Charlie, gave his elbow a quick, covert shake. Not covert enough, however, to avoid detection.

'Miles,' said Nicholas, 'for heaven's sake. It's siesta time.'

But Charlie, whom Adeline now suspected of not having been asleep at all, lifted the brim of his hat with one finger and rolled his head lazily to one side.

'Ah, at last,' he said. 'Are we going to have that swim?'

'Yes!'

'Miles, for God's sake stop being a pest – '

'Let me just go and dig out my bimmers. Honestly,' added Charlie to Nicholas, 'I've been looking foward to it.'

'It's up to you, of course.' Nicholas glanced at his watch. In that one small gesture he conveyed his boredom with and dislike of all of them. Peter lifted his head, opened his eyes briefly, smiled and dropped off again.

Charlie got up and stretched his arms above his head, fists clenched. 'Go on then,' he said to Miles. 'I'll see you in there.'

Miles ran off, adroit at removing himself from dangerously unpredictable adult company.

As the door closed behind Charlie, Adeline got up.

'Swimming too?' Asked Nicholas.

'Going for a walk.'

'You'll expire. Just relax.'

'I'm perfectly relaxed,' she snapped, causing Nicholas

to smile his close-lipped, sarcastic smile. 'I just want to stretch my legs.'

She put on her sunglasses and set out across the garden and down the hill. At the pool Deirdre sat on the edge in her bathing cap, her sturdy sun-reddened legs dangling in the water, while Miles splashed and exhorted her to come on in.

Adeline followed the path between the lavender bushes. Their scent, rising in the afternoon sun, was as rich and heady as wine. As she walked she drew a handful of the small, dry flowerheads off a stem and crushed them in her hand breathing in, on this baked Mediterranean hillside, the atmosphere of clean sheets and airing cupboards and handkerchief sachets in grey English houses. Bees droned over the bushes. She felt as though she were walking through a fragrant, tranquil sea. An enormous yellow and black butterfly with eye-marked wings sat sunning itself on a branch; she paused to watch it and the wings stared back at her. Below her in the valley a red-roofed farmhouse like a child's toy, with a barn and square white outbuildings, nestled amid neatly striped, cultivated fields. In one of these fields a wagon piled high with hay swayed behind a nodding black horse. A tiny figure in blue overalls and cap sat on the driving board. On the valley road a red sports car whined like a hornet on its way to Cannes. Above the farmhouse, on the opposite hillside, orange and lemon and fig trees basked in their appointed places between dry stone walls. Away to the north were another two houses, not dissimilar to the Villa Clemency, one pink, one white, both British owned, nestling in their prettily landscaped gardens like a couple of pampered kept women.

Though this was Adeline's first visit to the Villa Clemency, the Eyres had owned it for more than a year, and Fenella was constantly urging her to buy a place of her own down here. 'A home from home,' Fenella would enthuse, but that was just the trouble. Adeline wanted to escape. She did not care to be part of a smart set, an annual migration of well-heeled gypsies who left the smoke only in order to re-form their cliques and refurbish their reputations in new surroundings, no matter how idyllic.

Knowing from past experience that the attractions of the lavender would be less apparent on the steep climb back she did not go right into the valley, but described a wide arc across the face of the hill and then returned. She was due to go home in a few days' time, and she felt ready for it. She was becoming slightly bored and restless, and less tolerant of the others. With the exception of the new arrival, who had not yet had time to get on her nerves.

As she reached the top of the hill she could hear the splashings and whoopings of the swimmers, and when she emerged on to the lawn she could see Charlie and Miles fooling about in the pool like a couple of high-spirited dolphins. Deirdre Martin, her bathing costume wet, her cap removed, sat on a poolside chair reading a magazine a shade self-consciously, Adeline thought. Above and behind them the villa still slept behind its veil of vines. She herself walked round the end of the pool and sat down on the steps to watch. Two towels lay in a heap on the stone flags. One was pale blue and richly piled, the initials 'M. E.' monogrammed in one corner. The other was a threadbare, sun-bleached rectangle of cloth in danger of losing a Cash's name tape, 'C. V. Farrell'.

'Hallo, why don't you come in?' Charlie hoisted himself on to the side of the pool by his folded arms, his hair black and sleek like an otter's coat, his shoulders glistening with water. 'Deirdre's been in,' he added encouragingly.

'I can see that. Perhaps later.'

'Now's the best time, when it's really hot out. In fact – ' He ducked beneath the surface and burst forth again, eyes closed, spouting water – 'this is my idea of sheer bloody heaven.'

Miles climbed up the steps on the far side and pattered past Deirdre to the diving board, his feet leaving dark prints that were instantly erased by the sun.

'Hey look! Hey, Nanny! Adeline! Charlie look – I'm going to do a honeypot!'

He ran, bounced, rose and plummeted into the water,

his arms closed around his bent-up knees, eyes tight shut, teeth gritted and bared in a grimace of elation. The splash he made sent a shower of drops on to the pages of Deirdre's magazine. They all applauded. Charlie pulled himself up to sit on the side.

'*Bravo! Magnifique!* Now let's see a couple of widths of crawl.'

'Oh, *no*,' groaned Miles, delighted. 'Crawl's so *hard*, but I'll try!'

They watched as he ploughed, with flailing strokes, the width of the pool. Deirdre, perhaps feeling that she should be paying more attention, put down the magazine and moved her chair closer.

'Now a width breaststroke,' she suggested.

Charlie said: 'He calls you Adeline.'

'He calls you Charlie.'

'On my insistence. Who wants to be sir-ed in a place like this? But I'm amazed his father allows him to be informal with you.'

She described, briefly, her status. 'There's already one Mrs Marchant here, It'd be too confusing for the poor child. Before that, a long time ago, I was widowed. It seemed simplest to revert to my maiden name. And if you don't like being sir-ed, imagine being called Miss Gundry. It sounds like the driest, most emaciated and repressive governess.'

Charlie inclined his head and took his cue. 'Which you most certainly are not.'

'Thank you.'

Charlie reached for his towel. He rubbed his hair vigorously and then asked: 'Would it be impertinent to ask if a poor widow meets many eligible woodcutters?'

'I'm far from poor, so I meet plenty. Some woodcutters. Some frogs who turn out to be princes and some princes who turn out to be toads.'

Charlie spread the towel and lay down on it on his back, his fingers laced behind his head.

'Oh *Charlie*!' shouted Miles. 'Are you getting out for good?'

'No, just for now.'

'I'll come in again,' said Deirdre. 'Wait while I put my cap on.'

Adeline looked down at Charlie. There were two small white scars near his left collar bone – chickenpox perhaps? – and a fine, feather-shaped streak of dark hair ran from his navel to the waistband of his trunks. His ribs stuck out boyishly. She hoped her voice didn't give her away when she spoke.

'That child obviously thinks the world of you.'

'I don't know about that. Anyway, it's mutual. It's just that I sometimes think it would be more use to the little beggar if I played with him all day.'

She detected a note of seriousness, even of tenderness. Feeling that reassurance was required, she said: 'He's an only child, and he leads the kind of sequestered life that many upper-class children do. It's not such a bad life – I mean look at him now.'

Charlie tilted his head back to look up at her. 'Do you have any children?'

'Peter and I have a daughter of about this age.'

'And?'

'She's what my mother calls a hoyden. She means it as a compliment.'

'I'm sure she does.' He let his head drop back. 'I rest my case.'

Adeline agreed with so much of what was implied here that she was unable to decide on the exact nature of her response. She simply did not know him well enough.

'I do wish they'd let him wear his hair a bit longer,' she said tamely.

'Yes.' Charlie turned over on to his stomach. His own hair was a little too long, and curling as it dried. 'Yes, I have my own views about that.'

Adeline, though curious, was inhibited by loyalty to Fenella, and said nothing. Charlie continued unabashed.

'I realize it may not be true, but I've heard Nicholas Eyre has fairly catholic sexual tastes, and there's none so punitive as the guilty. All this steely rectitude is a sign of an unquiet mind if you ask me. Which very properly you don't.' He lifted his head and gave her his sudden intimate grin.

She said: 'You'll get nothing from me, young man.' A little too firmly.

The afternoon processed on its way. Fenella drove Pru and Paul down into Cannes to do some shopping. Nicholas and Peter talked business on the verandah. Charlie and Miles sat at the dining room table devising a timetable and playing battleships. Deirdre sunbathed. Adeline wrote a letter to Dora which would almost certainly arrive after she did.

That evening they went out to dinner, as they frequently did, this time to a new restaurant of Paul Hudson's choosing. Adeline was unclear whether Charlie had been invited or not, but at any rate he did not accompany them. The food was wonderful, too wonderful, as it always was. Adeline was beginning to feel that she could happily have murdered for a slice of toast with Gentleman's Relish. After dinner, when it was suggested they move on to a nightclub, she would have preferred to go back to the villa with Peter and Pru, but felt constrained to lend moral support to Fenella. Obligingly she drank more than she wanted to and danced from time to time with Paul, who tended always to hark back when in his cups.

'So you don't see anything of the Elverstones these days?'

'No, nothing at all.'

'I suppose you know she's bad again.'

'No. I really have no contact with them any more, I haven't for years, Paul.'

'You don't need to be sensitive about it, Adeline.'

'I'm not. But it was a very long time ago.'

'I'm afraid there'll be no more novels. That last one was a travesty, didn't you think? It could only have been brought out on the back of her reputation. If an unknown author had produced that it would never have seen the light of day.'

'We're lucky her reputation counts for something, then. She's still a remarkable writer.'

'Hm.' Paul swung her into a reverse turn. 'It's Neville I feel sorry for. He looks like absolute death at the moment.

On the way back to the villa, at two in the morning, Adeline felt exhausted.

And yet she was perversely glad to find Peter and Charlie still up, and playing cards.

'For money!' exclaimed Fenella, sinking down on the sofa and removing her shoes.

'Peter, you are the end.'

'It was his idea,' said Peter.

'But I'm losing,' added Charlie, 'so everyone's happy.'

Paul yawned. 'Just so long as no-one press-gangs me into playing. From boyhood games have always made me nervous. If you'll excuse me, I'm going to bed.'

'I shan't be long myself,' said Fenella. 'Good night, Paul.'

Nicholas poured himself a whisky and went out on to the verandah. Without looking up from his cards, Charlie asked:

'Do you play poker, Adeline?'

'No. I don't gamble.'

'Ah – you mean you don't play cards. Everyone gambles.'

Adeline laughed and sat down by Fenella, lighting a cigarette. 'You'll be saying "Life's a Gamble" next.'

'Well it is,' said Peter.

'What rubbish you men talk,' remarked Fenella sleepily.

Adeline, enjoying a second wind, asked: 'Then where does free will come into all this?'

'It's badly overrated,' said Charlie. 'There's far more satisfaction to be gained from putting yourself in the lap of the gods, or in the hands of fate and simply brazening it out. That's much freer than free will, that's real freedom.'

'Nonsense, it's base servitude.'

Peter chuckled. 'You're on a losing wicket, dear boy. This woman loves an argument. She wouldn't back down even if she agreed with every word you're saying.'

'I still contend,' said Charlie equably, 'That it's a dull man – or woman – who isn't susceptible to the fascination of gambling, even if they've never played a card or thrown a dice. It's an attitude of mind. A quality of spirit.'

'I'm off to bed,' said Fenella. 'Nick? Darling, are you coming?'

'Very shortly,' said Nicholas, without turning. But when Fenella had gone he came back into the room, closing the door behind him, and stood beside the card table, watching intently. His manner was more animated, thought Adeline, than it had been for some while. There was the old sardonic acuity, the air of detached and mocking interest.

'D'you want to sit in, Nick?' asked Peter.

Nicholas shook his head. 'Just looking.'

Not long after, Adeline fell asleep. She was awakened by the reluctant scrapings and stretchings of over-tired people turning in.

'God . . . what time is it?' she asked, looking at her watch. It was just after four.

'Not worth going to bed,' said Charlie.

'I don't agree,' said Nicholas. 'Good night.'

Charlie yawned. 'I'm going to get some air . . .' He walked out into the garden, hands in pockets, face lifted to the sky as if counting the stars.

'A fellow of nocturnal habits,' observed Peter comfortably. 'Unlike me.'

'He certainly sleeps a good deal during the day, which would account for it,' said Adeline. 'Who won?'

'That, if I may say so, is a typical woman's question. A non-gambler's question. Things are going my way at the moment, but then there's always tomorrow.'

'Peter, you ought to be ashamed of yourself, I bet he hasn't got a bean.'

'Not at the moment, no. In fact he's probably accounted for most of what Nick's paying him as well.'

Adeline was scandalized. 'Don't you feel at all guilty? And Nicholas was just standing there and watching. I don't call that the action of a responsible employer.'

'Come on, Addy, don't be so disapproving! Nick knows the ropes. For one thing Charlie will probably win it all back next time round, and for another I wouldn't dream of accepting his IOU, let alone calling it in. It's just a bit of fun.'

'It strikes me as both dull and dangerous and there aren't many things you can say that of.'

'True.' Peter clasped her shoulders and kissed her warmly on both cheeks. 'Night, Addy. Sweet dreams.'

'Good night.'

He left the room. Adeline walked around, turning off the lamps one by one, feeling the darkness and quiet close about her. She was no longer tired and she felt that timeless sense of excitement that accompanies being up before dawn, when the rest of the world is asleep. She thought how much rather she would watch the sun come up than go to bed and sleep through the fresh, golden morning. She walked to the verandah door and stood gazing out. Now that the room was dark the garden beyond seemed less so. With the approaching dawn the stars had faded and the air had a velvety, muffling intensity. She became conscious of the ripple and splash of water: Charlie was swimming.

She stood very still, listening to that secret sound in the darkness. In a moment he appeared on the diving board, his naked body luminously pale, silky wet. With the unselfconsciousness of someone who thinks himself quite alone he shook his head like a dog and bounced up and down a few times on the board experimentally. Then he walked to the end and stood staring down into the water as if uncertain whether to dive or not. Adeline imagined being in the cool, glassy water, naked, weightlessly meeting that young man's body . . . her own body bloomed with desire. She closed her eyes.

When she opened them she knew at once that he had seen her, or was conscious of her presence. He stood very still, his face turned in her direction, his arms hanging loosely at his sides, in an attitude at once passive and challenging. Her face burned. She held her breath. The fine thread of sexual invitation stretched taut between them, its pull stronger as she resisted it.

It was ridiculous, crazy. Vulgar. Undignified.

Adeline opened the door and walked out, stepping out of her shoes on the verandah and leaving them there. As she crossed the terrace she pushed the straps of her long red evening dress from her shoulders and felt the thick, warm night breathe on her skin as Charlie dived into the pool, with scarcely a splash.

CHAPTER TWENTY-ONE

1937

O N HER RETURN, Adeline swept down to Fording Place, scooped up Dora and Dorothy and drove back to London the following day. Her effect on the inhabitants was like that of a Mistral – they felt that they had been buffeted by some hot, unstoppable natural force which had unsettled them and disturbed their surroundings and roared on its way before they'd had time to adjust.

'You've got to admit she's in good form,' laughed Anne.

'God in heaven,' said Frank.

'It's the artistic temperament, you have to make allowances.'

Frank grunted. 'I'm not surprised she's still single – what sane man could live with that?'

'Now my dear, that isn't fair –'

'True though.'

Adeline, carried along on a racing, shining wave of happiness the like of which she hadn't experienced in years, was in no state to recognize the preoccupations of others. If she had been she would soon have realized that she was in the presence of a barely contained secret. As it was, her own secret – that of being in love – both filled and enclosed her and left no room for anything else. She was buoyant with it, protected by it, besotted with it. She felt, as one does, that the world centred upon her, and that everything pleasing in nature, every tree, flower, young man and maiden, was simply an extension of her joy. Her present separation from Charlie brought an edge of sadness to this joy which only served to intensify it. Here, she was the only custodian of their love. Gladly she filled that role, and felt that she had no other: it was her *raison d'être*.

Not for nothing had Dorothy spent thirty years *in loco parentis*. She recognized at a glance the symptoms of severe over-excitement, and knowing Adeline as she did she could hazard a fair guess at to its cause. Gazing out of the car window at the ripe, slothful late August fields, she permitted herself a philosophical thought or two on coincidence, and the symmetry of fate.

At nine, however, an hour seems an eternity and quiet reflection does nothing to alleviate the pangs of impatience. Over lunch in the George Hotel in Salisbury Dora's resolve finally gave way. Fortified with roast chicken and strawberry ice-cream, her tongue loosened by her mother's gaiety and nearly a pint of ginger beer, she released the cat from the bag with a flourish.

'Mummy, Dorothy's got something to tell you.'

'Oh yes?'

'Not now, dear,' said Dorothy. 'Another time will do for that.'

'For what?' Adeline directed a look of amused enquiry, even brighter and more penetrating than usual, at Dorothy.

'Nothing that won't keep.'

'She's getting married!' announced Dora, in a growling, grinning stage whisper. 'Mr Dance asked her, and she said yes!'

'Dora, I –'

An Imperfect Lady

'Dorothy! Really? Truly?'

Dorothy's blush of assent was at odds with her severe expression. 'I'm afraid Dora was speaking out of turn, I had no intention of mentioning anything just yet.'

'But why keep it to yourself? It's wonderful news! We should have champagne.'

'No, please – it wouldn't agree with me in the car,' muttered Dorothy.

'Then you must promise to give me a blow-by-blow account as we go along.'

'Yes, Dorothy,' said Dora, 'tell Mummy the whole thing.'

'The whole thing' amounted to a simple and affecting story of chaste and faithful patience. Or had it, Adeline wondered, simply been idleness on Chris Dance's part that had caused him to wait uncomplainingly for twenty, odd years for the woman of his choice to come within proposing distance? For that was what he had done. Indeed he could hardly have been said to have been waiting, for there had been no real obstacle to his popping the question at any time. Secretly, Adeline was dismayed at this passionless inertia, and a little surprised at Dorothy's acceptance of it, until she reminded herself that this was no callow young couple but a woman in her fifties and a man ten years older than that. The probability was that neither of them would have married at all, one through circumstance, the other through temperament, had it not been for this tardy reunion.

The moment she had known she was pregnant she had contacted Dorothy, and she had been with her ever since. During her marriage to Peter they'd lived in London and their visits to Fording Place had tended to be *en famille*. It had proved more difficult than she'd expected to push Dorothy out into the real world. Freedom had to be forced upon her. The provision of more time off was no guarantee that she would do more than remain in her room reading, knitting and writing letters, clinging obstinately to the habits of a lifetime. Adeline wondered if she harboured any of the romantic dreams which had so pervaded and coloured their days together in the nursery. Had they simply withered away, or were they still there, as bright and shining as ever, unclouded by experience? She hoped that the latter was true, but she also could not believe that this belated marriage of resignation (for that was how she saw it) had anything to do with the dreams. Since the divorce Dorothy often spent weeks at a time at Fording Place with Dora, and without Adeline. These visits had provided the time and the opportunity for willingness and patience to reap their small reward.

Later in the journey, when Dorothy had moved into the front seat so that Dora could stretch out and sleep in the back, Adeline said:

'You'll be wanting to leave us, Dorothy.'

'There's no hurry. I told you I wasn't planning to say anything just yet, we shan't be marrying till next year. I won't leave you in the lurch.'

'But Dorothy there *is* a hurry!' She was so keen to impart her own sense of urgency that she inadvertently pressed the accelerator and narrowly missed a fat man on a bicycle. 'Sorry! But Dorothy, you and Chris – you've waited so long, I don't think you should wait another moment if you can help it. You mustn't give another thought to us. I've taken up more years of your life than any one person has a right to, and now it's yours and Chris's turn. You *owe* it to yourselves, you really do. I mean – you have somewhere to live, don't you?'

'Yes. I can move into Christopher's cottage. It's plenty big enough for two.'

'There you are then. There's no reason to wait. Out upon waiting –' Adeline thudded to a halt at a crossroads. 'You must start your new life as soon as possible.'

Dorothy smoothed her skirt, looking, as she did so, at her neat, dry hands which had never worn a ring. 'What about your daughter?'

'If you start being reproving I shall have to start calling you Nanny again,' said Adeline.

'You lead such a busy life, and she's got no father –'

'Nonsense, she has an exemplary father as you very well

know. We're all much happier the way we are. She's the last one you want to worry about: there are so many people who dote on Dora she can take her pick. Quite soon she could go to boarding school. She'd love St Aggie's, for instance.'

'I dare say.' Adeline could not fail to catch the note of dejection.

'Oh Dorothy, we're going to miss you, we're going to miss you horribly, me more than anyone. I honestly don't know what I'd have done without you over the past few years – you've been a tower of strength. But now it's time you thought about yourself and your happiness. Do you see?'

Dorothy nodded. 'And what about you, then?'

Adeline recognized the emotion concealed by the severity. She said gently: 'I shall be fine. I'm a big girl now.'

Dorothy looked directly at her for the first time. 'Are you happy? Have you got what you wanted?'

Adeline beamed, and squeezed Dorothy's hand. 'Bless you. Do you know, I'm very happy. And I really think I have almost everything I want. The trouble is that if things carry on like this there'll be nowhere left for me to go but down!'

She laughed and began to sing, as she often did in the car. Her singing woke Dora, who joined in on the back of a yawn.

'Charlie is my darling, the young chevalier!'

Adeline did not usually care for London in August, with its dusty streets and stale greenery, the weary summer past its prime and the crisp colours of autumn still out of reach. But this year she felt so full of energy and optimism that she could hardly wait to lay claim to her neglected life in the city. Her surroundings, the home that was uniquely hers, assumed a fresh charm for her. Her answer to Dorothy's question had been nothing but the truth, and she blessed her good fortune. When Charlie returned, as she knew he would, she wanted him to find her at her best, not for reasons of vanity but because she wished to make

him a present of herself, her success, her style, whatever
it was she did well. He knew so little about her, she longed
to surprise and delight him. Nothing was too good for her
love.

She and Dora, with Dorothy and a Belgian 'bonne'
named Merle, occupied a spacious house in the Vale of
Health in Hampstead which Peter referred to affectionately as 'The Nunnery'. Adeline had chosen the house
for its position, and for its friendly and accommodating
nature. The Vale of Health was the closest thing to the
Devon countryside to be found in London. This little
enclave, almost a separate colony, of whimsical houses set
in a hollow on the western edge of Hampstead Heath, felt
perfectly secluded though it was no more than a hundred
yards from two busy roads. It was set in a sort of armchair
of land, with steep wooded slopes on three sides, and
before it a lake, to the south of which the Heath fell gently
away, before billowing up to Parliament Hill, where the
children flew their kites. Here it was possible for Adeline
to maintain a countrywoman's perspective on her adopted
city.

But most important was the house itself.

She was a great believer in the characters of houses and
this one was stylish, benign and flexible, like an experienced courtesan. In it she found aspects of those houses
she had most liked and admired to which she had added
the idiosyncratic colour and comfort which she herself
liked. It was a substantial house of considerable presence;
like Fording Place, a house that embraced riotous parties
but in which it was always possible to be alone. It was a
tall, secretive house like the one in Allerton Square, from
which people could come and go at will while she painted
in her top floor studio with only the view from her window for company. And like the Pink House it was a folly,
with a flat roof from which protruded a stubby tower
topped by a minaret. When she had first moved in, Adeline's neighbours told her that one of the house's earliest
occupants had been a naval officer who had never resigned
himself to living so far from the sea, and had erected the

tower so that he could scan the horizon with his telescope as if from the bridge of a ship. Before Adeline's occupancy the tower had simply been used as an extension of the attic, but when she had had the attic itself converted to a studio she had installed a black iron spiral staircase and turned the tower into a retreat. Now a padded seat ran round the walls at window height, baskets of plants hung from the roof, and a door led out on to the flat roof, which she had had surrounded with a balustrade. On the roof, perfectly secluded between the mellow mossy brick of the chimneys, Adeline would sunbathe naked in the summer, listening to the rustle and coo of the pigeons. On winter afternoons, stiff from painting, she would come up here as the spicy dusk drew in, and watch London, distantly surrounding her, come to light. She was a Londoner now, and yet her memories of her own childhood had brought her to this particular place, and it made her happy to see Dora, who was in any case a boisterous, tomboyish little girl, able to do on the Heath all those things which she had done at Fording Place – riding, swimming, climbing trees, tobogganing, flying kites. Sometimes she wondered what she had done to deserve the best of so many worlds.

And because the house was a happy one it acted as a magnet to Adeline's friends, none of whom were too far away. Peter and Pru lived in solid comfort in a St John's Wood mansion close to the flat of Peter's art school days. Duncan and Joel had a garden flat in Muswell Hill, looking across to Alexandra Palace, and Toni now maintained an immaculate establishment in a mansion block near the Edgware Road. These were still her dearest friends, the ties with whom had remained strong in spite of her concerted efforts to sever them. Weeks, even months, could go by and she would see none of them, surrounded as she was by newer friends, and acquaintances, and sitters and patrons and, she had to admit it, hangers-on. But then, one precious empty Sunday, Duncan and Joel would arrive at the door, having walked the six miles from Muswell Hill, Duncan coughing and smoking and complaining, Joel spry and fresh-faced. They would slip back into her life as if they'd never left it, spoiling Dora to death and charming Dorothy just enough to prevent her dying from shock.

Peter came as often as he could to see Dora, and about once a month he and Pru would collect her for the weekend. Just occasionally, when Peter was there on his own, and Dora had gone to bed, he would embrace her and say: 'What about it, Addy . . . for old time's sake?' But she had not the slightest difficulty in extricating herself with a laugh, and telling him she was more interested in the new times, and he should be too.

Toni was the least frequent of all her visitors. For some years after Bob's departure and Adeline's marriage to Peter, she had disappeared from Adeline's life, to lick her wounds in private. It was only since her reappearance that Adeline fully realized what Toni had been through, how long lasting its effects would be and what it had cost her to admit she needed Adeline's friendship. She was a proud, private person, who had dropped her guard, the sensible self-containment of a lifetime, when she fell in love with Bob. Till then, she had lived for her work; everything had been subordinate to her ambition, her urge for self-improvement. But as she gradually, almost unwillingly, relinquished her heart to what even she could see was the most unlikely of men, another cherished but long-hidden dream began to surface – that of a contented love match, home and children. Toni's own childhood had been a beleaguered, make-do-and-mend affair, but now she saw the real possibility of an idyllic family life, with children who were cherished by her and a husband she admired and respected. She was a one-man woman, both by temperament and upbringing, and she had no doubt that this was the man for whom Fate had intended her. Accordingly, she had relegated ambition to second place, only to find that Bob had done the same thing to her. She bore him no ill will – she still loved him, after all, and was sane enough to recognize her symptoms in him – but the pain and humiliation were so bitter that she could only hug them to herself until they passed, as it were, into her bloodstream and became part of her. This poisoning of herself was the only way she knew of coping with her misery. And the day that she read of Adeline's divorce, and sought her out, was the day she began to be partially cured.

Adeline was making a great deal of money. The thirties, her own and the century's, were her golden decade. She was in constant demand, not only as a painter but as a guest. The craze begun while she was still a student among a certain section of society was now a full-blown fashion. She was smart, she was chic, she was amusing, her calm divorce from her rich and amiably potty husband made her smarter still. Anyone who was anyone wanted a portrait by Adeline, and not primarily as an investment. When you bought a Gundry painting it was to hang on your wall, to be an object of entertainment and discussion amongst your friends. With the peculiar inverted narcissism of those who are too often in the public eye, the famous, the notorious and the talked-about yearned to see themselves as Adeline saw them, warts, idiosyncracies, weak chins and all. Now it was not merely the county set who commissioned her but actors, politicians, writers, singers – anyone whose pocket matched his or her ego.

An artist would have had to be possessed of an almost saintly integrity to maintain her original vision under the onslaught of so much material success, and Adeline was no saint. She worked fast anyway, and she never said no. The result was that she was permanently and direly over-committed. Little by little, in so gradual and insidious a fashion that it was hardly noticeable until it was too late, the style that had made her famous became the thing itself. Her portraits became scarcely more than cartoons or caricatures. The critics, who had never much cared for her, felt vindicated, and as such permitted themselves to damn with faint praise: this was fun, but not art. Like any craze, her painting sowed the seeds of its own demise.

But on her return from France in the late summer of 1937,

her popularity was still at its peak, and with the sublime confidence of a woman in the first raptures of love, she could not envisage a time when it might be otherwise.

They were greeted by Merle, fat, perspiring and emotional, and the only male occupant of the Nunnery, Adeline's Irish setter, Brody. Brody was the first dog Adeline had owned since the dear, departed Clancey, but at two years old he was a wild, charming, amoral delinquent who showed no signs of reforming and becoming a co-operative companion as Clancey had done. From the top of his sleek, red head to the tip of his flapping banner of a tail he was a hopeless case who stole, chewed things, and ran away. It was impossible not to love him for his beauty, his exuberance and his pathological devotion, but the four females loved Brody with a certain reluctance, knowing that it would do them no good.

Now, as he attempted to leap into Adeline's arms and lick the features from her face, Merle launched into a half-despairing, half-admiring catalogue of his crimes over the past month.

'. . .'E was up in the village, madame, I am beside myself with worry, what am I going to say to you if 'e is struck down by a car! I did not 'ave one wink of sleep, the next day a policeman bring 'im back. 'E 'ad been round the butcher's shop begging for meat – as if I do not feed 'im properly! – and 'e 'as stolen a joint of beef, the butcher 'as sent a bill for it, what could I do . . .?'

'*Brody*! You bad dog! Poor Merle – never mind, I'm back now.'

'Yes, madame.' Merle, a realist, did not seriously expect Adeline's return to make much difference to Brody's reign of havoc. On the other hand she worshipped her employer and was prepared to give her the benefit of the doubt. 'You 'ad a good holiday?'

'A heavenly holiday, thank you, Merle.'

'Come on, Brody!' Dora raced up the stairs to reacquaint herself with her room and her possessions and the dog hurtled after her.

Dorothy said: 'I'll go and get us unpacked.'

'Yes . . .' Adeline was looking through the thick sheaf of letters on the hall table. She glanced up. 'And after that why don't you ring Chris, Please. Tell him you're free as air.'

'We'll see,' said Dorothy.

Adeline left most of the letters on the table and took one into the sitting room with her. Merle hovered.

'Shall I make tea?'

'A cup of tea would be wonderful, Merle. Thank you.'

When Merle had gone she opened the letter. She could hardly believe it, and yet it was true. He was such a *fool* . . . she laughed to herself and shook her head, enchanted by his romantic gesture.

Yes [Charlie had written], I *did* write this before you left for England. Pretty silly I know, but I wanted you to find a letter from me waiting for you when you got back. I'm overcome with panic at the thought of your simply dismissing this as a fling, just one of those holiday things. I know what it's like when you get home to the trivial round, the common task – though in your case I suspect it's neither trivial nor common, which makes it worse. Life and work and family and friends reassert themselves with terrifying speed and firmness, don't you find? But please, my darling, darling Addy, keep a small space in your mind and your heart for me, at least until I come back. Then, if you wonder what on earth you were thinking of to take up with such a scruffy, callow bore, you can say so and I suppose I shall have to accept it. After what you've told me about your life in London I have this horrifying picture of you being swept away on a flood tide of admirers and dealers and gallery owners and glittering top-drawer people. Ghastly! On the other hand, as I write this, after lunch while Miles is having his nap, I can hear you talking to someone down on the verandah, talking and laughing, and you just don't strike me as the flighty type. For my part, I know I seem a bit of an idiot, but I *do* mean what I say. And in case you wondered, I don't make a habit of declaring undying passion to rich and famous older ladies after a few days' acquaintance. My life is pretty monkish, between St Luke's and tutoring, but writing this letter seems the most natural thing in the world. Just hearing your voice, I want you something fierce. How the hell am I to manage for another three interminable weeks after you've gone? And how have all these charming, clever people failed to notice what is going on right under their noses? Don't they wonder why you're more beautiful every day? Or why I'm so unaccountably bloody cheerful as I go about my Bob Cratchet-like tasks? I suppose it would simply never cross their minds that a bobby-dazzler such as yourself would stoop to conquer a no-account like me. But you have, you have, I must be the luckiest devil on earth! Even if you're deciding at this very moment, as you read this stuff, to send me packing, it will still have been worth it I promise you, my gorgeous darling. To think, all these years you've been around, lavishing yourself on other people. It makes me grind my teeth just to think of it. I love you, miss you, love you, and I shall be suffering the fires of hell till I see you again. Yours unashamedly, passionately, hopelessly enamoured – Charlie.'

'The fires of hell' indeed . . . Adeline smiled but her mouth was unsteady and there were tears in her eyes. A cup of tea had been placed at her elbow as she read, but she had not noticed. She put the two sheets in order again, and smoothed them. It seemed to her that they felt warm, as if the writer's ardour had transmitted itself to the paper. She lifted the letter to her face and fancied she could smell his sun-warmed skin, and the faint tang of lavender that haunted everything at the Villa Clemency . . . She lowered it again and studied his handwriting, which was large and many-looped like loose knitting. His signature hurled itself across the final page like a shout; she could picture him practising it over and over again as a small boy. She kissed it, and her body remembered other kisses and flowered in treacherous anticipation.

'Mummy?'

'Yes, darling.'

'Can I take Brody to the lake?'

'Only if Dorothy will go with you.'

'She says yes.'

'Then yes.'

Dora came to the side of the chair and stared at Adeline. Her eyes were round and perspicacious behind her glasses.

'Mummy? Are you all right?'

'Of course! Never better! Why do you ask?'

Dora hunched her shoulders in an exaggerated and faintly embarrassed shrug.

'You look very pretty, and very sad.'

Adeline heard them go, the skitter of the dog's paws in the hall, Dora's yell, Dorothy's token and automatic reprimand. She let her head drop back on the chair, her eyes closed. She pressed the letter to her heart and sat still and silent, suspended in a sensuous melancholy.

When she went to say goodnight to Dora that evening she knew at once that the child wasn't sleepy. She was lying on her back instead of her side, her bear clutched to her chest like the broadsword of a knight in effigy. It was dark now at eight o'clock, and Dorothy had left a nightlight burning on the chest of drawers. Dora's upturned face in the gloaming was like a pale pool into which Adeline dipped her own face as she kissed her.

'Sit down, Mummy.'

Adeline did so. 'What is it, Dolly?' She used the pet name to establish her seniority. For at this moment her thoughtful daughter seemed far older and wiser than her. Like many other aspects of parenthood, a mother's attitude of reassuring certainty did not come easily to Adeline. Her urge to protect was at odds with her reluctance to dissemble. At this moment, sensing an impending interrogation, she envied Dorothy her store of experience and her large collection of common-sense responses, one for every conceivable contingency. Or almost every one, for Dorothy was not Dora's mother.

To break the silence in which she felt that delicate and awkward questions were being formed, she said: 'It's nice to be home. And to have you back, I've missed you.'

There was a pause. 'What did you do?'

'Oh, all the usual things . . . Swam, and talked and ate and drank too much, and lay in the sun . . . nothing very exciting.'

'Is Daddy still there?'

'Yes. He sent lots of love. He'll come over and see you as soon as they get back.'

'Good.' Another pause. 'When will Pru have her baby?'

'In November. Three months.'

'Ages.'

'Not long really.'

'I can't wait to see it.'

Adeline laughed, but could make out no answering smile. 'It'll be no great shakes to look at, not at first anyway. You were as bald as a coot.'

Now, a smile. 'A swede, Daddy says.'

'He's right. Only noisier than a swede.'

'Gran showed me some pictures of you when you were a baby. You weren't bald, you had lots of black hair.'

'That's true. I was a rather fine specimen.'

'She said you were beautiful, the most beautiful out of you and Uncle Frank and Uncle Bob.'

Yet again Adeline felt her present life, so different and so very much her own, stirred by the soft, insistent ripples that radiated from the past.

'I don't know about that,' she said.

'You were just like your father, Gran said. What was he like?'

Adeline rose, and then stooped to kiss her daughter once more. 'Like me!'

'That's cheating!'

'It's all you're getting. Time you were asleep. Night, Dolly.'

'Night . . . I say Mummy –'

'Yes?'

'When Dorothy gets married, will I have to have another nanny?'

'Not necessarily.'

'Good,' said Dora. 'Only I'm getting a bit old for it.'

Adeline kept her face under strict control. 'That's settled, then. Sleep tight.'

It was late September before she saw him again, and the green of the heath was turning to bronze, edged here and there with a glint of copper. Her life and her many commitments swallowed her up, as he had predicted. If it hadn't been for his frequent letters – love letters, they didn't pretend to be anything more or less – she might have begun to think of him as a chimera, a hallucination brought on by the sunlit indolence of the Villa Clemency. But the letters buffeted her with their passion, and tenderness, and humour, and kept the image of the real man before her. For once, she was overwhelmed by another's directness. She felt almost shy in the face of such ardour, and her own letters seemed dry and stilted by comparison. She thought, it's ridiculous, I'm behaving like an inexperienced awkward young thing, instead of a woman of the world with two marriages, many lovers and a chequered past behind her. But this, she realized with delight, was one of the classic symptoms of love: there was nothing untoward about it, or about her. She was a walking cliché.

Dora went back to school up in the village, and Dorothy announced that the wedding was fixed for December. As to song and dance and celebration, she would have none of it. She and Christopher (as she alone insisted on calling him) were to be married from her brother's house in Enfield, and there would be a family-only gathering afterwards. She was deaf to Adeline's shameless cadging for an invitation, and to Dora's entreaties to be a bridesmaid.

'We're both too old for all that,' she said firmly. 'No frills, just a plain, private affair. I'll send you some cake.'

Adeline told Dora to stop pestering Dorothy, but privately she agreed with her daughter who complained bitterly that it didn't sound like a proper wedding at all but more like a funeral.

By mid-September she had begun a portrait she had been much looking forward to, of Francis and Nancy Herbert, a slightly down at heel, but grand, theatrical couple in their eighties. On the afternoons that they were sitting to Adeline they would walk, at a measured pace, from their house in Keats Grove to hers in the Vale of Health, he with much major-domo-like swinging of an ebony cane, she with her arm through his in a way that suggested partnership rather than dependence. Having sparred, amiably but loudly, throughout their sitting they would then allow Adeline to drive them home. Since they were notorious for their verbal clashes, Adeline had chosen to paint them as the devoted couple they plainly were. The fact was that in her present state she would paint nothing but love.

It was one evening when she was returning from Keats Grove in the Alvis that she became involved, through no fault of her own, in what might have been an extremely nasty accident.

She had just turned into the road that led down to the Vale of Health when she was narrowly overtaken by a large, gleaming motorcycle, travelling at speed. This alone, though dangerous and annoying, would not have been enough to enrage her. But having overtaken her the motorcyclist cut in sharply so that she had to brake, and had the nerve to shout and wave at her as though she were the offending party. Nettled, she blipped her horn. He shook his fist. She leaned on the horn again. They were approaching a steep bend in the road. The motorcyclist, obviously unfamiliar with the area, and anyway too preoccupied with hurling abuse at her, went into the bend far too fast and left the road with snarl and a crash, coming to rest in a smoking tangle on the grass verge, the front wheel of the motorcycle buckled against the trunk of a tree.

Seeing that the man sat up almost at once, and began struggling to his feet, Adeline let rip. Slamming the door of the Alvis behind her she advanced on him like an avenging fury.

'You idiot, you deserved that! Do you realize we might both have been killed? You were driving like a complete lunatic just then, and how you had the *nerve* to swear at me, I don't know! I'm just glad you wrecked that wretched machine! Now you can come back to my house and I shall take the greatest pleasure in calling the police to take the damn thing away, and you with it!'

'Don't worry,' said Charlie. 'I'll come quietly.'

Afterwards she could only remember saying, 'You fool, you silly fool . . .' as she kissed and kissed him, her righteous wrath dissolving into tears of bliss. He was filthy, with the dust of the road, and oil from the crash, and a certain amount of blood for which they at first could find no source until they discovered a small cut above his left ear. She was wearing a yellow shirt and wide, white matelot trousers, both of which became smeared with grime, but she welcomed these traces of him, and pressed herself against him, wanting to be marked as his. 'You're such a fool,' she sobbed, laughing, 'you could have been killed – *I* might have killed you.'

'I can't think of a better way to go.'

'No . . . no . . . but you'd have died with me hating you . . . thinking you were some stupid, ignorant stranger . . .'

'Instead of your stupid, ignorant lover,' he said. 'Christ!' There was something close to a sob in his voice. 'My bike! D'you know what that is?'

'A richly-deserved wreck. No.' She kissed his agonized face. 'Don't worry, we'll get it fixed.'

'Only a Brough Superior . . .' She thought he was like Mr Toad, poop-pooping away. 'A bloody Brough Superior SS80 . . . Christ!'

'And it will be again.' She very nearly laughed as she led him gently, like a child, back to her car. 'Don't worry. Come along.'

'Right,' said Charlie. 'Now then, are you sure you don't want to change your mind?'

Dora held the card in both hands, no more than six inches from her face. Her eyes moved from the card, to Charlie, and back to the card.

'No. I want this one.'

'So it was your decision, wasn't it. You had the chance to choose another card, but you turned it down.'

Dora nodded, giggling.

Charlie sighed. 'On your own head be it. Now put it back.'

She did so, and he shuffled, swiftly and dexterously, with a flutter and a whoosh like the sound of pigeons being released from a loft. Dora watched, spellbound. Adeline watched both of them: her two loves, an ill-assorted pair. Between them sat Brody, panting gently, his long tongue hanging from the side of his mouth. They formed a curious triptych, of which she was not part. She had to go out. She stood near the window in evening dress. It might have been possible to extricate herself from the party at this late stage, but a long-ingrained habit of independence had stopped her from doing so. Charlie would spend the night, he would be here when she got back, and they could be alone. She took a perverse pleasure in delaying that moment, in hoarding her anticipation.

Having shuffled, he looked up briefly at her and winked. She felt herself teased and she smiled and turned away for a moment. She had lied for him to the police. She must be mad.

'Now then,' he was saying to Dora. 'We both know your card is in the pack somewhere, but only you know which card it is. Yes?'

'Yes,'

'That's what you think. Now I'm going to find it.'

He began to deal the cards on to the floor between them. Dora kneeling, bent forward over her folded arms, her thick plaits brushing the carpet, her tongue protruding slightly. Brody copied, sniffing the cards and wagging his tail. Charlie pushed him gently out of the way and continued to deal.

'I have an idea I'm getting close,' he said. Dora glanced up at him, her face red from leaning over. 'Am I?' She shrugged, mystified. 'You don't know? I thought you were the one who knew. Still . . .' He dealt four more cards, each one more slowly. The fifth card he studied carefully, with furrowed brow, before laying it down.

'That's it. Two of hearts.'

Dora sat back on her heels. 'Crikey, that's *correct*. How did you do it?'

'Simple. It's hotter than the others. Your mind, your concentration, has made it hotter.'

'Charlie, you fraud,' said Adeline. 'Tell her how it's done, properly, so she can baffle her friends.'

Charlie looked aggrieved, one hand on his breast. 'Fraud? I'm wounded, Adeline, deeply wounded. Dora, feel this card.' He held it out to her. 'Tell this unbeliever – is it or is it not hotter than the rest?'

Dora rubbed the card between her finger and thumb. Her eyes met Charlie's. Then she turned to Adeline with a wide, disingenuous stare.

'Yes, Mummy – it's definitely hotter.'

'There you are!' Charlie stood up and stretched. 'Corroborative evidence and incontrovertible proof.'

'Rubbish.' Adeline picked up her handbag and moved in the direction of the door. 'You two are in cahoots. I must go. Dora, go to bed as soon as Dorothy tells you, and please try not to be a nuisance.'

'We're just going to play a hand of pontoon,' said Charlie. 'Dora, you shuffle.'

He followed Adeline out into the hall. Effortlessly, he had colonized her home and made it a place for his amusement.

'Merle's put supper out for you,' she said.

'Supper, cards, a house full of women – I don't deserve all this.'

'No,' she said, but she felt her face and body soft and sweet with loving him, 'You don't. I'll see you later.'

The party was a private view at the Canfield Gallery. Adeline knew about half the people there, not including the artist himself. He was a red-faced, shock-headed, furious-looking man, who, she suspected, had been handed a list of people whom it would be advantageous to invite, and who resented it bitterly. She sympathized with him more than he would ever know as he strafed the assembled company with a stare of barely concealed loathing. But his hostility was water off a duck's back to her. She drank, she talked, she smoked, she laughed, she knew from the way people looked at her that she was in sparkling form. Something radiated from her so that they wanted to be near her. Ida Rabone put it into words: 'You're stunning tonight, Adeline. What are you taking?'

'Loose living, Ida. You should try it.'

'I have, my dear, it wore me out . . .'

Paul Hudson beamed confidentially. 'Darling – did you know Neville's here? This graceless fellow is by way of being a protégé of his.'

'The paintings are exciting. I might even buy one.'

Paul raised his eyebrows. 'Adeline! Isn't that going a bit far?'

'I'm in the mood.'

She laughed and he laughed with her. 'That much is obvious.'

Not having considered it before, she did buy a painting, a cool, blue, empty landscape seen through a window. It was both tranquil and tantalizing, even a little threatening, as though the artist were deliberately refusing to show whatever else was going on in the room behind his back. On one side of the window the suggestion of a shadow fell on the wall, on the other there hung a mirror, reflecting only a half-open door.

'I wouldn't have thought that was your style at all,' said Ida.

'It's not. That's why I like it.' Something occurred to her. 'Anyway, it's a present.'

'Oh? May one know for whom?'

'A maiden aunt, Ida.'

At half past ten she left, pressing the hand of the angry artist and declining, with the utmost charm, the invitations of various acquaintances to go on for dinner. In the lobby of the gallery, as she put on her black taffeta coat with what Charlie had called its 'demon king' collar, she encountered Neville. His hair was greying, and he had put on some weight, but all in all he did not present the picture of suffering which Paul had described in France.

'Hallo, Adeline. How are you? I seem to see your name everywhere.'

'Neville . . .' She kissed his cheek. The other world that they had shared, the different air that they had breathed, swirled about them for a moment and then ebbed away. 'I'm well. How are you both?'

'I'm robust, as you know. Just as well, because poor Mary-Anne is very bad.'

'Neville, I'm so sorry.' He was staring at her with an expression of forlorn accusation. 'What can anyone do?'

His eyes shifted away from her face, he shrugged and pushed open the door for her. 'Nothing. I suspect I may soon have to admit defeat and put her into some place where they can at least banish the horrors.'

They stood on the corner of New Bond Street. Sleek after-theatre cars purred past them, and cold, rich clothes stood about in the windows of expensive shops. Adeline thought, I will not, not feel guilty. I will not take responsibility for this terrible thing which is not my fault. I loved her, I did what I could, and it was not enough.

And it had all been such a long time ago.

'Perhaps you're right,' she said. 'Maybe it would be for the best. Good night, Neville.'

They lay together in Adeline's bed. Their bodies still rippled and rocked in the wash of lovemaking. Slowly they were restored to the reality of each other, and of their surroundings. He stroked her and smoothed back her hair as if soothing a fever. She rediscovered the small scars near his collarbone.

'A duel,' he said. 'A very palpable hit, but the day was mine.'

'Chickenpox?'

'Mm . . .' He kissed her lightly, open-lipped, between the breasts. 'Hm . . . Everything about you is so much bigger and better and more sumptuous than anyone else.'

She shook with laughter. 'You're hopelessly partial, and I'm glad that you are.'

He propped himself on one elbow and admired her as she lay quite still and open to his inspection, on her back with one arm encircling her head.

'Your shoulders, for instance . . . splendid . . . Edwardian shoulders.'

'You have a polite way of putting it.'

'No. Oh no . . .' He bent and kissed her, and then lay down with his cheek against her shoulder. She felt him smile. 'Some nunnery! Terrific mother superior though, I will say that. What if Dora comes in when I'm doing . . . this?'

'She won't.'

His hand moved. 'I could make you yelp.'

'Charlie . . . ! The door's locked.'

A little while later they sat up against the pillows and shared a cigarette. Charlie, drawing her head alongside his as if pointing at something far away, indicated a picture on the wall opposite.

'I've been looking at that.'

'Liar.'

'No, honestly. Earlier, when you'd gone out and Dora was showing me around. Is it one of yours?'

'M-hm.'

'I like it, awfully. It looks back at you. Who is it?'

She made inverted commas with her hands. 'Portrait of an unknown young man.'

'What, really unknown? No. Who?'

She shrugged. 'Someone I met on holiday once.'

'You and your past. All the things and all the people and all the paintings, such a lot I'm going to have to find out about. I shall need plenty of time. Will you marry me?'

She didn't hesitate. 'Yes.'

Not long after that they turned out the lamp and he fell asleep almost at once. She felt his arm become heavy across her waist, and his breathing fade to a great distance. It was the distance of sleep but she saw it, suddenly, as that of youth. She was wide awake, staring and restless; he had dropped into slumber as swiftly and simply as a child. She lifted his hand, fondled and kissed it. It was warm and nerveless, hers to caress, and yet lost to her. Gently she restored it to him, slipping from beneath his arm and laying it at his side. He didn't stir. She could make out the slick black line of the cut above his ear, and was suddenly swept again by love and desire for him. But feeling older, as she suddenly did now, though she hadn't in France, she did not disturb him.

She put on her kimono and left the room, closing the door softly behind her. Then she went up the stairs to her studio, its familiar cluttered emptiness washed pale by the uncurtained moonlight. The old theatrical couple, half alive, watched her from the easel, their faces hovering above the still vague forms of their bodies.

She climbed the spiral staircase into the tower and sat on the seat, staring out, her arms folded tight against the cold. Pigeons, roosting on the sill only a few inches away, did not move. London was a distant black jumble, studded with lights.

She had meant it when she said she would marry Charlie. A thousand sane and sensible arguments cried out against it, but the heady sweetness of this love outweighed all of them. The arguments, what were they? Mere practical considerations, his youth, his comparative lack of means – well, she had money, plenty of it, and the means to go on making it. They had known each other for such a short while, indeed they scarcely knew each other at all – and yet it didn't feel like that, he occupied her heart and her life as though they had been kept warm for him all these years. She smiled to herself. He was disorganized, reckless, a fly-by-night. That might well be true. But then she was no saint and there were many people who'd testify to it. And this was something entirely new. The completeness of her love enveloped and blotted out all other considerations. She was strong, she knew it. She could make it work.

His hands slipped round her face, the fingers threading through her hair and then cupping her chin, tilting her head back to look at him.

'Are you changing your mind, all alone up here?'

She shook her head. 'No.'

He sat down beside her. 'I meant it.'

'So did I.'

'Then why did you leave me?'

She put her arms round him. 'You were sound asleep, and I couldn't sleep.'

'But you see,' he whispered into her hair, 'as soon as you were gone, I missed you.'

They sat still for a moment, and then she stood up and took his hand.

'Come on. You must go back to the spare bedroom. We both need to sleep.'

He beamed up at her. 'Yes we do. I'll need a lift to Victoria Station in the morning, I have to be back at school for a rugger match and the chap at your garage said the Brough would be a week at least. Would you mind awfully?'

'Of course not,' she said. 'Don't you know I'd do anything for you? I love you.'

CHAPTER TWENTY-TWO

1938

THE YOUNG VICAR bestowed a bright, patronizing smile on Elizabeth.

'Good morning, Mrs Gundry! You didn't walk all this way?'

Elizabeth did not return the smile. She stood in the church porch, the last to leave, pulling on her gloves with brisk, jerky movements.

'Certainly. I'm not entirely decrepit, you know.'

The smile grew larger still. 'Heavens, above, I wasn't suggesting that you were. But it's quite a step in bad weather.'

Elizabeth wondered why, as one grew older, the young adopted a special verbal style when they addressed you. She could not believe that the phrase 'quite a step' figured in Mr Crosby's speech when he was amongst his contemporaries.

'If you call this bad weather, Mr Crosby,' she said, 'you must have spent a trying winter. We natives consider we've got off lightly.'

Mr Crosby had been the incumbent at Tarrford for less than a year and was still making the common mistake of seeing himself as the shepherd of his dwindling flock. He was well meaning in a simplistic, unfocused way, but he was not alive to the nuances of temperament, status and seniority which informed his congregation. Neither did he have the ability to discern people as individuals. They broke down into the young, the elderly, the infirm, the absolute bricks and the frankly ungodly. There was a degree of overlap, of course, and a number of subdivisions, but by and large he was satisfied with this basic analysis. Elizabeth Gundry was elderly, and it was therefore important that she be shown the proper degree of solicitude. If Mr Crosby had had any idea of the intense irritation he caused by this behaviour he would have ceased forthwith. But he blundered cheerfully on.

'I can't offer you a lift?'

'No thank you. The exercise does me good, and I've precious little else to do.'

Believing this to be a complaint, Mr Crosby accompanied Elizabeth as she walked down the path. He even, for a moment, laid a pastoral hand beneath her elbow but she twitched away from him as if stung.

'Don't say that. You mustn't say that,' he soothed. 'I don't know where this village would be without you and your daughter-in-law. She was here at eight o'clock, her usual bright and cheery self. You're exceedingly lucky with your family, you know.'

This was too much for Elizabeth. She stopped, and confronted the vicar, staring down at him from her superior height, made more imposing by her large hat.

'It is not a question of luck, Mr Crosby,' she boomed. 'It's a question of breeding. Now, if you'll excuse me. Good morning.'

Marching rather too briskly on her way in her determination not to appear infirm, Elizabeth slightly regretted this assertion, not because it might have given offence to Mr Crosby – she didn't suppose it had given nearly enough – but because she wasn't sure that it was true. Elizabeth had always loved her children in an abrasive, unthinking sort of way, and she still did, but with increasing bafflement.

1938 had begun inauspiciously with her breaking her wrist, and the consequent deluge of unasked-for advice from all concerned, which had almost drive her to distraction. She had lived comfortably, happily and independently in the Dower House for the past thirteen years, but this infuriating accident had put it in everyone's head that she ought not to be living alone. Fortunately, the redoubtable Dorothy Dance was now on hand, and she had stepped into the breach with perfect competence and common sense before Anne – dear Anne, wonderful Anne, bossy Anne – could insist on her return to Fording Place.

All this, however, had paled into insignificance beside the latest bombshell from Adeline. Elizabeth was no fool. She did not expect her family to consult or defer to her, but she still believed that there were certain moves which it was appropriate to make. For heaven's sake, she had not even seen this man (and incidentally, what sort of person called themselves Charlie? – it was like something from the music hall), though Dorothy Dance had, and what she had said had done nothing to allay Elizabeth's fears. A schoolmaster in his twenties whom Adeline had met in France, apparently, and whom she had known for only a few months before marrying. When Dorothy had described him as very nice, quite charming and good looking, her heart had sunk still further. It was not that she disapproved – how could one disapprove of a man one had never met? – and from Adeline's letter it was obvious she loved him. Phrases like 'never been so happy' and 'seventh heaven' abounded. But Elizabeth had reached the conclusion that her daughter lacked judgement, as she herself had done. The difference was that in the days when she had married Richard she had known that nothing short of total catastrophe, she couldn't even think *what*, would 'put them asunder'.

When she had begun to find the marriage just a little irksome she had not, like many of her friends, launched upon a series of affairs, but attempted to inject some excitement into her life by other means – riding to hounds, and learning to drive, and being a match for a man on the tennis court. She loved Richard, whose sweet-tempered indolence she mistook for saintliness, and whom she secretly thought too good for her. She did not want to descend to the level of other couples of their acquaintance, whose extra-marital amours were an open secret, accepted by everyone, and whose marriages were generally acknowledged to be highly-polished, well-upholstered shams. It was not that she wished she had not married Richard, but that she wished she had not married, and there was nothing to be done about it either way.

It was only when they had met Howard and Cynthia Charteris at Newton Abbot races that she experienced despair for the first time. She had been pregnant with Bob at the time, and not feeling her best, but here was a man who, instead of being sympathetic or chivalrous, looked at her with a robust admiring greed. Their mutual desire had been instantaneous and terrifying, and had continued unabated from that moment onwards, fanned to an even greater heat by their long periods of separation. Telling herself that she could never have married Howard, because they would both have been at each other's throats within a year, was no consolation. The fact was that Howard confronted her with the irrefutable proof of what she had known, in her heart, all along: that she had made a wrong turning many years before, and there was no going back.

She'd known long before Adeline was born that the baby she carried was Howard's and had welcomed it as a blow struck for independence of a sort. This would be her secret, her triumph, and not even Howard would know. She had derived a jealous, sensuous pleasure from watching Howard's daughter grow up in the equable atmosphere of Fording Place.

Richard was the most unsuspicious of men, and if he did know anything he certainly gave no hint of it. On the contrary, seeing that Elizabeth was happiest when the Charterises were there, he prosecuted the friendship with, for him, considerable energy. Elizabeth saw no reason why things should not continue indefinitely in this way. The very last thing she had foreseen was Adeline's idiotic, misguided, pig-headed determination to marry the Charteris boy . . .

Elizabeth sighed, and stopped to take a breather. It was March, the last harsh bite of winter before the spring. A residue of snow lay in crusts at the sides of the lane, and in frozen rags on the tangled hedges. The air was cold, heavy with moisture. Elizabeth felt buried by the grey air, and the round, muddy hills, and the indignities of advancing age. She began to walk again, trudging this time, her sturdy shoes slapping down on the dank surface of the road. She still missed Howard. She often thought of him, as he had been, and of Cynthia, still alive, twittering and humming in her expensive nursing home: a silly, cold woman being fussed round and pampered as if she were a baby. Elizabeth raged at the injustice of it and slapped at the black twigs with her gloved hand.

Well, she had made her mistakes, and learned, literally, to live with them. But at least there had been no opportunity for further mistakes. When she saw Adeline flitting from marriage to marriage and with God knows what-all in between it looked dangerously like poor judgement given free rein. At least, thought Elizabeth grimly, when her daughter was married she was visible, you knew what she was up to. Asked for her opinion, which she never was, Elizabeth would have lamented the passing of Peter Marchant. He had seemed a really nice man – amusing, enterprising, no oil-painting, certainly, but personable enough, and clearly devoted to Adeline. The fruit of that particular union was Elizabeth's only grandchild (she didn't know what Frank and Anne were up to) and she doted on her. By rights Adeline's child should have been a mewling, neurotic clinging little thing, considering the shocks to which she'd been subjected, but she was turning into an absolutely delightful girl, bright, resourceful and good company. Elizabeth wondered what Dora made of this new alliance. Really, Adeline was the absolute end. She might well be the toast of fashionable London (even thinking the phrase made Elizabeth grimace) but what she knew about running her life could be written on the back of a postage stamp.

'Oh dear,' said Anne, who'd been looking out for Elizabeth through the drawing room window. 'Absolutely twitching with rage about something.'

'It's that bloody parson,' said Frank. 'I can't think why she goes to church when she knows he'll infuriate her.'

'She goes from habit like the rest of us.' Anne got up and glanced briefly and without much interest at her reflection in the mirror. 'But actually I doubt it is that. It's far more likely to be Addy's latest.'

'You're right. You and I will be put in the invidious position of sticking up for Adeline, as usual.'

Anne leaned her face into her husband's, twitting him gently. 'You don't have to, you know. Are you a man or a mouse?'

'I'm your husband. I toe the party line,'

Anne went out into the hall to open the door for her mother-in-law. She called over her shoulder. 'I'm very fond of your sister. She's only chasing happiness like everyone else.'

Frank didn't reply. Adeline, and Bob too – they seemed always to be chasing something. The mere thought of the kind of lives they led made him feel quite tired. He thanked God for his own good fortune. His marriage to Anne had brought him perfect contentment. He was sorry for his wife's sake that there would be no family, he knew it was her great secret sadness, but it didn't matter that much to him. He entertained no high-flown notions about the Gundry line. If there was one thing the war had taught him it was that one must make the most of the present. Frank read the papers assiduously, and spent a good deal of time alone during which he reflected on his findings. What point would there be in raising children if, as he gravely suspected, they were all going to be thrown into another war?

The women's voices drew nearer across the hall. As the drawing room door opened Frank squared his shoulders, removed his hands from his pockets and prepared to spend the next couple of hours fencing good-naturedly with his mother.

Joel sipped his coffee and gazed out of the kitchen window. Dear old Ally Pally, he greeted her like a friend. She took on the character of the weather, seemed to change with the seasons. This cold March morning she was steely and majestic, rising above the icy fog like a gigantic battleship. He'd looked out at her so often from his window as he waited for kettles to boil and eggs to cook and sauces to thicken, that now he half expected to hear the sonorous drone of a foghorn hailing him across the intervening space.

He sighed and washed his cup under the hot tap. And dried it. He was as meticulous about the house as he was about his person, and the more turbulent Duncan became, the more meticulous he was. This morning it was important to maintain order, and an even keel. Sunday or no, these few minutes by the kitchen window would be Joel's only relaxation. There was cleaning to do, lunch to cook, and Duncan to rehabilitate, in ascending order of difficulty.

It was unfortunate that they had received Adeline's letter on a Saturday, because it meant that Joel had had no way of dissuading Duncan from launching into a protracted bacchanal lasting from mid-morning until late at night with only brief intervals for snoring, troubled sleep. He had been by turn excited, euphoric, captious and maudlin, and finally extremely sick. Joel had outlasted him in order to clean up and tuck him in. It was his pleasure to do so, but he was weary of it – just plain weary. Adeline's letter, with its news of a fresh start, a young man, a new and special love, had reminded Joel of how long he and Duncan had been together. It was all very well for the snooty cat from upstairs to look at them askance, and move her arm out of the way if they passed in the hall, but did she realize she was looking at an old married couple? Seventeen years they'd been together . . . he wouldn't even know *how* to live with anyone else.

Talk of the devil, there she was. The woman passed by on the other side of the hedge, her atrocious felt hat bobbing primly up and down, proclaiming her righteousness as she set off for morning service at All Saints.

Joel went through to the bedroom and parted the curtains. Duncan moaned a little, but he was nowhere near conscious. Joel gazed down at him tenderly, and wistfully. The two of them had risked so much, for so long, by living together openly as they did. Of course they were oh, so careful, using euphemisms like 'friend' and 'colleague' and doing very little entertaining. They even left for work separately, and if they were going somewhere in the evening they tried to meet in Town wherever possible. As neighbours they were almost painfully quiet, orderly and conscientious, far more than any normal couple would have been. They did all this in order to remain together, but it was hard sometimes to remember why that was important. Duncan was deeply, savagely depressed. Apart from days like yesterday Joel had learned to gauge his mood by its shades of gloom, ranging from mild melancholy, through sulky glumness to tearful self-pity and beyond. Much of it would have been comical had Joel not known that the unhappiness was real enough.

He pulled the bedclothes up over Duncan's broad, fleshy shoulder. He felt a twinge of envy for Adeline with her new husband, her hasty and impulsive marriage. But he was needed here, and that counted for a good deal.

Toni noticed a lot about Bob and Louise in the moments before they saw her. They were all three of them in the foyer of the Haymarket. Toni, who was always early for everything, had already powdered her nose and bought herself some chocolates, but Bob and Louise were only just arriving. The first and most striking thing she observed was their closeness. They went together like hand in glove – so marriage hadn't cooled their relationship. Louise was, if anything, more beautiful than her photographs. Her face had acquired great character. She looked, thought Toni, as if she had learned a lot the hard way, but had emerged at peace with herself. As Bob took her coat Toni saw that she had put on a little weight, and her very simple blue dress displayed the sensuous womanliness of her figure. The sharp edge of expensive elegance had gone, but it had been replaced by something far more enviable and alluring which Toni, slim, smart and well-paid, knew she couldn't hope to achieve. For a second she was flooded by hot, sour jealousy which drained away as quickly as it had come.

Bob, returning to his wife's side, saw Toni, and smiled, raised his hand in greeting, and began steering Louise in her direction. Toni could discern no flicker of surprise or consternation in his expression. It was incredible that for him she was a tiny bit of the past, dulled and dwarfed by time and experience, whereas for her it was as though she had seen him only yesterday. Not that she showed it.

'Hallo!' she cried, before they had quite reached her, grasping the nettle.

'What an extraordinary coincidence!'

'Toni – I don't like to think how long it's been. Darling, have you two met?'

They shook hands. Louise's smile was warm, charming, completely unaffected; it was obvious she knew nothing.

'Can't we all have a drink?' she asked. 'Are you with anyone?'

Toni glanced at her watch. 'I'm not sure we have time, do we?' She didn't answer the second question. She preferred to come to the theatre on her own but would at this moment have killed for an escort, any escort, to disguise her singleness.

'Oh dear . . .' said Louise. 'What about the interval, then?' She seemed keener than Bob. The one-minute bell rang.

'Yes, a good idea,' he said. 'We'll see you in the bar, shall we Toni?'

'Lovely, I'd like that.'

As they parted company in the auditorium she knew, from the angle of their heads, that Louise was asking him who she was. And who, she wondered, was she?

'You were at the Slade with Addy,' said Louise, over drinks in the crush bar. 'I suppose you've heard her news.'

'Yes. I had a letter just the other day.'

'You haven't by any chance met him, have you?' asked Bob. 'My sister's just a comet zooming across the heavens now that we're down in the sticks.'

'I have met him, yes,' said Toni. 'I went up there for lunch one Sunday and he was there.'

'So what's he like? Apart from indecently young.'

Toni remembered how he had admired her for her straight talking. 'He's no match for her.'

Louise laughed affectionately. 'But which of us is?'

'I mean he's not worthy of her. I don't know what she sees in him, he's a lightweight.'

Bob raised his eyebrows. 'A searing indictment.'

'People don't fall for the right people,' said Louise gently. 'It doesn't work like that.'

'No, but . . .' Toni struggled to explain. 'I don't mean to make him out a monster. Actually I liked him, it's almost impossible not to. But all the time I wondered why? He's going to live off her – '

'Nice work if you can get it,' said Bob drily, not judgmentally.

'Not literally, I wouldn't know about that. I meant that he's a much lesser person in every way. He'll feed off her, drain her.' She paused. 'It's only what I think.'

Bob looked at Louise. 'Well, we did ask.'

Louise reached out and touched Toni's wrist. Her fingers felt warm. 'Thanks for telling us. You may well be right, but what can any of us do but wish them well? Love conquers all, as we know to our cost.'

In the ladies' Toni wept, though it was impossible to

tell from her reflection in the mirror. She still loved him. She begrudged him nothing, least of all his beautiful, loyal, courageous wife. But the unevenness of it took her breath away. All these years later, and her wounds were still fresh, while he bore not even the smallest scar. She applied more lipstick carefully. He was very thin on top and his nose seemed to become more prominent as his face got thinner. What with the limp, thought Toni, she was probably the only other person who could understand why Louise had left her rich husband and her sweet children to throw in her lot with Bob.

'She doesn't mince her words, your friend,' said Louise, as they sat down for the second half.

Bob stared at his programme. 'No. And she's probably right, too.'

'Let's hope not. But I liked her.'

The lights began to dim. 'Toni? Yes, she's a good sort,' said Bob. 'But getting a little spinsterish, I thought. She needs a man.'

He said it to annoy her, and to please him she pretended that it did. 'Don't be so damn vain,' she whispered.

The curtain rose. Louise wondered if her husband would have made his comment had he realized which man it was that Toni needed.

Nicholas and Peter were lunching in Simpson's.

'You're amazingly sanguine about it,' said Nicholas, watching his companion pour more claret, but covering his own glass with his hand.

'Why shouldn't I be?' Peter speared another small roast potato from the vegetable dish and popped it, whole, into his mouth. 'I like to see her happy. She deserves it.'

'Perhaps. I'm just astonished that you don't find the comparison insulting.'

'Comparisons are odious.'

'My point precisely.'

Peter mopped his mouth with a vigorous flapping movement of the napkin. 'Come on Nick, stop being so supercilious, you know it won't work with me. I'll always

be fond of Addy, but I don't own her, and I never did.
And she certainly doesn't owe me anything. I've got Pru
now, and the twins. Each to his own.'

Nicholas leaned back as his plate was removed. 'He's a
complete wastrel. Hopeless, useless.'

'Pudding? Of course!' Peter took the menu and scanned
it. 'I don't see why you should care either way. You've
never liked Addy.'

'I can see when something is entirely inappropriate.'

Peter chuckled. 'That's rich. What about you and Nella?' Nicholas did not reply. 'You for afters?' He shook
his head. Peter laid the menu down and leaned forward
confidingly. 'Guess what we're giving them for a wedding
present.'

'I couldn't. A revolving cake stand.'

'Close. A piece of the island.'

Nicholas made a whistling face. 'I just hope that idle
bugger appreciates it.'

'What does it matter? Addy will.'

'Which bit?'

'Whichever bit they like so long as it's not where we've
built our house.'

'It's extremely generous of you.'

'Isn't it?' Peter slapped his waistcoat, and looked up at
the waiter. 'Nothing for my guest. I'll have the profiter-
oles.'

In the Nunnery, Brody howled as the telephone rang.
When Adeline was at home she answered it at once: its
continued ringing was a desolate reminder of her absence.

Merle approached at a fast waddle. 'Shut up, noisy –
'allo?'

'Merle, it's Mrs Eyre. Is Mrs Farrell there?'

Merle's brow furrowed. Her breathing was stertorous.
'Who?'

'Your employer, Merle.' Fenella laughed. 'She did
marry Mr Farrell, didn't she?'

'Oh! Yes, yes, I'm so sorry Mrs Eyre, my apologies – '

'That's perfectly all right, it was something of a surprise to us all. Is she about?'

'No, no, no. They 'ave gone to the Windward Islands.'

'No, really? Where, do you know?'

Merle sighed and closed her eyes, making a visible effort of concentration.

'St Minerve? Mr Marchant 'as lent them 'is 'ouse, I believe.'

Fenella gasped. 'The absolute *swine*! He knew all along!'

'Madame?'

'Nothing.' Fenella began to laugh. 'Nothing at all. How is my darling Dora?'

'She is at school in Devon,' said Merle glumly. ' 'Ere is just me and the dog.'

'Oh *Merle*, cheer up. Look on it as a holiday. When will they be back?'

'Three weeks,' said Merle. She glanced down at Brody, who was chewing the telephone lead. '*Mon Dieu*, three weeks . . .!'

Adeline lay prone on the warm, moon-coloured sand. Charlie's cheek was cradled in the soft hollow of the small of her back, his arm encircled her buttocks. Both were naked. Their bodies were relaxed after swimming, and heavy with the sun. They felt as if they still floated, drifted in the heat between sleep and arousal. Between them and the idling sea, clothing, like flotsam, was sprinkled along the erratic twin trail of their footsteps.

Slowly Adeline lifted her head and rested her chin on her cupped hands. Sparkling grains of sand clung to her damp, brown skin. Her eyes were cat-like, drowsily narrowed.

Charlie stirred, and rolled his head in order to kiss the rising curve of her spine.

'What are you doing?' he asked.

'Nothing.'

'I can hear you thinking.' He moved so that he was alongside her, and in the same attitude. He licked her shoulder. 'Smooth, salty, nicely browned . . .'

'Don't. It makes your tongue rasp like a cat's.'

'Sorry . . .' He closed his eyes again and let his head fall on to his folded arms. His voice was wrapped around a yawn as he asked, 'Have I told you recently how mad I am about you?'

'Yes.'

'That's all right then.'

'Charlie.'

'Mm?'

'I've decided. This is the place.'

'Mm . . . .'

Realizing she'd lost him she got to her feet and stood, turning slowly, surveying her realm.

'Yes,' she said, this time to herself. 'This is the place.'

On the day they got married, a Thursday, Charlie and Adeline had made what Charlie subsequently referred to as 'a smooth get-away'. The hint of a clandestine and criminal act which this phrase carried was not lost on either of them. Adeline knew very well that there were those among her friends and relations who would feel affronted by her actions. But it was for this very reason that she knew they must be swift and sure. She did not wish to hear their well-meant warnings, their half-hearted best wishes and disparaging asides. She didn't want to see their worried frowns and head-shakings. So the day before the wedding she wrote and sent letters explaining the position, expressing her happiness and asking for nothing. When they read the letters, she reasoned, she and Charlie would be far away, and by the time they returned everyone would be reconciled to the idea.

They would both have preferred to be married long before this, but Adeline had insisted they wait, for Dora's sake. Dorothy was marrying in December, and Dora was due to begin at St Agatha's in January. Adeline had to know that Dora was happy with their plans and with her own life before she went ahead with anything. She had chosen to tell her daughter and her ex-husband on the evening not long before Christmas when he brought his presents over. She told Dora before he arrived. The child's face had been a study in rapid, concentrated thought.

'What about Daddy?'

'We'll tell him this evening.'

'Won't he be upset?'

'No! Why should he be? He's married to Pru now, and they've got the twins.'

'But he loves you best. Are you sure he'll be all right?'

This had given Adeline pause, but in the event Peter had reacted with perfect equanimity, betraying no sign of pique, disapproval, or self-pity. She could have wept for gratitude.

'And you won't tell anyone, will you?' she begged him.

'Whyever not?'

'Because there will be a hue and cry, as you very well know.'

'You don't care what they think, surely? That's not like you at all.'

'I don't wish to be exposed to all the inevitable busy-bodying.'

'You'll shock them a lot more this way.'

'Please, Peter – for old times' sake.'

He'd kissed her tenderly. 'If you put it that way.'

Charlie, somewhat precipitately in Adeline's opinion, had handed in his notice, and left St Luke's at the end of the autumn term. He had found himself another teaching job in a small and extremely expensive prep school in the East Heath Road, but had thought it best, as he explained to Adeline, not to take up the post until the summer term. She had agreed. They would be getting married some time in the early spring, and Peter had offered them his new house on St Minerve for their honeymoon. Not even Pru knew about it. They would be lost to the world. Inevitably, Charlie was left with a good deal of time on his hands. He took a furnished flat in Downshire Hill and paid the landlady an inflated rent for maintaining his few possessions in the bedroom, and the treasured Brough Superior under a tarpaulin at the side of the house. Most of the time he spent at the Nunnery, playing with Dora during the holidays, walking Brody for miles, and conducting a running dialogue with Merle in which he tried to persuade her to ride pillion. From time to time he simply disappeared 'into Town', reappearing with a self-satisfied air a day or so later, like a tom that has been out on the tiles.

In between these unexplained jaunts he seemed, as Dorothy would have put it, to be 'looking for mischief', and the mischief he sought most keenly was Adeline. His demands were urgent and frequently downright indiscreet but she could deny him nothing. Her passion for him was only matched by the tenderness that engulfed her when she was with him. She fancied that she saw him quite clearly, and that she loved the whole man, Charlie Farrell, without reservation. It was a good feeling, she felt wonderful and looked her best. Anyone who was this good for her, she reasoned, must be meant for her. All her past loves seemed poor, half-formed things next to this. With Simon, it had been a fantasy of romance that had withered before the realities of marriage. She had been enslaved by Marian, but that had been an obsession, an addiction which made her wretched and which, in the end, she had had to escape in order to save herself. Peter had been a strong and loving friend – and still was. But Charlie, no matter what anyone might say, or what she herself knew, was her true love, as she was his. Life was sweeter, better, more worth living now than it had ever been.

Nonetheless, their love made them reclusive. Once Dora was safely installed at school in the new year, Adeline had a commission to finish and arrangements to make for an exhibition in the early summer, her first for two years. She gave Merle three weeks off to visit her family in Brussels and they mewed themselves up in the Nunnery with the phone off the hook, plenty of fuel, and the Heath embalmed in snow all around. They both agreed that they had all they wanted, or needed, in each other.

St Minerve from the air was like a dark, pear-shaped ooze of oil lying on the turquoise silk of the Caribbean. A smudge, a breath of smoke, marked the position of the volcano Mont Cherasse. On the leeward side of the island the coast was rimmed with a ribbon of sand, darkening from silver, through metallic grey, to charcoal black; on the windward side it was fringed with a tangled boa of surf. As the tiny de Havilland Fox Moth circled and sank, shudderingly, preparing to land, they could see the satellite island of Larme des Anges, to the south of St Minerve. Encircling both islands at a distance of some miles was the dark rim of a coral reef, sometimes submerged, sometimes breaking the surface in a line of sharp black studs surrounded by flickering breakers.

The plane turned its nose to the west for its final precipitous descent. The sun was going down almost as rapidly, its rich last rays casting the volcano into floodlit relief, and turning the thin, floating ribbons of cloud to pink, amber and cardinal red.

The airstrip at Vieille Tour was one of the reasons Peter Marchant had chosen to pay a small fortune for Larme des Anges, instead of the smaller fortune he might have paid for any number of neighbouring islands. Though Vieille Tour was no more than a clearing carved out of the lush vegetation that rioted in the volcanic soil at the foot of Mont Cherasse, it did at least mean that one could make use of the small British contract plane out of Kingston instead of enduring an indeterminate wait for the lumbering flying-boat.

Even so, Adeline and Charlie, travel-shocked but wondering, had a bone-shaking half-hour ride in a pungent taxi from Vieille Tour to the landing stage at the southern tip of St Minerve, and then a short ferry trip across the narrow Monroe Strait to Larme des Anges.

In the back seat of the taxi they sat hand in hand. Their driver wore a pink and white striped collarless shirt and a gor-blimey cap. He drove his Ford with one delicate, *dégagé* blue-black hand, with the other he held the roof on. When he changed gear, which was infrequently, he abandoned the steering wheel altogether for the few seconds it took to move the lever. When he pressed the horn, which he did often and urgently as a pre-emptive measure on the entirely empty road, he did so with the inside of his wrist.

When they'd left the few lights of Vieille Tour behind they drove for perhaps a mile on a tarmac surface, before turning off on to an unmade road, with no appreciable lessening of speed. In the strangely luminous darkness they could make out palms on either side of the road, and beyond the trees to their right an endless, pale beach and the silken sea, fretted with light. When Adeline looked over her shoulder she could see a swirling, settling wake of dust hanging in the air. From time to time the driver turned his head and treated them to a gentle, collusive smile. Once, he spoke:

'You am going Lammerdange? Mr Marchant?'

Adeline leaned forward. 'We're friends of Mr Marchant's, yes. He's lent us his house for a few weeks.'

'Lammerdange ace-high. Ace-high house,' opined the driver, winking. It sounded exactly as though he were recommending an obliging bordello. Charlie made a stifled sound and Adeline laid her hand on his knee.

'You've been there?'

The driver favoured the road with a quick glance and a sustained blast on the horn. 'No, not me. Me brother am there long time, help build house.'

Charlie said: 'And you think we're going to like it.'

'For sure. It am very smart house, got everything people need.'

As they waited on the landing stage for the boatman to stow their cases to his satisfaction, Charlie put his arm around Adeline's shoulders.

'Look up.'

She did so, and caught her breath. She had never before seen the moon and stars hanging so close to the earth, with the soft radiance of lanterns. She felt that she could without difficulty have reached up and plucked one out of the sky. An enormous amber moon rested against the flank of the volcano. Around them the scented night vibrated with small sounds – the gurgle and slap of the water beneath the wooden jetty, the hiss of the waves on beach, the purr of insects . . . the persistent, crooning cry of some nocturnal bird in the trees beyond the shore line.

Still gazing up she said softly: 'Do you remember when I first met you? You said you thought you'd died and gone to heaven.'

'I still feel like that.' When she lowered her head it was to find him looking at her. 'And it wouldn't matter where we were.'

Lost in the Caribbean night, with the mountain behind them and only a shining mile of water between them and the Tear of the Angels, they sensed for the first time the reality of their freedom.

The crossing took only six minutes. They stood in the nodding prow of the boat as it puttered over the lilting water. They were the only passengers but the boatman was as beaming and benign as the cab driver had been before him. He stood at the wheel of his battered motor launch, a hand-rolled cigarette between his crooked stumps of teeth, a smeary bottle of rum at his elbow, with as much pride and aplomb as the Master of the *Queen Mary*. When they were halfway across the strait he emerged from the wheelroom and offered them the bottle, grinning encouragingly and wiping the neck and opening industriously in his cupped palm. Seeing their hesitation he took a swig, smacked his lips and again shook the bottle before their faces, meanwhile pointing with his other hand, like the Ancient Mariner, at their unseen destination.

'Lammerdange – !' he exclaimed throatily. 'Angels' tear!' He held up the bottle.

'Rum – angel's piss!'

His chuckle rose to a hyaena-like cackle. Charlie held out his hand and took the bottle.

'Since you put it that way.' He quaffed obligingly. 'Jesus! Je – sus!'

As Charlie fought for breath, the boatman returned to

his lair, almost dancing with glee. Adeline wiped the tears from her beloved's face. 'That'll larn you to go native.'

'Hell's teeth – ! Where's your womanly sympathy? You could kill weeds with that stuff! Mind you,' he passed the mouth of the bottle beneath his nose, 'it hits the spot.'

'Hey!' A cracked cry issued from the wheelroom. 'Lammerdange!'

They turned their faces to the south and saw, suspended between stars and sea, the dark, secret shape of Larme des Anges.

They were met at the quay by Auguste, the Marchants' general factotum, whose whole manner bespoke a superior calling. His gleaming white shirt shone like a badge of office, marking him out from the rest of the ad hoc reception committee which made a point of greeting every ferry.

'Mr, Mrs Farrell? Please come this way.'

With the haughty politeness of a butler he ushered them through the smiling, shuffling crowd to the Jeep, and drove off at the measured pace of one who is sensible of heavy responsibilities.

The tiny township of Angeville (of which the local pronunciation was irresistibly like 'anchovy') was no more than a single street, a few lights, a few people caught momentarily in the headlamps, waving as they went past – and an unmistakable scent. Unique as a set of fingerprints, and forever after as identifiable to Adeline, the web of smells that drifted round the Jeep that first evening fixed and imprinted Larme des Anges on her senses. She could not then separate and trace them – the flowers, the spices, the cloth, the people themselves and the fabric of their lives – but she knew that she was breathing in the essence of this place, and that it had entered her bloodstream. She felt for, and clasped, Charlie's hand, and he lifted hers to his lips and kissed it.

Auguste coughed in a soft, apologetic way, as if warning them of his intention to speak and thus disturb them.

'Everything is ready for you at Outlook Point,' he announced. 'Mr Marchant has sent his orders.'

'It's very kind of him,' said Adeline. 'Very kind of all of you.'

'You will enjoy this island very much,' he went on. 'It mostly belong Mr Marchant.'

'Yes – so we understand.'

'Not Angeville. Not the town. It not up to much,' added Auguste scornfully.

'Have you always lived here?' asked Charlie.

'No *sir*, not me. I come from Port Minerve. It's a proper town – you must visit Port Minerve while you're here.'

'I'm sure we shall.'

They went a little way in silence, slightly chastened by the declamatory guidebook manner of their driver. As before, the road had long since given way to a crunching, juddering track, and they were now climbing quite steeply with the sea to their left and some kind of rugged, rocky outcrop to their right. Again the introductory cough. 'Outlook Point is not far now. Nothing is too far on this small island.' It was impossible to miss the patronizing note of the man from Port Minerve.

'Tell me,' said Adeline, 'do you think we could use the Jeep, to drive around and explore?'

Auguste waved a hand, graceful and expansive with assumed largesse. 'Any time, ma'am. It no problem. Mr Marchant has said to make yourselves at home. There is a letter for you at the house from him.'

Charlie put his lips to Adeline's ear. 'Witness the long arm of your ex-husband . . . he's checking up on you.'

This, as it turned out, was a slander. The letter which awaited them in the large and splendid drawing room of Outlook Point was addressed to them both and was to the point.

Dear Both [it said], Welcome, and please make yourselves absolutely at home. The house and everything that goes with it is yours for the duration. Auguste is the major-domo and loves to be of service, just ask for whatever you want. I was much exercised as to what to give the couple who have everything, but it suddenly occurred to me that if you enjoy the island, you might like a piece of it for yourselves. Even if you never wish to see it again it's a valuable chunk of real estate on which you'll be able to realize a smart profit in a few years' time. The island's only five miles by three so you'll have no difficulty seeing it all. The only real road runs east-west, from Outlook Point to the other end, via Angeville, but there are one or two rough tracks leading north-south off that, most of which the Jeep can cope with. I own the whole thing except for Angeville and the old fort, but Auguste knows all about that. Don't feel obliged to accept, it's no skin off my nose either way. If you do decide on something, and you want to build, I can be of some assistance as I know all the local building-wallahs and can weed out the crooks for you and get the best possible deal.

Of course, as I write this Pru still has no idea what you're up to, but by the time you read it she will, and will join with me in wishing you all the luck in the world. If you're half as happy as we are you won't have done badly. Have a wonderful holiday, see you when you get back. Love, Peter.

'Well,' said Charlie, 'I utterly withdraw my earlier unworthy remarks.'

'Dear Peter . . . he has a flair for the expansive gesture.'

'What'll we do? I shouldn't know where to begin.'

'We'll explore at our leisure, and if we see something we like, it's ours.'

Charlie put his arms round her and spoke against her cheek. 'That's how I've always worked . . .'

She closed her eyes, and Peter's letter drifted to the floor. 'We'll know when we find it.'

'Absolutely . . .'

Characteristically, Peter had created in Outlook Point a

little slice of England in the middle of the Caribbean. The house, a spacious and opulent bungalow, was set in the centre of three acres of what was clearly destined to be a pleasure park, with a pool, a tennis court, a pitch-and-putt course, a private boathouse and landing stage at the water's edge. At present not all these amenities were completed, and the land had a stripped, raw look about it. Apart from the drive, handsome patio and pool it was, as Charlie remarked, rather like a luxury hotel in the middle of a quarry. Auguste showed them around on their first morning with the utmost pride and indicated exactly where everything would be when the work was finished, but pointed out that this had been suspended for the duration of their stay so that they would not be disturbed. He also explained that the site had been chosen for its easy access to the beach, for this was the only part of the island, apart from Angeville, which did not fall away steeply to the sea. Whereas here, he told them, they could stroll from the garden on to the sands and back without breaking into a sweat.

'You realize,' said Charlie, as they followed their guide, 'we are being offered a chunk of sheer cliff.'

'Cynic,' said Adeline.

The house itself was luxurious, well-appointed and comfortable, furnished and decorated in a chintzy, country-house style quite inappropriate to its surroundings. There appeared to be plentiful supplies of food and drink, but when they enquired about the availability of these commodities on the island Auguste was quick to dismiss the Angeville Store as 'no damn good'. He went shopping in Port Minerve once a week and placed large orders which were brought by ferry. Anything they wanted, he said expansively, anything at all, they only had to say – Mr Marchant's orders.

On their tour of the grounds they were shown the two tiny white bungalows which accommodated Jules, the cook, and Pierre the gardener, with their respective families. Auguste, a bachelor, had quarters in the main house.

Jules' wife, Corinne, did the cleaning at an unbelievably early hour for they hardly ever saw her.

Their every need, as Peter had promised and Auguste had indicated, was supplied. For the first three days, stunned by the journey and enchanted by their isolation, they remained at Outlook point, swimming, eating, drinking, and sleeping. They went to bed early and made love, and woke early to make love again. But as their energy returned so did their curiosity about their surroundings, and the full possibilities opened up by Peter's letter. With a spare can of petrol, a picnic, and many admonitions from Auguste, they set out to explore.

Larme des Anges was no more than a volcanic stutter, or comma, following on the great submarine eruption of St Minerve. It rose from the sea like a shark's fin, its central hill topped by the stone fort built by General Xavier Monroe in 1873. Both islands, though originally under French rule, had been tussled over by the French and English for a hundred and fifty years, and General Monroe had erected his fort in order to keep cannons trained on the harbour of Port Minerve. There was now an English governor in residence, but the essentially French heritage of the islands lingered on in the names of places, and of people, and in the patois spoken by the residents of Port Minerve.

But the charm of Larme des Anges, as they discovered, was that it belonged to no-one. Or at least, much of it belonged to Peter, but only in name. The east-west road, and that leading from Angeville to the fort, had been built by General Monroe to facilitate the landing and billeting of his troops; the other tracks, described by Peter in his letter, were no more than that. As Charlie and Adeline criss-crossed the island on their explorations they knew themselves to be driving, and walking, where scarcely anyone had been for decades. Often the tracks simply petered out, drowned in the tropical forest where the parrots fluttered brilliantly and screeched in the echoing leaf canopy, or abruptly emerging on to the lip of a cliff where the booming rollers raced in from the Atlantic to break on the coral reef and then smash and snarl on the rocks. Everywhere was a rich, rampant, untouched beauty such as neither of them had ever seen before. When they left the Jeep to walk, the vehicle was lost to view in seconds amongst the giant ferns and the tall, whispering walls of bamboo. The sea that encircled them was an electric jewel-blue. Once, far from the cliffs but within the embracing arm of coral, they saw a school of porpoises leaping and frolicking, describing great glistening metallic arcs in the sunlight, the embodiment of *joie de vivre*.

In the middle of the day they made their way up to the fort and leaned up against its warm, grey walls to have their picnic. Once it must have been a stern and imposing building but now, like some grim old missionary gone native, its severe outline was overgrown with palms and ferns, and brilliant with hibiscus and bougainvillea, poinciana and African tulip, jasmine, and frangipani. It was a paradise of flowers, of shapes from the most fragile and delicate star to enormous waxen bowls as big as birdbaths; and of colours from glowing crimson to luminous white, lavender and gold. The humid air seemed to droop and tremble with scent. When they had eaten they made love, beneath the golden eye of the sun.

It was late in the afternoon that they came to the secret path. They were at the western tip of the island, furthest from Outlook Point. The track along which they'd been driving became gradually narrower until they were obliged to stop.

'Shall we walk,' asked Charlie, 'or call it a day?'

'Oh, *walk*,' said Adeline, 'we must.'

They'd gone only a little way down the dwindling track when Charlie, who was wandering lazily at the rear, called: 'Hey, Addie – darling this looks interesting.'

It was a minute pathway, a mere thread between the trees but leading down in the direction of the sea. From the minute they saw it they followed it, quickly and in silence, enthralled with their discovery, knowing that somewhere just ahead the trees would open out and they would see the sea.

When they did, it was more extraordinary than they could have imagined in their wildest dreams. The path was winding and precipitous for several hundred yards, and then they were suddenly hurled out of the trees and on to a high, undulating ridge of ash-white dunes. Before them the beach sloped away, smooth, secret and untouched to the sea that glittered a fiery opalescent blue in the evening sun. The bay was perfectly secluded, for some small bubble in the mighty prehistoric upheaval which had thrown up the islands must have burst here, creating a small crater. Twin, curved promontories of rock embraced the cove, one of them hollowed into a natural arch about fifteen feet high. This arch stood astride the water's edge, and each lapping wave struck a faint, keening sound from it, a plaintive pervasive note that shimmered in the hot air.

Entranced, silenced by the beauty and strangeness of it, they advanced separately on to the beach. As they moved forward, so the path by which they had come was lost to view, and on three sides of the cove there was only the sultry hanging forest, closing them in with dense curtains of many shades of green.

Like children who are the first to step on a fresh fall of snow they walked barefoot towards the sea, slowly, as if engaged in a magic rite. The distant, gentle ringing of the rock arch rose and fell like breathing. They might have been in the presence of some benign and sleeping giant.

Adeline turned to Charlie. They were yards apart, but the remote beauty of this place conferred an intimacy upon them so that she spoke softly.

'Let's swim. We must swim here.'

'But we – ' He began to say something about the Jeep, about towels and swimming things but she was already pulling off her clothes.

'It doesn't matter.'

They shed their clothes and ran into the sea, swimming far out and then turning to look back, both of them somehow feeling that it might be different, that it might not still be there. But now that they floated in the still, blue eye of the bay they could see how the forested cliffs and the sweeping arms of rock encircled and protected them. The rock formation on the northern side was uneven and tapering where it ran into the sea, like the tail of a dragon. It was impossible for them not to feel that this place had a life, a heartbeat of its own, that beneath the rock and sand and water lay some watchful creature which had thus far jealously guarded its privacy but which had allowed them, and only them, to enter its domain. They were awed and privileged, but strangely safe.

When they came out of the sea they lay on the sand, still and spellbound, in the dragon's embrace.

And it was not long after this that Adeline stood, and said quietly to herself: 'Yes . . . This is the place.'

CHAPTER TWENTY-THREE

1939

'HAPPY ANNIVERSARY, old thing!' Peter kissed her. 'Lovely party! And it's a whole year longer than any of us thought you'd last!'

He laughed heartily and innocently because he, at least, didn't mean it.

'But where's Charlie?' asked Pru in her eager, straightforward, way. 'I was looking forward to giving him a big kiss!'

'Jezebel,' said her husband affectionately. 'I'm delighted he's AWOL.'

Adeline smiled serenely. 'You know Charlie, he's hopelessly unpunctual. He'll be here.'

She felt that her serene smile was pinned smooth and tight over the wretched disarray of her feelings. The noise of her party washed and broke against her assumed calm like waves on a cliff.

'Hey!' Peter thrust his glass at Pru and swept Dora into his arms. 'Who cares about Charlie, here's my favourite girl. By God you're getting heavy, what do they feed you

on in that institution of yours?' He put her down again.
Dora, who was self-conscious about her size, blushed with
embarrassment.

'Nothing – it's mostly foul,' she muttered, and was
rewarded with indulgent laughter. 'I'm surprised I haven't
wasted away.'

'Quick, Dora,' said Pru, whisking a plate of angels on
horseback from a nearby table. 'have one of these.'

Dora pushed her spectacles up her nose with her finger.
'Those are absolutely revolting.'

'All the more for me,' said Peter, taking two. Adeline
placed her hands on her daughter's shoulders.

'I thought I'd told you to go to bed. It's nearly midnight.'

'But you said I could stay up for the dancing.'

'It's getting too late.'

'Charlie's not here.' Dora's voice held the resigned note
of one who understood the sub-text.

'Come on,' said Peter, 'let your poor old father come
and tuck you in. How did you manage to be here, anyway?
Time off for good behaviour . . .?'

Adeline felt weak with gratitude. 'I'll be up in a little
while.'

'I'm sorry, Addy,' said Anne, 'but I'm going to have to
take him back to Brown's. We're simply not used to riotous living.'

'That's all right,' said Adeline, 'I understand.'

'Where's he got to?' asked Frank bluntly, putting on his
coat. 'I hope you're going to give him a piece of your
mind.'

'I shall, don't worry.'

'Anyway, it's a marvellous party,' said Anne firmly.
'We shall be dining out on it for months. Thank you,
dear.'

Adeline submitted to her sister-in-law's warmly affectionate embrace, and her brother's gruffer one. She felt
the taint of sympathy in the first, of disapproval in the
second. She kept smiling.

'By the way,' said Anne, doing up buttons and drawing on gloves, 'you look absolutely wonderful, doesn't she Frank? If this is what marriage to Charlie does for you after one year then I take my hat off to him.'

'I'm very happy . . . we both are.'

'Good. Glad to hear it,' said Frank.

Adeline opened the door. She was beginning to feel terribly tired. 'Give my love to Mother. I'm sorry you couldn't persuade her to come.'

'She's happier where she is, these days.' It was impossible not to infer that Frank felt the same.

She closed the door behind them. Her party seemed to be in decline before it had even properly begun. Brody lay panting at the top of the stairs, prostrate with over-excitement, waiting only for Peter to go before sinking into a deep and dreamless sleep on Dora's bed. In the dining room the beautiful buffet over which Adeline and Merle had toiled was now a deserted battlefield, the white cloth stained and littered with greasy, crumbling, tattered wreckage. In the hall, the carpet had been taken up, ready for dancing, the gramophone and records stood waiting in the corner. There was Joel, taking a record from its cover and polishing it on his sleeve. Without looking at her, he said:

'Feeling blue?'

'No, certainly not.'

He placed the record carefully on the turntable and began to wind the handle.

'Lots of wives would be.'

'I wouldn't know about that.' There was a tremendous burst of laughter from the other room. 'Duncan's in good form.'

'He likes parties.' Joel gave a little shrug of bafflement. 'I'm afraid he's blotto, but don't worry. I'll take him home before he becomes an embarrassment.'

'You're very good to him.'

'Well –' Joel placed the needle on the swimming rim of the record. 'It's no hardship. Shall we?'

A soulful voice began to declare, 'Love is the sweetest

thing'. For a minute or two they danced alone, graceful and quiet in their mutual understanding. Then the door burst open and Duncan appeared, red-faced, clutching Fenella by the wrist, laughing faces clustered in his wake.

'Ha! Caught red-handed hogging the music! Come on, sweetheart – ' He whirled Fenella into his arms. 'let's get this party moving! Addy darling, can't you put on something a bit livelier? Nella and I want to wear out shoe leather!'

It was no good protesting, for he'd already gone to the gramophone, and having removed the needle was busy selecting another record. The other guests, naturally drawn to his noisy exuberance, were taking his lead, and as the more up-tempo strains of ' 'Sactly Like You' made themselves heard, the hall was suddenly full of dancing couples.

'It's no good, I don't feel this energetic,' said Adeline. She spotted Toni standing in the doorway, and dragged Joel to her side. 'Look, you two dance together, I need another drink.'

The drawing room displayed that creased, trampled, desecrated appearance of a place recently vacated by a large number of revellers. Bob and Louise, with Ida and Paul Hudson, stood at one end, talking, and Adeline found a drink and a cigarette and joined them.

Louise pointed at a picture. 'We were discussing this, Addy. I rather like it but everyone else thinks its execrable.'

It was the eerie, bluish painting Adeline had bought the night of Charlie's arrival at the Nunnery. 'I remember when she bought it,' said Ida, as if in possession of some incriminating secret.

'I don't say it's execrable,' said Paul. 'It's not to my taste but he's an excellent investment.'

'It's Charlie's, actually,' said Adeline firmly. 'I bought it for him.'

'What does he make of it?' asked Bob, smoothly and quickly, preventing an awkward pause from developing.

Adeline laughed gaily. 'He thinks it's ghastly, but then

he doesn't know the first thing about pictures. He likes mine,' she added. For the first time she thought, how could you do this to me? When I want everyone to see how much I love you, how can you make them doubt that I do?

Ida fell upon this opportunity to steer the subject in another direction.

'Talking of which,' she said, 'are the commissions still pouring in?'

Adeline felt impatient with Ida, who knew very well that her last exhibition had been panned by the critics and poorly attended by the public. She herself was a realist; what she resented was Ida's treating her as though she weren't.

'Not pouring in, Ida, no,' she said. 'But trickling quite comfortably, thanks. Why don't you all dance? You should all be dancing.'

Ida, a little miffed, put her arm through Paul's. 'That sounds astonishingly like an order.'

As they walked away, Bob glanced at his watch. 'Do you think he'll be coming, Addy? Because we've got a hell of a long way to go.'

'Oh, I know, I'm sure he will – look, why don't you stay the night?' She could hear the note of desperation in her voice. 'Toni is – ' She stubbed out her cigarette with a sharp, pounding movement. 'I'm sorry, that was a bloody silly suggestion.'

'It wasn't at all,' said Louise. 'Bob, we could do that. The night is yet young.'

Bob's voice, when he answered, was light, but Adeline recognized the intense look he gave Louise as that coded message which passes from man to wife.

'It's a lot younger than I feel. Honestly, darling, I've got a mountain of writing to do tomorrow. I'd like to get back.'

'Is it my imagination,' said Louise to Adeline in her charming, confiding way, 'or do men become staid much quicker than women? I think you did well to marry your bonny young husband, Addy.' As she said this she looked teasingly at Bob, but squeezed Adeline's hand in a gesture of solidarity. 'Come on, Methuselah, you're not dragging me away till you've danced with me.'

Adeline followed them and, skirting the dancers, went upstairs to Dora's bedroom. Dora was asleep, but Peter stood by the bed, his hands in his pockets, and Brody lay draped over the end of the flowered eiderdown.

Seeing her, Peter smiled. 'Just gazing.' He nodded his head at the dog. 'Is that allowed?'

'It's ignored.'

She came to stand beside him. 'She hasn't undone her plaits.'

'Oh lor, should she have done? What will happen?'

'Nothing, it'll just be hell to brush tomorrow.'

'She seems full of beans. Never stopped talking, mostly about school.'

'She has a very fortunate nature.' Adeline slipped her arm through his. 'Like her father. I don't deserve her.'

'Nonsense, you deserve the best, the very best.' There was a brief silence as they stared down at their sleeping daughter. Then he said: 'What the devil do you suppose he's up to?'

'I don't know. He does this from time to time – well, quite often. I think he just meets people – complete strangers, sometimes – and they have a drink, and get talking. I know he plays cards.'

'Gambles?'

'I suppose so. I suppose it's partly my fault. He knows cards bore me to tears so he's bound to play somewhere else. But I don't really know. I hate to be a nag, an old witch, I'm frightened I'll drive him away – '

'A nag? An old witch? You?'

'You forget how much younger he is than me. And Peter, I love him so *much*, I don't think anyone understands how much. If I only saw him once a month I'd still think myself lucky – ' Peter was shaking his head. 'You think I'm mad.'

'Not more than you always have been.' He squeezed her waist.

'I'm angry with him tonight not because he's let me down, but because he's made everybody feel that they were right all along. He's let himself down, can't he see that? What's the matter with him that he won't protect himself?'

'I don't know . . . I don't know. He just doesn't see things in the same light as you or I might do . . . But Addy, one thing's certain: you don't do yourself or him any favours by putting up with all this nonsense. I was talking to Frank – '

'Oh, Frank.'

'He thinks the world of you, and he talks a lot of sound sense. If you and Charlie are to make a go of this then you've got to run the show. You're the one who can put things right. He may have no strength of character, but you've got enough for two. You must take responsibility, not just allow him to – to – '

'To do as he likes, as if he were an adult?'

'To do as he likes as if he were a *child*!' In his frustration Peter's voice rose sharply for an instant, and Dora lurched on to her side. 'We'd better go, we'll wake her.'

Outside the bedroom he said: 'I'm sorry, I didn't mean to shout. It's just that I hate to see you, I don't know, *humbled* like this.'

She had to smile, albeit ruefully. 'Perhaps a little humility wouldn't go amiss.'

He patted her cheek. 'Just take care, and take command – for your own sake and for Dolly's. Dance?'

'Why not?'

Adeline got quite drunk and danced with everyone. Her manner became excitable and cavalier and she declared, 'To hell with Charlie!' so loudly and often that no-one was left in the least doubt that she was badly cut up about his non-appearance. The party took on the air of a richly flamboyant wake, at which the most palpable presence is that of the absent departed.

By half past one almost everyone had gone. The hall and stairs had now acquired the ransacked look of the rest of the ground floor, over which the warm drifts and currents of the party floated like ghosts.

Adeline sat halfway up the stairs with a last glass of champagne cradled in both hands, and her shoes off. Her last remaining guests – Peter, Pru and Toni – all thought she looked the most beautiful they had ever seen her, none more than Peter, who experienced a sharp pang of longing even as he stood with his arm about his dear wife. To know Adeline, he thought, was to measure every other woman against her. She excited admiration for her gifts, and forgiveness for the extravagance of her mistakes. Her successes and her failures were on a grand scale. And what a body . . . he sighed and kissed Pru's flushed cheek, to armour himself against those lush bare shoulders, the proud and generous bosom, the vivid, vulnerable face with its broad, tender mouth and fiercely aquiline stare . . . How extraordinary and unfair that she should so worship the unappreciative young Farrell! But then Peter remembered that for five, mostly happy years she had been his wife, more time than he'd had any right to expect . . .

'We must be off,' Pru was saying.

'Of course . . .' Adeline rose from the stairs and walked over to them, her tipsiness if anything adding a stateliness to her carriage.

'Yes, you must,' she said. 'You must get back to your dear little boys . . . how are they, by the way?'

'Oh they're *fine*,' began Pru, 'toddling around and driving poor Nanny out of her mind with worry. Apparently twins are usually behind other children, but the paediatrician said ours are simply forging ahead!'

'How sweet . . .' Adeline's eyes filled unaccountably with tears. 'By the way, did I tell you the Dragon House is finished? Charlie and I . . . we're going out there in the summer. It's the loveliest present anyone ever gave me.' She kissed each of them in turn, and Peter took her by the shoulders.

'I'd consider staying there if I were you, Addy. There's going to be a war, as sure as eggs is eggs.'

'A war . . . I know.' Adeline closed her eyes for a moment. 'Must we think about it now?'

'Of course not!' said Pru. 'The thing is, Addy, are you going to be all right *now*?'

Toni came over. 'I'm staying. I'll look after her.'

When they'd left Toni asked: 'What about the mess?'

'Help comes in the morning.' Adeline collapsed on the sofa, her arms across her face.

'In that case I'll make us some tea.'

When Toni had left the room Adeline felt the last of her furious gaiety ebb away, and in the misery it left behind she found herself praying, as she had as a child: If only . . . if only he comes back, everything will be all right, and I'd never ask for anything again, ever. But please let him come back, *now* . . . The full enormity of what had just taken place hit her like a bucketful of icy water, restoring instant and wretched sobriety. Their first anniversary, the party at which she and Charlie were to have flown their flag and danced the night away together for all to see – it was all over, and he hadn't turned up. A tiny mouse of anxiety began to nibble at her mind. What if it wasn't his fault? What if he'd had an accident on the motorbike and was lying bleeding in some ditch, or dead and unidentified in a hospital morgue?

'Hey, hey – ' Toni brought a cup of tea and crouched down beside her. 'Drink this, you'll feel better, and then we'll go to bed. He'll turn up, you said so yourself.'

'Toni, he might have come off the bike! He rides it like a lunatic, it wouldn't be the first time – '

'No,' said Toni crisply, stirring sugar into her own tea, 'nor the first time he's gone off with no explanation, from what I gather. Drink up.'

'I'm not going to bed until I know where he is. Do you think we should ring the hospital?'

'Don't be silly, Addy. Which one? Where would we start?'

Tears began to course down Adeline's cheeks. 'Oh *God*, if anything's happened to him I'll never forgive myself, I do love him so, Toni – '

'I know.'

'I don't know what I'd do without him – '

'You'd manage, I expect. We all do.'

'Toni, I'm sorry, I – '

Brody heard the motorbike first, and came galloping down the stairs to the front door, but Adeline was only seconds behind him, flying across the hall, out of the door and down the steps in her bare feet. There was a cold, clinging fog in the air, but she found her way into his arms almost by instinct, and smothered his face with kisses.

'Charlie, oh thank God, thank God you're safe! I love you.'

He kissed her, smoothed her hair, drew her gently alongside him back into the house. When he began to remove his coat she tugged it from him and threw her arms once more about his neck.

'You bloody bastard, where've you been?'

Toni appeared on the stairs and he caught her eye briefly over Adeline's shoulder.

'I met some fellows that I know,' he said, his eyes on Toni's face. 'We had some drinks – and one thing led to another. I'm so sorry, my darling, I know it's unforgivable.'

'Oh it is, it is – !' Adeline planted her mouth firmly on his. 'I don't intend to forgive you, ever. I'm going to make you pay, Charlie Farrell, pay till your eyes pop out of your head . . .'

Toni heard him whisper, softly, 'My darling,' before he clasped her and pressed his face into her shoulder in an attitude of passionate remorse. They stood locked together, oblivious to everything but each other, swaying very slightly and murmuring, like a tree with twin trunks. Their flawed love, for all its faults and inequalities, seemed to lift them beyond the reach of reproach, and to bless them in a way that silenced all sensible criticism. Toni, watching, felt her own heart as dry and brittle as a dead leaf within her. It wasn't heavy, but light and insubstantial, floating in her inner emptiness. She was not, after all, needed here, so she turned away from them and went quietly up the stairs to bed.

'I've got something for you,' said Charlie.

She rubbed her face against his like a cat. 'I don't want your miserable peace offering. Come to bed.'

'Let me give you this first. Please. It's the first really special present I've got you. And very likely the last, so I should make the most of it.'

She brushed her mouth across his, and sighed. 'You flanelled me into it.'

'Close your eyes.'

'Why – ?'

'Do as you're told for a change.'

She closed her eyes. There was a silence, and then she felt the cool slither of a small object dropped between her breasts, followed by the warm touch of his lips in the same place. She began to melt with pleasure and desire, and she threaded her fingers into his untidy dark hair that was still damp and curling from the fog, and pushed his head away, saying gently: 'You have to let me see.'

She drew the tiny object from the bodice of her dress. It was a pale, almost milk-white opal, veined with fire and shaped like a drop of water just about to fall from its gold chain. She held it up, studying it in silence as it trembled in the half-light, and then looking past it at Charlie. His face wore an expression of anxious excitement.

'Do you like it? Do you really like it? I know it's not the kind of thing – '

'Yes, I like it.'

'Do you see what it is? Why I had to give it to you?'

She nodded. Holding the opal against her cheek with one hand, she held out her arm and drew him to her.

'My darling.'

'I can't compete with a ruddy island,' he whispered, his voice shaking. 'But I can give you an angel's tear, and it comes with all my love, for what it's worth.'

She nodded again, not trusting herself to speak, nor having any words that were adequate.

They fled to Larme des Anges that summer. They were escaping not just London, with its crowds and its rumours of war, but the feverish imbalance of their own lives. They needed time alone, time to themselves away from the suspicions and expectations of other people, and where there was no-one to offer Adeline well-intentioned criticism or advice.

They agreed this as they lay in one another's arms at night. They saw quite clearly that marriage had not conferred stability and respectability on their relationship. If anything, it had been taken by many to be an act of foolhardy defiance. And the curious thing was that they themselves did not feel married. There life together was attended by none of the usual and established developments concomitant with marriage. They were simply lovers living under one roof. Adeline's. What could they do? Charlie continued with his job at the school, but no-one could have been in the slightest doubt that it was Adeline's income that maintained them in style and comfort.

The strength of their love was wonderful, ridiculous, it never failed to astonish and delight them, but they knew, too, that there were gaps and weaknesses in the fabric of their lives which gave rise to talk, and for which they could summon no defence. Adeline took a great deal on trust. She allowed Charlie his other life, his unexplained flings and disappearances, and neither complained nor enquired about what he did. She felt lucky and privileged to have so much love, she would not be so mean-spirited as to reduce it to a matter of rites, duties and obligations. She adopted the same attitude with regard to their financial affairs. They shared a joint bank account, and she paid her finances as little attention as she had done for the past ten years. There was enough and more than enough to be comfortable, and to have fun. She refused to worry about money.

In spite of Peter's generosity in giving them the land, the Dragon House had cost them a small fortune. It was a modest enough house, only half the size of Outlook Point and with none of its conspicuous luxury. It was simply an unpretentoius white-walled, red-roofed, three-bedroomed bungalow, but Adeline had chosen to build it in the most spellbindingly beautiful and inconvenient position in the Windward Islands. The mere cost of transporting the building materials from Port Minerve to the site was astronomic. Neither cost nor labour were alleviated by Adeline's insistence on the wooded cliff remaining as unchanged as possible. No unnecessary felling of trees, no tarmac road, no crisply landscaped garden. It was, the builders agreed, 'one helluva pissentail sweat' just so the madwoman from England could live in a jungle, on a cliff, with a pretty view. Still, they had liked and been amused by Adeline when they had met her, so the work went forward.

Peter and Pru now spent four or five months of the year at Outlook Point, and in October Adeline had been out to stay with them and review progress. She had purchased a secondhand, bright red American pick-up truck in Port Minerve and gone back and forth across the island each day, inspiring and infuriating her workforce by turns and very often pitching in herself, carrying hods and mixing cement, blissfully happy.

Local interest in the Dragon House was intense. In the bar and at the store they shook her hand and wished her luck, pointing out she had picked a place renowned for its evil spirits which stalked and howled both day and night. They seemed highly delighted with the prospect of the fun and games to follow, but it was made clear to Adeline that she would have difficulty in persuading anyone from Angeville to work at the house. It was Auguste who came to the rescue by producing, like a rabbit from a hat, a brother in Port Minerve who worked as a chef at the Colonial Club and was more than prepared to be a cook-housekeeper in the unholiest spot for the wages Mrs Farrell was prepared to offer. Philippe had a wife and assorted children whom he treated with the utmost casualness, declaring that they could be fine remaining on St Minerve providing he shone the light of his countenance on them from time to time and supplied their modest needs. Auguste confided to Adeline that his brother had long been looking for just such an escape route, and that the devil himself would be small beer beside Philippe's monstrous wife.

Adeline had returned from that visit in early November exhilarated, enchanted with the progress of the house and longing to tell Charlie and Dora how wonderful it was all going to be. This she did, at some length and with the growing awareness that her audience was not, could not be, as enthusiastic as she was about an unfinished bunga-low on the other side of the world. It was half-term and they seemed to have formed some sort of unholy alliance in her absence. The place was extravagantly untidy. Brody was uncontrollable, and Merle spoke darkly of extra-cur-ricular cooking. Adeline came back to earth with a bump. She felt like the only adult in a house full of renegade children, and this sensation was reinforced when she opened her mail, which contained nothing but bills and a painfully polite letter from her bank manager pointing out that their joint current account was in overdraft, and did she wish a sum to be transferred off deposit to remedy the situation? The following day she rang the bank to expedite the transfer, and paid the bills. She realized that she had only one commission lined up, and that she had precious little interest in carrying it out. For twenty-four hours, as Charlie escorted Dora and Brody on lengthy foraging parties on the Heath to find material for a bonfire, she had felt alone, and old, and worried. But when she had mentioned her anxieties to Charlie that night, warm in his embrace, he had laughed gently at her and told her if she would run all over the globe building outposts of empire, then what did she expect? And anyway, he added, she wasn't exactly hard-up. She just had a temporary problem with cash-flow which she had already taken steps to allevi-ate. Good grief, he said, there were plenty of people who'd consider themselves lucky to have her problems . . .!

When he put it that way, she laughed too. She was easily comforted.

At the end of the summer term, slightly shamefaced,

she had taken Dora to Fording Place accompanied, as a palliative, by a school-friend. Not that Dora was in the least put out at not going with them, though Elizabeth did remark caustically that it was about time Adeline included her daughter in her holiday arrangements.

Adeline bridled. 'We need some time on our own, Mother.'

'I'm quite sure you do.'

'What's that supposed to mean?'

'It means your family situation isn't exactly orthodox –

'I see,' hissed Adeline, as she climbed into the car. 'And yours was?'

For the first quarter of a mile she drove at a furious rate, hot with indignation. Then she pulled in to the side of the road and burst into tears.

But when they lay in the shade of the trees, encircled by the sleeping dragon, with the throb of its heartbeat in their ears, they knew it had all been worth it. For the time being at least, they had escaped.

'Happy?' asked Adeline.

'Mm.'

She put her lips to his ear. 'Love me?'

'Mm . . .' He moved his hand, feeling for her, and she clasped it. Almost at once she knew he had fallen asleep, but it didn't bother her. There was something trusting about his hand lying quietly in hers. She did not feel as she sometimes did, deserted by him.

She heard the faint chuckle of sound high above amongst the trees which meant that Philippe and his fifteen-year-old son Nathan – a youth of melting, tongue-tied beauty – would soon be bringing lunch down to them. Life here was sybaritic as only a primitive life in fecund surroundings can be. There was no mains electricity on Larme des Anges, and unlike Outlook Point the Dragon House did not have its own generator. They used paraffin lamps and candles, and Philippe cooked on a wood-burnign stove not unlike the one used by Mrs Donaghue at Kenarvon. The pattern of their day was set by the sun, starting with breakfast at six, an immutably English affair of toast and eggs, with dark, fragrant local coffee. Lunch was more Roman feast than picnic. Cold roast pork, chicken, goat meat, frogs' legs and hare, with deep-fried plantains, baked yams and fresh avocados, and a cornucopia of fruit to follow – guavas, paw-paws, bananas and pineapple. With this they drank bottled beer, kept cool in a calabash filled with water. After a siesta under the trees they would climb the hill and take the truck to some other part of the island, to walk, or fish. Sometimes they drove to Outlook Point and played tennis, occasionally they borrowed the boat and circumnavigated the island. When they did this they were always struck afresh by the strange and secret beauty of the dragon bay, with their small white house suspended in the waterfall of lush green. In the early evening they had always to go back for one last swim in the bay, when the rocks were beginning to mellow in the brief, brilliant sunset. At each moment throughout the day they'd think, and say to each other, 'This is the best time', only to find it superseded by the next.

Supper was their main meal, when they sat on their verandah, with candles on the wooden table, and the soft yellow lamplight spilling through the door behind them. It was now that Philippe excelled himself. At Outlook Point the dignified Auguste had been trained by Pru to take due care with delicate British palates. Philippe had no such scruples. Released from the culinary restrictions of the Colony Club, and confronted by an amenable and captive clientele, he let rip.

On the first evening, when Nathan had served them, smiling shyly, Adeline asked:

'Nathan, what's he giving us? We want to know about it.'

The smile had grown even wider. 'It callaloo, ma'am. Father speciality.'

'Callaloo?' Charlie lowered his face over his steaming plate and breathed deep. 'it smells ambrosian.'

Nathan nodded.

> 'Fungi, Gundy, Callaloo,
> Plantains, Sea-grapes, Boiled Foo-foo;
> Paw-paw, Soursop, thick Goat Stew,
> Johnny Cakes and Jug-jug too.'

The smile threatened to split his face, and he withdrew, delighted with himself but also embarrassed by his daring.

It was the first of Philippe's apparently inexhaustible repertoire of exotic stews, containing pork, fresh fish, conch, crab, salted meat cooked with okra and spinach-like callaloo greens and garnished with dumplings made from plantains and cornmeal.

By the end of a week they had sampled everything in Nathan's rhyme and the half-hour before supper as they sat in the velvety dark, sipping rum swizzles, had become an orgy of greedy speculation and anticipation. And the food was so good and so rich that when they'd eaten they would often go down to the beach again and make love in the soft, sifting dunes. They were becoming like everything else in this place, glossy and richly coloured and bursting with sensuous juices.

Thinking about this, Adeline laid her arm across Charlie's shoulders and bent to kiss his neck, just below his ear. He at once rolled on to his back and grabbed her.

'Gotcha, you great big beautiful woman.'

She laughed and kissed him on the mouth now, her black hair falling round their two faces like a curtain. How could she not be weak and soft with him? He was so proud and eager and possessive. His love enveloped and blinded her with its sweetness.

He whispered: 'I don't know what we're waiting for.'

'Lunch . . . they're coming down . . .'

They got to their feet and pulled on a few clothes. They could hear the voices of Philippe and Nathan like a small stream flowing down through the trees, the sing-song patois they used to each other and sometimes laughter, and song, trickling and bubbling in the still, midday heat. Every sound took on a lazy, deliberate

quality as though it had arranged itself for their delight
– the call of the parrots deep in the cool leaf canopy,
the sleek plop of a fish jumping in the bay, the faint
insistent ringing of the sea in the rock arch, all were
simply the background music for their love.

That afternoon they swam right out to the rock at the
end of the dragon's tail. It was much further than they
thought, and when they dragged themselves out up on
to the rock itself they were gasping and laughing with
exhaustion. But Charlie was elated by the effort, and
scrambled from their rock to the next one, and then
jumped, slithering, to the third, which was far higher.

'I'm going to dive off here!' he called.

'Don't be silly.'

'Yes, why not? The water's beautifully deep, look at
the colour of it out here!'

'Charlie – '

She was only remonstrating idly, not really expecting
him to dive, but even as she spoke he took off with a
yell, arcing untidily away from his perch, plummeting
down perilously close to the rock face, it seemed to
Adeline, before crashing into the glassy violet surface of
the water and sending a shower of glittering splinters
into the air.

It was ages, too long, before he surfaced. Adeline
stood up, her heart thudding and her face cold. There
was perfect silence. For five or six dread-filled seconds
she thought him dead. And then he popped up right
beneath where she was standing, shaking the water out
of his eyes and gasping, hugely pleased with himself.

'Hey, what about that? How did I do?'

She didn't know whether to laugh or cry. 'Idiot! You
scared me half to death!'

'There was nothing to be scared of . . . I'm coming
out now.'

The incident had shaken her more than she would
admit. She thought it was because she was that much
older that she saw risks and dangers and terrible possi-

bilities where, for him, none existed. And yet even allowing for that there was running through all his behaviour a streak of pure recklessness which seemed to take no account of his own safety or of her feelings. Behind that dive, she felt sure, lay the same impulse which prompted his idiotic speeding on the motorbike, and his unexplained disappearances, and she feared it.

Her anxiety made her cool towards him, but it didn't suit her to sulk, and after a few minutes during which they sat side by side and awkward with each other for the first time, she turned and put her arms round him.

'I'm sorry,' she said. 'I was frightened.'

He stroked her back. 'You're always in such a hurry to kill me off.'

'Don't make a joke of it.'

'Now we're both sorry. A sorry pair.'

She drew away from him and sat with her arms clasped about her knees. 'Charlie, if there's a war, you won't do anything rash, will you?'

'What on earth do you mean?'

'You won't be too all-fired eager to do your bit, will you? I don't want to lose you.' Especially now, she thought, but she didn't say that. In this matter as in all others she loved him too much to pressure him.

He picked up the towel and rubbed his head with rapid, vigorous movements.

'We'll have to cross that bridge when we come to it. It hasn't happened yet. I suppose the time might come when I have to.'

She pulled the towel out of his hands and set it aside. 'But teaching – wouldn't that be some sort of reserved occupation?'

'It might be, I don't know. Look, why the hell are we talking about this?'

'Just promise me that you won't be precipitate. That we'll talk about whatever's going to happen. Please.'

She saw the smile begin, and then fade as he realized how serious she was. For once he didn't try to touch her, or to blur his words with protestations of love.

'All right,' he said. 'I promise.'

She was washed through, drained, by relief, and laid her forehead down on her knees while she fought for control. Now, some time soon, she would tell him about the baby.

After their return to England at the end of August, the inevitable happened so fast, and yet so unremarkably, that it was hard to believe that the war, so long feared and discussed, had actually arrived. Of course, the necessary motions were gone through. Sirens sounded, shelters were constructed, drills and contingency measures of all sorts were devised and instigated. Most people were affected by a sense of anxious anti-climax. Was this it? Perhaps the worst would never happen. Perhaps now that Britain had shown her hand the Germans would simply back down.

At the Nunnery, it was business as usual. Dora returned to St Agatha's and Charlie to Heath Court. Adeline, to her surprise and amusement, was approached by the governors of her alma mater to paint a portrait of the current headmistress, Miss Enid Marsh. It would be extraordinarily appropriate, said the chairman in his letter, if the traditional Head's picture were also the work of an alumnus of the school. He had not, he wrote politely, been familiar with her work until attending her exhibition the previous year, but she could now count him among her admirers.

Adeline went down to the school to make some preliminary sketches, and to arrange subsequent sittings at her studio at times convenient to Miss Marsh. She liked the Head, who was a large, serious woman without a mean or trivial bone in her body, and an appearance of such clean, wholesome plainness that Adeline kept thinking of a cottage loaf.

Dora, predictably, was horrified. 'You? Painting old Boggy? What for?'

'For money,' said Adeline briskly.

'But she's awful.'

'No she's not, she's a very nice, very brilliant woman who has dedicated her life to Philistine little ingrates like you.'

'You won't talk about me, will you?'

'Certainly not. Nothing will be further from our thoughts.'

Dora groaned. 'I'll never live this down.'

But whatever Dora's reaction, Adeline was happy to be gainfully employed. Still harbouring the lovely secret of her pregnancy, and feeling wonderfully well, she retired to her studio and began rationalizing the sheaves of old portfolios, some of them going back years. They were mostly pencil and charcoal drawings, scores of them. Peter, Toni, Duncan and Joel, from their Slade days . . . members of her family . . . Elizabeth with Richard . . . and with Howard . . . all those sketches she had done at Allerton Square, and in Cornwall, before Marian's orgy of destruction . . . Even allowing for the savage losses sustained then she realized that she had, in effect, a pictorial record of a whole host of people and associations. Latterly there were drawings of the Villa Clemency, with Charlie simply one of the group lazing on the verandah and by the pool, until he emerged as a subject in his own right, almost her only subject for the past year and more. Many of these later drawings, she realized, would probably scandalize Miss Enid Marsh, and she gathered them together in one folder which she placed behind many others.

Reflecting her mood and assisting her endeavours, the September sunshine poured into the studio as she pottered about, and the pigeons massed, strutting, rustling and crooning on the flat roof above. The sittings with Miss Marsh, too, proved to be strangely soothing. Here was a sitter as different from herself, and most of her other subjects, as it was possible to be, with almost no ego, and no personal interest in being painted. Also, the portrait itself had to be executed along certain prescribed lines – formal, dignified, straightforward.

'Just do what you can,' Miss Marsh would say, 'with such unpromising material.'

She made four trips to London, on successive Saturdays, always taking the six o'clock train back in the evening. During those days the two women established a friendship based on mutual respect and real liking. It was a careful, and a polite friendship, for each had profound reservations about the other which they could not, after such a brief acquaintaince have voiced without giving the gravest offence. Adeline's well-tuned antennae detected in Miss Marsh the distinct, if latent, sexual ambivalence of a lifetime spent in exclusively female company. Miss Marsh observed in Adeline the complete lack of sound judgement or objectivity which so often accompanied artistic gifts. Charlie she treated with a calm reserve as though, if she allowed herself to become more voluble, she might say something she would regret. Adeline could well imagine her quelling insubordination at St Agatha's: she was a woman of high and unbending standards.

Enid was only three years older than Adeline, but here the similarity ended. She disclosed a background and a life so different from Adeline's that it might have been the product of another planet: the clever, hardworking daughter of a Portsmouth butcher, who had gone on from grammar school to read English at Girton, and thence into teaching. Her antecedents, she was well aware, were far more humble than those of the girls in her care, but she was not ashamed of them. She also stated categorically, and a shade defensively, that her work and her girls were her life, and left little room for anything else. Her home was the headmistress's flat in St Agatha's. At Christmas and Easter she visited her widowed mother, and in the summer she went abroad, alone, to places of historical and archaeological interest. She listened to Adeline's description of the Dragon House with baffled admiration.

'But what made you choose somewhere so far away?' she asked.

'Ah, but we didn't choose it. It chose us.'

'Really? How curious. I can honestly say I have never been aware of being the object of such a choice.'

'Nonsense! You're a teacher,' (here Adeline recalled a remark of Charlie's). 'That's a vocation. It chose you.'

'Well – possibly. Does your husband regard himself in that light?'

'No, but then he claims he's a schoolmaster, and that there's a difference.'

'It's a nice distinction . . . but, yes, he may be right.'

It was clear that Enid Marsh was greatly relieved that such a distinction, however nice, existed.

Adeline decided to tell Charlie about the baby on the Sunday following Enid's last sitting. Since their return from Larme des Anges she felt that their life was on a more even keel. The yen for order and stability which her pregnancy had induced had been satisfied by these calm early autumn days, by the sunlit quiet of her studio with work in progress, and by the conversations with Miss Marsh. Perhaps, ironically, the start of a war would prove to have marked a sea-change in the tenor of their lives. They were going to be a proper family, Dora would have a brother or sister, Charlie would be a father. And what a mother she was going to be, this time around! She felt it in her bones, and saw it in her face when she examined it in the mirror – a serene maternal glow, the very essence of well-being.

That Saturday, she invited Enid to stay for an early supper, promising that she would drive her into Town to catch the later train. Enid demurred, but she brushed her protests aside, saying how pleasant and civilized these days together had been, and how nice it would be to round things off in a sociable manner. And Charlie, who had been refereeing a rugby match at Heath Court, would want to have an opportunity to say goodbye.

He was expected home at six, but when at seven he had still not arrived, they decided to go ahead. Enid was apologetic.

'I'm afraid I'm putting you out terribly, Adeline. I really think it might be best if I ordered a taxi and was on my way.'

'You mustn't do any such thing! He's only been held up, I'm quite used to it.' (Here Enid's expression indicated that she could imagine how well.) 'You and I will eat, and crack open a bottle of wine.'

'To be honest, I scarcely drink.'

'But you'll let this be one of the rare occasions.'

'I might have the smallest drop.'

Merle was bringing coffee when Charlie returned. There was the usual stuttering snarl of the motorbike coming too fast down the hill, then stopping too abruptly and being manhandled through the gate, all to the accompaniment of Brody's hysterical welcome. Merle rolled her eyes.

'Shall I bring Mr Farrell's supper up 'ere?'

'Not right away, Merle, we'll let you know.'

Merle rolled out into the hall as Charlie entered. They heard his distinctly informal greeting, her more guarded one, conscious of a visitor. Adeline could imagine the thumb jerked in the direction of the dining room. In a moment he looked round the door, unwinding his scarf. He looked flushed, his manner was boisterous.

'Hallo darling, mea culpa. Evening Miss Marsh, you still here?'

Enid's face assumed an expression of gracious restraint. 'Yes, but not for very long.'

'Oh, don't dash off – ' He disappeared momentarily to deposit the scarf, and then reappeared, going to kiss Adeline and inspecting the bottle. 'Celebrating, I see?' He sat down between them and poured himself a glass. 'Well here's to it, whatever it is.'

'I finished the portrait,' explained Adeline. 'I knew you wouldn't mind us going ahead, only I have to take Enid for her train in a minute.'

'No problem. I went for a drink with Alec Brotherton. I am refreshed.'

'So we see,' said Adeline, not reprovingly.

Enid rose, laying her napkin on the table. 'I shall go and collect my things together.'

Charlie beamed at her. 'Don't mind me.'

When she'd left, Adeline leaned across and kissed him, laughing. 'You mustn't tease her. She doesn't know how to take you, it's not fair.'

'I didn't seem rude, did I?'

'Not rude, not actually rude.' She ruffled his hair. 'Who won?'

'Oh, it was cancelled. Opposition have got a measles epidemic, every third boy is laid out, apparently, I hope to God we don't get it.'

'So what have you been doing all this time?'

'I told you – I went for a jar with Alec.' He glanced at her mischievously.

She felt entirely indulgent towards him.

'And then?'.

'I was coming to that.'

'Well get to it, I demand an explanation.'

'We signed on!'

She laughed. 'You did what?'

'Signed on, as jolly Jack Tars. It's been a fantasy of mine for as long as I can remember and now that the war's official this seemed like just the moment. It's no good, I can't just sit around in the staff room while everyone else does their bit. The school'll probably be evacuated anyway. So Alec and I moseyed on down to the recruitment office, and the deed is done! Basic training in Cornwall, starting next month.'

She lowered her coffee cup very carefully into its saucer. She felt cold and wooden. 'You're playing a joke on me.'

'No joke. Honour bright.'

'But you promised you wouldn't do this. You promised.'

'Yes, but Addy – ' He moved his chair closer to hers and clasped her hand. It was then she realized that he had never meant the promise. 'Addy, there is actually a war on now. It may not feel much like it at the moment, but it sure as hell will when things get going. I want to be there.' He tilted his head to look into her face. 'I thought you'd be proud of me.'

She shook her head, unable to speak for the disappointment, and for shame at the violence of her reaction. She actually felt sick.

Enid appeared in the doorway and remained there, discreetly.

'Just to say I'm quite ready when anyone's ready to take me,' she said quietly, 'or of course I can take a taxi . . .'

Charlie stood up. 'How about the motorbike? I'll get you there in no time!'

Adeline pushed her own chair back and rose. 'Don't be silly, Charlie. Come along Enid, we'll go now.' She left the room avoiding his eyes.

When she got back an hour later he was still sitting in the dining room, though the table had been cleared.

'Have you had something to eat?' she asked.

'Not hungry.' He was rather drunk she realized, another means by which he had put distance between them.

'Charlie – I was going to tell you something.'

'Tell me now.' He reached out an arm for her but she didn't go to him. He scrubbed at his head with both hands in a gesture of desperation. 'Look, I'm *sorry* . . .'

'I'm expecting a baby.'

'*What*?' The astonishment, and then the joy, on his face was like a sunrise.

She had to smile too.

'I said I'm pregnant. We're going to have a baby.'

'A *baby* – oh Addy, Addy . . .' In seconds his arms were round her and he was kissing and kissing her, laughing aloud though she felt his tears on her face. 'I love you so much, and now we're going to have a *baby* . . .! I can't believe it . . .'

He lifted her high, kissing her neck and swinging her

from side to side. When he set her down again she could have drowned in the love in his face.

'You're wonderful,' he said. 'Wonderful.'

Later, as she lay back against his shoulder, she asked softly: 'Why did you do it? Can't you get out of it? They don't need you.'

'Perhaps not,' he murmured, falling asleep. 'But maybe I need them.'

CHAPTER TWENTY-FOUR

1939–1940

CHARLIE WAS HAPPY. He was not, at the worst of times, a man much given to worry or care, but he had at certain periods in his life been aware of the worries and cares of others, and that had clouded his horizon. The weeks preceding his arrival at HMS *Raleigh* in Cornwall had been such a period. He could not understand Adeline's dismay at his decision to sign on. It was unlike her to be timid or anxious, and though he was flattered by her concern he also felt weighed down by it. His excitement and delight about the baby had to some extent been deflated by her reaction. She'd said nothing more, but there had been the silent reproach of real unhappiness in her eyes, at the back of her voice, in the very set of her shoulders. He had no idea how to cheer her. Reversing his decision was out of the question even had it been practicable. He couldn't believe that she had really not expected him to do it. The circumstances under which she had exacted his promise had been so utterly different. Would she, of all people, really have wanted him to sit on his hands when there was a war on? He was baffled. When he made love to her the night before his departure he could scarcely imagine the long weeks without her and the rapturous welcome of her swelling body. And yet when he and Alec Brotherton boarded the train for Cornwall he realized that he was not just leaving, but escaping from her.

This was a matter for curiosity rather than guilt, and even the curiosity didn't last beyond the time it took them to get talking to the other men in their compartment. Charlie had a pretty fair idea of the regime that lay in store for him, but no matter what its rigours, restraints and restrictions it had, even this journey had, the flavour of freedom.

The flavour remained, the sensation endured. Used to the minute network of rules and the relentless regimentation of prep schools, Charlie did not have the slightest difficulty in adjusting to the curious land-locked introduction to Naval life. Accustomed to the somewhat half-hearted enforcement of petty regulations, he found it soothing to be subjected to such regulations himself. He found the routine, imposed from above, both familiar and freeing, and he enjoyed the opportunities for guile and resourcefulness afforded by this circumscribed existence.

There was, for instance, the abiding issue of cash flow. His own married man's pay of three shillings a day, cushioned by the existence of ample resources at home, was quite adequate for the limited demands upon it. But a young single rating on two shillings a day, paid fortnightly, with five shillings hived off at source into a post office savings account to pay for fares home, and with cleaning equipment and uniform replacements to be bought from the remaining nine bob, was distinctly hard up. The obvious solution was for the better off to buy the services of the less fortunate in such areas as cleaning, dhobying, and keeping weapons up to scratch. In Charlie's case this arrangement in turn allowed him the extra time to instigate a card school. With only the NAAFI ale bar for competition, the school flourished. Charlie had found himself a niche. Alec was not so sure they'd done the right thing.

'What are we *doing* here, old boy?'

'Serving our country in her hour of need.'

'I feel entirely out of place.'

Charlie could not resist teasing Alec. 'Think how you'll feel when we get to sea.'

'Exactly!'

'Where's your spirit of adventure?'

'I strongly suspect I don't have one.'

Poor Alec, he was not happy. He was a slightly scatty bachelor Latin master, several years older than Charlie. A gifted teacher, he had nonetheless spent his staff room years sedulously avoiding exercise. Unfortunately for such as he, the daily round at HMS *Raleigh* was designed to promote obedient minds in fit, strong bodies. Alec was prepared to be obedient, but fitness was quite beyond him. The endless square-bashing, the running and the rowing were bad enough. But the prospect of 'Jankers', a draconian punishment involving a stiff run followed by several circuits of the parade ground at the double, with a rifle held horizontally across the shoulders, had him almost gibbering with fear. For a man who had not broken out of a walk since his teens – and there were many of them on the course – such a punishment could result in complete physical collapse.

'It's inhuman!' moaned Alec. 'I'd rather be shot!'

'You only have to keep your nose clean, for God's sake.'

This Alec did. No recruit could have been more law-abiding, or more anxious to avoid reproach, but to his intense relief the dreaded Jankers was abandoned not long after that for all men aged forty and over.

'Only three more years to go,' he confided to Charlie. 'If I can last that long.'

Charlie on the other hand, accustomed to taking games and supervising Hare and Hounds on the heath, was reasonably fit. He had no problem meeting the physical demands of the camp and the food was better and more plentiful than that in the average prep school. All in all, he'd never felt better.

Their first week – during which, symbolically as it seemed, their civilian clothes were sent home – was given over to the recruits' induction: medical and dental check-ups, the distribution of pay and identity books and discs, introductory lectures and inoculations. In many cases these 'jabs' tested the recruits' susceptibility not only to illness but to Navy life. As their arms swelled and throbbed, so their spirits sank. It was during this period that Charlie, lying awake at one in the morning, first heard a grown man sobbing with homesickness. He was non-plussed. He had comforted dozens of small boys suffering from the same thing, but what the hell would you say to a fully-grown insurance clerk, weeping helplessly for Esher?

For an hour or more the sobs continued, and Charlie remained awake, bearing the poor chap company. Once he said quietly, 'Cheer up, mate, a week from now it won't seem so bad,' but there was no reply. Eventually the sobs became less frequent, and finally petered out. At last, Charlie slept, unaware of how many times, and in how many dark, distant places, he was to hear that sound.

The course got into its stride, and the days passed more quickly as they gathered momentum. In the morning they rushed to divisions, were inspected by slowly strutting, ramrod-stiff 'brass', and were then dismissed to training sessions. They learned to fire rifles and revolvers in the butts, to identify enemy ships by silhouette, to splice rope, and, incessantly, to drill. They ignored at their peril the strict, minute, and rigidly applied forms of naval discipline. They called a bed a 'billet', the floor 'the deck', the wall 'the bulkhead' and ablutions 'the heads'. They submitted to endless kit inspections. When they sallied forth, resplendent in new uniforms, to the local pubs on their nights off, they referred to it as 'taking the liberty boat'.

The intensive but benign indoctrination worked.

Gradually they felt a little less like the mixed bag of private citizens they actually were, and more like the men of the fleet they hoped to become. By the time they were five weeks into the ten-week course, even the most dismal among them were cottoning on. Stiff penalties were inflicted for failure to write home, but they needed no prompting. Their letters, which at first had been full of tender, tear-stained solicitude for loved ones left behind, took on a breezy and self-confident note. Morale improved generally. Gradually but steadily they stopped looking over their shoulders and began to scan the horizon, eager to go to sea.

When the course was completed there would be ten days' home leave over Christmas. Then Charlie and Alec were bound for HMS *Victory*, Portsmouth barracks, to await draft.

Adeline read Charlie's cheerful, funny letters with mild astonishment. His passionate concern for her and for the baby came warmly off every page, but so did his enthusiasm for naval life. He was evidently sublimely happy, but it was impossible to feel any resentment. What he had said was right: would she really have wanted him any different? She shook her head, smiling, over the anomalies that beset her. It was impossible to overlook the similarities between these letters of his, and those of Dora's from St Agatha's. Both were distinguished by an engaging and disingenuous boastfulness, a catalogue of happenings rendered opaque by jargon, heartfelt expressions of affection and anticipation, and requests for cash.

Still, she missed him horribly. When in early November the baby began to move, she could hardly bear him not being there. She imagined his boyish delight and curiosity, the admiring, concentrated stare, the touch of his hands. In bed at night she clutched a bolster and thought, achingly, of his smooth, murmuring warmth. She missed the version of herself that he reflected back at her, a gentler, more indulgent, more womanly Adeline, always soft and sensuous, always with a twinkle in her eye. Her body felt neglected without his unabashed revelling in it. No-one had ever made her feel so lovely, so loving nor so loved. It was as though, in his absence, he came more clearly into focus, so that she knew precisely what it was in him she loved, and how greatly she prized it.

The changes in her body took on a different aspect from that of her first pregnancy. Then she had been happy and healthy but young, too, and uncurious. Peter's attitude had been robust and matter-of-fact. They had taken it all for granted. This time there was a magic for her in this slow sea-change, this enlarging and ripening. She was conscious of herself as a vessel for their love, hers and Charlie's, a vessel soft and pliant, but strong and resilient too. She lay in bed and listened to the strong beat of her heart, and pictured their baby growing, secret and protected. She longed for Charlie's rapt and wondering celebration of her state, his ecstatic crowing over their combined cleverness. She missed him. She missed him.

She sought diversion and consolation, as she always had done, in the plain, daily good things of her life. She walked Brody, she cooked for her friends, she selected a room for the baby and she and Dora spent a weekend choosing things for it. She appeared content and self-absorbed, but there was a part of her that remained secret and detached, waiting for Christmas and Charlie's return.

For Adeline during this period her body was a citadel. She lived within its walls, the custodian of her growing baby, deliberately isolating herself from the war and its implications. Her concern, as she saw it, must be with life, not death. She would give no credence to the posters and the barbed wire and the dug-out shelters. She would not allow herself to be threatened.

On Peter's advice she had reluctantly put herself under the supervision of the same Harley Street consultant as before, a man of awesome and patrician presence, to whom she was paying large sums in order to be told that she was fighting fit.

'It's ludicrous,' she complained good-naturedly. 'I don't

need all this attention, I don't know when I've felt so marvellous.'

'That's not the point,' insisted Peter. 'At your age you need keeping an eye on.'

'Well!' exclaimed Pru. 'The perfect gentleman! Addy's not altogether decrepit just yet, you know darling!'

'Thank you, Pru.'

'You know perfectly well that's not what I meant,' he said testily. 'It's just that it pays to be sensible. If you won't consider yourself, consider Charlie.'

'I do little else.'

Pru laughed, but Adeline glimpsed the momentary hurt on Peter's face and felt remorse. She would not normally have hurt him, for all the world. But lately he had been uncharacteristically pompous and irritable. She found his misplaced solicitude trying, though she understood at least part of the reason for it – he wanted to do his bit, but had so far been turned down. He had already, to Nicholas's disgust and against his advice, converted two of their West End interests – the Cabin and the Pandora – into service clubs where off-duty soldiers, sailors and airmen could eat, drink and dance at halfway reasonable prices from midday till midnight. Adeline hardly liked to mention the irony of this attitude in a man who, at twenty, had fought tooth, nail and paintbrush to avoid going into the army. She could not, however, fully appreciate his concern for her and his jealousness of Charlie who not only had her, but had joined up with the cavalier ease and confidence of youth.

He was constantly urging the placid Pru to remove to Larme des Anges for the duration, and now he directed this line of attack at Adeline, too.

'You'd be mad to stay here, and you'd be safe as houses on the island. Particularly if you both went –'

'We'd be able to play bridge and hold Dorcas parties,' muttered Pru.

Adeline's main objection to the idea concerned itself with Charlie – when would she see him? But not wanting to turn the knife in the wound, she said: 'I dare say it would be sensible, but I don't want to run away. This is my home, stand and fight, that's the thing. I'd rather be smashed to smithereens in the Nunnery than live an old maid's existence in paradise.'

'If I may say so, Addy, that is a hopelessly pig-headed attitude.'

'Yes and it's *my* attitude and *my* problem, and I'm too old to change.'

Poor Peter, he was suffering agonies of frustration which were in no way alleviated by his business partner's refusal to take the least interest in the war except as a means of making money. While Fenella, caught up in a whirl of aristocratic good works, was scarcely visible to the naked eye, Nicholas was at his most chilly and detached.

'We should do what we're good at,' he contended drily, 'and what Peter and I are good at is business. People are going to want to enjoy themselves, the more so as things get worse, and the people who can afford to pay will still be able to pay then. And there are bound to be shortages – if we can fill the gaps in people's lives and make a profit, everyone's happy.'

Peter mumbled darkly and ineffectually about profiteering, but their relationship had always been an uneven one, and at this moment Nicholas was in the ascendant. For others, the war had as yet brought few changes. The advertising agency was shrinking round Toni with the departure of most of the up-and-coming young men, but she continued to go in punctually each day, smart, efficient and self-possessed, relishing her greater responsibilities and the chance to be absent for longer from her increasingly spinsterly flat.

Bob, prevented from making his pacifist protest by virtue of his gammy leg, had been allotted a free-ranging home-front brief by the *Courier*. He was to chronicle the actions, reactions and day-to-day lives of ordinary civilians in the major cities, and especially the capital. Honour was thus satisfied, and while others removed out of London Bob and Louise moved back in, to a flat overlooking the river at Hammersmith. It was a particular pleasure for Adeline to see more of her sister-in-law, whose serene, worldly composure lent the illusion of a logical pattern to the vagaries of life.

Since returning from Larme des Anges she had seen only a little of Duncan and Joel, enough to know that the onset of war had simply brought their troubles more sharply into focus. Joel was frankly terrified of being obliged to leave Duncan, whose alcohol consumption had increased in direct ratio to his deepening depression, and whose erratic behaviour was now giving serious cause for concern.

'If I get call-up papers,' he confided to Adeline over lunch at l'Opera, 'I'm damned if I know what I'll do. I simply don't know how he'd manage. I can only hope that something comes up which will enable me to be usefully employed here in London.'

Adeline covered his hand with hers. Careful, competent, clever Joel. Successful Joel. Poor little Joel from Newcastle who learnt to ballroom dance in the front parlour and then been ambushed by his own nature.

She was so fond of him, of them both. 'Shall I tell you something?'

He gave her an upward, sidelong glance, and removed the spectacles he now wore. 'You're going to anyway.'

'You and Duncan were the first couple I'd seen who were really in love. I envied you then, and I still do, because you've lasted.'

Joel's pale cheeks turned rose-red. A middle-aged man who could still blush. 'You make us sound like a monument.'

'Well you are in a way!' She laughed and took out her cigarette case, offering him one. 'A monument to love and fidelity, and here's to you. I know it's not been easy.'

He shook his head and glanced away, with a shrug. 'No-one makes me stay.'

'I know. That's what I mean.'

He looked back at her, smiling, his composure restored. 'And what about you, and your handsome, unreliable Charlie? Is this love here to stay?'

'Oh yes,' replied Adeline with perfect confidence. 'Oh yes, it is.'

Charlie, travelling home by train for Christmas, discovered how great was the ineluctable charm of the naval uniform. In the rumbling carriages going east, and in the teeming darkness of blacked-out London, no-one knew that he and Alec were mere raw recruits. All the world smiled upon them. Station waitresses called them ducks and bus conductors called them mate and slapped their shoulders. Everyone, it seemed, regarded them with the fond indulgence normally reserved for lovers.

Adeline and Dora surveyed their handiwork, and saw that it was good, or at least Adeline did. In the past, generally speaking, she had attempted to give some theme and cohesion to her Christmas decorations, but this year she had said to hell with all that, and had let rip in a riot of paper chains and holly wreaths and cardboard lanterns and frilly crepe paper bells. The bold and well-defined lines of her house and its decor were submerged beneath a tide of cheerful, cheeky ephemera. No picture, however imposing, was without its sprig of holly, and Adeline had teetered terrifyingly on a step ladder to hang a spray of mistletoe from the light in the hall.

She was enormously satisfied with the result. In the drawing room, with her arm across Dora's shoulders, she said: 'Doesn't it look nice?'

'Yes.'

'I'm glad we put the tree in here, not in the hall. It's nice to be able to see it all the time. And I do so like the *smell* of a Christmas tree.'

'Yes.'

Adeline looked at her daughter – her clever, sturdy, perspicacious daughter. Happiness, she realized, was a very insulating state, and pregnancy even more so. She turned Dora to face her.

'Dolly . . . what's the matter?'

Dora gave a shrug; lips compressed, face red, fingers

fiddling urgently with a strand of tinsel so that a tiny, glittering snowstorm floated to the carpet. Adeline sat down on the sofa and forced Dora to sit down by her.

'Out with it.' Dora shook her head dumbly. 'Come on, Dolly, you must. There's no sense in bottling it up.'

Dora looked away, chin bravely lifted. She blurted out: 'I'm worried about you!'

Speaking, of course, made the tears come, and she released a great, groaning, embarrassed sob. 'Oh, damn . . .!' She pulled off her spectacles and dashed at her eyes with the back of her wrist. 'I'm sorry! I can't help it – I'm worried about you.'

Adeline didn't know what to say. She was touched and baffled. She put her arm round Dora, who felt solid and stiff, awkward with her unaccustomed feelings. Brody interposed a questing, sympathetic nose.

'Oh darling . . . darling Dolly . . . Come on, mop up, and cheer up. You *mustn't* worry. You're as bad as your father!'

Not to be talked out of it, Dora shrugged her off and said, with a kind of broken dignity: 'I don't like you being all on your own here, with the war . . . and everything.'

'But I'm *fine*! And I've got Merle, and this fool –' She patted Brody. 'And Daddy and Pru aren't far away. I'm *fine*.'

'Can't I stop going to St Agatha's and go to school somewhere here again?'

'No, Dolly. You know you love it there, and it's so much safer to be out of London –'

'I know, but I want to be with you!' Another storm of tears. Dora buried her face on her lap, her arms round her head. 'I want to be with you!'

For several minutes she was inconsolable. Adeline could do nothing but sit by her, rubbing her back and stroking her plaits as one might fondle a dog. She was awed by this display of concern, and didn't feel worthy of it. The decorations on her colourful, over-dressed tree twinkled in the firelight. It looked suddenly vulgar and sentimental.

The next day Charlie came back, and the longed-for Christmas began. So great was Adeline's emotional investment in the whole thing that it was hardly surprising if the festive season took on a certain feverishness. Amidst the bright, glittering rubbish with which, as Charlie observed, she had turned the Nunnery into Father Christmas's grotto, they made merry and played at Christmas with the furious absorption of children. Adeline laughed a lot, but all her laughter was perilously close to tears. She was aware, but unable to prevent, the strange contradiction in her behaviour which meant that her carefully maintained tranquillity during Charlie's absence had been bought at the price of panic now that he was here. His presence in the house meant that there was only his departure to look forward to, his departure into the unknown. Desperately she played the game at which she'd become adept as a child, of stretching each successive day a little further, to make this short time together seem longer than its natural span.

She was aware that she did this alone. Charlie was as sweet and loving as ever, but he came to her armoured in his new life, enthused and diverted by the exclusively male world he now inhabited. Adeline knew she should acknowledge that world, ask him about it, admire and inspect it, show an interest, but it was beyond her. To do any of those things would be to admit the Navy's just claim upon him and that she couldn't, wouldn't, do. The strain of her many conflicting feelings tired her. The only time she truly relaxed was at night, when they had made love and she lay with her back tucked against him, his breath on her neck, his warm arms and hands encircling and stroking her breasts and stomach. Then she felt her breathing quieten, her heartbeat slow: he was here, and he was with her.

'What's the matter, Addy?' he whispered one night. 'What are you frightened of? Tell me.'

But she was too ashamed to tell him that it was him she feared. That there was something in his nature that she couldn't reach, or touch, or understand. She feared his absence, not just of body but of spirit, and she despised herself for it. She had never felt like this before, never craved or expected any man's whole attention, but then she had never before been so much in love.

Things were made no easier by Dora, who was growing up. There was no repetition of her earlier outburst, but she seemed to be observing them to an uncomfortable degree, and to be uncertain about whose side she was on. One moment she was giggling hysterically over some foolish game with Charlie, the next she was flying up the stairs to her room in a tearful rage. At one moment she was colluding with him, the next she could scarcely bring herself to speak to him.

It was very exhausting. When the day came for them both to leave – for Charlie was escorting Dora part of the way on her journey to Devon, where she'd be met by Anne – Adeline did not feel she had the strength to bear it. She wanted Charlie simply to be gone, abruptly, spirited away, so that she could close the door and give in to the shameful, healing, inexplicable tears that had threatened her for days.

She stood in the hall watching as Dora did up her coat, flicked her plaits out from beneath her collar, pulled on her gloves. She smoothed the brim of the dark grey felt Aggies' hat, and handed it to her. The silence between them was tense, churning with things too complicated to put into words. When Charlie came down the stairs, terrifyingly alien and jaunty in his uniform, they both turned to him as though he might, magically, be able to say something to put things right.

He took Adeline's hand and laid it over his heart, holding it there with both of his. He was good at these simple, affecting demonstrations of love.

He said: 'I'll write and tell you the minute I know where I'm going to be! The very minute.'

'Yes,' she nodded and smiled. 'Please do that.'

Still holding her hand with one of his, he put out his other arm and drew her against him, almost as if they were dancing. Dora dropped her eyes, then turned to look in the mirror and adjust her hat.

'We're embarrassing young Dolly,' he said, to comfort both of them. 'But you must promise me you'll take good care of yourself. Do what the doctor orders. Let people make a fuss of you. Promise?'

She nodded.

'I didn't hear you. Did you hear her, Dora?'

'I promise,' said Adeline quickly.

'Goodbye then. Or *au revoir*.' He pushed her from him with deliberation, as if she were resisting, whereas in fact she was merely numb.

'Goodbye. And goodbye, darling –' She turned to Dora and swamped her in a great hug, the hug she had not trusted herself to give him. 'Look after each other and give my love to everyone down there.'

'Come on,' said Charlie, 'our carriage awaits.'

She went into the drawing room and watched from the window as they went down the steps and into the waiting cab. When he turned and looked up at her, waving, she managed to raise her hand and to arrange her face into a smile. But as the taxi pulled away she bent her head amongst the tired and tattered decorations and wept like a child.

Charlie was only a week at Portsmouth before he received notification of his draft to HMS *Cambridge*, presently anchored off Grimsby. He left the Portsmouth barracks with relief, for there was considerably less room per man than there had been at Torpoint, and pilfering was rife. On the journey north he experienced again the excitement of a new start, and the warm surge of approval and encouragement from everyone he encountered.

He and the rest of the new, untried, anti-aircraft gunnery unit, all composed of ex-civilian volunteers, made the queasy journey from harbour to ship in the ship's cutters, and in the kind of English winter weather which rusts metal and corrodes the spirit. Sleet, whipped from Siberia on the back of a freezing wind, lashed their faces as the cutter clambered and swooped through a mountainous sea beneath a tumultuous, threatening dark sky. The three-badge able seaman at the helm took a villainous delight in these conditions, grinning foxily as the boat teetered and rocked on the summit of each wave and then smacked down sickeningly into the churning trough on the other side. Nothing in their brief sea-going experience had prepared the recruits for this, and most of the faces which had been bright and eager on the quay were slack and fish-belly white by the time they reached the *Cambridge*. They boarded her, chastened and nauseous, via a shuddering, slapping rope ladder that seemed possessed of independent life.

The arrival of this phenomenon, a complete gunnery unit composed of HO (Hostilities Only) volunteers, was greeted with leering disbelief by the ship's company of regulars, who gathered at every vantage point to watch. Charlie, though frozen and soaked like the rest, was non-etheless not sick. Catching sight of the amiably sceptical faces on the sidelines he recognized the gleeful mockery that's directed at every new boy, and which could probably be deflected by a willingness to accept, for a while at least, the status of lowest form of life.

The deck tilted steeply and a sheet of icy water rushed over the cruiser's low freeboard and on to their feet. In the late afternoon dusk the stern grey walls of the bridge and the gun turrets were like the battlements of a sea-borne castle, prodding the sky. A few scouting gulls mewed and wheeled crazily, riding the wind. Alec, standing on Charlie's left, made a stifled moaning sound through pressed-shut lips.

Their welcome, mercifully brief and to the point, was delivered by the ship's gunnery officer, Lieutenant Gold-ring, flanked by a couple of chief petty officers whose expressions held the tender concern that a wolf reserves for a goat. Goldring introduced himself, and pointed out that in thirty-six hours they would be on active service, as flagship of four anti-aircraft cruisers operating out of the Humber as a protective escort to east-coast convoys. He hardly need point out, need he, the importance of settling down, mucking in, and getting on with the job. The CPOs, he said, indicating Merriman and Pitt, would show them the ropes. Dismissed, they began to shuffle below, and Alec bolted for the rail.

The *Cambridge* was not a ship in the prime of life, but one of several Ceres-class cruisers commissioned in 1918, and subsequently converted to an anti-aircraft role with the addition of ten high and low angle guns and half a dozen multiple mountings. It was the resulting top-heaviness that made the adapted World War One ships among the most unpopular in the fleet. In severe weather – and the winter of '39/'40 was terrible – she could tilt to an angle of thirty degrees from the sea's surface. Her motion, it was graphically explained to new arrivals, was like that of a bucking bronco trying to unseat its rider: she appeared to pitch and roll simultaneously, with a lurch that was quite capable of knocking even an experienced seaman off his feet.

As Charlie and his whey-faced companions made their unsteady way down two levels to the mess-deck it was almost possible to feel nostalgia for the bitter wind above. The air, as they descended in the wake of CPO Merriman, grew thick enough to cut. Given time, most of them would cease even to notice the rank, stifling atmosphere of the lower deck, but to new hands already debilitated by sickness it was like the odour of hell itself that afternoon.

The seaman's mess-deck, when they reached it, would with little modification have been recognizable to a jack tar of Nelson's fleet. An area twenty-five feet by fifteen, and no more than eight feet high, designed to accommodate forty, now comprised the entire living space for sixty men. Six scrubbed wooden tables stood at right angles to the bulkheads, flanked by stools. At the inboard end of each table was a large wooden bread cask that doubled as a seat for the head of each mess. There were, as they would soon discover, only a limited number of slinging billets for hammocks, long since claimed by the regulars, and the rest of the men had to sleep on or under the tables. When hammocks were slung, it was impossible to walk upright. The ablutions consisted of four basins, two showers and three lavatories, the inadequacy and inefficiency of which added to the smell. The air was stale and dank. Condensation streamed down the bulkheads.

CPO Merriman turned out to be quite fatherly in a gruff and abrasive way. 'It'll soon feel like your mother's boozum,' was what he kept saying as he showed them round and demonstrated (presumably for future reference) how to 'sling an 'ammick'. They were almost ignored, now, by the men who sat about, playing cards, reading dog-eared magazines and writing letters. Charlie suspected that this aloofness was not necessarily hostile, but the natural result of living cheek-by-jowl with other men for days on end.

Their first evening was a nightmare of confusion. Bludgeoned by messages over the ship's tannoy which they were unable to understand, buffeted by the ceaseless movement of the ship, and completely disorientated, only Charlie and a couple of others had any stomach for supper. Because the *Cambridge* was still moored at anchor, and freshly supplied, the food wasn't bad – mutton stew, carrots, spuds, and a vegetable that was to become infamously familiar, tinned 'pusser's peas', overheated to a khaki sludge. This was followed by jam suet pudding. The sight of the gash buckets afterwards, filled with these mixed plate-scrapings, was not calculated to settle queasy stomachs.

As they lay in their wretchedly uncomfortable billets, Alec put his arms over his face. His voice was querulous.

'God help me . . . I'm not cut out for this . . .!'

Charlie fidgeted irritably. He was disinclined to be Alec's nursemaid. 'Which of us is? We'll settle.'

'It's all right for you, you're not ill . . . I feel like absolute bloody death!'

'Shut up, Alec, and try to sleep.'

'Jesus Christ!' Alec hauled himself up and stumbled mis-

erably, hand over mouth, in the direction of the already
hard-pressed heads.

Five days later they had become, if not hardened, at least
resigned to shipboard life. The waves which had nudged
their stomachs into their throats lying at anchor off
Grimsby were as nothing to those they encountered in the
North Sea. Many of the HOs, with neither sea legs nor
sea sense, and with their morale at an all-time low, were
prostrated with seasickness. They got no sympathy,
everyone knew it was something that passed with time.
The only attention they received was a general clearing of
the path to allow them to use the heads rather than the
deck. The severe weather, which on dry land it would
have been possible at least to jeer at from time to time
from the comparative warmth of a house, at sea became a
personal and relentlessly cruel enemy. As the *Cambridge*,
with her fellow cruisers *Curlew*, *Clamorous* and *Conway*,
shepherded their merchantmen up and down the east
coast, the men forgot what it was to be warm and dry.
Other than regulation oilskins, almost no special foul-
weather clothing was issued, and the HOs, without as yet
the foreknowledge to bring a plentiful supplement of their
own garments, went about their work with the oilskins
over nothing more than overalls. Coming off duty provided only a brief sense of relief, for the battened-down
mess-deck was increasingly dank and comfortless. The
floor where Charlie and Alec slept became slippery and
noisome with water, the contents of spilled gash buckets,
and worse.

Charlie, however, did sleep. He was curiously at peace
with himself. Not that he was by any means immune to
the discomfort. He was as damp, cold, and dirty as the
next man. He joined with the others in speaking nostalgically of home, but he was at home here. He participated
in the general good-natured blagging of the officers, but
was not envious of them: the life of the mess-deck exactly
suited his nature. Here there were neither expectations
nor responsibilities beyond those precisely laid down. The

lack of privacy, which favoured no-one, afforded a certain kind of anonymity that he relished. He found that he was looking forward to their first real action.

Adeline would have been shocked to know how vague was her husband's mental picture of her when he was at sea. Charlie was more realistic. Safely immured in the *Cambridge*, he was able to admit that he should never have married her. He loved her, oh yes. When he was with her he was overwhelmed by her, as he had been on their first meeting, and the other women he'd known, before and since then, were diminished by her. There was no-one like Adeline, and his proposal had been the only way he could think of laying claim to her. But now that he had her he was unnerved by the strength of her passion for him, her unstinting love, her unswerving loyalty which God knows he had tried and tested to the full, only he knew how much. How could he live up to that? How could any man, least of all he himself? The greater her love, the greater his shame, and the worse his behaviour. He had even, he recollected with distaste, on the night of their anniversary given her a necklace bought by another man for that other man's unknown wife. He'd won it at cards, and then so perfected his story that he had almost reduced himself to tears when he'd given it to her. She wore it, he knew, always, though it wasn't her sort of thing. Every time he saw that opal laying small and pale on her breast he experienced a spasm of rage at the mess they'd got themselves into.

And now the baby was coming. Ironically she'd been more beautiful than ever at Christmas, a different Adeline, tremulous and fecund, an earth-mother. And Dora, gaining on them, sizing them up, playing them up. It had been unbearable. His desire for Adeline was undiminished, but his enthusiasm for their marriage had died. The war had come just in time, just as he was about to create, by whatever means possible, an escape route.

Without actually planning it, he built up the case against himself. Every few weeks when they put in to re-stock and refuel at Immingham, the ratings of HMS *Cambridge* took the liberty boat, enduring not just the rigours of the cutter trip but a swaying, lurching tram ride to enjoy the fleshpots of Grimsby. Charlie did no more than many others. He got roaring drunk at the long, bleak bar of the Rats' Nest pub, he won and lost a few bob at cards in the upstairs room, and he consorted briefly and urgently with the cheerful, businesslike ladies of the night. He enjoyed all these diversions, the more so because they were innocent of emotional ties and obligations. Fights, friendships, fornication, all were short-lived, and undertaken with a gusto fed by the prospect of the long haul back to the ship at eleven o'clock. Whatever ills afflicted the ratings on the swaying, overcrowded, dimly lit tram, or on the lurching liberty boat, conscience wasn't one of them.

The baby was due at the beginning of April. In the middle of February Adeline made an appointment to see Sir Victor Tuzoe, an appointment that was outside her pattern of regular visits.

Determined not to allow her entire day to centre on her small kernel of anxiety she drove early into London and sought out Fenella, who was engaged in the receiving and packaging of woollen garments for servicemen at a drill hall in Kensington. She looked quite lovely and happier than Adeline had seen her for ages, standing among the piles of ancient, felted clothes in an exquisite cream shantung suit with a fox fur collar. Adeline imagined, wrongly, that she herself more or less blended into her surroundings in an old black cape, baggy trousers and red and black shawl tossed over her head and round her shoulders. She was mildly surprised when Fenella spotted her at once and cried out rapturously:

'Addy! Over here! Don't you look simply marvellous?' Fenella was always less cautious when not with Nicholas. 'It can't be long now, surely?'

'No, only six weeks. I'm getting a little tired of the waiting. Are you completely indispensable or can you have lunch?'

'I can have lunch, of course.'

They sat over tea and wads at the WRVS canteen near the door of the hall. Adeline realized that her impulse to see Fenella, rather than any of her other friends, had not been simply fortuitous. Fenella was, without doubt, the person least likely to ask searching questions about her life, herself, or about Charlie. No questions, and no advice: no-one was better versed than Fenella in the art of sublimating troubles. Today she was sunny and talkative. The war had benefited her by giving her a sense of purpose, and of her own usefulness outside the ambit of Nicholas and their various homes. The slight sadness, the strain of being always controlled, which had covered her face like a fine veil for years, had lifted today. She talked, relieving Adeline of the need to do so.

'Look at us,' she said, 'two married ladies. Did you ever think, back in Gower Street in that dismal room of yours, that you'd be sitting in a place like this with me nearly twenty years later? And expecting another baby at your age? It's a disgrace.'

'They say it keeps you young.'

'Not me!' Fenella shook her head. 'I'd have been an old lady if I'd had any more, all that worry, and struggling to please Nick. No, it's getting easier all the time at the moment.'

'How is Miles?'

'Miles is *fine*. He's coping with school so much better than I'd dared to hope. It's funny about children, isn't it? They're so much stronger than one imagines . . .'

Adeline reflected on this as she stared at a pre-war copy of the *Lady* in Sir Victor Tuzoe's richly furnished waiting room. Children were tougher than one thought, and their toughness, what was more, was in inverse ratio to their size. Wasn't it a well-known fact that babies abandoned on doorsteps in the middle of winter survived, and cried until rescued?

Silently, the crisp, immaculate nurse appeared in the

doorway. 'Mrs Farrell, would you like to come through now?'

Adeline followed her. Stealth and wealth, Adeline always thought when she came here. Footsteps were muffled by thick carpets, traffic noises barely heard beyond closed windows and voluminous curtains, voices were hushed, manners were restrained. She hated it.

In his consulting room Sir Victor had numerous pictures, including one which Adeline had painted of Lady Tuzoe years ago, when she'd been married to Peter. She very much doubted that Sir Victor would commission anything from her these days, and she suspected that the appearance of his wife's portrait in the surgery represented a demotion. He bought pictures only as investments, and was a crashing snob. But none of that mattered. It didn't matter one bit as long as he earned his money this afternoon.

It was Sir Victor's great talent to be soothing. Soothing was an art in which he was pre-eminent, and he persisted in the notion that it was what expectant mothers most desired – more than medical advice, more than medicine, more, in his view and his experience, than the truth, as often as not.

He listened to Adeline, checked her notes, asked her a few questions in his soft, rich voice that was like the furry drone of a giant bumble bee. Then he removed his spectacles, steepled his fine hands together and addressed her.

'I have to say, Mrs Farrell, that you seem wonderfully well to me. I suspect that there's nothing to worry about. You're due quite soon, and there is very often a quiet time, a rallentando as it were before the great crescendo of birth.'

He smiled at her. He had limpid brown eyes, the lids of which drooped at the outer corners, assisting his air of mournful, aristocratic wisdom. Adeline wanted to shout at him not to patronize her. She wanted to shake the expression of calm complacency from his face. Instead, she smiled back.

'I see. It's just that there's been such a lot of activity and now I haven't noticed any for more than a week.'

Sir Victor leaned forward and put his spectacles on again. 'Why don't we just have a little look to see how the baby is lying?' he suggested mellifluously.

He never issued instructions, let alone orders. The patient was always right. On the couch, Adeline stared up at the exquisite white moulding of scrolls and flowers on the ceiling, and felt Sir Victor's warm, politely confiding hands on her stomach.

'Mm . . .' he murmured wonderingly, and then: 'M-hm,' more decisively. He gave her stomach a little pat. 'Right, Mrs Farrell. Get yourself comfortable again and then if you'd join me . . .'

When she emerged from behind the screen he was sitting in his chair, legs crossed, hands holding the arms expansively, like a king on a throne.

'Do sit down, Mrs Farrell.' He watched smilingly as she complied. 'You're quite right, he's quiet at the moment, but I see no cause for concern. He's a fine big chap and the head is engaged. It seems to me that he's quiet because he's ready to be born.'

'But it's so early,' she protested.

He referred to her notes. 'Yes . . . yes. You were quite certain about the dates?'

'Reasonably certain.'

'At any rate it doesn't signify,' he soothed. 'He may simply be getting in position early.' Adeline wished he would stop referring to the baby as 'he'. 'You're probably going to have a very easy time of it.'

The gunnery crews of HMS *Cambridge* had not yet fired a single shot in anger. The enemy so far had been notable for his absence. They were all prey to a certain anxious tension, as though each unremarkable day that passed was storing up trouble for the future. They were all edgy. When would it happen? they wondered. What would it be like? Most importantly, how would they react?

In late February, whether as a direct result of their winched-up nerves or simply by chance, they encountered death – its possibility and its reality – on more than one occasion, with no assistance from the enemy.

On the first instance one of the older, regular hands was put in detention for leave-breaking. Jack Collins was a popular and kindly man, an able seaman with fifteen years' service behind him. He was a sort of Naval recidivist, who did little but complain about the harshness of Navy life, but who couldn't have lived any other kind. Generally speaking, after nights on the town in Grimsby, one or two of his messmates would see to it that he was bundled on to the tram, cleaned up and stood upright for the benefit of the First Lieutenant. On this one occasion that his oppos had failed to catch up with him, he turned up on the quay next day, sick and repentant, and was exposed to the full grandeur and severity of King's Regulations.

The detention cells were situated right forward, and one deck below, so that anyone in them was subjected to the full force of the ship's movement in rough weather. To prevent any prisoner doing away with himself, shaving was barred, and clothing was restricted to a plain canvas suit, without belt or braces – or even shoelaces. The bed was a six-foot block of wood, with a wooden pillow at one end: a blanket was only forthcoming if the temperature dropped below thirty-two degrees. For his first three days in the cells a prisoner's rations were confined to three ship's biscuits and two mugs of water a day, gradually returning to something like normal by the end of a week, but minus puddings. His task was the dreary and laborious one of picking two pounds of oakum per day. Conditions were harsh, but not cruel. A prisoner's only real fear was that he would be forgotten when the ship went into action, and be entombed in his six-by-four foot steel cell if the ship went down. To prevent such a thing happening it was the first duty of the Master at Arms to release all prisoners the moment the signal for Action Stations was sounded. On Jack Collins' fifth day in detention Action Stations was called. Footsteps pattered and scurried on every side as men hurried to their appointed positions, but as yet no-one came. Moments later the main armaments opened up and the cell plating groaned and vibrated with their thunder. Jack, who had until that moment been awaiting release with his usual phlegm, began to panic. He howled and hammered on the cell door, but no-one came. Sure that he stared a hideous death in the face, he pre-empted it by having the massive heart attack which had been waiting for some years to ambush his ill-treated frame. After three quarters of an hour the firing ceased as abruptly as it had begun. It had only been an exercise, but no-one had told Jack Collins. He was dead.

Only a few days later, in seas so high that the men of the *Cambridge* felt like submariners, one of the HOs who had come aboard with Charlie and Alec and been terribly ill ever since, was swept overboard. He had been hurled against the wire rail with such force that the sea-soaked weight of his body had snapped the wire. The alarm was given, but within seconds he had been engulfed.

As a result of these accidents morale was low, and yet the urge to confront the enemy was stronger than ever. If they could give the Hun what for, at least they would have justified the rigours and dangers of shipboard life. They were in the mood to bloody a few noses and had so far been denied the opportunity. Frustration and anger were building up.

At about eight o'clock one morning, Charlie had just come off watch and was on the mess-deck, shaving and washing before breakfast. Above the ship's company had stood down from Action Stations and the defence stations crew of the eight-barrelled pom-pom were about to clean the gun. Nearby were a few HOs, Alec among them, cleaning the decks. The captain of the crew led his team to the front of the mounting to sponge out the eight barrels, unaware that a firing switch circuit in the pom-pom's director had become corroded.

This particular gun was known as the Chicago Piano on account of its characteristic sound. At the moment the first man touched the first barrel that abrupt bark was heard, and a torrent of contact-fused shells ripped through the gun's crew. Where five men had stood there was now only a sickening debris of human flesh, and reddened shreds of clothing lying in a slick of blood and viscera. A single shell ricocheted, and found Alec, almost severing his head and killing him instantly.

The men who witnessed it could at first do nothing. Moments of horrified paralysis were broken by the arrival of CPO Merriman issuing orders. Like a bushfire the word of what had happened went round. By the time Charlie reached the deck the hoses were being unreeled and those with strong enough stomachs were beginning to clear up the human mess with deck brooms and shovels. They were just covering up Alec's body, but he was glad he hadn't seen it. Still dressed only in overalls and plimsolls he set to, oblivious to the cold. The gruesome job had assumed for all of them an importance far beyond the simply practical. As Charlie swept, and sluiced and scraped the sodden remains into a pile he could think only of the afternoon they'd signed on, as carelessly pig-headed as a couple of schoolboys.

Alec had taken a double first; he'd had a brilliant mind but a soft, biddable nature. Charlie was sure that Alec would never have been here if it hadn't been for him. He experienced a body-blow of shock. This was his fault. His own stupid words to Adeline came back to him: 'It's always been a fantasy of mine . . .' For the first time since boarding the *Cambridge* he was violently and agonizingly sick.

When the dreadful pile was complete, the men's hammocks were brought and the 'sails', and Charlie, with frozen, blood-caked fingers, divided what was left of the gun crew between them and sewed them up. The five small, misshapen packages, weeping blood, were carted to the quarterdeck for the ceremony of burial at sea. At least, thought Charlie, Alec's body had retained its form . . . it had not been rendered so much un-recognizable carrion.

When next he wrote to Adeline he did not mention the accident. He found that he could not express it in any way that was adequate. And in some less innocent way he hoarded this experience that was entirely his and which, he was certain, she could never understand.

The nurse was a nice woman, not past shedding a tear. Her plain, kindly face was strained with sadness as she said:

'Would you like to hold her for a moment?'

Adeline shook her head. She was exhausted and she hurt. Blood and fluid trickled down between her legs – her body was crying, even if her face couldn't manage it. The nurse came closer, offering her once more her perfect, and perfectly dead, baby daughter.

'Just for a moment?'

Adeline held out her arms. She did not hold the baby close, but a little distance from her. She dared not love her any more, or make the loss any worse.

They had thought it would be a boy, they'd thought of a lot of boy's names . . . only Clea, for a girl. And yet – she remembered her anger with Sir Victor, constantly referring to the baby as 'he' – perhaps Clea, with her last minute breaths, had registered an objection. Now she lay, wrapped tight in a shawl, serene and passive in her betrayal.

'Shall I . . .?' The nurse reached out to reclaim her and Adeline let her go. She knew that the three of them had been left alone for a minute out of kindness, so that the worst, at least, of the appalling indecencies of grief might be got over in understanding female company. If she could have obliged, she would have done. But the pain was too great. Instinctively, her mind had applied a tourniquet to her emotions so that she would not bleed to death: she knew her worst suffering was still to come, she could not imagine that it would ever end.

One question she had to ask, and would not ask Sir Victor for fear of being soothed.

'Nurse . . .?'

'Yes, my dear?'

'Do you think she was in pain?'

'No, no.' The answer came immediately, and very matter of fact. All very quiet and peaceful. She adjusted the bundle in her arms. It seemed to have changed its character, become entirely inanimate, horrifying. Adeline turned her head away. Clea, their little Clea . . . she was now a slightly embarrassing item of hospital property.

'You have to take her,' she whispered. 'It's all right, go on.'

The nurse hovered. Outside in the corridor came the creak of footsteps.

'Yes,' she said, 'I will now. Doctor's coming back to see you.'

Adeline kept her head averted. She heard the murmured exchange in the corridor, the rustle of the nurse going away. She felt an agonizing spasm of pain and her body ejected a fresh gout of blood as though the baby were being ripped from it. She closed her eyes. Outside in the blackout the air-raid siren sounded, rising over London like the howl of a wolf.

It was the fourth time Charlie had read the letter. He sat at the mess table with his head in his hands, studying it. He was trying to absorb its contents, to feel something, but it was like a cry from a distant hilltop, just scratching his consciousness.

. . . counted as a real person, you see, so there was a birth certificate, and a wretched, horrid little funeral. People wanted to come for my sake, but I wouldn't let them. The only person I could have borne to be there was you. Anne came to stay with me after I came out of hospital. She is an absolute brick and kindness itself, but I didn't want her there. I couldn't even write this letter till after she'd gone. Sympathy's all well, but I'm afraid I despised them for sympathizing when they couldn't possibly understand. You're the only person can do that.

He raised his head for a moment as if coming up for air. Then he turned the page and read again the last few lines.

> . . . your daughter, she was absolutely beautiful, with dark hair and long fingers. I'm so sorry, Charlie, so terribly, terribly sorry . . . and I love you so much, always. Adeline.

Frowning, he folded the letter and smoothed it.

One of his messmates, Reg Dix, was sitting further along the table.

'Oy, Charlie – it'll never happen.'

Charlie put the letter in his pocket. 'I'm afraid it has.'

'Sorry, mate . . . bad news then?'

'My wife lost the baby.' There it was. Five words covered it.

Reg shook his head. 'Missus all right?'

'Yes.'

'Women are tough,' said Reg. 'And look at it this way, you still got each other.'

'That's true.'

'Always a next time,' said Reg.

Charlie smiled briefly. He didn't reply, for he knew that there would be no next time. And perhaps, after all, since Adeline had coped so bravely, this was all for the best.

CHAPTER TWENTY-FIVE

1944

FRANK SAT AT the corner table near the window in The Plough and Harrow with Chris Dance. His usual table, he realized rather glumly. When exactly had that happened? He remembered how, before the first war, he and Simon Charteris had used to laugh, not unkindly, at the dullness, the quiet, the inherent staidness of this pub, and now here he was: a regular.

Chris Dance was saying something about the bomb damage in Exeter, and how he'd had the devil's own job finding that good shop which sold the only boots he was prepared to wear, because it had moved to new premises in Gandy Street.

Frank was more or less listening. He managed to nod and made sounds of intelligent agreement, while noticing that he was the youngest man present: and he was bloody nearly fifty! It made you think. Chris was sixty-five and looked, thought Frank, like every child's idea of a jolly Farmer Giles – ruddy of face, generous of girth, bald of pate. For some reason, Chris's appearance caused him a spasm of irritation.

'Another?' he asked, to escape for a moment.

'Don't mind if I do – just the other half, thanks.'

Waiting at the bar, Frank wondered if it was because Chris looked so exactly how he himself ought to look – bucolic, expansive, content. Whereas he was feeling dull, and out of things. He was restless. Since the war – the other war, his war – he'd not had the slightest desire to travel, but recently that had been changing. There were signs that the show might be over soon, it was going the Allies' way. When things were back to normal he was going to take Anne away for a holiday somewhere – away from Fording Place, away from Tarrford, away from all her blithering committees and organizations and good works. He might even take Addy up on her offer of this house of hers in the Windward Islands. A few weeks of rum punch in the Caribbean sunshine . . . it would make a nice change from the corner table at the Plough, and he would have his wife to himself for a bit.

He carried the beers back. It was seven-thirty, mid-July, and the sun had dropped just enough to send long golden beams through the window, exposing the dusty drabness of the pub with its handful of elderly men.

'Cheers,' said Chris, raising his glass. 'Your very good health.'

'And yours.' They supped in silence. Then, 'How's Dorothy?' enquired Frank.

This was a good way of setting Chris off since, like most men who come to marriage late, he was deeply uxorious and talked about his wife as if she were some rare creature in captivity. On a rather baser level, it also occurred to Frank that after this final burst he could reasonably excuse himself and go home for supper. In the way of these things, when the two men met at the Plough at seven o'clock, Chris Dance had already eaten, but Frank had not.

He listened with half an ear as Chris rattled on. No

doubt about it, he was well under Dorothy's thumb. As long as he didn't have to listen to too much of it, Frank was amused by the whole set up. He was fond of both of them, and owed each of them a debt of quite different sorts. But whereas Chris was a genuine innocent, Dorothy had got everything exactly as she liked it. She had a home, a husband, independent status, and she had a stake in Frank's life. With no hint of vanity, Frank knew that Dorothy had always doted on him – more than that, she was in love with him. As a child, and even as a young man, he'd played up to it shamelessly; now he simply accepted it. Besides (and this was where the debt came in), it had been Dorothy's firm bosom, bouncing rebelliously behind her starched apron-bib, that had provoked his body's first sexual response, and the ripe swell of her bottom bustling about the nursery which had kept him in a bursting agony of lust for one whole Christmas holiday when he was twelve.

Though he had neither wanted nor been able to analyse her allure at the time, she had epitomized womanliness, a figure both motherly and provocative, intensely, unbearably close and yet untouchable, nurturing and seductive. The tension between them had been truly awesome. His dreams had become extravagantly, uncontrollably lubricious. And then, during the course of a term, the fever passed. For him at least, but not for Dorothy. There was still more than a trace of it about her now. All these years she'd been carrying it about with her, but nothing had ever been said. Officially, none of these feelings, so passionate and sinful and tumultuous, had ever existed.

He glanced at his watch and smiled regretfully at Chris: 'Well, this has been very pleasant as usual, but I must be off.' He patted his midriff. 'Inner man's making himself felt.'

'Of course, of course, you cut along,' agreed Chris. He looked at his own watch. 'Shan't be much longer myself. I want to get back to listen to Bob. We never miss.'

'No, indeed,' said Frank, rising and collecting his stick and cap from the corner.

He didn't much care himself whether he missed his brother's broadcast or not. Anne tuned in loyally, but he quite often managed to find pressing business in another part of the house. Bob's talks, which the BBC broadcast under the title 'The Rest of Us', were extremely popular, but Frank could without difficulty detect the faintly bolshy tone which had informed so much of Bob's activities over the years. It irritated him past all telling, all that exaltation of 'ordinary people' and 'the working man'. Not that he had anything against it *per se*, but it was a bit rich coming from a chap with all the benefits of a comfortable upbringing, an expensive education and who'd put the Gundry name on the front pages for running off with the wife of a millionaire.

'Good night, then,' he said to Chris. 'See you in the morning. Regards to Dorothy.'

Chris made a cap-tipping gesture. 'Good night. Oh yes, she'll be up at the house tomorrow, I've no doubt.'

No doubt, thought Frank as he emerged into the evening sunshine and released Molly, his Labrador from the boot-scraper. Mo Atkins, the local ARP man, and Colin Pedder from the shop were just on their way in. Frank exchanged greetings with them, considering he had had a lucky escape. He really didn't think he could have stood their amiable self-importance, or their war-according-to-Tarrford, tonight.

He began to walk at a measured, comfortable pace, along the high street and then up the meandering lane that led to Fording Place. It was a long walk, but he enjoyed it, and would have undertaken it even if 'Shanks's Pony' had not been the patriotic form of trans-port. And in spite of his present restlessness he still derived a good deal of pleasure from surveying the land – his land – the soft hillsides now covered in sturdy arable crops. He missed the cattle. They'd only retained a very few, and replaced the rest with pigs, which were economical, and produced a quick, high yield.

There was the drone of an engine behind him, and a lorry roared past. As it receded a cluster of tanned faces stared back at him – German POWs. One of them blew a kiss and there was a burst of laughter as the lorry disappeared round a bend in the road. Infernal bloody cheek, thought Frank, but he wasn't really offended. He could well imagine what they thought of him, a plodding stay-at-home, and he didn't hate them for being German. Perhaps that was a legacy of the first war, when they'd still from time to time had to engage the enemy hand to hand. Once you'd seen the other fellow's stubble, and his pimples, and his eyes bloodshot with tiredness, it was hard to regard him as anything other than just one more poor bloody foot soldier, who happened to be in the wrong uniform. You killed him just the same, but it was an awful, stomach-turning thing to do. This time round none of them got a look at the chaps they were firing at. In fact the women, children and old men of Tarrford had probably seen more of the enemy than most servicemen had. Very often, as they passed through the village in a lorry or on foot, they whistled at the girls, and the girls, Frank noticed, had no objections.

Reflecting on the war brought him, inevitably, to the contemplation of those of his acquaintance directly involved in it. They'd had a letter from Adeline this morning. Poor old girl. He worried about her rather, though she seemed to be putting a good face on things as usual. Frank had precious little time for that Peter Pan of a husband of hers, but she certainly thought the sun shone out of his backside. And since she'd lost the baby – terribly bad luck that, you wouldn't wish it on your worst enemy – she had if anything become even more devoted to him, as if she'd stored up enough love for two and then found herself with only one person to lavish it on. And he was never there.   Frank applauded the patriotic impulse wherever he found it, but that fellow had joined up with almost indecent haste, off to play sailor-boys (not prepared to carry any responsibility, Frank noticed) with the ink barely dry on the marriage certificate. Frank, an Army man, belonged to the 'Navy-gets-the-gravy' school of thought. The Navy was doing a good job – as far as it went. But that job was not to be compared with the necessary dirty work done by the Army. He didn't burden his sister with these views: she had enough to contend with. All her own fault, of course, but he acknowledged that she was too long in the tooth to change now. Such a pity that with her ability – and looks, even – she chose to squander them on the featherweight Charlie Farrell.

He paused, and shouted at Molly, who had been waylaid by some smell in the hedge. When she'd caught up, he walked on, automatically picking up the thread of his ruminations. At least Adeline had something to keep her occupied now. Some chum of hers, a chap she'd known ever since art school, had landed a cushy job in the Min. of Info., and had got her appointed an official war artist, with special reference to women at work. She seemed to enjoy the job. Just as well, for there were precious few other outlets for her talents these days. In retrospect, it had all been a flash in the pan, though one which had made her a packet. She'd kept the pot boiling (her typically robust phrase) over the past few years with some run-of-the-mill commissions – generals, industrialists and academics – but the golden times were over. Frank had always taken a pretty dim view of women working, but in his sister's case it was a very necessary distraction from the distressing shambles of her private life. And young Dora was turning out so sensible and grown-up, almost too much so for a young thing of sixteen: with her mother's example before her she probably looked on life as a minefield of hazards and potential catastrophes. She had her sights set on an English degree, but Frank did hope she'd find time for a little fun.

Frank turned into the drive of Fording Place. A large area of what had once been lawn, where they used to play badminton, cricket and croquet, was now given over to the growing of vegetables, whose homely, regimented rows gave the house a serviceable look. Between the vegetables and the wood a group of galumphing boys in shorts and plimsolls ran about in pursuit of a football. Their urgent, distant shouts reached Frank on the evening air. Evacuees: surely one of the reasons why he had become a regular at the Plough. There were eight of them at Fording Place, four boys, four girls, and Anne, God bless her, loved each snotty, swearing, homesick, incorrigible one of them as though they were her own. Though he didn't share her tender feelings, Frank didn't dislike the evacuees, and understood that having them was the useful, sensible thing to do. It was just that they were always *there*. And periodically their mothers would descend, like creatures from another planet. The mothers he did find difficult. They were so loud, so extreme, altogether too much in every department. Not only that, but the children always behaved appallingly when their mothers visited, and it would take Anne and Dorothy several days after their departure to get the household back on an even keel. In the fervent but futile hope of integrating the evacuees into the local community, Anne had founded the Tarrford Children's Salvage Corps, comprising locals and townies. The Corps roamed the village in search of unwanted metal, paper, cardboard, and pig food. So far from the bright-eyed young patriots of Anne's imagination, the Corps had assumed the aspect of a gang of marauding bandits in which the evacuees were pre-eminent. They seemed possessed of a fiendish cunning and energy in the execution of their task. If the relevant bins were not left out they simply took what they could find, to the fury of the householders. Frank had twice to deal with the local constable on this particular issue.

' 'Allo, Mister!'

'Oy, Mr Gundry, give us a game!'

Frank raised his stick and waved it. 'I'm going for my supper! Another time!'

'Can Molly play? 'Ere Moll! Moll, good dog, over 'ere!'

Frank allowed her to go, and she gambolled over to the boys, tail waving. It was rather touching, the way their initial terror of the dog had given way to passionate devotion.

But really, *soccer*! In July, too. He frowned, and then thought: I'm turning into a pompous bastard. What the hell does it matter?

'See you later!' he called.

At about the same time that Frank was returning from the pub for his supper, Adeline was riding from Willesden to the Vale of Health on Charlie's motorbike. She'd been outside all day, drawing a group of housewives who were converting a bombsite into allotments, and she'd caught the sun. It was a pleasant feeling, riding home in the dusty, golden evening. She promised herself a bath, a walk with Brody, some supper, and perhaps an hour pottering in the garden: simple pleasures, to help her pass the time, and to sleep well.

She enjoyed her job, though if she were truthful it was more for the opportunity to meet people than for its artistic possibilities. She knew it was possible to produce good, even great work under these circumstances, but her heart wasn't in it. She did her best, because Joel had used his influence to get her the job and she didn't want to let him down.

The motorbike was her great delight. She felt as free and happy riding round London on it as she had when she'd bought her first bicycle at the Slade. The Alvis spent most of its time in the garage these days. As the war went on she became more and more convinced that she was suited to the simple life. She lived in trousers and shirts, she ate vegetables grown in her garden, she used the motorbike or walked for miles. In the winter she and Merle lit one fire, in the kitchen in the basement, and shared their evenings with perfect harmony and contentment, though real warmth, she had to admit, was one luxury she did miss. She often thought longingly of Larme des Anges, built on such a tide of optimism, and neglected for so long. An acquaintance of Peter's from Port Minerve was keeping an eye on things for them, and Philippe was in residence, and doubtless living high on the hog. She only hoped he wouldn't effect a reconciliation with his fearsome wife and move her and the rest of the family in with him. It all seemed, as the song had it, so long ago and far away, but she promised herself that their very first treat when the war was over would be to go, with Dora, and have a long, long holiday there. On cold, lonely winter nights in the blackout she'd gone further than that: she'd dreamed that they might sell up and go to live there. Was it written on tablets of stone that you could only have so much happiness and beauty and peace? Did paradise, if you found it, have to be rationed like so much else, for the good of your character? She was quite prepared to answer an emphatic 'no' to both these questions. And yet she knew the idea would remain a dream, because Charlie wouldn't be able to stand it. The place that meant freedom to her would become, after a short while, as bad as solitary confinement to him, and she knew where her happiness lay. She also sensed that her hold on that happiness was more tenuous these days. Perversely it was when he was with her that she realized most clearly how thin the thread was that linked them. When he was the other side of the world facing God knows what danger – as he had been now for over a year – he seemed more truly and wholly hers than when he was home on leave. His proximity highlighted the threadbare patches in their marriage which in his absence she did her best to ignore.

She passed the pond and went into the small churchyard at the top of East Heath Road, parking the motorbike against the green metal railings. They had only been retained on the road side, the others were long since gone to make aeroplanes. She came about once a week, just to pass the time of day with Clea. The grave was unassuming: a small square of grey stone set into the ground, with the words 'Clea. March 1940' engraved on it. Instead of a headstone she'd planted a viburnum tree, which at this time of year threw a puddle of leafy shade, and in winter was covered with pink-white flowers. Adeline left no other flowers, nor did she kneel, or pray, or weep or touch either the stone or the tree. She came as she used to go to Dora when she was tiny and sleeping in a bassinet, to look in and check that all was well, that was all. If the vicar appeared she fled, unable to bear his avuncular concern and good fellowship.

Today it was all very quiet and peaceful in the afternoon sun. There was an air of seclusion of which Adeline approved – something like a nursery, a place in which a tiny child could be free and untroubled. The city was being terrorized by rockets and buzz-bombs, but she could honestly believe that no such fiendish device would come near here. It seemed a spellbound place. A blackbird hopped across Clea's stone and gave her a bright, sidelong look.

She went back to the bike and pushed it a little way, not wanting the snarl of the engine starting up to destroy the sunlit serenity of the churchyard. Charlie had only come here once, and that, she knew, only for her sake. His attitude on that first leave after it had happened had been one of almost too philosophical acceptance. There had been the smallest hint of impatience: he'd wanted her to recover, to put it behind her, to forget. She'd been quite unable, so soon afterwards (and even now) to do any of those things, but she had tried her best to be as he wanted. They should have been so close, but it had been the start of the awkwardness between them. She blamed herself. What was it, after all, that she required of him? That he be as destroyed by grief as she had been? What purpose would that serve? And anyway, it was impossible. How could he feel the same as she had, who had carried Clea inside her for nearly nine months?

She arrived at the Nunnery, parked the motorbike at the side of the house and went in. The bath she had promised herself she postponed under the onslaught of Brody's delirious welcome. Walk first, bath later. She called to Merle that she'd be back in an hour, and set off, moving up the hill and through the trees in the direction of Kenwood House. She passed two couples sitting on a rug – very young girls with airmen in uniform. She caught the eye of one of the girls and smiled, but the girl gave her a hard stare as if she were being nosey and she quickened her pace, rebuffed. She felt keenly her isolation. Often, recently, when she'd been with a group of women in a companionable atmosphere of mutual understanding, she'd been unable to align herself with any of them. They were all so plucky and practical, or downright opportunist. None of them seemed as hamstrung by love as she undoubtedly was, so she kept uncharacteristically quiet in their company. She heard them say, the ones whose husbands and fiancés were away, that you just had to hope the men'd come back safe and sound, alive. That was the most you could hope for, a secure and settled future. But sometimes, in some secret place in the furthest recesses of her mind, Adeline found herself wondering if it might not be better if Charlie's ship were torpedoed, or if a VI landed on the Nunnery, so that the two of them might never have to face the uncertain agonies of peace.

Beyond the trees, a bus was halted at the side of the road. Its side bore the legend: '*Your* courage, *your* cheerfulness, *your* resolution WILL BRING US VICTORY.'

Not mine, she thought.

The *Cambridge* was docked for a couple of days at Alexandria, for refuelling and to give the lower deck in particular an opportunity for shore leave. The ship had seen nearly eighteen months continuous service, with no home leave during that time. They'd done a bit of patrolling up and down the east coast of Africa, which had been peaceful, had been peaceful, but putting in at places like Mombasa and Durban had afforded more enjoyment to the officers than the ratings. Endless cocktail parties, dances and receptions had been laid on for the upper-deck by the ex-patriot locals, but there'd been precious little for the rest of them to do. When there had been a dance on board the *Cambridge* at Cape Town, for which the lower-deck had to provide the band, the food and the service, not to mention a complete sprucing up of the ship from top to bottom, mutiny was in the air.

So Alexandria was a sweetener. No other port offered a more varied and plentiful supply of 'booze, bum and baccy', nor such unrivalled opportunities for debauch and corruption, especially for the younger seamen.

Charlie had availed himself of these opportunities on more than one previous occasion, but he didn't care for Alexandria. She was a bitch of a place, brightly coloured and strongly scented, gilded in the sunshine, but diseased through and through. There was no pretence here, everything was for sale, and it was pressed on you the moment the liberty boat got in. In Alexandria a mirror was held up to the side of your nature that you might prefer to forget, and you were challenged to deny it.

This burning, glittering afternoon he hung over the rail with his oppo Gus Cleary. Gus never went ashore, preferring to stay on board and supplement his income by doing other men's dhobying and mending. He had a troop of children back home in Cork whose welfare exercised him greatly. He was a nice, sentimental man. Having once heard that Charlie's wife had suffered a stillbirth he had befriended him, unable to believe that anyone could get over such a tragedy.

They'd received mail on arrival at Alexandria, so thoughts of home preoccupied them. There had been the usual sprinkling of Dear John letters, men swearing they'd never touch another woman as long as they lived, then off ashore tonight to eat their words and give themselves the granddaddy of a hangover. Adeline's letter to Charlie had been long, and funny. She had enclosed a snapshop of herself on the motorbike, and he showed this to Gus.

'By God, she's a looker,' was Gus's comment.

'Terrific bike. Brough Superior SS80.'

'You know what I mean. The missus. Don't you worry about her?'

'She knows how to ride it.'

'I mean with the men, Charlie, the men!'

Charlie smiled and reclaimed the snapshot. 'Don't give it a thought.'

'Cocky bastard.'

'She's not the sort.'

Gus shook his head. 'They're all that sort if they're lonely.'

'Not Adeline.'

'You're a lucky man then. I hope you're good to her.'

Charlie didn't reply. He was fond of Gus, but the other man's dogged niceness rattled him sometimes. What the hell did he know? The answers that he elicited from Charlie made Charlie himself feel increasingly hedged about with obligations. A lucky man? He knew that was how it looked, but he felt like a rat in a trap. The two men took a turn round the lower deck. The sea off Alexandria was pure and crystalline, all ranks were encouraged to go swimming. It was ironic, therefore, that as they strolled down the starboard side Gus put his hand to his face and grimaced.

'Jesus, the stink!'

The stench was terrible, overpowering. Charlie looked over the side.

'Poor sod,' he said.

They were berthed alongside a 'dumb light', moored in position by civilian contractors to receive all the waste from the *Cambridge*. They had inherited the lighter from another ship, so its noisome hold was already piled high with every kind of refuse thrown out by the individual messes.

'I'm off,' said Gus, who couldn't bear to look.

Charlie remained, fascinated. Over the reeking mountain of trash crawled an emaciated youth – he could have been anything from twelve to twenty – with a withered leg that dragged behind him. His job was to salvage any bottles or cans from the swill and put them in one of a couple of sawn-off oil drums that stood on the lighter's deck. His terrible creeping, insect-like progress was interrupted frequently as he came across a large enough lump of discarded food to squirrel away in a tin can for sale, or consumption, later on.

Sensing someone's eyes on him, the boy looked up towards the ship's rail and grinned hopefully, his mouth a dark gash in his wasted face. Charlie spread his open palms. He had nothing to give, and the smile was extinguished instantly. The crawling examination of the rubbish continued.

With a sort of horrified admiration, Charlie continued to watch. Perhaps that was the way to be: no pride, no expectations either of yourself or of others. Then no-one got hurt, and there was nowhere to go but up.

The *Cambridge* – old, battered and top-heavy – had survived thus far against all the odds. After the east coast at the beginning of the war she'd been part of an escort in the North Sea, sometimes going as far north as the Arctic Circle, running the gamut of the U-boats around Bear Island. The conditions had been so bad that the mess-deck was permanently awash with icy water, and they'd had to chip the ice off the gun mountings with picks. Then she'd been on the infamous Malta run, where she'd suffered some damage, but never enough to take her out of service. Men who'd hated every nut and bolt and plate of her had, over the years, conceived a grudging affection for the old tub and her ability to stay afloat.

Nonetheless, there was a feeling, as they set out from Alexandria, that they were pushing their luck. She couldn't go on for ever, and the Mediterranean was still highly dangerous.

Disaster came swiftly and sharply out of a cloudless

blue sky. Ship's company was still at defence stations, twenty-four hours out of port, when a radar report came through of enemy aircraft in the vicinity. At the same moment as the bell for Action Stations sounded, a dozen JU87s plummeted down from nowhere, catching them on the hop. Charlie, running like a rabbit towards his action station on 'B' Gun, was deafened by the scream of the aircraft and the whine and thunder of the bombs that seemed to be falling round them in a curtain. The ship was violently shaken, as though she were being worried by an enormous terrier. The Fight Director Officer was screaming like a madman as the planes came at them from every direction. Charlie was only yards from 'B' Gun when he looked over his shoulder to see Gus chasing after him, struggling with his lifejacket (which he should have been wearing all the time at sea), and beyond him a row of evenly placed water spouts rose from the surface of the sea. Charlie yelled something, already far too late, at Gus, but as he yelled the next two bombs in the sequence struck the *Cambridge* fair and square. There was a terrific double-barrelled jolt, a blinding flash of hot, white, light, and then a torrent of black smoke. Charlie was lifted off his feet and thrown violently backwards against metal casing. He struggled upright, winded and bruised and as he did so he realized that the deck was listing beneath his feet. The grand old lady was a lifelessly tilting hulk, a liability.

He was disorientated and nauseous. Shouts and screams mingled with the black smoke, figures pelted past, visible for an instant and then swallowed up again. Beneath the shouts and cries, and the snarl of the JUs could be heard a dull roar.

The smoke began to clear and he stumbled forward, leaning against the incline of the deck. Where 'B' Gun had been was now just a chaos of twisted girders and bent and shattered steel plates. A fire had taken hold in the fo'c's'l and others could be seen, leaping and flaring amid the wreckage like jack-o'-lanterns. About a third

of the ship had been shot away. They were wrecked,
and burning fast.

Charlie saw Gus lying where he had fallen, with his
legs buckled under him as though he'd been caught in
the act of praying. He ran over to him and squatted
down at his side. There was a blackened, blood-soaked
hole at the top of his chest but he wasn't dead. His eyes,
red and watering, stared up beseechingly at Charlie. He
grabbed his wrist in a tight, relentless grip,

'Don't leave me, Charlie, for Chrissake . . . !'

'I wasn't going to. Take it easy.'

A swift purposeful movement overtook them, men
running astern. The ship gave a rending groan and listed
a little further. An officer – the captain – stopped by
them and put his hand on Charlie's shoulder.

'Abandon ship, lads. Every man for himself, and good
luck. Abandon ship.'

'Yes, sir. Good luck, sir.'

The formalities had been observed, the hierarchy
maintained. What the hell next? Instinctively he glanced
upward. Above the smoke the sky was a brilliant,
smiling blue, against which the JUs circled watchfully,
like vultures.

'I'll be back,' said Charlie. 'I won't be long.'

He didn't want to try and move Gus till he knew
exactly what he was going to do and where he was
heading. There was no hope of any boats being launched;
they were completely smashed, either by blast or flying
debris. Survivors in the less badly damaged area of the
ship were throwing overboard life-rafts, floats, planks,
locker lids, any damn thing that would float. A few men
had gone below to comb the belly of the ship for trapped
and wounded men. A ladder had been thrown over the
side, but the younger and more terrified men were just
jumping for it. Near the rail was a collection of some
ten pairs of boots and shoes, stood in neat rows as if
their owners half expected to return. Once in the water
it would be up to the survivors to make their way to
one of the destroyers in their convoy by whatever means

they could. The rescue operation was always a risky business, for the enemy aircraft would keep swooping and sniping for as long as they could, and often it wasn't possible to pick men out of the sea till nightfall.

He ran back to Gus. He felt, as always, very clear-headed and purposeful. His heart raced with excitement. He could have threaded a needle with a steady hand. On the way he accosted a white-faced ordinary seaman of about twenty, who was standing, paralysed by panic and indecision.

'Hey you, I need you! Quick!'

They got back to Gus, and took an arm each. 'This is going to hurt,' he warned.

They struggled to the ladder, with Gus howling and protesting with every staggering step. The young rating looked as if he might be going to cry.

Charlie propped his two charges against the rail.

'I'll get on to the ladder, you help him on to my shoulder. Take the strain till I say!'

For about thirty seconds Gus, in agony, screamed blue murder as they manhandled him into position. Then suddenly he became a limp, uncomplaining weight, leaking blood down Charlie's back as they lurched painfully down the ladder. In the water below was an inflatable dinghy, crowded with men, but staying close to help them out. Hands reached up and eased Gus clear of Charlie's shoulder and into the dinghy which lurched and rocked violently. Already it was so overcrowded that there was scarcely any freeboard.

'Sorry, only one more!' There was an officer on board – fortuitously the ship's doctor. 'We've got two more wounded on here!'

Charlie was in the water now. The young seaman clung in an agony of fear to the bottom rungs of the ladder.

'Get this one in,' he said. 'I'll swim for it.'

'Make for the *Denby*!'

Somehow they pulled the young man into the wallowing dinghy and began paddling with lumbering slowness away from the *Cambridge*. Slowly, but still ten times faster than Charlie could go. He took a few heavy, lunging strokes and grabbed hold of a slab of wood, a table-top from one of the messes, it looked like. He pushed it ahead of him, working his legs furiously. The destroyer *Denby*, which had looked quite close from the deck, now seemed a hundred miles away. A plane ripped through the smoke and swooped low overhead. Any minute they'd bomb the *Cambridge*, to sink her.

He was already left far behind by the dinghy, and the chances of rescue for an isolated man were remote. He realized, with a peculiar detachment, that he fully expected to die. While going through all the motions of escape, he was anticipating death. There was a tremendous boom behind him and he was punched by a shockwave as the JUs began to deliver the *coup de grâce*. A fresh pall of smoke the shape of a gigantic oak tree rose above the dying ship. Beyond it the destroyers circled helplessly like a pack of animals when one of their number has been shot.

Each waves of bombs seemed terribly close, to be falling just short of his struggling, waterlogged legs. He didn't look back again but kept kicking his legs. The *Denby* crept closer, inch by inch. He could make out the dinghy, which had reached her, and the men beginning to climb up her ladder like flies on a flypaper. The sun was hot on his head and his face burned, but the rest of him was starting to be numb. He was perfectly calm. In a moment there would be an explosion, light, then darkness. No pain, just an ending.

When at last he was almost there he paused, his lungs heaving, and lay on the slab of wood for a last look at the *Cambridge*. With a thunderous growl she up-ended and began to go down. For a moment Charlie was reminded of an illustration he'd seen in *Morte d'Arthur* – the mysterious arm, holding the sword, breaking the surface of the lake, and then submerging once more . . . the sense of the water reclaiming its own.

For almost five years the comradeship of the cramped

and cheerless mess-deck had been his home, his security, his life. He'd known there both friendship and freedom, enhanced by constant shared danger. Seeing the *Cambridge* go down he felt utterly abandoned, and betrayed.

He'd have welcomed death now, but it didn't come. His body, tenacious of life, continued to struggle clumsily through the water. He reached the bottom of the ladder and began to climb. As he dragged his legs from the water his waterlogged overall trousers pulled heavily at him. He felt beaten, unable to move either backward or forward, just hanging on stiffly, hoping something might happen. People were shouting at him from far above but he couldn't make out what they were saying, let alone act upon it . . . The shouts grew more urgent, his body heavier. He let go with one hand and the ladder slapped against the side of the ship. He wanted only to drop, and be done with it. Then suddenly the ladder was shaking violently. A man came down to just above where he was and yelled at him to get a fucking move on, a large, hard hand hoisted him beneath the armpit and he was moving again, his plimsolls slipping and jerking on the rungs.

At the rail he was almost catapulted on to the deck by the urgent waiting hands. The tenor of the voices changed to one of concern and congratulations, shadows passed between his closed eyelids and the sun, a blanket was put over him. He heard his voice saying over and over again, in response to enquiries, that he was all right. He knew he should get up, move, go somewhere, do as he was told. But for a moment all he could do was lie there, eyes closed, and try to come to terms with the fact that he'd survived.

It was one of those curious, glancing, chance meetings that happened in wartime. Peter was passing through Victoria Station on his way back from Sussex, where Pru and the boys were billeted for their greater safety. Since the Army had seen fit not to send him into the teeth of the fighting he'd created a niche for himself, running the best, the cheapest and the most stylish servicemen's club in town. In retrospect, it had also been prudent to remain where he could keep an eye on Nicholas, whose buying and selling and 'supplying demand' struck Peter as sailing pretty close to the wind.

Preoccupied, and feeling harassed after the usual tedious and erratic journey, he would certainly have walked straight past the man on the bench, except that he dropped his paper, and as he stooped to pick it up he glimpsed a face he recognized.

'Charlie – ? My dear chap, I don't believe it!'

Charlie looked up and then rose rather stiffly, as if he'd he'd been asleep. Peter wrung his hand vigorously and slapped him on the shoulder. He took in in an instant the wear and tear of war – the slight tightening of the face, an older and wiser look in the eyes that was at odds with the jaunty rating's uniform. Still, seeing Charlie again after an interval of over a year and a half, Peter was forced to concede all over again that he was a handsome blighter. For Adeline's sake he was genuinely, hugely, glad to see him.

'It's been ages – far too long. What made them suddenly relent?'

'Survivors' leave. The poor old *Cambridge* finally bought it.'

'God, I'm sorry. You're all right, though?'

'You know me, I lead a charmed life.' He smiled, and it made him look ridiculously young. It was impossible not to like the fellow, in spite of everything. On his day he could charm the birds from the trees.

Peter chuckled. 'So, which way are you heading? I mean, are you going home or going back?'

Charlie hesitated before answering: 'Going home.'

'Me too. Monday to Friday I lead a bachelor existence in St John's Wood. Why don't we share a cab?'

'I would, Peter, but I've a couple of things to do in Town.'

'Fair enough. Look, keep in touch, won't you? I saw

Addy just recently, tearing about on that motorbike.
Marvellous! But then you know that.'

'Yes.'

'Bye for now then. Enjoy your leave. I'm absolutely
delighted to have seen you.'

They shook hands again and Peter continued on his
way. Just as he left the station concourse to join the
queue at the cab rank he glanced back and saw Charlie
sitting down once more on the bench, lighting a cigarette. He looked for all the world like a man killing
time.

It was the following day, another hot, settled, late summer's afternoon, that Dora opened the front door of the
Nunnery to find her stepfather on the doorstep with a
bunch of roses in his hand.

'Charlie!'

He smiled, but put his finger to his lips as he came
in. She shook her head.

'It's all right, you'll surprise her, I'm all on my own
here. Merle's got the afternoon off and Mummy's out
with Brody. Oh Charlie, she'll be so pleased, she'll *die*
when she finds you here!'

'I hope not.' He dropped his kitbag and held out his
arms. 'Give us a kiss.'

Dora kissed him carefully, putting her hands on his
shoulders to resist his hug. She was self-conscious with
him, she didn't want him to feel how much there was
of her these days. And he, as always, was so easy and
unconcerned, and his very lack of awkwardness
increased hers.

'Let's look at you,' he said. 'You get more grown up
all the time. And clever, they tell me. Much too grown
up and clever for card tricks, I suppose.'

'Not at all.' She knew she'd gone red. Whatever she
said tended to sound – inappropriate. 'Do you want to
come out in the garden till Mummy gets back?'

'Why not?'

He followed her, still carrying the roses. Outside in

the sunshine she thought her rug and her book, her cardigan rolled into a pillow, looked embarrassingly self-indulgent.

'I was just lazing about,' she explained.

'Quite right.'

'Do you mind the rug?'

'I don't even mind the grass.' He flopped down at once, his hands linked behind his head. His face was brown, but where there were lines, around his eyes and running from nose to mouth, they showed white. He squinted up at her, one eye closed against the sun. He was the only person she knew who made her wish that she was pretty. If she resumed her place on the rug she didn't know what she would say to him. She was sure she would be boring. She thought of all the girls in her class who would think him absolutely gorgeous and terribly attractive and would give their right hands to be where she was now, but the thought only made things worse.

She caught sight of the roses, lying on the grass in the sun, and snatched them up.

'I'll go and put these in water, the poor things.'

'Thank you, Dolly.'

His eyes were closed, so she breathed in the scent of the flowers. 'They are lovely.'

'Think she'll like them?'

'Oh she'll love them, of course she will.'

'Good . . .'

She left him and went back to the house and down-stairs into the kitchen. There was a small terrace outside the kitchen window, but it was below the level of the lawn, so she couldn't see him. She ran cold water into the sink and laid the roses in it, to have a good drink before putting them in a vase. As she did so she heard the front door open, and the patter of the dog's feet in the hall. She was almost sure they'd come straight down here as they practically lived in the kitchen these days. She was excited to be the bearer of good news, but also conscious of a certain anxious dread, something she always experienced in connection with her mother and Charlie. Apart from Peter they were the two people she absolutely loved most in the world, but it wasn't easy to be with them because of all the *feelings* that swirled around them. Still, she told herself, as Adeline came down the stairs to the kitchen, she would probably grow out of all these worries.

Adeline came in. Dora knew that some people thought her mother beautiful, and others thought her peculiar. She herself thought that Adeline changed from day to day. This was one of her good ones. With her black hair and her brown skin and her bold piratical face it was hard to imagine any other woman, however lovely and elegant, who wouldn't have appeared simply wan beside her.

'Glorious day!' she exclaimed. She embraced Dora. 'But the roses – who from?'

'Guess,' said Dora.

'Daddy's been here.'

'No. Guess again.'

'I can't. My brain doesn't work.'

'Charlie, Mummy. He's out in the garden.'

Dora listened with a mixture of indulgence and envy as Adeline raced up the stairs again. She filled Brody's water dish and put it down for him. He lapped noisily. She was glad of his ordinary, thirsty, unemotional presence. Looking up, she caught sight of herself in the glass front of the crockery cupboard – a sensible, rounded girl standing in the kitchen, coping with things. Her phlegmatic appearance did not accord with her feelings. She took off her glasses and cleaned them vigorously on her skirt.

She did not go out straight away, not for reasons of discretion but because she did not want to expose herself to their reunion. When she did open the garden door she rattled the handle a good deal to advertise her arrival. But they were way down at the end of the garden with their backs to her. Charlie's hand rested on the nape of Adeline's neck, beneath her hair. Dora knew exactly how that must feel. She did hope that some day a man would touch her in exactly that way. Anxious that they should know she was there, she called:

'I say, would anyone like some tea?'

It was Charlie who turned first, with a big grin. 'Dolly! Are you offering? You're a saint.'

'I know.'

'Need a hand?'

'No thanks,' she said rather curtly. 'Any fool can put a kettle on.'

Just the same, he began strolling back down the lawn towards her, and Adeline remained where she was for a moment before following. Her face shone with that awful naked vulnerability of what Dora supposed was love.

CHAPTER TWENTY-SIX

1950–1951

ADELINE'S ATTITUDE TOWARDS cards hadn't changed. She was still bored and disturbed by them, the more so as Charlie's enthusiasm for gambling had increased. The exclusivity that emanated from any group of people sitting round a card table infuriated her, and she had long ago decided that the best means of combating it was to absent herself altogether from the proceedings.

On Larme des Anges this presented little difficulty. The atmosphere of excitable preoccupation in the drawing room of Outlook Point offered no competition to the scented, moonlit darkness outside. She left the house, and walked around the corner to escape its light. At once the night embraced and befriended her, she was included in its gentle celebration of ordinary daytime things.

The gardens of Peter's house, now that they had matured, were spacious and elegant and full of diversions for the Marchants' numerous house guests. In this they contrasted sharply with the environs of the Dragon House, which Adeline had steadfastly refused to prune, trim, 'modernize' or 'improve'. A tract of land that had exerted a powerful fascination over her was what she had chosen, and that was how she wished it to remain. This not changing things had taken on the importance of a sacred trust to Adeline, now that each time she came back here the island seemed smaller, besieged by progress. During the war, and in the years since, Larme des Anges had ceased to be an isolated paradise. The old fort where Adeline and Charlie had picknicked among the flowers was now a spruce, up-to-date American weather station. The bumpy track which had led from the harbour at Angeville to the fort was a glossy black tarmac road, the grassy rock-strewn slope before the walls had been levelled out and turned into an immaculate gravel sweep where sleek black Cadillacs basked in the sun. The windows of the fort were glazed, the battlements were freshly rendered and white-washed and from the central tower a radio mast prodded the sky alongside the sparkling red, white and blue of the Stars and Stripes.

To Peter's satisfaction, and Adeline's horror, the Americans had built a causeway linking Larme des Anges to St Minerve. Of course it was far more convenient – commissions of every sort could now be accomplished with no difficulty whatsoever – but the advantages were two-way. Adeline was not a despiser of her fellow man but for so long the Dragon House had existed as a sanctuary, and now it shocked her to see the cars and lorries plying back and forth on the causeway, breaching her precious barrier of seclusion.

The house itself, thanks to Philippe's conscientious ministrations, had survived her long absence well. It had remained dry, and basic maintenance had been carried out to its fabric. Since the war had ended she and Charlie had been out as often as possible, in the school holidays. This was the place where she breathed more freely, knowing that here there would not be the long, anxious periods of waiting, the uncertainty and dread exhaustingly concealed, which increasingly marked their life in London. Though Charlie liked to cross the causeway to the

Colonial Club, and to various rackety, disreputable establishments down by the docks, all she wished to do was to live the life of a beachcomber.

She knew he was wretched, much of the time. God knows, he took little pains to conceal it. She also realized that he was testing her, almost, but not quite, beyond endurance. She knew that if she once failed the test and lost control, their problems would become all her fault, and he would have the pretext he sought to abandon their marriage. Staunchly, she resisted. She held out. She would not ask where he went, or enquire what he did. She forebore to mention the steady erosion of their finances. She continued to tell him that she loved him, which was, surprisingly, still true. Because carefulness and pretence did not come naturally to her, she placed herself under considerable strain. She was still doing some painting, but she had little heart or energy for it, and Charlie's salary from Heath Court was not large. The Nunnery was a big house, expensive to run, and they neither of them possessed the habit of thrift. Charlie had told her with a kind of bitter defiance that he was unlikely now to be elevated beyond his present status. He was forty next birthday, no longer a young man. The comfortable niche he'd found for himself after leaving university, and of which he'd boasted to her so long ago at the Villa Clemency, had become first a rut, then a trap from which there was no escape. The job for which he'd evinced a fortuitous aptitude had left him neither suited nor qualified for anything else. He'd been reprimanded twice by the headmaster, the second time in writing, for 'sliding standards' of dress, of punctuality, of behaviour and of teaching. At the same time there had been expressions of appreciation for his talents and his good relations with the boys. The clear implication was that it would be sad and regrettable if Heath Court had to let him go, but that they would not hesitate to do so if necessary.

Adeline might have borne this more easily had she not been able to see all too clearly what was happening. She knew very well that others, notably Frank, considered that she was being a doormat. He'd actually said as much, claiming that it was his duty and responsibility to prevent her from ruining her life any further. In response she had simply smiled and pointed out that she and Charlie had been married now for nearly thirteen years when no-one had thought they'd last for one, so they were not doing badly, and that whatever *modus vivendi* they had worked out for themselves was no business of anyone else's.

Of course that was the truth, but not the whole truth. Their *modus vivendi* suited neither of them. When she forced herself to compare it to the comfortable, happy existence she had enjoyed with Peter, from which she had so simply and ruthlessly extricated herself, she saw just how desolate it was. And yet she was powerless to change it, for one very good reason. She loved Charlie deeply, completely and helplessly, with a love that still retained the inexplicable ecstasy of its beginnings. Like a magnet Charlie drew all the different kinds of love she had ever felt – the protectiveness of the mother, the unquestioning adoration of the daughter, the passion of the lover and the loyalty of the wife. He completed her. And curiously she never doubted his love for her. When they were alone, their door locked and bolted against the world with its temptations, its threats and its good advice, she knew that he cared for her, and that if only they could stay close they could make it.

She did not concern herself about the possibility of other women. If they existed she did not wish to know about them, and she believed, without vanity, that what he felt for her was the most he was capable of feeling. She had the best of Charlie emotionally, and must make the best of it. No, it was his restlessness and boredom which were the enemy. His stupid gambling, which drove her to the very edge of her patience, was only an attempt to inject an element of risk into an existence which he found intolerably predictable. The blue painting she had given him had already gone. Having hocked it he'd asked her, sheepishly, like a small boy, if she minded. She'd replied that it had been a present and was his to do with as he liked – if selling it had helped get him out of a tight spot then it had served its purpose. She was never angry or hurt.

An additional aggravation to Charlie's gaming was the involvement of Nicholas Eyre. No-one as rich and smart as Nicholas could properly have been called a spiv, but Adeline knew, like everyone else, that there was no material difference between him and the men selling nylons, sheets and make-up out of suitcases in the West End. Nicholas had grown fat off the war and Peter, in his easy-going way, had turned a blind eye to it. They had gone their separate ways in the end. While Peter had opened the doors of the Cabin and the Pandora to service-men of every nationality, laying on shows and plays and investing his own money to keep prices low, Nicholas had made Renaldo's and the Fulbourne famous – or infamous, depending on your point of view – for maintaining a stan-dard and ambience that were strictly non-wartime. What you couldn't get at Nick's places wasn't worth worrying about. Adeline had been to the Fulbourne with Charlie when he'd been back on his survivors' leave, in '44, and she'd hated it. Hated the smirking, soignée women and the loud, confident men; hated the drinks, food and music that seemed cynically to mock the making-do and mend-ing that was the order of most people's day.

Still, she could have ignored this, or had nothing to do with it. It was a couple of years after the war that Nicholas had begun to hold gambling parties. He presented them as the last word in civilized entertainment, and to begin with that was what they seemed to be. Eight or ten couples would be invited to a dinner party, and treated to one of Fenella's most faultlessly planned and exquisitely executed meals. The company would be tolerable, and even richer than the food. And yet there was an emptiness at the centre of it all which Adeline attributed to the Eyres' strange marriage of mutual tolerance. She would sit there, drink-ing too much but failing to get drunk, and watch Charlie winning hearts. In this stuffy company he shone, he seemed boyishly friendly and charming, warm, humorous and altogether delightful. The wealthy, hard-boiled men

guffawed obligingly at his jokes, and hearty young heir-
esses in frumpy dresses and fabulous jewels simpered and
blushed. Adeline was proud of his success, she liked him
to be the person to whom others were irresistibly drawn,
she even enjoyed the sidelong glances and covert observations which marked them out as a curious and slightly
exotic couple.

It was after dinner, when a game or two of something
would be proposed, that the evening became intolerable.
The game was usually 'chemmy' – chemin-de-fer – and
though it was chiefly the men who accepted the invitation
there were usually one or two of the older women who
would join them at the table. The younger girls, attracted
to what they believed to be the glamour of gambling,
would cluster round, giggling and admiring. Later, when
one or two of them were slightly drunk, they would attach
themselves, like self-appointed mascots, to whoever happened to be winning at the time. By the end of the first
hour the atmosphere round the table would have changed.
The conversation grew thinner, the smoke thicker, the
most distinctive presence in the room became the game
itself. Of all those present it was Nicholas, the instigator
and the bank, who remained the most cool and unconcerned, furnishing drinks, chatting to the tipsy girls and
generally giving the impression that the whole thing was
a homely diversion with little at stake. Which may have
been true for him, for although considerable sums changed
hands it was the bank that stood to gain most in chemmy,
and to gain more the longer the game continued.

Adeline never stayed to watch. She would leave them
to it, retiring to the drawing room with Fenella and the
other non-participants. Occasionally, as they talked, a
groan of despair or a roar of excitement would float
through to them. They always ignored it.

To begin with she had always hung on until about two
am and then indicated to Charlie that it was time to go.
Half an hour after her signal he'd leave the table, to the
accompaniment of a good deal of ponderous ribbing from
the other men, and they'd go home together. The first

alteration in this pattern was on the evening he looked up and said: 'I'll hang on for a bit, darling, if that's okay. You carry on – I won't be long.' She'd seen him again the following morning, bleary-eyed and unshaven.

It had seemed neither profitable nor prudent to ask whether he had won or lost, and she did not do so.

From here it was only a short step to leaving alone every time, and without reference to Charlie. The gambling parties ceased to pretend to be anything else. She attended less and less frequently, and then only to see Fenella who loyally disdained to make any comment on the proceedings.

Soon Adeline gave up going to the parties altogether, while Charlie became a regular, whose attendance required no invitation. Concerning his fortunes at the chemmy table she still did not enquire. She did not assume that the ebb and flow would be very great, since Charlie did not have large sums to play with. Despite the removal of the blue painting she was confident he would never gamble with anything that was not specifically his own, and he had so few possessions. She had never met anyone less acquisitive. To her knowledge the only things of any value that he had ever bought were his beloved motorbike, and the white opal pendant which she wore always. On a material level he was the same carefree fellow whom she'd first found asleep in the sun, and who'd been quite happy to lose his last fifty-franc note.

Adeline sat down on the wooden seat next to the tennis court. The flat, empty surface of the court beyond the blur of wire was soothing. It was restful to be in this deserted place which was usually noisy with some hilarious game in progress, and where a large group of bibulous spectators invariably barracked from the sidelines.

From the house came a burst of laughter. They were happy. She and Charlie were safe here. She sat quietly. She had brought no drink with her, and no cigarette. The warm, clear moonlight lapped against her. She thought of the Dragon House and knew that no matter how late they got back tonight she would walk down through the trees and across the singing sand to the water's edge.

She heard voices, quieter and closer, and footsteps. There were Dora and Miles, walking across the lawn on the far side of the court, thinking themselves alone. There was nothing in the least amorous in their manner. They were not holding hands. In fact Dora's gesticulated enthusiastically as she talked, and Miles's were thrust into his pockets as he listened, head inclined, to what she was saying. Adeline knew that their voices were lowered not for secrecy, but privacy. She wondered if she should cough, or call to them, just to let them know that she was there, but since she couldn't hear what they were saying there seemed no point.

It had been so touching, so interesting, the growth of this relationship. They were such a serious young couple. Not a hint of frivolity attached to their liaison. While they'd all been here this Christmas, Dora had been off over to Outlook Point almost every day, but it was more rare for Miles to return the compliment. Adeline couldn't understand this, and she knew that Charlie was hurt by it. She could only conclude that Miles, who was shy, was embarrassed by the two of them.

One way and another, Miles was a study. He had never been as academically bright as Dora. Charlie's coaching had got him into public school, but could do no more, and once there he had failed to distinguish himself in any field. But this had not prevented him going out, innocent of qualifications, and securing himself a job as ASM with a provincial rep near Oxford. With the Pavilion Players he was blissfully happy. It didn't take a psychologist to see that among the would-bes and has-beens of the small theatre, cushioned by their extravagant and spurious warmth, their 'darlings' and 'sweeties', their ready and meaningless demonstrations of affection, Miles was enjoying the sort of indulged childhood he had never had. What was more, he was displaying, to Adeline's amusement and in the face of his father's caustic disapproval, a certain mild tenacity. When Nicholas expressed dismay at

the turn events had taken, Miles simply smiled and refused
either to retaliate, or to alter his chosen course.

He was full of surprises, for now quite suddenly and
without preamble he put his arms around Dora and kissed
her firmly – one might almost have said briskly – on the
lips. Adeline caught her breath, in sympathy with her
daughter. For an anxious moment she thought that Dora
might be about to resist, to make some objection, or push
him away, she could be so *crushing*. But no, her arms went
round his neck and the kiss, undergoing a sea change,
became less workmanlike and more leisurely. Adeline
released her breath. She was relieved and gratified to see
that it was a practised kiss. She sat perfectly still until it was
finished, and Dora and Miles went on their way, down in
the direction of the sea.

About ten minutes later Adeline returned to the house.
The game of poker was still in progress. Peter and Charlie
were playing with Hugh Campbell, the Marchants' friend
from Port Minerve. Around the fireplace where burned
a pretty, but unnecessary, driftwood fire, were gathered
Fenella, Pru and Isobel Campbell, Hugh's wife. The thir-
teen-year-old Marchant twins, Adrian and Mark, were
sitting out on the verandah in their pyjamas, reading. At
least, they had books with them, but Adeline knew they
were doing what Frank would have called 'keeping all
fronts under observation'. She didn't doubt she had not
been the only one to watch with interest as Miles and Dora
kissed. They were nice, solid, fair-haired boys, young for
their age, and allowed to do pretty much as they liked at
Outlook Point, particularly at Christmas.

'Hallo, boys,' she said. 'Still up?'

'Yes, we are,' replied Adrian, in the kindly tone of one
obliged to answer an incredibly stupid and obvious question.

'I'm sure it's high time you were in bed,' said Nicholas,
appearing from just inside the french windows. The boys
returned, unperturbed, to their books and Nicholas turned
to Adeline. 'Been for a stroll?'

'Oh, just sitting . . . the night's so lovely.'

'Yes.' He made it sound like 'no'. 'I prefer a more – occupied landscape myself.'

'I know you do.' As always Adeline had to make a conscious effort not to be provoked by him. 'So does Charlie. I love it here, but I always get the feeling he's waiting for whatever-it-is to happen.'

'Mm . . . and now,' said Nicholas, 'I suppose you are come to take him home.' Always, if only by implication, he characterized her as the bossy, managing wife. The injustice of it riled her.

'I don't take him, as you put it, anywhere. But, yes, we must go quite soon.'

'Ah . . .' He lifted and lowered his head in a slow nod. He never pursued arguments beyond the opening sortie, he wouldn't give her the satisfaction. Adeline suspected that her relationship with Nicholas Eyre would be radically improved by a good fight, but fights – in which, after all, real feelings would be involved – were not his style. She sometimes wondered how Fenella, so fragile and faun-like, and Nicholas, so cold, had managed to produce Miles at all.

She caught Charlie's eye and he raised his hand to tell her to hang on for a moment, he'd be with her presently. To escape from Nicholas she went over to sit on the arm of the sofa next to Pru.

'Pru – are you sure it's all right if Dora stays tonight?'

'Of course! You know we love having her, and they're so sweet together, aren't they Fenella?'

Fenella obliged with a faint smile. Nicholas had come to stand behind her. Hateful and unworthy thoughts crossed Adeline's mind: that the two of them had finally found something they agreed on, the unsuitability of their son's attachment to Dora.

Charlie pushed his chair back from the table and came over to them, yawning and stretching. His hair was untidy, he carried his jacket over one shoulder. Isobel cast him a glowing smile; she was hopelessly charmed by him.

'Oh, you're not *going*?'

She held out her hand in a vague, graceful gesture of constraint, and Charlie took it and handed it gently back to her lap as if it were a bird, or a kitten.

'We must, we must.' He looked at Adeline. 'Must we?'

'Yes.'

'Where's Dora?'

'She's staying.'

'Ah. Good.'

Peter and Hugh joined them, they said their farewells and their thanks, plans for the following day were discussed. The boys came in from the verandah and sat perched on the back of the sofa like monkeys on a branch. The Outlook Point party were going on a maroon next day, taking the motor launch right round St Minerve to one of the beaches north of the volcano, but Adeline and Charlie were not going. Everyone said how very sorry they were about this, and wouldn't they change their minds? But Adeline would not, and carefully avoided Charlie's eye.

As they climbed into the truck with Adeline behind the wheel for the drive back, Dora and Miles reappeared and came over to say goodbye.

'Been skinny-dipping?' asked Charlie.

'Certainly not,' said Dora.

'Just walking by the sea,' explained Miles. He smiled his shy, sidelong smile and rubbed assiduously at some invisible mark on the bonnet of the truck. Though not especially tall, he was a gangling young man, whose wrists and ankles seemed always to protrude from his clothes. Adeline liked him enormously.

'Goodnight my dears.' She kissed them both. 'Going on the picnic tomorrow?'

'We might,' said Dora. 'And then again we might not. One has to feel extremely enthusiastic about those outings. 'Night, Charlie.'

'Night Dolly, sleep tight.'

'Don't call her that, she hates it,' said Adeline automatically.

'I am here, you know Mummy.'

'I'm sorry. I am becoming an officious elderly parent.'

'Oh no . . . you could never be that,' said Miles.

As they drove off, Charlie chuckled and kissed her cheek. 'Fishing for compliments again.'

'Who, me?'

'You know he thinks you're the cat's pyjamas. I reckon he'd marry Dolly just in order to be your son-in-law.'

'Tosh. Anyway, you mustn't keep calling her Dolly, now that she's put away childish things.'

'She needs teasing a bit. She's so serious, your daughter.'

'There's nothing wrong in that.'

'I didn't say there was.' He kissed her again, this time more purposefully, and the truck made a small detour over the grass verge. 'I'm glad *you*'re not too serious,' he added.

'For heaven's sake – ' Adeline frowned and smiled. That sweeping generalization was typical of him, and it infuriated and disarmed her simultaneously. It obliged her to go along with his picture of her, the picture that suited him at any given moment. To take issue with him would have been simply too arduous and complicated, she had no stomach for the fight.

When they got back, and had parked the truck, she said: 'I'm going down to the beach.'

'Private party, or can anyone come?'

'Anyone.'

They went down the narrow path which hadn't changed since the day they first discovered it, and emerged on to the grey-white dunes. The air and water were so still tonight that the dragon made scarcely a sound, only the faintest ringing note like the reverberation of a tuning fork.

'Oh how I love this place . . .' Adeline sat down, halfway between the dunes and the sea, her chin resting on her knees. 'I love it.'

'I know you do.' He went and stood some way in front of her. He'd picked up a stick, and now he began to break pieces off and throw them into the water. His restlessness

plucked at her desire for peace, as a child tugs on the sleeve
of a preoccupied adult.

'What about me?' he asked.

'What about you . . .?'

'Still love me?'

'Yes. Of course. What do you mean, "still"?'

He was silent. Wearily she got to her feet and went to
him, putting her arms about his waist and laying her cheek
against his back.

'Charlie . . . darling. I don't know why you say these
things.'

'I'm a bastard.'

'I've always known.' She made a joke of it.

'I'm serious.'

'Yes, but I'm not, remember?'

He hurled what remained of the stick into the water,
and the movement jerked her head back. He began to walk
along the sand towards the rock arch, his hands in his
pockets, and she walked beside him, keeping pace.

'This is silly,' she said. 'I don't want to have this ridiculous conversation. I love you. Take it or leave it.'

He turned his head away from her, as if he were saying
something to himself which she was not intended to hear.
She wished she could pinpoint when his mood had
changed from one of sprightly good humour to this
exhausting, demanding petulance. This was the sort of
sulkiness she'd have found unconscionably tiresome in
anyone else. But with Charlie she was always careful.

'Charlie . . .?' Now it was she who pulled at his sleeve.
'Please. Don't be like this.'

Suddenly, he stopped walking and turned towards her.
Relief washed through her, weakening her. She had said
and done the right things, and her reward was his smile.

'I'm sorry, Addy. Really.'

'What for?'

He kissed her and she thought: I am fifty years old and
I have learned nothing. Thank God.

Events over the first few months of 1951 would have been

enough to demoralize the sturdiest and most emotionally secure of women, let alone one like Adeline who was engaged in a day-to-day struggle to maintain an even keel. Towards the end of her life, when she looked back on these months she wondered if they might be categorized as a period of natural disaster, an act of God, arbitrary and devastating and yet necessary to provoke a cataclysmic change. Perhaps a crisis had been necessary to resolve an untenable state of affairs.

To begin with, Charlie was summarily sacked from Heath Court. He was out all that Friday night, and when he came back next morning Adeline was up in her studio, putting the finishing touches to the managing director of a tinned-food company. She knew better now than to go to the head of the stairs and greet him. After the front door was closed she heard his sluggish footsteps wandering down the stairs to the kitchen for coffee . . . returning to the drawing room. He'd lie there on the sofa, she knew, sipping his coffee, looking and feeling terrible, trying to rally his forces and subdue his guilt until he was ready to face her. She made a wry little face as she reflected that he probably didn't realize how strong was her instinct to rush and comfort him, to tell him it didn't matter. The game had become the reality.

About half an hour later he emerged and came heavily and haltingly up the stairs to the first floor. Here he called up to her, tentatively.

'Addy . . .?'

'I hear you callin' Lord.'

'I'm back.'

'So I gather. How are you?'

'Bloody awful.'

'Come up and see me, why don't you?'

'In a tick.'

Taps ran, the lavatory was flushed, she heard him in their bedroom, changing his clothes. Then he came up the last flight of stairs and appeared in the doorway, shivering and clasping himself.

'Christ it's cold in here.'

'I don't notice it. It's because you're tired, and you've got a hangover.'

'Maybe.'

She continued to paint. He didn't come near her but prowled about the edges of the room, sometimes behind her, sometimes in her peripheral vision. The clear, oblique February light was unkind: he looked terrible.

He came to stand just behind her right shoulder and leaned forward as if scrutinising this dull portrait in which he could have no possible interest.

'Well,' he said, 'I'm out of a job.'

It was a relief, almost, to hear it said, to have come to the crunch. She laid down her brush, carefully, waiting to tune her reaction to his.

'Oh, Charlie – why?'

'I finally said my piece to that bastard.'

'Lyall.'

'That *fucking* bastard!' he yelled, and drummed both fists against his forehead.

She took his wrists and held his hands against her. His face was contorted with anger and shame.

'To hell with Lyall,' she said. Lyall was the new, young headmaster at Heath Court, the same age as Charlie himself. A brilliant, able man who was going places in his profession. Charlie had ignored the warnings at his peril. The best, the only, present she could give him now was some remnant of dignity, however spurious.

She said: 'Don't worry, you'll find something else. It's their loss. You're so gifted – the boys worship you.'

'The boys!' He wrenched away from her and went and leaned his head against the wall. 'But he told me I was a bad influence on the boys. Unpunctual, disorganized, I don't maintain discipline or inspire respect, they're not learning anything in my classes, apparently. Apparently I've become a figure of fun.'

'Did he say that? In so many words?'

'He implied it.'

'It's unforgivable!'

'So I have my marching orders. Half term, and that's it.'

She heard the venom in his voice and knew that she didn't care about the job, or about Lyall, or even about Charlie's humiliation. She simply did not want this conversation to turn into something else, and to find her self trapped.

She went and stroked and comforted him and they went and climbed into bed, not making love but simply lying close together, hidden from the world.

They pretended to put it behind them. They even behaved as if they had. Charlie obtained another job, at the church primary school which Dora had attended. He was one of only two men on a staff of twelve, and the other was so old and infirm as scarcely to count. Charlie joked about it, but Adeline knew he was unhappy and rebellious, and could not imagine that it would last. At least twice a week he was out all night at gaming parties run by Nicholas, or one of his crowd. She was witnessing his self-destruction but had systematically robbed herself of the weapons with which she might have fought it.

Sadly, Brody had to be put to sleep. On one of his habitual wanderings he picked up a thorn in his ear which developed overnight into a huge abscess that affected his sight, hearing and balance. He was nearly crazed with pain, and bit Charlie when he tried to get near him. When she'd got Brody to the vet the infection had spread inward, and there was no hope of operating successfully. She'd taken the decision and left him there, gone home and burnt his rug and his slipper, put away his food and water dishes, thrown his basket in the cupboard under the stairs, made the weeping Merle a cup of tea.

In late March, Merle was taken very ill. A heavy cold turned into acute bronchitis and she had to be in hospital for two weeks. When she did finally return it was on the strict understanding that she did no work for a month, and was then led back into it very gently. During Merle's convalescence Adeline hired a daily cleaning woman, but she became more and more convinced that the Nunnery was becoming impractical, a drain on their resources and a millstone round their necks.

Finances were a continuing problem. They were beginning to live off what capital she had accumulated in palmier days. Even this, she realized ruefully, had only been saved on Peter's advice, and now she was simply not doing enough work, nor was Charlie bringing enough in to redress the balance. She had a sense of the structure, the framework of her life breaking down and floating away, beyond her control. There was no point in trying to discuss her fears with Charlie. The only money he understood was that which actually jingled in his pocket – or a mere number, a meaningless collection of words spoken over playing cards. For money as a fact and condition of everyday life he cared not a jot, and he laughed at her anxiety.

'Come on, Addy, stop behaving like a shopkeeper! Look at us, we're not exactly church mice.'

'Exactly. I think we ought to adapt to circumstances at bit more.'

'A retrograde step, Never say die!'

She knew this was nonsense, and tried to economize. The black Jaguar which had succeeded her beloved Alvis was now itself replace by a humble bull-nosed Morris. She frantically sought commissions and churned out a series of workmanlike, mediocre portraits destined to hang in offices and on stairs, and in echoing hallways where people waited.

Then she lost her opal necklace. It wasn't by any means the first time the chain had broken, but in the past she'd always found the stone, confounding the theory that opals were bad luck. This time her exhaustive and continued searches produced no result, and she was heartbroken. She experienced the loss in a physical way, her hand would go instinctively to her throat to touch the necklace and she would experience a shock to find it gone. She hated to think of it, the symbol of their love, lying in some dark corner, forgotten and broken.

Charlie was altogether more philosophical. 'Don't upset yourself so, darling,' he said, 'it was never that special. Cheer up, one of these days I'll buy you another one.'

She couldn't decide whether he didn't understand, or whether he understood all too well and was consequently disconcerted by her reaction. She stopped mentioning the lost opal, but continued to hope against hope that she would find it.

Besides, she knew her problems to be trivial compared to those faced by others. Joel had finally conceded the futility of trying, singlehanded, to contain and absorb Duncan's drinking habits, and Duncan had been sent to dry out in an exquisite converted manor house in Hertfordshire, near Ayot St Lawrence. It was costing Joel a packet, but as he explained to Adeline and Charlie when they went to visit, only the best would do.

'It's bad enough for him having to go through all this. Since we have the cash he may as well do it in comfort.'

They walked across a large, light, elegantly furnished lounge, then through glass doors, beyond which the garden glistened in spring sunlight, lit by drifts of snowdrops and early daffodils. In the lounge and conservatory dazed and exhausted-looking people sat about with their hands in their laps, as if trying to reconcile themselves to the shock of unclouded reality.

As they emerged on to the lawn, Charlie asked: 'Will he ever want to go home? That's the thing.'

Joel looked slightly reproving. 'Oh yes. He's desperately homesick.'

They walked across the lawn and down to an artificial lake bordered by a path. At once they saw Duncan, sitting on a green bench in his curiously inappropriate dark, fur-collared overcoat, feeding bread to a group of cacophanous mallards. Joel laid a restraining hand on their shoulders.

'One moment . . . I'll just go and tell him you're here.'

They watched as Joel approached Duncan and bent to speak to him, gesturing in their direction. At once Duncan stood up, mallards scattering and quacking, crusts raining to the ground, and flung his arms in the air.

'Advance, friends, and be recognized.'

It was curious to see the change in him. For one thing he was thinner and paler, he had aged. The unhealthy high colour and febrile exuberance which had been so typical of him were now gone; the expression 'drying out' seemed exactly to describe what he had undergone. He looked wrung out, sucked dry of the juices which had both sustained and been destroying him.

Just the same, he was overjoyed to see them.

'Addy . . .! Charlie . . .! How dear of you to come and visit the old dipso in captivity!'

'Don't say that,' said Joel, sharply.

'I was being friendly, Jo!'

'You know very well what I mean.'

Duncan kissed them both extravagantly. 'You're a tonic, the pair of you, a sight for sore eyes, and they don't come much sorer than mine. Shall we take a turn?'

As they walked, they split naturally into two pairs, with Joel and Charlie moving more briskly in front and Adeline and Duncan walking slowly, arm in arm, behind them. In spite of the sunshine a nippy, bustling breeze wrinkled the surface of the water. The ducks sculled alongside them for a while, hoping for more bread.

'Do you feel better?' Adeline asked.

'No. If you want to know I feel worse. I feel atrocious. Palsied. Stinking bloody awful.'

'I wish you wouldn't beat about the bush so, Duncan!'

'I'm sorry. I dare say I'm infinitely healthier, but I feel wrecked. Wrecked and chastened.'

'I suppose it's all part of the process. Are you going to be able to keep it up?'

He sighed a deep, wavering sigh. 'I shall have to try, shan't I? I've terrorized poor Jo and embarrassed the rest of you for long enough, and all this – ' He waved an arm at his surroundings – 'is costing a king's ransom. Jo's a saint, don't think I don't appreciate the fact. A saint for putting up with me the way he has.'

She was touched. They were such old, dear friends, and misfits that they were they accepted her and Charlie lock stock and barrel. She was grateful to them.

She said. 'He's not a saint, Duncan. Far from it. He's better than that. He does what he does for you because he loves you and cares about you. He complains like the very devil sometimes, but he reckons it's worth it.'

Duncan's eyes filled with easy tears. 'I don't deserve him.' He dashed at his eyes with his coatsleeve.

'You don't have to deserve it,' said Adeline. She realized as she spoke how ironic were her words. 'Love's not a reward. It's a fact.'

The wedding of Dora and Miles in May stood out like a good deed in a naughty world from the depressing events that preceded it. It didn't much matter that it rained, or that Nicholas was sour-faced, or that Elizabeth was cranky and domineering – the young couple were happy enough in each other. Where blessings and congratulations were forthcoming they accepted them gratefully, but they didn't actually need them. Adeline was full of admiration for them and their quiet, unassuming strength.

Nevertheless, a whole day of family, friends and relations, with all the accompanying shoals and cross-currents, left her exhausted. Elizabeth, Frank and Anne, and Bob and Louise, all spent the night at the Nunnery and it was three in the morning before she and Charlie crawled into bed. She found, suddenly, that she was tearful. Everything had gone well, she had no regrets or misgivings, and yet she was left with the irrefutable fact that Dora was no longer primarily her daughter, but Miles's wife. No matter how happy Dora was, no matter how sensible and confident, there were bound to be difficult times, times when *she* would lie in the dark and cry, and feel alone, and not know where to turn. Adeline hoped that Dora would turn to her, but feared that she would not. For what kind of example had she presented? One of chaos and turmoil and instability. Perhaps her daughter, in trying to be as unlike her as possible, would settle for second best, would put up with too much in the interests of constancy.

'I'm sorry,' she wept into Charlie's warm shoulder. 'I'm behaving like the mother of the bride.'

'You are the mother of the bride.'

'I do so wish I'd been a better parent.'

'You've been you. She'll never forget that.'

'That's what I'm afraid of!'

'Come on Addy . . . Addy! This isn't like you.'

'I don't know what is like me, that's the trouble.'

'Calm down. It's been a lovely day. You've been marvellous.'

She raised her face and kissed him. 'So have you.'

'Me? I just let it happen round me.'

'No, you did more than that. You were very sweet to everyone, and it can't have been easy. When I see everyone together like that I see just what a pig's ear I've made of my life.'

He shook with laughter. 'I'm trying to work out whether that's meant to be a compliment.'

'Oh yes, it is. I love you so much . . .'

He rocked her gently against him and stroked her hair. With all his many weaknesses he had always had the ability to comfort her. Soon she slipped into sleep, trying not to think how long it had been since he had told her he loved her.

Charlie knew, almost to the day. His breaking, one by one, of the threads which tied him, was steady and deliberate. And as the summer of 1951 dragged on he knew that soon they would all be severed and he would stand free, and be able to walk away. He dreaded the doing of it, he longed for it to be over. He had no wish to see Adeline, whom he loved, unhappy, and yet the responsibility for her happiness was one he could no longer bear. Her extraordinary tolerance, her capacity to sustain and absorb injury, were a source of wonder and fascination to him. Sometimes, very occasionally, they had caused him to question his own behaviour, but in the end the urge to escape was more powerful than the pangs of conscience.

At eight o'clock one Saturday morning in early July, he sat on a small, hard chair in a café opposite the bus terminus at South End Green. There was a large black coffee on the table in front of him, and he'd propped his newspaper against the brown china salt and pepper set. He was so tired that he felt brittle, as though if someone were to brush against him he might simply crumble into a small heap of dry fragments.

He tried wearily and ineffectually, to confront the implications of what had just happened to him. He had lost. Lost seriously and spectacularly. At a house in Mayfair he had handed over a meaningless IOU to a genial young man in evening dress, whose name he could not even remember. It had all been exquisitely gentlemanly, he knew it could be months before the matter was mentioned again. Still, it represented a watershed, an ultimatum. His ability to pay, no matter how late, would be scrutinized: it was a test he had to pass if he wished to remain *persona grata* at the tables he frequented at present. He had never owed so much before, and thanks to Adeline's forbearance their joint resources had always been sufficient to see him right. The blue painting and the opal had seen him out of a couple of other tight corners. There had been a certain aptness in the opal returning whence it came: the chain had broken and he'd found it in the hall when he came in the small hours one morning. It had presented itself to him and he's accepted it gratefully. It had been not stealing, but justifiable opportunism. This time he didn't know what he'd do.

He sipped his coffee and felt the bitter, black liquid flow revivingly down his gullet, the only real sensation he could manage. On the other side of the road a tramp emerged from the underground gent's lavatory by the bus shelter. He paused at the top of the steps, mumbling and gesturing, his head and shoulders questing this way and that as though trying to pick up some scent, the scent which would lead him to his destination. He appeared to make a

decision and took a few headlong, shambling steps to the
south – dreaming, perhaps, like Dick Whittington, of a
West End paved with gold? – but the impetus wasn't sustained and he slumped down on a bench, his chin on his
chest, his hands hanging limply between his legs. A man
sweeping the pavement swept round him as though he
were an inanimate object. Charlie identified with the
tramp. Only a matter of a few bob separated them. It was
just a question of degree.

A little boy of about eight – one of his pupils from the
church primary school – passed the window of the café
carrying a copy of the *Daily Sketch*: probably been sent
out to buy the paper. Unable to resist looking in at any
unguarded window he glanced into the café as he passed.
Charlie automatically straightened, made those adjustments to his bearing and expression which were a natural
reflex on confronting a pupil. But the boy's eyes slid over
him quickly and uninterestedly: he hadn't been recognized. He realized with a shock that bad luck had made
him invisible.

He picked up the newspaper and gave it a shake to
straighten it, but also to reassure himself that he could hear
the snap and rustle of the pages. He opened it, scanning
each page quickly and without interest. Then his attention
was caught for a moment by a small photograph in the
obituary column. He was sure he recognized the woman's
face from somewhere. Not really curious he began to read
the obituary. Of course, it was the novelist Marian Elverstone, none of whose books he had read, but whose face
must be familiar from other pictures in other papers. He
had an idea that she and her chums had struck a good
many *outré* attitudes between the wars. She had a cold,
supercilious but arresting face. The novels were listed,
there was a reference to her marriage to Neville Elverstone, the artist and critic . . . she had died, apparently,
aged sixty-seven, in the Green Hayes Home for the Men-
tally Ill in Roehampton, South London, where she had
been a resident for eleven years. Christ . . . eleven years in

a loony bin when you'd been a celebrated literary lioness, it hardly bore thinking about.

Two pages further on there was something else about her, a more informal photograph of her with her husband. Charlie's head ached and his eyes were beginning to feel gritty with tiredness, but he read the piece to stop himself thinking about anything else. Suddenly Adeline's name leapt off the page at him. He went back and re-read the passage.

'Throughout the twenties,' it ran, 'the Elverstones surrounded themselves with a coterie of artists and writers who shared their attitudes not only to art, but to life and love. Membership of this unconventional but elitist group was much sought after but rarely granted. Among the favoured few were . . .' here followed a list of names, and then, '. . . and, for a brief period, the fashionable portrait painter Adeline Charteris. It was thought by many who knew her that it was the ending of the novelist's attachment to Adeline Charteris which precipitated the final mental breakdown from which she never fully recovered.' Charlie read this particular sentence twice. Attachment? What was implied by that? He ran his eye down the rest of the piece with less interest. 'Last night Neville Elverstone described himself as "desolated and utterly bereft". He said: "Though she had been seriously ill for a long time she still exerted a powerful hold over the affections of all who knew her. Even over the past year she has had moments of perfect lucidity which made her illness more painful both for her and for those of us who witnessed it. She was a wonderful writer and a remarkable woman".'

There was more, but Charlie laid the paper down. A single, persistent, but elusive notion flittered around in his head like a bird trapped in an empty building. He was too weary and shell-shocked to pursue and lay hold of it, but it was there, and he knew that eventually it would settle.

He finished his coffee, pushed the rolled-up paper into his jacket pocket and left the café. The tramp had gone from the bench by the bus shelter. Two little girls giggled and piped, 'Good morning, Mr Farrell,' as he crossed the road to the Heath.

By the time he reached the Nunnery he felt much improved. The house was welcoming in the morning sunshine. The pigeons clustered like plump grey fruit along the parapet of the flat roof. It was only when you got very close that you could see the signs of dilapidation – the window frames were blistered and cracked, the brickwork was pitted, the black and red tiles in the porch were sunk. He remembered the glossy handsomeness of the house as he'd first seen it when Adeline had brought him here blackened and bleeding after falling off his motorcycle. Then it had seemed like an extension, in bricks and mortar, of Adeline herself – large and stylish and generously proportioned. Now it had seen better days.

He let himself in and went straight up the stairs. Merle came into the hall and called up after him.

'Mr Farrell, is that you?'

'Yes – where's Mrs Farrell?'

'She is gone away.'

He felt sickly and cold with fear. 'Gone away?'

'Gone to Devon. She is talking to the girls at Founder's Day, at 'er school.'

The relief made him almost dizzy. It was extraordinary how he dreaded to hear that she had left him, when he was planning to leave her.

'Of course,' he said. 'I remember.'

'You want some coffee, Mr Farrell?'

'No thanks, Merle. I'm going to wash and have a nap. Heavy night.'

He listened to her shuffling creakily back down the hall towards the kitchen stairs. Then he went up to the bedroom, pulled off his clothes and put on a dressing gown. In the bathroom he splashed his face, head and neck with cold water from the running tap, and cleaned his teeth. When he caught sight of himself in the mirror his reflection gave him a shock. With his hair slicked back by the water he looked haggard, and strangely hunted. His frantically active, searching brain was at odds with his appearance.

Back in the bedroom he flopped prone across the tapestry bedspread and at once felt his body slow and regulate itself, in relief, for sleep. His last thought as his eyes closed was that there was precious little for him to lose now, except Adeline's love.

When he woke it was early afternoon. The sun had moved round and was pouring in through the window to the right of the bed. It fell with kindly brightness on the picture that hung on the opposite wall so that as Charlie rolled stiffly on to his back it was just as if Lady Luck, who had so signally deserted him last night, had decided to make amends by showing him a way out.

With sudden energy he reached across, pulled his jacket from the back of the chair and took the newspaper from the pocket. He thrashed through it, found the obituary column and threw the rest of it to the floor. Looking again at the photograph of Marian Elverstone he felt as though a window had been opened revealing a strange and hitherto undreamt of landscape.

He folded the sheet of newspaper until it formed a frame for the photograph, and then rose from the bed and went over to the picture. It was unmistakably the same person. Even this close to the portrait, with every swirl and scrape of the brush clearly visible, you could see what an excellent likeness it was. Charlie went back to the bed and lay with his hands linked behind his head, staring at the Portrait of an Unknown Young Man. The portrait of Marian Elverstone. The portrait, undeniably, of an attachment.

The newspaper lay, folded neatly, on Enid Marsh's coffee table. Around it, sipping post-prandial coffee, stood an Anglican bishop with a high complexion, a Tory MP, the headmistress with four senior members of her staff, and Adeline. Adeline knew Enid too well not to realize that she would have read the paper, and she had too great a regard for her intelligence to suppose that she had drawn any but the correct conclusions.

Already, from the direction of Big Hall, there could be heard the chattering roar of hundreds of young voices as the girls assembled for prize-giving. Did they, these days, have access to daily newspapers? When she'd been at St Agatha's 'news' had been simply what Rose Daniels had seen fit to disseminate via the noticeboard in the corridor. But would she in a few minutes have to confront three hundred knowing faces, perhaps smirking, perhaps disgusted, or downright shocked? She didn't think she could bear it, not for her own sake, but for Marian's. The last, the only thing she could do for her was to protect her. Not from embarrassment, or humiliation, or shame, because Marian hadn't known the meaning of those things. But simply from misunderstanding, which her precise nature had so abhorred.

She caught Enid's eye and the headmistress came over to where she stood near the window – the same window from which Miss Daniels had summoned her to tell her of Richard's death.

Enid's expression was sympathetic. Like many women who have never appeared young, she seemed scarcely to have changed since the days when she had sat to Adeline in the studio of the Nunnery. One of the advantages, thought Adeline ruefully, of living a cloistered life.

She laid her large, pale hand on Adeline's arm. 'My dear . . . I'm sorry.'

'No, no – ' Adeline shook her head. She did not wish to indulge in the sharing that seemed to be invited by sympathy, no matter how discreet and well meant. 'Enid, I feel as if I could be exposing you – all of you – and the girls, too, to an awkward and embarrassing situation. I think it might be best if I stepped down.'

'Please don't do that, Adeline, I beg you. So many of the girls will be bitterly disappointed.'

'They might also be downright horrified. And though you're too polite to say so, you have your parents to think of.'

'That bridge can be crossed if and when we come to it.'

'Do the girls read the papers?'

'There's a copy of *The Times* left each day in the library. I suspect only about half a dozen members of my sixth form even glance at it. Please don't go. I asked you to initiate and present this new art prize because you are an artist and an old girl of the school. Those are good reasons and they hold good. If the newspapers choose to make something out of some long forgotten youthful excess – '

'No, Enid!' Adeline's face assumed the expression of hawkish fierceness which had quoshed many presumptuous assertions but which it had worn less often of late. The bishop glanced over his shoulder and the MP looked at his watch. 'Enid, it wasn't youthful excess and it has never been forgotten. I loved Marian. I feel as bereft now as if I'd only seen her yesterday. I haven't the least intention of concealing anything or pretending that nothing happened. I am simply offering to go if you think that what is in the papers today will cause any distress or awkwardness. And because I cared far too deeply for Marian to allow her to become some sort of topic for salacious chit-chat, either in the dormitories or in the staff room.' She glared at the bishop's back view. 'Or anywhere else.'

Enid's cheeks showed two patches of blush-pink.

'In that case,' she said, as she turned away, 'are we all ready to go through?'

Afterwards, Adeline asked Enid if she might call London. By one of those curious coincidences he picked up the phone at once, as if he'd been standing by it, waiting for her to call.

'Yes?'

'Neville . . .? It's Adeline.'

'I see.' It was impossible, from his tone, to gauge his reaction.

'I just rang to say how terribly sorry I am about Marian.' She couldn't say the word 'death'.

'Yes,' He seemed to reflect. 'It's all very sad.'

'Is there going to be a service . . . a funeral?'

'There has to be something, unfortunately. I'm going to see to it. She'd have hated anyone to be there.'

'I understand.' There was an uncomfortable silence. 'You're absolutely right.'

'And you, Adeline. You're well?'

'Yes, I'm fine.'

'Good, good . . .' His vagueness, more insulting than rudeness would have been, stood between them. He was allowing her no claim to intimacy, no right to an explanation.

She said, more abruptly than she wanted to: 'It was unfortunate, I thought, the innuendos in the paper – unnecessary.'

'Innuendos?'

'About Marian and me. I am sorry about that, Neville, I assure you it was none of my doing.' She had rung for comfort and was apologizing to him.

'Really Adeline – ' He gave a short laugh. 'What an extraordinary thing to say. It was all perfectly true. We must learn to live with our peccadilloes, mustn't we?'

She saw that her delicacy and her apology had been entirely wasted. Whatever had been implied in the press had been implied with Neville's knowledge. Only when she had replaced the receiver did she say: 'Goodbye, Neville.'

When Adeline got back to the Nunnery at eleven o'clock that night she was exhausted. Her day had been a harrowing blend of inner turmoil and outward composure. Duplicity was not her strong suit and she was almost quivering with strain as she got out of the cab. She had been shocked, on leaving the school in the late afternoon, to find a reporter from the *Western Mail* hanging about in the front drive, wanting to know if she had any comment to make. Outraged and, if she was honest, fearful, she had given him the shortest possible shrift and swept into the waiting taxi with the sound of her heart thundering in her ears.

In the same compartment as her on the way back to London had been a bluff elderly gentleman reading the paper. She had been irrationally terrified that he might spot the story, perhaps make some comment – he looked the type. What should her reaction be? The very last thing she wanted was to call down a storm of unsavoury and prurient attention on herself, or Charlie, or Dora and Miles. And yet neither was she prepared to dissemble, to creep away and hide and beg to be overlooked. She was bitterly resentful. Her grief over Marian's death was being diminished and stunted by all this hateful nonsense. Her grief clamoured inside her, demanding a hearing, but there seemed to be no place for it. The only appropriate behaviour was icy dignity, which did not come naturally to her.

She wished terribly that she had told Charlie. In the taxi from Waterloo she promised herself that if he was waiting for her she would tell him everything, straight away. She was sure, certain, that he would understand, and then she would have the strength of his love to help her bear this loss.

She was aching in every joint as she climbed the steps to the front door and let herself in. She could hear the phone ringing as she did so, a hard, peremptory intrusive sound, but by the time she was inside Charlie had answered it. She closed the door quietly, but he knew she was there and held out his arm to her as he listened to whoever it was. Wearily she went to him and laid her face on his shoulder, feeling his hand warm and confiding on the back of her neck, beneath her hair. Tears of sheer debility welled and oozed from her eyes and feeling them he stroked her.

'No,' he said sharply, in a voice unlike his own. 'No, sorry. Nothing at all. Thank you.'

He said 'thank you' in a brutally rude and dismissive tone. Then he depressed the cradle once, and laid the receiver, buzzing angrily like a fly on its back, on the table. Adeline had had enough of being rude and dismissive herself. To hear Charlie doing it for her was like receiving the most romantic of gifts.

'Thanks . . .' she whispered. 'Thanks. God, how I hate them.'

'They're only doing their job.'

'Don't defend them!'

'It's you I'm trying to defend.'

'I know and I'm sorry. I'm sorry you had to find out in this way what I should have told you long ago.'

'Ssh . . .'

His arm round her waist, he led her up the stairs and into the bedroom. It was in darkness and he didn't turn on a lamp.

'Come on,' he said, 'take your things off and get into bed.'

She pulled away from him, rubbing her eyes and forehead, summoning her resolve.

'I don't want to sleep just yet, I want to talk!'

'Sleep for a while, then. You'll talk better if you do. Phone's off the hook and I'm here to look after you.'

He slipped her jacket off her shoulders and tossed it on to the chair and then knelt to coax her feet out of her shoes. There was something in the sight of him kneeling there, doing her this small, tender service, which unmanned her completely and she gave herself up to his ministrations, his undoing of buttons and zips, his slipping her nightdress over her head. She thought she'd never loved him more, and it was when she needed to love him the most. The rightness of it was a comfort to her. As she slid down between the sheets she asked:

'What will you do?'

'I'm not tired. I had some kip earlier. Don't worry, I'll be here whenever you wake up.'

In fact, she slept until six, when brilliant early morning sun fell full on her face to wake her, and though Charlie wasn't beside her she could hear him downstairs, clinking cups, making tea. She felt lapped and protected by his care. Rested now, in the early, sunlit morning, she'd tell him what she had to and they'd begin again.

Charlie watched his own hands as they put the tea things
on the tray. They were perfectly steady, the movements
precise and delicate. He felt slightly distanced from himself. It was like being drunk, except that he was clear-
headed. He was so absorbed in his own problem that
he felt no conflict between his sympathy for Adeline and
his urgent need to capitalize on her predicament. His
only niggling concern was that the eliciting of this last
kindness from her might postpone his departure. So fine
was the balance between loving and leaving Adeline that
he could scarcely distinguish between the two. He
carried the tray up the stairs, and nudged open the
bedroom door with his foot. Adeline was sitting up
against the pillows, the back of her right wrist against
her forehead, as if shading her eyes: she was smiling.
She looked beautiful, and tired. Her beauty tugged at
Charlie's heart, but seemed also to vindicate him. After
all, he was a swine. She deserved better. He'd be doing
her a favour by going.

His footsteps sounded on the stairs and he came in with
the tea tray and put it down on the table beside her.
He'd pulled on his shirt and trousers of the night before,
but his feet were bare and his hair rumpled. She caught
his hand and kissed it.

'Thank you. Thanks for everything.'

He went and sat down on his side of the bed, facing
her. He took a cigarette from the packet on the floor
and lit it, striking the match on his thumbnail. It was a
trick that still amused and delighted her. But when he
doused the match with a quick, wringing movement of
his hand she saw how drawn his face was.

She pulled herself up against the pillows, holding her
teacup in front of her.

'Did you read anything?'

He shrugged, exhaled, exhaled smoke as if blowing
away a fly. 'A bit. Enough. I dare say they'll lose interest
eventually.'

'It was so important to me. One of the most important things in my life, something that changed me.'

'All right. I wasn't trying to imply that it was trivial. It's just that it's over and done with, so why rake it over?'

She was hurt. 'I'm not raking it over, Charlie. I just regret having seemed to keep it secret from you.' He jerked his head back in a silent laugh. 'Why do you laugh?

'The double standard in operation. I do little but keep things from you, but you must be a spotless paragon of honesty.'

'I didn't say anything like that.'

'I know. I know.'

It seemed that the basis of the conversation, its emphasis and mood, had altered and she had not noticed it happening. The pleasure and confidence she had felt in his company seeped away and she felt cold and uncertain.

'Look,' she said, trying by force of will to steer things her way, 'I want to tell you about Marian for my own sake, because she's still very much with me, she isn't – wasn't – someone you could just set aside and forget about. I find it very hard to believe she really is dead. I can't imagine her allowing death to happen to her. I told someone yesterday that I loved Marian, but now I'm not sure that I did. I was infatuated with her, bewitched by her, but I didn't know what love was then. I didn't know until I met you, Charlie, that's what I'm trying to say!' It hadn't been, but now it seemed imperative to get across this single, simple message.

He drew on his cigarette, using the movement to turn slightly away from her.

'You were lovers, you and this woman?'

'Yes. Does that shock you?'

'No.'

She tried to alter the tack of the conversation, to divert him. 'That picture – the one you say you like – that's a painting of Marian.'

'I realized that.'

'We were on holiday in Cornwall. Sometimes we dressed up for fun, as a joke.'

'Adeline – ' He stubbed out his cigarette with a violent, screwing motion and turned to face her, fixing her with a disturbingly searching stare. 'Adeline, there's something I need to tell you, too.'

Thank God, she thought. Thank God there's a reason for this.

'Anything,' she said. 'Please tell me.'

'I've lost a lot of money.'

For a moment she didn't catch the sense of what he was saying. She pictured him dropping a wallet, losing a jacket with small change. 'Where?'

'No, I lost it the night before last. At chemmy.'

'Oh I see. How much?' He had never mentioned his losses to her before. She felt strangely honoured that he was confiding in her now, and she was eager to help. But he didn't reply, so she asked. 'Really a lot?'

'Yes.'

'Tell me.'

He did so. She laughed, in complete disbelief. 'But darling, you don't – we don't – have that to lose!'

'I know.'

'I can't take it in . . .' She pressed her hands to her face, shaking her head. 'Are you sure there hasn't been some mistake?'

'No mistake.'

'Surely no-one would call in a debt like that from someone who simply didn't have the money?'

'It won't be called in. But I shall be expected to pay.'

'You can't, Charlie. We can't pay.'

He said, in a cool, matter of fact voice. 'We may not have the cash to cover it, but we have the assets.'

'Assets . . .?' She couldn't keep pace with him, she was struggling in the undertow of the wave, blinded, deafened and disorientated, without clues to guide her to the light and air.

He put a hand on her wrist, but it was a hard, emphatic hand, not a gentle one.

'There are things we could sell.'

'I suppose so.'

'You do understand,' his voice became more urgent, 'I absolutely have to pay. I've had a run of bad luck recently, it happens. The law of averages says it can't continue.' He laughed. She pulled away from his hand, and swung her legs stiffly out of bed, wrapping herself tight in her dressing gown. The sunshine that had seemed so benign now glared into the room like an inquisitor. She stood looking down at Charlie. He looked a little better, as though he had been relieved of a burden. She couldn't have called it a moment of truth, for she didn't know what the truth was, but it was certainly a new perspective.

'What are you staring at?' he asked.

'Nothing. You.'

'Same thing.' He laughed again. She felt quite ill with the strangeness of it. The sudden loneliness was like vertigo.

'Obviously,' she said, 'I'll do what I can to help. Does it all have to be paid at once?'

'No, I just have to show good faith. The gambling fraternity's very gentlemanly. I can't think why they put up with me!'

She couldn't smile, as he did. She was ashamed for both of them.

'We'll do whatever has to be done,' she said.

'Thank you.' He got up and moved not towards her but to the picture. 'You know,' he remarked conversationally, 'this would be worth quite a bit.'

'I doubt it very much. It's one of mine.' She thought, I sound bitter. Her shame deepened.

'Yes, I know it's one of yours, and it's bloody good . . .'

'I'm out of fashion, Charlie.'

'It's a painting of Marian Elverstone, though.'

Suddenly she saw what he was getting at, saw exactly how it had been. The run of bad luck, culminating in the heavy loss . . .his return to the empty house . . . the story in the papers . . . a sleep on the bed, and then the awakening, the realization that here before him hung a painting which had acquired, in an instant, a glitter of desirability.

'It's my picture, Charlie. I painted it for myself, and I kept it.'

'Adeline, I've never asked you for help before – '

'No, you haven't – you've just taken!'

'But I am *now*!'

'You're being unrealistic. This one painting would scarcely begin to see off that debt.'

'Perhaps not, but we do have some money – and you're got a lot of other pictures, all those sketches, they go back years. There are people who'd kill for those now, I'm prepared to bet!'

The exquisite irony of his choice of words struck her at the same time as their force. Her confusion began to recede, to be replaced by an unpleasant lucidity.

'Yes,' she said. 'I dare say it might be possible to make quite a killing by plundering my past life.'

'You're putting it very crudely.'

'Well, it's a pretty crude business, isn't it?' He reached for her but her hand flew up to ward him off. 'Don't!'

'Addy – '

'No! How could you? How could you ask me to part with it, now, when I've only just heard that she's dead? How could you bring yourself to ask me, Charlie? I don't believe I can ever have known you.'

'Steady on . . . I was in a fix. I am in a bugger of a fix. I'm worried sick and I was asking for your help – '

'You asked having already worked it all out. You took it all for granted, didn't you? You knew I'd help, I said I would, I wanted to help, but you couldn't even wait, you couldn't even see why what you were asking was wrong. You're stupid, Charlie! You're stupid, and so am I for putting up with you!'

She could hear herself, she was screaming now, and there were tears crawling down her cheeks and she knew how ugly and grotesque she must look, and she was perversely glad. Let him feast his eyes on the other side of her, let him be repelled, appalled, shocked.

'Look,' he said, turning his back and walking away from her, 'I'm sorry. I didn't mean to hurt your feelings. It was only a thought and, as you point out, the ruddy picture would be a drop in the ocean with the kind of sum we're talking about – '

'Yes, and that's the important thing, of course. This ridiculous squalid situation you've got yourself into with your bloody games-playing. If you want to behave like a bloody fool from now on, Charlie, then go ahead, but don't expect my sympathy or my admiration for it – '

'For Christ's sake, Adeline!' His voice rose suddenly, to a harsh shriek, as he rounded on her, and now she saw *his* rage, and *his* ugliness. In the sound and sight of him she witnessed the pent-up resentment and frustration of years, and it shocked her. 'Stop lecturing me! Stop behaving like a fucking sanctimonious cow! I've *never* asked you for help, never made demands on you, this is the *very first* time! You make me sick with your "Oh I love you Charlie" "I'd do anything for you, I won't ask questions" – perhaps you should have asked a few more fucking questions and then you'd know me better!'

Now he had given her something to fight against. His face, thrust towards hers, was taut and strained with fury like a flag caught in a gale. He was no longer her handsome darling but a middle-aged man in a tight corner, fighting dirty.

'You're right,' she said. 'I've been too tolerant, I've been had for a mug. No more, Charlie, I promise you. From now on your problems are your problems. I should have seen this coming – '

'What? Seen what? Must you be so priggish? I can't see – '

'No, Charlie, you can't see anything, and never have been able to. Go. Go on, get out of my room. I don't want to see you in here, I want to be on my own.'

' "I want to be alone!" ' he mimicked cruelly. 'This is my room, too, for better or worse, for richer for poorer. Yes?'

'No, it's not. It's *my* room, in *my* house. You've never wanted any part of it or showed any interest in it until now, when you need to pay your debts. So get out of it now.'

'All right. I will.' She heard in his voice that he was pleased to go, and she was disgusted.

In a flat voice, she said: 'We'll sort the money out somehow. We can sell the Gwen John, and some of the watercolours. We can sell the house. It's too big for us anyway. We'll sort things out. But I shall decide how for this one last time. I decide this time, and then you're on your own.'

'Yes,' he said. He dragged his jacket off the chair and pulled it on. 'I will be. We should never have got married, Adeline, and we've both known it for years. Everyone said so behind our backs, and everyone was right. I'm not cut out for it, and you – you're still carrying a torch for that whey-faced lesbian bitch!'

With a great lurching, violent movement he lifted the portrait from the wall and threw it flat on to the ground between them. It made a tremendous noise, like a gun-shot. It lay between them like a corpse.

'Go away,' whispered Adeline. 'Go.'

She half expected him to say 'don't worry, I'm going' – they had sunk so low, become so enmeshed in hateful, lacerating clichés – but he said nothing more. He went out of the room, leaving the door open behind him, ran down the stairs and out of the house. There was no sound of that door closing, either, no crash like a full stop, just the sunny, breathing silence.

Merle called tremulously: 'Madame? Madame, are you all right?'

'Yes thank you, Merle. I'm sorry. I'm going back to bed for a while.'

'You want anything?'

'No thank you.'

She closed the door of the bedroom, quietly and firmly. One voice for Merle, one for Charlie. She picked up the painting heavily but gently, as though it were a child, and replaced it on the wall. He's been right, it was good. She had captured perfectly the assumed rakishness, the mixture of mercurial cleverness and timidity which had typified Mr Goodbody. The eyes, slightly shaded beneath the rim of the hat, stared unforgivingly back at her.

CHAPTER TWENTY-SEVEN

1955

PETER MAY HAVE owned most of Larme des Anges, but once Adeline took up permanent residence there it became her island. Quite unintentionally, and without realizing it, she set her stamp upon the place. It was odd, for she had never sought to colonize or alter her small part of the island, but simply to blend in and enjoy it. And yet her tall figure in highly coloured shirt, baggy white trousers and vast, battered straw hat became part of the scenery in the Angeville store, and Danny's bar, and buzzing round the roads in her smart new American Dodge.

Because they had grown fond of her, the locals protected her. Her privacy at the Dragon House was universally respected. The very fact that there was no gate, nothing to keep the world at bay, promoted a certain delicacy. All were welcome, but none took advantage.

Not that she was any recluse, or latter-day Miss Haversham. She was cheerful, energetic, gregarious – and happy, in a way. It was simply a different kind of happiness, one that she had determinedly fashioned for herself. She had done it before, during the bad times in Ireland, and following the loss of her baby. She simply went back to work on her life.

To begin with, her finances had been at their lowest ebb and this had actually assisted her climb from the abyss. There had been something cleansing in the ruthless stripping down of her circumstances, the settling of Charlie's debts and the reassessment of what was left. She had sold the Nunnery and the four months, May to August, which she spent in England each year she spent at the Dower House, Elizabeth having removed under protest back to Fording Place with Frank and Anne.

At the Dragon House, she did her most serious painting. Her time in England she regarded as an opportunity firstly to be with her family, secondly to see friends and, a poor third, to remind her contacts in London that she was still about. On her occasional sorties to town she looked up Bob and Louise, and Toni, the Marchants if they were about, and Fenella though she generally avoided Nicholas. Duncan and Joel, after Duncan's emergence from the clinic, had cut their losses and moved to Suffolk.

Professionally, her fortunes were once more in the ascendant, though she regarded this upswing with a certain amiable scepticism. When the small flurry of prurient interest about herself and Marian Elverstone had died down, she had coolly and deliberately decided on a course of action which she knew would make or break her artistic reputation. She had assembled all those private sketches she had down over the years – of her family, of Simon, of Marian, of Dora and of Charlie – and had painstakingly selected the best from each group. From these she had made a further selection of personal favourites and used these, with photographs, as the basis for a series of portraits. The work had been a cathartic and a healing process. It had helped in some small measure to make sense of the chaos of the past. She had thought a great deal of Howard as she worked, and she had the sense of making reparation for her ignorance.

When she took the first of the paintings, and their

accompanying sketches, to Max Dyer at the Canfield Gallery, he had been warmly enthusiastic.

'They're splendid, Adeline. Truthful, not whimsical, like some of that early stuff of yours that was so popular. I do congratulate you. But I'd have thought you'd have had enough of people picking over your private life.'

'I have. That's precisely why I'd like these viewed openly and publicly. These are paintings of people I've loved, and who've influenced me profoundly, they're not smutty secrets, least of all Marian. I hope that people may see them, and me, in a different light. But really I don't give a damn. These pictures are for my satisfaction, and I'm glad you think they're good.'

Max did, and he was not alone. The exhibition, in late '52, was a personal triumph. Even the critics, never friends of Adeline's, applauded the candour and directness of the 'private portraits'. She had obtained excellent prices for those she had sold, and her favourites, including the Portrait of an Unknown Young Man, she kept for herself. She was once again offered more, and more interesting, commissions, but accepted only as many as she could easily manage during her annual sojourn at the Dower House. At Larme des Anges she continued to work on her portraits and even began to reconstruct the group study of the Elverstones with their friends at Allerton Square. The many years which separated her and her subject matter were actually a help. She found that her view of those people was sharpened by time, and she had a greater degree of objectivity.

By the same token, the person whom she was least able to capture on canvas was the most recent. Try as she might, she could not distil a truthful and complete picture of Charlie from the dozens of glancing, elliptical sketches she had made. The real man was still too close, and too powerful a part of her. She could not pin down in clumsy paint his quick, flashing charm, his elusive young/old good looks, the sweetness – it was the only word she could find – that had been his peculiar characteristic. She could not paint the reasons why she had loved him. It caused her

great personal agony that others almost certainly attributed this difficulty to an unwillingness on her part, when
nothing, nothing, could have been further from the truth.

How she wished they would not make these unspoken
assumptions which were so wrong, and against which she
had no defence. They saw with fond interest how she had
recovered from the split with Charlie, and how brilliantly
she had risen above it. They were encouraging, affectionate, and most of all, approving. She knew so well what
they were saying, as they looked on. Just look at the difference in Adeline. She's a new woman, working again, successful, living where she's always wanted to live, getting
about and seeing people. It's only a wonder she put up
with it as long as she did. It was always a mistake. We
knew it, and at last she's seen sense.

What hurt most was that they were saying so much of
what she herself had screamed at Charlie on that terrible
morning. She had demeaned herself then, by believing for
a moment their version of events, when the truth was that
she loved him, and would always love him, and felt the
desolation of his absence every single day. But she neither
complained nor explained. She let them believe what they
would and kept her own counsel. The fact was, she
expected him to come back. In her better moments she
told herself that he would return because he loved her. In
her worst moments she reflected that he owed it to her –
for the hundreds of unexplained absences, the small, casual
betrayals, the wilful secrecy against which she had never
fought. With hindsight she saw just how great the gulf
had been across which they had clutched hands. She forced
herself to acknowledge that Charlie had been merely waiting for a chance to spring himself from a situation which
had become, for him, gradually more intolerable. The
blind eye she had so determinedly turned in the hope of
keeping him had prevented her from seeing the truth –
that he was trapped. And all she had done to express her
love, and deserve his, had made the trap close in.

She had seen him again, of course. He had come back
the very next day, much the worse for wear, but terrify-

ingly rational, saying he was sorry, that the worst mistake he'd made had been staying as long as he had. He'd said the money was his problem, he'd arrange a loan, he was sorry he'd ever assumed . . . the pain of hearing him talk like this had been unbearable. They'd embarked on another wicked, wounding argument. Finally they'd reached a compromise. She would pay off half the sum by whatever means she could, and the other half would constitute a personal loan from her which he could pay off over an indefinite period, without interest. This he had accepted with reasonable grace – he had little choice – but he had pointed out that the loan must not be regarded by either of them as some sort of hostage. That had finished her. She simply agreed, and let him go.

They were not divorced. For a while she'd heard something of him from time to time. He had left, or been relieved of, his job at the primary school. Nicholas had seen him at a party, Peter had seen him at London Airport 'propping up the bar with some ghastly looking people' as he put it. After a while he had disappeared. She threw away the few clothes he'd left, and locked up the beautiful old motorbike in a rented garage. There were no other reminders of him, his disappearance had left no trace in her life, only in her heart.

She became, in the winter of 1952, the world's most doting grandmother. Patrick Eyre weighed in at nine pounds and was the apple of his parents' eye. Miles and Dora had bought a terraced house on the outskirts of Oxford, where Miles had got a new job at the Playhouse. On becoming pregnant Dora had given up working in a bookshop and had had some small success selling short stories and poems. Her heart was set on writing a novel, and Adeline was sure she would do it.

Both she and Peter admired the two of them for exactly those things which Nicholas most deplored. They were stubbornly independent, materially unambitious and quietly, unselfconsciously unconventional. It was by no means unusual for Miles to cook meals and push the pram while Dora wrote. They had no interest whatever in making a good impression for its own sake, and had no intention of having Patrick christened, or of putting his name down for public school. Adeline felt sorry for Fenella, whose loyalty prevented her from being as demonstrative towards her grandchild as she might otherwise have been. Nicholas was cold and aloof, washing his hands of the whole dismal business.

Adeline was surprised by the strength of her love for Patrick. She loved him passionately, physically, adoringly, she thought Dora the cleverest girl in the world for having produced him, she could almost have stayed nearby for ever, just to be of use to them, and look on as Patrick grew in beauty and brilliance. But she knew better than to entertain such a notion for more than a second. They had their life, and it was utterly different, from hers, thank God, and must be allowed to remain so.

Always, when she was in London, she went to the leafy churchyard at the top of East Heath Road to visit Clea. Often she would simply sit on a seat under the trees keeping her daughter company and sometimes as she sat there people she didn't know and had never seen before would pause at the tiny grave and make kindly, dismayed remarks over the baby who had died. She never spoke to them, but she was enormously grateful to these sympathetic strangers, and liked to think of similar scenes being enacted when she was thousands of miles away in Larme des Anges. Once she'd found a bunch of lilies of the valley laid on the grave. Clea had friends.

At the Dragon House she had Toni, and Duncan and Joel, to stay as often as they could manage. It was quite like old times when they all sat out on the verandah in the evenings, talking and laughing, but the enduring nature of these friendships forged so long ago pointed up the changes in her own life and sometimes she'd leave them when the conversation was in full swing, and walk down by the sea, alone.

Duncan and Joel were doing well, taking things a day at a time. They'd bought a small arts and crafts shop, with a flat over it, in Framlingham and were managing to make a go of it in spite of a seriously under-developed business sense and the initial mistrust of the locals. Duncan was not naturally suited to country life, but Joel had no wish to be a civil servant for the rest of his life and after Duncan's rehabilitation they'd decided jointly that it would be better for both of them if they found some means of earning a crust in which they could engage together. So in Well Cottage Crafts Joel sat at the table by the till, in his gold-rimmed half-spectacles, reading Jane Austen, while Duncan fussed, fumed or was happy according to the number of customers and suppliers who called in. But he'd remained sober, and they'd gradually built up a social life centred on the local dramatic society, which had never had such splendid scenery.

The hotel business was Peter's latest enthusiasm, and his favourite toy was an exquisite Cotswold manor house which he was having converted. He and Pru and the boys sailed through their comfortable, wealthy, placid lives not beginning to comprehend, nor able to imagine, what horrors other people suffered through wrong decisions, and foolish actions, poverty, and misplaced love.

Adeline had been in Devon for the Coronation. She was deeply moved by the procession and the ceremony, which they watched on one of two hired television sets placed at either end of Tarrford village hall. About a hundred and fifty people had crammed in, the lucky ones on metal and canvas chairs, the rest sitting on the floor or standing. The rain had beat thunderously on the roof and turned the windows into waterfalls, but they'd all been spellbound. The air grew thick with the smell of damp hair, and gaberdine, the steam from wet clothes drying out, the swirl of genuine sentiment. The tremendous ceremony had been punctuated by coughs and sniffs and throat-clearings. Adeline had felt her throat fill and her eyes smart as she watched those flickering blue-grey images of the young Queen, so slight and stern-faced, dwarfed by the magnificent setting of which she was the centre and focus, almost trembling beneath the weight of the crown.

'Good luck to her!' Elizabeth had said in her loud, auto-
cratic voice. 'Good luck to Her Majesty!' and there had
been an answering murmur of unaffected goodwill from
the rest of the transfixed audience.

Afterwards they'd gone back to Fording Place, and after
lunch there was a party to mark the occasion, to which
every child in the village had been invited. Frank, as host
and chairman of the Parish Council, had presented com-
memorative mugs to each child. This ritual, and the tea
and games which followed, had been planned for out of
doors, but in view of the still-torrential rain the entire
exercise had been moved indoors. Anne and Dorothy
were in their element. A wartime spirit of pluck and enterprise pervaded the proceedings. Adeline confined her
involvement to doing as she was told and going from time
to time with Frank and Chris to take nips from the whisky
decanter in the dining room. She watched in genuine awe
as Anne and Dorothy persuaded fifty children of
between five and eleven to play grandmother's footsteps
with Elizabeth as the grandmother.

At the end of it all, as they sat with their feet up in the
drawing room, she said to Anne: 'I don't know how you
do it, I really don't. I couldn't cope.'

Anne waved both hands in the air. 'But Addy, I love it,
you know I do! I can't tell you how I miss our evacuees.
I still correspond with one or two of them. Shirley Palmer
got married the other day – Married! It makes me feel a
hundred! And besides she was such a sour-faced little so-
and-so when she arrived here. I think we did her a lot of
good. When she left she was happy.'

Adeline reflected that her sister-in-law might truly be
termed a really good woman. But it was not in her that
she felt compelled to confide her deepest feelings. That
summer of 1953 she had Bob and Louise to stay several
times at the Dower House. It was the first time for many
years that she had the time and emotional freedom to enjoy
their company and she was astonished at how relaxed and
happy she was in their company. Perhaps because they
had felt the lash of general disapproval themselves, they

displayed no trace of criticism, nor of satisfaction that her marriage to Charlie was over. Bob, trailing an impressive mantle of radio fame, was still capable of the occasional devastating shaft of sarcasm, but he had mellowed. And Louise – Adeline felt ashamed when she remembered how, as a jealous little girl, she had watched her with Simon and dismissed her as an empty beauty. She had been so young, no more than a girl herself, though Adeline could not have been expected to understand that at the time. And she had become, without doubt, a lovely, generous, sympathetic woman.

She asked the questions Adeline most longed to answer. One Sunday as they walked by the river, where now a new pair of swans nested on the island, she said:

'Do you miss him, Addy?'

'Yes. Yes, I do. Terribly.'

'You love him.'

'Yes.'

Bob said: 'Remember we used to lurk in these branches and give visitors the fright of their lives?

'I do.' She knew he was not changing the subject, but trying in his oblique way to comfort her by reminding her of their shared past. All three of them paused and looked up through the layer on layer of rustling green, brightening towards the sky. 'I often used to think that when we were all grown up, or immeasurably old, as we are now, that life would be a piece of cake, because we'd have learned all the answers.'

'Absolutely,' said Bob. 'I so looked forward to being someone who *knew*.'

'And look at us,' Louise linked her arms through theirs. 'Still baffled, still searching, still hoping – '

'Still fooling ourselves,' added Adeline, 'still scared.'

'Thank God,' said Bob. 'What the hell is there left if you've got all the answers?'

They walked on, and Adeline talked some more about Charlie and how she hoped, and believed, that he would come back.

'I know one thing,' said Louise, 'and that's that no-one could have done more than you to ensure that he does.'

'But Louise, I sent him packing. I said some terrible things, they haunt me. And besides, he loathed being married, I know that now – something I *do* know.'

'Yes, but you loved, and you still do. It's your great talent, Addy. It's a gift. And I can't believe that anyone with whom you've once shared the gift is going to be able to live without it.'

Bob cleared his throat and Adeline peered round Louise at him, smiling. 'Sorry brother. Women's talk.'

'Not at all,' he said. 'I was about to say that I whole-heartedly endorse my wife's view. But now, of course, I shan't bother.'

Peace was something she valued more these days. Not quiet, necessarily, but peaceful surroundings, space. The days when she'd loved being a Londoner were over, and the place where she was happiest was Larme des Anges. She felt that in some curious way if she were not sur-rounded by too many people and distractions she could give out a signal, a bat-squeak of communication to Char-lie, to let him know that she was there. Sometimes in a crowd she experienced a surge of acute anxiety, would see a vivid mental picture of him banging on her door, beg-ging to be let in, unheard, while she was surrounded by these other people who meant nothing. This never hap-pened but that an hour later, when she returned, she would suffer a sickening sense of disappointment. For he was never there, and she was more alone than ever.

On Larme des Anges she'd bought a pinky-brown Weimeraner puppy from an American family – the man worked at the weather station. Unlike her previous two dogs, Gypsy, a bitch, was as sweet and soft and supple by nature as she was in appearance. She was so eager to please that she scarcely needed training, and she clung to Adeline like a lissome shadow.

It was in the late autumn of 1955 when Adeline was walking Gypsy on the beach and planning the Christmas she would arrange for Duncan and Joel, that she received one of those bolts from the blue that shook her view of the world. She had almost reached the rock arch, and Nathan's calls, frantic but faint, were at first almost lost in the ringing of the water. When she did hear them she turned idly and began to meander back with Gypsy cantering in the edge of the surf beside her.

When Nathan emerged on the crest of the dunes, flapping his arms madly up and down in his brilliant white shirt, she knew she must run. Gypsy careered away, thinking it was a game and Adeline ran more heavily, the sand sucking and dragging at her bare feet.

'What is it?'

'Telegramme, ma'am, you got a telegramme!'

'Thank you.'

She took it from him and sank down, sweating and out of breath, the dog lying next to her.

'You going to open it, ma'mm?'

'Don't worry, Nathan, I shall in just a moment when I've caught my breath.'

'Okay ma'am.'

Visibly disappointed Nathan trailed away up the path. Adeline turned the telegramme over in her hands. She was shaking with excitement. All she could think of was that it might be from Charlie.

The truth was like a punch in the face.

'Adeline. Stop. Accident Bob tragically killed. Stop. Call booked seven your time. Stop. Louise.'

Bob . . . ? Adeline let the paper go and it rolled and danced lazily across the sand. She laid her face down on her lap and thought of her brother. Accident Bob tragically killed. Bob who'd cried angry, humiliated tears by the river . . . Bob who'd sulked jealously when Frank had first come home in uniform . . . who'd put up with her and Clancey in his well-ordered bachelor flat . . . Bob that Toni loved, and who loved Louise . . . Accident, Bob tragically killled.

She was alone at the house, and there was no-one at Outlook Point. There was no-one to turn to, or share her memories with, no shoulder to cry on. She put her arms around the warm, panting dog and sobbed.

When she at last returned to the house and told Philippe what had happened his face became a mask of distress.

'Your brother, I'm so sorry ma'am. What can I do?'

'Nothing, Philippe. My sister-in-law, his wife will be ringing me later this evening.'

'You like anything to eat?'

'No thank you.' She was touched by his desire to minister to her.

'A drink? I get you a swizzle.'

He was so eager to provide her with something that she let him bring her the drink, and in fact it was welcome, if only because she could hold the cold glass against her face, and turn it between her hands. She could do nothing else. She simply sat, motionless, waiting for it to be time for Louise to ring.

She both longed for and dreaded the call. Such a great distance, and so little time. What state would Louise be in? Much as she loved her sister-in-law, there was an inherent awkwardness. Whose loss was greater, who must be the stronger? Adeline felt as though a piece of her past, the backdrop against which her present life was played, had been torn away. But Louise had to face the awful, awesome present.

But when Louise rang, her voice faint across the hissing, crackling distance, she was composed. She didn't weep, but she began speaking urgently and at once.

'Addy? Oh hell, I wish you weren't so far away, we need each other, don't we? It's so sudden, so terribly sudden. He went out in the car to drive to Langham Place, he wasn't more than a few hundred yards from home when it happened. You know he's not the smoothest of drivers, with his funny leg – a dog ran across the road, a *dog*, Addy, and he had to stop sharply, and he broke his neck. It was so eerie: when I went to identify him, he looked just the same as he had a few hours earlier, absolutely unmarked, absolutely himself. They told me he'd have felt nothing it was so quick. I can't believe it's happened, Addy. How can such a terrible thing have such a silly, trivial reason? . . . but Addy, I wanted to speak to you as soon as I could so that you knew everything, from me . . .'

Now she stopped speaking and Adeline was overcome with gratitude for the largeness of spirit which had prompted Louise to speak to her so soon, when her own grief must have been terrible.

'Thank you, Louise,' she said. 'I feel so far away, and helpless. When's the funeral?'

'The end of the week, here in London. I'm hoping your family won't mind, but he wasn't a sentimentalist, and this way more of his friends will be able to come. Ronnie Farmer from the BBC rang me and said they would like to hold a memorial service for him, so I suppose we shall do that if I can bear it – ' Again she broke off, and now Adeline cried with her.

'Louise . . . ? Louise you must have someone with you.'

'Yes, it's all right, I have a friend here. Look Addy, we only have about another minute. Don't think of coming over, just think of me on the day, and remember Bob, and write to me soon. He was so fond of you, so proud of your talent and your courage, I know he'd want me to say that.'

'Louise . . . I wish I was there, I do wish I was with you!'

'And the other thing I must say for him, he was so sorry about Charlie. We liked Charlie, he was a sweetie and he made you happy. You should be glad your Charlie's still alive. While he's alive there *is* hope. And now I must go. I don't . . . I can't talk any more . . . I just wanted, you know, to hear your voice and to let you know exactly what happened – '

Their time was up, they shouted goodbye, they were summarily disconnected. Slowly, Adeline set down the receiver, and at once Gypsy came over and climbed on to her lap. It was strictly forbidden, and she was far too big, but now her warm weight was a comfort.

Adeline stroked the dog. It was quite dark now, and in England it would be midnight, but Louise would not be sleeping. She'd be facing the grim, unrelenting loneliness which would not yet seem quite real, but which would never go away.

Somewhere out there Charlie *was* alive, and she was glad of it. But she entertained little hope.

CHAPTER TWENTY-EIGHT

1963

CHARLIE FARRELL EXPERIENCED a moment of truth. It happened at the hotel in Singapore where he was staying with Maude Bingham. The day had followed its usual pattern; he'd spent the morning on the golf course and was now sitting in the foyer waiting for Maude to come down for lunch. There was a two-day-old copy of the *Daily Telegraph* open on his knee, but he wasn't reading it.

The slow-turning fan churned the humid air above his head. He had on a clean white shirt and a freshly pressed lightweight jacket and trousers, but already he could feel the sweat collecting beneath his arms, around his crotch and between his shoulder blades. He never felt clean in the Far East except when he was in the pool or on the beach. He drank gallons of iced and diluted alcohol without ever managing to get decently drunk. He played cards afternoon and night without ever becoming excited. When there was no alternative he made love, if you could call it that, to Maude, squeezing and stabbing her fat body until she gasped in ecstasy, not realizing he wanted to kill her.

He had grown to hate Maude, for reasons that were wholly unfair, but up till now he hadn't hated himself. In the last few years he'd had money, and what many men would have considered an easy life. When he'd first left Adeline he'd done assorted jobs – private tutoring, selling insurance, dealing in more tangible commodities as rep for a firm who made novelty china goods. He'd also done kitchen portering and washing up at several large London hotels. And he had become, through a steady but almost imperceptible process, a full-time gambler. He had carried out his lowly responsibilities with the minimum effort required to retain the confidence of his employers, and the salary needed to fund his other life. The loss of self-respect had been an insidious business. Charlie's looks, his pleasant manner, the way he spoke – these things saw him through the better jobs for a while. Most of the people who employed him considered him an asset and the customers were charmed by him. He almost succeeded in charming himself, in believing that he was younger, cleverer and more honest than he was. But not quite. In quiet moments, as he drove along deserted B-roads late at night, or lay awake in the small hours in his bleak service flat or some anonymous hotel room, he recalled Adeline, her face and voice, with frightening clarity, and was reminded of what he had lost: not just the woman herself but her capacity for seeing what was best in him and making him see it too. At these moments misery, like a sharp physical pain, would tighten his chest and stomach and make sweat burst out on his face and in his palms.

Only shame had prevented him from going back. He had told himself that when things were better, when he could hold his head up and hand back most of the money he owed her, then he'd return. But the right moment had never come, and time had slipped away. The characteristics, mental and physical, which he had thought to be assets, now seemed liabilities. He began to be conscious of the mild disdain in which he was held, the suspicion with which people viewed a well-spoken, educated, middle-aged man who had done nothing with his life. They

no longer thought him charming and amusing but a failure, albeit a likeable one. He saw it in their eyes when
they were listening to him, and in the way they kept him
waiting just a little, with no apology. He sensed it in the
manner of some men, which was both jovial and peremptory, in the way women glanced over his shoulder to see
who else was in the room.

He'd met Maude and her husband in Monte Carlo in
1959 and he and Maude had at once forged an unholy
alliance. She was rich, very rich, open-handed and happy-
go-lucky. She adored gambling and could afford to lose
a great deal and scarcely notice. Her carefree generosity
cushioned Charlie from anxiety and paradoxically his fortunes took an upswing, and he began to win. 'I'm your
lucky charm, Charlie boy!' Maude would cry, enfolding
him in an embrace that was treacherous with diamonds.

Commander Bingham was a thin, grey, cold man, who
treated his wife with a bloodless courtliness and Charlie
with icy politeness. He made it plain by the very set of his
shoulders that his wife's predeliction for Charlie was the
final proof of her innate vulgarity. When she patted Charlie's cheek and straightened his tie it was as though pins
were being driven into Commander Bingham's spare,
upright figure.

But Maude loved to gamble, and so did Charlie. They
became glued together by their shared obsession. If one of
them won especially handsomely they'd pool the win-
nings to fuel further gambling. They travelled about, on
the continent, on cruise ships, in the Far East. They
became well-heeled nomads, and Commander Bingham,
at home in Godalming, quietly and ruthlessly filed for
divorce, citing Charlie, which was legally true.

'Oh! You've done me such a favour, Charlie boy!' she
cried, and swept him off on a transatlantic liner.

Charlie soon forgot what it was to work, both the effort
and the dignity. He tried to avoid thinking of himself as a
kept man, but that was what he was. He frequently made
enough at the table to last any reasonable man for months,
but the money was no longer necessary to him. Maude

fostered and funded his gambling, and expected nothing
in return but that he escort her into dinner, light her cigarette, fill her glass, laugh at her jokes, and pleasure her in
bed.

It was all very easy except the last. He disliked feeling
so little when she felt so much. He disliked doing it at all,
and sometimes his anger would imbue his performance,
so that Maude would shriek, and afterwards would call
him 'Tiger' with ghastly coyness.

He realized one day, through some remark of hers, that
she was a year or two younger than Adeline – only sixty
– and it had stunned him. He had never even thought of
Adeline in terms of her age, but there was no other way
of thinking of Maude. The rich woman's tactics which she
employed to keep the rising tide at bay cruelly emphasized
this fact. Her face was lifted as her body sagged, her hair
was regularly teased and highlighted, but was becoming
increasingly coarse and sparse; the skin on her face was
soft and fragrant, but on her throat, beneath her arms and
across her stomach it was dimpled and puckered like crepe
paper. She was not an ugly woman, and on her day she
could look quite glamorous and sassy. But she was not,
nor ever could be, an Adeline. So Charlie pitied her and
his pity, along with his self-loathing, were the chief factors
in his inability to leave.

'Excuse me – I wonder – might I ask you . . .?'

Charlie, recalled abruptly to the present, looked up to
see Maude's diametric opposite standing before him in
an attitude of polite supplication. This was a thin, eager,
pastel-pretty young Englishwoman in a dull but expensive
powder-blue suit. Her hair was fair and limply fine, her
face pink and a thought chinless. She looked rather sweet
and distrait. Charlie rose at once.

'I do apologize, I was miles away.'

'Oh no, it was me . . . not at all . . . I wonder if I could
ask you a rather awful favour?'

'Ask me any kind of favour at all, please.'

'Oh lor, how nice of you! I've just done such an extraordinarily stupid thing. I think I've left a bag, well a little vanity case really but it's got all kinds of treasures in it, in the loo at the airport. We're only staying here for a couple of nights, we're meeting my husband, and then we're going on to Perth for Christmas . . . heavens, I seem to be telling you the story of my life.'

'Not at all.' Charlie had all but forgotten Christmas. 'You'd like me to go to the airport and retrieve your case.'

'Well no, actually, the thing is – it's in the ladies' anyway, but I thought if perhaps you wouldn't mind standing *in loco parentis* for a little while I could just jump in a cab and see . . . It's not the end of the world if I lose it, but I'd quite like . . .' She tailed away, slightly embarrassed, perhaps, at wanting her 'vanity case' so much. Charlie couldn't imagine what such an apparently unadorned girl would carry in the case.

'Don't worry,' he said. 'I'm entirely at your disposal.'

He smiled at her and she blushed fierily.

'Look, they're over there – boys!' She called with the sudden, unselfconscious stridency so typical of the English. 'Boys, come here, will you?'

Two boys aged about eight and ten rose from nearby chairs. They wore the unmistakable grey shorts and shirts of prep school, though they had discarded red blazers, caps and ties, which they now carried. They looked hot, and a little world-weary, as though this kind of situation were not unfamiliar to them. The smaller boy wore spectacles.

'Hallo there,' said Charlie.

'How do you do, sir,' said the older one.

'That's Harry,' said the mother, 'and this is Michael. And by the way, how silly of me, I'm Angela Prescott –' They shook hands. 'So I'll just dash, shall I, and be as quick as I can? Jonathan – my husband – should be here before too long, probably before I get back. He's always ticking me off for being disorganized!'

'It's the sort of thing that can happen to anyone,' said Charlie. 'You go and sort it out, we'll be fine.'

'Bless you, I'm so grateful. The boy has taken our cases

up. We've got two double rooms, I can't remember the numbers . . .'

Her brow began once more to furrow. Charlie took her elbow and turned her gently in the direction of the main door.

'Off you go.'

'Yes, I'll dash, thank you so much. Bye-bye boys –' She aimed a glancing kiss at her sons' impassive faces. 'Goodbye –'

'Charles Farrell.'

'Goodbye, Mr Farrell. Right! I'll go and see what I can do . . .'

She bustled off, half running, her thin legs splaying out beneath the restrictive hem of her straight skirt. The two boys watched her go, not so much wistfully but in order, Charlie sensed, to avoid looking at him.

'Now then,' he said, 'what shall we do?'

Reluctantly they turned their heads. 'We don't mind, sir,' said Harry.

Charlie had forgotten what it was like to be addressed in this way, and found it curiously touching, both for the assumption that lay behind it and his own unworthiness.

'Please,' he said, 'don't bother with the "sir". School's out.'

Harry smiled a small, polite smile. Michael rubbed his eyes behind his glasses with two travel-stained index fingers.

'I tell you what,' said Charlie, 'let's go and find your rooms and then you can dump all those stuffy togs and get a bit more comfortable. Do you fancy a swim before lunch? You've got trunks with you?'

'Yes . . .' There was indecision in Harry's voice. 'But he can't swim.'

'Shut *up*!' Michael was red with mortification.

'It won't matter either way,' said Charlie, 'the shallow end's very shallow.'

At the desk he told the exquisite Malay receptionist that he was taking the boys to the pool, and that if either Mrs Bingham or Mr Prescott should enquire they were to be directed there. Then he collected the room keys, his own and the Prescotts', and they went up in the lift to the second floor. Charlie felt mental muscles long unused beginning to creak back into action. His schoolmastering days were over, but boys didn't change that much. And neither did parents, he reflected, opening the outer door of the lift and ushering Harry and Michael out into the silent corridor. The innocent callousness with which the English packed their young children off to boarding school also allowed them to entrust their offspring to complete strangers at the drop of a hat. Charlie wondered what on earth his unspoken credentials had been and concluded that he had been English, had spoken with the right accent, and had been available. Did some vestiges of schoolmasterly reliability still cling to him? he wondered. He doubted it, somehow.

He let the boys into their room. Their cases had been placed at the foot of the nearest bed.

'There you are,' he said. 'Can you cope all right?'

'Yes, fine thanks,' said Harry. Michael bounced on the bed on his knees.

'You get your trunks on, then, and I'll do the same and pick you up in five minutes.'

When Charlie returned he wore only shorts over his trunks, and a towel round his neck. The two boys, deeply conservative, had replaced all their clothes, but he made no comment.

'Who are you going to see in Perth?' he asked on the way down.

'Oh it's our aunt and uncle and our cousins,' replied Harry. 'They've been to stay with us, but we've never been to stay with them before.'

'I expect you'll have a marvellous time.'

'Our cousins are called Dale and Paula,' said Michael suddenly, with more than a hint of infant snobbery. 'They're older than us and they're both girls.'

Charlie entertained a fleeting mental picture of the two tanned, no-nonsense Australian maidens with these careful, socially aware English boys. He withdrew on to the safe, high ground.

'What does your father do?'

'He works for the Hong Kong and Shanghai Bank,' said Harry with the practised casualness of pride. 'Next holidays we'll be going to Hong Kong. Mum's going there after we go back to school.'

'Hong Kong's a terrific place,' said Charlie. 'You'll really like it. And there are hundreds of English families there, so you'll probably find your flights to and fro are full of chaps like you, doing the same thing.'

They didn't respond to this, and Charlie deduced that he had unintentionally diminished their sense of their own importance by referring to this horde of ex-patriot children.

They went through swing doors at the side of the foyer, across the covered terrace with its white chairs and cane and glass tables, and down the path, flanked with frangipani and hibiscus, to the pool. The water glowed a dazzling electric blue. There were not many other people there, but a few children chirruped, scampered and jumped around the water's edge like tropical birds.

Charlie felt the boys' tension, the pull between stiffness at the sight of the other, already wet and confident children, and their own longing to swim. But once they'd found poolside chairs, and got undressed, the tension evaporated. It was impossible for boys of their age, once freed from restrictive clothing and immersed in clear, sparkling, tepid water, not to enjoy themselves. There was no loss of dignity for Michael, for two of the other pool-users were non-swimmers of about his age, sculling about in rubber rings. While Harry bounced and hurtled, spreadeagled, from the low diving board, Charlie remained with Michael in the shallow end, and listened to him talk. His conversation consisted of an intermittent monologue, rather as if the water were washing out various small particles of information which had been stuck in the corners of his mind.

'I don't want to go . . . they'll want to do masses of

things I can't do, and we'll never be on our own . . . they're terribly busy. And bossy. Bossy and busy. I wanted to go and stay with Anstey but Mum said I couldn't possibly go there for two months so I've got to go to Aunt Jan's . . . I say, I can *almost* swim, shall I show you . . .? Well I nearly can, I know my foot touched the bottom a bit there, but it wasn't bad! My best subjects are maths and woodwork, I made some good bookends the term before last . . .'

In the end Michael truly did swim a couple of strokes and Charlie was quite surprised at his own genuine delight at this achievement. Harry was summoned from the diving board, and repeated demonstrations were given to an accompaniment of much splashing and spluttering. Charlie was reminded of that time in the south of France, with Miles, and Adeline . . . .

The grown-ups at the poolside began to drift away, dragging their unwilling offspring with them, and Charlie realized that it was after one. On the grass at the far end of the pool was a wooden chalet selling snacks – hot dogs, chicken in a basket, dollops of sweet Malay curry with rice, ice creams, and fruit. Rather than trail back upstairs, get dressed, and sit in state in the dining room, Charlie took the boys to the bar and let them order iced Coke in bottles, with straws, and hot dogs with fried onions and ketchup. He himself bought a cold beer and a curry, and they took their lunch back to one of the tables and sat in their bathing trunks, eating and drinking, and letting the sun dry them.

Michael and Harry were now quite themselves, bragging and scoffing enthusiastically, largely ignoring him in the nicest possible way. Charlie realized that he was entirely happy in their company, which was the absolute opposite of what he had become used to over the past few years. He felt more relaxed, more genial, more at peace with himself and the world than he had done in ages. In fact he would have lost track of the time altogether had not Maude suddenly hove in view, fluttering her fingers flirtatiously. She wore an expensive shantung shift dress,

splashed with large pink and blue flowers, pink high-
heeled sandals and chunky gold necklace, bracelets and
earrings which looked like costume jewellery but which
Charlie knew to be real. She carried a brimming glass of
gin and tonic.

'Charlie . . .! There you are!'

He rose to greet her and the two boys did the same,
regarding her with undisguised curiosity.

'Hallo, dear. You haven't been looking for me, have
you? Didn't you get my message at the desk?'

'Oh, the little girl did say something . . .' She plumped
down in a chair and beamed, pop-eyed, at Harry and
Michael. 'Now tell me who your new friends are!'

'This is Harry Prescott, and Michael Prescott, who have
just been keeping me company while their mother goes
back to collect something she mislaid at the airport. This
is a very good friend of mine, Mrs Bingham.'

'But "Maude" will be absolutely fine!' cried Maude,
over their muted how-do-you-dos.

'So what have the three of you been doing?'

'We've been swimming, and eating lunch –'

'Oh, so you've *had* lunch, you sneaky thing!' Maude
tapped the back of Charlie's hand reprovingly. 'And
there's me, I've come all this way to collect you.'

'Sorry about that, but we were all hungry. Why don't
you let me get you something from the pool bar?'

'No, no, it's too hot for me here. I shall finish my drinkie
and wend my weary way back to the dining room. Do
you know, boys,' she added confidingly, leaning well forward so that her gold necklace clanked on the tabletop,
'I'm very prone to do silly things like your mama. I'm
forever putting my handbag down and wandering off
without it and then, panic stations! Ask Charlie, he's
chased back to fetch it many a time!' As she spoke these
last words she gave Charlie's hand another pat, this time
a proprietary one. To extricate himself he bent over the
side of his chair and took his cigarettes and lighter from
the pocket of his shorts. He did wish Maude would go

away and have her lunch. She was spoiling things. Already he fancied the boys were seeing him in a different light.

'Don't make yourself late,' he said.

'I wasn't going to,' she said, and then laughed loudly and gaily. 'But I know when I'm not wanted! All boys together, I know the score!' She drained her glass and rose. Sometimes Charlie wondered if she was as stupid as she made out.

'There's no need to dash off,' he muttered with poor grace.

'Oh but I must, I hate to outstay my welcome.'

'Mr Farrell?'

They'd all been so taken up with Maude they hadn't noticed the tall young man approaching their table. He had receding brown hair, deep-set eyes and a managing manner.

'Yes, that's me.'

'Hallo, Dad.' Harry stood up and half extended a hand to be shaken. His father gave his shoulder a manly, approving squeeze and ruffled Michael's hair with a cuffing motion.

'I'm Jonathan Prescott, I got your message. Sorry you've been troubled with these two savages.'

Maude chuckled. 'I shouldn't worry your head about it, the three of them have been having the time of their lives!'

Prescott gave a cool, enquiring smile.

'I'm sorry, how rude of me – this is Maude Bingham.'

'It's hallo and goodbye. I'm off to have lunch, all on my ownsome, Mr Prescott,' declared Maude and teetered off, holding her empty glass aloft. Michael craned after her.

Charlie said: 'Won't you let me buy you a drink? You've only just arrived, haven't you? You must be exhausted.'

'Not really. I'm very used to flying.'

'But you'll have a drink?'

'No, thanks awfully.'

'Well –' Charlie smiled down at the boys. 'I hope you didn't mind my taking them for a swim.'

'Not at all, not at all. Children and other ranks are best

kept employed as my father used to say,' said Prescott, apparently unaware that he had said anything that might be construed as offensive. 'Anyway, I'll take them off your hands now. Grab your togs, you two.'

'It's been no trouble. I've enjoyed it.'

'Something tells me you're not a parent, Mr Farrell.'

'Well – no.' He was going to mention the schoolmastering but thought better of it, adding lamely: 'No I'm not.'

'Thought not. Now then, you chaps ready? How about some lunch, eh? I dare say Mummy'll be along soon.' He turned to Charlie. 'Angela is hopelessly scatty. I'm surprised she even got herself and the sprogs this far, let alone the baggage.'

Charlie laughed politely, and then said: 'As a matter of fact they have eaten. I bought them a snack from the pool bar. I hope that was all right.'

He glanced at the boys, hoping for some kind of endorsement, but their faces had resumed the look of closed watchfulness that had characterized them earlier.

Prescott smiled, but his eyes were chilly. 'Is that so? That was very kind of you. I trust you were properly thanked.'

'Thanks weren't necessary – but yes, I was.'

'Good. Anyway, they might as well come along now and keep Angela and I company.'

The boys moved dutifully to their father's side. It was on the tip of Charlie's tongue to suggest that they stay here, with him, for a little longer, which would be more relaxing for both parents and children. But Prescott had already laid hold of a shoulder with each hand and was beginning to steer them away from the table with a steely, jocular firmness.

'Here, don't forget this.' Charlie picked up a striped towel from under the table, and handed it to Michael. 'Keep up with the swimming.'

'Swimming at last, are you? That's a mercy,' was Jonathan Prescott's comment.

Harry said: 'Thanks very much for looking after us, sir.'

'My pleasure.'

'Yes, most civil of you – um, do I owe you anything? They could eat a hole in anyone's pocket.'

'No, no. You don't owe me a thing.'

'Thanks so much. Have a good Christmas. Goodbye.'

Prescott shook Charlie's hand briskly, and the three of them walked away. The father's hands still rested on the shoulders of his sons, lightly enough, but unmistakably frogmarching them towards the hotel.

Charlie sat down heavily and stared at the lilting blue of the pool, where one dogged elderly man was doing lengths of breaststroke. His head rose and fell rhythmically, chin high, mouth spouting water. A solitary old man, killing time, keeping himself in trim. Charlie was fifty-two. It was a shock to realize that Prescott, the brisk, affluent family man was probably twenty years younger than he. He recognized the type from his schoolmastering days. They took a firm line with 'the young' as they called them, as though they were lion, or wildebeest, and they expected you to do the same. They had perfect faith in you – they had to, really, since they were forking out all the money in order that you could take over. They went to great lengths not to know too much, they took an astonishing amount on trust, but should some misdemeanour or trace of mismanagement force itself on their attention they were terrible in their wrath. They had paid handsomely for peace, and they expected to get it.

Charlie suspected that once the ice had been broken Harry and Michael would have a splendid time in Perth, under the kindly, if scatty, auspices of their mother. They'd probably be quite different children by the time they got back to school and would need to be brought firmly and kindly back into line by those persons with whom Jonathan Prescott had entrusted their education.

Charlie was aware, again for the first time in many years, of those things for which he had a modest gift, those things he was good at. It was comforting to know that the gift was still there, but chastening to know it was being wasted.

The old man came up the steps of the pool, water trickling off his wrinkled stomach and bent shoulders. Charlie rose quickly, before he could strike up a conversation, and headed back in the direction of the hotel.

'Changed your mind about a decent tiffin?' enquired Maude, encountering him as she left the dining room.

'No, absolutely not. I'm going up to my room for a bit.'

'But you will come to the lounge later on?' Maude liked to play bridge for peanuts in the afternoon and Charlie usually joined her. Their more serious and expensive habits were indulged in the evening. Today Charlie could think of nothing he would loathe more than retire to the dim, silent lounge, with its greenish, underwater murk and its little tables surrounded by preoccupied people.

'Would you excuse me?' he said. 'To be perfectly honest,' (how often that was the prelude to a lie), 'I'm a bit bushed. I think I might have a sleep.'

'You poor old thing,' said Maude. 'That'll teach you.'

He couldn't be bothered to ask what it would teach him. 'See you later.'

'Would you like me to come and give you a knock around four?'

'No, that's all right. I'll rouse myself by degrees.'

Maude kissed him. 'I'll see you in the bar at six, then.' Her day was plotted out like a smallholding into these separate and distinct areas. 'I think I'm going to be lucky tonight,' she added. She always said this, and when it proved to be true she took it as evidence of a mystic prescience. 'Toodle-oo.'

As Charlie neared the end of the short corridor which led from the dining room to the foyer he saw Jonathan and Angela Prescott. It was obvious she had only just got back from the airport, for she carried a small grey case and was looking pink and damp with perspiration. Her husband's manner was brisk and censorious. Something in their attitudes made Charlie hang back. There was a table with copies of the *Straits Times* and foreign magazines and he paused here, looking down at the coloured covers, listening to the Prescotts.

'So stupid of me, absolutely typical . . . I could hardly believe it when I found out, but the woman had put it aside for me, so no harm done . . . sorry darling . . . where are the boys?'

'Gone up to their room for a bit.' Prescott spoke more quietly, but with sharper emphasis. Charlie could hear every single word. 'You know, Angie, you really shouldn't have left them with a total stranger.'

Angela laughed breathlessly. 'But he's English, and he's staying here. He seemed a very nice man . . .' Charlie realized he had been perfectly correct in his assessment of her criteria. 'And he simply couldn't have been nicer or more obliging about it.'

'I dare say, I'm sure he was, but it would have been more sensible to ask some nice married couple, someone else with children of their own instead of latching on to that Farrell fellow.'

'But Jonathan, really –!' She was fighting back, but tempering her retaliation with a shrill, anxious laugh. 'From what you say they had a simply wonderful time.'

'They enjoyed themselves, yes. But little boys are no judge of character. I didn't care for him. He's the sort who buys children drinks at the bar and thinks it's amusing when they get tipsy.'

'But you said they had Coca-Cola!'

'Possibly. I'm simply telling you that I know the type. And when I turned up he was with the most awful woman. The two of them just weren't the kind of people I want my children mixing with, that's all.'

Charlie's face felt red hot, and his head was pounding. He could no longer see the print or the pictures on the magazines. He leaned his fists heavily on the table to support himself, for his knees were like jelly. Angela Prescott, good company wife that she was, was beginning to concede that she'd made a mistake. As they walked away in the direction of the lifts, her voice floated back to Charlie.

'Oh dear, I'm sorry, I suppose it was silly of me . . .
but nothing like that even crossed my *mind* . . .'

Prescott, having established his authority in matters of
child care and social judgement, made some soothing
remark. The status quo was restored, and they were
friends again.

Charlie straightened up. He was a little unsteady on his
feet and a Malay waiter going in the direction of the dining
room hesitated fractionally and gave him an enquiring
look. He felt slightly nauseous and though his face was
still hot his hands and feet were cold. He'd never fainted
in his life but he was afraid he might do so now.

Breathing deeply he collected himself, crossed the
foyer, retrieved his room key and began to climb the stairs.
He couldn't face the little carpeted box of the lift, the mir-
rors which forced you to stare back at yourself no matter
where you turned. Every few stairs he stopped and leaned
on the banister. On the first floor landing there were a
couple of sofas and he sat down for a moment. An American couple, dressed to the nines, crossed the landing and
ran their eyes over him in the way the child had done that
morning, long ago, after he had lost so badly. It was the
same thing. There was something about misery that made
you invisible. He struggled on. As soon as the door of his
room was closed behind him he began to shake like a
leaf. He recognized the symptons: he was in shock. He
collapsed on the bed. The bedspread was a slightly rough
Madras cotton with a distinctive Far Eastern smell. A
bamboo blind was drawn about halfway down the french
windows. Two Malays, hotel staff, were talking in the
garden beneath the balcony, and the sing-song chuckle
and chatter of their conversation floated up to him like the
sound of jungle birds, incomprehensible, the language of
another world.

He lay there, shaking and sweating, for about half an
hour, and then fell into a heavy sleep full of terrible half-
caught dreams which slipped away without making themselves known. When he awoke, it was much later. The
light had changed and it was raining, that flat, heavy, dense

downpour of the tropics. The room was cooler, and the air held the sharp, plaintive scent of wet greenery. The big red tiles that covered the floor of the balcony seemed to wrinkle and dance beneath the onslaught of leaden drops.

Charlie sat, then stood, stiffly. He was still shivering, but now he was cold. He was still wearing only shorts, with his swimming trunks underneath. He removed the shorts, and his trunks, and went out on to the balcony. He stood with his head bowed, letting the drilling rain pound on him like a powerful massage. Then he went back into the room, rubbed himself down with the towel and pulled his trousers on. The rain started to slacken off, and the sky began to look yellowish. Soon it would be hot again.

On an impulse he took his soft, new wallet from his jacket pocket. The phone number he wanted was on the back of a creased and dog-eared black and white snapshot. He sat down on the bed and lifted the receiver of the phone on the small table, dialling the hotel switchboard. His hand still shook, but this time with nervous excitement.

The switchboard answered, he made his request, and the girl expressed some doubt but said she'd do her best and call him back.

While he waited, he could do nothing but sit on the edge of the bed. He realized that he was a little light-headed. The decision having ambushed him as he slept, he was stunned by the ease with which one could make things happen, how simply one could knit up the holes in one's life if one had the will to do so.

After about six minutes the phone rang, and the girl said that the number he wanted was ringing. She sounded grudgingly surprised, but Charlie himself felt no surprise. He was being impelled forward.

The line was bad, but on the far side of a tide of hissing and crackling he could hear the phone ringing on Larme des Anges.

Now someone answered.

'Hallo? Dragon House?'

He said: 'Who is that, please?'

'This is Adeline Farrell. Who's that?'

He stood paralysed for a second, while the receiver crackled in his hand. After so long, she had used his name. Their married name.

'Sorry, who?' Her voice rose, trying to penetrate the jungle of interference.

Slowly, he replaced the receiver. She was there. He could reach her. And she was still his wife.

There was a light knock on the door as he buttoned his shirt and he paused, holding his breath. He heard Maude's sigh, and rustle. She knocked again and said in a wheedling voice: 'Charlie . . . Charlie boy? Are you awake?'

He didn't answer, or move.

'I'm off to have some tea. Shall I see you down there?' Again he heard her move, fidgeting impatiently, her straw handbag rubbing on her silk dress, her gold bracelets clinking. Then she gave a little grunt, of annoyance or acquiescence, and went away.

Charlie never wanted to see her again.

Quickly now, afraid that his mood and his sense of purpose wouldn't last, he finished dressing and packed the smaller of his two cases. When he went to collect his wash things from the bathroom the hard, white strip of light over the mirror revealed him unflatteringly to himself. For a moment he saw exactly what Jonathan Prescott had seen – one of those young-looking not-so-young men, with nothing to commend them but a certain charm and facility. Everything from his haircut to the expensive watch which Maude had given to him, and the soft, pale shoes he'd had made here in Singapore – everything bespoke a slight, necessary vanity. He saw that he had become the tawdry, suspect misfit of Jonathan Prescott's imagination.

He switched off the bathroom light, put the remaining things in his case and locked it. Then he left the room without a backward glance.

As the sun broke through, the hotel, which had closed in on itself in the rain, began to blossom once more. Huge, tepid drops of water swelled and splashed from the room, from balcony rails, from every leaf and petal. The scent of flowers was rich and sweet. Steam rose from the lawns. Voices murmured and called, making arrangements for the evening. As Charlie waited for the lift a Chinese chambermaid in a short white cotton overall and slapping flat sandals went along the corridor with a trolley on which were soaps and piles of soft towels. She gave him a broad, gold-splattered grin.

Just as the lift appeared, so too did the entire Prescott family, and got in with him. The boys avoided his eye and did not say hallo, the parents were a little too eager to do so.

'I'm so glad I saw you,' cried Angela Prescott, 'because I haven't yet had a chance to thank you for looking after Michael and Harry.'

'There's no need. I was only too happy.'

'You're off, are you?' enquired Prescott, glancing at his case.

'That's right.'

'UK?'

Charlie hesitated. 'Perhaps. I don't honestly know.'

'Footloose and fancy free,' commented Prescott. Charlie smiled obligingly. He would never see these people again: who cared what they thought?

'Goodbye, then,' said Angela Prescott, holding out her hand. 'And again thank you so much.'

'Not at all. Have a good holiday in Perth. Bye, boys. Good luck.'

He heard the slightly too-intense silence just behind him as he stepped first out of the lift. They were being careful not to let slip any stray comments while he was still within earshot.

He glanced around, but Maude was nowhere to be seen. There were one or two people with suitcases, otherwise the foyer was deserted. Maude would be in the lounge, or in the garden, having her tea, thinking him still asleep. He glanced at his watch. It was half past four. At least three quarters of an hour before she went back to her room to get dolled up for Happy Hour.

He went over to the desk. It crossed his mind for a second that he could simply go, and leave Maude to pay the bill, which she quite often did anyway. But he stamped on the impulse as unworthy. A clean break, a fresh start, that was the idea, and he could at least begin by doing the decent thing, and not hurt her more than she was going to be hurt already.

He was flush at the moment, with a substantial amount in cash and a healthy supply of traveller's cheques. All he didn't have was any security. What he had was all there was. He had become so used to the buffer zone of Maude's wealth, he had forgotten what it was to view funds in finite terms. Monopoly money, fun money was what it had become. Still, he estimated that he had enough for his purpose.

He settled up – it was so simple – and walked out of the main door into the hot, glaring afternoon. Three taxis stood pulled up to the right of the door. The drivers of the first two, Chinese in brightly checked short-sleeved shirts, were playing dice on the bonnet of the first car, but as soon as he appeared they scooped up the dice and stood back to allow the taxi to shoot forward.

'Where to?'

'Airport please.'

'Airport!'

The taxi shot forward again, pausing perfunctorily between the elaborate stone gateposts topped with pine-apples before attaching itself, with much use of the horn, to the snarling stream of traffic.

Charlie loosened his tie and leaned his head back on the seat. Hot, moist, noisome air from the driver's open window played on his face. His stomach fluttered uneasily with each sharply taken corner and squeal of brakes. The cabbie's elbow protruded from the open window while his fingers rested with suicidal delicacy on the steering wheel. When Charlie met his eyes in the rear-view mirror he gave him a strange knowing smile and nodded, as though he knew what his passenger was thinking. Charlie wished there was a blind he could pull down between the two of them. Instead, he tried to throw up a barrier of formality by leaning forward and saying: 'Look, could you take it easy? I'd rather arrive in one piece.'

'You've got flight to catch?'

'No, I've not booked anything. Slower. Please.'

'Okay.'

Charlie leaned back his head once more and closed his eyes. He could hardly believe he'd got this far, and that it had been so easy. He was exhilarated, but afraid.

In the terminal building the air conditioning turned his sweat to a clammy chill in seconds. Here, surrounded by people who had made arrangements, who knew what they were doing and where they were going, his confidence flagged. He went to the bar and ordered a beer while he took stock once more of his finances. In his bank account in England he had, he thought, just over a thousand pounds. On his person this afternoon, in various currencies and in traveller's cheques, about seven hundred and fifty. The further away he got from Maude the less the money seemed. His heart began to race. He drank the beer quickly and ordered a whisky. Fortified by the Scotch he got moving again. He went to the flight desk and booked a ticket. No flight till the following evening, a stop-over in Los Angeles, a change of planes in Florida, and two-thirds of the money gone. It was still a bugger of a journey. He only hoped the travelling wouldn't prove to have been the easiest part.

Still in his heart he carried, like a knight who wears his lady's favour, the fact that she had used his name.

CHAPTER TWENTY-NINE

1963

Duncan and Joel were on the rock that formed the left-hand, western pedestal of the rock-arch in the bay of Larme des Anges. Below them in the turquoise water Adeline's eleven-year-old grandson swam and swooped like a dolphin. The faint gloops and splashes made by Patrick's swimming were curiously intimate, cutting them off from the rest of the beach.

Near her shack at the edge of the dunes, Adeline was perched on a canvas chair, sketching. She wore a long, red and green robe, and a sun visor bearing the Coca-Cola motif borrowed from Patrick. In her left hand was a cigarette in a holder and when, as happened from time to time, she looked in their direction, she waggled the cigarette as though it were an antenna, picking up messages.

'It's God's little acre, and no mistake,' sighed Joel. 'It's just a pity it's so far away.'

'Ah, but that's chief among its charms,' said Duncan. 'No-one can reach you here.'

'You wouldn't want to live here, though. Not you personally.'

Duncan heaved himself on to his back. 'Don't tell me what I personally would or wouldn't want. Presumptuous thing.'

Joel prodded him. Swimming was the only form of exercise Duncan liked, and he always went home from Larme des Anges looking fit and well. His hair, which had been grey from his twenties, was still thick and curly. Stretched out on the rock wearing only what Joel considered to be obscenely brief swimming trunks, his pensionable years sat lightly on him.

Joel couldn't swim, and his fair skin burnt painfully unless he was careful. He wore light blue jeans, a blue and white cheesecloth shirt and a white straw hat. 'Very Cecil Beaton,' Duncan called the hat, but without malice. He had the scruffy person's uneasy admiration for the naturally elegant.

'There he goes,' said Joel. 'Heading for the shore.'

If his grandmother was anywhere about, Patrick liked to seek her out at regular intervals. Of all his grandparents, Adeline was the one he felt most drawn to. It was a mixture of closeness and strangeness. He basked in her indulgent and admiring love, but he also felt emanating from her, the more thrilling allure of something foreign and exotic. Not just her face, her hair, the funny things she wore, though they were colourful enough – but her past life which he sensed was fretted and fraught with fascinating complications. She was a great one, as everybody said, for enjoying life and living in the present, but you'd have had to be a fool not to realize that there was a great tangle of secrets in the past. He walked across the warm white sand to where she sat. She didn't look up, but when he was a few yards away she said: 'There you are. Come and tell me what you think.'

She sought and valued Patrick's opinion. He was always straight with her. Now he stood by her shoulder, looking at the drawing, and she sat smiling, looking at his face.

'It's fine,' he said.

'Oh dear, bad as that, eh?'

He laughed. 'That's not fair.'

'You don't usually flannel me.'

'I wasn't flannelling!' He was stung. 'It's okay. There's nothing the *matter* with it. It looks like what it's supposed to look like. I just prefer it when you do people.'

Now it was Adeline who laughed, heartily. 'Yes, I do too – prefer it when I do people. Still, the occasional landsape is a useful exercise, a good discipline.'

'Boring, boring, dull, dull.'

'Horrid boy! How was the water?'

'Fab. The trouble is, going back to the grim, grey English sea again.'

'And you don't miss English Christmas weather?'

He shook his head. 'Golly, no. Mum and Dad a bit,' he conceded, 'but nothing else.'

'That's the style,' said Adeline. She stood up and folded her chair. 'Be a lamb and put this in the shack. Time I was going up, with the Outlook Point lot coming to supper.'

'The Crazy Y gang.'

'The Fab Four.'

'Showing off how groovy you are.'

Bickering amiably they packed up, Patrick and Adeline, perfectly in tune with each other.

'They're going back to the house,' said Joel. 'Time we did the same.'

'Mm.'

Adeline waved, and made drinking motions. Patrick put his hands to his mouth and yelled something. Joel removed his white hat and flapped it in the air.

'I wonder if she's happy.'

'Adeline . . . ?' Duncan struggled into a sitting position, rubbing his eyes. 'I'm sure she is. She's better at it than most people.'

'That place of hers could do with another lavatory,' said Nicholas irritably, slapping on shaving lotion.

Fenella, who was putting on earrings at the dressing table, looked at him over her own reflection.

'There's no need to get crusty about it. If there's a queue you can go in the bushes. It's the way she likes it, it was never intended to be luxurious.'

'It lacks basic amenities.'

Fenella shrugged. 'Don't go if you don't like it. Stay here and eat in solitary, luxurious state.'

'Don't be silly, of course I'm going. Apart from anything else it's only by going over there that we'll get to see our grandson this Christmas.'

Fenella rose from the dressing table. 'He just likes it there. It's not a fiendish plot against us, or anything. If you remember, Dora always used to come to Outlook Point.'

'I'm not in the least interested in what Dora used to do.'

'But I am. You know me.'

Nicholas, looking at Fenella, wasn't at all sure that he did. They had been married for thirty-five years, which was incredible enough in itself. Marrying Fenella Marchant had been a ploy. He had despised her for what he saw as her gullibility, and he had bullied and belittled her in many subtle, and some not so subtle, ways. And yet, though he had been no sort of husband to her, she had always been a wife to him.

It was Neville he'd coveted. But Neville's outward show of devotion had been misleading, for beneath it all he'd been bound to his wife with hoops of steel. Even in recollection Nicholas could recreate the confused desire and rage that had typified that time, the state of permanently suppressed jealousy which only Neville, with a smile or a touch, could dispel. And Adeline's arrival on the scene – that it had been by his agency still made him grind his teeth – had heralded the end of it.

In marrying Fenella he'd cocked a snook at the whole pack of them. But there was something he hadn't allowed for – she loved him. She had never been a sensual woman, her sexual needs were simple and few, for which he had been grateful, and yet in other ways she wanted only to please him. She had bent before his unkindness only to spring back, and she had cherished their son while never openly taking his part against Nicholas. The possibility of their marriage failing was not one she had ever entertained. It would have been easier for her to take refuge in a group of friends who could have supported and sympathized with her, but she had never done so. The result was that though he could not honestly say that he loved her, she had made her presence indispensable to his well-being.

'Ready then?' she asked. She was standing at the door of their room, still slim and ridiculously young-looking in a green and white shirtwaister and a cheap shell necklace she'd bought in Angeville.

'Ready.' He went and stood before her, and their eyes met. They shared few confidences but sometimes each felt the other's complex store of secret understanding.

'Ready,' he said. And then added. 'You look very pretty. As usual.'

'Oh God!' wailed Pru. 'Nick and Nella will be waiting for us. We always keep them waiting.'

'Let them wait,' replied Peter. 'Breathe in.'

He gave the zip on his wife's dress a final tug and at last it shot up over her plump back.

'Any hooks and eyes?'

'I can't remember.'

'Doesn't seem to be . . .yes, here's one . . . hang on . . . there we are.'

'Thanks, darling. Now then bag, bag . . .'

'What do you need a bag for?'

'I suppose I don't, really.'

'Of course you don't.'

'No. Well that's me then, I *think*.'

Peter sat placidly in a chair as Pru wandered about the bedroom, wondering if she wanted this or that. She was right, Nicholas and Fenella would be waiting, but what the hell? This was his house, he came here expressly not to be hurried. Pru slid back the wardrobe door and selected a pair of shoes. Bending over to put them on was an effort.

'I simply must go on a diet.'

'Why? I like you as you are. Something to get hold of.'

'How delicately you put it, darling?' She laughed and fluffed at her hair with her fingers. 'The boys are always on at me about it.'

'Thank heavens they're not here then.'

'What a *horrid* thing to say . . . ! Right, off we go.'

As Peter held the door for her she whispered: 'I hope Nick won't be rude to Addy all evening, it's so exhausting.'

Peter shrugged. 'For you, perhaps. She can take it.'

'I sometimes think she's had to take such a lot.'

'Maybe she has, but some people are designed for that, and she's one of them.'

Patrick sat on Adeline's bed as she selected which jewellery to wear. She had changed into a long black and white checked skirt and a plain black shirt and was now rummaging through what she referred to disparagingly as her 'bits and pieces'.

Patrick was writing a letter to his parents the paper resting on a book. Their mutual silence was completely companionable.

'It was the strangest thing,' she said, pouring coffee and handing the cups to Patrick to pass round. 'He just asked me who I was and then rang off. It was quite tantalizing, really.'

'Well I think you should have had it traced,' remarked Peter. 'You're all on your own here most of the time, prey to any crank.'

'If I was in London I might expect a certain number of unsavoury calls, but not here, somehow. Anyway, I don't think it was a crank. He didn't ask me what my underwear was like or anything, I'm sixty-three, for heaven's sake.'

'It was definitely a "he", was it?' asked Joel.

'Oh yes, At least I think so. The line was apalling, as if he were calling from the other side of the world.'

'You'll be lucky to have a line at all by tomorrow,' said Nicholas. 'They'd put the storm warning up at the fort when we came over.'

Patrick sat on the rug, next to Gypsy. Fenella leant over and tapped him on the shoulder. 'No swimming tomorrow. Why don't you come and spend the day with us?'

'Thanks very much. I might.'

Nicholas turned to Duncan. 'How's business, by the way?'

'Middling. We keep our heads above water, don't we, Jo?'

'It must be fun,' enthused Pru, 'selling nice things to nice people all day.'

Joel smiled. 'The things are nice, certainly, but not all the people are, and we're not exactly rushed off our feet.'

'I think you chaps are too bogged down with the admin.,' opined Peter. As he enlarged on this, the telephone rang.

'Excuse me.' Adeline went out into the hall, closing the door behind her.

'Hallo? Dragon House.'

There was a series of confused sounds, as of someone trying, unsuccessfully, to ring from a call box. In the silence that followed she said, again: 'Hallo?' But there was only the buzz of the empty line.

Puzzled, she returned to the living room, where all faces, most of them smiling, were turned towards Peter, who was telling a story against himself.

'. . . So there it was, they'd got me, bang to rights. That's the Germans for you. They're always working, always thinking, even when you could have sworn they were just enjoying themselves. I was taken for a mug, but you have to admire them for it. And of course they're reaping the rewards, they've more or less left the rest of Europe for dead . . .'

Adeline sat down. 'Nobody,' she said. 'Wrong number.'

Now that he was so close to his destination, Charlie was afraid again. He had intended to make himself known on the phone this time, to say 'I'm here' so that she would come and rescue him. But then he realized that that was not how he wanted it to be. He wanted to arrive, not to be fetched. He wanted to reappear on his own terms, and not cry for help. There wasn't a cab in sight at the moment, they'd all been taken by other passengers off the same flight, and he knew from experience that they wouldn't be back tonight. If he waited till morning he could take a taxi bright and early, and he'd feel better then, less tired, more buoyant.

He walked across the tiny airport building in the direction of the gents' cloakroom. On the outside of the glass door was a huge moth, transfixed by the brilliant light. Its outspread wings, yellow pattered with black, were like a painted mask, staring in at him.

He went into the cloakroom and washed his face with cold water. Then he returned to the bench and lay down. He didn't worry about being moved on. With the rush of incoming passengers processed, the airport staff were laughing and talking, drifting away. An enormous policeman in shorts was drinking a soft drink from a can. With the cool but slightly sticky plastic of the bench beneath his cheek, Charlie's last thought before going to sleep was that he was too old for this sort of thing. But as he eyes closed no-one paid him the slightest attention.

Adeline slept briefly, and not all that well – one of the penalties of getting older. Because of the storm warning, the others hadn't stayed late, and yet when she woke she realized that it still hadn't broken. The air was sticky, and a restless wind prowled round the house. Gypsy, who usually slept at the end of her bed, was lying near the door, trembling.

She looked at her watch: just before five. She got out of bed and dressed in cotton trousers and shirt, and a sweater, with an old pair of canvas shoes.

'Come on, old girl,' she said. 'Let's go and take a look at it.'

Before leaving the house she looked into the living room. A whining snake of a draught was lifting the fringe on the dhurrie and rattling the leaves of the plants. The remains of last night's white wood ash was scattered on the tiles, sifted and combed into rippling patterns like desert sand. She pulled up the blind and exposed a dark, racing sky just beginning, half-heartedly, to lighten.

She turned to see Patrick in the doorway, still in pyjamas.

'Morning,' she said. 'A wild one.'

'Are you going out?'

She walked over and kissed him. 'I'm going to walk round the road and look at the causeway first, and then take the dog on the sand for a minute.'

'Can I go down with her now?'

'All right. But don't go out on the rocks. When the wind starts to get up it's really not safe. I'll be there myself soon.'

'Great!'

Patrick ran off to dress. Adeline went to the back of the bungalow, to her studio, which was really just an enclosed area of the verandah. It was in the teeth of the wind, and already her easel had been blown sideways against the wall, and the earthenware pot which held her brushes had tipped over. She righted these, and closed and fastened the shutters. Then she went to the kitchen where Nathan was finishing the previous night's washing-up, and told him she was going for a walk.

'There's a storm coming,' he said fearfully. 'It no good for walking, ma'am.'

'I shan't be long.' She knew he was not so much warning her as begging her to stay. He was terrified of the high wind. 'And anyway I'm not sure we're going to get the worst of this one. It's been too long coming.'

He didn't look comforted, but she left him and went back to the hall, where Patrick now stood in jumper and jeans. She handed him the dog's lead.

'Put her on this till you get down to the beach, or she won't go with you.' She glanced in the direction of Duncan and Joel's room. 'Any sounds from them?'

Patrick shook his head. 'They must sleep jolly heavily with all this racket going on.'

As he spoke, some stray object that had been left out of doors was dislodged by the wind and trundled with a crazy clatter against the walls of the house. Adeline and Patrick went out of the screen door and on to the front verandah, where the bougainvillea now streamed into the air like tangled hair.

Adeline patted Gypsy, who was no longer nervous now that she was out of doors. She put her hand on Patrick's shoulder.

'Sure you'll be all right?'

'Of course, it's great.'

'Don't do anything rash, this weather needs treating with respect. If it gets any worse than this come back to the house. Otherwise I'll come down to the beach in a few minutes and meet you.'

'Okay. I'll be okay! Come on, Gypsy!'

As she turned into the road the wind pounced on Adeline, snatching and tugging at her so that for a moment she was breathless, and almost lost her balance. When she looked back at the Dragon House it was no more than a glimmer of white between the dark trees that leaned and heaved like horses pulling a heavy load. She could feel the island tensing and bunching itself, preparing for the onslaught.

Away down to her left the sea was a surging grey, fretted with white. She could hear, faintly but unmistakably, the howl of the wind and waves in the rock arch. As she came round the shoulder of the hill she could see the causeway, a thin, pale thread like an umbilical cord linking the smaller island to the larger one. It was still, at the moment, passable, but she was sure it would be closed to traffic within the next hour. To her surprise, a solitary set of car lights was moving towards the southern end, in the direction of Larme des Anges. As she watched, they disappeared beneath the rim of the hill into Angeville.

Having seen the causeway, she would have turned back, but the wind was less fierce now that she was in the lee of the hill, and she was drawn, too, by the pale light in the east, an evidence of nature's good faith, a promise that the bad weather would eventually end, and order be restored.

As always, she felt in less danger out here than she did in the house. She identified so closely with this piece of land, and had been at pains not to despoil it. She had struck a bargain with Larme des Anges, and expected that it would be honoured.

She realized the car was approaching before she saw it. She could identify a sound that was man-made, not part of the storm. Then she caught the fitful blink of the headlights between the whipping trees. She thought that it must have taken a wrong turning, for this road led nowhere but the Dragon House. She was convinced it must be someone wanting to get up to the weather station, and she stopped at the side of the road to flag the driver down and give any help she could.

In fact, the car stopped just before it got to her. She was temporarily dazzled by the headlights. If it had drawn alongside it would have been safe. As it was, the enormous, whitened dead branch that came spinning out of the darkness, struck and pierced the roof at an oblique angle, shattering the yellow glass sign that read 'TAXI'. The crash of tearing metal and splintering glass was shrill above the booming clamour of the wind. The car's headlights remained on, staring fixedly ahead.

Adeline dashed forward and bumped into the driver, who was howling with shock, but unharmed.

'Are you all right?' she yelled. 'Are you all right?'

'I told him it no good, I told him the weather no damn good, but he made me come! What I going to do?'

'Who else is in there?' She glanced over his shoulder and saw the pale smudge of a face in the back seat. 'Look – ' She took the driver by the shoulders. 'Have you put the handbrake on?' He nodded, sniffling. 'My house is up there, the white house, you walk up the hill and fetch help.'

'No, ma'am! I stay here with you!'

'Oh – damn you!'

Adeline ran to the rear passenger door and pulled it open. It was partly jammed by the impact of the branch, which had entered the roof above the front passenger seat and travelled diagonally. One crazy gnarled, grey limb protruded from the rear windscreen.

She looked down and saw Charlie, his eyes vividly dark in his white face. For a moment she could not hear the wind, or the moans of the driver, she was deafened by a thunderclap of emotions. In the same second that her heart filled with joy, she knew with certainty that he was dying.

The dark interior of the car seemed to be filled with the rough, unyielding form of the branch, the jagged end of which had impaled Charlie just above the waist on the left side. She knew she mustn't move him, and she could not make out the extent of the damage. Frantically she pulled off her thick, oiled-wool sweater and laid it over him, and then felt desperately for his right hand. When she found it he clasped hers with surprising strength. His blood covered their joined hands in a warm, sticky caul.

'Adeline – Adeline – '

'My darling. Don't!' She bent and kissed him. 'We're

going to get help, it's going to be all right, I promise, don't move or talk.'

The driver, panic-stricken, wailed at her. 'We need go, ma'am! You and me go fetch help from the house!'

She turned her head awkwardly, not wanting to hurt Charlie, and put as much furious emphasis as she could into her voice.

'Look, you bloody stupid man, *you* go! Go up to the house, my friends are there. Fetch help, and get someone to call an ambulance from Port Minerve before it's *too late!* Do you understand? Go!'

Moaning, the man ran off into the half-darkness, weaving drunkenly as the wind caught him.

Adeline turned back to Charlie. She sat as best she could on the edge of the seat beside him, her knees wedged against the open door. Very carefully she slipped her free arm behind his neck so that he could rest his head on her shoulder. His eyes never once left her face. She knew that whatever hope there was for the two of them was vested in her, and she felt inadequate.

'I love you,' was all she could think of to say. 'I never stopped loving you.'

'Addy . . . I'm sorry.'

She wouldn't cry. She kissed him on the forehead. 'Help's coming,' she said. 'Just hang on to me.'

He did, his grip on her hand tightened fiercely. His body against hers felt hot and stiff, skewered by pain. The branch jutting through the roof of the car acted like a sail, which the wind caught and dragged. When Charlie yelled she didn't know what she could do but hold him tighter. It was the level on which they had always been able to communicate, this simple, physical level, and now there was no other means left to them.

'I love you,' she kept on saying. 'Hold on, my darling, hold on to me, I'm here.'

She thought of all the years that they'd been apart – and she could not even ask him where he'd been, what he'd been doing, what had brought him back. She couldn't ask him now, and she'd probably never know.

All she could do was try and hold his body and soul together, but she could feel the unnatural heat beginning to ebb away from him. Where her clothes and his were pressed together they were sodden and matted with his blood, like a shared skin.

She put her mouth to his ear. 'I kept your motorbike,' she said. 'It's good as new.' But he showed no sign of having heard.

The sky was lightening. The storm, as she had predicted, was moving away. But like a bully that aims a final kick at a fallen victim it hurled one last tremendous gust of wind that shook the car like a terrier shakes a rat. Charlie's jacket, which had been lying on the floor, and which Adeline had displaced when she got in, was snatched away, and tumbled across the road. A handful of banknotes came out of the pocket and flew away, whirling crazily on the back of the departing wind.

She felt a slight tug on her hand. Terrified, she put her face close to his. His skin was damp, his eyes more intense than ever with the effort of speaking.

'Yes? Yes, I'll hear you. What is it?'

She hoped, she prayed to God that she *would* hear, that somehow she would absorb what it was he wanted to say through his skin, through his blood.

Then quite suddenly he seemed to rally. He took his hand from hers and, lifting it, placed it on the back of her neck, beneath her hair.

'Addy – I didn't come because of the money,' he said. His voice was clear, completely audible. 'I came because I love you. I'm not worth anything without you. What I owe you is everything but money.'

She touched her cheek against his, unable now to prevent the tears coming, and as she did so she felt his hand slip from her neck, and his body relax for the first and last time, free from pain.

Patrick raced up the path from the bay, with Gypsy galloping in front of him. It was great, wonderful! The dragon had really lashed its tail, and howled and raged, but now the sun was coming up. And he was hungry.

He expected to meet Adeline coming down the other way, as she had promised. But when he reached the house there were Duncan and Joel, with another man, heading down the road. Joel was still in pyjamas, with a jacket over the top.

Philippe appeared on the verandah and called to him. Gypsy was already there, wagging her backside and jumping up, asking for her breakfast.

'Philippe!' he shouted. 'Where's Gran?'

He could tell by the hesitation that something had happened and he ran full tilt after the others, overtaking them.

Adeline hoped they wouldn't come too quickly. She wanted these moments to hold him really close as she hadn't been able to do before, to breathe him in, to imprint him on her memory. She wasn't sure that she would be able to let him go when she was asked to, she wasn't sure she could bear it.

She heard the brisk slap of footsteps careering head-long down the hill. She knew it was Patrick before he arrived at her side.

'Gran?' he whispered, frightened. 'Are you all right?'

And then, when she nodded and reached out a hand for him he asked: 'Who is it?'

ENDPIECE

PATRICK GOT UP slowly, and slid his camera bag to the ground. Kicking off his shoes he walked out as far as Lindy and then called over her shoulder to Adeline.

'Hey, Gran – what have you been saying to her?'

Adeline raised both hands. 'Me? Nothing.'

Lindy glared at him. 'Don't blame her – I'm the one who's talking to you!'

'You're disturbing the swans,' said Adeline. All three were now in the water, gliding away with disdainful grace.

Lindy and Patrick lowered their voices. Patrick put his arm around her, turning with his back to Adeline so they couldn't be heard.

Adeline lit a cigarette and closed her eyes. She was tired this afternoon, but not unpleasantly so. Heavy, drowsy . . . lethargic. She put it down to struggling down the steep bank, carrying her chair. She hoped she'd feel more energetic tomorrow so that she could sparkle on the chat show as she wanted to. She thought of the red, black and gold dress and smiled to herself.

When she opened her eyes, Patrick had gone and Lindy was making her way towards her. She was grim-faced, but her manner had altered.

'Sent him packing?' asked Adeline.

'We're going to drive down to Tarrmouth for a swim. You don't mind if we skip the tea, do you Adeline?'

'Don't be silly. Swimming's much nicer.'

Lindy picked up her shoes and stood before Adeline with them dangling from one hand. 'Bye, then. Perhaps we could pop in this evening . . . say goodbye.'

'You do what you like, my dear. It's been lovely to see you.'

'Yes. And you.' Suddenly Lindy bent and kissed her. For a moment Adeline felt the smooth brown arms round her neck, the nudge of the tight stomach on her lap, the brush of frizzy curls on her eyelids.

Then the girl was off, marching across the ford with long, determined strides, clambering out on the bank, disappearing between the trees.

Adeline sat quietly. After a few minutes the swans returned, but this time they remained in the water. Almost motionless, their reflections upended beneath them like the images on playing cards.

Suspended between sleeping and waking Adeline felt a light touch on her shoulder. When she looked she saw that a leaf had drifted down and settled on her. Everything was so dried out, barely hanging on. But the touch had seemed firmer, more deliberate than simply that of the leaf. She felt not that she had been left alone, but as though someone had just come to her side. She felt relaxed, and safe, quite unwilling to move.

She was glad they had gone together, to swim in the sea.

A FLOWER THAT'S FREE

Sarah Harrison

Kate Kingsley – an exotic flower from the harsh soil of Kenya, blooming in London, in sun-drenched Malta, in decadent Berlin. Amid the turbulence of World War II she confronts personal danger, faces conflicting loyalties, loves two different men, aches over the heart-breaking choice and finds a kind of freedom at last. Beautiful, restless, impulsive, Kate is an unforgettable heroine to capture every heart.

'A compelling and intriguing book, the work of a fine storyteller'
Catherine Cookson

'Full of unforgettable people, places and passions'
Woman's World

'You'll love it'
Woman's Own

FICTION

☐	Both Your Houses	Sarah Harrison	£6.99
☐	The Flowers of the Field	Sarah Harrison	£5.99
☐	A Flower That's Free	Sarah Harrison	£6.99
☐	Hot Breath	Sarah Harrison	£4.99
☐	Cold Feet	Sarah Harrison	£4.99
☐	The Forests of the Night	Sarah Harrison	£4.99
☐	Foreign Parts	Sarah Harrison	£4.99
☐	Be An Angel	Sarah Harrison	£5.99

Warner Books now offers an exciting range of quality titles by both established and new authors. All of the books in this series are available from

Little, Brown and Company (UK),
P.O. Box 11,
Falmouth,
Cornwall TR10 9EN.

Alternatively you may fax your order to the above address. Fax No. 01326 317444.

Payments can be made as follows: cheque, postal order (payable to Little, Brown and Company) or by credit cards, Visa/Access. Do not send cash or currency. UK customers and B.F.P.O. please allow £1.00 for postage and packing for the first book, plus 50p for the second book, plus 30p for each additional book up to a maximum charge of £3.00 (7 books plus).

Overseas customers including Ireland, please allow £2.00 for the first book plus £1.00 for the second book, plus 50p for each additional book.

NAME (Block Letters) ....

....

ADDRESS ....

....

....

☐ I enclose my remittance for ....

☐ I wish to pay by Access/Visa Card

Number ☐☐☐☐☐☐☐☐☐☐☐☐☐☐☐☐☐☐

Card Expiry Date ☐☐☐☐